The
Barrister
and the
Letter of
Marque

Books by Todd M. Johnson

THE
BARRISTER
and the
LETTER OF
MARQUE

TODD M. JOHNSON

BETHANYHOUSE

a division of Baker Publishing Group
Minneapolis, Minnesota

Published by Bethany House Publishers
11400 Hampshire Avenue South
Bloomington, Minnesota 55438
www.bethanyhouse.com

Bethany House Publishers is a division of
Baker Publishing Group, Grand Rapids, Michigan

Printed in the United States of America

Library of Congress Cataloging-in-Publication Data
Names: Johnson, Todd M. (Todd Maurice), author.
Title: The barrister and the letter of marque / Todd M. Johnson.
Description: Minneapolis, Minnesota : Bethany House, a division of Baker
    Publishing Group, [2021]
Identifiers: LCCN 2021004792 | ISBN 9780764212369 (paperback) | ISBN
    9780764239137 (casebound) | ISBN 9781493431502 (ebook)
Subjects: GSAFD: Legal stories. | Mystery fiction.
Classification: LCC PS3610.O38363 B37 2021 | DDC 813/.6—dc23
LC record available at https://lccn.loc.gov/2021004792

Scripture quotations are from the King James Version of the Bible.

This is a work of historical reconstruction; the appearances of certain historical figures are therefore inevitable. All other characters, however, are products of the author's imagination, and any resemblance to actual persons, living or dead, is coincidental.

Cover design by Studio Gearbox
Cover image of Victorian man crossing bridge by Mark Owen / Arcangel

21 22 23 24 25 26 27   7 6 5 4 3 2 1

In memory of Robert C. Dickerson II

*One of the finest men, finest lawyers, and best friends
I've ever had the privilege to have known.*

Letter of Marque and Reprisal

On behalf of his Majesty King George III, by the grace of God,
King of the United Kingdom of Great Britain and Ireland,
defender of the faith,
To our trusty and well-beloved captain,

Greetings:

scoundrels and enemies of the Crown commit many
depredations on the seas against the interests of the Crown
and its possessions about the world, and the Crown, being
desirous to prevent these mischiefs—in particular the practice
of smugglers violating the Crown's license to the East India
Company for tea trade in China and lands thereabout—
Does hereby grant you, this date,

a commission as a private man-of-war, with full power and
authority to seize said vessels wherever you meet them upon the
seas or coasts, and empower you to take all such merchandise,
money, goods, and wares as shall be found on board,

From those who willingly yield
and those you are forced to compel to yield.

Given at our court,
the twenty-first day of November 1816,
the fifth year of our regency, on behalf of His Majesty,
King George III.

Prince George Augustus Frederick, Regent to the King

PROLOGUE
SUMMER, 1797

CASTLE KITTLESON
WILTSHIRE COUNTY, ENGLAND

Early evening shadows blanketed the study lit only by desk candles and a sputtering fire in the hearth. Eighteen-year-old William Snopes watched his father from the entryway, hunched over stacks of papers on his desk.

Exhausted from the long ride, chilled in his damp riding clothes, William gathered himself in the entry before stepping fully into the room.

His father rose from his chair and approached.

"What on earth are you doing home?" he demanded.

William had grown during his last term at Oxford but had imagined more growth than was the truth. His father, a hint of graying at his temples and iron in his eyes, still looked to exceed him by several inches and at least fifty pounds. He seemed even taller with his granite posture.

The hours of preparation on his ride fled.

"What did you do to her?" William said, more inquiry than demand. It was all he could muster.

"What did I do to *whom*?"

"To Mary. What did you do to her?"

"What impudence! Interrogating me without even a hello? You *will not* address me in that tone."

A year before, those cold eyes would have unmanned him, sending him sulking away. At least he was standing his ground tonight.

"What did you do to her, Father?" he said more boldly.

"Who in blazes told you I did *anything* to *anyone*?"

"Our tenants, the Blengens. What did you do to their girl? What did you do to Mary?"

Discomfort rippled beneath his father's stolid eyes.

"That *farm girl*?" he bellowed. "Their comings and goings aren't my concern." He paused, raising a thick hand to his chin. "Though perhaps I heard that her family sent her north to live with relatives for a time. Is that your meaning?"

The hesitation, the false ease. He'd seen it in his father's lies before.

The fear that had floated in him finally took anchor.

It was true.

"Sent north to relatives?" William grew stronger. "Father, Mary's their only child. The Blengens would die before they'd willingly part from her."

Silence. A hateful glare. No shame. No denial.

Sad fury carried William away.

"How *could* you, Father?" he said through a sheen of tears. "She's sixteen years old! Mother's only been gone these ten months. You've always demanded your way with everyone, but this . . ."

The blow came from William's left.

He dropped hard to his hands and knees, shocked. Lightning split his vision. His left cheek and ear pulsed with terrible pain. Blood ran along his cheek in a rivulet down onto the rug.

Overhead, his father's furious breaths filled his ears.

A full minute passed before he even tried to rise from his knees. Slowly he stood.

At full height again, something had changed. The last fear had vanished. Taking with it the final filaments of respect for his father.

He clenched his fists behind his back and stared unflinching into his parent's futile, indignant glare. "You shame me, Father. You shame Mother too."

"Your mother isn't alive. *I'm* your only parent now. Measure your next words carefully, William. Another of these insolent accusations, *one single word . . .*"

The threat passed over him, powerless.

"I'm leaving," William said.

"No, you're not. You're returning to Oxford and your studies. And in the spring, when you graduate, you'll take up your commission in the Guards as planned."

"No. I'm leaving."

"Leaving? Leaving?" Laughter. "To do what exactly?"

"I'll study to be a barrister."

"Why, for heaven's sake, would you do that?"

"To be someone different from you."

The stare faltered. "If you leave, you'll no longer be part of this family. I'll disinherit you."

William turned and left the room for the staircase.

An hour later, he returned from his bedroom, a small bag over his shoulder. His face still pulsed. A trace of blood lingered in his mouth. He left the manor house through a door that avoided the study, opening onto the garden. Through thin shadows cast by the half-moon, he walked toward the stable.

Unbearable shame and anger filled him. He had no capacity for anything more. Just a cloud of fury, all else emptiness.

Until, slowly, chords of Haydn's Symphony Number 100 rose in his mind. It was from the last concert he'd attended with his mother, the previous summer in London. They were seated near the front that night, holding hands, both knowing that she was dying. The powerful notes permeated him now, like the palliative of his lost mother's touch. The arpeggios and triads rose from the hidden vault of mind and heart where lingered every musical note William had ever heard performed—a treasure that sounded at William's call or seemingly for no reason at all. Stored beyond anyone's reach, particularly his father's, whose final touch would be the backhand that had emancipated his only child.

With Haydn dulling his disgrace and setting his pace, William crossed the estate's dark, manicured lawns to the stables, avoiding the glow of light that still came from the windows of his father's study.

Notes were ascending in the symphony's third movement as he neared the outbuilding when William stopped abruptly. His heart plummeted. Haydn faded into despair.

Two stable hands sat on stumps near the doors, a lantern at their feet.

His father had anticipated his flight because he'd stupidly announced his plan to leave. If his father couldn't hobble him, he could at least deny him a horse, so many miles from town and many more to London.

What would he do now without a horse?

"Master Snopes?"

A familiar voice with an Irish brogue startled him. William looked about.

The bearded stable master stood beneath a tree, thick hair rising with the gusts of wind, hands grasping the reins of William's favorite bay, already saddled.

William went to him.

"Forgive me, lad," the stable master said, "but I was about on the grounds and overheard the row. You were very clear with your da about your intentions, and knowin' your father's likely desire not to aid you, I thought I'd sneak Delilah here out of her stall in case you be needin' her again tonight. She's fed and rested."

William's heart picked up a beat of hope. "It's dangerous for you to help me, Aeron."

Aeron shrugged. "Danger and the Irish are old chums. Besides, I'm responsible, aren't I? Sendin' you word about Mary and all?"

"I'm glad you did. I needed to know."

The stable master frowned. "Well, surely someone needed to know. But havin' fueled your fight with your da, I need to ask if you're sure about this, son. It's a hard world. Tough as it is doin' your father's biddin', it'd be a much easier path than the one you're considerin'. And I heard the curse by which your da told you that you'd never have his support again if you left."

"Mary Blengen's condition didn't do this. This had to happen anyway."

"Maybe so, Master William, but you can still be a barrister without leavin' in this fashion. There's no shame in turnin' back. I can slip Delilah back into the stable in the mornin' if you choose, with none the wiser."

"I'm going," William declared.

Aeron nodded, a sign of approval—maybe even pride. He held out to William a cloth bag. "If you're certain, then here's a roll with food and a few crowns. I'll be bettin' you snuck out with little more than a change of clothes, didn't you, sir?"

"I can't take your money, Aeron."

"You can and you will. If you're wise, you'll use it to finish school. And when you get to London, there's a priest who can help you make your way. Father Thomas at St. Stephen's Church. Not my cup of tea, mind you—an Anglican—but I come to know him in Belfast. For a soul not respectin' the pope, he's still solid as oak."

It was all suddenly overwhelming, dizzying even. The pulsing pain and the weight of what he was about to do.

"I'll help you when I can, Aeron. You know that."

The stable master nodded. "Sure you will. Now be gettin' along before you change your mind again. And since you're so determined now, I'll admit that I thought you should've done this last year, after your dear ma died."

"I won't forget this."

"Just make somethin' good out of your life, boy," Aeron replied, shaking his hand. "It's a thing easier said than done in this world."

Feeling hollow, William hoisted himself into the saddle. With a last farewell, he turned the bay to ride down a slope toward a grove and the back trail that would take him to the road.

Before he entered the trees, William slowed and looked back. The candles of his father's study still burned faintly. He thought of his father there, bent over the estate books, putting William and any other distraction out of his mind. Still certain he ruled the world.

A trace of bloody phlegm had gathered in his mouth. William spat it to the ground and turned the bay away.

He rode off, the hollowness relenting a little as he heard again the call of the C trumpets of Haydn's symphony rising gracefully toward its percussive climax and triumphant timpani roll.

A Winter's Evening

FEBRUARY 1818

MIDDLESEX DISTRICT
LONDON

In evening fog, thirty-eight-year-old William Snopes, barrister, strode up the quiet street to Clerkenwell Green. His tall top hat, the closest thing to current fashion he permitted himself, fit snugly, preventing the cool air from touching his forehead. He walked quickly, as was his habit, sometimes silently counting his steps or humming a tune while crossing a bridge or square to keep his mind from running too far or fast ahead.

The Middlesex Courthouse loomed ahead through the mist. How long had it been? Two months since he'd last been here, at the previous court session. As he approached the edifice, he admired once more its Greek pillars, arched windows, and unmistakable gravitas. Trial would start here in a week. The thought of it—the anticipation—sent a foot tapping out the rhythm of a Strauss waltz he'd heard at Green Park the previous fall.

It was good to visit the courthouse before the press of trial preparation made it difficult or impossible. It mattered not the case or even the chance of success. A visit steadied his mood, as usual a mix of defiant optimism and excitement. As Edmund, his junior, had reminded him, their defense was shaky, their client's demeanor a mixed blessing, and William's plan for the day's evidence risky. But they'd done all they could. The rest was up to the judge, divine Providence, and the fortunes of luck in the jury they drew.

He reached out a hand to the courthouse façade to touch the cold, moist flagstone.

"I'll be back soon, Middlesex," he said softly. "Treat me kindly."

He turned about and headed home.

The Strauss piece measured his long strides all the way back.

THE ROYAL RESIDENCE, CARLTON HOUSE
LONDON

A slender girl with midnight-black hair walked the unlit halls of Carlton House, the royal residence of King George III and his son, Prince Regent George Augustus Frederick. Its cavernous splendor was subdued in the dark of early morning. Head down, the girl passed through the quiet grand dining hall to the kitchen, crept past stacked pans and pots awaiting the coming day, walked silently down a hallway to the rear of the residence, and finally stepped out a back door into the cold, mist-speckled moonlight of London.

She strode through the chill for the few yards necessary to reach and take the steps leading into St. James's Park. Through grounds crisp from winter frost and guarded by tall rigid pines, she hurried on to a dormant flower bed covered with snow. Halting there in the silence, her limbs began to quake.

"*Here, love,*" a high voice hissed behind her.

A man stood amid a stand of birch. His right eye drooped nearly onto his cheek. His mouth displayed a white-toothed grin that reflected the moonlight. He crooked a finger to summon her, and she reluctantly obeyed.

"The papers?" he demanded.

She untied her bodice to remove a sheaf of pages to hand to him.

"Mmm, still warm." The man's grin broadened as he stepped forward. "Come, my love. It's such unnatural cold for the season. Give us a kiss to warm us."

"Stay away, Lonny," she said and pushed him back.

His brow furrowed. "Ah now, Isabella, you don't wanna be bitin' the hand that feeds you. Don't be forgettin' who got you your job and what you owe for it, missy. Has it slipped your mind that these are hard times? Hard times that don't know favorites? Why, I could tell you stories about even the flouncy upper-crusters who dress like sheikhs but haven't a spare shillin' for hay for their horses—drained by the king's taxes these past twenty years. You should be thankin' me every day for the position I got you! Livin' and workin' amid the lucky ones that never miss a meal."

"Sure," Isabella said, shivering again. "So I could steal from them."

Lonny clucked his tongue. "Is that what's botherin' you now? A bit of conscience? Shall we bring you back home to the streets, then? Is that what you'd prefer?"

Isabella's stomach tightened, and she shook her head. "I did what you asked, Lonny. I brought you your papers. Are we done now?"

"We're done, my love." He laughed. "Go on home to your royals."

She hurried off.

Lonny's grin disappeared. He drew a length of rope from a pocket, sliding the papers into a cloth bag that he tied about his waist beneath his coat. Then he turned in the direction away from the retreating girl.

His own chilly meandering passed through places alive with London's nighttime plunderers, drunks, and lost ones. Some recognized and avoided Lonny, while others gave him a frosty glance of disinterest and dismissal. Two hours followed, through back streets ghostly and quiet, sleeping markets and jagged alleys, over the Thames bridges and back again, alternating between smells of fetid decay in neighborhoods dark and narrow to the clean woodsmoke rising from town homes glowing with gaslights.

Finally, he circled back to the riverbank once more to stop at the base of the towering London Bridge. It took a moment to spot the young boy who awaited him, standing in the shadows. Lonny neared, pleased at the fear in the boy's eyes. Untying the bag, Lonny passed it on.

"Get along now, Tad, my boy," Lonny growled. "Don't dawdle, but don't cut it short. Do all of your route to be sure no one's followin', then get to the office and leave the package or you'll pay for my disappointment."

Tad nodded nervously. He slid the bag beneath his coat and hurried away.

Crossing the bridge's span over black swirling waters, Tad rushed through broad streets in the sleepiest hours of the night. Avoiding the rabbit warrens and narrower alleys where a young boy like himself might be robbed or worse, he passed Westminster Cathedral, then St. Paul's. Fog crept close. For a time, before dawn rose, Tad was forced to stay an arm's length from shop windows dismembered by the mist to keep to his route.

Early sun flowed red through cracks in the fog as Tad rounded a final corner to his destination: a fine Mayfair neighborhood with newer brick town homes and shops. The outer door to the finest building—two stories high, its stoop freshly washed—was unlocked. Tad pushed inside, padding up the stairs to a door, the sign on the door declaring in bold paint, *Mandy Bristol, Solicitor.* Removing the papers from the bag, Tad slid them with a push beneath the door, then knelt down and peered with one eye to be sure they couldn't be retrieved.

He sat up, heaving a sigh. He'd done his job. No beating should await him when he returned to Lonny in Whitechapel. Only twenty shillings, a pat on the head, and a shove out the door to get to his usual day.

He spat on the wooden floor and rubbed his stomach in thanks for his good luck.

Then he stood and returned to the streets that were his home.

ON THE THAMES
PORT OF LONDON

Captain Harold Tuttle unwrapped the scrolled paper at his sea desk and read in the fitful light of a candle. Only a single piece of paper and yet it was capable of extraordinary might. Just ink and parchment, but with the seal of the English Crown, a source of power for a captain of only thirty-three years to act with the authority of the greatest empire on earth.

Such was a Letter of Marque.

Harold set the Letter down. Out the stern cabin windows of the *Padget*, the harbor waters rippled as the ship edged toward the London dock to the rhythmic tugs of the oarsmen off the bow. The midnight moon split the Thames into streaky lines that ducked and weaved amid the crowd of scows, schooners, brigs, and warships docked or anchored on the river. The scents and sounds of London grew stronger the nearer the *Padget* drew to the quay: the waste of the city floating in the river, tempered by sweet sawdust of lumber cut for ship repairs; the bodies of sleeping sailors packed on the anchored boats they passed; the lapping of waves; the howl of a dog; the angry voice that shouted it down.

It was good to be home. In hours—at most a few days—he'd be back with his Rebekah. This time, on bended knee.

Harold locked the Letter of Marque away in his cabinet, pocketed the key in his trousers, and went up on deck.

Quint Ivars, the first mate and ship's physician, was at midship watching the landing. Harold patted his shoulder.

"Ready for dry land, Mr. Ivars?"

"Aye, Captain." The first mate smiled. "A year and three months is a long time to be away."

"It could have been much longer. You served under Admiral Jervis in the Royal Navy. Surely you were out longer than this under his command?"

"No, sir. All Atlantic duty. The longest time at sea was eight months, sir."

"Then you'll be as glad as me to get ashore."

"Aye, Captain. That's for sure."

Ivars's service under the esteemed Admiral Jervis—a demanding taskmaster who ran a tight fleet—was part of what had attracted Harold to the man. His first mate was no complainer.

Still, he heard in the man's words an undeniable echo of the misery of their first year on the voyage now ending. Down the coast of Africa, nearly foundering around the Cape, circling impatiently in the Indian Sea in fickle winds. The Letter of Marque was powerful but without purpose if they couldn't find what they were seeking: a fat French merchantman subject to the authority granted by the British Crown. Whole months had passed in search of such a prize, until every officer and crew member had resolved themselves to the likelihood of returning to London empty-handed.

Then arrived that blessed day when the French ship came sailing out of the fog in the wake of a typhoon off the coast of Ceylon, Atlantic bound, crammed like a Christmas goose with two hundred tons of Chinese tea and a mere ten twenty-pounders measured against the *Padget*'s twenty. She'd been taken without the loss of a single man on either ship, and the *Padget* had at last turned for home, the poor luck of their voyage behind them.

Harold drew himself to ramrod posture. This was no time to

recall the hardship, nor to let down the military standards that had kept the *Padget* shipshape throughout the voyage. Besides, all was well now. The investors would be celebrating soon; the crew would receive their shares.

His own sweet love, Rebekah, would receive his proposal.

"When shall I tell the lads they can go ashore?" Quint asked.

"After we're unloaded and the cargo safe—not a minute before," Harold commanded. "Make sure that's *very clear*. The share of any crew member who disobeys that order is subject to forfeiture. Prepare them to wait two days at least." He hesitated. "To soften the blow, I'll arrange for fresh food and some rum to be brought aboard."

"The wait will be torture, sir. But the rum will be appreciated. I'll pass the word."

Torture? Maybe. But they wouldn't leave the ship unmanned until its hold was empty and the tea stored safely ashore, in the warehouse of a consignment merchant. *"Never furl a single sail until the last enemy ship is out of sight or beneath the waves,"* his last commander had warned repeatedly. He'd been right.

Harold was scanning the wharf when someone brushed his side. He looked down.

A boy had appeared, hair so white he looked like a candle in the night.

"Going ashore, sir?" the boy asked. "Won't you be wanting your pistol?"

Harold patted the boy's head. "Yes, young Simon Ladner. I'd say that's a good idea for anyone walking in London this time of night. Get it for me. Loaded. And be quick about it."

The towing boats slid the *Padget* into berth with the ease and skill of a salty crew. A few others of the crew began wrestling the gangway into place, knowing the captain was departing. The oily dock shimmered in the moonlight; the wharf lay silent with the late hour. Harold rubbed moisture from his hands in the briny air.

He sensed a presence at his side again and looked down.

Simon had returned, pistol in hand.

"Loaded, Simon?" Harold asked sternly.

"Aye, Captain."

"Good boy." Harold grunted and took it. "When I return from shore, I'll bring some peppermints. And if you keep to your duties, Simon, you'll be the first ashore to greet your father."

Simon smiled as Harold took the pistol.

A light creased the night, followed instantly by the explosion of a gunshot from ashore.

Harold reacted instinctively, dropping behind the gunwale and pulling the boy after as the zing of a ball cried out. As he dropped, the pistol, barely in Harold's grasp, clattered uselessly to the deck in his surprise.

His pulse thundered in his ears as he looked frantically about. The small crew on deck, unprepared and unarmed, had hit the deck for safety as well. Harold glanced at Quint, who lay prone only a few feet away, eyes wide.

"Cease firing!" a voice cried from the darkness ashore. "*Cease firing!*"

Harold edged an eye over the gunwale.

Shadows about a warehouse just beyond the *Padget* had parted, and figures were emerging. Several wore constable uniforms with the band of an arresting party on their forearms. With them marched half a dozen soldiers in scarlet tunics, flintlocks in their hands.

Harold reached out and took up his pistol from the deck.

"Shall I call the crew to arms?" Quint hissed low, glancing about.

"In London Harbor?" Harold exclaimed. "This isn't rotting Calcutta. Can't you see? These are constables and soldiers of a king's regiment."

The squad of men onshore had reached the end of the gangplank and were coming aboard.

"Oh, Captain!" Quint's voice broke into Harold's raging thoughts. "Simon!"

Harold looked to his side.

The boy was crumpled in a ball, blood leaking through his tunic, forming a black circle at his chest.

Harold reached to raise him, but Quint had already crossed to lift the boy up, cradling him in his arms.

A sheriff appeared at the top of the gangway, leading the rest of the party.

Setting the pistol back on the deck, Harold stood to confront him. "Why did you fire?" he cried out. "You've shot him!"

The sheriff took in the sight.

"Sergeant Rhodes," he said over his shoulder to one of the soldiers. "See what you can do for the boy."

"No! Our Mr. Ivars here serves as ship's doctor. He'll take him belowdeck."

The sheriff hesitated, then nodded his assent. The first mate hurried away with the boy.

"Are you Harold Tuttle?" the sheriff demanded.

"*Captain* Harold Tuttle. Are you insane? Firing at my crew? Boarding without permission? What is the meaning of this?"

"I gave no order to fire. But I saw myself that you were holding a weapon. And the meaning of this, Captain Tuttle, is that we were ordered to arrest you and your crew for piracy."

The night had descended into madness. "Piracy? That's absurd."

"Did you take the brig the *Charlemagne*, September last? A French tea merchant in the Indian Sea?"

"Yes. Under authority of the Crown. I hold a Letter of Marque."

"Every smuggler and pirate pleads the Crown's assent."

"It's true. We were given authority to take French smugglers. I was empowered to harass any French tea brigs I found in the region."

The sheriff shook his head. "Show us this letter, Captain."

"I want to see after the boy first."

"Later. I'll see that letter now."

It was a terrible thing, taking orders from this man. But Harold reluctantly led the walk to his cabin, each step a hollow wooden echo threatening the satisfaction he'd known only minutes before. The ship about him grew stiff and quiet as he marched, the deck crew watching in bewildered silence.

In his cabin, Harold could hardly light a candle, his hand shook so with a smoldering rage. As the shadows receded, he drew the key from his pocket.

The drawer unlocked. He pulled it open.

It was empty.

Impossible.

"It was here!" he shouted. "I read it only minutes ago!"

The sheriff's men gripped Harold's arms.

"Wait," he said with bewildered despair. "Wait, please. This is all some terrible mistake. The Crown will confirm my letter. And you needn't arrest my crew. They only followed my orders."

The sheriff raised his chin with an air of indifference. "That's unfortunate," he answered. "Because it appears that your orders have led them all to the gallows."

There was a scuffle. A voice called out from the steps to the main deck—Quint Ivars's voice.

"That's my first mate," Harold called.

"Let him through," the sheriff said.

As he stepped into the captain's quarters, Quint's face was the pallor of the yellow moon, shining low through the stern windows.

"Captain," he said in a strangled voice, "the boy Simon . . . he's dead."

2

MIDDLESEX SESSIONS
MIDDLESEX COURTHOUSE
LONDON

Still several blocks from the courthouse, young Edmund Shaw, barrister, clutched his cloth bag with one hand and impatiently pulled up his collar against the cold drizzling rain with the other. The royal carriage, following in the wake of a mounted guard, was passing slowing by, impeding Edmund's journey across the street. Edmund caught a glimpse through the carriage window of portly Prince Regent George, wrapped in a deep-blue robe, staring disinterestedly out at his subjects. Some of those subjects rewarded his gaze with stares of their own. Several even stretched for a better glimpse.

Edmund would have none of the exchange. The prince regent was a fat fop of a man. Likely en route to see one of his mistresses. A Whig by politics, Edmund had little love for the throne regardless of who occupied it. But he was particularly disdainful of *this* man. At least the regent's father, King George III, had made an effort at ruling before insanity struck him down. His son, the next King George, now having ruled in his mad father's stead for seven years, spent his time and the country's money on new palaces, balls, finery, and actresses—while the poor were an ocean about him.

"A pox on the lot of them," Edmund said aloud.

The carriage and guard were past. Edmund hurried across the street, sidestepping muddy puddles and worse. A few blocks along and the Middlesex Courthouse loomed. Edmund rushed inside.

Catching his breath, he looked about the high-ceilinged court-room, packed tight and warm against the cool air outside. Like a freshly heated griddle, its occupants released a menagerie of smells: sweet-spice merchants, pungent horse traders, earthy tea sellers, gently perfumed ladies. All gathered for a day's entertain-ment at the quarterly docket of civil and criminal charges. Includ-ing the criminal trial of the gypsy tinkerer now sitting in the dock, the elevated space reserved for defendants. To Edmund's eyes, their client appeared as lonely as a solitary pawn on a chessboard.

Edmund removed his wet overcoat and made his way through the swinging door of the bar to take a seat beside his boss and mentor at counsel table, where he placed his bag beneath the table.

Focused on the proceedings, senior defense counsel William Snopes barely registered the arrival of his junior, Edmund, as the young barrister took his seat at William's elbow. William wore the oldest gown and wig in the courtroom—the latter a mop that splayed horsehair strands like a nest of overturned spiders, while Edmund's was as new and neat as his certificate of passage of the bar.

The senior counsel took to his feet "Objection, my lord," Wil-liam intoned.

Judge Plessing looked to the barrister. "Objection, Mr. Snopes?"

William nodded. "That is the case, my lord."

The judge leaned back, easing the pressure on an ample stomach. "And what, pray tell, was objectionable about your opponent's question?"

"His question assumed the guilt of my client, your lordship."

The judge leaned forward and smiled. "As does everyone in the courtroom, Mr. Snopes."

The gallery burst into laughter. Avoiding playing the brunt of the joke, William joined in with a light laugh of his own.

"Of course, my lord," he replied when quiet returned. "But may I ask the court's indulgence until the matter of guilt has been settled to the satisfaction of the jury?"

"Yes, yes," the judge replied. William smiled, hoping that he'd blunted the judge and jury's prejudices for the moment.

The magistrate pointed to their opponent. "Prosecution counsel, Mr. Periwinkle, shall refrain from assuming the guilt of the accused by the nature of his question."

The cross-examination of their client, young tinkerer Patrin Cooper, went on. It was a grand torture, being forced to listen while sitting there stone-faced, appearing unconcerned for the jury's sake. Excruciating. His junior, Edmund, was barely able to contain himself as the prosecutor, old Lawrence Periwinkle, far past the prime of a modest career and clearly the worse for "lunch" at the pub, had a field day with his cross-examination of Patrin.

"So then, you left your wagon and went into the chemist's shop, correct?" Periwinkle articulated with only the slightest slur.

"Aye. I needed a bit of poppy for my wife's headaches."

"And your accusor, Master Tenbome, was already in the chemist's shop?"

"Aye."

"And Master Tenbome's wagon, with his cache of goods bound for his London warehouse, was parked outside the chemist's place of business."

"I saw it, yes."

"And Mr. Tenbome greeted you in the chemist's, correct?"

"Yes."

"And he let you make your purchase while he awaited his—that's a correct statement of the facts, is it not?"

"Aye."

"Then you left the chemist's."

"Aye."

Periwinkle leaned across his table to level a malevolent gaze at Patrin. "And on your way back to your wagon, you *lifted* from the Tenbome wagon a case containing Chinese figurines and placed it in your wagon, didn't you, sir."

"No, sir. I did nothing of the sort, sir."

"Was there anyone else in the street when you exited the chemist's?"

"No one I saw."

"But you heard Mr. Tenbome's testimony today that he saw you, through the shop window, busy yourself at his wagon before going to your own."

"Aye. I saw that a case was sliding out from under the straps and so pushed it back onto the bed of Mr. Tenbome's wagon. That was all."

"The case with the Chinese figurines, Mr. Cooper? The one that was missing by the time Mr. Tenbome returned to his wagon?"

"No. I mean, I don't know. I didn't look in it."

Eight pound and six. That was the value Tenbome had placed on the stolen goods. Not enough to warrant a hanging, but enough to transport their client aboard a pestilent ship to Australia for the rest of his days. William glanced at their client's mother and wife, seated, pale-faced, in the front row of a gallery that had grown quiet with the testimony. He scanned the rest of the crowd. A woman who was covered completely but for her eyes. A sailor with a smoking pipe clenched between his teeth. The local parish priest and his friend, Father Thomas, sitting solemn and still. Was this only entertainment for the lot of them? Did they appreciate or care about the consequences hanging in the balance?

"You are a gypsy, are you not, Mr. Cooper?" Periwinkle inquired. Their client hesitated. "I am."

"I see the brand on your thumb. Thievery?"

"I was fourteen."

"Thievery?"

"Aye. But never again. My mother and wife'll tell you I'm clean as a lady's kerchief, and 'ave been since that day. I didn't take that man's goods—"

"Mr. Periwinkle," the judge interrupted. "Can we move this along?"

The prosecutor nodded graciously. "Of course, your lordship. I've nothing further for the accused."

The justice of the peace presiding, Magistrate Alfred Plessing, settled back in his chair, waving a hand toward William.

Judge Plessing was not a bad man. His manor lay just a few miles west of London. William knew for a fact that he was good to his people, to the village that relied upon him, to the local parson of his diocese. He did his duty as a magistrate each quarter, prodding justice along at a reasonable and measured pace. But he was no scholar of the law, nor master of his own biases. And William could see that he'd already lost patience with this proceeding, with two more cases scheduled for the jury yet that afternoon.

"I've no questions at this time," William called.

"I call as my final witness Mr. Keyes," the prosecutor declared.

The most critical witness was now taking the witness box. William glanced at Edmund, seeing a trickle of sweat trace a trail along his temple. William looked to the gallery, where the managing solicitor of the case and Edmund's close friend, Obadiah Cummings, was seated. The solicitor returned William's nod with a hopeful shrug.

Edmund leaned to William's ear, thrusting his nose amid the wig fibers. "Are you sure of this strategy, Mr. Snopes?" he asked.

William looked back at him with widened eyes. "Am I sure? Of course I'm not sure. This is a trial, not a mathematical equation."

Edmund heaved a breath and nodded.

"And you've got the goods?" William asked in return.

Edmund gestured toward the bag on the floor.

"Good."

William rose. "My lord," he called, "I wonder if we may approach the bench?"

The judge looked perturbed but nodded his assent. Edmund followed in William's wake, joining Periwinkle beside the raised table where the judge presided.

"My lord," William began, leaning in at a whisper, "I understand that Mr. Periwinkle intends to call an eyewitness to the theft. A Mr. Daniel Keyes."

"That's correct, my lord," Periwinkle acknowledged, the fumes of his lunch at the pub dominating the air about them. "He will unequivocally identify this Mr. Cooper as the thief."

"Given the importance of this testimony," William replied, "I request that my client be permitted to leave the dock and sit at counsel table. Just for the short time needed to consult with him regarding Mr. Keyes's testimony. It would, I believe, save time from me seeking an adjournment to confer before my examination of this witness."

The magistrate shook his head. "Highly irregular, Mr. Snopes. Highly irregular."

Periwinkle raised a confident eyebrow. "Ah, but your lordship, I have no objection."

The judge looked them all over. "Well then. So be it. Your client may join you at counsel table, Mr. Snopes—only for the duration of this witness, mind you."

"That is very gracious, Mr. Periwinkle," William said. "Thank you, my lord."

They returned to their seats at counsel table. Young Patrin Cooper left the dock and moved to join them as Periwinkle called out again, "The prosecution calls Daniel Keyes to testify."

It took no more than several ticks of the ancient clock hanging above the jurors for the new witness to appear from a side door. But in those few moments, Edmund stood, ushering their client into the seat beside William, then seated himself two chairs farther away. In that same instant, Edmund procured a well-groomed horsehair wig, identical to his own, from the cloth bag beneath the table and placed it on Patrin's head.

Periwinkle, focused on the new witness in the box, took no notice.

"Mr. Keyes," Periwinkle addressed the new witness. "You are a hostler, are you not? You care for horses at the Inn of Grey Gables near the chemist's shop?"

The witness coughed to clear his throat, then thrust his chest out importantly. "I do indeed, master."

"Were you at your job the day there was a theft of goods in front of the chemist's shop last month?"

"Aye."

"And what did you see?"

"I saw a man come out of the chemist's and reach in and take a wooden crate from a large wagon there—plain as can be. Then he put it on another wagon, got aboard, and drove away."

"Very well. And is that man seated at counsel table?" Periwinkle waved an arm in the direction of defense counsel. "With Mr. Snopes?"

"Aye, plain as can be."

"Thank you. Nothing further."

William rose instantly to his feet. "Which one, Mr. Keyes?"

The witness stiffened. "Which one what?"

"Which one? Which of the gentlemen seated at my table was the perpetrator of the theft?"

Periwinkle's eyes shifted to the table, where Edmund had now slid off his robe, resting it behind Patrin's chair.

"Why, I object!" Periwinkle shouted, seeing the three wigged men.

The magistrate stared across the room, taking in the sight.

"This is most inappropriate, Mr. Snopes," the judge bellowed. "You've cloaked the accused as a barrister."

"My lordship, I cannot see why that would offend. While a barrister must be properly wigged in the courtroom, I know of no admonition against a party wearing such a wig as well."

"But you're clearly attempting to confuse this witness."

"Not at all, your lordship. I'm simply trying to determine whether this witness—*critical to the prosecution*—really knows who he is accusing of the serious crime of theft."

The magistrate hesitated.

"Mr. Plessing, this is simply not done!" Periwinkle objected.

The judge's eyes shifted to sear the prosecutor like hot coals.

"I am *Justice Plessing* today, *Mr. Periwinkle*. Or *your lordship*. However you might address me at a club or at a card game, you will kindly not forget to address me appropriately in this setting."

"Your lordship," William chimed in. "Perhaps a compromise might be agreed upon. What if you were to direct both the accused and my assistant to stand and remove their wigs. That would provide Mr. Keyes a fair chance to view them as he would have seen the culprit that afternoon."

Perhaps he wouldn't have agreed minutes before. Now Judge Plessing contemplated the room like a circling hawk, his nasal breaths filling an expectant silence in the gallery that a parson would have envied.

"Very well," the magistrate said. "The two gentlemen at defense table besides Mr. Snopes will stand and remove their wigs."

Edmund and Patrin were nearly the same height, but as Edmund rose, he crouched just a bit where he stood, still several chairs down from William. His hair beneath his wig was deliberately grown out and cut ragged, while their client's was coiffed and oiled. Patrin's shirt was finely pressed and spotless; Edmund's, now fully revealed, carried stains of several meals.

"Why, it's him." Keyes squinted. "Surely as the sun rose this morning!" He extended a finger pointed directly at Edmund. "That man stole the other'ns goods from that wagon. I saw him with my own eyes. Plain as can be."

"This is unfair! This is an ambush!" Periwinkle cried out amid gasps and shouts from the gallery.

Leaning across their client to address Edmund, William allowed himself a small smile. "I believe that's the best summation I've ever heard old Periwinkle give," he said.

RED HOUND PUB
FOUR BLOCKS FROM THE MIDDLESEX COURTHOUSE

Edmund's stomach was coiled with frustration, his jaw tight, his fingers tapping a repeating rhythm on the table. Barrister Snopes glanced at him over a sip of beer. Solicitor Obadiah took them both in before opening his mouth to speak.

"It's not port, Mr. Snopes," Obadiah declared. "You're sipping it as though it were. Beer doesn't get better in small quantities. In fact, knowing the quality of the beer at this place, I'd venture the opposite is true. You'll be here tomorrow at this time if you keep at it that way."

"You and Edmund may drink your beer any way you wish, Solicitor," William Snopes replied. "It's a free country. But gulping beer has always seemed to me like swallowing without troubling to chew. Now leave me to my own preferences."

The table grew quiet.

"Edmund, you're unusually subdued," Snopes spoke up. "Disappointed with this afternoon's jury verdict against young Patrin?"

"I'm fine." Edmund smiled weakly, taking a draught of his own beer.

"Objection!" Snopes called. "This man is lying!" He grinned at

Edmund. "Don't be naïve about the outcome today. Our strategy proved very effective."

His pent-up dissatisfaction burst. "Effective? Truly? Mr. Snopes, they found Patrin *guilty*."

"And the good magistrate fined him when he could have transported him."

"But it was clear our client wasn't guilty."

"Was it?"

Edmund could hardly credit his ears. "Of course! You heard that Keyes witness. He had no idea who really took the figurines."

Snopes shrugged. "What of Mr. Tenbome's testimony about seeing our client stop at his wagon after he left the chemist's? Patrin admitted he'd done so—even that he'd placed his hands on a chest on the Tenbome wagon. Our client also admitted there was no one else near enough to take the goods."

Edmund stared at Mr. Snopes in shock.

"Sir, then you think Patrin was guilty?"

"No. The truth is, I'm not sure. Come on now, Edmund. I understand your disappointment. But you're twenty-three now, not fourteen—and a trained barrister. You must know by now that believing someone is innocent and being able to prove it to the satisfaction of a jury are not synonymous. Don't allow your belief in a client's innocence to cloud your judgment as to how hard it might be to prove it."

Though his chest ached, Edmund tried another smile, raising his beer in toast to his mentor and employer. "Of course, sir," he declared.

Except he wasn't disappointed. That was too small a word for it. Seeing that bloated excuse of a regent today on the street, thinking of all the toffs and scions of wealth in Parliament, only reminded him that the jury system was his last hope as an Englander. Now to lose a trial on such flimsy evidence threatened the collapse of even that tender faith.

He gulped another mouthful of beer.

"Anyway, the jurors couldn't possibly see the truth, Mr. Snopes," he burst out. "They were already biased against Patrin because he's a gypsy."

Obadiah, who seldom strayed from Edmund's side in an argument, nodded his agreement. "I'm with Edmund on this one, sir."

Mr. Snopes shrugged, unfazed.

"Of course they were biased! And don't forget that he'd been convicted as a *thief* as a young man! Did you think the jury would be unmoved by such things? You can't banish what people believe when they step into the jury box—nor can you afford to despise them for it. Our job isn't to save the jurors' eternal souls but to guide their hearts and minds on the precise matter of our client's guilt or innocence. Disdain for the jury will stink like sulfur, and the jury will sniff it and despise *you* and your client in turn. Who will wish to please someone with a congenial verdict if they believe that that someone holds them in contempt? If you want to win the jurors, Edmund, you must love them as children. Like children, they'll be inclined to reciprocate. If they love you enough, they may hesitate before displeasing you. Love. That's the bond that good barristers employ to sway jurors, Edmund. Now that you've completed your apprenticeship, you should know that."

"As you say, Mr. Snopes." Edmund nodded, silently refusing to agree.

"No, Edmund," Snopes continued. "Not as I say. As I have *observed*. And as for today, I had few illusions we could move this jury—yes, with all of its biases—to find young Patrin Cooper innocent. I'd hoped, however, that we could seed enough doubt in the mind of our fine Judge Plessing so that, if the jury found Patrin guilty, he would refrain from imposing the terrible sentence of transportation. As I told you at the outset, our magistrate today is, at heart, a good man. And that latter goal, young Edmund, we achieved."

Eight pounds six. The judge's fine was intended to match the value of the stolen goods. Snopes was right. That fine paled against the prospect of a life sentence after a voyage to the far side of the world.

Still, how did one compromise with injustice?

"It will take Patrin a year to save up so much money," he said.

"Far better than the alternative," Snopes rejoined. Then he reached into his pocket and withdrew a handful of coins. "Which reminds me. Here's your portion of the fee."

The pile of coins sat on the table for a long moment. Heart aching at his weakness, Edmund gathered them up and thrust them into a pocket.

"A better wage than Judas received," he muttered. Rising, he bumped and nearly overturned the table in his haste to go.

William watched Edmund's retreat in silence.

"He's unbending, Mr. Snopes," Obadiah said.

"You've been his friend longer than my acquaintance," William replied, disappointed. "Have you ever known him differently?"

"Never."

"Unbending in a very windy world. Passion and idealism are wonderful, until they drive their host mad. He'll break if he isn't careful."

"You know where it comes from, Mr. Snopes."

"Yes. Still I worry. Perhaps you should follow him."

"Not tonight," Obadiah said. "It's too fresh. I'd only annoy him further. But about those coins you've given Edmund and me, Mr. Snopes. Patrin told me that you refused any fee on his case."

Snopes shrugged. "So?"

"Paying us when you'll accept no fee is a generous act. You should tell Edmund. It might mollify him."

"And risk his turning it down in a proud gesture of his own? No. Refusing the fee was my decision. I won't have it impoverish you or Mr. Shaw."

"My wife and I thank you. Still, I believe you should've told Edmund—"

"Ah, Master William Snopes and one of his band of legal knights! Fresh from another joust in court!"

Startled, William turned.

A man had appeared at Obadiah's shoulder—a dark-haired priest, narrow-faced with resolute but not unkind eyes.

"We don't joust, Father Thomas," William answered. "Wrestle, perhaps. We grapple with the inscrutable truth. Yes, I prefer that metaphor."

The Anglican priest, Father Thomas Neal, went to the bar, returning with his own mug of beer.

"Take my seat," Obadiah said, standing. "I've got to be getting home. Suzie promised pigeon and kidney beans tonight, along with a mince pie."

"Don't blame you a bit," William said.

"Mr. Snopes." Obadiah addressed the barrister once more. "It was good work today. Edmund will come around to see it."

"Thank you, Solicitor. Now enjoy an evening of rest. And my best to Suzanne."

The priest sat silently at William's elbow, working at his beer as the pub grew louder with the deepening evening. The tall fire molded wavering shadows about the patrons that filled the space.

William waited until it was clear that the priest wouldn't launch his point without an invitation.

"So, what did you think about the trial today?" he asked at last.

Appearing relieved, the priest looked to William. "I believe you should be looking after your charge's spiritual life."

"There it is! I was curious what your lecture points would be today."

"Edmund's path was dark enough for many years."

"Edmund's a brilliant young man. He'll work out his own eternity, thank you. I'm certain with your fine help."

"William, you may have chosen a spiritual desert for a career, but you should steer Edmund away from your profession while you still can. Before its inherent contradictions break him. At least shelter him from the *methods* you employ. He would listen. The boy looks up to you."

"As I said. A brilliant young man."

"I'm serious. Your profession is fraught with danger, William. Trying to help the guilty go free can damage a soul."

"So you've said on many occasions. And I respond the same: everyone deserves a defense."

"Yes. But Barrister William Snopes goes beyond just delivering a defense, and you know it."

"Why so serious, Father? When I saw you in the gallery today, I knew I was in for a verbal lashing. You clearly thought young Patrin was guilty. Well, he was found guilty. You should be satisfied."

"You nearly achieved a finding of innocence."

"Nearly so. As I've told you before, my friend, innocence is a relative thing in the world of law—highly dependent on the prisms through which jurors view their own lives, and the quantity of hard work and skill a barrister applies to achieve it."

"That's not correct. Innocence isn't achieved and it isn't relative. Your client either did the deed or didn't. It's an objective fact."

"Yes, but one known with certainty only to God, who has ignored my every request to take the witness stand. In this fallen world, innocence is what the jury or judge says it is. It is our difficult task to help them see the matter as clearly as possible."

"You mean favorably to your clients."

"Of course."

"Sinners are sinners, no matter your skill in achieving a wrongful verdict."

"Yes, our clients are sinners in a fallen world—as are we. Yet doesn't our Lord Jesus defend us before our Father despite our guilt?"

"Don't twist Scripture to suit your purpose, William. It's not the same, and it's beneath you to contend it is. And please, please don't compare yourself to the Christ. At least not when I'm raising a mug within earshot."

William smiled, taking another sip. "Fair enough. I suppose your lecture came with some Scripture for me to contemplate as usual? Come on now. Out with it. Then we both can enjoy our beers in relative peace."

Edmund left the pub, walking for over an hour through a chill mist; ambling beyond the shops and dwellings that welcomed the barristers of Middlesex Court until he reached the darker corners of London. Seeing Patrin's trial, where his client had so little chance of true justice, Edmund wanted to take satisfaction from Mr. Snope's explanations. Instead, his mentor's words flowed over him tonight like polluted water.

Snopes was a good man. A very good man. But he hadn't spent two years in a debtors' prison, languishing there as his parents passed away; hadn't spent six years in a boys' home, working alongside street gangs like an indentured slave, as he and Obadiah had. If he'd had a lick of that kind of life, he'd be just as impatient as he and Obadiah were with the idea of half justice.

Edmund spat on the ground.

No conscious decision guided him after leaving the Red Hound Pub. Awash in disappointment at the day's verdict, his feet chose the familiar direction he traveled. Going to the place of sweet release of mind and spirit.

An alley opened before him. He muttered a vague and ineffectual protest to himself, then continued.

At the end of the alley was a door pitted and thick as a castle wall. He raised a fist and knocked.

A hole opened, and two eyes appeared. "Mr. Shaw?"

"Yes."

"You're outta credit, Mr. Shaw."

"I've money."

"Let's see it."

Hating himself, Edmund dug into his pocket, raising a fist of coins.

Metal latches slammed back and the door groaned inward.

Past the stubble-faced doorman, Edmund saw pipe smoke smothering the candlelight on chandeliers over men at tables or along a bar in the far corner.

Edmund looked about. "Tables for brag tonight?" he asked.

"Aye," the door steward answered. "Those two card tables on your left. If you like, four to penny's over there. Good games of dice in the corner."

A ripple of anticipation smothered his last hesitation. Edmund took a step into the room.

Thick fingers curled about his wrist. "You'll be needin' to bring yourself flush in the back first, Mr. Shaw," the steward said.

Edmund shook off the grip. "All right," he muttered.

The door slammed tight behind him. Edmund weaved through the crowded room to the back, expectancy and the heat of the fireplace already raising perspiration on his forehead.

BROOKING STREET
LONDON

Trudging home from the Red Hound Pub, Obadiah Cummings tugged up his coat collar. The freezing drizzle transformed cobblestones into quivering reflections of the gaslights overhead. Puffs of wind shook tree branches, setting loose more frigid showers.

Cold and hungry as he was, it seemed to the solicitor a perfect and typical winter evening for London.

But then, he cheered himself, it had been a good day at court, showing the best and worst of English justice. How fortunate he was to serve as a solicitor in such an age of broadening minds and stunning change. A period of revolution in thinking and practice. Twenty years ago, a victim of a crime would have no representation at all, nor likely the assistance of the courts—unless he or she could afford to pay a constable to arrest the suspect and try them. It was the same with defendants charged with a crime, who were unlikely to enjoy any representation at all. Now a barrister of William Snopes's skill could protect a young man from the horror of transportation. And, Obadiah reminded himself, another young boy, an orphan destined for a life on the streets, could instead rise to the rank of solicitor and win the hand of a fine woman like Suzie.

Buoyed, Obadiah's thoughts returned to Suzie's promised meal. With lengthened strides, he crossed an empty road. On the far side, the walk was blocked for street work so he retreated into the street.

His foot dropped into a puddle, rising above his ankle.

"For the love of . . . !" he exclaimed.

In that instant, a carriage passed, pulled by a single horse, the wheels whipping a cold, filthy spray across Obadiah's back and neck.

Another curse crossed his lips.

"Whoa!" came a high voice ahead. Obadiah froze.

To his surprise, the coach had slowed to halt only a few yards farther along. A gloved hand waved from the carriage window.

"Mr. Cummings?" It was a woman's voice, calling again. "Mr. Cummings? May I speak with you?"

The voice was unfamiliar. Obadiah approached carefully, stopping before the window.

It was a four-seat family coach, old and in desperate need of paint. Its family crest was worn nearly invisible with age. Its driver, as ancient as the coach, gave Obadiah only the briefest glance from his perch.

"Please get in, Mr. Cummings," the woman said through the window.

"Begging your pardon, ma'am? You say you want me to get into your carriage?"

"Yes. We'll drive you home. It's a miserable evening, and the driver knows the way. In fact, we were given directions by the clerk of court and were en route there just now. Please get in. I need to discuss some urgent business with you."

Such a long day it had been. A long week, helping Mr. Snopes prepare for trial. A small hearth fire and Suzie's fine cooking awaited him. A quicker journey was welcome. It was a bold and odd gesture, but Obadiah nodded his head and grabbed the pull to go aboard.

The carriage lurched off. The lady watched Obadiah as he shifted uncomfortably in his seat, producing a *squelch* from his waterlogged boot.

He looked up and made an effort to smile at her.

The lady wore a clean but outdated hat and scarf, hiding all but her eyes, which were sharp and clear and hinting of youth, concealed by her cloth-muffled voice. She sat straight-backed yet relaxed—in Obadiah's experience, a trick mastered only by the upper classes. Otherwise, he could glean nothing of her. Except that she also looked strangely familiar.

Then the covering of her face reminded him.

"I saw you in the gallery at the trial today," Obadiah said.

"Yes. I've been attending the Middlesex trials the past week, looking for a barrister. Someone in the gallery told me that you're the solicitor who refers work to barristers William Snopes and Edmund Shaw."

Obadiah nodded. "I make such referrals, yes. But Messrs. Snopes and Shaw are not tied only to work I send them. Perhaps you aren't familiar with the legal professions, miss. Solicitors such as myself prepare contracts, form corporations, draft wills and trusts—all manner of work requiring legal drafting skills. The sole work we do not perform is in the courtroom. Trying cases and appearing before judges and magistrates is the exclusive realm of barristers. Solicitors refer such work to the barristers of our choice, but for their part, Messrs. Snopes and Shaw are free to accept case referrals from any solicitor who sends it to them."

"I'm fully aware of the English legal system," the young lady answered curtly—just as the carriage rocked hard on the cobblestones, displaying the full extent of its failing shocks. "But tell me: does Mr. Snopes tend to socialize in the upper circles?"

It was an odd question. "What do you mean?"

"Well, my research indicates that Mr. Snopes's father is Lord Kyle Snopes. Does that mean Mr. Snopes mixes in upper society?"

Obadiah fidgeted in his seat. "Mr. Snopes is not . . . closely associated with his father."

The lady nodded. "I see. But these are, as you know, hard times. Jobs are scarce, taxes and tariffs high. Surely it would be much easier for Mr. Snopes to prosper as a barrister if he were ingratiated to those in upper society."

Where was she going with this?

"What I might know of Mr. Snopes's personal life is not for public consumption."

She nodded again. "Commendable. But answer this: Messrs. Snopes and Shaw may be permitted to accept cases from other solicitors, but a man in the gallery told me that you're the source of most of their cases. Is that true?"

"I wouldn't know about that, ma'am. I'm not privy to every source of the gentlemen's business."

"Well, I believe the speaker was implying that Mr. Snopes isn't terribly popular in the bar and has a limited number of referring solicitors."

Obadiah bristled. "He's a fine barrister. I'd say one of the very best in London."

"He may be the best barrister in all of England, but is he well-liked? You've already implied that his father is not a patron of his practice, and you've also implied he does not get significant work from the higher levels of society. There must be a reason for that. Is it true that some criticize his methods?"

"My lady, I can't speak to Mr. Snopes's popularity. So far as I know, he has no interest in running for Parliament. But I've never seen his better in trial. And I've known his junior, Mr. Shaw, most of my life. In fact, I am pleased to call him my dearest friend. He's nearly as young as myself but quick as a whip, with great prospects. Now, if your purpose is to malign these good gentlemen or have me betray their confidence, I'll make the rest of my way home on my own." Obadiah rapped a fist on the ceiling of the carriage.

The carriage didn't slow. "Davidson, my driver, is inexperienced at his present task, Mr. Cummings," the lady said. "Forced into this service by me. He's more at home with cutlery and linens, I'm afraid. But you mistake my point. The fact is, I don't like attorneys, whatever their specialization or background. I've seen them cheat and grasp and it's been my conclusion that, beneath a very thin veneer, they're in the business of serving themselves more than their clients. So I'm not looking for a barrister I could hope to like, nor one good at ingratiating himself to colleagues or magistrates or those of privilege and power. In fact, I'm looking for the rare one who's unconcerned with such things."

Obadiah stiffened. "I don't understand," he muttered.

The shawl slipped a little, revealing fresh skin about a mouth youthful yet mature. Perhaps thirty, he estimated, though her eyes seemed older and now deeply serious.

"Let me be perfectly clear then, Mr. Cummings. I'm Lady Madeleine Jameson of Heathcote Estate in Essex. My cousin has been imprisoned for deeds he did not commit, and I stand in danger of losing my estate as a consequence. I'm in need of an excellent barrister. One willing to fight men of great resources, not answer to them. A barrister unafraid of using any tools he must and not hobbled by concern for status. Is that your Mr. Snopes?"

5

Edmund took the interior steps of Gray's Inn, bleary and awash in self-recrimination. A stone of the pyramids was strapped to his back; he could swear it. His pockets were empty. He hadn't changed from his court clothes—hadn't even been home to do so—and they still carried the food stains on his coat. At least this day following Patrin's trial should be quiet, he told himself. It should be so if Mr. Snopes followed his usual practice of taking a day off following a trial.

The door into the foyer to the offices creaked far too loudly. Voices carried from Barrister Snopes's chamber. The barrister himself. Then Obadiah. Then a female voice.

"Come along, Edmund!" shouted Snopes, calling out to him, his voice booming like the salute of a cannon. It was his senior's new-case voice, Edmund recognized with dismay.

"Hurry now," he heard Mr. Snopes call again. "You're late!"

Standing, William watched Edmund come reluctantly into his office, stooped with fatigue. He stifled his embarrassment at Edmund's

45

clothes, still stained from the day before and even more wrinkled. Edmund's eyes, red and lined, signaled worse yet. Obadiah had related that this potential new client, Miss Madeleine Jameson, was already a skeptic about barristers and solicitors. Edmund's appearance couldn't be improving her impressions.

"Edmund Shaw," William said with a nod, "meet Lady Madeleine Jameson of Heathcote Estate. That's in Essex. Mr. Shaw is my junior at the bar."

As Edmund greeted her and they all took their seats, William caught the disquiet in Lady Jameson's eyes, surveying Edmund's disheveled clothes and weary face. "Lady Jameson has come to us through Mr. Cummings," William went swiftly on. "Please, my lady, continue with your story."

"Of course," she said. "A little over a year ago my father invested a large sum of money in a merchant ship. It was a brig called the *Padget*. We agreed to finance the acquisition and outfit the ship, to be captained by Harold Tuttle, a cousin just a few years older than myself and a former officer in the Royal Navy. There were two other investors as well. The ship sailed for the Indian Sea and was gone for fifteen months until its return last week."

"A successful voyage, yes?" Obadiah prodded.

"Yes. The *Padget* returned with a hold full of tea from China. "

"That should be worth a princely sum," William said. "Captain Tuttle was trading under contract with the East India Company, then?"

Miss Jameson shook her head.

William thought for a moment. "The East India Company holds a monopoly on British trade in that region, under supervision of the Crown. That includes the tea trade with China."

"Yes, I know."

William began to protest when Obadiah stepped in.

"Describe your legal matter, Lady," he said. "Mr. Snopes, allow her to explain what's happened and these points will become clearer."

Lady Jameson nodded. "The *Padget*, with its cargo, was seized in London Harbor, nearly the minute of its arrival eight nights ago."

"Seized?" William asked. "By whom?"

"By London constables, supported by Crown soldiers."

"On what charge?"

"I was informed confidentially by one of the arresting constables, after Harold was taken away, that the charge is piracy."

William leaned closer with interest. "If the *Padget* wasn't trading through the East India Company, how did it acquire tea in that part of the world—and why return it here? The company's monopoly on trade east of the Cape of Good Hope is governed by Royal Charter, which, I understand, accounts for over twenty percent of England's taxes and the Crown's support. Your captain surely didn't violate that charter or attack a company ship, then boldly sail his prize into London Harbor."

"The *Padget* did no such things," the lady said.

"Then what, and from whom, did the *Padget* pirate its cargo?"

"The *Padget* pirated no one. Captain Tuttle and his crew took the cargo from a French vessel."

"A private vessel?"

"Yes."

"A private vessel?" Edmund muttered, antipathy and impatience rising in his raspy voice. "Seizing *any* other vessel in a time of peace would be piracy. That would be true whether the victim was operated by the East India Company or not."

"This was not an act of piracy," Lady Jameson stated, matching Edmund's vehemence. "The French vessel taken by my cousin was itself a smuggler, violating the East India Company's contracts with its tea suppliers."

"My lady," William rejoined, flashing Edmund a stern glance at his tone, "what gave the *Padget* the right, as a private vessel, to make that judgment and take the French ship's cargo?"

"The *Padget* and my cousin Harold and his crew were operating in the Indian Sea under the authority of the sovereign to take French smugglers."

"What sovereign?" Edmund said overly loud.

"Surely ours, Edmund," William answered instantly at the rude outburst, sending his junior another hard look. "I presume, Lady Jameson, you mean that the Prince Regent George, as caretaker of his ill father the king, granted your cousin authority to take French smugglers on behalf of the British Crown?"

"That's precisely right," Lady Jameson said. "Captain Tuttle was operating under a Letter of Marque from the Crown granting just such authority. It was signed by the prince regent and approved by the High Court of Admiralty."

The room grew silent. Like the quiet after a bursting rocket, William thought. Or the hush after a lunatic's outburst.

"With all due respect, Lady Jameson," he said patiently, "do you understand what a Letter of Marque is?"

"Yes. It's a letter originating with the Crown granting authority to a private vessel to take other nations' ships, by force if necessary, as if the holder of the Letter were operating as part of the Royal Navy."

The lady had done her research. It was a definition right out of a legal treatise.

"Yes," Edmund erupted again. "But such letters are nearly always issued in time of war to privateers to engage them as adjuncts to the Crown's Navy. You're now expecting us to believe that the regent issued a Letter of Marque for your privateer to take French vessels, even though we're no longer at war with France?"

"Yes. To capture French smugglers."

"Impossible!" Edmund nearly shouted. "I've never heard of such a thing! Letters of Marque are a tool of war."

"Are you calling me a liar?" the lady shot back.

"Enough!"

William rose to his feet. "Edmund, I'll complete this inquiry. You will go to your office. Now."

Edmund straightened, looking shocked at William's scolding, staring at him as if through a fog. He blinked several times. Then he stood and quietly left the room.

When the door had shut, William turned to the lady as he sat once more.

"My apologies, Lady Jameson. Edmund seems to be . . . tired from the labors in a trial just ended."

The lady's youthful face was red, her lips tight. "Too tired to change his clothes?"

Snopes looked to the floor, momentarily embarrassed. "Did your father know the details of the *Padget*'s mission when he invested?"

"Yes."

"So your father knew that your cousin claimed he would be seizing French vessels, operating under a British Letter of Marque?"

"Yes."

"Did you or your father actually see the Letter for yourselves?"

"No. But we had assurance from my cousin that he'd received the Letter and that it was genuine."

"And you say there were other investors?"

"That's how we acquired the Letter of Marque. After we purchased the *Padget*, we were in need of additional investors to finance the merchant ship's operation. In response to an advertisement, my cousin was approached by a solicitor named Mandy Bristol, representing owners of a corporation. Mr. Bristol informed us that those investors could supply a signed Letter of Marque authorizing the taking of the cargo of French vessels, and would do so in exchange for receipt of twenty percent of the profit of the first voyage."

William straightened, his chest tightening. "Did you say Mandy Bristol handled your business arrangement with the investors?"

"Yes. Do you know him?"

"I do. Did you personally meet Mr. Bristol's clients?"

"No, they wished to remain anonymous. My cousin dealt with Mr. Bristol alone."

William settled back in his seat. "All right. Please go on. And I'd next like to know why, if your cousin has the protection of a Letter of Marque justifying his actions, he's been detained at all."

"I don't have an answer to that. You see, Mr. Snopes, I can't find my cousin."

The room grew silent once more.

"I don't understand," William said. "You said he was arrested."

"A more appropriate description would be that he's disappeared. The ship remains in the harbor, with the crew gaoled aboard her, though my cousin was taken ashore. I was at the harbor when the arrest occurred. After receiving news via a Gibraltar mail packet that Harold had arrived there and expected to reach London this month, I'd traveled to the Thames harbor with a good friend each night of the previous week until a very late hour, hoping to greet my cousin's return. My carriage had just arrived on the harbor road when I saw the soldiers leading Harold from his ship. By the time I'd inquired of the constables remaining at the ship, my inexperienced driver was unable to locate the soldiers' wagon carrying Harold in the fog. Since that night, I've asked at every constable's office, garrison, and prison in London for over eight days, and no one admits to any knowledge of my cousin or his arrest."

William looked quizzically to Obadiah, scribbling notes in the corner. The young solicitor looked up at William and shrugged.

"You checked at Newgate Prison, then?" William asked. "It's the most likely destination for such an offense."

"It was the first place I checked. I've been back twice more."

Obadiah groaned. "We all should pray he isn't in Newgate Prison. It isn't a fit place for man or dog."

"Or woman," William added, fixing his gaze back on the lady. "Something's obviously wrong here, but I can't believe your cousin has simply disappeared. There must be some administrative error."

"So I thought. But it's been eight days."

William pondered a moment. "Do you realize that, as owners

of the vessel, you and your father are at risk of arrest and prosecution yourselves?"

"I do."

"And you know that piracy is a capital offense? Punishable by hanging?"

"Yes. My father and I know the risks. Now I would be pleased if you'd tell me if you'll take the matter on. My cousin took this voyage in hopes of settling his fortune and supporting his marriage to a young woman. He has always been too good a man to even conceive of perpetrating fraud. His naval career grew him in discipline and honor. Before he sailed, Harold left a note with the very friend who accompanied me to the harbor last week, confirming his receipt of the Letter of Marque. Mr. Snopes, I know my cousin well; he wouldn't have sailed without the Letter, nor would he have taken a French ship without legal leave granted by that letter. He and his crew were operating under authority of the Crown. They don't deserve any punishment for their actions."

The clarity and firmness of the statement impressed William. The lady was harder than her youth and beauty would suggest. Despite her skepticism of attorneys, her adamance stirred William with concern for her.

"I trust that loss of the ship and its cargo would work a hardship for you and your father as well as your cousin?"

"Of course. With the funds advanced to buy the ship, it would be a devastating blow. The ruin of our estate, in fact. But my first concern, and that of my barrister, must be my cousin's freedom."

William looked again at the solicitor, who stared back uncertainly.

"Lady Jameson," William said at last, "all I can say at present is that I don't know if I will accept your case."

The lady looked as though she'd expected the rebuff. "I assume that it's a matter of payment . . ." She reached into a valise at her feet, withdrawing a small bag that she dropped onto the desk. "That's nearly one hundred pounds. I can, of course, provide more."

"Keep your payment," William said, seeing surprise in the woman's eyes. "Keep it until I've made up my mind."

Downcast with disappointment, Lady Jameson retrieved her bag as William glanced out the window at gray skies. With Crown involvement, this case had the potential of fire. Uncontrollable once started.

He doubted she fully appreciated the depth of her trouble.

"If you claim it's not the money, then why do you hesitate? Do you believe my cousin has a poor case?"

"I believe that your case carries much risk, even beyond the courtroom. Resisting a challenge from the Crown, Miss Jameson, usually carries a cost."

"Your solicitor implied that you care little about public opinion or the repercussions of a public case."

William smiled tepidly. "He said that? It's a foolish barrister who would invite hostility from the public that will sit as jurors to judge his future clients. The people love and despise their sovereign. Taking a case against the Crown's interests, big or small, is always a throw of the dice. And a case of piracy will make a headline in every paper from here to Paris. Many of your strongest detractors, Lady Jameson, you will find among your own social circles."

"You don't know my social circles, Mr. Snopes. I don't care about public opinion. If you do, then perhaps I've come to the wrong man."

"Perhaps you have. There are far more prominent law firms in London, with counsel who thrive on representing people of station, or cases awash in politics."

"Mr. Snopes, as I told your Mr. Cummings, I'm not looking for a barrister of prominence. Whoever took the ship has the authority to summon constables and soldiers and the apparent ability to hide my cousin from me. I don't know why they've chosen the *Padget* for their attack. But I'm afraid I won't be able to match their power or gold. My only hope for success is superior skill in a courtroom. Where a jury is the arbiter of truth, and money and connections don't matter."

William shook his head. "Where money and connections may matter less, perhaps," he corrected. "How can you be reached once I've made a decision?"

Her shoulders fell beneath a look both crestfallen and confused. William refused to be moved.

"I need to return home to care for my father," she answered. "It's at least a four-hour ride, on the main road to the Essex coast, near the village of Staunton. I've already sent my manservant ahead with my carriage."

"Very well. We'll reach out as soon as practicable."

"I'd prefer we meet here in London. If you send a messenger, I'll come straightaway."

"As you wish."

She rose to go, Obadiah and William rising with her. Her face had lost the challenge she'd arrived with, now looking disappointed and drawn.

"Please consider the matter seriously," she pleaded once more.

"Of course."

The office door had barely closed behind her when Obadiah turned to William.

"Since when did you become such a respecter of the Crown?"

"I'm turning over a new leaf, Obadiah," he said, then winked. "I'm concerned for the young lady, but I won't be pressed into a decision on such a case."

Obadiah shook his head. "Pressed into a case? You mistake me. I thought you'd decline it on the spot. Since I've known you, you've always declined political disputes. You've refused to get mixed up with the high-and-mighty. Though I admit this would certainly be a substantial financial case, Mr. Snopes. Purchasing and outfitting a ship must have run the lady and her father twenty thousand pounds or more."

"It would very much be a political dispute, Obadiah, one already staged with constables and seizures. And to answer your question, of course it gives me pause."

"I wonder where the lady will find help if we're unwilling. She'll discover that one hundred pounds goes a much shorter distance than she imagined in a matter like this."

"It will be difficult," William admitted.

"What of her cousin's disappearance? What do you make of that?"

"Disturbing, but not the greatest warning sign. A ship accused by the Crown of piracy, docked in London Harbor, and a fortune in tea impounded? Eight days have passed and the newspapers haven't printed a sentence about it. News like that should run through London like wildfire. Why so silent? Silence and discretion can be much more expensive than a good barrister. If this is a Crown prosecution, as is most likely, has the prince regent quashed any word of these events in the press? Why so? And another thing: why haven't we heard the least stir among our colleagues at the bar? Wouldn't the other investors, the ones who supplied the Letter and hold a twenty percent stake, have gotten counsel of their own by now?"

"You'd think so," Obadiah acknowledged. "Though you should at least have taken the retainer. What if she goes to someone else while you're deciding? With Patrin's trial over, things are slow just now."

"If she goes elsewhere, then we'll find another case or take a well-deserved rest. Now fetch Edmund. Despite his display, his doubts about the lady's story weren't wrong, and you know he can sense a liar from three courtrooms away. Fill him in on what he missed and bring him back."

Moments later, standing before the desk, Edmund looked like a defiant dog that had just been beaten with a stick. William stared up at him without flinching as the mantel clock ticked off a full minute.

"What was that display?" he finally demanded. "Attacking a prospective client like that? And a young lady, no less? You come in here today looking like you've slept in your clothes, if you slept at all, and proceed to keelhaul her. Explain yourself."

Edmund remained silent.

"Edmund, I will say this only once. You will never again, in my office or in my employment, attack a person who's entered this office seeking our assistance—especially a young woman. Whether they reveal it or not, clients usually arrive at our door in fear and under oppression. You will not use whatever skills you've learned under my tutelage as weapons to probe their weakness. Good grief, man, I shouldn't need to say this to you. You and Obadiah aren't in the boys' home any longer, and I've never been your headmaster. But you *are* less than a year beyond the bar—far too soon to disguise moodiness as wisdom. Your conduct reflects on me as well, you know. So if you won't say what's troubling you, at least straighten up as my junior. Do you understand?"

Edmund nodded reluctantly.

"Good. Now, you made it very clear what you think of the lady. Set aside your prejudices and tell me what you think of the lady's case."

Edmund shook his head, responding slowly. "It makes no sense, sir. When has the Crown issued Letters of Marque in peacetime the past century? And against the French? We're only a few years past a long war with Napoleon. The royal treasury's exhausted. The London markets are in tatters. Even the wealthy are cinching their belts tightly these days. Our prince regent is no genius, and he may not like King Louis, but he can't want another war so soon. Loosing privateers to prey on French merchant ships is inviting one."

"A single privateer, so far as we know."

"Even one. And another thing: why would she and her father invest with partners her father doesn't even know—putting his estate at risk to do so? The rich can be fools, but that smacks of lunacy."

"Maybe they had little choice. You saw how modestly she

dressed. A product of the financial problems you mention, perhaps? This *Padget* may have been serving as a single roll of the dice to save all."

Edmund shook his head again. "I don't believe it. Are you seriously considering taking her case?"

"Perhaps. I thought you had a heart for the downtrodden, Edmund."

"Yes, sir, for the downtrodden. Not for the wealthy, weeping for their diminished fortunes. And besides, Obadiah said she offered a hundred-pound retainer. What desperate victim does that?"

"Do you have any idea what it costs to operate an estate? Especially in these hard times? A solvent owner would have offered much more."

"She's also lying," Edmund rushed on, growing more passionate. "Or at least telling us only a fraction of the truth. No, she's of the same class as those who'll prosecute her unfortunate cousin."

"Maybe at one time," Obadiah chimed in. "But her carriage says otherwise. I've a feeling that a hundred pounds is quite dear to her."

Edmund wasn't wrong. Nor was Obadiah. It would be a political battle such as he'd avoided so many years now. But features of the case made him reluctant to simply walk away.

William took a breath. "Well, gentlemen, I've decided to at least investigate this further. For a start, I want you to canvass the prisons, Edmund, as Lady Jameson claims to have done. See if you can learn whether and where Captain Tuttle's been imprisoned. If so, interview the man or at least arrange for a visit."

Edmund's eyes widened, though William noted, to his satisfaction, that he held his peace.

"Don't look so put upon, Edmund," William said. "I haven't asked you to defend the lady, only to assist in finding her cousin. Obadiah, I'd like you to go to the East End wharves and confirm the existence of this treasure ship full of tea. And for now, try to do it without arousing notice of our interest."

"There must be hundreds of ships docked this time of year, sir, and I neglected to ask the lady the *Padget*'s specific whereabouts."

"Given that it's unaffiliated with any shipping companies, it's likely in the Metropolitan docks on the northern side of the Thames. Let's plan to meet in the morning to discuss what we've each found. Do you still belong to the Union Club, Obadiah?"

"I do."

"Good. Pick me up at my room in the morning and we'll go there for breakfast."

"And you, sir?" Obadiah asked.

"Me? Did either of you recognize the Mayfair solicitor Lady Jameson identified as the agent for the silent investors?"

"Mandy someone," Obadiah replied. "No, I didn't."

Edmund shook his head as well.

"I'm not surprised. He keeps a low profile as a solicitor. It's been many years, but I handled a case referred to me by Mr. Bristol when I was a young barrister. Back before he'd gained a reputation for representing a certain class of client that paid well and demanded great discretion. I plan on visiting the man now."

6

HOME OF DOROTHY EMERSON MARKS
WESTMINSTER, LONDON

"I wish you hadn't arranged this," Madeleine repeated to her friend. "I really need to be getting back to Heathcote this evening."

Dorothy stood before a tall mirror, toying with curls that fell to her cheeks. Her skin was fresh and young, her eyes wide and untroubled. She was a loyal and goodhearted friend, and Madeleine loved her deeply. But she couldn't help wondering, despite her expressions of concern, if Dorothy could even begin to understand the troubles surrounding Madeleine's family and the Heathcote Estate—or the financial woes of so many others, even of her own class in these stormy times since the war. Dorothy's countenance reflected life sheltered by prosperity and a "proper marriage" at age nineteen into a family that enjoyed the favor of the Crown.

"My dear, *dear* friend," Dorothy replied, "I won't hear another protest: I insist you stay one more night. You've been treated unfairly, Madeleine. And for what? Just because your family has suffered a few financial setbacks? It's a temporary state of affairs, I'm quite sure, and not the fatal disease people make of it. You *must* stay, I insist. We'll show all the world how foolish and shortsighted they've been about you and your family. They'll embrace you and love you once more, just as I do. You'll see."

Treated unfairly? Madeleine produced another smile for her friend. Dorothy's innocent spirit rendered her genuinely incapable of acknowledging even the evidence before her own eyes. Madeleine had deliberately withheld from her the full details of her family's plight and hadn't whispered a word about her visit to the barrister's office. Dorothy had accompanied Madeleine the night of Harold's disappearance—even witnessed the *Padget*'s seizure—and still acted as though tonight's dinner party was the most important matter in the universe. Such an incapacity to see beyond her privileged surroundings was a trait beyond Madeleine's understanding.

Yet Dorothy had never wavered in her friendship with Madeleine and her family, even after invitations to social events for London's winter gatherings or the rest of the year in the country-side had ceased arriving at Heathcote Estate. Her isolation made Dorothy's friendship that much more precious to her.

"I fear you'll be embarrassed," Madeleine said. "Especially given your guest list tonight. The Fetterlys are kind but deeply prejudiced. Sir Ethan Covington isn't kind or forgiving and a bulldog about social propriety. Dorothy, I don't want you to be muddied by the same waters as my family."

"Nonsense. You'll dazzle as always. Will you play your flute? Did you bring it as I asked? Could you play one of Bach's solos? At least find occasion to use your French."

"You're a good and loyal friend," Madeleine said, hugging Dorothy from behind. "But no, I did not bring my flute. After all these years, you know I'm not a performer." *And in any event,* she thought, *I would never play to win the hearts and minds of those who've treated my family so poorly these past years.*

"You must make an exception tonight. We could borrow one."

"No, Dorothy," Madeleine repeated. "Besides, Sir Ethan wouldn't care the tiniest bit if I played flute like a master or spoke a thousand languages. He and his wife will only see a dress three seasons out of date, worn by a destitute lady past a responsible marrying age."

"Stop that! You paint yourself and your family terribly and unjustly! You're lovely beyond words. Come. We'll find a dress that suits you. One that will satisfy even the Covingtons."

Sweet Dorothy, Madeleine thought, afraid and saddened as her friend took her arm to lead her to the wardrobe. *What will happen to our friendship when the prosecution of my cousin for piracy becomes widely known? When word of our investment in the* Padget *reaches the whispering crowds at galas and balls? When the reason for my father's absence is fully exposed?*

What will you think of me then, Dorothy?

It was drawing near dinnertime, and Madeleine chafed for the evening to be over.

The older man standing before her, Torrance Fetterly, continued his ramblings about his exacting management of his country estate. At least his single-mindedness allowed no questions from his audience, including Madeleine. She nodded politely again and stifled a yawn as the speaker regaled her with the latest theories of crop rotation and the proper care of recently sheared sheep.

Her eyes wandered. Mr. Fetterly's wife stood in a corner with Lady Helen Covington and Dorothy's husband, Daniel, all safely away from Mr. Fetterly's boring salvos. Dorothy had left the room to see to dinner details. That accounted for everyone except Sir Ethan Covington. He was the man Madeleine most feared this evening.

Sir Ethan was eyeing Madeleine from a chair by the fireplace. From reputation and experience, Madeleine had no wish to be cornered with the man.

The party was called to dinner. Even seated, Mr. Fetterly continued dominating the conversation. His rolling lecture continued through early courses of oysters and asparagus. Not until the soup had arrived did Sir Ethan's wife, Lady Helen, finally wrest the talk to the theater, her patronage of the Lyceum, and the latest music from Vienna—all topics which permitted Madeleine to maintain her courteous silence.

"Madeleine?" Dorothy's voice interrupted her welcome solitude in the midst of the fourth and main course.

Madeleine toyed with the venison on her plate, not looking up.

"Madeleine?" Dorothy called again.

Madeleine smiled at her friend. "Yes, Dorothy?"

"Do tell us, have you had an opportunity to travel to France recently?"

Please no. She shook her head. "Why, no. I've never had the opportunity."

"That's so unfortunate. I know you speak French brilliantly."

Sir Ethan stirred, seated across the table from Madeleine.

"On the topic of traveling," he picked up loudly, "I have another question for you, Miss Jameson."

The dragon had been awakened. "Yes, Sir Ethan?"

"Have you sailed anywhere recently?"

"No, Sir Ethan. I haven't traveled much lately."

"I see. Well, what do you think of sea travel?"

This thread was leading somewhere. Madeleine's chest tightened. "I think it's the wonder of our age, Sir Ethan."

"Yes, yes. Essential to the trades, of course. Which raises another interesting question. Do you have an opinion on the subject of trading?"

From the corner of her eye, she saw Dorothy's brow furrow with uncertainty and worry.

"What on earth could you mean, Sir Ethan?" the host intervened.

"I quite agree, Sir Ethan," Mr. Fetterly added. "What would the young lady know on that topic? Now, if you're talking about agricultural exports, I can say from no small experience—"

"It's a simple question," Sir Ethan shot back, his eyes fixed on Madeleine. "And an unobjectionable one. I simply asked the young lady's thoughts on trading."

The table grew quiet.

"Trading?" Madeleine replied.

"Yes. More specifically, what do you think of a gentleman becoming engaged in foreign trade?"

She avoided Sir Ethan's stare. "I suppose it depends upon the circumstance."

"Well, say a gentleman acquired a ship to procure goods abroad and sell them in England. Do you think that engaging in the merchant trade through such means is an appropriate vocation for a gentleman?"

The other guests looked on, perplexed and curious.

"I would say it depends upon the nature of the trade," Madeleine answered.

"That is a politic answer, Miss Jameson," Sir Ethan replied. "For myself, I see no circumstances when trade would be appropriate for a true gentleman. Our ordained role must be the maintenance of our estates for the betterment of the people who depend upon us, and the governing of England and its growing empire. But let me narrow my inquiry. What would be your opinion if that ship were used for illicit ventures?"

Madeleine took a bite of her venison, her fingers tingling.

"Why on earth are we wandering into such serious topics?" Dorothy mercifully demanded. She looked to Lady Helen for aid. "What were you saying, Lady Helen, about the concerts at Vauxhall Gardens we can expect this spring?"

Sir Ethan was unrelenting. "Let me be even more direct, Miss Jameson," he pressed on. "Is it true that your father has taken an interest in a trading ship?"

There it was. What did he know?

"That's not true, Sir Ethan," she answered carefully. "My father has done no such thing."

"Well, that's settled," Dorothy said. "Lady Helen? Vauxhall Gardens?"

Sir Ethan waved his table knife like a rapier. "Truly? Because my sources seemed quite certain. I was told that your father purchased a brig and used it to launch himself into trade in the Far East. Wouldn't you agree, Miss Jameson, that becoming a trader is no solution for poverty borne of poor farming? And that trading in illicit goods is worse still?"

"Sir Ethan!" Mr. Fetterly exclaimed. "I insist that you cease your interrogation of the girl!"

But Sir Ethan would not be deterred. Besides, the subject was too far engaged.

Madeleine set her napkin on the table. "Sir Ethan, as I've already said, my father has not acquired a ship for trade."

"Well, I'm very pleased to hear of it," Sir Ethan said, though his eyes declared her a liar.

All the days of searching for her cousin. The worry and fear for his welfare. Concern for the fate of the *Padget* and all it portended for the estate. Her inability to hire the barrister she'd chosen. Now those eyes. The fear and weariness crumbled into anger: a fuming, roiling cascade of emotion that drove Madeleine beyond her last restraint.

"But I've acquired such a ship myself," Madeleine added, almost to her own surprise. "And apart from your reference to illicit trade, I've done all that you described."

A curtain of silence covered the room. Even Sir Ethan looked surprised at the sudden admission he'd been seeking.

"Your attempt to defend your father's actions is admirable, Miss Jameson," Sir Ethan said at last. "But that's impossible. Your father is still alive. You're not an heiress yet."

"You are incorrect once again," Madeleine said. "If you must know, my father made me heiress to Heathcote Estate two years ago, before his declining health rendered him unable to care for our holdings. Any ill thoughts you bear for the actions of my family you may assign to me. Is your curiosity fully satisfied now? Or have you other questions about my affairs?"

"No, I'm not satisfied." Sir Ethan matched her stare. "I've also heard that your family mixes socially with members of your town, Staunton, and that your social circle there includes a woman said to abet the smuggling trade in Essex County. Is that true as well, Lady Jameson?"

There were several gasps. Mr. Fetterly and his wife joined Sir Ethan's stare, awaiting a response. Lady Helen looked away in shock. Dorothy and her husband seemed bewildered.

Madeleine's own breaths began coming deeply and fast.

What purpose lay in preserving the last thin threads of connection with these people and all the others who would swiftly learn of tonight's dinner?

You will regret this and soon, a voice whispered inside her.

I don't care.

"Sir Ethan," Madeleine began, her face as hot as her pounding heart. "Do you know where your servants acquire the sugar that sweetens your tea and coffee? The tobacco that fills your pipe? The molasses that adorns your table and fills your cookies and tarts? You set budgets and leave it to your staff to meet them, not worrying about how they do so. Well, they acquire those goods from the smugglers you decry. They must do so because the Crown's taxes prevent the filling of your ample larder by any other means. Taxes which you bear with difficulty, but which crush the tenant farmers and shopkeepers without discrimination or empathy—people who would simply do without if not for the quarterly arrival of the smugglers' prows. Those taxes were raised to impossible heights to pay for the recent war with France, which impoverished the Crown and the state, and which are now necessary to keep the regent and his coterie in finery and new homes. Wars in which neither of your sons found reason to fight, but in which my brother, Devon, died for England on a foreign field under Wellington's banner."

Sir Ethan's visage was taut and unforgiving. Had she really believed she could move him?

"You failed to answer my question, Miss Jameson," he said. "Are you engaged with such people as I described?"

Strength and resolve faltered. A glance took in the white face of Dorothy and reminded Madeleine that her words this evening did not only affect herself. She held back her intended response.

Her hands clasped together to avoid trembling, Madeleine rose. "Nor did you answer mine, Sir Ethan," she replied. Then she turned to Dorothy. "Thank you so much for dinner. I believe I'll be returning to Heathcote this evening after all."

7

VILLAGE OF STAUNTON
COUNTY OF ESSEX

It was well past midnight when Madeleine rode her mare Gypsy at a walking pace into the empty streets of Staunton. The evening fog enveloped hedges, trees, and buildings she'd known her entire life, rendering them strangers. The absence of anyone on the street painted the scene a town of ghosts, rising to mock her for her failed performance under Sir Ethan's attack.

Madeleine clasped the reins tightly, huddling low over the horse's damp mane.

The sign for the chemist's shop emerged from the gray to her right. Madeleine coaxed her mare to a halt and slid from the saddle, tying the reins to a post. An alley took her over slippery cobblestones to a door at the back of the shop, and a shiver shot through her as she knocked gently.

Candlelight appeared in the window overhead. Moments later, the door before her opened inward.

"Keep it low" came the croaky voice of the chemist's wife. "Samuel's sleepin' light these nights. And you're very late."

"The fog," Madeleine answered as she entered. "I hadn't planned to travel alone and at such a late hour."

"That's right, you shouldn't have. But I was meanin' you're *days* late, girl."

The chemist's wife lit a match, and two candles soon sputtered to life. The pair of them, set on a table, tossed shadows at tins, mortars and pestles, and glass bottles half full of powders. The aproned woman, her thick ginger hair tied back, gave Madeleine another stare. Then she reached out to take Madeleine in a crushing hug.

"You look bad," the woman whispered in her ear. "You look worried."

Feeling the approach of tears and ashamed at her weakness, Madeleine drew away. She took a deep breath of the strange, familiar smells of the place that always comforted her.

"Some business matters in London, Roisin."

"As you say, dear," Roisin said, eyeing her carefully. "Did that ship of yours come in at last?"

"Yes. But not as I'd hoped."

Madeleine told about the charge of piracy and seizure of the *Padget* and its cargo.

"Oh, good Lord in heaven," Roisin burst out, making the sign of the cross. "And you indebted to Solicitor Rooker and all. Not to mention the American too. What are you plannin' to do?"

Deadened by the worries she'd been contemplating for over eight days, Madeleine only shrugged. "As for Solicitor Rooker, I've no choice. I'll ask him for more time to repay his loan."

"Really? You know old man Rooker, girl. He'd dig up a grave if he thought a client had taken a farthing into the ground with 'im. He'll take full advantage of this, mark my word."

"I know, Roisin, I know. I don't trust him. I've simply no choice."

"Listen now, girl, I've some money I can give you to tide you over. Enough to satisfy that graspin' Rooker for a bit anyways."

"No." Madeleine's answer was firm. She wouldn't shame herself twice in one evening by accepting Roisin's help. "You'll not tie this shop's future to the problems of our estate. No, I'll convince Solicitor Rooker to extend the loan somehow."

"That'll be a feat. But even if you do, what'll happen when the American hears of this? He carries half your debt, and smugglers have ears everywhere. The takin' of your ship will be no secret for long to someone in his profession."

"I'm sure he'll get no wind of it until the trial has started," Madeleine answered, trying to sound convincing. "By then, I can talk him into waiting until it's over."

Sir Ethan's words about her family's connection to a smuggler drifted back to Madeleine. "I'm worried all of this will bring attention to you," she said aloud.

"And what have I done that I'd fear such a thing?" Roisin asked innocently.

Madeleine smiled at the dear woman before her, and the defense she'd nearly made to Sir Ethan came rolling out. "Not a single thing. You've only kept the folks in Staunton and the rest of the county in goods they couldn't otherwise afford with the Crown's tariffs. Storing and distributing molasses and sugar and coffee and tea that the American smuggles in past the King's Navy—at no profit to yourself. That's all you've done. If the king cared half as much for the people in the countryside as you do, Roisin, the American would have no market for his goods at all. And you also introduced me to the American when I so desperately needed more funds for the *Padget*."

Roisin looked away. "Stop makin' me out to be Joan of Arc. I get first pick of the goods, don't I? And as for the American, don't bring that up as a prized decision. I wish I'd never introduced the two of you. Let me make it up now. Please, take the help I'm offerin'."

"No. You've helped enough."

"You're as stubborn as when you were ten." Roisin sighed, throwing up her hands. "And too brave for your own good."

Madeleine's insides quaked with shame, recalling how she'd wilted under Sir Ethan's attack. "I've no courage at all when it really matters."

Roisin took her arm. "You've a saint's courage, girl, fightin' as you do to save you and yours. My offer to help stands, girl. But if you won't accept it, what are you going to do about gettin' your ship and tea back?"

"I'm hiring a barrister. Someone to represent my cousin Harold—and myself if necessary. I saw him at work in a trial in London. He's very good."

The older woman reached out and took Madeleine's hands. "It saddens me to see you this way, and with no mother awaiting you at home to talk to. Or a father well enough to help. I'm glad you stopped by. Very glad. You know you'll always have me and Samuel. Ever since you wandered in off the street, daughter of his lordship, wonderin' if we sold candy and what were all those interesting smells and a dozen other questions. That day you became the child Samuel and me never had. It pains me so to see you lookin' like the devil's chasing after you. It breaks my heart. Go home now. Go see after your father. Get some rest."

She'd longed for a word of encouragement from Roisin since the instant of seeing her cousin taken away at the docks. She smiled, momentarily released from her blanket of solitude and worry.

With a final hug, Madeleine left as she'd entered.

Back in the saddle, Madeleine walked Gypsy through the remaining streets of town. Only a few miles now. It was foolish to ride home tonight without an escort. She should have waited until her manservant, Davidson, could come to pick her up. Yet she couldn't stay another night at Dorothy's home, not after the terrible dinner. Regret and distress began filling her again as the chemist's shop retreated behind her. The infuriating judgment of Sir Ethan and all the others like him. The wearisome years of struggle.

Renewed fear for her cousin and the *Padget*.

Her horse whinnied worriedly.

Madeleine sat up. What had troubled the mare? The thickening fog? Even leaning forward and straining, she could barely see the road under the horse now. The ground began to rise with the *clip-clop* of the mare's hooves on the arched wooden bridge. It marked that she was leaving town, passing over the gurgle of the stream beneath as though she and Gypsy were floating across the water. Until they were back to the quiet of the dirt road beyond.

Another quarter mile passed.

The horse whinnied again.

Madeleine listened. From a distance behind her came the clatter of another horse trotting the planks of the bridge. Who would be out in this fog who didn't need to be? And why did they sound as though they were moving so quickly?

Blind in the fog, she stopped the mare beneath some low-hanging branches to listen again. Wind passed through the trees, playing a chord of creaking wood and shivering leaves. A pheasant's wings launched the bird toward a nearby field. Then the sound of hooves rose again, close enough to hear the other horse's panting through the fog.

Her chest tightening, Madeleine tugged the reins to force Gypsy off the road and down a shallow ditch, then up the far side into a stand of trees. A few feet into the woods, she reined her in and slid to the ground.

The following hooves came abreast on the road, invisible only yards away. Their sound was passing.

Relief seeped in.

Then the horse and rider slowed.

Halted.

Madeleine stroked her mare to silence with trembling fingers. The horse on the road backed up and snorted.

"Whoa," a low voice came through the fog.

Silence.

The fog and trees shrunk around her like prison walls. The woods behind her were too thick to flee through, and only marshland lay beyond that. The road with the rider offered the sole escape.

A long minute passed.

The voice clucked to the horse on the road, and they began to walk away.

Madeleine let out a long breath. She waited until the road had become deathly quiet, then reached for the cloth sack of coins in her saddlebag. Taking a handful that she slid down into the depths of the saddlebag, she knelt to scrape a hole in the damp earth, where she laid the sack with the remaining coins. Covering the hole with dirt and leaves, she took off her scarf and tied it around the nearest sapling.

Then she stood and huddled for warmth against the mare.

She waited what seemed an hour. When her teeth were grinding and her body shaking, she finally pulled herself stiffly into the saddle and walked Gypsy back onto the road.

The sound of the other horse and rider had disappeared. She tried to clear her mind over her shivering. The wood where she'd hidden had to be the small thicket near the drive to the manor house grounds. Another mile or so and she'd be safely home.

She kicked the mare into a walk.

Half an hour passed. A small hedgerow signaling the manor drive emerged from the fog to her right. Madeleine turned her horse onto it.

Home. A fire. Embracing her father. A bath. Her body began to relax.

Gypsy whinnied and sidestepped with alarm. Madeleine looked up.

Another horse and rider had appeared out of the fog ahead.

Madeleine gasped, yanking Gypsy to a sudden stop. She peered at the figures through the wisps of gray. The man looked huge, seated calmly atop a black stallion. A scarf was drawn across his chin and mouth. A hood covered his head. One hand gripped a pistol.

"What do you want?" Madeleine forced out.

The man and horse stood quietly in the mist.

"If you've no business with me, then get out of my way," she commanded, her voice lifeless in the wet air.

"Your saddlebag, miss," the man called in a London accent. "Tie it loose and drop it to the ground."

Her mind and body were riven in two.

"Were you sent by the American?" she asked.

"American?" The man snorted. "What American? Now drop the bag to the ground as I told you."

She had no choice. She couldn't reach the manor without passing within an arm's length of a pistol shot. If she rode the other way, the race in the fog would be more dangerous than the pistol.

Madeleine reached down to obey, untying the saddlebag and letting it slide to the ground.

The man threw a leg back and dropped from his horse. Ambling to her side, he retrieved the bag. Reached in.

She heard the tinkle of coins.

The man looked up with his covered face. "Off the horse and step away, miss."

The wall of fog seemed to echo the man's words.

"You're stealing my horse now?"

"I said *off*."

She did as he commanded. Landing hard on cold, deadened legs, she took a step back.

Pistol fire split the night from the far side of the horse. Gypsy reared, let out a heaving squeal, and collapsed hard and unmoving at her feet.

Horror engulfed her. The man walked back through the eddying gray to his own horse to remount. He reined the stallion by her through the fog.

He slowed to lean down.

"Don't be hanging about the Inns of Court looking for any more barristers, miss," he said through his mask. "And you'd best be leaving that ship in London for your betters to sort out. Or next time that'll surely be you."

8

NEWGATE PRISON

Heavy drizzle drained the sky as Edmund strode busy streets beneath his umbrella.

The darkness and close air suited his mood.

He forced his head up. *Come out of it, you sniveling child. Mr. Snopes hasn't taken the case yet.* Even if he did, the woman didn't seem the worst sort of her class. Why rip into her or fight a battle with his senior that he might not have to? It wasn't their fault that his head and legs ached; they didn't put the cards in his hand that lost him every shilling of the pay Mr. Snopes had given him.

If only he had a different vice. Like gluttony. At least he'd be able to pay the rent on time each month.

A stone made its way into his shoe. Perfect. Edmund lowered his umbrella and stopped abruptly, kneeling to empty it.

A man only a stride behind shifted quickly to move past, coming so close that Edmund saw a thin white half-moon scar above the man's left eyebrow, overseeing an eye that drooped like a low-hanging chestnut onto his cheek. Edmund stood and walked on. Up ahead, the man turned a corner and disappeared.

Since the lady's appearance, Edmund had been to every prison except the most obvious. None of the others had record of the arrest of a Captain Tuttle. He'd deliberately left this one, Newgate Prison, for last, hoping a trip here wouldn't be necessary.

The building came into view ahead, making Edmund shudder with his reluctance to go there. Dark brick walls with arched windows stood several stories tall. Pestilent and filthy, five hundred inmates crowded a building that might safely hold half that number. A gust of wind brought its smell, and Edmund nearly gagged. Ahead, the coroner's wagon pulled away from a barred exit. Filled with those who'd earned the "black reprieve," no doubt.

No matter his mood, no matter a prisoner's crime, Edmund couldn't muster the hardness to wish anyone be locked up here. It echoed of memories of his time with his parents in debtors' prison yet was far worse. He put a handkerchief to his mouth as he neared the visitors' door.

A single clerk sat at an elevated table in the entryway. Bundled against chill and dampness that his small coal brazier couldn't dispel, the pale young man was inking entries in a journal.

"Your business?" the clerk demanded. In a deliberate display of insolence, the young man didn't even look up.

"I'm here to visit a prisoner." Edmund leaned his umbrella against the table. "Captain Harold Tuttle."

"We've no prisoner of that name here."

Such a long and fruitless day after a long and fruitless night. The answer gave him the perfect excuse to turn and leave.

Except he wouldn't do that to Mr. Snopes. And the clerk's voice and look riled him.

"Truly? You know that without consulting your journal?"

"I know my business."

"Well, do me a kindness and look anyway, will you?" Remembering William's lecture, he tried to sound congenial. "He would have been admitted seven or eight nights ago."

The clerk pulled the journal closer to reluctantly comply. "Your name?"

That tone again.

74

TODO M. JOHNSON

"Why would you need my name? You haven't even confirmed there's anyone for me to visit."

"If you want me to search, I'll need your name first."

Ridiculous. And intentionally provocative. Edmund felt his back and arms stiffening.

"Edmund Shaw. I'm a barrister."

The clerk made a show of turning back several pages in the journal.

"No one of the name Tuttle here."

"Do you have any prisoners brought from a ship called the *Padget*?"

"No."

"Again without looking?"

"I can't help you. Now, if you'll *excuse* me."

He'd stand here all day before he'd be dismissed this way. "I want to speak with the warden."

"He's got no appointments available for several weeks."

Edmund raised a finger and pointed. "Then you'd better tell him that I'll be back with a writ of habeas corpus for Captain Tuttle's release in the morning."

The clerk sneered at the naked bluff. "A writ gets a prisoner released if they're wrongfully imprisoned, *Mr. Barrister*. I've already told you: I've no record of your captain even being imprisoned here."

The bureaucrat knew his law, and it burned in Edmund's stomach. Before he used his fists that ached to respond, he was out the door and into the rain in three long strides, fuming as he walked up the street.

Was it plain, if galling, disrespect, or was he hiding something?

Edmund pulled up his collar to keep out the rain—and recalled: he'd left his umbrella behind with the clerk. He turned back reluctantly.

A man slammed into him, sending Edmund stumbling backward.

"Your pardon," Edmund murmured, catching his balance.

The other man grunted and pushed quickly past. He soon disappeared from view behind several other walkers.

Strange. Edmund had caught his face and seen the scar and drooping eye. He was the same man who'd nearly collided with him *before* his visit to Newgate.

Edmund shook his head woefully. A losing night at the brag table. Facing the dark prospect of Mr. Snopes taking on a case defending a rich family's fortune—the kind Edmund had sworn to himself he'd never support. Nearly run over twice by the same man in a matter of minutes.

All unforeseen outcomes. Coincidence? Fate? Luck? Whatever its name, Edmund wished chance would deliver more favorable winds.

THE THAMES DOCKS
EAST END, LONDON

It would be dark soon. Obadiah stood in the light rain amid warehouses and stacked cargo on the wharf. There it was, the *Padget*. Resting in the waters of the Thames, a brig, docked and lying low in the water. Two men with constable's armbands were lounging on its deck amidships.

Obadiah began a slow walk down the busy waterfront, weaving between stevedores and sailors. He passed the *Padget*, noting faces looking out of the gunports. Likely the crew, locked belowdecks. He also noted a group lingering ashore in the shadows. More guards, Obadiah concluded.

He reached the end of the dock. The ship directly behind the *Padget* was the *Boreas*. He turned about.

Passing the men standing about onshore, Obadiah took a breath and approached.

"Eh, chaps?" He smiled. "Sorry to trouble you. I was supposed to meet a mate here who works the docks. If I was late, I was to meet him at a pub. Can't recall the name, but my mate said it was the best one hereabouts. Can you guide me?"

Blank faces greeted him. From the back of the group, a thick man with a walrus mustache emerged.

"That'd be the Rusty Scupper," he said in a growling voice. "Cross Corning Road and go east."

"Thanks kindly." Obadiah tipped his hat and moved on.

Not a man there, except for the big one, knew the local pubs. Those were no local seamen. Likely they were more constables assigned to watch the ship. Guards keeping a low profile.

It was all consistent with Lady Jameson's story of her missing cousin.

The Rusty Scupper was where the gruff one said it would be. Obadiah entered into a wall of sound.

"Guinness," he ordered at the bar, looking about. When the pub manager returned with his beer, Obadiah said, "Say, do you know whether any sailors are here from the *Boreas*?"

The manager looked down the bar at a young man seated alone. "I heard him and a few mates talkin' about the *Boreas*."

"Thanks kindly."

Obadiah looked to the young sailor. His glass was nearly empty. Taking his foam-capped beer, Obadiah went to a seat beside the boy.

"Son," Obadiah began, though he looked only a few years younger than Obadiah, "let me fill that for you." Before the boy could respond, Obadiah whistled to the bartender, who came to oblige.

When the bartender was gone again, Obadiah leaned in. "That beer's for the favor you'll be doing me in a moment. I'm from the Union newspaper. I was sent to follow up a rumor that the *Padget* got boarded by some constables when it docked next to the *Boreas* a week or so ago. Would you know anything about it?"

The boy blinked blankly several times. The beer Obadiah had replaced wasn't nearly the boy's first this night.

"Well, *I'm* from the *Boreas*," the sailor said unsteadily. "You're from a newspaper? Anybody in trouble?"

"Nah. Don't worry yourself on that account. I'm no constable. I'm just looking for a story."

The boy took a long drink of his beer.

"Sure, that 'appened."

Obadiah smiled his interest. "Why, good! What did you see?"

"Didn't see it meself. But Steven, he was on deck. He knows just what happened. HEY, STEVEN!"

Obadiah cringed. A chair at a table nearby scraped the floor.

"WHADDYA WANT, JESSE?" a voice boomed back over the crowd noise.

"THIS MAN HERE WANTS TO KNOW ABOUT SOME-BODY BOARDIN' THE SHIP NEXT TO OUR'N LAST WEEK!"

Oh, sweet Mary. Obadiah looked about. The bar went quiet to make way for the shouted exchange.

"WHAT IN BLAZES DOES HE WANNA KNOW?"

"Whaddya wanna know?" Jesse asked Obadiah.

Obadiah glanced over his shoulder, preparing to move to Steven's table, but he was unable to pick out Steven with his booming voice.

But then he did see the big man from the group at the dock—the mustached one who'd told Obadiah about the Rusty Scupper. The man had appeared in the door and was scanning the room earnestly.

"It's all right," Obadiah said to the young sailor, hearing the crowd noise rising again. He took a gulp of his own Guinness. "I've got to go. I'll look you and Steven up next time I'm back."

Lowering his head, he made his way through the crowd toward a side door.

Once outside, he ran as fast as he could away from the port.

PARK STREET
MAYFAIR DISTRICT
LONDON

William stood on the street corner, his umbrella thumping with the tempo of the falling rain. With his toes he tapped the rhythm of a waltz he'd heard performed at Vauxhall Gardens the previous summer. Hearing the name Mandy Bristol again had reminded him of his younger days when he'd been considered a good dancer, especially the cotillion. He wondered how he'd fare with the more modern waltz, a step he'd never actually tried at a ball. Dancing was one of the few things he sorely missed from his days of youth before leaving Oxford, predating his move to London to experience the solitude of a modest professional income.

He glanced up and down Park Street. When he'd first settled in London, the city had seemed a delicious cauldron of people and commerce and energy. Despite his limited means, he'd tried to explore every inch of it—naïvely and sometimes at great risk. Park Street in those days was home to orderly shops, teahouses, and bakeries, though in the past twenty years it had grown into an even more settled haven of affluence, with handsome town homes and estate houses bordering streets where professionals could buy or sell their goods and services in safety. Only a few miles, but a world away, from the narrow roads and alleys where the honest poor fought to survive gangs, pickpockets, and purveyors of illicit pleasures. London was excitement and grinder all at once, the years had taught William. But oh, how he loved its people with all their imperfections.

"Lookin' for a shop, are ya, mister?" a voice called.

A young boy had appeared at his feet. Ten or eleven likely.

"Easy to get lost here, sir," the boy went on. "But me, I know this street like a compass. Just half a quid, sir, and I'll see you to where you're going."

William's colleague at the Inns of Court had sworn that Mandy Bristol's present office was near this intersection. Maybe it was, but half an hour's search had revealed no solicitor's sign in any window.

William put on a look of serious consideration of the boy's offer. "Half a quid? You look too young to be a highwayman. A shilling. That or I'll ask at the millinery shop over there."

The boy's eyes flashed displeasure. "The shilling first, sir."

William reached into his pocket and handed over the coin. "I need to know the way to the office of Solicitor Mandy Bristol."

A glint of surprise came into the boy's wide eyes. "That door right behind ya. Second floor."

The boy was out with it and running away before William could thank him, as though he suspected William might try to retrieve his coin.

The slap of his wet shoes was soon accompanying William up the building's wooden stairs to the second floor.

Mandy Bristol, Solicitor, a hand-painted sign on the door announced. The sight of it raised a note of old anger in William. He raised a hand to knock, then thought better of the courtesy and simply marched in.

The front foyer had been decorated to convey success. Two doors led away to back offices. In the middle of the foyer stood a double-sized solicitor's cabinet, open on one wall. A barrister's desk and chair occupied its center, the desk surface and chair back lavished with riveted dark leather. Twin padded client chairs faced the desk. Hunting landscapes graced every wall.

"I beg your pardon!" a voice called through the door leading to an inner office. "Isn't it still customary to knock? We're open only by appointment. That door should have been locked."

William stepped closer to the inner office door until he could see the man who'd called.

The stout solicitor was dressed as stylishly as his office. Beneath a bald pate that rose above his ears like the Matterhorn, a mutton beard overhung a coat with long tails at the back, set higher in front, a square-cut waistcoat showing beneath it. The lining of the shoulders and chest of the coat was quilted to fit, and William detected a boned corset rendering a smaller waist on the man. It was a feat accomplished with an effort.

"Don't you remember me, Mandy?" William asked coolly.

"William?" The man's eyes surveyed him, taking in William's older trousers and simple jacket as he stepped into the foyer. "Is it my Mr. Snopes?"

"Yes, Mandy."

"My, my, my," he exclaimed, approaching. "How long has it been since we spoke last?"

"Nearly twenty years." A vein in William's temple began to throb. "So long I'd almost begun to think you'd caught a ship for Australia."

Mandy's eyes narrowed, measuring the penal colony reference for a jest or an insult.

"In fact," William went on, taking one of the cushioned chairs without invitation, "I don't believe we've spoken since I tried that case you referred. Back when I was in my twenties and we were all still answering to our third King George."

Mandy took his own seat behind the desk, growing uncomfortable. "I recall the matter," he said curtly.

William nodded. "Good. Do you ever cross paths with Mr. . . . what was our client's name? Hawk? Pigeon?"

"Lord Finch."

"That's it. Do you ever see Mr. Finch these days?"

The solicitor squirmed, reaching an unconscious hand to adjust his corset and taking a deep breath.

"*Lord Finch*. No, not since you achieved his acquittal. I understand he moved to Greece."

"That was my first major acquittal, Mandy. And so unexpected! A red-letter day for a young barrister."

Mandy pinched his lips. "What *precisely* can I do for you, William?"

"I've often wondered about your career, Mandy." William's blood now stirring, he would not be hurried. "You've clearly enjoyed a successful one. Yet, since that day we marched triumphantly out of The Old Bailey, I've seldom seen you at the Inns of Court. And in all candor, it isn't often that I hear your name bandied about by others of the legal profession either."

"Yet I hear about you often," Mandy said, his voice rising. "Still handling street cases and shopkeepers' affairs. Dressing more like your clients than your colleagues, I see. Still running the race in your own fashion. As for me, I've chosen to focus on a select clientele."

"Like your Finch, I imagine," William replied flatly. "I suppose I should take offense that you've never referred another matter to me."

"I believe you made your view perfectly clear about accepting future cases from me, William, as we were exiting the courthouse the day Finch was acquitted."

William snapped his fingers. "Now that you mention it, I recall that I did."

"Are you planning on telling me why you're here, William?"

"Of course. I have prospective clients who entered into an investment with one or more of your clients. A Lord and Lady Jameson. Father and daughter."

Mandy's eyes grew opaque. "I'm not sure I recall that surname."

"Oh, you must. They partnered with a corporation owned by two of your clients for the voyage of a ship called the *Padget*. You were the solicitor and agent for your clients in the matter."

"It doesn't sound a bit familiar." The answer was unwavering, but a faint flush came into Mandy's cheeks. "You said 'prospective clients' previously. Now you say clients. Do you represent these Jamesons or not?"

"We're working out the details."

Mandy ran the back of his hand along a whiskered cheek. "Well, I'd be happy to look through my records to see if I have any notes on the matter."

"That would be appreciated. The ship has been seized by the authorities, you see, and accused of piracy."

"Piracy? Now that's unusual these days. What kind of piracy?"

"Taking a French ship in the Indian Sea. But the captain, a Harold Tuttle, claims to have the protection of a Letter of Marque from the Crown, with instructions to take French smugglers. A letter your clients had arranged for him."

"Does he really claim that? And the Crown disagrees, I take it?"

"They must. We assume from the captain's arrest that they're the ones pursuing a prosecution. Would you know anything of the matter?"

The solicitor shook his head. "A Letter of Marque? I know nothing of that. And I'm sure I'd recall a vessel acquired for the purpose of merchant shipping in the Far East."

"Yes. Please do review your records, though. Your clients would certainly wish to know of these developments."

"Of course."

William rose, placing a calling card on the desk. "I'll let myself out. Please give my regards to Finch." He paused at the door, unable to restrain himself a final time. "Just out of curiosity, Mandy, have you had occasion over the years to see Colonel Slatterly as well?"

Mandy rose. His face and his hairless white head were turning pink. His chest puffed with rising anger, rendering an appearance that he might burst from his corset entirely.

"No. Why would you ask that?"

"Hmm. I just thought that a man of such talent—such uncompromising *sincerity* as a witness—would be an asset in other legal proceedings than just Finch's. False testimony, delivered with eloquence, can be hard to come by."

It took a moment for Mandy to get out his reply.

"What . . . are you . . . insinuating?"

"You give me too much credit, Mandy. Insinuating requires creativity and deflection. I prefer to speak right to the heart of the matter."

"William?"

"Yes?"

His face grown nearly purple, Mandy's eyes had lost the last pretense of courtesy or restraint. "Sly, clever William Snopes, son of a lord, and yet he defies family and station to pick up strays off the street. Flea-infested dogs who've lost their masters and their way. With such instincts, it's a wonder you've survived so long in your profession without being badly bitten. You may wish to show more discernment in choosing clients in the future."

"Never been bitten?" William returned a glacial smile. "You clearly haven't stayed abreast of my career. But experience has taught me that masters with their leashes are far more dangerous than the few poor hounds who manage to slip away. In any event, I'll make my own decisions about whom I'll represent. Good day."

10

SOMERS TOWN
LONDON

William looked out the window of his second floor flat onto a street surprised by morning sunshine. Roads were dry, jacket collars turned down. A hackney cab rolled past, the horse's head lifted. Even though a cold snap was settling in, everything and everyone below seemed unburdened by the rain's lifting and the freshened air.

He reached for a cup of tea, cool from the night before. The milk had settled. He sipped, choosing not to mind rather than troubling to get fresh tea, marveling at his own laziness. He wished he felt the same refreshment as the people in the street apparently did. Maybe then he'd bother with preparing a new kettle of hot tea. After a night of little sleep, he *felt* like Edmund had *looked* the day before: as though a knife had been slipped between his ears and a fist of gravel deposited in his stomach.

It was Mandy Bristol. Mandy . . . Bristol. The man didn't even have the character to lie well. All the trappings of success that money could buy. Bright, clever, and deeply corrupt. His benefactors must be many or very well-heeled—or perhaps both. Since the solicitor lacked social station by birth, he'd always envied the status and probably earned those benefactors through abject willingness to cut legal corners. Obliterate them, more likely. Just as he'd done in the Finch case so long ago.

"How could I have been so stupid as to let that man use me back in the day?" William fumed aloud. To blazes with Bristol and his paid witness Colonel Slattery. Let them all rot.

Nearly twenty years gone by and it still festered like an open wound. He'd seen enough wealthy men of his father's cut—entitled, grasping—to hold them all in high suspicion. But it was Mandy Bristol's case, rife with corruption and special status on both sides of counsel table, that first drove away any wish to represent the wealthy of London.

William physically shook himself to shed the feeling, knowing that the act must make him appear like an old dog. He wished he could let it go so easily as that. Besides, he'd accomplished his purpose with Bristol yesterday. He'd sought him out to learn about the lady's new case, and while Bristol believed he'd told him nothing, by his poor lies he'd told William all he needed to know. He'd communicated that nearly every word the lady had told them was true. There was a ship. There were investors. There had been a taking of that ship in harbor, and almost certainly a pending charge of piracy. There was a missing captain. There was a controversy surrounding a Letter of Marque.

Which meant the lady's case was very real. And with Mandy Bristol involved—at whatever level—likely one with the political grist and backstabbing that fed William's legal nightmares. The kind William had told himself he'd never undertake again, not after his last encounter with Solicitor Mandy Bristol, Lord Finch, and their hired witness Colonel Slattery.

Yet here he was, considering representing one of that class again. An upper-class family against the Crown. Why? True, if Lady Jameson spoke accurately, a man's life was at stake. And there was the strange issue of piracy.

What of the young woman herself? Such an odd mix of grand

pride and commonness. Humility even. Why did she stick with him? Was it the way she'd stood up to Edmund? The strength of her resolve?

"Sir?" A voice interrupted his thoughts.

In his hat and coat, Obadiah stood in the open doorway to the stairwell.

"Don't you knock before you throw open doors?" William replied testily, embarrassed at his appearance and surprise.

"I did, sir. A dozen times, sir. We're going to be late to the Union Club. I've a cab waiting downstairs."

William set down the cold tea. "I'll only be a moment."

Retreating into his bedroom, he dressed quickly in a simple black suit—fine enough to satisfy Obadiah's club members. He was about to return to the solicitor when he saw, resting on the dresser, the papers Father Thomas had given him when they'd parted at the pub after the trial.

He picked them up and glanced at them again as he walked back into the living room.

"What are those, sir?" Obadiah asked.

William looked up. "These are from Father Thomas. Whenever he has the ambition to teach me a lesson, he leaves papers with biblical arguments supporting his propositions. These are a renewed condemnation of my career and craft, and its impact on young Edmund."

"You're bringing them with you?"

"No. I've already reviewed them. Don't tell Father Thomas. He's certain I ignore whatever he gives me. I wouldn't want to overly encourage him."

William dropped the Father's papers onto the couch, then grabbed his coat and umbrella and joined Obadiah at the door, setting the matter aside as he took the stairs down to the street and walked out into bright sunshine. It was too fine a morning. He would enjoy the carriage ride with Obadiah in peace.

Except peace eluded him. For the length of the ride he was

hounded, as he had been all night, by a bitter memory of the fatherly face of Colonel Slattery—testifying before Mandy Bristol that day, seated in The Old Bailey's gallery, knowing that William Snopes was winning the day on the back of lies the young barrister only learned as he waded through the colonel's testimony on the stand. And when, late in the day, William had realized it, he hadn't mustered the courage to acknowledge them to the court or jury.

All of that whirled in his head against a backdrop of an orchestral theme. One which, astonishingly, given the usual habit of his gift, he couldn't quite make out.

Plaguing him far more than the morning's sunshine could dispel.

⊲══⊳

THE UNION CLUB
CENTRAL LONDON

"Two shillings, gents!" a young boy with a cloth cap called out as William and Obadiah exited the cab. In his hand was a thin paper-covered book. A bag over his shoulder was filled with more.

William contemplated the boy for a moment, then reached into his pocket and paid the price.

Obadiah looked shocked. "You read *penny dreadfuls*, Mr. Snopes?"

"Of course I do. Half of London reads them. We've twenty newspapers in London, and I'll wager these volumes sell better than most of them on a given day."

"Maybe. But they've barely any truth to them at all."

"That's what makes them so stirring. Tell me, Obadiah: do you think it's a good idea to look down your nose at books that set life's expectations for half the potential jurors in town?" He held the book up. "*The Thames Mystery*. A timely title given Lady Jameson's matter, I think. My favorite was *The Life and Times of the Highwayman Jack Thackery*. Are you really telling me you don't read them?"

Obadiah's eyes grew guarded. "Well, maybe now and again."

They found Edmund seated at a table Obadiah had reserved. Though his face was still lined with fatigue, he was better dressed this morning. William's apprehension for his junior lowered a bit.

The Union Club was poorly attended, the white-coated servants moving slowly amid only a few members present. Another sign of the times, William thought. The two-story home on Bleeker Street was very modern. This included, in the evenings, the novelty of bright light from interior gas fittings unknown in most London homes. William admired the modernity of the feature, though he still preferred the softer light and intimacy of a hundred candles spread about walls and tables. How did Obadiah keep up appearances at the place, meeting the dues on the scarcity of cases he'd referred to them of late? Was he referring cases to other barristers as well?

It seemed very unlikely. Young Obadiah had weaknesses like any man: despite how hard William knew he'd worked in his solicitor's apprenticeship for that slave driver Foster, he still struggled to draft a commendable brief, for example. But along with a bulldog's tenacity, he'd never swerved from a stubborn strain of loyalty— toward William, but particularly toward Edmund.

Through a light meal, Edmund told his story about his visit to the prisons and garrisons and, at the last, to Newgate.

"You sound as though you believe the clerk was lying about our Captain Tuttle's presence at Newgate Prison," William said as Edmund finished.

"The way he insisted on knowing *my name* made me believe that the mention of Captain Tuttle's disturbed him. I admit, that implies to me he had something to hide."

"Anything else to share about your visit?"

Edmund shook his head no.

"What did you find at the docks, Obadiah?"

The solicitor described his night, which ended with his long, serpentine race home from the docks to avoid being followed.

"The crew must be gaoled below the *Padget*'s decks. It's locked up very tight."

"Which certainly confirms the lady's story," William said.

"What did you learn from the solicitor?" Edmund asked William.

"Bristol? The man still struggles with the truth. He said he knows nothing of the *Padget* or the Letter of Marque or the captain for that matter. Yet when I goaded him at the end, he implied a threat if we took the case. No, I'm fairly confident that every word the lady shared with us was confirmed by Solicitor Bristol yesterday."

"Why would the solicitor, if he does represent the investors, remain silent about Captain Tuttle and seizure of the ship?" Obadiah asked. "Don't his clients also lose from the impoundment of the *Padget* and its cargo?"

William shrugged. "I've wondered the same. Still, any matter which engages Mandy Bristol is likely stained with corruption. Perhaps he's trying to avoid getting his clients drawn into an investigation."

"Fine. But why would the Crown be keeping this all a secret?"

"You have me there, Obadiah."

"This business of arresting and hiding the captain without an indictment is serious, sir," Obadiah went on. "There's no legal exemption permitting the Crown to jail a man for so long without a public charging."

"Yes, we're past that legal nicety, all right," William answered. He glanced at his junior. "Edmund, you still appear skeptical."

The young barrister toyed with stirring his tea. "Shouldn't we consider the possibility that Lady Jameson also struggles with the truth, sir? I'll admit to the clerk's evasion at Newgate and that you heard threats from Bristol, but what proof do we have about any of this—other than a ship at dock that appears to be under guard?"

"How about the retainer Lady Jameson offered?" Obadiah demanded. "Why would anyone offer a hundred pounds to a barrister for a case that doesn't exist?"

"I don't know," Edmund replied. "But I'm certain there are people willing to part with money to pursue a claim that's only vapor. She may have other motives for hiring us."

"Perhaps," William acknowledged. "Even so, remember the other oddity here: the silence of the newspapers. As I said before, if the lady's story is correct, we can assume the perpetrators have either been successful in preventing the newspapers from hearing of it or they have sufficient clout to silence the editors. Either possibility implies great resources, social station, or both. Gentlemen, we can chase our tails in this conversation for hours, but to determine whether there's a true and defensible case, we have to first find Captain Tuttle and interview him."

"How?" Obadiah asked. "Assuming he's being hidden, what means do we have to flush him out?"

William smiled. "The boy vendor out front has given me an idea. The people holding Captain Tuttle in custody want the ship's seizure and the arrests to remain quiet, so they must fear public knowledge and reproach. We need to force our adversaries to produce the captain and start the legal wheels rolling—where we can engage them. To do so, we need to pierce the silence, create public interest."

"I don't see how," Edmund grumbled. "The newspapers aren't likely to accept our word on events, even if they aren't being silenced. And we can't print the story ourselves."

"Ah, Edmund, that's where you're wrong. I believe we *can* print the story ourselves, and must. The newspapers haven't the only presses in town."

"True. There is the Church. But I doubt they'd lend us their machines."

"You miss my meaning." William reached to the floor and picked up the book he'd just purchased, opening to the title page. "Publisher Wiscomb and Sons," he read aloud.

Edmund shook his head. "Hire a book publisher to print broadsheets? Who'd pay attention?"

"Again you miss my meaning," William replied. "I'd publish this story as a penny dreadful."

Edmund and Obadiah looked on as though William had declared himself for Parliament.

"You're joking!" Edmund cried at last. "You'd publish this tale as such trash? Who'd believe it? They're less than a third factual on a good day!"

"And everyone's secret pleasure," William rejoined. "And you're wrong: the public will believe it—or at least want to know if what it says is true. I already have the title: *The Appalling True Story of the Unlawful Seizure of the* Padget *and Her Brave Crew, and the Imprisonment of Navy War Hero Harold Tuttle*. I'll write it myself. Perhaps with a little of your youthful energy to help."

"How quickly could we get it released?" Obadiah asked, looking enthused.

"If I subsidize it, I'll bet they'd have a volume on the street in two days."

"We'll be sued for slander if we can't prove our facts," Obadiah said.

"That won't be possible. You can't sue for slander if nobody names you as the bad actor, and we don't even know the guilty parties. But we *will* need funds to feed the serial every day or two with new editions—at least until we shame the newspapers into taking up the story or force our opponents to respond. It won't be cheap."

"I like it," Obadiah said.

"I don't," Edmund declared.

"So you've made clear, Edmund. Nevertheless, I'll need your help for a couple of days getting this publication out."

Edmund made no effort to hide his disappointment. "Sir, please help me understand why you're considering taking such a case, with so little to warrant the commitment. You've passed on these kinds of cases before. Here's one that might implicate the Crown itself. Isn't this the 'political tar' you've always avoided?"

William stared at Edmund, momentarily helpless in the glare of an excellent question. He replayed the arguments he'd faced in the late evening hours about the emotional and professional costs of such a case, then weighed the pounding and public reproach the case might bring.

What was different about this case that would lead him to keep considering it?

Maybe he just wanted to challenge Mandy Bristol after all these years. Hadn't he felt a powerful yearning to take the case the instant he saw the solicitor framed in the doorway of his office? Hadn't that yearning grown as they parted?

What of that Jameson woman?

The inner arguments quieted. He'd say nothing of them to Edmund and Obadiah. There was another truth he could state more safely and persuasively.

"Because our opponents' ability to sidestep the legal process with the kidnapping of the captain," William began, "and the brazenness of the matter anger me. Combined with a young man's life at stake, and the appearance that this Lady Jameson, her father, and Captain Tuttle may be greatly outnumbered and out-funded. No, I can't shake the case off like mud from my boots. Even if, Edmund, you hate the fact that our clients may have their roots in the upper class."

The young barrister appeared embarrassed. "I don't hate them. Not precisely," he said, then drifted into silence.

His retreat seemed a good sign to William. At least he was thinking and not just reacting.

"I'll accept that for now," William answered. "But whatever your feelings, I'm determined that we're at least taking the next step. Let's get started on drafting our first penny dreadful."

11

JAMESON ESTATE
HEATHCOTE MANOR
COUNTY OF ESSEX

Even in full morning daylight, the return ride into Staunton refilled Madeleine with the terror of the evening. Sidestepping the horror of her stricken mare still splayed on the drive, she rode away from the estate grounds, soon finding the woods where she'd hidden the coins the night before.

Tying off her horse, she walked into the trees. Her scarf was undisturbed.

She knelt and dug at the earth. The cloth bag was still there, inches below the surface. Deeply relieved, Madeleine placed it in her saddlebag and rode on.

It wasn't until she was riding over the bridge into town that Madeleine felt a respite from the fingers of fear at her throat. Even then, a rider passing from behind startled her until she saw the face of a familiar farmer. He acknowledged her with a tip of his hat.

Solicitor Rooker greeted her in the entryway of his law office with sad eyes—his mortician's eyes, she'd always called them, steeped in formal, cold empathy. How her father had put up with the man and his thieving fees for so many years, she'd never know. She never would have come to Rooker for help to buy the *Padget* if she'd had any other choice.

Madeleine steeled herself as the solicitor led her silently into his back office.

"How is your father?" Rooker asked when he'd sat stiffly behind his desk.

"Fine, Mr. Rooker, thank you. I'm afraid I'm here because I need an extension on the estate's loan."

Rooker's eyebrows rose. "An extension? On the eve of its maturity? What on earth for?"

"The return of our investment has been . . . delayed."

"I see. I see. I do hope you appreciate that the risk I've . . . we've undertaken on that loan is considerable. I don't see how we could permit such an extension."

"You could because my father was a client for thirty years and supported you with legal work through the worst economic times. I'm not asking you to forgive our debt, only to delay repayment. And only for three months."

She set the soiled bag on the solicitor's desk. "That's a little under one hundred pounds. Consider it a first portion of the loan repayment."

Rooker didn't even look at the bag. "Lady Jameson, that represents less than one percent of your debt."

"I know. But it's a good-faith payment."

The solicitor sighed and stood to pace. "Please recall, Lady Jameson, that I am only an agent for the loan. As I explained to you at the time, it would have been impossible for me to lend such a sum myself. Your loan came from a consortium of professionals and colleagues. Even with your father's power of attorney enabling you to pledge the Heathcote Estate against the ten-thousand-pound sum, I and my colleagues agreed with *great trepidation*. As for myself, I participated only as an accommodation for an old client. Extending the loan now would only add to my risk and that of my colleagues."

Most of what she heard was lies, Madeleine was sure. She could never understand her father's blind spot for Mr. Rooker and others with professional licenses. The penny-squeezing solicitor could easily have made the loan himself and most certainly did. He was only refusing the extension in his greed to acquire Heathcote Estate.

"Then arrange for me to meet your consortium so I can try to convince them."

"Impossible. Simply impossible. They prefer anonymity."

Rooker found his seat again. "Lady Jameson, you're but twenty-nine and inexperienced with such business matters. Let's convene tomorrow with your father—"

"Mr. Rooker, you know perfectly well the state of my father's health. He'll have nothing to add to our discussion."

She had only a single card left to play to Rooker's greed.

"I'll agree to an additional five percent interest on the loan in exchange for a three-month forbearance."

The solicitor's eyes grew lidded. "I don't know that—"

"Six percent and two months."

The pained expression and show of hesitation disappeared. "Ten percent and two weeks," the solicitor replied.

"Seven percent and one month."

"Agreed," Rooker announced. "I'll draw up the papers . . . uh, on behalf of the consortium. It will take half an hour or so. You may wait in the client room."

Standing, Madeleine reached to the desk and took the bag of coins. Solicitor Rooker looked on, startled.

"But I assumed—"

"You'll get *all your money* in a month," Madeleine said and marched from the office.

An hour later, Madeleine entered the chemist's shop, empty of customers. Roisin came out of the back room.

"Madeleine! Back to town so soon? Is everything all right?"

Madeleine felt the soiled bag bulging her pocket. "I had to wrestle old Rooker for an extension on the loan."

"Better get it in writing, dear. I wouldn't trust that vulture to prune my hedges without the arrangement bein' signed and witnessed."

"I did." She looked into her old friend's eyes and dearly wanted to share—with anyone, but especially Roisin—the terror of the night's attack. But Roisin would insist that Madeleine heed the threat and abandon any lawsuit. She hadn't the strength to argue the point now.

"I just wanted to ask that you take care. Please be especially careful with your work with the American just now."

"I will, girl. Don't fret about me. Save your thoughts for your father and yourself."

Madeleine said good-bye with a final hug and walked out to her horse. Nearly a hundred pounds were in the bag in her pocket, another five hundred hidden at home. All the cash she and her father had in the world. It was only February, and those funds would never carry the estate or the farmers dependent on them until spring. Their creditors would drown them by summer.

Proving the existence of the Letter of Marque was her only way to save Harold. But it was also the only way to get the cargo released and sold before her world came tumbling down.

And now, with her agreement with Solicitor Rooker, she had precisely thirty days to do so.

12

Arriving late, Solicitor Mandy Bristol climbed the mountain of steps to the towering front door of Lord Beau Brummell's mansion, moving so quickly that his legs grew rubbery and his breath came hard. A single knock and the chief butler greeted him with stateliness, then turned to lead him deep into the gilded house—beneath chandeliers sparkling with artisans' handicraft, past suits of armor, between portraits of stern family stock unmistakably dressed for service to Crown and country. Huffing to keep up with the butler, Mandy was finally ushered through twin doors into a library, where leather-bound books lined shelves from floor to ceiling and an engraved oaken desk stood majestically on pillared legs. An arched window behind the desk framed a garden and pines beyond.

The butler disappeared. Mandy was still breathless when booted footsteps joined him in the room.

"Solicitor Bristol," an affectionless voice greeted him.

Mandy turned to his host. "Good morning, Lord Brummell. I came as quickly as I could when I got your message."

"Thank you so much," Lord Brummell replied dryly. He walked past Mandy to the chair behind his desk.

Lord Brummell seldom failed to surprise Mandy with the opulence and modernity of his attire. Always dressed as though he was about to be presented at a ball. Today it was split tails and a short-cut front, with black velvet lapels, large buttons front and back, and a stiff cravat high and tight on his neck, signaling indifference to comfort.

Given his loyalty to style, Mandy wondered if the lord even slept in such clothes.

"Have you seen this?" Lord Brummell asked, lifting high from the desktop a paper-backed book.

He knew it instantly. "Yes, I have, sir. "

"'*The Appalling True Story of the Unlawful Seizure of the* Padget *and Her Brave Crew*,' et cetera, et cetera," the lord read at arm's length. He looked to Mandy. "What do you make of it?"

"Tripe, sir. Street trash. No one will pay it any attention."

"Really? Have you seen Volume Two from Monday? Or today's Volume Three?"

"Yes, sir."

"And I should ignore it? That is my solicitor's sage advice?"

This was the kind of verbal trap Brummell liked to lay. But there was no way around it. "Yes, m'lord. These penny dreadfuls are for the lowest of the masses. It will go nowhere."

"And yet here it is! On my own desk! I caught my groom reading the first edition in the stable yesterday. I sent the butler to acquire the second and third, each filling in more salacious details of brave Captain Tuttle's daring and innocence. I'm afraid I must disagree with you. In fact, it's my belief that every storekeeper, factory hand, deliveryman, and lady's maid with the capacity to do so will have read them all by tomorrow. And they'll be joined by half of the noblemen, members of Parliament, and lords and ladies of London—either because they secretly have their servants sneak them copies of the publications or because they discover them as I did, in the hands of their staff."

"Sir, everyone knows these things are the basest form of fiction.

Even if they read them, your contemporaries will pay them no mind."

"Ah, my contemporaries. But what of the masses?" The lord turned the pages slowly to near the back of the book. "'The strong but graceful lines of the brig the *Padget* still occupy London's docks as these words are recorded, her brave and stalwart crew gaoled in its belly for crimes they did not commit, cruelly unrewarded, even punished for acts of heroism against the scourge of smuggling.'" He looked back at Mandy. "Not your typical penny dreadful, is it? More like a call to arms. And you think this will not result in half of London traipsing to the docks to confirm with their own eyes the presence of the *Padget* in all her glory? Her crew gazing plaintively from the gunports? Outfitted and staged to confirm every word of injustice described in this book for the tourists who come to see her? My men at the docks tell me the pilgrimages have already begun."

The books of the library seemed to hang close in mocking attention. The trees outside garnered Mandy's jealousy, safely on the far side of the glass.

"This is the handiwork of that barrister you told me paid you a visit a week or so ago, isn't it?" the lord added.

"Snopes, sir. William Snopes." He cleared his throat. "It's possible."

"Possible? The parting of the Red Sea was possible. Hannibal's crossing of the Alps with his elephants was possible. The publication of this tome is not an ancient event; its authorship should not be difficult to confirm. I pay you to know *what is and what is not*."

"I can check. I *will* check, my lord."

"Good. Now tell me about this Snopes."

His feet growing sore, Mandy stretched on his toes, hoping for an invitation to sit. His host ignored his discomfort. "Well, sir, he is the son of Lord Kyle Snopes."

"Don't tell me what I know. I preside with his father in the House of Lords, man. Tell me what I don't know."

"Of course, sir. Forgive me, sir. William is Lord Snopes's only son. He's rumored to have ruled William with an iron hand. Soon after his mother's death, William rebelled and left home. I believe he was not yet twenty at the time. There are many rumors about the reasons for his departure. One has it that he discovered his father had murdered a servant and secretly buried him on the estate. Whatever the cause for William's leaving, it does appear true that his father wanted him to serve in the King's Guard and follow in his footsteps managing the family estate before entering Parliament. William refused and found a barrister willing to sponsor him for apprenticeship to the bar instead."

"I'd heard some of this before. How do we know any of it to be true?"

"Barrister Snopes handled a case for me not long after he passed the bar. I made it my business then to run down information about him before hiring him on the matter, my lord."

"That's better. What else?"

"He's unmarried, sir. I believe he had a sweetheart when he worked on my case, but I'm aware of no other dalliances with courtship or marriage. He seems entrenched in his career."

"All right. More."

"Since that one case, I've not attended any of his trials, yet it's said that he's developed a style of conducting them in . . . an independent way."

"What do you mean? Doesn't he know the rules?"

"He knows the rules; he just interprets them differently."

"And he gets away with that?"

"It depends upon the magistrate, sir. And though he seems to have shied away from controversial cases, he's willing to take matters that other barristers might find distasteful. Difficult cases."

"Does he win?"

"Surprisingly often, my lord."

"Has he a weakness? Money? Hubris? Ambition?"

"I don't know at present. It is rumored that his junior, Edmund Shaw, has a gambling habit."

"You learned this how?"

"I've had people researching since Barrister Snopes's visit to my office last week, my lord." *And I thought I'd have more time to complete that research before this interrogation.*

"That's good. The man you paint is unlikely to respond to a bribe."

"Agreed, sir," Mandy said, his feet and knees aching.

"Is it a certainty he will take Captain Tuttle's case?"

"Unknown. You'll recall that, after I learned a Lady Jameson, the captain's cousin, had visited the Inns of Court, I arranged for delivery of a message to dissuade her from retaining any barrister at all. I didn't know at the time that Snopes was the barrister with whom she spoke. If she persists with legal representation regardless, I can't say what Barrister Snopes's inclinations will be."

"Yet this recent publication would seem to indicate he's accepted the representation or is likely to do so."

Mandy grew silent.

"You've reassured me repeatedly, Mr. Bristol, that our arrangement regarding the *Padget* would never come to light."

"This is a brief complication, Lord Brummell. Nothing more."

"Yet I'm also informed that the discussions between Captain Tuttle and the Crown's prosecuting barrister, Sir Barnabas, are failing to reach their intended conclusion."

"Is that so, sir?"

"Yes, it is so. Enough of this waste of breath. I want you to speak with Sir Barnabas yourself and ensure that he speaks with Mr. Snopes directly. I want Sir Barnabas to determine if Mr. Snopes is now representing Captain Tuttle. If so, learn whether Snopes will attempt to convince the captain to accept our proposed resolution of the *Padget* problem. If all that still proves unsuccessful, the Crown will have no choice but to proceed to prosecute the piracy charge."

"As you wish. Sir Barnabas will, of course, have to reveal the captain's location to Barrister Snopes then, my lord."

"Certainly. It's time to do so anyway, before the captain's disappearance gets out and creates its own rumors."

"I'll see to it, my lord."

"Good. Oh, and I want you to prepare stories for our contacts at the newspapers to counter these street books. Degrade this Snopes fellow personally. Paint him as a drunkard—or worse, a traitor to Crown and country. I also want stories running this *Padget* aground as a traitorous scow full of brigands and thieves. And find some dirt on this Jameson clan as well. Hold on releasing anything, though, until we see the outcome of Sir Barnabas's meeting with Snopes."

"Yes, my lord."

Lord Brummell's eyes grew flinty. "Mr. Bristol, do you fully appreciate the continued need for secrecy as to the role that I and my partner play in these matters? And how critical it is that we continue to enjoy anonymity from whomever you employ to assist you in your dealings with this Lady Jameson and her counsel?"

More scolding. *Let me get out of this inquisition chamber and about your business.* "Of course, my lord."

"I hope you do. Now leave me." Lord Brummell picked up the paper-backed book once more. "I hadn't quite finished this thing. This Snopes begins to vex me. But if this is indeed his writing, he has a certain flair with words."

13

Edmund entered William's office, shutting the door to the foyer behind him. "There's someone here to see you," he said. "A barrister." He set a card on William's desk.

William raised it to the light. "Do you know whom we have the pleasure of meeting this morning, Edmund?"

"I didn't look closely at the card."

"Our visitor is Sir Barnabas Fletcher. *King's Counsel*."

Edmund's eyes betrayed his surprise. "He's a KC?"

"That's right. One of the king's own, appointed to serve His Majesty when called. Do you know how many KCs there are in the entirety of the English bar? Thirteen. Eight of those legal lions are hopelessly past their prime. Sir Barnabas is in the midst of *his* prime, and I've seen him at work in the courtroom. He's very good."

"As KC, he can't represent any interests against the Crown, correct, sir? So he must be here as either private counsel or on behalf of the Crown."

"Yes, Edmund. They're free to do private work—simply not against the Crown. I can think of no matter we're handling that would attract the interest of an exalted KC other than the Crown's prosecution of Captain Tuttle, which means we've driven them out of the tall grasses. Bring him in. And leave the sparring to me for now. Don't speak unless I ask you a direct question."

Edmund was nervous, which surprised William. He usually seemed unimpressed or openly hostile to all nobility or those near it.

Perhaps it was because this nobility consisted of a higher rank in his own profession. The highest, in fact.

Sir Barnabas followed Edmund into William's office. Likely in his fifties, he was square-jawed and closely shaved, cheeks pink with the vitality of a younger man. Sir Barnabas greeted William before taking a seat.

"Mr. Snopes," Sir Barnabas began, "we haven't had the pleasure of meeting in a courtroom, have we?"

"I'm sure that I would remember the experience." William smiled. "To what do we owe the honor of this meeting?"

"I've learned only today that you may represent Lord and Lady Jameson in the matter of the pirate ship the *Padget*."

William nodded. Where would he have gained that knowledge? Mandy Bristol? Edmund's visit to Newgate? Each had its own implications.

"We don't acknowledge acts of piracy," William said. "But, at least preliminarily, we're seeing to the Jamesons' interests—as well as those of Captain Tuttle."

"And this is your junior?" Sir Barnabas gestured to Edmund.

"Correct again. Edmund Shaw, Esquire."

"I understand you've recently passed the bar," Sir Barnabas said to Edmund. "My congratulations."

Edmund nodded stiffly.

"Well then," Sir Barnabas declared, "to business. I've been retained by the Crown to pursue a piracy prosecution of Captain Tuttle and his crew."

"I see. Has there been a formal indictment of Captain Tuttle?"

"Yes. Though piracy cases are ordinarily heard by the Admiralty Court, due to the unique circumstances in this case, the Admiralty Court has waived jurisdiction in favor of the Central Criminal Court, which issued the indictment. You would have been informed earlier except that no one was aware you were serving Captain Tuttle's interests as counsel. In fact, Captain Tuttle was indicted two days past."

You didn't know of our involvement because the man has been hidden from us, William wanted to say, but withheld. He flashed Edmund a sidelong glance to do so as well.

"Now that we know of your role, I've been granted authority by the Crown for a proposition we hope you will convey to Captain Tuttle."

"Which is?"

"That Captain Tuttle admit his guilt. In exchange, we'll seek court approval of punishment that avoids the gallows."

"What punishment would that be?"

"Transportation to Tasmania."

William looked at Edmund, who was barely stifling a response. "And the crew?"

"They'd be freed, under the presumption they were following Captain Tuttle's orders. So long as they remain silent about the whole affair, they won't be prosecuted. If any breathes a word, they'll all be fully prosecuted, without the good fortune of the option of transportation. I'm confident the court would approve this proposition."

William nodded. "Sir Barnabas, are you aware that Captain Tuttle claims he operated under a Letter of Marque from the Crown itself?"

"So I've been told."

"Do you acknowledge that, if true, Captain Tuttle and his crew are innocent under the law?"

Sir Barnabas shrugged. "I acknowledge nothing. If there was any truth to Captain Tuttle's claimed Letter of Marque endorsed by the Crown, do you think I'd have been retained by that very Crown to prosecute him now? The Letter of Marque is a fiction, and one which does not concern us."

"Um-hmm. If that *fiction* doesn't concern you, why are you offering an arrangement at all?"

"Mr. Snopes, the truth is that the prosecution would be a messy affair."

"Because of the Letter of Marque?"

"No. Because of the prospect of twenty-one bodies, captain and crew, displayed on the gallows. Guilty or not, that would not be a favorable image for the ruling regent. I'm informed that it would also present a challenge to the Crown Pardon Council, discerning upon whom and how many—if any—to bestow the Crown's mercy of a reprieve."

"Don't forget the practical difficulty of so many hangings at once now that Tyburn scaffold is no more," William said matter-of-factly. "I know for a fact that it could accommodate twenty-four, Sir Barnabas."

The barrister stared as though trying to confirm if William was being humorous or insulting.

"Yes, of course," Sir Barnabas answered at last. "And there is also the matter of the nature of the crime. I happen to represent the Crown and its servants in many cases. This case impacts England's relationship with France. I'm informed that our regent and his counselors have been able to keep King Louis and the French government mollified and mum about Captain Tuttle's taking of a French merchantman in a time of peace, but only on the promise that the Crown will prosecute him and his crew. However, with the recent publication of a fictional work about the *Padget*, a penny dreadful, both the French king and our regent are losing latitude to compromise. Once the details of the piracy reach the streets of Paris—particularly a piracy claimed to have been sanctioned by our own Crown—it will ignite an outcry among the French citizenry, forcing King Louis to action. Perhaps even to war."

"Hence the silence in the London papers about the seizure of the *Padget*?" William asked. "Our good regent's doing or yours?"

"I'm not privy to the Crown's relationship with the press," Sir Barnabas said with a shrug. "Nor have I lowered myself to speak to the clamoring gossips who've titled themselves journalists. Anyway, that's irrelevant. What *is* relevant is that higher considerations dictate against fully punishing Captain Tuttle and his crew. Hence my offer and, I'm informed, the willingness of the court to support the offer."

Edmund stiffened. William leaned forward to enforce his junior's silence.

"In order to consider your offer, you do realize we'd need access to our client," he said to Sir Barnabas.

Sir Barnabas's eyebrows rose. "Access? Have you had a problem meeting with Captain Tuttle?"

If he was lying, he was much better at it than Mandy Bristol.

"Sir Barnabas, in the nearly three weeks since the ship's taking, we haven't even been informed of the captain's whereabouts."

"Come, Mr. Snopes! That's no secret. He's in Newgate Prison."

Edmund's face was on fire now. William felt his own growing hot as well.

"That's good to know," William somehow managed to say calmly. "I do hope that we'll have no further trouble meeting with him."

"I will ensure that you will not, although I confess I've already put this proposition to Captain Tuttle myself. If only I'd known of your representation earlier, I would never have spoken to him directly. Do forgive me."

"Of course," William replied evenly, knowing further protest was useless. "Tell me: have you been in touch with the other investors?"

"Other investors? Whatever do you mean?"

"It's my understanding that the Jamesons were not the only investors in the *Padget*'s voyage. I'm informed a portion of the ship's profit was to go to a corporation owned by two investors."

Sir Barnabas shrugged. "So?"

"As I asked: have you been in touch with them?"

"No. Unless you've proof that your investors sanctioned your captain's illegal actions, I'm not interested in commercial squabbles. The prosecution of blatant acts of piracy is my concern."

"Then what are your intentions for the *Padget*—if Captain Tuttle agrees to your terms?"

"It will be sold to pay damages to the French, of course."

"The ship and cargo?"

"Certainly."

"You'd need Lord and Lady Jameson's approval for that. As the ship's owners."

"Yes. I should hope they'd readily agree. You know that we could try them for piracy as well, since they hired this Tuttle to captain their ship. They should be very grateful there's been no suggestion of prosecuting them—so far."

Edmund took a step forward. William raised a hand to halt him.

"I must add, Mr. Snopes," Sir Barnabas went on, "that we will require your clients' response within two days."

William blinked. "Two days? Why?"

"Because, if I'm unable to achieve a settlement within that period, I've been instructed we must proceed to trial, and very soon."

"That's impossible!" Edmund finally burst. "We haven't had an opportunity to interview witnesses! To prepare!"

Sir Barnabas glanced at Edmund, unfazed. "That's what I've been informed by Magistrate Raleigh."

"Raleigh? At The Old Bailey?" William straightened. "You're sure he's been assigned as judge in the matter?"

"Yes. As with Captain Tuttle's location, I'd assumed you'd heard."

"How could we?" Edmund nearly shouted. "We weren't even permitted access to our client!"

Frustrated, William raised a hand once more to silence Edmund. His junior mercifully obeyed.

"We'll be requesting a few months to prepare," William said with an even tone. "Until May at the earliest."

"You may certainly seek it. But I believe the judge thinks this matter should be resolved . . . as soon as possible. He appears sensitive to the difficulties this has caused the Crown vis-à-vis the French. He also wishes to quell defamatory beliefs that the public might adopt from the penny dreadful I mentioned. Have you heard of it, by the way?"

"In fact, I have. A marvelous bit of writing, I'm told." William stood. "This has been most interesting. But it appears we have some work to do."

Sir Barnabas stood and nodded his *good day* with a light smile.

When the outer doors had closed shut, Edmund turned to William, livid.

"An accelerated trial? Curse whoever's behind this."

Still reeling himself, William resisted the urge to admonish Edmund for his outbursts in front of the barrister.

"That's not our greatest problem," he replied instead. "Old Judge Raleigh made his reputation as a hard-nosed barrister in the western counties. Since he's been appointed a magistrate to The Old Bailey, he's become a hanging judge of the first order. We'll get no quarter from him."

"This is outrageous! Little chance to prepare. Little chance even to speak with our client. And a KC on the case! You said he's good?"

"He's very good. Works hard and is persuasive. Especially to judges, who wield so much power over the proceedings. I wonder if Mandy had some role in Sir Barnabas's retention."

"But your Mr. Bristol represents the investors," Edmund said. "Why would he support a prosecution? I can't even understand why these supposed investors are staying hidden at all. You'd think they'd join in defending the *Padget* and her captain and crew, if only to protect their profits. If they'd come forward and acknowledge providing Captain Tuttle with a Letter of Marque, then the captain and the lady's problems would be over."

"Agreed," William said. "But they haven't. And not yet knowing the investors' identities, we're left to explore other avenues of defense. I'm going to start by testing Sir Barnabas's assurance that we can actually speak with Captain Tuttle."

"Mr. Snopes," Edmund said warily, "you know of my distaste for this case. Still, you're not seriously going to suggest that Captain Tuttle agree to their terms, are you? You know as well as I that the Tasmanian colony is the worst for transported prisoners—assuming he even reaches there alive. He may be trading one form of execution for another. If he's innocent, that's a terrible bargain."

William nodded. "That will be up to Captain Tuttle. And in making that decision, he must know that he also bears the burden of the risk to his crew if he refuses."

"Maybe so. Still, I hope he turns it down."

"His choice," William emphasized again. "I'll find out when I meet with him."

Though in his heart, he hoped precisely the same.

14

NEWGATE PRISON

Standing before the clerk, William refused to acknowledge the chill in the prison entryway. Even his oversized coat couldn't protect him against it. He stared down at the seated man fitting Edmund's description, young yet cold as a cod and with a similar complexion. At least he hadn't denied knowledge of Captain Tuttle this time.

"Follow me," the clerk said, standing and motioning.

They walked down a passageway through locked doors, each manned by a guard, then into the heart of Newgate Prison itself. Striding along dank, stinking corridors between barred cells, William observed whole families—prisoners joined by wives and children—with the walls about them ascending to tiny apertures of sunlight, their only source of illumination besides torches and small coal fires for warmth. Farther along were separate quarters for single men or women, many clothed humiliatingly in rags or worse. The healthy were barely separated from the ill and had little chance of remaining healthy due to the lack of heat. It was, William thought in disgust, the rankest symbol of England's slow march toward modernity.

They reached a staircase that descended beyond the reach of

sunlight. William turned to the clerk with alarm. "The captain's in the isolation cells?"

"Yes."

"What violence has he committed?"

"I'm not the warden."

Shaken, William followed the clerk down, their footfalls echoing into darkness ahead, rounding until they reached a subterranean hallway where torches threw shadows across a long row of cells. The clerk led William to a spot only a few cells from the end.

"This one," the clerk said and pointed, but he made no motion to unlock the door.

"I want to go in."

"No one's given entry to these cells."

"You'll let me in or I'll see the warden."

"He's a very busy man," the clerk said. "Fifteen minutes with the prisoner."

Not awaiting a response, the clerk ascended the steps, leaving William stunned and alone in a silence broken only by the skittering of rats.

There was movement in a shadowed corner of the cell William faced. A figure shuffled forward into the torchlight.

It was a man, his clothes torn, his face bruised, cuts healing over each eye. He looked an ancient thirty-five, though he held himself proudly erect.

"Captain Tuttle?" William asked.

"Yes. Who are you?"

The smell of the corridor was revolting. "A barrister. William Snopes. I've been sent by Lady Jameson."

The captain stared as though the words sank in slowly. "My cousin? I'd begun to think she'd no word of my arrival. Or that she'd given up on me."

"She hasn't, I can assure you. Neither she nor we were informed you were in this prison until today. Captain, your face. You've been beaten. The jailors?"

"No. Other prisoners. Several were in this cell when I was first locked up. Some tried to steal my clothes. I assure you, I gave as well as I got."

"This place is barbaric," William muttered.

The man looked weak, laboring even to talk. "Your experience, Mr. Snopes?"

"Fifteen years past the bar. Though this is my first case defending an assertion of piracy." William reached into a deep pocket on his bulky coat and pulled out a flagon of wine, a half loaf of bread, and a handful of carrots. "Enough experience to know the meager rations in this place. It's not much, Captain. Still, I suggest you eat slowly."

"God bless you," the captain said, reaching for the food. "I fear I'll get scurvy with the food they provide."

Gratified at the captain's appetite, William gave a half smile. "I'll arrange for more and regular food. Captain, I must tell you that I haven't accepted your representation—at least not for trial of your case. Nor that of Lady Jameson and her father. I need more information to make my decision."

The captain nodded. He took several bites of the bread and a long drink of the wine. William waited patiently until the captain slowed.

"What do you need to know?" the captain asked at last.

"First, are you aware of the specific charges against you?"

"Only that I was arrested as a pirate. It's absurd. I'm not a pirate, nor is my crew."

"I was told by Lady Jameson that you seized cargo from a French ship in the Indies. Is that true?"

"We did. The *Charlemagne*. Smuggling tea out of China."

"Before we discuss that, tell me about yourself and how you came to captain the *Padget*."

Captain Tuttle took another bite of the bread before looking up.

"After England sent Napoleon to his retirement, many British sailors and officers were retired from England's service as well, including myself. I'd walked the docks for months looking for a decent berth. Jobs were scarcer than saints, for ex-sailors at least. I was desperate. There is a young woman, you see. One I'd hoped to betroth. Then I learned the *Padget* was for sale, an old brig out of service after the war. They wanted nineteen thousand pounds for her. I decided to buy her for trade in the Americas but had nothing like that kind of money. I told my cousin Madeleine about my need. I knew the Jameson estate had suffered hard times for many years, even before things worsened in England since the peace. My strongest hope was that Madeleine might know someone with capital to invest. A week later she surprised me, saying she and her father could find the money to buy the brig. We agreed I was to receive twenty percent of the profit on the first voyage and fifty percent on future voyages, once the ship was paid for."

"And what of money to pay for a crew? Provisions? To acquire cargo for trade?"

"We agreed we'd advertise in the papers for investors to cover those expenses."

"This voyage was a risky affair financially then?"

"Yes. But risks must be taken if a man wishes to better his position."

"And there is the young lady."

"Yes. I'm not ashamed of my ambition, Mr. Snopes, nor the reasons for it. Rebekah will forever be the love of my life. But her family won't sanction a match with a former naval officer without prospects. I don't blame them."

"A solicitor responded to your advertisements, correct?"

"Aye. That devil Mandy Bristol. He met me at the *Padget* one afternoon and told me he represented a corporation with two investors behind it. The investors insisted on staying anonymous. They offered little money, but Bristol claimed they had something better: a Letter of Marque from the Crown to hunt down French tea smugglers violating the East India Company's contracts with Chinese tea merchants, signed by the regent himself. Tea is gold these days, as you know, Mr. Snopes, and I couldn't have asked for a more hopeful prospect. Bristol said that the regent wanted to help the East India Company chase tea smugglers crossing the Indian Sea and end their theft, which was cutting into company and Crown revenue. Bristol made a point, though, of saying that the taking of smugglers was to be done without public fanfare. We were to teach the French a quiet lesson."

"And you never met Bristol's investors?"

"No. The solicitor presented the proposal and handled the details. It was all worked out between Bristol and myself."

"And you believed him? About the Letter?"

"To be honest, we had no other choice. Even so, I insisted to Bristol that I wouldn't sail without the Letter *in my hand*. I pressed to meet with the regent's counselors who prepare such documents, or better still the regent himself. Bristol refused, saying the political sensitivity of the matter prevented it, that he and his investors must act as go-betweens with the authorities. Weeks passed while Bristol failed to produce the Letter. At last, already bleeding wages to my assembled crew and with launch of the voyage at risk—in fact, the day before our intended sailing date—Bristol finally brought the Letter to me. I never told Bristol, but I'd already secretly retained a solicitor in Chelsea, a man who used to work at the Exchequer and at Carlton House and knew the King's Seals. It cost me nearly my last shilling, but the man examined the Letter and seal and said they were genuine."

"Who was that solicitor?"

"Ryan Mortimer. On Hampstead Road."

"All right. Now tell me about taking the French merchantman."

"It was good fortune, really. We'd all manner of problems getting to the Indian Sea, from doldrums to storms to a raider shadowing us around the Cape. We made it to India but had no luck once there. At anchor in Calcutta, we were down to the last provisions we needed to get back to England. Then we finally got word from an East India Company man I'd befriended about a French merchantman rumored to be anchored at Ceylon with smuggled tea, bound for the Americas. Sure enough, we'd only trolled the sea lanes a few days when a schooner sailed out of the eastern sea, her masts tall, rolling low and fat in heavy waters, a French tricolor snapping from her jack staff. The *Charlemagne* was settled so deep I knew she had a full hold. Near to five hundred tons of tea, as it turned out. Better still, the schooner had only ten guns against our twenty."

"So you attacked?"

"I did. Turned out she had enough men and arms to put up a fight. We had but a skeleton crew ourselves, barely enough to man our own guns, and most every man serving at least two jobs. Regardless, at a thousand yards we put two shells across her bow, and she heaved to. Didn't lose a man on either ship."

"You say a full cargo?"

The captain nodded. "Yes. Their papers made clear they'd acquired the tea illegally from the East India Company's vendors. The taking represented triple the profit we'd have known from my plan to trade in the Americas."

"Then you sailed for home?"

"Yes, with a couple of stops along the way. The last was two weeks in Gibraltar for water and repairs we'd tried to hold off until we returned to England. While there, I sent a mail packet ahead to Madeleine with a departing ship, letting my cousin know of our planned arrival date—and the good news about the cargo. Then, once repairs were done, it was back up the coast, into the Thames, and home."

There were no hesitations by the captain, no sensitivity even about the unusual elements of his story.

"Tell me about the seizure of your vessel here in London," William requested.

The captain was growing weary, but after another drink of wine he described the midnight arrival of the soldiers and constables, followed by the disappearance of the Letter of Marque he'd held only minutes before the boarding. At the last, the captain described the killing of a cabin boy named Simon Ladner.

William started. Had he heard correctly? Lady Jameson hadn't mentioned it, so she couldn't have known. But surely Sir Barnabas had been told when he was retained for the prosecution. Why hadn't *he* mentioned it?

"How old was this boy?"

"By the day of our return, perhaps fourteen."

"You're sure he was killed?"

The captain's face collapsed into sadness. "Yes. My first mate was a sailor named Quint Ivars. I'd served with Ivars early in my naval career, aboard the *Pelletier*, and he'd seemed a good enough seaman. But when he presented himself for a berth aboard the *Padget*, he said he'd gained experience as a physician's mate as well. Medical officers are a rare commodity aboard small trading brigs such as ours. I leapt to hire him. It was Ivars who saw to the boy after the shooting. The boy's death was especially hard on Mr. Ivars. It was he who'd brought the boy aboard in the first place, at the request of his father, a friend and cobbler from Whitechapel who'd lost his wife in childbirth. Young Simon learned very fast and never complained or slacked. Everyone in the crew cared for him very much. The soldiers and constables should never have fired on us, Mr. Snopes. There was no reason to do so and harm the boy."

There was a stirring in a cell even deeper in the darkness, followed by a hollow cough and a shuffling of feet.

"It's obvious, Captain Tuttle," William began again, lowering his voice, "that the proof of your innocence lies in establishing the existence of the Letter, which you say was missing when the soldiers took you to your cabin. Where did you keep it, and who knew of it?"

"It was locked in a cabinet above my cabin desk. I'd shown it only to Mr. Ivars. He knew where it was kept—in case I didn't survive the voyage. But he couldn't have taken it; he was on deck with me between the time when I last saw the Letter and when I led the soldiers to my cabin. And I had the only key. As for the rest of the crew, they were told I had the Letter, which was a necessity to ensure they obeyed my orders for taking French ships. But I didn't advertise where I kept it, any more than where my other valuables were locked."

"Why do you believe the Letter was stolen?"

"It's obvious, isn't it? To destroy my defense to the charge of piracy."

"Who would have a motive for such action?"

"I don't know."

William thought a moment more, then continued, "We're running out of time, Captain, and we've something more to speak of today. The prosecutor informed us he offered you a resolution: a guilty plea in exchange for transportation to Tasmania—and your crew not facing charges."

"Yes. He's been here twice, threatening me to accept his offer."

"Are you innocent, Captain Tuttle?" William asked. "Did you truly have a genuine Letter of Marque when you took the French ship?"

The captain looked through the bars with steady eyes. "Yes. I swear on everything holy to me. I swear on my love for Rebekah."

"You do know that your innocence doesn't guarantee our ability to prove it, yes?"

"I'm aware of that."

"And that the judge could order your execution if you're convicted."

"Aye."

"And you also know, if you refuse the offer, that you put your crew at risk of prosecution?"

"That's the hardest part in this, Mr. Snopes. But yes, I realize that."

"Then what do you want me to communicate to the prosecutor?"

The captain took a grip of the bars. "I'll tell you the same thing

I told that smug Sir Barnabas. If they hadn't killed the boy, I'd take their damnable offer. It'd be a lie and an injustice that would drive me mad, but I'd take it for the sake of the crew. But if I accept their offer, Sir Barnabas said I'd also have to agree there'd be no future prosecution of anyone—including whoever killed Simon. Let them hang me if it comes to it. Do all you must to protect my crew. But I can't let someone walk away from killing that innocent boy."

The captain's steadfastness was unmistakable. William's belief in the man and his story intensified. Who would accept the risk of hanging if they were truly guilty and offered this bargain? Still, the weight of risk the man was willing to take dropped onto William's own back like a sack of flour.

"Do I understand correctly, then," William asked, "that if we accept your case, you'd want us to prosecute the boy's death, as well as defend the case against you and the *Padget*?"

"Yes, if that can be done. Though I've no idea how I could pay you for it, especially rotting in this pit. Every penny I've got is tied up in the *Padget*."

It would be a singular fight, with so much at stake. Not only for Captain Tuttle, but for himself and for Edmund and Obadiah.

And for Lady Jameson.

His next words would be disappointing, as they had been for the lady. Still, William leaned close and said the only thing he could. "Captain Tuttle, I will honor your resolve with a decision about trial just as soon as I'm able."

William removed his coat and gave it to the captain as they parted. As he started up the stairs leaving the captain behind, he heard it again: the orchestral piece that had plagued him in the morning hours on his ride to Obadiah's club for breakfast. Louder now. Still torturing him, its identity just beyond reach.

Why couldn't he recall the tune?

15

SOMERS TOWN
LONDON

Ending a long and thoughtful walk, William arrived back at his flat. Ascending the stairs, turning at the final landing, he started and caught his breath.

A man in a black cassock and white collar was seated on the step before his door.

"Father Thomas," William spoke as his heart slowed. "What spiritual failing has God sent you to correct in me today?"

The bony man stood. "Nothing in particular. Though from your surprise, I take it you've a guilty conscience. That's a good start anyway."

William led him into his paper-strewn sitting room. "I'm afraid I've no time to debate today. I've a new case I'm considering and several errands to run."

"As I've heard," the Father said, taking in the typhoon about him. The priest studied William's face. "Are you really so shocked I'd know your business? While you seldom stray from life among heathens, Obadiah and Suzanne often grace the parish church, as does Edmund."

121

"If you're aware, then you'll excuse me for bidding you good-bye."

William rooted about in his papers looking for better walking shoes. When he looked up, the Father stood his ground.

"I'll be gone in a moment," he said. "I wanted you to know that someone came to see me yesterday." There was unmistakable seriousness in the priest's voice.

"Who's that?" William asked reluctantly.

"Suzanne, actually."

"Obadiah's wife?"

"The same. She came to speak with me."

"Then I'm sure that's a confidential matter."

"Ordinarily. Except that *you* were the topic of our discussion. You should know that Suzanne is afraid."

William stopped to face the Father. "Afraid of what?"

"Of this case you're thinking of taking."

"Thomas, I'm happy to debate the moral failings of the judicial system, but I *won't* subject my decisions to your judgment as to which cases to accept or reject."

The Father held up his hands. "Hear me out, William. I thought you should know the substance of Suzanne's concerns."

She was a good and level-headed woman and Obadiah was fortunate to have her. William stopped his search among the papers. "Which are?"

"That you are giving serious consideration to defending a case against the Crown that may have great political ramifications. And that there have already been threats made against you should you take the case."

"Suzanne needn't worry. If I choose to take it, I'll manage just fine."

"Perhaps. But yours aren't the only legal cases I've observed at The Old Bailey. You've gained a reputation for clever advocacy, William. That cleverness may prevail with your typical clients—debtors and wronged tenants and the poor, such as that boy

Patrin—but high crimes like piracy are far more serious affairs, which could embarrass the Crown. There can be consequences for engaging in such things. Politics has a much broader reach than the courthouse."

"I'm not an adolescent, Thomas. I've been weighing those considerations already."

"Have you? Then have you considered that piracy charges can stir popular discontent as well as professional? You're not a popular man already among certain classes of businessmen, you know."

"If you mean moneylenders, debt handlers, and bankers, that's true. I've tended to represent their accused victims."

"Precisely. And the Crown has the means to encourage much unrest against you, foster a popular cause against you, perhaps even enflame the masses and the street mobs against you. Your career could be at risk, not to mention your safety. I frankly don't understand why you're still giving consideration to the case at all. You've had opportunities with upper society disputes in the past and declined."

Once again, William marveled, unhappily, at how Father Thomas could strike at his own underlying concerns.

"Nothing like this, Thomas. There's a flavor to this I don't like."

"Then you've decided to take the case?"

"No, I have not. Now, thank you, Thomas. I'll take your worry under advisement."

The Father made no motion to leave.

"Another point, William, is that the case could represent a threat to Obadiah and Edmund as well."

"If Obadiah has such concerns, he should bring them to me directly. Same with Edmund. They're both fully grown men and certified attorneys. They should speak for themselves."

"It would scarcely occur to Obadiah that you might make an error in judgment on such matters. He'd follow you into Hades, with Edmund only a few steps behind. They think that much of you."

"Praising with faint damnation, are you, Thomas?"

"I'm quite serious."

"I know. I'll take all you've said into account."

Father Thomas gave a familiar stare of dissatisfaction. "William, the day you graced my parish door in your flight from your father's estate, I feared your experience would compel you to use your barrister's position to seek revenge against others of your class. Then there was the disappointment that followed in your search for your half sibling that your father had banished—"

"You promised to never speak of that."

"And I haven't, up to this very moment. There's been no need. Because, until now, you've shown no signs of a vengeful sentiment."

"And why do you think that might change now?"

"I don't know. A feeling. A stirring in my prayers. The fact that you're still considering the case."

William hovered between affection and anger at the Father's words.

"You needn't worry," he finally answered. "My grudge, then and now, implicated one man, not his whole class. I won't succumb to despising the wealthy in general or the Crown in particular. Unlike Edmund, I understand their place, so long as they act with propriety. I'll take each case as it comes, on the merits and without emotion. Including weighing the dangers you speak of in the present one."

"So you say. But be careful. This piracy matter would be a dangerous case to take to satisfy rebellious sentiments."

"You needn't concern yourself. I'm not inclined to martyrdom."

"I hope so," Father Thomas said skeptically. "I'll be taking to my knees for you and your companions about your decision."

"Most appreciated."

Father Thomas nodded, then turned to leave. Once at the door, he halted.

William waited for another ax to fall. The Father looked over a shoulder at him.

"Can't you afford an occasional cleaning maid, William?"

"Good day, Thomas."

Soon back out the door again, William's walk to Chelsea was long. He preferred such treks on foot, especially when he had much to think about.

On this occasion, William spent the distance silently railing against Father Thomas and his visit an hour before. The man was positively taking up residence in William's brain. The priest needn't keep descending like a harpy to remind him of his responsibilities, he thought. *Leave my conscience. Let me get about my business my own way.*

By the time he'd reached the Chelsea address, the air was filled with a misting rain. *Ryan Mortimer, Solicitor* was on the door before him. Likely the man's residence as well as his office, William thought, looking about the neighborhood.

He knocked.

The door was opened by a young maid.

"I'm looking for Solicitor Mortimer," William said. "Is he in?"

"It's very late, sir. After his business hours."

"Please. The matter is urgent."

"I can see if he's available. Your name, sir?"

William handed her a card. "Barrister William Snopes. Please inform Solicitor Mortimer that I'm here about a mutual client, Captain Harold Tuttle. I only require a few minutes of his time."

The maid curtsied and turned about, closing the door behind her.

In a moment she returned. "Mr. Mortimer will see you in his office. Please follow me."

Solicitor Mortimer joined William in a small, neat office. Apologizing for arriving without an appointment, William explained the reason for his visit.

"May I take it, Mr. Mortimer, from your willingness to meet with me, that when you met with Captain Tuttle before his voyage the year before last, you gave him positive news about his Letter of Marque?"

The solicitor was middle-aged with black hair, long fingers he cupped on his lap, and a firmly professional demeanor.

"Mr. Snopes," he replied carefully, "you must appreciate that I can't comment on attorney-client discussions."

"Of course. But Captain Tuttle has been detained, so he can't give you permission to speak with me—unless you're amenable to visiting him at Newgate Prison. Let me limit my question to this: is it true the captain asked you to examine a document in the nature of a Letter of Marque for its genuineness? I needn't know, at this time, what your advice was on the matter. I'm sorry to press the point, but there is some urgency."

The solicitor's gaze remained on William as he pondered. If eyes were any measure, he was a decent man. Cautious, as most solicitors were—more judicious and prudent like Obadiah, as against the passion of a risk taker like Edmund. Likely weighing what he'd stepped into and how far he was willing to go for a client he'd only represented briefly and once, over a year before. Especially if there was now controversy about the very opinion he'd rendered for that client.

At last, the man slowly stood. "I will agree to this much, Mr. Snopes. I will, by the day after tomorrow, visit your office and inform you as to what I may or may not say in this matter."

William understood the gesture, and he rejoiced. The solicitor was signaling his intent to get permission to speak. That could only mean he planned a trip to Newgate, a trip only necessary if Captain Tuttle was in fact a client. And why would he trouble with such a trip if he hadn't advised Captain Tuttle, before the voyage, that the Letter of Marque was genuine? If he had originally informed the captain that the Letter was not real, the solicitor wouldn't now bother to gain permission to tell William such damaging information.

The sum of it was as near to an acknowledgment of the truth of the captain's story as William could have hoped for—and key evidence to win the captain and the lady's case.

"Thank you," William said, buoyed. "I'll look forward to hearing from you."

Lady Jameson would be pleased with this news, he thought as he left the office and looked up and down the street for a cab. Now, one more task to round out a full and successful day.

It was nearing one o'clock in the morning when the carriage William caught in Chelsea brought him, after a long ride, within a few blocks of the Thames docks.

"You'll have to walk from 'ere," his hunched driver said. "A big cargo or two must've come in. Streets are too busy tonight to get tangled in traffic closer to the river."

William paid the fare and exited.

The driver was right. Despite the hour, stevedores and sailors mixed in a swirling crowd along the waterfront. From Obadiah's description, William knew precisely where he needed to go. Even so, bumped and jostled in the light of torches lining the water, it took nearly half an hour to reach his destination.

In a corner of the London shipyard, William finally stared at the docked ship, ghostly quiet in the night. Rocking low at anchor, the brig seemed smaller than he'd imagined.

He walked onto the broad quay leading to the brig. Halfway there, a man stepped from a warehouse into his path. He had no weapon in his hands, but a constable's band wrapped around his left arm. Several more men, dressed the same, were seated in the shadows.

"The rest'a the dock's restricted," the constable said. "You'll turn about now."

"I'm a barrister," William tried. "One of the men jailed on the *Padget* is a client of mine."

"Don't know what you're talkin' about, mister. The dock is restricted," he repeated.

William thought for a moment. Who aboard was most important that he see? "Can you at least confirm that the *Padget*'s first mate, Mr. Quint Ivars, is aboard her?"

The constable spat. "The whole swillin' crew's aboard her. Now be movin' along or you'll join 'em."

Arriving empty-handed, without the cover of an Order of Compulsion from the court, William had no tools to apply. He made his way back to the shore.

At least he'd seen the ship with his own eyes. And if the constable spoke the truth—if no one had been released—then First Mate Ivars would still be there, available when the time was right to speak with him.

Not as satisfying as his visit to Solicitor Mortimer, but good enough. With the first mate aboard the ship, they'd get to him eventually. And if he took the case, they'd compel the man's appearance at trial. Assuming Ivars confirmed the Letter of Marque, that would make two witnesses to the Letter besides the captain.

If that wasn't enough to win the jury, he should find a new calling.

William turned away and headed up the quay.

The busy docks soon gave way to quieter streets. No gas lamps lit these thoroughfares, leaving the way home, under cloudy skies, as dark as the countryside.

Maybe he should walk home to Somers Town. It was a tempting chance to clear his head. He glanced about. The dark covered the shabby homes and closed shops like a fist. A walk through this district would be a foolhardy decision if he valued his pocketbook and his life. Best that he find a busier road to catch a late night cab.

William reversed direction and crossed over the road. The sodden street was empty of carriages and people going either way, except for a man on the far side, traveling the direction William had just abandoned. The man's eyes were locked ahead as William passed him near enough, even in the dark, to see a battered flat cap pulled down on a sloping forehead and, on his left side, a low eye beneath the furrow of a white scar.

William hurried his pace.

Something about the man made him glad for his decision to find a cab.

16

OFFICE OF THE LORD PRIVY SEAL
CARLTON HOUSE

"Lord Hollins will see you now, Mr. Snopes."

William followed the fresh-faced, neat-as-a-pin bureaucrat down a wide portrait-adorned hallway. Since his visit to Solicitor Mortimer, it had taken two days to get this appointment, then today, nearly a two-hour wait. If not for his satisfaction with the meetings with the solicitor and the constable at the quay, William would have been livid. Yet things were going too well for him to be peevish. A bit more good fortune today and most of his fears about the case would be put to rest.

William had observed in his practice that recently decorated British government offices tended toward the stern and practical, reflecting the lean times. Not so in the office he now entered. Lord Hollins's room was dressed in the French décor popular before the recent wars with Napoleon. Sumptuous, artistically inclined paper on the walls, graceful wood furniture about the floor.

And, William noted, looking up, they matched Lord Hollins's dignified bearing, seated behind his desk.

"I understand from my clerk," the lord began, "that you're inquiring about evidence of a Crown document supporting your client's mercantile venture. I'm afraid the regent can't grant you an audience on the matter, particularly given the pending prosecution."

"I understand," William said. "I don't need to speak with the regent. I only want to review your records regarding the document. I know that this office maintains a registry of all the Crown's private correspondence, and that a Letter of Marque is considered a form of such correspondence. I merely want to see the registry."

"I'm afraid, Mr. Snopes, that it's not the policy of the Crown to permit review of its private letters or the registry. Perhaps you could inquire at the Lord High Admiralty office. All Letters of Marque are affirmed there."

"I already went there. They told me that the records of affirmed Letters of Marque are only maintained in the registry here."

"I wasn't aware. Well, I'm sorry but I can't accommodate you."

"I can arrange an Order of Compulsion."

"Which we will refuse to honor. This is business of the Crown."

So much for smooth sailing and another good day.

"Lord Hollins, my client is being prosecuted for acting illegally, when he states that he acted in reliance on a valid Letter of Marque issued by Prince Regent George on behalf of King George III."

"Then your client should simply produce the Letter in his defense."

"He no longer has it."

"I'm sorry. There's nothing this office or the Royal authorities can do."

"And you're saying that the regent won't acknowledge his own signature on a document—either here or in court?"

"I'm saying precisely that. If the Crown could be compelled to certify in court every document he signed, either our regent or myself would never leave the courthouse. That's the primary reason for affixing the Royal Seal, held here at Carlton House. It is all the evidence necessary to affirm the Crown's actions."

William nearly rose out of his chair. "You're talking in circles, man. My client no longer *has* the Letter. How can he affirm its seal? All I ask is to see whether a Letter of Marque was registered as provided to my client."

"I'm sorry."

Now he did rise. "My lord, a man's life is at stake, and you're arguing formalities!"

Lord Hollins looked back with frosty indifference. Solid. Unmoving.

"Very well, Mr. Snopes. This once, under the circumstances, I will make an exception."

Shocked at the turnabout, William was still replaying the words in his mind when the lord rang a bell.

No one answered.

He rang again.

Just as his face was registering frustration, a young woman came into the office.

"I'm sorry, my lord," she said shyly, "but Jonathon has stepped away."

"Isabella, why aren't you with the king?"

"He's asleep, my lord. I was passing in the hall when you rang. Is there something I might do for you?"

"I doubt it." The lord shrugged. "Ah, very well. Do you know where the document registers are kept, Isabella? For the king's private seal?"

"I do, my lord."

"All right. I want you to bring a volume recording an official document, a Letter of Marque, which was issued . . ." He turned to William. "When do you claim that the document was issued?"

"November of 1816, my lord," William answered.

"November 1816. Bring me the volume for that month and year."

They waited in awkward silence, William staring off through the windows overlooking St. James's Park, the lord growing impatient.

At last the young woman came back into the room. She held a

volume so large she had to grip it in both hands. Giving William a nervous glance, she handed the book to Lord Hollins.

"Thank you, Isabella." The lord laid the volume on his desktop and began to page through it. He reached a point where he turned back and forth several times, scanning several pages carefully in each direction. Then he rotated the volume on his desk for William's review. "Here, Mr. Snopes."

William ran a finger up and down the page for each of the weeks of November 1816. Next he examined the spine of the book to see if any pages had been removed. "Thank you, my lord," he said at last before rising and walking hazily from the building.

He was halfway across St. James's Park before he became conscious that he was walking in the wrong direction and turned about.

For all his belief in Captain Tuttle's sincerity, there was no Letter of Marque recorded on any date in November of 1816.

17

William had journeyed on foot to The Peacock. The restaurant and teahouse on High Islington Street was built of dark-green wood and yellow brick. The place served only passable fish and chicken. But William was having neither today. He was content with the restaurant's excellent tea.

He took a long, troubled sip. What had he expected with his visit to the Lord Privy Seal? Had he really thought that the Crown would start a piracy prosecution even if their own records showed the regent had issued Captain Tuttle a Letter of Marque?

It seems he had.

It had been a stupid notion.

If the government didn't issue a Letter of Marque, yet Solicitor Mortimer was satisfied that Captain Tuttle's letter was genuine, what could he conclude? That the captain's letter simply wasn't properly recorded? That there was an excellent forger involved? If so, who forged it? Mandy Bristol's so-called investors?

The case spun him like a dreidel.

Even if the document wasn't genuine, did that matter? Wouldn't

134

Solicitor Mortimer's certification of what he saw be enough for a jury to acquit? What jury would send a man to the gallows who had relied, in good faith, on an excellent forgery?

He took another sip of the cooling tea. Where did this leave him? If he was so confident of the evidence, why hesitate to take the case?

The politics, of course.

Then if he was so uncertain of the politics, why was he so slow to walk away?

Could his hesitancy be with Lady Jameson? She too had hovered in the back of his mind since her visit. Born into comfort yet facing terrible consequences. Unlikely to find another decent barrister if he declined the case. The first woman of upper society who'd approached him with such a case. Difficult to forget.

He sensed it: that tune again. It rose unformed from his memory, as impossible to grasp as smoke. He knew it, but still it eluded him as no piece ever had. It was so . . . painfully familiar.

William shook his head and looked about for distraction's sake.

The Peacock was the site of rare, good memories from his youth. Aeron had introduced him to it when William accompanied the stable master on his trips to London to trade horses for the estate. The gentle chief groom seldom frequented pubs. But he'd introduced William to tea at The Peacock and to conversations surpassing any William was raised to believe possible from an uneducated man. Over hot pots of tea, Aeron had taught him of horses, of the joys of unhurried afternoon talks, of the potential corruption of privilege, and of the perils of underestimating a "common man."

He'd never brought a colleague to The Peacock, preferring to come alone. Alone with his thoughts and memories. Those memories included his pain at Aeron's disappearance the morning after William departed—fired, as William had feared, for the crime of bringing a saddled horse to aid his escape. Even after twenty years, on each visit William longed to see Aeron again.

What he wouldn't give for the chance to simply thank him to his face once more.

A copy of the *Courier* sat on the next table, left there by a customer. William picked it up, reached for his tea . . . then stopped.

The headline of the lead article, front page and above the fold, read:

SLY BARRISTER WILLIAM SNOPES CHALLENGES CROWN
Barrister Claims Pirates Acted with Crown Authority

"Oh, good Lord." His stomach turned as he read on.

> *Barrister Snopes, rumored in past cases to have suborned perjury to protect murderers, forgers, thieves, and worse from transportation or the gallows, is now selling his skills to pirates, who claim permission to take French vessels on the Indian Sea. . . .*

The article rambled for two full columns. Terrible accusations. Certain to set him up for censure from the bar. The article even took aim at "all barristers who, in their avarice, act as though they have license to justify any depredation, whether by sleight of tongue or outright lies."

Near the end of the article, the writer even identified the location of William's flat.

No, no, no. This was no article, but an intentional and malicious attack. Designed to either force him away from the case, endanger William and his potential clients, prejudice a future jury, or all of those possibilities.

And it signaled what he'd feared and Thomas had warned him about. This would be no ordinary case. There was special danger lurking here.

That wasn't the end of the newspaper's attacks. On the next page was a separate article dedicated to Lord and Lady Jameson of Heathcote Estate, who "on good accounts, are involved in the thriving smuggling business in Essex and supporting the pirates' trade in the coastal county."

The paper dropped to the table. William looked about, half expecting a crowd to be gathering to take his head.

He'd dawdled too long and lost the luxury of time. Rising, William rushed toward home and the stable where his horse was kept.

18

JAMESON ESTATE
ESSEX COUNTY

Riding his bay up the drive to Lady Jameson's estate, the late afternoon sunlight threw William's shadow far ahead.

The hours of riding in cool, fresh air hadn't fully cleared his head as he'd hoped. Still, he'd made up his mind.

Edmund and Father Thomas were right. He owed no duty to Lady Jameson or her cousin. The lady was, by title and property, one of the class into which William had been born, and he knew that it was light duty. He wouldn't put his own career and those of Edmund and Obadiah at risk by leading them against the Crown in a volatile case. He wouldn't charge the cannons leveled against them.

Still, it was cowardly to convey his decision by messenger. And before he pronounced it, he wanted to see her in her own setting, the Heathcote Estate. He needed the reminder that she was no small business person or laborer or debtor he need pity or protect.

William had expected a fine estate like so many he'd known as a young man. Yet, even on the ride up to the manor house, he could see signs of disrepair. Statuary near the entrance was gone, leaving behind empty pedestals. A thin layer of gravel on the drive showed through under patches of a recent snowfall. A short distance from the drive entrance, William could see where something heavy had been dragged from the drive, tearing up the lawn in a trail toward some woods.

The three-story manor house appeared as ancient and stately as any he'd seen. Two wings rose about a central portico. To one side, a slope rolled down to a bridge, which vaulted a wide now-frozen creek. The outline of fallow gardens stretched far behind the home to tall hedges.

All appeared to be unprepared for winter and had a look of sad decline.

William reined in the bay before the house and dropped wearily from the saddle.

"Identify yourself, sir!"

Startled, he glanced about. The front door was closed. No one was at the surrounding windows. He took a step back.

A man with long gray hair and thick facial stubble was leaning out of a second-floor window.

"I'm William Snopes," he called.

"What brings you to my door at this hour? Are you a poacher? A highwayman?"

William sighed. "Not unless you believe today's *Courier*, sir. I'm a barrister, here to see Lady Madeleine Jameson."

The man retreated, then returned just moments later with a long-barreled musket at his shoulder. "The lady of this house is Lady Catherine. Madeleine isn't more than fourteen! What business could you have with my young daughter, you scoundrel!"

There was a flurry of voices through the window. Hands took the man's shoulders, pulling him back over shouted protests.

Soon the front door flew open.

Lady Jameson stood there, eyes wide, her hair wild. She was dressed in working clothes, soiled from use. A floor brush was in one hand.

William could easily have mistaken her for one of the staff.

"Mr. Snopes!" she protested. "I wasn't expecting anyone. I thought I made clear we should meet in London."

Embarrassment flooded him. "I'm so sorry. I just thought this more . . . efficient. I could return to Staunton, and we could meet tomorrow if that's convenient."

"No, no. It's just . . ." She glanced over her shoulder. "Please come in."

Down a staircase behind Lady Jameson came a man as old as the one wielding the musket, dressed in a butler's livery.

"Lord Jameson's back in bed, miss," he said. "Miss Kendall is watching him. He's had a sleep draught."

The lady nodded self-consciously. "Set the table for dinner, Davidson. Mr. Snopes and I will be in the dining room tonight. Then see to his horse."

William followed her into a study, his regret at his surprise visit growing.

"Lady, this is a great imposition. There's no need to feed me. I'd planned to return to London tonight in any event. Our business won't take long."

"No," she said, recovering herself. "You just surprised me at this hour, that's all. I insist you stay the evening. It will be very cold tonight, and your horse looked tired."

The resolve that had driven him here was disintegrating. William nodded. "I hadn't planned to come today, you see, so I got a late start. I don't think—"

"Come now, Mr. Snopes. It would be foolish to return to London until your horse is rested," Lady Jameson repeated.

When she visited his office, he'd noticed her fair skin and intelligent eyes. Caught unawares, the natural elements of her beauty were confirmed by the pleasing shape of her mouth and blue eyes and the spirit coloring her cheeks.

William realized that he'd made no reply and was staring. He looked away and nodded his yes.

"Sit. I'll be back very shortly." She left the room.

He looked about the study. It might have been a looted room. Open spaces on the walls spoke of missing frames and paintings. The floor was too large for the furniture still here. The fireplace was stoked but not burning, despite the room's chill air. The study was long, with a magnificently high ceiling. But the dust-covered books and candelabras looked rigid and lonely from disuse.

It must have been grand once. William felt stirred by the same combination of awe and discomfort he'd felt since he was a boy when surrounded by the dimensions and plumage of wealth.

Except this place seemed humbled.

Coming here had been a mistake. He felt as though he'd stumbled on to a family secret.

Lady Jameson reappeared minutes later, better dressed but still modestly. Her hair was put up, her face pink from being washed.

They sat before the unlit fireplace. Awkward silence immediately descended.

William pierced it, getting to the point. "I've located your cousin. I visited him recently."

"*Thank heavens*. Is he all right?"

"Yes . . . although he's in Newgate, I'm afraid. I've asked Obadiah to bring him food and a daily change of clothes. He's also interviewing the captain to assemble a crew list."

"What did Harold say about the piracy charge?" Her voice was very anxious.

"He confirmed taking the French vessel's cargo but insisted he held the promised Letter of Marque. You should also know that the Crown's prosecutor reached out to us and offered an arrangement to avoid your cousin's prosecution." William explained Sir Barnabas's visit to his office in full.

"Transportation to *Tasmania*?" she exclaimed. "Harold declined it, of course."

"Yes. Though for reasons you might not suspect."

"Which are?"

William straightened. "Your cousin asked us to represent him

141

and your interests in the *Padget*, but he also wishes us to prosecute the death of a cabin boy."

"A death?" Lady Jameson reddened. "What cabin boy?"

"Captain Tuttle said a boy was shot while standing at his side, by a constable or soldier who'd come to arrest him. He's adamant that the responsible party be prosecuted. Yet the offer of transportation requires that your cousin give up that option."

"Harold wishes to prosecute the death?"

"Yes. And he hasn't the money to support it."

"I see."

"As I told Captain Tuttle, we'd need court permission to try the boy's murder along with our defense of the captain. I'd prefer to do so, if we can determine the shooter. Not only would justice be better served, but the shooting by the constable will help nullify the jury's sense of unease with the charges leveled against your cousin. I informed your cousin we'd discuss the financial issues later. I've other news to share as well." He explained his visit to Solicitor Mortimer and the docked ship.

"That's wonderful news!" She brightened. "Doesn't that assure an acquittal?"

"I thought so too, at first. But I followed those events with a visit to the office of the Lord Privy Counselor in charge of the Royal Seals. I hoped for confirmation that the prince regent signed your cousin's Letter of Marque. Sadly, all I confirmed was the *absence* of any record of the Letter."

Lady Jameson stared, seeming lost. "I don't understand. What does all this mean?"

"Our best hope? Either there was an administrative error, or your mystery investors provided your cousin with a forged Letter of Marque—one so well prepared that it even fooled Solicitor Mortimer."

The lady searched him thoroughly with her eyes. "Which do you believe?" she asked.

"I don't know," he said, noting her disappointment. "And that brings me to another reason for my visit. My lady, the newspapers have learned of your cousin's prosecution. They've unanimously taken the tack that I'm a corrupt barrister and that the case against Captain Tuttle is solid."

Lady Jameson's face grew white.

"Newspapers? More than one?"

"Yes."

"Did you bring any with you?"

"Two, in my saddlebag, though there are more. One newspaper attacking your cousin and myself is understandable. So many, all singing the same song, reeks of collusion."

The lady grew silent.

There was no point in holding anything back now.

"You also must know," William continued carefully, "that the newspapers accuse you and your father of involvement with smugglers here in Essex."

"I see," Lady Jameson murmured.

"Frankly, you have a strong defamation claim. We may also wish to raise that in the action defending your cousin and the *Padget*."

She looked away.

Unease gripped William. Where was the outrage? What was the source of the fear he saw instead? "Are you all right, Lady Jameson?"

Silence.

He weighed again the evidence of the room surrounding him. "My lady, are you concerned with being able to fund your cousin's defense?"

She turned on him in anger. "Is *that* why you've visited? Did you want to see our home? Did you come because you doubted I could afford your services?"

"No," he replied gently. "That's not why I came."

The woman dropped her head in her hands. "Since everyone seems to know our business, Mr. Snopes," she began, "I might as well share with you. As you've now seen with your own eyes,

143

our estate has suffered from bad harvests and the ravages of taxes and tariffs since my mother's death five years ago, as well as my father's decline, which you witnessed. I have but three staff, along with part-time help from families of our tenant farmers. Only two servants remain with us at all times: Davidson, who does nearly everything within the limits of his age and experience, and Miss Kendall, who cooks and cares for my father."

"I'm sorry," William said, uncertain how to reply.

"Don't be. I don't seek your pity. I still live far better than most do in these times. But I'm determined to do what I must to rescue the estate, as much for our tenants as for myself. That was the reason we took the risk of the *Padget*."

Davidson entered the room before William could respond.

"My lady, I'm sorry to interrupt. Your father is still awake, and I require some guidance."

The lady nodded at William. "Please excuse me."

Sudden quiet fell in the wake of Lady Jameson's unexpected confession of decline. William stood and began pacing the room, not knowing what to do. In the farthest corner, he saw a grand piano. He went to it.

A flute stand with an eight-keyed flute was beside the piano. William pressed the piano's ivory keys. He ran his fingers through a scale.

Notes from the piece that had plagued him for weeks returned to mind. They were clearer now. An ascending tempo and scale. A symphony for certain.

With his right hand, he traced on the keyboard one of its movements—for strings, he thought.

Footsteps approached.

William looked up at the lady. Removed his fingers from the piano.

"Do you play?" Lady Jameson asked.

"Uh, no. Well, I did. Nothing that would merit a royal performance. But I do have a great love for music." He waved a hand toward the flute and piano. "Do you play?"

"Yes. Mostly the flute. I know the flute's an unusual instrument for a lady; you needn't say it. But I insisted and my parents relented. My brother was a gifted piano player, and we used to play duets together. I haven't been able to part with either instrument."

"Your brother?"

"Yes. He died in the war."

"I see. I'm so sorry. And for the death of your mother that you mentioned earlier."

She nodded, seeming to relax a bit.

"My brother, Devon, was killed at the Battle of Tarragona in 1813. His death weakened my mother, who was always frail. She died of typhus soon after. Despite the faith in which our father raised us, those losses destroyed him as well. You saw him at his bedroom window when you arrived. He's not himself these days."

William looked about, feeling a welling of sympathy.

"I apologize for my outburst earlier, Mr. Snopes," the lady went on. "Of course, you must assure yourself of my ability to pay your fees."

"I didn't come today to challenge you about the fees, Lady Jameson." He paused. "You manage the estate alone, do you?"

"Yes."

"How?"

"Through a power of attorney granted by my father when he was . . . more able to make such decisions."

"May I ask," William went on, "how you managed to invest in the *Padget* with your financial challenges being what they are?"

She took a deep breath. "We . . . I borrowed the funds."

"Borrowed? Banks are very skittish in these times."

"From our family solicitor. Mr. Snopes, you say you are not concerned about my ability to pay your fees, yet you continue to ask questions about my finances."

"My compensation is far less important than trusting my client," he said.

"I don't understand."

"Lady Jameson, particularly with these charges in the newspapers and the financial plight you acknowledge, I need to confirm that neither you nor your cousin have engaged in any illegalities regarding the *Padget*."

The servant Davidson appeared.

"Dinner is served," he said.

The lady looked to William, her eyes giving no answer.

"You must be very hungry. We can speak as well over food in the dining room as here in the study."

Dinner, served by Davidson and Miss Kendall, began as quietly as their first greeting at the door. It was a simple meal: quail, which the lady said she'd shot herself earlier in the day, preserved blackberries, cream, pudding, and red wine.

Neither William nor the lady spoke a word until late in the meal.

"This new barrister prosecuting Harold," the lady said at last, "is he experienced?"

"Reluctantly, I admit he is. In fact, he's a King's Counsel."

She clearly knew what that was, as disappointment flooded Lady Jameson's expression. William felt an urge to defend his own experience but didn't.

"Mr. Snopes, do you have family?"

"I've never married."

"And your father. He's in the House of Lords, I understand."

"Yes." He set down his spoon. "Some people seek me out assuming my father's status will help their case. I work very hard to ensure that they realize the truth: that my father's wealth and position will do nothing to advance their cases. In some instances, perhaps the opposite. I've been independent of the man since age eighteen."

"Of course," she answered immediately.

To his astonishment, she seemed completely at ease with his answer.

It dawned on William that he'd managed to prolong a brief visit, intended to confirm his sentiments and leave, into hours, with lengthy questions implying he might represent her after all.

Why didn't he tell her his refusal of the case and be gone?

Still he sat, picking at his quail with a knife.

The question he'd previously asked: suddenly William realized he very much wanted an answer.

"My lady, I need an answer to the question I raised in the study. Is there anything in your business dealings with the *Padget*, your background, in the loan—anything which would compromise your cousin's defense? Any illegality at all? Your answer is important to your own safety, as well as your cousin's."

Her voice grew resolute. "What does it matter? The landed patricians in neighboring estates—once our friends—already avoid us as though we were infected with the plague. Since even before my father's physical decline, they have acted as though our misfortunes were deserved, from incompetence or worse, I believe it enables them to pretend that their estates and positions are gifted by a higher power, and they could never suffer as we have. News reports of misconduct will only confirm people's disdain. My father is beyond caring, as am I, but I love this land and our tenants. I love the town and parish—as all of my family has. I am all that remains between our survival and bankruptcy, and its impact on the farmers and people of Staunton who depend on us. That's why I made the investment in the vessel, even with borrowed funds. I'd do it again."

Mr. Snopes nodded sympathetically. "A well-stated defense," he pressed softly. "But not an answer to my question."

She set down her cutlery. "I don't see why your representation should subject me or my actions to your scrutiny or approval."

"It must, because your defense may prove a very difficult affair. For myself and my staff as much as for you and your cousin."

The lady's face grew still.

"Yes," she said quietly. "I suppose it will." She paused, then added, "Very well. I'll answer your question. I've done nothing illegal as regards the *Padget*."

A tight fist of empathy occupied William's chest. He still couldn't seem to muster the resolve to decline her case. She seemed so deeply sincere. Sincerity—or the ability to feign it—was the most important quality of a good barrister. She would have made an excellent one.

William pushed back his chair and stood. "Thank you for dinner, Lady Jameson. I think I should retire now. I plan to get back to London tomorrow. I'll give you my decision regarding representation in the morning."

More disappointment filled her eyes.

"Of course" was her reply.

The servant appeared.

"Davidson will show you to your room."

William nodded, then followed the servant up the staircase and into a room looking over a side lawn. His small case already rested on the bed. Twin candles created pools of light in the darkness. As Davidson withdrew, William walked to the window, opening it slightly.

The fist of empathy still gripped his chest. Anger joined it, passing through him as he considered the forces likely directed against this solitary woman and her cousin. Someone intended to crush them. Her hands were empty of any real weapons to fight back—even financial ones.

He'd come to observe her wealth and follow Edmund's and Thomas's lead by declining her. He hadn't planned on seeing such a crumbling edifice of an estate. He hadn't planned to be touched by the resolution of the lady herself.

The movement he'd traced on the piano returned. A little louder now. He almost had it. It would drive him insane if he didn't recall it soon.

The movement stayed with him until he fell asleep.

Coarse smoke reached William through his dreams. It was wispy and vague at first, then strong enough to rouse him. He sat up in bed fully awake. Walked to the window he'd left ajar.

The sky was dark in the early hours of morning. Through the trees beyond the lawn, sparks flew high above the branches, like shooting stars retracing their paths home. Occasional surges of flame rose from the woods to the west, revealing smoke that billowed as a black scourge against the blue-black sky.

William quickly dressed and hurried downstairs, heading outside in the direction of the trees. A cold wind penetrated his jacket as he crossed the lawn in the dark, then a field where dead winter grasses brushed him as he walked. William felt the first drops of a winter rain on his forehead. Past the field, his steps took him into a wide break in the trees where the soil was broken. Footsteps traced a path across muddy ground. He followed them through the woods to a broad clearing.

A bonfire roared in the middle of the clearing. The smell of kerosene and burning flesh hung over a scene of dancing, towering flames. Heat pulsed against his face.

William stepped near enough to see that the heart of the fire was the outline of a horse, its flesh melting over crackling bones.

"What are you doing out here?"

William started.

On the far side of the fire, he made out Lady Jameson, robed and hooded.

He rounded the fire to her side. "The smoke woke me," William said uncertainly. "What in heaven's name is all this?"

"A few days ago, my horse died . . ." she began, trailing off momentarily. "One of only three that remained to us. Davidson used our other horses to drag it here yesterday, before you arrived."

Rippling flashes of orange revealed tears on her cheeks.

"You're crying."

"It's the smoke," she said unconvincingly. She rubbed them away.

"Why burn the animal at night? Now? In the coming rain?"

"I couldn't wait any longer. Gypsy—she was my favorite. I couldn't leave her to be eaten as carrion. And we hadn't enough help to bury her."

"But now? At night?"

"I didn't want to be seen."

"Seen by whom?"

Pause. "By you."

"Why?"

She hesitated again.

"A man killed my beloved horse at my feet, Mr. Snopes," she said with sadness and anger. "A giant of a man. It was the evening I returned from meeting with you. I must have been followed from London. On the drive to the manor, he shot my mare and warned me not to pursue the case to protect Harold and the *Padget*."

"Why didn't you send word?"

"I was worried you'd refuse to represent us. I feared what you'd do if you knew we'd been threatened with harm."

There was thunder from cracking wood or bone, followed by another black cloud taking to the sky.

William was stunned. Could the hidden investors have done this? Surely not agents of the Crown.

He thought again of Captain Tuttle. Despite what he'd learned from the Lord Privy Seal, he believed the man.

Recalled again his visit to Mandy Bristol.

Thought of Lady Jameson.

The orchestral arrangement finally burst through. The piece that had eluded him these past weeks came fully alive.

It was Haydn's Symphony Number 100, with all the tumult of its final movement that he loved. He hadn't heard the piece, in person or memory, since the night he'd fled his father. When he'd been so alone and uncertain. Defenseless. Defiant.

He looked again at the lady.

Those were precisely the sentiments he'd felt about Lady Jameson ever since she'd come to his office. Without allies, but determined. A child of the upper classes who no longer belonged there. All these days, from the hearing through his investigation, she'd floated in the backwaters of his mind on the ebb and flow of the Haydn piece he couldn't identify.

William looked toward the house, invisible through the trees. A manor held in place by courage and will. Lady Jameson should have been well married years before. Seeing and hearing her passion to save that manor and her family's estate, he didn't need to ask why she wasn't.

It felt suddenly foolish to be standing here in the rain, when the truth was that he'd made his decision the moment she answered the door wearing a servant's clothes.

"Lady Jameson," he said, "you've judged me wrongly. Return to the house and get some rest. I'll watch the fire until it's safely down. Tomorrow I'll interview you at length, then ride back to London. We've a great deal of work ahead of us if we're to win your case."

19

OFFICE OF BARRISTER WILLIAM SNOPES
GRAY'S INN
LONDON

"So you're actually taking the case?" Edmund said, seated before William's desk.

William glanced from his junior to Obadiah and back again. He'd already reviewed what he learned the past several days, and the atmosphere in his office was as he'd expected. Obadiah, always game, the committed optimist once a decision had been made, was ready and eager. Obadiah's friend, Edmund, creative to brilliance but too often brooding and suspicious of decisions which were not his own, certain of unseen predators waiting to pounce.

For the benefit of both, William would show no doubt.

"Yes, Edmund. There's always contrary evidence; there are always wrinkles. With Solicitor Mortimer's testimony certifying the Letter, I believe that either Captain Tuttle held a convincing forgery or a genuine Letter of Marque when he took the French ship. Either way, he doesn't deserve transportation or execution. I'm troubled by the mysteries surrounding the matter. Still, I intend to proceed. That includes prosecuting the killer of the cabin boy."

Edmund grew resigned. "Where will you have me start, then?"

"Actually, Edmund, I've decided not to have you involved in this

152

one. I'll need someone to manage other matters while I proceed with Lady Jameson's and the captain's case."

A short pause, then, "But I'm your junior, sir."

"And as my junior, it's best that you keep my practice afloat while I handle the Jameson case."

"Then Obadiah will still assist you?"

"Yes. I'll need his help gathering evidence, briefing and such. The usual solicitor's chores. Of course, I'll miss your presence at counsel table."

Edmund shifted in his seat. Obadiah looked back and forth between them. "Uh, sir," the solicitor said, "do you believe the lady's story about someone killing her horse and threatening her?"

Always the peacemaker, changing the subject, William thought. "I do. Or she went to impossible lengths to deceive me."

"This is all new for me, sir, even in a capital case," the solicitor admitted. "The newspaper articles. Shooting a horse. Destruction of evidence. I've never seen or heard of the fight spilling out of the courtroom quite like this before."

"Nor I. But the case will still be won or lost *in the courtroom.*" William looked to his junior. "There'll be other cases, Edmund."

Caution ruled Edmund's expression as he looked back at William. "Will there be, sir?" He rose and walked from the room.

When they were alone, Obadiah shook his head.

"What is it, Obadiah?"

"I just don't understand why you won't tell Edmund."

"Tell him what?"

"Why, it's obvious, isn't it? To anyone but Edmund, that is. It's clear you don't want him involved to protect him from the attacks you're experiencing. Bullheaded barrister that he is, Edmund assumes you lack confidence in him."

The solicitor's clarity of insight surprised William once again, especially regarding Edmund. It was little wonder, given what Edmund and Obadiah had been through together for years before William had found them. But with Obadiah's small stature and usually expressionless face—William swore he'd seen him sit in the court gallery for hours without revealing an ounce of reaction—it was easy to forget the young man's uncommon talent for reading people.

"Because, my dear Obadiah, that would only stiffen his determination to be involved." He paused to let that sink in. "Besides, despite the personal attacks, with Solicitor Mortimer to confirm Captain Tuttle's letter, and the hope of more helpful testimony from the first mate, from now on we'll mostly be seeking witnesses from among the remaining crew members to corroborate what the captain told them of the Letter's existence."

A slight twist of the mouth signaled that Obadiah was unconvinced.

"As you say, sir," he replied. "That reminds me, though. At Newgate, when I brought clothing and food to Captain Tuttle, he told me his Solicitor Mortimer had already been to see him. The captain granted him permission to speak freely to you."

"Excellent. I should hear from him shortly, then."

"Yes, sir. What are your intentions about pursuing the investors to prove a forgery?"

William shook his head. "Without the Letter itself, the investors can lie about its authenticity without fear of challenge—if they admit the Letter's existence at all. We don't dare risk what they'd say to a jury."

"Very well. Where do I start?"

"By preparing a brief for a continuance. We haven't gotten official word on a trial date, but given Sir Barnabas's warning, we should anticipate little preparation time. Request at least two months from today's date. Though the evidence is trending our way, until we interview the crew and first mate, I won't feel comfortable."

"Yes, sir."

There was a knock on the office door. Obadiah rose to answer it. To William's surprise, the door opened to a young boy, perhaps ten or eleven. To his greater surprise, the boy looked familiar, though he couldn't place him.

"I've papers for Barrister Snopes," he squeaked nervously.

"You've found him."

The boy dashed to the desk and put the papers in William's hand.

Obadiah watched worriedly as the boy spun and rushed away. "What do they say?"

William scanned the pages in his hand. Then scanned them again.

"Sir?"

"Don't bother with the continuance brief just yet, Obadiah," William grunted.

"Why?"

William looked up, trying to hide the unease stabbing his chest. "Because these papers are from dear Judge Raleigh. Besides containing the formal indictment of Captain Tuttle, I'm ordered to meet with the judge and Sir Barnabas at The Old Bailey this very afternoon. The court is entertaining a petition from Sir Barnabas to hold me in contempt for publishing our penny dreadful. And to refer me for disbarment."

20

LONDON CENTRAL COURTHOUSE
THE OLD BAILEY

So much for the fantasy that he was in control, William thought as he sat at counsel table. Clearly, Sir Barnabas was determined to prove otherwise.

William hated the harpsichord in all its forms. Particularly now, as the stubborn notes of a harpsichord piece by Babell played discordantly in his head. He looked up at Judge Raleigh, leaning over his desk on the raised dais, preparing for the hearing like a descending hawk. He remembered Raleigh as a grim, uncompromising barrister whose glare would curdle milk. As a judge, he was far worse. Humility was lost, restraint banished.

"You should take my offer."

Sir Barnabas stood at William's shoulder, staring down with the solicitude of a corpse. William searched his face for a hint of malice. He saw none. Amazing how thin this *gentleman's* veneer truly was. Today he'd brought a motion threatening William's very right to practice law. His absence of emotion only made him seem a greater predator.

"It isn't an offer," William replied. "It's a death penalty for an innocent man."

"Hmm," the barrister said. "Well, the offer stands until I leave the courtroom today."

The judge cleared his throat, instantly quieting the room. "So, what do you have to say for yourself, Mr. Snopes?" he growled. "How do you answer Sir Barnabas's charge? Publishing a treatise to influence future jurors in a criminal case? That's a serious violation of your duties as an officer of this court. I plan to report the result of this contempt hearing to your Inn for discipline, including disbarment."

William stood, determined not to allow his anger to show. "My lord, the publication Sir Barnabas claims to be contemptuous was published before I was even aware that formal charges had been made against Captain Tuttle. Not only that, but the good captain was, I strongly believe, being deliberately hidden from us to prevent our conferring with him."

"Now you dare to impugn the reputation of a fellow barrister, Mr. Snopes? A KC no less? Are you also slandering the admitting clerks at Newgate?"

"Of course not, my lord," William answered, wanting to thunder his fears and suspicions to the contrary. "We've no idea who was responsible for hiding Captain Tuttle at Newgate Prison—only that he was. We do believe, however, that Captain Tuttle's presence at Newgate might still be secret but for the very publication Sir Barnabas claims was so defamatory."

"My lord," Sir Barnabas nearly shouted, standing, "this is preposterous! How can Mr. Snopes seriously make such a statement? I myself had no difficulty gaining access to Captain Tuttle on multiple occasions."

"That's true," William followed, pleased at the expected response. "And deliberately meeting with another barrister's client seems to me a much greater ethical lapse than the publication which troubles Sir Barnabas."

"Except I had no knowledge of your representation of Captain Tuttle when I met with him."

"Precisely. Just as I had no knowledge of any pending charges against my client when I prepared the publication. Only that he'd been detained—and apparently unlawfully so."

Stick that down your throat.

William could see that his argument had caused even Judge Raleigh to pause. He'd as much as told the magistrate that if he found William in contempt and referred him for discipline by his peers at Gray's Inn, William would lodge his own complaint against Sir Barnabas before the KC's peers at the inner court for his improper meetings with the captain. That would certainly slow the judge's precious race to the captain's trial.

Judge Raleigh pondered in silence.

"Mr. Snopes," he declared at last, "reluctantly I'm going to withhold judgment on your contemptable publication—so long as you don't attempt any such strategy again. Nor will I recommend disciplinary action by your inn at this time. They may make their own judgment in that regard. But consider yourself on a very short leash indeed. Gentlemen, I'll see you back on Monday, March the nineteenth, to begin trial. That is ten days hence."

Ten days? William's heart sank. "My lord. Regarding that date—"

"You can stop right there, Mr. Snopes." The judge scowled. "Because of your publication, this story is out there for all to read. The impacts on the esteem of the Crown and the daily conduct of our government's business, as well as the chance for unbiased justice in this case, are considerable. I'll hear no request for a continuance. You'll be here on the date selected, prepared to commence trial on the charge of piracy against Captain Tuttle."

We're contemplating ending a man's life, William wanted to argue, *and you're worried about a few days?* But it would do him no good with Raleigh.

"My lord," William said, his alternative argument prepared, "my purpose wasn't to ask for a continuance for time to prepare the defense."

The eyes of Sir Barnabas and his coterie clung to William.

"Then just what were you intending to ask?" Judge Raleigh replied.

"We request, my lord, the right to prosecute a man among the arresting party for the murder of a young cabin boy, Simon Ladner. Given the overlap in evidence, I presume the court would prefer the murder prosecution be conducted simultaneously with Captain Tuttle's piracy trial. That would, regrettably, require additional time for a fresh indictment. And though I'm sure the court knows that this complex case is already likely to be a long trial, the Ladner boy's murder prosecution would require even more trial time and preparation."

The room became a tomb.

Judge Raleigh turned to William's opponent. "Sir Barnabas, I wasn't informed of a killing associated with your case against the captain. Is this true?"

Sir Barnabas stood slowly. "I believe there was a death on the occasion of the arrest."

"Why wasn't I informed? Was the Crown intending to prosecute the matter?"

The barrister shook his head. "We've no information that the death was intentional. Assuming an unintentional or accidental death, it is the Crown's conclusion that it should be prosecuted as a private matter. And I've not been retained to do so."

Judge Raleigh pierced William with his stare once more. "Are you saying you're prepared to prosecute this death, Mr. Snopes?"

"Yes, my lord."

"Against whom?"

"Against the constable and sheriffs who conducted the arrest, my lord. We're still investigating who fired the fatal bullet."

The judge shook his head. "Always complications," he murmured, perturbed. He grew silent again.

William's heart began to pound with hope.

With a suddenness that startled, the judge straightened and shot a fresh hard look at William. "You are a clever one, Counselor. Very clever. Coming up with this argument so late in the day. Well, I'll have none of it. The prosecution of the boy's death will have to wait, and there will be no continuance. But I will concede this much, Mr. Snopes. You have three days to complete the trial rather than the customary one."

His heart drowning in disappointment at the near triumph, William shook his head. "Given the nature of this case, my lord, I fear three days will be inadequate—even without the murder prosecution."

"You'll make it adequate. Three days."

The judge and his legal staff disappeared through back doors out of the courtroom. William stared at the empty bench.

Ten days to trial. No more than a breath in time. If he hadn't the assurance of Solicitor Mortimer's testimony to clinch the case, it would be impossible. As it was, even in the shadow of the gallows, he'd be trying this one on the fly, with limited chance to know what many of Sir Barnabas's witnesses would say before they were sworn to testify.

"Final chance," Sir Barnabas called from his table.

William didn't look in his direction.

"Good day, Sir Barnabas."

"In that case, you should know we've released the *Padget*'s crew. A decision regarding their prosecution will await the result in this one."

William's last calm melted. "You've released them before I could interview them? With so little time to trial? They could be anywhere now!"

"Perhaps you need more help than your solicitor and your hot-headed junior can provide? But don't worry. A number of the *Padget*'s crew will be testifying for the prosecution, so you'll hear what they have to say at trial. A few are even quoted in this afternoon's papers, I'm informed. The *Gazette* seems to have taken a particular interest in this case and its characters. Have a restful week, Mr. Snopes."

William watched the barrister and his juniors withdraw.

The imposing courtroom, garnished with dark and solemn wood, fell especially silent, like a field after the passing of mounted cavalry. William looked about the room; the space he knew and loved so well seemed charged with something unfamiliar. As though it were awaiting no legal case at all—no measured arguments on law or fairness, guilt or innocence—but the drums of war and inevitable death.

In such a struggle, did he have any chance of protecting the lady and her cousin?

William pulled off his wig and made his solitary way to the door, his blood hot.

He'd be hanged himself before he'd roll over.

If it was war they wanted, then it was war they'd have.

21

HEATHCOTE ESTATE
ESSEX COUNTY

Davidson entered the dining room with the air of calm that Madeleine had known her entire life. "The carriage is ready, my lady."

Madeleine took a deep breath, sorely tempted to delay leaving the only home she'd ever known. Before her return, the manor house could vanish from her life. The loss of the *Padget* could make it so. Solicitor Rooker could seize the grounds to repay the loan. The prosecutor could come for her and her father as conspirators to piracy.

It all made parting both perilous and sorrowful.

"One moment," she answered Davidson. "I'll be right out."

She took the stairs to her father's room, entering to the soft light of an overcast sky through the window. He was seated in his favored rocker, with sweet Miss Kendall nearby.

It was her father's preferred place from which to survey the grounds. Waves of white hair reached to shoulders once strong enough to hold her and her brother at the same time. His once-keen eyes were now clouded and emotionless. If they took him from this house, he'd be lost forever.

She leaned down and hugged him. "Father, I'm doing all I can.

I've hired the best barrister possible. Pray for us, as I'll be praying for you."

He didn't stir as she released him. She kissed his pale forehead, then nodded to Miss Kendall and returned downstairs.

The carriage took the drive to the road under low gathering clouds threatening snow. A single horse was tied to follow. In the interior, Madeleine pulled her scarf closer. Passing fields and woods she'd explored since she could walk, her thoughts wandered to possibilities she didn't want to consider. She was still staring when staccato bumps beneath the carriage awoke her to the wooden bridge into town.

Davidson halted the carriage before the chemist's shop, where Lady Jameson got out and went inside.

The shop was empty—neither customers nor Roisin nor her husband were to be seen. Madeleine took a moment before calling out, "Roisin?"

All was quiet.

Had she gone shopping? She usually left a sign on the door. Madeleine considered leaving but badly wanted to speak with Roisin to ask if she'd had any contact with the American. She stepped around the counter to the door leading to the preparation room in back.

In the center of the back room, Roisin stood frozen. An apron wrapped her thick body. Her hands were white with powder. Her eyes were wide.

"Go away, Maddie," she hissed.

Before Madeleine could move, a man stepped from the dark of the pantry closet.

"Lady Jameson," the American said in the clipped Yankee accent Madeleine so disliked. "You were the chief topic of our conversation."

"Leave her be," Roisin commanded. "I told you. I'm speakin' for the lady."

"Is she now?" the American asked Madeleine. "Is the chemist's wife your agent now? As I remember, Roisin here negotiated our loan arrangement, but the money all went directly to you."

She remembered the man vividly, though they'd met only once: on the chilled sand of the seashore at Crispin's Point. Staring at him now, fear engulfed her. She wanted only to say yes and walk away.

But she couldn't—she *wouldn't*—leave Roisin this way.

"No," Madeleine managed. "I'll speak for myself."

"Good. That makes things much easier."

The American stepped around Roisin to face her. "I've learned that your ship is docked in London Harbor. Where's my money?"

They'd spoken only briefly when the gold was delivered, dragged from a dinghy onto the shore as the smuggler's schooner rocked at anchor a hundred yards offshore from the point. He'd tried to intimidate her then by standing close, testing to see if she was afraid of him. It had worked. She'd been unable to hide her fear.

He intimidated her as much now. His voice seemed like a storm piling into rocks. His smile thinly concealed an air of brutality.

Except she had even fewer choices now than she did then. And fear was no longer such a stranger.

And she knew she needed to draw closer to the man—not shy away—if she was to convince him to extend the loan.

"If I'm to do business with you directly," she said, "I must know your name."

The American's stare hardened. For an instant she thought he might strike her.

"Only my crew and my friends know my name."

"Does Roisin know it?"

He nodded. "She's a friend. And she knows how to keep her mouth shut."

"She's my friend too. And she'll tell you I also know how to keep a secret."

The dark smile again.

"All right. It's your hanging if I ever learn you've spilled it. My name's Grayson. Grayson Turner. Now tell me why I don't have my money."

"You know why I haven't the money, Mr. Turner," she answered as boldly as she could manage. "Your sources will have told you."

He took in her face. "Yes, I do know. Then tell me what we're going to do about it."

"I'm sure Roisin has already told you what I can do. I'll need another three months."

"I'm to accept this why?"

"I'll pay you two hundred pounds now."

"The loan was fifty times that. Then there's the interest."

"It's what I can give you. You'll get the rest of your money with the interest when we sell the *Padget*'s cargo."

"*If* you sell the cargo. From what I've heard, that's not guaranteed."

"We will. If we fail, you can keep the *Padget*."

"I don't need a brig, my lady. I need my money. And if you fail, I doubt they'll let you keep her anyway."

"I'll add five percent to the interest on the loan."

Reaching behind his back, the American pulled a pistol from his belt. "Maybe I should just go back to your house and start taking my repayment in goods now."

"My lady said five percent, sir."

The American turned.

Davidson stood in the frame of the back doorway. Madeleine's father's Brown Bess musket was in his hands, leveled at the American's chest.

The American slowly lowered his hand with the pistol. "Just who are you?"

"He's my servant," Madeleine answered, relief and gratitude flooding her. She looked to the smuggler. "Davidson can retrieve the two hundred pounds now. That and an additional *ten percent* interest from this point forward for your forbearance."

The American shook his head, giving a sigh. "That'll buy you one more month. The problem with your ship should be settled by then. But if you lose your brig and cargo, Lady Jameson, there'll be hell to pay—servant or not. I'll be back in two hours for the coin."

He brushed past her to leave the shop.

Madeleine felt her legs give out. She found a stool and dropped.

Roisin stood staring at her, grinning. "Well, it seems you won't need me doin' your negotiating from here on out, that's for certain," she declared. "I'm proud of you."

Madeleine took a deep breath. "Davidson!" she cried out. "Thank you. I had no idea you'd brought Father's musket."

The servant nodded. "My lady will understand that I couldn't leave it at home with his lordship. It also seemed a foolish thing to be without it, given how things are at present."

"I owe you much."

She thought a moment as her heart began to slow. "Davidson, return to Heathcote and bring the two hundred pounds. You know where I keep it."

"Yes, miss."

"Then, after you accompany me to London, I'll want you to return to the estate rather than stay with me as planned. I'll keep the spare horse for myself there."

Roisin's grin faded.

"Now, there's a rott'n plan, Madeleine, considerin' what we just saw."

"No," Madeleine replied, still shaken but feeling strength returning to her voice. "No. I believe the American—Mr. Turner—will allow us our month. I worry more about those pursuing Harold and the *Padget*. In London, I'll have my barrister and his team nearby for protection. For the duration of the trial, I'd feel better knowing you were at home, Davidson, protecting Father and the estate."

"As you wish. I'll return to Heathcote now for the funds."

When he was gone, Madeleine turned to Roisin. "I'll need your eyes and ears and prayers while I'm in London. Please keep a watch out for any passing strangers who might pose a risk for Father, the staff, and the home. Get me word of anything that should worry me. I'll be staying with Dorothy."

"Is there somethin' you aren't tellin' me, child?" Roisin asked, squinting at her.

She still declined to tell her of the attack on her mare. "No. Nothing you need worry about."

Roisin shook her head. "I don't know that I believe you, but I'll do as you ask. And you know I can count on most of your farmers and the folks of this town to help any way they can. They know what you've done for 'em, forgivin' rent and loanin' money about."

"Good."

She hugged Roisin, nearly groaning at the strength of the older woman's squeeze.

They sat and spoke for another hour, Roisin flowing with optimism to buoy her until Davidson returned. Madeleine left the funds for the American with Roisin while Davidson tied up the spare horse behind the carriage once more.

Then they started for London.

The carriage rocked to the sway of the rough country roads as the finality of what was happening overtook her again. She had no real idea what awaited her in London. At least the barrister had accepted their case. She'd have sworn from their conversation before dinner and at the table that he was going to refuse to represent them. Then he'd agreed with a passion and a strength that encouraged her.

Why had he changed his mind? What realistic chance did he have of saving her cousin and the *Padget*?

Successful or not, she now knew that the estate wasn't the only thing she risked losing.

Pondering the encounter with the American, she hardly recognized who she was becoming.

OFFICE OF BARRISTER WILLIAM SNOPES
GRAY'S INN

Flush-faced, William burst through the door into his office, a copy of the *Gazette* under one arm.

"Oh, you've seen this afternoon's papers, Mr. Snopes," Obadiah said, seated behind William's desk with several newspapers of his own spread across it. "Is that the *Gazette*? It's the worst of them."

"Yes. But every one's got some angle on the 'pirate ship *Padget*.' Our penny dreadfuls raised questions, but these stories spout pure fiction as gospel truth."

"And they're ugly, Mr. Snopes. Very ugly. You'd think the *Padget* flew a skull and crossbones and Captain Tuttle was Blackbeard come back to life."

"And that we're all a nest of Jacobins trying to overthrow the king and both houses of Parliament."

"What happened at the hearing, sir?"

William took a breath to slow his heart and explained.

"Oh, that's not good news, Mr. Snopes. Not any of it, sir."

"That statement's short by a mile. The way the hearing was going, I crown it a victory that the judge didn't enter his Order of Contempt. Though I'm very disappointed we can't pursue the cabin boy's death just now."

William heard the scuffling of shoes and the creak of Edmund's door. He looked over his shoulder as Edmund entered, his coat over one arm.

"I heard you talking from my office," his junior said.

"Yes. The hearing was grim. Much like the papers."

"Did I hear you say you're not pursuing the boy's death after all?"

"I will in good time. But in his wisdom, our judge has ruled we can't prosecute it simultaneously with the piracy charge. Worse, he's given us only ten days until trial."

"I heard that part, sir. It's impossible. Surely you'll need my help now."

William nodded reluctantly. "Yes, Edmund. I want us all to meet here in the morning. I plan to send you both out to search for the crew, and especially this First Mate Ivars that Barnabas has sprung with the rest of them. He's the best one to support Solicitor Mortimer's testimony about the Letter of Marque. For tonight, though, go home and rest. Over the next fortnight I'll be needing your services twenty-four and seven."

An hour after Obadiah's and Edmund's departure, William left the office as well. Clutching his briefcase, his steps took him out of Gray's Inn to the corner of Gray's Inn Road and High Holburn in an evening mist. A cab approached. William waved his umbrella, gratified as it slowed and halted. He shouted his address to the driver as he stepped aboard, and the carriage lurched forward.

William wiped rain from his face and let out a deep sigh. He'd made up his mind to do just as he'd instructed Edmund and Obadiah. He'd get a final good night's rest before that luxury ended.

Two blocks rolled by. Barnabas's face filled the wet alleyways and silent shop windows they passed. Mandy Bristol's face followed. *Where are your grimy fingers in all this, Mandy?* William asked himself. *What's your role here?*

Ten days until trial. William's heart burned at the unfairness of it all.

He rapped the roof and leaned out the window.

"The Thames shipyards instead!" he shouted. "Get me to the Municipal docks."

The driver shrugged at his improved fare and whipped the horse to turn about.

When they arrived stevedores and sailors mixed in a swirling crowd at the port along the river. Though the driver dropped William only a short distance away from his destination, it took nearly half an hour to reach the ship, bumping and jostling in the light of torches rimming the riverbank.

In a corner of the London shipyard, William stared at the docked ship. Rocking low at anchor, the *Padget* seemed smaller than he remembered only days before. The constables in the warehouse shadows were gone—secrecy no longer necessary, he guessed. A man was seated at the top of the gangplank on her deck, a lantern glowing at his feet. With such valuable cargo in its hold, a single guard seemed an oddity.

William had given himself no time to plan, reacting to the urgency of the impossible schedule and Barnabas's statement that the *Padget* crew was gone. "'*Boldness be my friend*,'" he recited in a whisper, then gathered himself and walked up the plank.

The man on deck was a uniformed soldier. He stood as William reached the top of the gangplank. A thick mustache and muttonchops rounded a sun-seasoned face over broad shoulders. He wore the double-breasted coat of a sergeant. William saw a brace of pistols in his belt.

"You're on guard duty, Sergeant?" William asked.

"Aye," the soldier declared. "And the ship's off-grounds."

"Not to me. I'm the barrister representing the captain of this vessel. I'm here to tour the ship in preparation for the upcoming trial."

The soldier regarded him a long moment. When he spoke again, a cockney accent surfaced. "Well, that's as may be, but none's allowed aboard, sir. Doesn't matter what you do for a livin'."

William reached into the cloth briefcase at his side. "What's your name?"

"Nathaniel Rhodes."

"Well, Sergeant Rhodes, I've a court order allowing me access." He thrust papers into the soldier's hands.

The soldier stared at the writ of trespass that William had produced randomly from his case. From experience, William knew it was a fifty-fifty proposition whether a sergeant in the ranks could read. William prayed no superior officer was about for the sergeant to consult with.

"I don' rightly care what it says," the soldier said, pushing the papers back toward William, his other hand straying to the handle of his pistol. "You can't come aboard."

"Judge Raleigh will be very disappointed. You're stationed in London, Sergeant? What regiment and billet?"

"Portman Street Barracks, Marylebone. The Twenty-ninth Regiment of Foot."

"The Twenty-ninth. You boys fought in the Peninsular campaign."

The soldier's hand slipped from his pistol. "That was before my time."

"Perhaps. But I happen to know that Judge Raleigh served in Spain with your regiment early in the war. He'll be very disappointed to hear one of his own unit refused his subpoena. I'm sure it will pain him to imprison a man from his old regiment for disobeying a court order."

The shouts of men struggling to haul cargo aboard a nearby ship filled the silence that followed. Waves lapped against the *Padget's* hull as the sergeant fidgeted at William's lies.

"I don't see why you need to walk the ship anyway," he muttered at last. "The crew's all been let go."

"Is that so? Then it's so much easier! I just need to view the captain's cabin and the cargo hold and then I can be on my way."

This door's about to open, William thought. In silent confirmation, the sergeant gave a sullen shrug, lifted the lantern, and led William slowly toward the stairs heading belowdeck.

Moments later, William paced the interior of the captain's cabin under the sergeant's watchful eye. By the glare of the lantern light, William saw that the room, clean and orderly, was lined with rich wood paneling. It was smaller than William had imagined. But then this was a brig, not a galley, he reminded himself. Nearly all the ship's tight space beyond the twenty guns must have been intended for cargo.

It was simple to pick out the locked cabinet and drawer where Captain Tuttle said he'd kept the Letter. William fidgeted with the handle in a futile effort to open it. He leaned close. There was no sign of tampering around the keyhole. Nor was there any damage to the cabinet itself. If the Letter was inside the drawer when the captain left the room before the boarding, then someone used a key to withdraw it—or did a masterful job of picking the lock.

"Let's see the hold," he told the soldier.

The cargo hold below the crew's quarters was low-ceilinged, damp, and musty, its interior packed closely with wooden chests stretching the length of the ship. From where William stood, he'd have to crawl over them to count them all. All appeared tightly shut, though their contents were no secret: the heady smell of dried tea filled the cargo space, competing only with the odor of flotsam from the Thames outside.

At the last, William walked the main deck. Stopping beside the gangplank, he imagined Captain Tuttle's description of the constable and soldiers approaching—the captain hearing the unexpected gunshot, dropping his own pistol with surprise, then learning that the boy had been struck at his side.

The distance from where William stood to the shadows was less than two hundred feet. Could one of the approaching soldiers have seen the captain's pistol at his side in the full moonlight that night, as the sheriff told the captain? Could he really have mistakenly believed the captain was raising it in defense?

It seemed unlikely from this distance and in the dark.

"Sergeant," William called, "what are your orders here?"

"Guard and protect the ship and her cargo."

"Until?"

"Until relieved."

"Only you tonight on duty?"

"No. Three constables as well. It's quiet now, so I sent them to get some supper."

William hesitated before his next question, expecting a protest. "Were you here the night of the boarding?"

The soldier had grown accustomed to speaking, but the pointed question stiffened him again. "I don' know if I should be answering that."

"Come now. It's a simple question. The order requires you to answer my questions, whether in court or not."

"Yes," he said reluctantly. "A squad of my regiment was ordered to help the local constables take a prisoner from aboard this ship to Newgate."

"By whom?"

"No one said. I just did as I was told."

"Who was in charge of the detail?"

"A sheriff. I was the ranking soldier in charge of the troops."

"It's my understanding someone from the detail fired a shot. Was it a musket round or pistol shot?"

The soldier grew quiet.

"Sergeant, I can take this up with Judge Raleigh if you'd prefer."

"I believe it was a pistol, sir."

"And who fired?"

"Don't know. No one talked about it after, and I didn't investigate."

"And a boy was harmed?"

"Yes."

"Why didn't you investigate then?"

A long pause. "The captain appeared to have a weapon, sir. It seemed to me . . . it seemed to be self-defense, so I chose not to single the soldier out."

If only he could present this event to the jury, William mourned once more. It would gut their opponents' appeal to passion about the claims of Captain Tuttle's piracy.

"Thank you, Sergeant Rhodes. I'll be sure to tell Judge Raleigh how cooperative you were."

The barrister left the gangplank and disappeared up the quay and onto a street headed west toward central London, humming a low tune. The soldier watched from the *Padget*'s deck until the last hint of his figure was gone. Then, with a grunt, he went to a sack at the base of the mast and pulled out a book, seating himself on the gunwale to read by the lantern light.

An hour and more passed before three men appeared at the end of the quay, all with constable duty bands on their forearms. One was swinging a cloth bag over his shoulder. They ambled to the *Padget* and climbed the gangplank.

"Thankee for the break, Sergeant," the lead constable called. He dropped the cloth bag to the deck at the soldier's feet. "Brought back some dinner for you."

"Thanks," the soldier muttered. "But I've got to get back to barracks. I'll have it there."

"Anyone come by?"

"No," the sergeant answered.

"Get your inspection o' the cargo done?" another of the men asked.

"I did. It didn't take long."

"What's that yer readin'?" the third constable asked, pointing to the book.

"Byron."

"Never 'eard o' him."

"I hear the trial about this ship is starting soon," the first constable said to the sergeant. "You be testifying?"

The soldier stooped to pick up the bag with his supper. "I believe I will," he said as he began his descent of the plank. "Yes, I do believe I will."

22

HOME OF DOROTHY EMMERSON MARKS
MAYFAIR DISTRICT
LONDON

Madeleine stood on the top step of the town home in the deep dark of late evening, her travel chest resting on the landing beside her. Davidson was a step down, waiting to bring it inside.

Leaning forward, Madeleine knocked hard on the front door again.

The interior through the windows was as dark and silent as the street. Why was Dorothy or her staff not answering?

"What could it be, Davidson? I sent word I'd be coming and might be late."

"My lady?" Davidson said. "Perhaps we need to find you a hotel room."

"No," Madeleine answered firmly. "I know your meaning. But Dorothy's a good friend. Someone will be to the door shortly."

The door suddenly opened into darkness. A manservant stood in the shadowed entryway with tousled hair.

"Philip!" Madeleine called out. "I'm so sorry we arrived this late."

The servant's eyes were a cold barrier. "I've been directed to tell you that regretfully, my lady, it will not be possible for you to stay at the residence this evening."

Her chest hollowed. "I don't understand."

"Those are my orders, my lady. Now if you will excuse me . . ." The door closed.

Madeleine stood motionless. "The newspapers," she muttered to no one.

She heard Davidson lift the chest and walk it back to the carriage on the street, then return to gently take her elbow. "It's chilly, my lady. Let's get you back into the carriage."

He guided her to the street and up the step into the carriage, nestling a blanket across her knees. "I'll drive you to a hotel, miss," he said through the carriage window.

"No. No. I won't be in public."

"Then where? Back to the estate?"

Where? Dorothy had been her only remaining friend in London. Her world felt as empty as her heart. Other than her lawyers, there was no one in London who would take her side.

"The solicitor," she recalled reluctantly. "Mr. Obadiah Cummings. The one whose home we visited when we were here last. Do you remember it?"

"Of course, my lady."

Shame swept her, no matter how hard she hated herself for feeling it.

"Drive me there now. And please stay with me in London a day or two longer after all."

William awoke to bleak morning light through the window. He arose with a suddenness that took his breath away.

He'd been so terribly tired the evening before, so relieved at avoiding the judge's contempt charge, that he'd overlooked the obvious: Sir Barnabas's supreme confidence. It was much more than professional self-assurance. It was a heady certainty of *triumph*. Telling William about the release of the *Padget*'s crew had been a gift from a man convinced it would make no difference as to the outcome.

In fact, it was nearly a bold invitation to William to go see for himself.

How could Barnabas be so completely convinced that William would fail to prove the Letter of Marque's existence? As though he was aware of the source of William's confidence in the case, and already knew how to counter it.

William put his feet on the floor, straining to think clearly. When Sir Barnabas confronted him in the courtroom, for an instant he'd been tempted to blurt out Solicitor Mortimer's anticipated testimony. Anything to wipe the smugness from the man's face.

He'd assumed it would be a total surprise to Sir Barnabas. It would have, wouldn't it? Captain Tuttle had said he visited Solicitor Mortimer alone, and that even Mandy Bristol had no knowledge of the man and his authentication of the Letter. If that were true, then how could Sir Barnabas possibly know of Solicitor Mortimer and his anticipated testimony? How could he possibly overcome it?

His chest felt as if an anvil had been surgically planted there. There had to be a reason for Sir Barnabas's grand confidence. William couldn't wait another day, even another hour, to confirm Solicitor Mortimer's testimony.

His head pounded from the rush of blood as he pulled on his boots and raced to the door.

The cab trip to Chelsea took over an hour through crowded streets. William nearly threw the coins at the driver before sprinting up the steps to Solicitor Mortimer's door.

The maid appeared on his third set of frantic knocks.

"Please, I must see Solicitor Mortimer," he begged breathlessly.

"I'm sorry, sir," the maid said. "Mr. Mortimer is away."

"When will he be back? It's terribly important that I see him."

"I'm afraid Mr. Mortimer won't be able to see you for some time."

William's heart began to gallop. "Please, miss. I need to know where Mr. Mortimer has gone and for how long. You see, the solicitor and I represent the same client, and he was going to consult with me about that client—today I'd believed. If you could just see your way to telling me when he'll be back."

The maid sighed. "Well, seein' as how it's business, I suppose I can tell you. A gentleman hired Mr. Mortimer yesterday to prepare a will and other papers for a family estate in Edinburgh."

Edinburgh? "How long will he be away?"

"Two to three weeks, what with the travel time. It was all done in such a rush, you see. The gentleman bringing the business arrived carryin' a ticket on a steam packet to the coast, and they had to get there right away."

William nearly crumpled. "A gentleman hired him?"

"Aye. A well-dressed gentleman. Said he was an agent for a client in Scotland. Come to London to hire the best solicitor he could find to do the estate work. Price was no object. Odd look about him, though, for an agent of finer folks."

"What do you mean, *odd*?"

"Well, he had an eye, you see, that hung down a bit on his cheek. Hard not to look on it, if you take my meaning."

It took a moment to recall the image: William's brief encounter with the man he'd passed on the street near the docks only days before.

"Was there a scar above that eye? His left eye?"

"Garn! You know him, do you? I know it's a sin to speak ill of folks, but the whole of it gave me a real shudder when I opened the door."

She continued speaking, but William had already turned away.

Their best witness had been lost to them.

What would he tell the captain?

What would he tell Lady Jameson?

178

23

OFFICE OF BARRISTER WILLIAM SNOPES
GRAY'S INN

Leaving behind the midday traffic, ascending the steps at Gray's Inn, William strode slowly to his office, head down.

Lady Jameson was seated there, along with Obadiah and Edmund.

"We were wondering why you were late today, sir," Obadiah said.

Just seeing Lady Jameson, whom he'd disappoint momentarily, William felt the monumental weight on his back grow.

Still ignorant of his news, she seemed to brighten at his entrance, though he thought her tired.

"I'm very glad you made it safely," he said with a nod.

"Thank you."

Ever vigilant Obadiah squinted at William. "Something wrong, Mr. Snopes?"

"An understatement." William dropped his hat on a hook. "I feel as though I've been around the world twice since we parted last night, dragged every inch of it." He paused for a long breath. "This morning I drove to Solicitor Mortimer's office to confirm his authentication of the Letter of Marque. I'm sorry, Lady Jameson, but the man is gone. Left for Edinburgh. Not likely to return until long after the trial."

Edmund buried his head in his hands.

Obadiah groaned. "That can't be true! He's the rock of our case! Oh, Mr. Snopes, this is terrible luck."

"Not a matter of luck at all, I think," William said, taking his seat. He described the man who'd hired Solicitor Mortimer. "I'm sure I saw the same man the night I first visited the *Padget*. I believe he was following me that evening. I wonder if he hasn't been ever since."

Edmund sat up. "I saw the man too," he joined in. "When I visited Newgate Prison the first time, I encountered him—twice actually. With that eye and scar, it has to be the same man."

Lady Jameson had grown white. "This solicitor now absent. Obadiah informs me the first mate and crew are gone. That only leaves my cousin's testimony. He'll never be believed with the Letter gone. Who are these people? Why are they doing this? *What do they want?*"

William remained silent a moment, pained at the lady's despair and having no good answer.

"Lady Jameson," he began at last, "I'd hoped to achieve an acquittal by simply proving the existence of the Letter through Solicitor Mortimer and the first mate. Our opponents have contrived to deny us the solicitor's evidence and, by releasing the crew, possibly the first mate's as well. We have no choice but to try to unravel the mysteries surrounding the affair if we're to convince the jury of your cousin's innocence. Mysteries from the Letter's theft to the identities of the strange investors to the reason the constables and soldiers were so eagerly awaiting the *Padget*'s return."

"How do we even begin?" the lady exclaimed. "It's all too preposterous. Who would fight so hard to prove my cousin's guilt?"

"I wish I knew," William answered.

"Just tell us what to do, Mr. Snopes," Obadiah said. "You must have some thoughts."

William took a breath to steady himself. "We immediately commence an intense search for the crew and particularly the first mate. This Ivars fellow is our last independent witness to have seen the Letter of Marque, while the rest of the crew must contain our thief. Obadiah, work with the *Padget* crew list Captain Tuttle generated. Visit shipping offices along the Thames. Review crew manifests for every ship planning to sail soon. Since the *Padget* crew was released without final pay, many will have already signed with other vessels. Find as many as we can to interview. Also visit the Central and Middlesex Courts to learn if any of the crew have been convicted of crimes—particularly theft."

"Of course, sir."

"Edmund, I want you to learn about the workings of the Lord Privy Seal's office in preparing and recording official documents. Try to determine whether the absence of an entry of the Letter might have been deliberate."

Edmund nodded. "So we're assuming the Letter was purposely stolen to frame the captain as a pirate?"

"With all that's happened, I lean with the captain in that direction. Though the Letter would hold value to forgers, and so we must at least consider the possibility of a thief simply stealing the Letter for profit once the *Padget* docked—with disastrous timing for Captain Tuttle. I'd also like you, Edmund, to inquire with any sources you have about forgers of official documents in London who might have coveted a copy of a real Letter of Marque."

"But if the Letter truly was stolen to make Harold appear a pirate," Lady Jameson said, "wouldn't that mean the theft of the Letter of Marque and Harold's arrest were planned even before his voyage began? Is that even possible? And if so, why?"

William shrugged. "I've thought the same. And consider this detail: I visited the *Padget* last night and talked my way aboard. I saw no signs that the lock in Captain Tuttle's cabin had been picked. Would a thief intent on quick profit have gone to the trouble of acquiring a spare key? Would he also have relocked the cabinet when he was done? Those facts imply, however oddly, that the Letter may have been part of a larger plan for the captain's arrest for piracy."

Lady Jameson shook her head, looking as lost as he'd seen her at the bonfire.

"My lady," William said, "that leads to a request I have of you: your aid in learning the identities of Mandy Bristol's investors behind all this. Assuming the Letter was a forgery when provided to Captain Tuttle, it's likely they had a role in acquiring or preparing it."

"How can I help with that?"

"Whoever has influenced the newspapers must have money and power, an assumption made even more likely by the arranged departure of Solicitor Mortimer. If it is the investors, and they have resources and connections, they likely reside in your circles. Use any resources you have to plumb facts, rumors, or gossip about persons interested in the voyage of the *Padget*."

The lady grew red. "It should be quite clear to you, Mr. Snopes, that I have no such connections anymore. None of my friends left in London will even associate with me. If not for the kindness of Mr. Cummings and his dear wife, Davidson and I would be in a hotel at present."

William cleared his throat, regretting forcing the lady to more painful candor, especially before others. "Of course, my lady. But please try." He turned to all of them. "We must all take a turn at visiting Captain Tuttle as well. We must keep the lady's cousin alive and strong in that hellhole of a prison. When he testifies, he must present confidently and with strength about the Letter. Any other appearance risks being viewed by the jurors as a sign of guilt. Bring him supplies, but just as important, keep him involved in the case."

"Once again, you've kept your own plans for last, sir," Obadiah said.

"I'll be busy with two tasks. Given that our judge refuses to allow us to prosecute the shooting at present, he'll likely also exclude any evidence of the boy's murder during Captain Tuttle's defense. On this latter point, I want to change the judge's mind and find a way to educate the jury about the shooting. To that end, I plan to go to Whitechapel and locate the murdered boy's father."

"And the second task?" Edmund asked.

"Even before Whitechapel, I will return to Mandy Bristol to learn more about his investors. When I last visited, I was able to confirm your story, Lady Jameson. This time, I'll flush out more information if I have to strangle it from him."

24

Edmund left Gray's Inn with a hard, purposeful walk. The meeting just finished with Mr. Snopes, Obadiah, and the lady had set his mind on fire. Mr. Snopes had given him a task, and he'd get to it. But first he had to see to another errand.

Mr. Snopes was a powerful advocate. But he was a fencer, not a boxer. Even if his senior couldn't see it, this was a fight of fists now. The man Mr. Snopes described, with the odd scar and the dangling eye, had to be the man he'd run into at Newgate when he'd first gone to visit Captain Tuttle. Even a passing glance proved this one was a thug. A tactic like shipping away Solicitor Mortimer was no contest of feints and thrusts. It was a fight of bloody noses and broken jaws.

He knew a bit about that kind of fight.

Seven years past, Edmund had been sixteen years and a month old the afternoon he was led by the headmaster to the small back-yard of the boys' home. Obadiah was with them, only a step behind, silent and taciturn as always. Edmund's eye was swollen large from a fight the night before; Obadiah's lip was split in two from the same contest. Both their backs bore welts from the beatings the headmaster had laid on them after the fight was broken up.

They'd stopped near a tattered garden at the fence line. Waiting there was William Snopes, Barrister at Law.

A barrister coming to the boys' home usually meant a boy in legal trouble. When Edmund was told that this one had come to interview for an apprentice, he hadn't for a moment believed he had a chance for the job. To the boys, barristers were "crispers"— dandies favoring high, tight collars with judgment behind their eyes, especially for a boy like Edmund who couldn't hold his anger and whose only education since age twelve had come through the tutor at the boys' home once a week.

Standing at the garden with both hands behind his back, Mr. Snopes had seemed younger and plainer than Edmund expected, dressed in a simple black suit with no wig or powder in his hair. As they approached, the man was tapping a toe and humming a tune in a low rhythm.

In the next few minutes, everything else about Mr. Snopes would surprise him as well.

"I'm told you've expressed a wish to apprentice to the bar," Snopes had said, looking him in the eye.

The headmaster stifled a chuckle.

"Yes," Edmund answered defiantly.

"You'll address him as *sir*," the headmaster growled, whacking Edmund's back with the stick in his hand. The blow struck a wound, and Edmund flinched.

Snopes raised a hand. "It's all right. He can call me whatever he wishes. He's not my apprentice yet." The barrister's stare took in the injuries to Edmund's face, and his chin held high. "Headmaster," he said, "I'd like to have a word with the boys alone."

The headmaster looked uncertain. "They're fighters, these two. The tall one at least. And the short one never lets on what's on his mind, but does whatever Edmund tells him. I'm not sure it's a good idea to leave you alone with them."

"I'm no such fighter," Snopes said, looking Edmund in the eye. "I have no skills in boxing or wrestling, and while I'm good with a blade, I've left mine at home today. Still, I think I can handle these two. If not, you'll hear my shout."

The headmaster grunted a final protest, then walked away.

Snopes turned to Edmund again. "Why do you want to be a barrister?"

"I've my reasons," Edmund said.

"Is one of them that your father died in debtors' prison four years ago? You and your mother were living in the prison with him at the time, weren't you? And your mother died soon after, I understand."

Edmund's rage at this barrister even mentioning his mother nearly bubbled out. He stood his ground and said nothing.

"Come on, boy. Talk to me. Was your father there lawfully? Was there anything illegal in his punishment?"

Silence.

"I take it from your reticence that you believe your father didn't deserve his punishment. So now what? Do you wish to become a barrister to take out your sense of wrong on the whole of the judicial system?"

He couldn't hold back at the taunt. "The system deserves it," he said, hotly. "My father was the one wronged."

"Oh? Why is that?"

"He never signed the note they jailed him for."

"Really? I looked into the matter. I understand there actually was a signed promissory note."

"No. My father signed the note for his boss, who claimed it had to be done while he was away and would be sorted out later. It was a fraud, mister. The boss took the money and left town, leaving the debt for my father. He never should've been the one jailed."

"I see. Well, do you have any objection to debtors' prisons in general? Apart from your father's jailing? Something must be done with debtors, mustn't it?"

"Yes, I've got an objection."

"And what's that?"

"There's no crime in losing your job through no fault of your own, or running up a debt for having someone in your family sick. We call ourselves Christians. Well, that's against every Christian notion. As I've read it, we're supposed to forgive people in debt. But those that have the money not only scratch coin out of other people's hides, they throw them in jail where they can never make it good."

The barrister smiled gently. "Young man, do you realize that you've just offered at least three legal arguments? Fairly good ones too. You could strike more long-lasting blows with those arguments than in any fight of fists."

The barrister turned to the other boy. "Obadiah. I'm told you're interested in being a solicitor. Are you Welsh?"

"Yes, sir."

"Lost touch with your parents, who sailed for America, I was told. You were left with an aunt here in London, who died when you were eight?"

"That's right."

"Took up with a theft ring for a year or so in Piccadilly, before being arrested and sent here?"

Silence.

"We now have an inkling of why your friend Edmund wishes to be a barrister. Tell me, Obadiah, why you'd like to be a solicitor."

Obadiah glanced at Edmund, who nodded back.

"It's a very good job, sir," Obadiah answered. "And quiet-like."

"True. Quieter than a barrister's job."

"And he's very smart," Edmund chimed in. "Smarter than me by a step."

Snopes looked to Edmund, then back to the smaller boy. "And you wish to follow your friend Edmund here in choosing a legal profession? Is that it?"

Obadiah looked to the ground. "Yes, sir. I do wish it."

"He just doesn't think it's possible," Edmund burst out again. "Coming out of this home, there's no decent profession will take us."

Snopes grew silent for a moment before turning back to Edmund. "Are you prepared to work harder than you've ever worked before?"

Edmund began to laugh, then stopped as he saw that Snopes wasn't smiling. "Harder than being hired out to street builders to dig ditches twelve hours a day?" he challenged. "Because that's our lot in here."

"Yes, much harder, though not in the same way. Penned indoors, looking out at sunlight you can't enjoy, day after day, until you no longer believe the sun is real. Studying so hard and long you'll think your head will explode, then studying more. Memorizing half of *Black's Law Dictionary*. All of Sir Edward Coke. Boy, you've no idea how little you know—and how hard it will be to catch up. You'll be derided by other students of the law mercilessly—for your background and for your ignorance—and you'll be powerless to use your fists to stop it. Twelve hours of work in a day will be a holiday for the next six years of your life, and humiliation and self-doubt will be your daily companions. And in the end, even if you succeed in passing the bar, no matter how much you wish it, you'll never right the wrong done to your parents."

Edmund couldn't believe his ears. Was he being offered an apprenticeship? After all these years telling himself it was what he wanted, could he really do it?

Snopes sensed his hesitation. "Your headmaster doesn't believe you're up to it. He laughed aloud when I asked if he had anyone here with the ability and desire to enter the profession. Perhaps he was right."

"He wasn't, sir," Edmund said sharply. "I know I can do it."

Snopes took his measure with a long stare. "Perhaps," he said.

The barrister then looked at Obadiah with a note of sadness. "I admire your loyalty to Edmund, son. Truly I do. You're well-spoken, given your background, and I fear the truth of your prospects. But I'm afraid I've no place for training a solicitor. It will be difficult enough to house and feed a single barrister apprentice."

Edmund looked at Obadiah at his side, the split lip reminding him that Obadiah had earned it for jumping on the back of a boy twice his size, one of the four who'd pounded on Edmund the evening before.

"I can't go with you if Obadiah doesn't come." Edmund could hardly believe he'd said it—though he intended every word.

Snopes's eyebrows lifted. "Really? The headmaster told me you've claimed a wish to be a barrister's apprentice since you arrived here at age twelve. Do you think barristers are rushing the gates of this boys' home looking for candidates? Do you really think you'll have another chance?"

"No. I know this won't happen again. I don't see how it could happen now. But Obadiah's taken a beating more than once for me, as I have for him. The others will come after him once I'm gone. The same boys who did this." He gestured to Obadiah's swollen lip. "I won't leave him to that."

The barrister walked around the two boys, then stopped before them once more. "Well, we can't punish that kind of loyalty, can we?" he replied. "I tell you what, Edmund. You accept the barrister apprenticeship, and I promise my very best effort to locate a solicitor who can manage your friend. Agreed?"

Edmund looked to Obadiah, who nodded. "Agreed."

"Good. Now go pack up whatever belongings you have while I speak with your headmaster. And both of you, be prepared to learn how to fight with your mind and your words instead of your fists from this day forth."

The memory slid away as Edmund reached a familiar street. Well, he'd learned not to use his fists all right. Mr. Snopes had seen to that. But he'd never shed the fight inside that fueled them. He doubted he ever would.

Today he was glad for it.

Edmund turned into an alley and strode to the door of his favorite gambling hall.

Seated with a beer he'd nursed for hours, Edmund watched, in a mirror over the bar, the three tables hosting cards. The house was bursting tonight, the noisy dice games filling the room.

But at the card tables, players slumped silently, focused on their hands of brag. Half were known to Edmund—more by their sullen stares than by names. Edmund took another sip of beer to settle himself.

His target, Phineas Hardacre, sat to the left of the dealer. A beat-up top hat hung from a hook behind him. He wore a greasy blue suit. His luck at the table had risen and fallen twice since he'd sat down. Now nearly the last of his chips were again in the center of the table.

"You've been called, Mr. Hardacre," the dealer said.

Hardacre dropped his cards faceup for those at the table to see. Another player grinned as he set down his own cards, and Hardacre let out a loud groan.

"You've been a lucky Irishman all night long," he said and cursed. As the winner pulled the pile of chips toward him, Hardacre gathered his few remaining ones, grasped his hat and coat in disgust, and headed for the door—cashing out before he left.

Edmund waited until he was outside, then followed him.

The man was a block from the gambling hall, making his way up the rain-doused street, when Edmund drew near. "Hardacre!" he called.

The man slowed, turning. His eyes took in Edmund and widened. He began to run.

Edmund was younger and much faster. In four strides he'd caught the lapel of Hardacre's coat and dragged him back against the brick wall of a nearby building.

"Why so shy now?" Edmund demanded. "That article in the *Courier* about my senior, I take it that was yours?"

"Nah. Not me."

"Hard to believe. It's your beat and your sloppy style."

"Come on, Eddie. Even if it was, have a thicker skin."

Edmund slammed him against the wall again. "What's this slander about Mr. Snopes? 'Disowned son of Lord Snopes.' 'Relies on perjury in the courtroom.' 'Enemy to the Crown'?"

"You've got your sources; I've got mine."

Edmund's breath was ragged. "I'll forgive you, Hardacre, this once. If you tell me who's behind this. Tell me who kept the *Padget* out of the papers until now, then pushed this crock of a story in the *Courier*. Convince me or you'll be crawling home."

"You're seeing ghosts, boyo. There's nobody pulling strings here."

"Really? Then why'd they print Snopes's home address? With everything you accused him of, you might as well have torched the place."

"Aw, come on. Even if there was somebody pushing this, you think I'd know them? I write the stories; I don't hobnob with the editors or their pals."

Edmund braced the man's neck against the wall with his forearm. "All right, then, if that's your plea, I won't beat you after all. But I'll make it so you can't show your face in a card hall from here to Manchester. I'll spread word that you cheat. Want to bet that the Nash brothers you beat at brag last month won't come looking for their money back?"

Hardacre blinked, gasping for air. "Who'll believe *your* word?" he croaked. "You lose every time you go into the place."

Edmund stared at his prey for a moment. "You read that penny dreadful about the *Padget* and Captain Tuttle?"

"'Course I did. Everyone did."

"I helped write that. And I'll tell you the title of the next one: *The Gambling* Courier *Journalist and His Sleight of Hand at Brag.* I know enough about you and how it's done to make it stick. See who believes it then."

The journalist's eyes widened. "I'd sue you."

Edmund grinned. "Take me to court? Please! You'll be dancing in my hall then. In fact, I'll start writing the piece tonight. I can have it on the street by Sunday."

Some of the defiance went out of Hardacre's eyes.

Edmund released him. "Fly away, little bird. See you in print."

"Ah, just slow it down, Eddie," the man muttered. He leaned down to retrieve his battered hat. "Give me a few. I'll see what I can find out."

With a final hard glance at Edmund, he hurried up the street.

25

OFFICE OF MANDY BRISTOL
MAYFAIR DISTRICT
LONDON

William watched as short, stout Solicitor Bristol alighted from his cab, paid the fare, and marched across the street to the building housing his office. The solicitor's dress today was even gaudier than the last time he'd seen him, the waist and neckline too high, the suit cut too short. A bright red waistcoat and French cuffs. Shoulders padded. The man had become an undeniable dandy in the years since William tried the case for him.

William waited only long enough to be assured that Mandy had ascended the stairs to his office, then followed him in.

The solicitor was visible in his back office as William entered the foyer. "Mandy?" he called.

The solicitor turned. The light in his eyes went dark. "What do *you* want?"

"We need to talk."

Mandy came out and stood beside the desk. "I don't think so."

"You never got back to me about your investor clients."

"What investor clients?"

"That won't do, Mandy. I've got witnesses ready to attest to the Letter of Marque your clients gave to Captain Tuttle. There's no point hiding the investors any longer."

"Really? Witnesses? And who might they be?"

Was there a hint of gloating there?

"That's my business. But I have a proposition for you and your clients, Mandy. I'll represent them and their interests as to the *Padget*, in this or any future legal proceeding, and I'll do so without charge. I'll also see that my clients increase *your* clients' percentage of the profit from the *Padget*'s voyage to thirty percent. In exchange, they simply need to come forward and tell the truth about the Letter of Marque and attest to its authenticity."

Mandy ran a hand along his chin and sideburn. "You continue to miss the point, William. I deny any knowledge of these *investors* you say were involved in your captain's sordid affair."

"Based on all that you told him, Captain Tuttle will say otherwise."

"Captain Tuttle is a pirate."

"Very well. Then hear this. I think your investors provided a forged document to Captain Tuttle. I also know that a young boy was killed during the boarding of the *Padget*, a lad by the name of Simon Ladner. I intend to prosecute that death, including the liability of your investors, based on their interest in the *Padget*. When I make those charges, I'm confident the court will force you to go under oath to divulge your clients' identities."

There were so many twists in the logic of his statement that even William had to concentrate to sound resolved.

Mandy went silent for a moment before shaking his head.

"What tripe!" he burst out. "Where is this magical Letter of Marque you claim my mystery clients forged? And if you prosecuted these investors for the boy's death, you'd have to prosecute your own clients on the same grounds. We're done here, William. And I'll thank you to make an appointment the next time you want to see me. I won't have you barging in as you please. Good luck with that trial, eh? Just eight days I hear?"

There was movement behind him. William turned.

It was the boy who'd served the contempt of court papers on him only days before, and now William realized he'd first seen the boy in the street when the urchin had given him directions to Mandy's office. He stood nervously in the doorway, a stack of newspapers under his arm. William wondered how long he'd been there.

"Get out, Tad!" Mandy shouted at the boy. "Now!"

The boy scampered away. From the speed of his exit, William guessed he'd felt the back of Mandy's hand before.

"Good day, Barrister," Mandy said tightly.

William refused to be dismissed. "There's a man's life at stake, Mandy. And a family's fortune. I don't know what you and your clients' full purpose is in this scheme, but I'll find them. When I do, I will not only destroy the scheme, I'll burn this filthy practice of yours down around your ears."

William marched back down the stairs to the street. Stepping outside, he realized that he hadn't even removed his coat.

He took a deep breath to calm himself. Glancing up, he saw thick clouds crowding directly overhead. Whether rain or a wet snow, William didn't care. He'd walk home despite not having an umbrella with him. He needed the time to think. He needed the time to cool off.

Something bumped him and he looked that way.

The boy from Mandy's office was standing beside him. His eyes were wide and looked as though he'd been crying.

"He can be impatient, can't he, son?" William said. "Tad, is it?"

Tad turned and raced away up the street.

Watching him disappear, William thought about Mandy's reaction in their brief argument. He hadn't learned much, but two key points became clear. Mandy hadn't even blinked at hearing about the murdered boy, even though the news hadn't appeared in a single paper or in the penny dreadful he and Edmund had published before learning of the event. Only one person not present at the *Padget* that night had admitted to knowing of the shooting: Sir Barnabas.

Then there was Mandy's knowledge of the trial date.

It all spelled a passage of information between the Crown's prosecuting counsel and Mandy. But why?

He couldn't imagine.

He'd instinctively assumed Mandy's involvement with the prosecution. This was the first direct proof of it.

The confirmation worried him greatly.

Nerves still lit, William decided to hail a cab after all. As he stepped inside, he reached to confirm the location of his wallet in his breast pocket.

It wasn't there.

He searched throughout his pockets but without success.

He must have left it at home. Unless . . .

William looked off in the direction of the disappeared boy.

Had the scamp dipped his pocket? Was he that sort? If so, he'd get little for his effort, as William carried little of value in his wallet.

He should be angry, but William couldn't help but feel sorry for the boy, seemingly a street thief as well as in Mandy's employ. He thought again of the child's tears.

Strange. From all appearances, young though he was, the boy seemed too hardened to be brought to tears by a single shout from Mandy Bristol.

HOME OF OBADIAH AND SUZANNE CUMMINGS

"Are you certain, my lady?"

Davidson looked his usual calm self, save perhaps for the skepticism in his eyes. Alone, seated in the small, tidy sitting room of Obadiah and Suzanne's home, Madeleine nodded her response.

"Yes, Davidson. You know as well as I that the back staircase is better informed about social goings-on than their employers. I'd like you to speak with any friends and acquaintances among staff in London for the winter. Learn whatever you can about aristocratic knowledge or interest in the *Padget* or my family's affairs. I'd also like you to glean what you can about Solicitor Mandy Bristol and the social circles he keeps."

"Aye, my lady. Am I to leave immediately?"

"Yes, though first I'd like you to drop me at Dame Baltimore's."

Her servant's eyes widened. "Dame Baltimore? Are you sure, my lady?"

"Yes. We both know she's the spider at the center of the social web of London, gathering gossip from her wheeled chair. She'll have picked up any vibrations on these topics within fifty miles of London."

"Yes, my lady. If she'll accept you in her parlor, of course."

"She'll see me, Davidson. If only hoping to learn some juicy tidbits for herself."

Davidson cleared his throat, then proceeded gently. "May I suggest, my lady, that you prepare yourself for what you must be willing to give away?"

26

HOME OF MANDY BRISTOL
THE STRAND
LONDON

The broad yellow carriage, inlaid with the Brummell coat of arms, slowed to a stop on the street in front of Mandy Bristol's town home. Watching from an upstairs window, Mandy thought it resembled a massive lemon tart. No one could possibly mistake it for anyone else's transport than that of Lord Brummell—which was almost certainly the point.

That fact, and Mandy's anticipation of soon being inside it, made this evening that much sweeter. He headed downstairs.

Lord Brummell was the origin of nearly all of Mandy's social invitations, but never before tonight had he offered to ride together to an event. Only weeks ago, Mandy had worried about a falling out with his client and benefactor. But tonight's gesture signaled that he'd clearly misread the man. If Lord Brummell was angry about the *Padget*, why take him to a dinner where the lord had also arranged Mandy's invitation?

"Tad!" Mandy cried out as he descended the staircase. "You'd better have finished shining those boots!"

The boy came running into the foyer, boots in hand, worry on his face. Mandy snatched them away and examined them carefully.

The leather was creaseless and supple. Mandy's face looked back at him in the deep shine. "It'll do," he muttered. Pulling them on hastily, he shouted to his servant that he'd be returning late, then pulled his cape across his shoulders before stepping out into the chilly evening.

He was at the carriage door when the boy's footsteps approached from behind.

Mandy whirled, enraged that Lord Brummell might see the ragged child emerge from his home.

"What is it, boy?" he shouted.

Tad held a briefcase in his hand. "Your servant, sir, said you wouldn't want to forget this."

Mandy snatched it away. "I don't want you here when I return. Get back to Mr. McPherson. Tell Lonny I've no other tasks for you this week."

He grabbed the pull to enter the carriage, taking a seat with a smile for his benefactor.

The carriage seated six comfortably, though only Mandy and Lord Brummell were to ride tonight. Which was why Mandy was startled at the third person present.

"Solicitor Bristol," Lord Brummell said, "this is Princess Charlotte."

Mandy was speechless.

"I'm so honored to meet you, Your Highness," he managed.

The princess nodded back at Mandy, then looked out the window.

The carriage rocked along the London streets for nearly a mile without a single word exchanged. It scarcely mattered to Mandy. Lord Brummell was introducing him now to royalty. *The pinnacle of society*.

What could it mean? At the very least, Brummell had fully forgiven him. More optimistically, the lord was making a show of his full confidence in his solicitor.

Mandy looked again to the princess.

Only twenty, Prince Regent George's only child was next in line for the Crown after her mad grandfather and her father who ruled in his stead. Now that he was becoming an expert in fashion through Lord Brummell's tutelage, Mandy marveled at the princess's green gown with its low waistband, the fitted bodice and boat-style neckline, all so magnificent and modern. Jewels—green, red, and gold—encircled both wrists and neck. So transcendent! How her youth accentuated her beauty!

He could barely remove his eyes from her.

The princess turned to face him.

"Solicitor Bristol?" her voice commanded.

"Yes, Your Highness?"

"Would you grant me a favor?"

"Of course, Your Highness. You need only name it. Anything at all."

"Would you please explain how you managed to cock up this business of the *Padget* so completely?"

He mustn't have heard that right. "Your Highness?"

"It is a feat I would have thought impossible. Your stupidity rivals that of my grandfather, the king. He, at least, has the excuse of insanity."

Mandy sat back. "I . . . don't understand." He looked to Lord Brummell. "What does she know?"

The princess looked to the lord as well. "What kennel did you find this one in, Lord Brummell?"

Brummell fixed his own withering stare on Mandy. "Mr. Bristol, don't look so stupefied. Given the present troubles, I suggested to the princess that it was time you met my investment partner. The princess agreed only to help you to understand the gravity of the situation you've created."

Mandy's stomach turned to liquid. "The princess is your partner? Your partner in the *Padget* matter?"

"In *all* the ventures that you've managed for us, including the

Padget. How else do you think we were able to arrange access to the documents we needed? How do you think we were able to arrange your communications with Sir Barnabas?"

"You two? I . . . I mean, sir, I thought—no disrespect my lady—it's just that I thought, after all this time, that your partner was a fiction."

"Close your mouth, Mandy. No. It's always been we two."

A growing fog in Mandy's mind was displaced by crushing disappointment. So his introduction to the princess was an instructional moment. Nothing more.

"I . . . I don't even know what to say," he stammered.

"Nor what to do, apparently," the princess said. "In only a few weeks, you've managed to put a four-year venture at risk and turn a highly profitable business into a debacle which now threatens to destroy us all."

"But, Your Highness," Mandy rushed to defend himself, "it wasn't my fault that the boy's shooting stiffened Captain Tuttle's resolve. Such a thing had never happened before. And I assure you that matters are still firmly in our control. We've kept the trial on a very short schedule. Mr. Snopes won't have nearly enough time to properly prepare. And—"

"Enough," Lord Brummell intervened. "I have other sources than yourself, Mr. Bristol. I know what transpired at the court hearing."

"Then you must know that—"

"Mr. Bristol," the princess interrupted, "do you grasp how important it is that the Letter of Marque, the cargo, the taking of the ship *not be in the public eye?*"

"Of course I've understood that, Your Highness. And I know that this whole public airing is truly unfortunate. But the Crown's prosecution is certain to win the day. In the end, the public will place no credit on Captain Tuttle's claim about a Letter of Marque. I'm sure you're disappointed with the complications of the arrest and the release of that book by Snopes and his bunch. But I believe—"

"Disappointed?" The princess rolled her eyes, and Mandy felt the last of his infatuation with her beauty and appearance of innocence dissolve. "Why it appears that we've discovered your intellectual gift after all, Solicitor: a marvelous talent for understatement. You don't seem to comprehend that the Crown's prosecution has dragged Lord Brummell and me too close to the heat and light of the fire—something you and those you've employed were to prevent. Are you aware that Barrister Snopes visited the *Padget* a few days ago—and was let aboard?"

Mandy smiled. "Yes. In fact, I arranged that."

"Arranged that? How? Why?"

"When I learned that Sir Barnabas had released the *Padget* crew, I knew that Snopes couldn't resist going to see for himself. I reached out to our man in the ranks to assist on this. If Snopes tries to use what he learned on board at trial, he'll be in for a grave surprise."

"You really should have checked with me first," Lord Brummell said.

"I believed that you'd approve."

"You think you're one step ahead of him, don't you?"

"My lord, the man has a reputation for clever advocacy, I'll grant you. But Sir Barnabas firmly bested him at the hearing."

"Mr. Snopes was *surprised* at the hearing," the princess replied. "And he still avoided a contempt order and a disbarment investigation. In fact, he still nearly achieved a continuance."

"Mr. Bristol," Lord Brummell added, "too much has already gone wrong with the whole *Padget* scheme. We mustn't underestimate Snopes any longer."

More argument would do him no good. That much was clear.

"Of course," Mandy answered.

"And now," the princess said, "I want you to listen to me very carefully. Steps must be taken. We want you to immediately end and eliminate any trace of the ventures that could come back upon us."

"Any trace?"

"Yes. Beginning with placing all your employees out of reach of these court proceedings. I want them relocated *now*. I don't care if you have to ship them to Jamaica."

"So soon? But we were preparing for another—"

"No, Mr. Bristol. You're not listening. We want everyone far beyond the reach of any court order to testify, and far beyond William Snopes's ability to find them. And we want their exile to be permanent."

Mandy heard the firmness of the order. "If you insist on curtailing everything at this juncture, and with such certainty, it could prove quite expensive."

"We don't care. Pay what you must. And as to this trial, we must take the fight to Snopes and his group on all fronts—personal and professional. If we lose the case, matters won't end there. A loss would certainly lead to more investigations about Captain Tuttle's Letter of Marque."

Lord Brummell bumped his walking stick against the roof of the carriage.

The driver called "Whoa!" and the carriage slowed.

"Now," Brummell said, "we believe that your time would be better spent complying with our request than attending this evening's dinner. Don't plan on the ball at the Rutledge home later this week either, I'm afraid."

"I . . . I already informed the Rutledges I would be there."

"I'm co-hosting the ball and will pass on your regrets. Assuming your success at trial, Mr. Bristol, you can be assured of many more social opportunities in the future."

Mandy looked down at his suit. Sculpted to mimic the latest fashion trends Lord Brummell was always modeling, it had cost him nearly ninety pounds. His invitation to this particular dinner had been a coup. To think that, for a moment, he'd even thought he'd be arriving with the princess. Now he was, quite literally, being tossed to the curb.

Bile coated his tongue.

"Of course, Lord Brummell," he answered—the only reply he could make. He glanced at the princess, but she was looking out the window once again.

With a tip of his hat to the turned cheek of the princess, Mandy climbed to the street.

The carriage rolled on as Mandy watched bitterly, his unopened briefcase with details of the court hearing in hand.

The princess is Lord Brummell's partner? Why? How?

The emphatic orders of the lord and the princess echoed in his head. He'd always known the lord was an inch of skin hiding a foot of cruelty. But the princess? Mandy wouldn't have thought such malicious resolve possible in someone so young and fair.

Mandy stomped angrily up the street in search of a cab home. They were cruel perhaps. But it was a cruel world, and not of his making, so he'd always strived to suffer less than the next man. With so much at stake—with all the progress he'd made in his own stature these past few years—he would carry out his patrons' wishes to the absolute letter.

With no lost sleep over the price.

NEWGATE PRISON

"They executed five today." The captain was speaking lifelessly. "Marched them up the stairs and away, I'm told, to a courtyard where the deed is done. A jailor told me yesterday that it's precisely six hundred twenty-seven steps from that staircase to the executioner's shed. Men can count the vanishing thread of their lives with that much certainty."

There was hissing from coal on the small brazier behind the captain, the only source of heat in his cell. The man looked pale today, more so than three days before when William last visited. Weary, lacking hope, rambling.

Seated just beyond the bars, William stiffened at the cruelty of a jailor who would torture a prisoner with stories of executions.

"I intend to spare you that walk, Captain," he said, nodding to emphasize confidence.

"Really?" the captain replied. "With only six days to trial? From everything Madeleine has told me, and all that your solicitor would not, I gather you'll have difficulty keeping that promise."

"The loss of Solicitor Mortimer's testimony was a blow, I grant you," William rejoined. "But we have more evidence to present— including the testimony of your First Mate Ivars."

"If you can find him." The captain looked away. "You'd think that my naval service would count for something in all this. The granting of your continuance at least, though I scarcely even know if I want that. I'm not certain I can last another day in this place, let alone six. I'm used to open skies and fresh air." He paused, then added, "I met Lord Nelson once, you know."

"Truly?" William said, pleased that the captain was enlivened at the memory of the naval hero.

"Oh, yes. Not in the service, of course. I was much too young for that. It was, I believe, 1800. I was thirteen and already certain I wanted a life at sea. Lord Nelson had accepted an invitation to a party at the Jamesons' winter town home here in London. I was staying over since my parents were also attending, and I'd heard the servants talking excitedly about the lord admiral's visit. After dinner I snuck downstairs to hide behind curtains in the music room next to the piano as the ball guests arrived. I hadn't had a chance to creep nearer to the main gathering before Lord Nelson came into the very room where I hid, accompanied by his wife, Fanny."

"That's extraordinary. Did you get any hint of the man?"

"To my eyes, he had the bearing of a god. Straight-backed. Resolute. Just as I'd imagined him to be. In my heart, I swore he could have sunk Napoleon's frigates with lightning bolts from his eyes. Until they began to argue, that is."

"Argue?"

"Yes. Lord Nelson and his wife. In a heated whisper, but near enough that I could make it out. It was . . . deflating, really. How could Lord Nelson have a dispute with his wife? Wouldn't he be beyond such pettiness?"

"What was the argument about?"

"That also was dispiriting. Even to a young boy's ears I made out that Lord Nelson had a mistress. His wife was imploring him to leave the woman behind. He was refusing."

The captain's shoulders had dropped, but William was too far in to abandon the story. "How did it end?"

"Lord Nelson's wife left the room in anger while the admiral remained a bit longer. Then the strangest thing of all occurred. Though he'd given no hint of seeing me, the admiral turned and looked directly at me where I stood peering through a crack in the curtains. A stare that pierced me."

"Did he say anything?"

"No. But he winked. He'd lost an eye in the service, you know, but he winked the good one. And this is the wonder of it: it wasn't playful. It was, if anything, a sad gesture. I thought, How could one such as he be subject to such low emotions as I'd just witnessed? Yet there it was. If Lord Nelson could be haunted so, shadowed by sin and cruel melancholy, what hope was there for the rest of us? I tell you that my belief in any certitude of happiness, or even justice, faded some that day."

The cells grew quiet as William contemplated how to turn away from the story he now regretted encouraging.

"Has your young lady visited you, Captain Tuttle?" he asked.

"Hmm?"

"I asked, has your young lady visited?"

The captain shook his head. "Rebekah? No. Madeleine tells me her family forbids it."

"Captain, you really mustn't despair," William said, frustrated that every word he uttered only lowered the captain's spirit more. "We'll find justice for you in all of this, I promise. And to that end, I must ask your help. Have you any more thoughts about where your first mate may have gone after being released from detention?"

The captain shrugged. "Not really. As I've told you, I knew Mr. Ivars from my early days in the service, though I hadn't seen him for many years. When he appeared dockside in the last few days before the *Padget* sailed, he touted a wealth of experience I couldn't ignore, especially as a physician's mate. I took a chance and appointed him first mate. He never let me down throughout the voyage, though he was a closed man. Did I tell you that he's originally from Bath or that region? I know little more about his background than that. If he stayed in London looking for more work, you might check the Sailor's Home on Dorsett Street."

Of course, they'd already checked there—plus a dozen other lodging places in the east end catering to sailors.

"Thank you," William said. "Please take heart, Captain. You're not alone in this."

The captain returned a wan smile. "Cousin Madeleine has said nearly the same, and she's the only living person in the world I completely trust. She's also told me she firmly believes in you, your integrity, and your counsel. With such an endorsement, I'll try to do as you ask."

HYDE PARK

"Must we meet like this?" Obadiah asked, his teeth chattering as they stood beside a frozen pond. "This is such an unseasonable cold."

Edmund stomped his feet for warmth at the solicitor's side. "If we must meet outdoors, Mr. Snopes, couldn't it be closer to the Inn?"

Yes, it was cold. Before leaving for the prison, he'd seen the frost decorating the windows at his flat and a thin layer of snow blanketing the street below and the temperature must have fallen another ten degrees since then. Late winter was the worst, laying on punishment for the season's early mildness.

But William was in no mood for grumbling after visiting the captain at Newgate only an hour before.

"You'll have to put up with the cold," he said. "I want a clear field of vision to see if that strange man is following us any longer. I don't trust walls or fences, even of our office. We've been overmatched by our opponents' spies thus far, and that must end. Tell us what you've discovered, Obadiah, so we can move on."

The solicitor leaned stiffly down and pulled a fistful of papers from the briefcase set on the snow at his feet. "As you asked, Mr. Snopes, I canvassed every shipper I could. You were right about the *Padget*'s crew looking for work. I've already located fourteen— well over half of them. Edmund's been helping me interview them. They've not too much to tell on the topic of the Letter of Marque, sir."

"I see. And you've reviewed their names with Captain Tuttle?"

"Yes. The captain eliminated seven as beyond the type of mischief we're investigating, mostly men he'd long known in the service. As to the remainder, he's skeptical about their being thieves as well—though I think our captain is the trusting sort. Still, all the crew members we've found so far left addresses with the companies they're shipping out with, and I've been planning on running them all down."

"Remember," William emphasized, "to focus particularly on finding this Quint Ivars fellow, the first mate. What of criminal records among the crew members?"

"Making slow progress there as well, sir," Obadiah said, his breath producing clouds between them. "Two of those I found were convicted of crimes. One for public drunkenness and property damage. The other for breach of promise."

"Neither sounds like who we're seeking." William sighed, disappointed.

"Have you gone yet to Whitechapel to search for the boy's father?" Edmund asked.

"Not yet. But I still plan to."

"Do you really think there's a chance the judge will allow evidence of the boy's shooting to be admitted?" Obadiah asked.

"I don't know. But among the other papers you're preparing for trial, please add a brief supporting the admissibility of the boy's shooting. Argue that it's relevant to proving felonious intent by the arresting party."

"Felonious intent, sir?" Obadiah asked. "Intent to do what?"

"Intent to steal the Letter of Marque."

"Are you really going to accuse the arresting party of that?" Edmund asked. "We've no evidence to support it."

"I'd accuse them of intent to steal the Crown Jewels if it would move the judge to allow the boy's shooting into evidence," William snapped.

Obadiah and Edmund went silent.

Regretting his outburst, William took a slow breath. "Edmund, what have you learned at the Lord Privy Seal's office?"

His junior shook his head. "Not much, sir. The document records are kept in a fairly public place. The entry of a Letter of Marque issued to Captain Tuttle could have been assigned to any number of clerks."

Another disappointment.

"Have either of you heard any word from Lady Jameson on her efforts to ferret out people showing interest in the *Padget*?"

"Only that she left soon after our meeting yesterday, telling Suzie she'd be gone all day," Obadiah replied. "She disappeared early again this morning, before I even saw her."

"Did she tell you what she was trying to accomplish?"

"No, sir."

William felt a cold rush of anxiety at the image of the lady traveling about London for long hours alone. At least it was likely she was visiting the more affluent corners of the city. He only wished she'd informed him of the details of her plan in advance.

He shrugged to hide his worry. "Well, then. I'll continue my preparation of examination questions at Gray's Inn. Let's meet at the office in the morning—say at eight—to compare notes once more."

HOME OF DAME BALTIMORE
CHELSEA

Perched at the edge of a cushioned settee, teacup in hand, Madeleine distracted herself by imagining the quantity of information that must have come into the parlor where she now sat. Only a coffee table away was Dame Baltimore, seated on a gilded, cushioned, wood wheeled chair, made in the French design the dame clearly favored. Surrounded by a cloud of vanilla and gardenia fragrance, the dowager held her own teacup in one hand, a Chinese fan in the other. The host's eyes were blank above a distant smile, as though she expected nothing of interest to come from this conversation. It seemed a practiced appearance, well played.

Except for her forehead and chin, Madeleine thought. Her forehead was knitted as tightly as a firmly tied shoe, her chin raised with expectation.

Madeleine had been right about gaining entrance to this parlor. She might be persona non grata with the highest of society, but to those like the dame, who counted their wealth in their knowledge of others' affairs, Madeleine was a prize who couldn't be turned away.

"And your father? How is his health?" the dowager asked as she raised her cup with measured care.

"He's well, thank you."

Dame Baltimore sniffed, a sign of displeasure at the short response. "Is that so? I haven't heard of him attending any events the past many months. It might even be years since I recall him at a party or dinner."

"Oh, Father has been very busy with the estate. We've added more livestock, and he is meticulous as to their care and marketing."

Dame Baltimore sniffed twice this time. She set the fan on her lap and rested a hand on one of the wheels of her invalid chair.

"You know," Madeleine began, fearing she was being dismissed, "there's an old acquaintance of my father's whom we were discussing just the other day. A solicitor here in London who seems to have disappeared. I was wondering if you might have seen him about, given the breadth of your friendships in London. A Mr. Mandy Bristol?"

A sip of her tea, taken at a languid pace, signaled the dowager's unwillingness to engage. "I really couldn't say, Lady Jameson."

"That's too bad. We had a bit of business we wished to bring him."

"Is that so? Well, you'd be better off seeking such information at the Inns of Court," the dowager replied.

Madeleine was swept with sudden dismay. She'd thought a reference to needing legal assistance would coax the lady into helping. Even in her own parlor, with a guest before her, she showed no inclination to do so.

Except, Madeleine realized, recalling Davidson's advice, that was her mistake. She was in no parlor at all. She occupied a market, where bargaining was as expected as in the West Smithfield meat emporium. Where currency was necessary to acquire the goods she sought.

Fortunately, she had a bucketful of such coin just now.

Madeleine swallowed to overcome her reluctance. "I don't know if you've heard, Dame Baltimore," she began, "but my family has engaged in some litigation in The Old Bailey."

A fire stoked in the old woman's eyes. "I do believe I've heard something of this."

"Yes. We've retained an attorney. A Mr. William Snopes. Perhaps you've heard of him?"

The fires banked higher.

"So you're truly proceeding with the matter? I admit to seeing something of this in the newspapers, though I didn't know whether to give the stories full credence. Mr. Snopes, you say? Why, I believe I've heard of him. Son of Lord Kyle Snopes."

"Yes, that's the one."

The teacup went down on the table. "What do you know of the man, Madeleine?"

She hadn't intended to bargain for such information—Bristol was her target—but Madeleine found herself suddenly interested.

"Not a great deal," she teased for a response. "I know that he and his father are estranged."

The dowager smiled. "You know, there are many rumors as to why that is the case. Murder. Espionage. I happen to know the truth of the matter."

Madeleine had no need to feign interest now. "Yes?"

"Yes. The fact is that Lord Kyle Snopes fathered an illegitimate child with the daughter of one of his tenants. William learned of it and left that very day."

A note in Dame Baltimore's story harmonized with Madeleine's image of the man, recalling him standing by her side at the fire in the rain.

"How do you know this?" she asked.

"I know it because my niece, Lady Sherrod of Winterfall Manor, just a few miles south of the Snopes Estate, learned of it through a tenant on her own father's estate. I also know from other sources that William Snopes, after he became established as a barrister in London, lived in a dingy flat south of Belgravia for the first five years of his practice to enable himself to spend every penny he earned in a vain attempt to find the lost child—who was, after all, his half sibling."

"A vain attempt?"

"Yes. In fact, the poor young girl whom Lord Snopes had so mistreated was shipped off to have her child far from the Snopes Estate and died in childbirth. It's rumored that her surviving baby was a girl, and that she was sent to America or Canada—into the care of a distant relative. The young Mr. Snopes was devastated by the loss and his inability to locate his sister. When he finally gave up his search, he vowed in his fury to never represent a member of his father's class again."

The dowager leaned forward, and her cloud of vanilla and gardenia encircled Madeleine. "Yet it would appear that you are an exception to that vow, young lady."

The story moved her, and for a moment Madeleine didn't

respond. But how could this aging fountain of gossip and rumor have gained such detailed knowledge? Did she dare believe it?

And if so, why had William consented to represent her?

Madeleine picked up her own teacup. "An exception? Perhaps. Although our cause is a just one."

"Is that so?" the dowager said, slowing the flow of her response in reaction to Madeleine's curt and clearly unsatisfactory reply in the game they played.

Madeleine had completely forgotten about the point of her visit, which came rushing back to her now. It would require more painful admissions but necessary ones. To build the fires again, she leaned back and placed a frown on her face.

"Dame Baltimore, I have a confession to make. My father isn't so well. I said otherwise out of shame for his condition. He is, in fact, quite invalided. And he has given me mastery over the estate."

It was weak fare—she'd admitted as much already at Dorothy's party. But the dowager perked up.

"And I will also admit," Madeleine grudgingly added, "that the claims in the newspapers—the ones that say that I and my father purchased a ship now accused of piracy—are equally true. Not the piracy, of course! But we do own the *Padget*, recently referenced in a penny dreadful. A ship that did take a French ship in the Indian Sea."

This was better currency, Madeleine could see. The old woman nodded, looking to her lap with a near return of her smile.

"Did you say you were interested in Mandy Bristol?" Dame Baltimore asked.

Madeleine sat straighter expectantly. "Why, yes. Perhaps you know something of his acquaintances or friends through whom we might find him. People with whom he mixes at social events?"

"I'm afraid I can't help you there, young Madeleine," the dowager answered to Madeleine's powerful regret. "With my affliction and the entrapment of this chair, it's uncommon for me to attend society events in person any longer, and I've not inquired as to who

214

might accompany Solicitor Bristol. The fact that I know so little of him is strange to me."

Dame Baltimore paused.

"But I can tell you that these past two years, he's been heavily engaged in the social scene. And it's said that his precipitous rise in society is because he has patrons. In very, very high places."

28

It had grown dark long before the time that William neared home on weary legs.

Since his morning visit to Captain Tuttle and midday meeting with Edmund and Obadiah, it had turned into a frustrating day, yielding little information. He was desperate for a cup of tea and a few minutes' respite before bed and an early morning to follow.

Voices ahead brought his eyes up.

Throwing shadows from a gaslight, a crowd of men milled about in groups of three or four near the entry to his upstairs flat. At first glance, William took them for customers of the tobacco shop on street level. Except, as congenial as the proprietor was, William had never seen more than a few customers an hour patronizing the place. Besides, the shop should have closed hours before.

He came nearer. There was a drunken tilt to the gathering. Gin-fueled anger flowed amid rising and falling voices. Like a smoldering fire poised for a breeze.

Not slowing his pace, William walked past, eyes lowered.

Only a few strides beyond a voice called. "Ain't that him?"

William didn't look back. He began to sprint up the slippery, snow-covered road—shouts following close behind. Sliding, struggling with his heavy coat and fatigue, at his first chance he turned onto a narrower street that he knew sprouted several more. The mob was still in sight when he chose yet another turn, then an alley branching out behind his horse's stable, for the first time putting him beyond sight of his chasers. A dozen strides more took William past several outlets before steps descended near the rear entrance of a pub. Just beyond the pub door, the alley dead-ended at a low wooden wall.

William jumped, got purchase on the top, and pulled himself over.

His breath coming in gasps, he knelt to slow his heart and listen.

Several seconds passed. Then footsteps sounded in the alley beyond the wooden fence.

"Must've gone the other way," a panting voice called.

"I'm goin' in here," said another amid puffs, most likely meaning the pub.

The fire had gone out of the weary voices. Holding his breath, William waited until the footsteps led away, back toward the pub and beyond his hearing.

William rose, shaking his head. Now he was exiled from his own home, which included all the work he had spread about there. Father Thomas had warned him this might be coming. Each day's newspapers labeled him everything from a puppet of the pope to a gold-grubbing barrister out to topple the Crown. Even with so much fodder, he still bet that the mob had organizing help or at least pub money to support them.

William reached and pulled himself up to peer over the wall. The alley was empty. He climbed wearily up and dropped to the other side.

Walking carefully away, avoiding the direction of his flat, he thought of Mandy Bristol and what role he might have played in driving him from his home.

With each step, he grew angrier.

He'd find the means to pay Mr. Bristol back.

HOME OF OBADIAH CUMMINGS

"You're very kind to let me stay the night," William said again to Obadiah and Suzanne, seated at the small dining table in their home. "Tomorrow I'll ask the good Father to retrieve some clothes for me, as well as my papers from my flat. I can set up quarters at Gray's Inn for the duration."

With Davidson retired to a small, tidy attic overhead, Lady Jameson sat across the room on a settee near the window. To William's surprise, he'd caught her making curious glances toward him.

"It's nothing, sir," Obadiah said as Suzanne brought William a glass of mulled wine from near a lively fire.

"We're just glad you're safe." Suzanne smiled through worry-filled eyes.

William sipped the cinnamon-and-cloves brew, attempting a relaxed manner. "Obadiah, I've been thinking. I'd prefer you limit your role in this case going forward. Edmund and I can cover things quite well."

"Oh, no, you don't," Obadiah answered. The fight in his voice reminded William of the young lad in the boys' home. "You already tried this with Edmund, sir. Suzie and I talked this over, haven't we, love? Mr. Snopes, you and Edmund are the ones on the front line, for sure. The gallery is always the solicitor's lot in trial. But I'm seeing this through with you whatever you do. And if it comes to it, I'll man the barricades at your side."

William looked down, warmed yet embarrassed his sentiment would show. He glanced to the lady again.

"I hadn't yet expressed it, Lady Jameson, but I'm also very pleased you've returned safely."

"Thank you. And I've some news as well. I've come from a meeting with London's most expert gossip, Dame Baltimore, and have a suggestion for locating Mandy Bristol's mystery investors."

"Which is?"

"As you know, I've never met Mandy Bristol. You've described him as ambitious and eager to curry favor. I was surprised that Dame Baltimore had little information about the man. But she did share that he's had a meteoric rise in society the past two years, with sponsorship from 'very high patronage.' If that's true, then it seems possible that these investors are the very patrons my source hinted at. Which means that Mr. Bristol may have been seen in the investors' company at the social events he's attended."

"You're right, Lady Jameson," William said. "Very good. So how do we learn who Mandy has been hobnobbing with at social events?"

"This is London's winter ball season, after all," the lady replied. "I haven't attended a ball in years. But at my request, Davidson called on friends among staffs of families now in London. Apparently, there's a ball only two days from now, at the London home of the Rutledge family. Davidson even managed to see the guest list. Solicitor Bristol was invited and has signaled his attendance."

"That's brilliant!" William sat up. "We might learn a great deal if we could gain access."

"I'd hoped you could manage that," the lady said, her eyes growing more cautious. "Though you're independent of your family, the Snopes name must still ride high in such circles, particularly here in London."

William shook his head firmly. "I haven't attended a ball in over twenty years. I was but eighteen when I last did. And I'm confident my reputation as a barrister would make me a poor risk as a guest."

"As I just proved in my visit to Dame Baltimore, curiosity can be as important as station in garnering an invitation."

"So you want me to volunteer to be the trained bear?" William smiled and thought a moment, taking another drink. "All right. I'll see what I can do." He paused a moment more, then took the lady in his gaze. "But only if you accompany me as my guest."

Madeleine's face flushed. "That's not a good idea, Mr. Snopes. I'm a pariah."

"As you've pointed out, Lady Jameson, what's important is that, like me, you're a *curiosity*. Everyone in those circles will know from the papers that I represent you. That should make us the perfect pair for the evening."

A full smile slowly formed on her face and her eyes lingered upon him.

William realized, to his delight, that it was the first such open smile he recalled seeing on the lady.

"Very well," she said. "I'll send Davidson tomorrow to retrieve a gown."

They sat another hour before the fireplace, content with the quiet. Suzanne finally rose and took William's cup.

Madeleine joined her, taking plates and cups to the washbasin in the corner while Obadiah showed William upstairs.

"How long have you known Mr. Snopes?" Madeleine asked when she was alone with Suzanne.

"Since before Obadiah asked me to marry him. I believe he wanted Mr. Snopes's approval, though he never said so. Mr. Snopes isn't so old himself, but he's been the nearest thing to a father to Obadiah since my dear husband separated from his parents at age eight."

"I can't make out what drives the barrister," Madeleine said, setting the cups down. "A force in the courtroom. Then nearly shy tonight in a living room. It seems very odd for one who chose a career as a barrister."

Suzanne smiled. "He can be shy at times, it's true. He's known many crosscurrents in his life. The only thing certain to rile his judgment is being lied to. Edmund made that mistake early in his apprenticeship and was nearly turned out. No, Mr. Snopes runs deeper than most men I've known. But shallow waters can grow dull, don't you think?" She looked Lady Jameson squarely in the eye.

Madeleine looked away. Suzanne surely thought it was embarrassment at personal feelings, and perhaps she was right. But just as powerful was the painful talk of lies as Madeleine recalled the half-truth she'd told the man about never committing an illegality regarding the *Padget*. It was true, she supposed: borrowing from a smuggler probably wasn't illegal. But it wasn't a direct answer to what he'd been driving at.

And yet even that wasn't what bothered her most.

Are the stories Dame Baltimore told, attesting to Mr. Snopes's character, true? she wanted to ask Suzanne. *Tell me what kind of man is now responsible for protecting our lives and fortune.*

"If it's his performance in the courtroom that genuinely concerns you," Suzanne began again, "you needn't worry. Mr. Snopes may be restrained in matters of the heart, but he always manages a lion's roar when it's called for before a jury."

Suzanne took another glass to wash while Madeleine picked up a drying cloth.

As Madeleine accepted the glass from her host's hand, the twitch of a smile at the corners of Suzanne's mouth signaled the questions she was refraining from asking as well.

29

THE LANYARD PUB
EAST END, LONDON

William jostled Edmund, who'd grown silent after his last question. *Padget* sailor Seymour Little, seated across the table, looked on quizzically.

Edmund stirred and turned to his notes for his next question.

William looked about, waiting for Edmund to begin again.

This pub was grimmer than most and a far cry from the cozy warmth of the Red Hound near the Middlesex Courthouse. More dedicated drinkers, William thought, and a more transient class of customers so near the dockyards.

Edmund continued his paper shuffling. His junior's loss of concentration had grown the past two days as he alternated with Obadiah assisting William's interviews of former *Padget* crew members. The young man's heart just wasn't in it. An uncharacteristic sign, William believed, of deep discouragement.

It was terribly frustrating, particularly when William most needed Edmund's usually energetic assistance, but he understood its source. Edmund and Obadiah had finished checking crewmens' criminal records, returning to Gray's Inn to announce that not a single crewman had been charged with theft—except this one presently seated across the table. Petty theft at age eleven, Seymour

Little's record showed, and a brand on his thumb recorded the transgression. Still, he seemed too simple to have conspired to steal the Letter of Marque.

Mr. Little was dipping into his second beer, foam painting his mustache white, when Edmund finally spoke again.

"Then no one, other than perhaps the first mate, ever actually saw the captain's Letter of Marque?"

"Aye, so far as I know. Though I don' think anyone thought the cap'n was lyin'. He was a straight one, even when things looked sorely bad. And if we hadn't believed him, no one would've manned the guns to take on that Frenchman off the coast of Ceylon."

"Mr. Little, is there anyone else in the crew, if you were forced to point a finger, you think capable of stealing the Letter?"

"Garn, no. Good crew, that. I suppose if I had to pick someone, I'd point the finger at Luckless Joel Brine. Or his pal, Mike Finnister. Bit 'o larceny in that pair. Always holdin' back when work was to be done, for sure."

The same two crewmen, Brine and Finnister, had said the same about Mr. Little. Petty likes and dislikes were all that Edmund and William had gotten out of the crew so far.

"Mr. Little, you have a history of theft, do you not?" Edmund asked at last.

The man hardly blinked. "Aye. That's when I was a lad. It weren't nothin'. Took a pair of hobnailed shoes, for no good reason other'n I liked 'em. I paid my price for it, though," he said, holding up his branded thumb.

If this man were a thief, he'd make a poor one. And if he were working for others to set up Captain Tuttle on a piracy charge, he'd be a terrible choice. Over thick shoulders and behind his wind-beaten face, the man had the mind and disposition of a child.

"Shame 'bout that boy bein' shot," Mr. Little went on. "He was a good 'un. Everyone said so. Worked hard, kept to himself. Scrambled to it."

"Yes, it was a shame," Edmund agreed. He glanced at William as if to ask, *Are we done here?*

Four days until trial. *Only four days.* Seaman Seymour Little was the twelfth *Padget* crewman they'd interviewed. They'd learned nothing helpful. Most disappointing was the consistent answer each gave as to the whereabouts of First Mate Ivars—who'd seemingly disappeared.

William decided to touch that subject now. "Mr. Little, do you have any idea where Mr. Ivars went after being released?"

"Quint took off like a racehorse the afternoon they let us go. Like he'd got a real purpose, I'd say. Not that we all weren't want'n to climb out the gunports after all that time gaoled belowdeck. Most of the smart 'uns went straight up the wharves to find more work."

"And that's where First Mate Ivars went?"

"Nah. The big shippers are east of where the *Padget* was docked. Most of us scrambled that way. When he reached the shore wi' the rest of us, I remember Quint turnin' west. Back toward town. Don't know why."

"And you haven't seen him since?"

"Nah."

"Thank you, Mr. Little."

It was the same answer a handful of the others had given: the first mate headed away from the Thames and the shipping companies where he might have landed work. Each response tore away more of William's hope of finding Ivars, the last independent witness who could corroborate the Letter of Marque.

William paid the bill. They left the pub under cloudless skies full of faded-blue winter sunshine. Catching a cab back to Gray's Inn, they rode silently in shared disappointment.

"I need to check on something," Edmund said as they reached the Inn. "Just an hour or so. I'll be back on task tonight."

Despondent, William didn't protest. "That's fine, Edmund. We'll talk later."

OFFICE OF BARRISTER WILLIAM SNOPES
GRAY'S INN

When William entered his office, he found Father Thomas standing in the foyer.

He nodded at the priest. "I can't thank you enough for your help, Father," William said, unlocking his door and taking a bag of papers from one of the priest's hands and clothes off the Father's other arm. "Was anyone at my flat when you arrived?"

"A few vagabonds hanging out near the door to the staircase. They eyed my coming and going, but no one dared a word."

"Well, it's most appreciated."

"Of course, William," Father Thomas replied. "I'd also planned to retrieve your evening clothes for the ball tonight as you asked, but those in your wardrobe were abysmal. The likes haven't been worn since the coronation of Henry VIII. I've brought you some others borrowed from an up-to-date parishioner instead. They should fit well enough, and you'll look as though you belong in this century."

As much as his pride made him want to refuse, he knew the Father was right. And he didn't wish to look foolish with Lady Jameson on his arm. "Thank you again, Father."

The priest nodded, glancing around his office. "This truly is a month of firsts. Like your apartment, in all the years we've known each other, I've never been inside your office."

"Nor I in yours. Some secrets must be maintained, I suppose."

"Um-hmm. Have you had any second thoughts about your involvement in this piracy matter—in light of the riot?"

"No," William replied as he took a seat at his desk. "And it wasn't a riot."

"Only because you've retained some foot speed over the years. It's a wonder the mob didn't circle back and burn your flat to the ground."

"Too many distracting pubs along the way, I imagine."

"You joke, but you also look worried, William."

William nodded. "That's so. We're facing a wall in this case, created by people intent on my client going to the gallows. Edmund, Obadiah, and I have been working for a week of eighteen-hour days preparing for trial and can't seem to garner any favorable testimony."

The Father looked on, uncommonly serious. "I suppose I should let you get back to your preparations, then, William."

"Yes. But before you go, Father, I'd like to ask a favor."

The priest looked instantly suspicious. "What kind of favor?"

"It's not for me, but for my client. I wonder if you could visit Captain Tuttle at Newgate."

"Has he asked it?"

"No. Not directly. But he's in a desperate place. I'm trained for the earthly struggle of the courtroom. He requires consolation and wisdom more in your field."

"Surely you're not admitting to the possibility that you might lose the trial."

"I'm deadly serious here, Thomas," William said sharply.

The priest looked startled at the tone William had never used with him before.

"I'm very sorry," the priest replied. "My jest was a poor one. Of course I'll go. This very afternoon."

"It would mean a great deal to me. And I have one more favor to ask."

"What is that?"

"I'd like you to attend trial. This case will take some difficult turns. I'd benefit from your keen eye and discernment. I'd also like you to acknowledge me in the courtroom each morning immediately before we begin, and each afternoon after we return from noon recess."

The Father stiffened. "Are you asking me to endorse your case for the benefit of the jury?"

"No. Through me, I'm asking you to endorse *my client* for the benefit of the jury. I only ask this of you if you believe it's warranted after you meet with Captain Tuttle—and I promise I'll never ask such a thing of you again in my career."

"It's an extraordinary thing you're seeking, William. Especially given my objections to your methods."

His methods. He recalled his words to Obadiah and Edmund in the park about the lengths he'd go to win this case.

Over a long pause, William thought matters over.

"What I say next must never leave this room, Thomas," he said at last. "As my earlier comments must make clear, despite my sincere belief in Captain Tuttle, as the evidence currently stands, I fear the outcome of this case more than any before. I've never told anyone, but as a very young boy I snuck away from our London town home on a damp winter day and visited the Tyburn gallows. I'd overheard that it was to be the last execution day conducted at Tyburn, and I didn't want to miss it. A single poor soul was marched to the ropes on trembling legs. You could see him looking about, foam on his lips, praying for the King's pardon to arrive. It never did, and he met his fate. Despite my zeal to be there, the image of what I saw that morning has never left me. Recently I've had terrible dreams of the captain in those straits."

The Father stared before clearing his throat. "You honor me, William, with your confession. Very well. I'll give you my answer to the latter request after meeting with Captain Tuttle. And if, *this one time*, I agree to do this, I'll throw in an additional favor you haven't requested—presumably because you're too stiff-necked to ask."

"What's that?"

"I'll pray each day for you. As well as for Edmund and Obadiah. The Lady Jameson. And particularly for your poor Captain Tuttle."

30

HOME OF SIR AND LADY RUTLEDGE
WESTMINSTER DISTRICT
LONDON

Determined to be his most optimistic for the evening, William shrugged off the cold, took a deep breath, and pulled himself aboard Lady Jameson's carriage outside Gray's Inn.

"You look lovely," he remarked as he sat across from the lady.

His resolution to be upbeat tonight was driven partly by his belated realization of how difficult it must be for the lady to enter the hostile setting where she once was welcome. If he'd considered it more thoroughly, he never would have asked her to accompany him.

Still, the compliment came effortlessly and with a sincerity that surprised him. Dressed in a loose, naturally flowing gossamer gown with a Medici collar and train, and a necklace with a large black pearl about her neck, she displayed the simple elegance that he always preferred.

The carriage lurched away. "Thank you, Mr. Snopes." The lady touched her necklace with a gloved hand. "Do you like the necklace?"

"It's stunning."

228

She smiled. "And I'll admit that it is quite valuable, the very last of my family's jewels. A gift from my brother, sent home from Spain. I couldn't bear to part with it. Still, you must know that I'm woefully out of fashion."

"I know nothing of the kind."

"It's true. This dress is the Parisian style, acquired by my mother years ago. But hoop skirts are still the rule in London. I've refused to wear one since I was twenty—not that I've had reason to don any ball gowns the past several years. Hoop skirts always made me feel as though I were standing in a barrel."

William laughed, enjoying her candor. "Then we'll be scandalous in more than one way."

"Yes. And you'll also note that I have no feathers in my hair."

"Should there be?"

"Of course. Ostrich, if available. Another fashion I refuse. I won't adopt plumage I wasn't born with."

To blazes with fashion. Her hair had a soft center part, framing her face in a series of small waves, with a crown—all so fine and breathtakingly natural. He could hardly take his eyes from her.

"You appear most modern yourself, Mr. Snopes."

"If that's true, then it's thanks to a friend. He described my clothes as 'hopelessly out of date' and managed to purloin these for me for the evening."

She laughed. "I admit I'm nervous. But a part of me is enjoying this. I know I shouldn't, given our purpose and what's at stake for my cousin."

"I suppose. But we've got very serious days approaching. Maybe it isn't so bad to be at ease tonight."

The carriage arrived at the towering Rutledge Town Mansion, lit by torches about the entryway. William recognized the place. He'd been sixteen—no, seventeen—when he attended a dinner here with his parents. He remembered the Rutledge family as near the peak of the London scene. A self-consciously proper family. Though, as he recalled, they were not unkind.

"Lady Jameson," William said before they left the carriage, "having never met him, you won't recognize Mandy Bristol if he's here tonight, while I won't recognize many faces familiar to you. I suggest we circulate individually as well as together and see what whispers we can pick up about Mr. Bristol. I've something I plan to use to try to gather information." He went on to explain his idea.

"Good. Let's try that," she said, nervousness creeping into her reply.

Davidson opened the carriage door, and they stepped out. With Lady Jameson on William's arm, they ascended the steps to the front entrance, which was flanked by liveried servants.

"Here we go," Lady Jameson whispered.

"Like any other plunge into cold water, we'll get used to it," William replied.

He felt her hand tighten about his arm.

The ballroom was resplendent in the soft, rapturous light of a thousand candles. William used to dislike the conformity of dress among the guests at these events, but tonight the interplay of color and movement dazzled. The chamber orchestra was crisp, the dances lively, varied, and fully attended. It all seemed more remarkable than he remembered.

In the nights before this evening, William had practiced the dances he'd so loved as a youth. Then he'd taken the precaution of purchasing a book on modern dances, which he convinced Lady Jameson to practice with him late into the evening at Obadiah's home. The cotillion and allemande of his younger days, the book made clear, had been replaced in popularity by the quadrille and the controversial waltz—born of a music which William loved.

The book was right. Within the first hour in the ballroom, he saw that most calls to the floor were for waltzes to the exclusion of other dances. The flowing guests gathered and parted and regathered like swans in a pond before William's and Lady Jameson's eyes. As the evening progressed, William surveyed the crowd from every angle, keeping a close eye on the entrance to see who was arriving. To his great disappointment, Mandy Bristol was nowhere to be found.

He'd grown to hope that tonight they'd emerge with a list of candidates for Mandy's hidden investors. Yet neither Mandy nor information about him was to be found. At most, William saw a few barristers he knew among the large crowd and noted occasional contemptuous or surprised glances from people he'd known in the distant days when he was a young fish in this pond.

After a while, Lady Jameson left him, moving to another corner to test the waters among a group of old acquaintances. William did the same until, growing weary, he accepted a glass of champagne from a passing servant, determined to find a seat.

"William!"

The caller was one of the barristers William had noticed early in the evening, Gregory Severson. A fair trial attorney, William registered, though the man was hampered by his background and wealth and an overly amiable personality, which, in William's estimation, denied him the necessary edge of a top-notch barrister.

"Good to see you, Gregory."

"Didn't think I'd ever see you at one of these affairs, William."

"A colleague convinced me to come—though I can't seem to find him. Don't suppose you've seen him, have you? A solicitor named Mandy Bristol?"

"Old Mandy? Haven't seen him tonight. Which is unlike the man, I should add. He's become a regular in the ball circuit."

"Has he? Mandy's asked me to handle a discreet matter for a couple of his closer clients. A very scandalous affair." William leaned in. "I can't share their names, of course, but I'll give you a hint: they're here tonight."

"Really?" Gregory looked about. "Afraid I don't run in Mandy's circles, so I don't know who that might be. But tell me, William.

I heard you've a case launching in a few days. It's all the talk at
The Old Bailey. Up against Sir Barnabas, eh? Watch out for him.
Sharp elbows. Doesn't like to lose."

"I'm sure he doesn't. If you'll excuse me, Gregory, I see someone
I must greet."

William wandered away. He'd used the same line a dozen times
that evening among the men he'd spoken with. None had volunteered who Mandy's clients might be. If Mandy was attending
social functions, it seemed he was avoiding obvious association
with the clients William and Lady Jameson were searching for.

Ah well, he told himself. It had been nearly an hour since he
last circled to Lady Jameson. Perhaps she was having better luck.

"Mandy Bristol?" Lady Pamela said in answer to Madeleine's
statement. "With clients engaged in a scandalous lawsuit? Clients
who are here tonight?"

It had taken a long while for Madeleine to catch Lady Pamela
alone. She was, so far as Madeleine recalled, the most versatile
and learned gossip in London, second only to Dame Baltimore.

"The *most* scandalous," Madeleine replied, leaning close.
"Please don't press me. I really shouldn't share the particulars. It
will be in all the papers within the week, at any rate."

The disadvantage of being considered scandalous, Lady Jameson had learned, was that few of the women she approached would
stay to speak with her beyond a word or two.

Pamela appeared to be an exception.

"I wonder who his clients could *possibly be*?" Lady Pamela said,
surveying the room. "I suppose it could be Mr. Fennelworth. The
man has been seen in the worst parts of London. Or Sir Scott.
Repulsive fellow. Has an actress as a mistress. Am I warm?"

"Um, I really shouldn't say."

"Surely not Pastor Martin of the Sacred Heart Church?"

"No. Not at all."

"In fairness," Lady Pamela said, "I can't recall seeing Mr. Bristol in either Mr. Fennelworth's or Sir Scott's company. Frankly, it's hard to imagine *who* Mr. Bristol's circles might include. I'd never heard of the man before the last year or two, and now he seems to gain invitations to so many events. Nearly as many as myself! It's a wonder how he manages it."

Madeleine remained with Lady Pamela for as long as she could stand it. When certain no more information was forthcoming, she extricated herself and stepped away.

She was making her way back to William when she saw Dorothy. Her old friend was standing near a window, her husband at her side. She should have expected it, though she'd hoped Dorothy wouldn't attend this evening.

She noted that husband and wife stood alone.

Madeleine couldn't help herself. Worried how she'd be received, her steps took her across the room to her friend's side.

"Dorothy," she began, "I want to apologize about the other night at dinner. I couldn't tell you because—"

"Apologize?" Dorothy's hardened eyes froze her. "This is the first event we've been invited to since that dreadful evening. The Rutledges are kind people. It may be the last."

"It wasn't my purpose to embarrass you."

"Embarrassment? It was betrayal. You should have told me. You should have refused the dinner."

"*I tried*. You insisted. And I didn't expect the reports in the newspapers. They're all lies, Dorothy dear. This lawsuit isn't what it seems. My cousin isn't guilty of the charges. We'll prove it in court."

"I *defended you*, Madeleine. Against all the rumors and attacks, I stood by you. Then to learn from your own lips that they were all true! You've stained my reputation forever. Don't ever speak with me again. *Never*."

Dorothy's husband took her arm. They walked away, leaving Madeleine to stand alone.

Stunned, Madeleine suddenly felt unable to catch her breath. Her friend was right. She'd lied to Dorothy with her silence that night. Just as she'd lied to Mr. Snopes to win his representation.

It was becoming so easy and so easy to excuse. In her effort to save her estate, who would she hurt? How much worse would she become?

She deserved her suffering.

For the first time in all the months and years of work and degradation, she finally felt herself succumb. Hollowed to her core.

All the faces and eyes surrounding her and she hadn't a single wall remaining to conceal her.

William saw the lady across the room, standing with a man and woman. He watched as the young woman mouthed words to Madeleine that he couldn't hear, then walked away on the arm of the man.

A startled, downtrodden look registered on Madeleine's face, unmistakable, even from a distance.

William crossed the floor to be at her side. "Lady Jameson, are you all right?"

She didn't respond. Her eyes appeared lost, almost glassy. "I can't do this any longer," she said in a low, strained voice.

"I know," William answered to lift her spirits. "Everyone's waiting for us to brandish weapons and demand their money or their lives."

The lady didn't respond to his jest. Her distant eyes remained fixed.

A man strode past, a woman on his arm. He stepped so close that he brushed Lady Jameson's gown.

She stepped backward, startled.

"Sir?" William called.

The man walked on.

"*SIR.*"

The man halted, turning slowly. "Are you addressing me?"

"Apologize to the lady," William said.

"What lady?"

Willian stepped forward, feeling Lady Jameson's hand reach out and restrain his arm.

"Your name?" William demanded.

This was a mistake. Ruinous to their purpose this evening.

He couldn't stop himself.

"Zachory Leader."

The man sneered, his face flushed with wine. William didn't care. This was one of the class he'd left behind, one of those who sniggered and smirked and wouldn't know a day's work if it smashed them in the nose.

He glanced to Madeleine's pale visage, and his hands began to tremble with rage. "Mr. Leader," he voiced deeply and loudly, "I suggest we discuss this out of doors. I wouldn't want to stain these magnificent floors."

Another man dressed in dark gray appeared at Leader's side. "That's William Snopes," he said, his tone low.

"So?"

"He knows his way around a blade, Zach. At least he did as a youth."

"I don't care. It's an abomination that he and that woman are here."

William pulled free of the lady's hands.

A taller man appeared. His dress made him impossible to ignore: a jacket exceptionally well-fitted, full-length tailored trousers, a high red cravat about his neck.

"Mr. Leader," the tall man said, "I saw what just happened. You'll apologize to the lady at once."

Zachory's eyes widened. "Lord Brummell, I can't possibly—"

"You'll apologize, and you'll do so this minute or I'll stand as this man's second for the duel you seem to be inviting. Though I don't think he'll require me. You won't be pleased with the out-come."

Zachory swallowed hard, then blinked as if rising above his inebriation.

"My apologies," he said with a stiff bow toward Lady Jameson.

"Good. Now go off and get drunker someplace else."

Eyes lowered, the man and his friend withdrew.

The tall man bowed. "As one of the hosts of tonight's ball, please accept my apologies as well," Lord Brummell said, addressing himself particularly to Madeleine. "Mr. Leader is a pig. I'd avoid his presence altogether, but he might harm himself if he wasn't invited."

Still looking shaken, Madeleine nodded and made an effort to smile.

"Thank you, Lord Brummell," William said. "I recognize your name, though I don't believe we've ever met."

"And I recognize yours. Your father, as you know, is one of my esteemed colleagues in the House of Lords."

"Of course."

"It wasn't our intent to create a stir this evening," William said.

"A stir? Not at all. If you're creating such a thing, I'd say it's in the courtroom." The lord leaned close to William. "You know, I'm rooting for you both in your upcoming trial. In fact, I'm considering attending myself."

"Thank you, Lord Brummell," William replied, surprised. "I doubt there are many here tonight who share your sentiments." He thought for a moment. "May I ask a question?"

"Of course."

"I was hoping to have an opportunity to speak with a gentleman I was informed would be here tonight. I wonder if you've seen him."

"Who might that be?"

"A solicitor. Mandy Bristol."

There was a pause. "Mandy . . . Bristol. I've heard the name. In fact, yes, I know of the man. You say he was supposed to be here? Even as one of the hosts, I'm not assured of personally knowing *every* guest invited."

"Do you know whether Mr. Bristol has any particular persons with whom he attends these events?"

The lord thought for a moment. "I can't say that I do. I don't recall if I've actually met the man."

There was a gentle tug on William's arm. William looked to Lady Jameson, still standing beside him.

Her pallor had grown even whiter. She seemed near tears.

"I'd like to leave," she said softly.

Shocked at the change in the lady, William looked about the room.

The music had stopped. In gathered groups about the hall, most eyes were fixed on William and Lord Brummell. At least of those who weren't staring at Madeleine.

William took a deep breath.

He should never have brought her here tonight. The woman had suffered threats, social exile, the potential loss of her home—and far worse, the death or crippling of those dear to her. Her own cousin's fate hung over her daily. Through it all, she'd remained unbroken. He'd admired her strength, and somehow assumed she was impregnable.

What foolishness. No one was impregnable. Every form of courage had its limits—and its moments of doubt. He wondered what she'd experienced this night that had finally brought her down.

They should leave now.

Except.

He looked about again. The eyes still stared at them; the mouths still moved in their common judgment.

William's heart pounded. He refused to retreat before this gathering that was no better than any other mob, no matter their attire. He wouldn't allow Madeleine to suffer such humiliation.

"I'll only be a moment," he said gently to Madeleine, then excused himself from Lord Brummell.

He crossed the room to the orchestra. "A waltz," he said to the conductor.

The conductor looked across the floor to Lord Brummell, who nodded.

The conductor called the dance, then turned to the orchestra and raised his hands. The musicians straightened. The violins began in three-quarter time, joined swiftly by rising violas. A cello. Then the pianoforte.

William crossed the floor to Madeleine. He extended a hand. "My lady?"

She looked at him, still cowed.

He looked back firmly, putting on his best smile of courtroom assurance.

"Mr. Snopes," she answered tentatively, taking his hand.

They danced the waltz, filling the floor from side to side, their wide sweeps and turns claiming every inch of it. They danced alone, followed by the disapproving eyes of the ballroom guests, not slowing from start to end—gliding, smooth and unfaltering. Her soft, shapely eyes remained fixed on his. It was, he thought, magnificent. As though they'd waltzed together their entire lives.

The orchestra finally stilled. William released her. He bowed. Madeleine curtsied, rising with gratitude in her eyes.

Only then did he lead her from the ballroom floor and out into the night.

31

WHITECHAPEL
EAST END, LONDON

Mandy walked the full length of the alleyway through thick mist. At least the winter fog covered the filth of the place, he thought, though it didn't dispel the smell. At the alley's end was a short staircase descending to a basement level door. He knocked out a rhythm—two knocks, three, one.

The door opened inward.

Decrepit wood furniture occupied a dank, cheerless room. Windows set high at ground level were covered with oiled paper. Several candles barely lit the small place, while two doors led deeper in. Like the open maws of snakes, Mandy thought, disinterested in going there.

He nodded at the man who'd opened the door and who now gestured him to a seat.

"No need," Mandy replied, not wanting to soil his suit. "This will only take a moment. I'm here to end our ventures."

Lonny McPherson smiled, taking a chair for himself. His teeth were magnificently white, even in the shadowy room. Mandy suspected that Lonny believed the feature deducted from the startling visage of his drooping eye. To Mandy, the discordant eye and teeth were equally appalling.

"End the ventures?" Lonny said. "I'd guessed as much. When I got your message from young Tad to meet, it was the only reason I could imagine for you dirtying your shoes at night to come to my humble office. Your partners worried about the coming date with the judge?"

"Reasons don't matter," Mandy insisted. "Speed *does* matter."

Mandy reached deep into a coat pocket for a large bag of coins. "I have here five hundred pounds. A hundred is for your troubles. The remaining is for your two workers, Tad and Isabella, to settle them into life away from London."

Lonny leaned back in surprise. "Two hundred pounds each! That's quite a sum for such young souls."

"It's to ensure that our wishes are satisfied. We never want to hear from these people again. You must impress upon them that this is to pay for a one-way ticket each."

"Tad's awfully young to be away from my fatherly care," Lonny said, clucking his tongue. "And Isabella? Alone in this harsh world?"

"I'm sure you can find likeminded colleagues in Edinburgh or York or Manchester to take them under their wings. This is a very serious matter. It must be done, and soon."

Lonny smiled again. "It took a great deal of effort to set up my part of our little business that you now want to end. No one else in London could've prepared Isabella to work with the royals at Carlton House as I did, caring for our dear crazed king. No one else could have assured safe transport of the papers she pilfered."

"Yes. It was a coup. Remarkable work. I applaud you. We've all profited. Now it must end."

"One hundred pounds *for me*, on the other hand, seems a paltry sum." Lonny crossed the room to pocket the bag, then returned to his chair. "This venture has cost me dearly, and now you're asking me to bleed more to end it. For only a hundred pounds."

240

"Cost you dearly?" Mandy said, regretting he'd parted with the money.

"Yes. I deal in human capital, Mr. Bristol. I take young folks as have potential—folks discarded by your society—and I train them into a skill. Then I launch them to practice that skill—to their profit and to mine. Simon Ladner now gone. Tad, a lad always eager to please—nearly ready to fulfill his role—sent away. And lovely Isabella, a dear girl who could've been my daughter. All used up and discarded. You want me to send them off where they'll be no profit to me ever again. And don't plead poverty when it comes to my wages, Solicitor. I know who's behind you. That fop Beau Brummell and his whelp, the Princess Charlotte."

Mandy was floored. "You're wrong," he blurted out.

"You think after working together all these years, I wouldn't know who's pulling the strings? But we were discussing the fairness of my compensation."

Mandy could barely assemble himself.

"You selected these *young folks* for the tasks," he managed. "You've been paid handsomely for their services. And now you're being paid handsomely for their send-off."

"What's handsome enough, I wonder, when the cost is so high—and your own profits so great?"

Silence settled between them.

Lord Brummell and the princess could never know that this man had learned their involvement. Which meant Mandy could never use this grotesque man again. He wondered if it showed in his eyes.

"There will be other ventures," Mandy lied. "Don't let your greed overcome you if you want to be called upon again. Will you finish the task as requested?"

"I took the money, didn't I?"

It was hardly a yes, but Mandy was anxious to be gone. "Good. When can you have Tad and Isabella resettled?"

Lonny considered a moment. "Before your trial begins. Three

days from now, isn't it? You know it'll be hard to ever set something like this up again. It's been a sweet rounder, it has."

"Just get it accomplished, Mr. McPherson."

"Of course, Mr. Bristol."

HOME OF OBADIAH AND SUZANNE CUMMINGS

Madeleine lay in bed clutching her pillow. Her emotions alternated between shame at her collapse at last night's party and the deadening sorrow and regret she felt for all she'd done. Her limbs were lead, her eyes red with periodic bursts of tears.

How could she go on?

An image of her mother arose. Her brother. Her heart burned to have them back.

Her father's face came. Strong and smiling, from before his failing health.

An image of her home before its decline. Playing with her brother in the gardens or far over the fields where their horses would carry them.

Roisin—then and now. At risk because of her efforts.

There was a knock at the door.

"Lady Jameson?" Davidson's voice called her.

She didn't respond.

"Lady Jameson. You wanted me to drive you to Newgate Prison this morning, to bring the captain food and clothing. Shall I ask Mr. Cummings to go in your stead?"

She wanted to cry out yes.

Then she recalled the kindness of William. Over recent years, she'd grown unaccustomed to such compassion. Carrying her with his words and voice—and then the waltz. Leading her from the ball through her daze.

"Don't yield to their judgments," he'd said, trying to console her in the carriage ride home from the ball, even though she wouldn't

242

tell him what had upset her so. *"You're a good woman, undeserving of the punishment these gentlefolk would inflict on you."*

His words had kept her from slipping into a chasm from which she felt she'd never return. Because of him, she'd left the ball without the worst of the shame the others wanted to exact; gripping the lifeline of William's arm with some of her dignity remaining—though she could scarcely imagine that she deserved it.

Only William seemed to believe she did.

Who was this man?

She cleared her throat. Took a full breath.

"No, Davidson," she called. "Prepare the carriage. I'll be going to Newgate as planned."

Madeleine ascended the steps leading to Newgate's entrance. The jailor knew her by now. She silently signed the log and then followed him into the chill and darkness surrounding Harold's cell.

William's kindness the night before, at the ball and after, had gotten her through the night. But the truth was that they'd learned nothing at the ball. Only that Mandy Bristol had become a common guest at dinners, balls, and hunts, yet no one could identify his closest companions or even a source for his invitations.

Though scarcely sleeping, she'd awoken this morning to harsh, unwelcome clarity. Not only about herself but also, with her first conscious breath, the sorrowful knowledge that Harold could be convicted. Somehow she'd expected the evidence of his innocence to arrive, but now, only two days from trial, she could no longer deny that it would take a miracle for William and Edmund to convince a jury to acquit. They lacked even one witness to the Letter of Marque besides her cousin. They lacked proof of the conspiracy woven around the *Padget*'s voyage.

Once they reached the lower cells, the jailor turned to leave. Alone, Madeleine tried to banish her mood from her face and voice before stepping from the shadows to the bars of Harold's cell.

"Cousin, I've brought you your clothes for trial," she said with a smile. "And some food too."

Harold emerged from the deep shadows of the cell to take the bag she offered. "Thank you, Madeleine," he said softly.

She saw instantly how low Harold was today. He moved slowly, stared at her through lidded eyes. In his weakness, she found herself searching for her own sources of strength.

"Did Father Thomas come again today?" she asked. "You said he's been coming nearly every day."

"Yes. And he no longer interrogates me about the voyage as he once did. He reads Scripture now. We chat. It helps. He seems to believe in me."

"As well he should."

Her cousin pulled a stool over to the bars and dropped onto it. "How is trial preparation going? Mr. Snopes hasn't been by for several days, and his solicitor, Obadiah, continues to play the sphinx when he's here."

"William is confident," she lied.

Harold's eyebrows lifted. "William, is it?"

"I'm sorry," she said, looking down. "Mr. Cummings's wife, Suzanne, has been telling me about the barrister, and I forgot myself."

He waved a hand in the air. "It's all right, Madeleine. I caught him in a similar slip last week about you. Besides, none of the formalities seem relevant anymore."

Her worry grew. "Has your Rebekah come to visit?"

"No. I sent word through Mr. Snopes telling her not to visit, even if her family relented and permitted it. There's no point in staining her reputation."

"Mr. Snopes has sent a messenger to Edinburgh to try to locate Solicitor Mortimer and speed his return," Madeleine said to raise his spirits. "He says he has high hopes."

"You're a terrible liar, cousin. We both know it's a twelve-day journey in the best of circumstances. And we don't even know where our good Solicitor Mortimer was bound. I've placed greater hope on your locating First Mate Ivars. How has that gone?"

She despised having nothing but poor news.

"We hope to find him at any hour," she said buoyantly. "Obadiah has been checking every last shipper in London, as well as every independent merchant ship on the Thames. Edmund has been helping. They've located nearly all of the crew, so I'm sure we'll find your first mate as well."

"Quint falling from the map makes no sense."

"Are we missing anything in our search, Harold?"

"No. Not unless Ivars took a smuggler's berth. And then we'd have no means to find him."

Madeleine felt a jolt. "A smuggler's berth?"

"Yes. Smugglers require crews as much as anyone."

"How would someone locate a smuggler's ship?"

Harold shrugged. "They make regular stops delivering goods like any other merchant. The trick is knowing when and where they stop. Not often in daylight, or anywhere on the Thames. Too much traffic along the pier."

Madeleine's heart picked up a beat. "Harold, I'm sorry, but I need to shorten our visit today."

"Of course. You must have many matters of your own to attend to. I've been miserably self-absorbed. Please, before you go, tell me how is your father? And the estate? How about old Davidson?"

"They're fine," she said, though she knew nothing about home the past week—another source of anxiety. "And you shouldn't concern yourself with such things. There will be time enough in the future. Please tell me, though, if I were to encounter your first mate, how would I know him? I mean, beyond doubt."

Harold thought a moment. "He has a tattoo on his upper arm, the left. Of a schooner he once served on."

"Thank you. Please stay hopeful, cousin."

"Wait," Harold said.

Stepping back into the darker part of the cell, he returned with a stack of papers. "These are letters to Rebekah. I've written every day but didn't want to send them only to have them discarded by her family. Please see that she receives them. Particularly if things don't go as we hope."

Tears gathered in Madeleine's eyes.

"Things will go exactly as we hope and pray, Harold," she said. "Mr. Snopes is the best barrister in all of London, perhaps all of England, and now I know him as a good man too. He'll win your case. I'm certain of it."

Madeleine strode the London streets, diverging from Newgate, rushing through the moving crowds even though she didn't know where she was going.

How did she navigate this?

If the first mate had taken to a smuggler's ship, she could try the docks once more, inquiring from that angle. She'd need to get her horse and ride to the docks to do so.

But if that failed, a better though more difficult source of information would be the American.

Except all of this created a dilemma. She couldn't tell William about the American without admitting her earlier lies. Perhaps she'd be willing to do that, hoping he'd forgive her: confess to William and Obadiah and Edmund and risk the death of any esteem they had for her.

But she couldn't risk William assuming that Harold had also withheld information about the American smuggler—even though it would be a false assumption. If William was so sensitive to lies as Suzanne had said, she couldn't risk the loss of William's belief in Harold and the dampening of his enthusiasm for his defense.

She turned to the street, raising a hand to hail a carriage. A two-seater came into sight and moved across traffic toward her.

"Your destination, miss?" the carriage driver called from his perch.

"I've no idea," she murmured, then shook her head and gave the driver the address for Obadiah's home where her horse was stabled.

WHITECHAPEL
EAST END, LONDON

William faced the bar in the tavern on Leman Street.

The snowy road was befouled by passing horses, coal-fire soot, and pools of garbage water thrown from upper stories and store-fronts alike. His feet ached, and his nose was numbed by the chill and the odorous assaults. He'd already walked half the Whitecha-pel streets that flowed like marsh water through a district where so many squeezed out a living on the nearby docks.

It occurred to him as he walked that he'd not heard the notes of a single piece in his head for days. Not since his epiphany at Lady Jameson's home.

He missed it. Even a funeral dirge would be welcome over the deafening silence.

He'd finally gotten to this task—searching for the boy Simon's father—spending five of his precious few remaining hours in the last days before trial. William had visited seventeen pubs and tav-erns, yet not a single manager admitted to hearing of a cobbler named Ladner—let alone one who'd recently lost his wife and apprenticed his son to the *Padget*. William's last visit with the captain had heightened a growing anxiety at their failure to find helpful evidence. Would he also fail to overcome objections to the jury hearing of the boy's killing?

The latest pub manager began as dismissively as the prior ones.

"Sad story, that," he said. "But never 'eard of him." He turned to stack a small barrel behind the bar. "Two weeks since the boy died, eh? He'd likely be in the groun' by now, right? Anyone bringin' the boy's body to Whitechapel would've delivered him to his kin, or the local undertakers who'd try ta *find* the kin. The undertaker'd give it a go, hopin' to find a relative willin' to pay for the boy's disposition. But if they 'ad no luck, in a couple of days they'd collect the smaller city fee for layin' him in the potter's field. The undertakers, they'd have a record of the poor souls that picked up the boy's body."

William was stunned by the simple brilliance of the observation. "Who are the local undertakers?"

"Two in Whitechapel hereabouts. Blackstone up on High Whitechapel Road and Stein on Peek Street."

He slapped a coin on the bar. "Your ale should be blessed for the remainder of your days. You've been helpful beyond words."

The sign on High Whitechapel Road announced *Blackstone's Mortuary and Undertaking Establishment*. Rising over a main road through the district, the place had an air of prosperity compared to the businesses buried on the narrower, darker streets William had slogged through all afternoon. Seated in a small parlor inside the shop, William faced the man who'd greeted him when he arrived: older, all in black, a tall top hat resting on thin wisps of gray hair. He'd paid respectful attention to William after surveying his suit, which was clean at least.

"Name again?" he asked William.

"Ladner. The boy's name was Simon Ladner."

"Uh-hmm. I do recall that name."

The undertaker disappeared into the back, returning with a thick volume he set down to page through.

"Two weeks ago, the casket was brought here. A boy's casket. Quite light it was. Paperwork said he died of a gunshot wound. The casket was sealed, and the accompanying paperwork instructed against opening it."

"That's it," William said. "Did you find his father?"

"His father? Hmmm." The undertaker ran a finger along the volume. "No. But this is coming back to me now. The casket was delivered without instructions as to kin. As is my practice, I planned to put an advertisement in the local, but a day later, the casket was collected."

"What was the collector's name?"

The undertaker surveyed William once more. "It doesn't say," he replied slowly. "Could have been anyone."

William reached deep into his coat pocket, in his haste and impatience producing a full pound's worth of coins to lay on the volume.

"The casket was picked up *by whom*?"

The coins were gone in an instant.

"Man didn't give a name. Didn't have to. He was Lonny McPherson."

"Where does this Mr. McPherson live?"

"Don't know. Just know of him."

"How do you know him?"

"Mr. McPherson's well known for his . . . business pursuits. Here in Whitechapel and in greater London. A bit under the board, if you take my meaning."

"Do you know why he came for the boy's body?"

"Didn't ask. All I know is he paid the fee and collected the casket."

"What does the man look like?"

"Oh, you can't miss him. He has a scar about here. And a droop of the eye below it."

William stared, hardly believing. "You're sure?" he asked stupidly.

"'Of course I'm sure. You can't miss it."

William walked out of the parlor, ignoring the undertaker's plea for more pay for the "extra bit of information."

Lonny McPherson was the man who'd been following them. And he'd also picked up Simon Ladner's casket.

William walked along, dazed. He'd assumed the man following them and arranging Solicitor Mortimer's departure was a paid hand, rendered dangerous only if he had also arranged for the killing of Madeleine's mare. He'd planned on merely trying to avoid the man, considering him a distraction from discovering the real bosses behind the piracy prosecution and theft of the Letter.

Now he wanted to talk to him. *Needed* to talk to him.

At least for that, William knew exactly where to go.

NEAR THE TOWER OF LONDON

William surveyed the yellow brick building in the dusky light, new enough not to be blotted by London's characteristic gray coal-smoke veneer.

No sign adorned the front. It wasn't necessary. Everyone in the city knew that this was the office of the Bow Street Runners, the only detection agents in all of London.

His knock was answered by a squat young man with a flowing mustache.

"Yes?" the man asked.

"I'm Barrister William Snopes. Is Joel Carver in?"

Eyebrows went up. "Joel? Uh, it's late, Mr. . . . Come back—"

"Snopes?" someone called from inside. "Is that your voice I hear? Stand aside, Pidger. Let a real English barrister through!"

The door opened wider. A familiar man as skinny and tall as a ladder burst through to give William a long-armed hug. William reciprocated uncomfortably.

"Come in, William, you old shyster," Joel declared. "Getting ready for that trial coming day after tomorrow? It's the talk of the courthouse. Come along to my office. Pidger, you come along too. You might learn a thing or two from this man."

William was soon seated in a room larger than his own office at the Inn. Crates were stacked and piled in every corner, overflowing with paper. Dusty shades were pulled tightly closed.

"Seems you're busy enough, Joel," William observed.

"Busy? You'd think they'd emptied the jails of every thief and scoundrel, we're kept so busy. Not just here. We've got agents now in every city in the realm. But never too busy to spend a moment with my favorite defense barrister. You seldom come our way, my friend."

"I know most of your work is for prosecutors, Joel, and I don't want to put you in a bad light."

"Don't worry about that."

He leaned toward Pidger, who was standing in the corner, and waved a hand for the man's attention. "When this man was still a youngster of a barrister, I did the investigation for prosecution in a trespass case against Snopes's client. He represented a farmer, who swore it wasn't *his* goat that got into the study of a banker who just happened to be foreclosing on the farmer's land. The creature had eaten most of the banker's furniture in a single night. My investigation had the farmer *dead to rights*—even to a witness, who saw him leading a goat across the heath toward the banker's house under a half-moon that night. Then this man here, Barrister Snopes himself, gets up and cross-exams me, pointing out in the process that the six-month-old goat in the banker's study hadn't been castrated, like everyone knew the farmer did to *all his goats* at twelve weeks. Embarrassed me to no end! The jury found against us. Had to waive the fee to my client when we lost."

"A highlight of my young career." William smiled lightly. "But you and your Bow Street colleagues don't have to return many fees, do you, Joel."

"That's a fact. But tell me now, what's troubling you that you'd cross the line to speak to one of us?"

"In the last twenty-four hours, I've come across a name I'm unfamiliar with. I wondered if you've heard of him and could tell me how to find him. The name's Lonny McPherson."

Joel let out a whistle, pointing to his colleague in the corner. "You've had a run-in or two with old Lonny, haven't you, Pidger?"

The squat man nodded. "Aye. A slippery one. Has his hands in many pots. Known to be engaged in some dubious enterprises."

"Has he been prosecuted?"

"A few times," Pidger answered. "But the man's got a ruthless streak. We did an investigation for the Central London constables a few years back. We had a key witness against Lonny turn tail and refuse to testify, making the prosecution fall. Word had it that Lonny skinned the man's dog and pinned it to his gate, then promised the same to his family if he took the oath against him."

The image of such a man or his proxy threatening Madeleine at her estate made William blanch with instant worry.

"Mr. McPherson picked up a casket a few weeks back, containing the body of a young boy named Simon Ladner," William said. "The boy was about fourteen years old. He was killed aboard a ship docked on the Thames. Don't suppose you ever heard of him."

"Can't say that I have," Joel replied.

Pidger shook his head. "Not at all."

"Any idea why McPherson would do such a thing? Does he have family that might have included the Ladner boy?"

"Not that I've heard," Joel said.

"Could've been from his canon," Pidger added.

William was startled at the reference to a pickpocket gang. "Lonny McPherson runs a canon?"

"Surely does," Joel said. "Runs a very loyal and very frightened crew. Lonny finds the vulnerable ones living on the street and wraps them up tight. Becomes something between a devil and a father to them. Sometimes he pairs 'em off, like siblings, to cement their loyalty to the canon. Maybe this boy had some connection to Lonny's crew."

William thought a moment. "Joel, is there any chance you could help me locate this Lonny McPherson?"

"Is this about your trial?"

"It is."

"Consider it done."

William thought again of the Letter of Marque and the absence of any record of its being issued by the Lord Privy Seal.

"Joel, my case may also involve a very good forger. Could you check who might be involved through your sources? This forger would specialize in government documents. In particular, a Letter of Marque. They'd have to be first rate. The forged document in our case passed inspection by an expert."

"That narrows the field considerably. I don't believe there's a forger of that quality this side of Newgate's walls at present. But I'll ask about."

"I'd be eternally grateful. And I'd pay any fee involved."

Joel waved his hand again. "We'll discuss that later. Find you at your office?"

William smiled wanly. "Unless you have news by this evening, I'll be at The Old Bailey."

Bundled against the chilly damp of early evening, Edmund leaned on the alley wall across the street from the newspaper office. It had been several hours and not the first time he'd awaited

Hardacre—both there and at the gambling hall. The man had disappeared in the week since Edmund threatened him. Apparently, a threat the writer didn't take seriously.

The door to the building opened and shut, and Edmund scrutinized the face.

Not his man.

The trial starting in the morning would fail, as things were, with disastrous consequences for Captain Tuttle. Edmund had helped Mr. Snopes prepare the examination and had been assigned some of the witnesses as his own—and all that was *good*, as far as it went. But all the hard questioning in the world couldn't overcome the absence of evidence of the Letter of Marque.

He stomped his feet on the ground and blew on his chilled hands. Maybe he'd been dragged kicking into this case, yet the only thing he disliked more than the preening classes was losing a case to one of them. Like Sir Barnabas who, he was ashamed to admit, had intimidated him on their first meeting.

But unless they were dealt a good hand soon, losing was exactly what would happen.

He'd even started liking the captain, bringing him food at Newgate. And the lady wasn't nearly so bad as he'd thought either.

The door opened again. A man with a top hat emerged, looked both ways, then started up the street. It was the hunched shape of Phineas Hardacre.

Edmund stepped out to follow on stiff legs. Whistling his way through a street thinning by the hour, the reporter made several turns. They were approaching a park ahead.

Edmund hurried his pace to draw nearer.

The reporter entered an empty passage running under the street. Edmund began running, catching him only a few yards from the far end.

"Hardacre!" he shouted, grabbing the man's coat.

The man turned. The frightened gaze of a stranger stared back at Edmund.

"Sorry," Edmund muttered.

"My wallet," the man stammered, reaching into his pocket. "Go ahead. Take it. You can have the money."

"Keep your money," Edmund growled back. "I'd only lose it at cards."

34

OFFICE OF BARRISTER WILLIAM SNOPES
GRAY'S INN
LONDON

"You're sure of this, Mr. Snopes?" Obadiah asked, nearly bobbing in the client chair in his uncommon display of excitement.

"Yes. This Lonny McPherson picked up Simon Ladner's casket and is the same man who followed Edmund and myself. Also the one who'd arranged for Solicitor Mortimer to leave town before trial. I'd wager he had some role in threatening Lady Jameson at her estate as well."

"And the Bow Street Runners were sure he's a leader of a pick-pocket canon?"

"Without question. Why would the leader of a bunch of trained diggers care about the Ladner boy? How would he be engaged with the *Padget* affair at all, for that matter?"

"I've another question, sir. What happened to the boy's father in Whitechapel?"

William shook his head. "He sounds like a fiction. Which makes me wonder whether the first mate knows this or was deceived as well."

"Could this Lonny McPherson be one of Mandy Bristol's investors?"

"Unlikely. He's exactly the sort Mandy tries to disassociate from. I'd wager McPherson is employed by the bosses in this affair, whether they're the investors, the folks behind the Crown's arrest and prosecution, or someone else. It's a jumble. But if we can run this McPherson to ground, we should learn a great deal."

"Then how do we proceed, sir?"

William pondered a moment longer.

"While we await the Bow Street inquiries, let's keep focused on trial preparation. Was our application for the Order of Compulsion approved?"

"Yes," Obadiah answered. "For the eight witnesses. All the subpoenas have been served. I have the list right here."

William looked it over, muttering, "Without the first mate, this adds up to a wagonload of hearsay."

"Should we seek an order compelling Solicitor Bristol to testify?"

"He'd resist it and merely lie if he was put on the stand. No, to stand a chance of success piercing this fog, it's obvious we still need McPherson or First Mate Ivars—or we must locate the forgers responsible for Captain Tuttle's letter."

There was a knock at the door. Obadiah's wife opened it cautiously to peek through.

"Suzie?" Obadiah called. "Why are you here?"

Suzanne brushed fresh snow from her coat. "I'm sorry. I know you're readying for trial, but I needed to tell you that Madeleine has left."

"Left?" William erupted. "Why? To where?"

"She wouldn't say. Didn't even tell Davidson. But she was out the door soon after you, Obadiah. Said it had to do with the case and she hopes to be back the day after tomorrow or the next."

"That's two to three days into trial," William said, irritated that Madeleine would add still more chaos to the case.

"No mention where she's gone?"

"None."

"We're unlikely to need her testimony for the first day or two anyway," Obadiah said.

He was right. And the truth was that her testimony was a sideshow anyway. If he was honest with himself, his true worry lay in her state of mind since the ball—and a powerful tug of concern that she'd left once again, traveling alone.

"Leave me now, Obadiah," William ordered, hoping the strength of his sentiment wouldn't show through. "I'll let you know if I hear from the Bow Street Runners. In the meantime, we still have much work to be prepared for trial in the morning."

CHEMIST'S SHOP
STAUNTON
ESSEX COUNTY

Roisin shook her head. Her white fist was wrapped around a pestle she was working so hard in the mortar that Madeleine thought she'd break it.

"No, Madeleine," the woman insisted. "I tell you again, I won't do it."

Madeleine's own face and hands were pale with chill, her riding dress muddy from the hard ride from London on treacherous, snow-sloshed roads.

"You have to, Roisin," she answered as firmly. "I spent the afternoon at the docks trying to find out who might know how to reach local smugglers and learned nothing. This is my only hope."

"It was foolish to go to the docks alone anyway, girl. Even in daylight. Boneheaded and foolish."

A shudder ran through Madeleine as she recalled the stares of some she'd spoken with on the quay. "I had to try. Now I need to meet with the American. Please."

"Madeleine, darlin', listen—even though it's not in your nature. That man will have his pound of flesh if you go askin' more favors of him. You don't want to meet him again until you've got the money to repay him."

"Which won't happen unless we can find Harold's first mate," Madeleine answered. "Do you think he'd know if this Quint signed on with a smuggler's ship in these waters? It would've been only in the past week or a little more."

"Maybe. I don't know. The American seems to know everything about his business, and the sea is his business. But you say the trial starts tomorrow? We could never find this sailor you're searchin' for in a single day."

"We don't need him for the first day. I think we have two, perhaps three days to bring him to court. But we're going to lose the trial without him, and oh, Roisin, that means Harold could die on the gallows. No one wants to say it aloud, but it's *true*. Do you know where the American is or don't you?"

Roisin squinted her eyes in a look of agony. "Ah, girl, I never could resist you. Yes, yes, I know *exactly* where he is, or at least where he'll be. He's comin' with a delivery a' sugar tonight. Out by Kilton's farm. Midnight or thereabouts."

Madeleine's heart rushed at the first stroke of luck in memory. "Thank you, Roisin. I'll go with you to meet with him."

"Like I or anyone else could stop you. We'll leave from here, at eleven. That's three hours. Now you get on home and rest. But know that if you're not back here by eleven, I'll gladly go without you."

35

ST. JAMES'S PARK
LONDON

"Darlin'," Lonny said, "you know we take care of our own, don't you?"

Standing near a thicket of trees in the heart of the park, young Isabella wrapped her arms around her coat. The snow reflected blue from the spruce, the slice of moon overhead, and the bitter cold of the early morning hour.

"What's all this about, Lonny?" she asked, teeth chattering. "You keep saying things I don't understand. Why have you dragged me out in the middle of the night?"

Lonny reached with outstretched fingers as he stepped closer. "You know that I'm right, don't you, darlin'? About caring for our own?"

The girl shook her head, her eyes narrowing. "Yes. Whatever you say. Now tell me, what's this about?"

"Only this, darlin'. I mean to be compensating you for the good work you've done." He took another step closer as he pulled a bulky sack from beneath his coat that clinked with coins. "I've got two hundred pounds in here with your name on it, Isabella. Relocatin' money, you see."

"Relocating? What's that?"

"Movin' you to a better place. Setting you up for a better life."

She took a step backward, alarm in her eyes. "Moving me? Moving me where?"

"To York, darlin'. I've made arrangements."

She fell into stunned silence. "You'll give me two hundred pounds if I move to York?"

"Aye. The same for young Tad, who should've been here by now."

She scuffed her foot on the frost-hardened ground. "Are you saying I'm done here at Carlton House?"

"Aye, darlin'. That's all over."

Her eyes flashed recognition. "That's what you said happened to Simon, isn't it? You told me he finished his work and you moved him."

"Aye. He moved on. For his own protection. Just as we're doing for you, darlin'."

He drew closer.

"Lonny, wait. I . . . I've got to think about this. I need some time." Her voice grew raspy with cold and fear. "Now I've got to get back to the house before someone knows I'm gone."

"Only a bit longer," Lonny urged. "The lad should be here any moment."

"You've never parted with two pounds at any time in your life," Isabella said angrily. "Now you'll give me two hundred?"

He shook the sack in his hand. "Aye. The folks we've done a service for, you see, they've asked that you and Tad leave London for a while. And darlin', I'll be square with you. If you need more, there'll be more. I'm sure of it."

Isabella shook her head. "York?"

"Are you deaf? Yes. York. Just for a while. *Where's that Tad?*"

"Everyone I know is here in London."

"We're your family, darlin'," Lonny said, reaching out to take her arm. "We'll stay in close touch, and we'll bring you back when it's safe." He looked around. "*Where . . . is . . . that . . . boy?*"

263

"I'm going to be missed at the house. I have to get back." She shook off his hand and stepped away.

Lonny cocked his head toward the woods behind her.

A thick bear of a man emerged from the shadows. In two long strides, he threw his arms about Isabella, a bulky hand covering her mouth and nose.

She wrestled wildly, squealing a muffled but terrible scream.

Lonny looked away, humming to himself. Only when the girl's struggles ceased did he look back again.

This pained him—really it did. But it was that solicitor's fault. How did Bristol expect him to be passing on *four hundred pounds*, a sum bigger than any they'd offered him for any single job before? Did they think he was a banker, willing to let that kind of coin just slip through his hands? Especially when the job could be done so much cheaper? Offering up that kind of money, Bristol and his bosses might as well have done the killing themselves.

The big man lay Isabella's still body onto the frozen ground.

"Get the bags, George," Lonny ordered, sliding Mandy Bristol's coins back into his jacket. "We'll have to look for the boy and drop her in the Thames along the way. *Garn, it's cold.* Let's hope the river's not frozen this night or you'll be chipping a hole for an hour to dispose of 'em."

Tad squirmed in his own skin knowing how late he'd be, hurrying through empty, frost-covered streets.

It wasn't his fault. Lonny's message reached him long past when he could've made it on time. The lad tasked to deliver it was the foul-up. He never should've gotten pinched near the station by trying to pick a gentleman on the way, then only finding Tad after he'd wriggled out of a constable's arms.

It didn't matter that the other boy was at fault, though. He'd take a beating for it. The message said the meet-up was of "topmost importance," which meant an extra hard one for his being late. Maybe Lonny had more papers to deliver—though Tad had never been sent this far to collect them before. Or maybe he'd tell Tad what happened to Simon, like Tad had been pestering Lonny about for over a year, and especially since he'd overheard about Simon being dead—it couldn't be true—in old man Bristol's office.

Whatever the reason for meeting, Tad wanted to run away and hide until Lonny cooled about his being late.

Except running always made things worse.

He rounded a corner and hurried across the road to St. James's Park. The park grounds shifted to blue and gray under the faint moonlight from the green and black of the streets. He trotted down some steps and over frosty ground on ancient shoes barely covering his frigid feet. Rounded a thicket of trees.

There, Tad stiffened and stopped.

Just ahead, Isabella lay on the ground. Her head was turned at an odd angle. Her eyes were open wide and still.

Lonny stood beside her, a long cloth bag in his hands. Lonny's muscle, Big George, lifted the girl's feet in the air, readying to put her in the bag.

A strangled yelp came out of Tad before he could stop it.

Lonny looked up. His droopy eye caught him.

"Get him," Lonny muttered to George.

George dropped the girl and took a big step toward him. Tad lit out the other way through the park as though demons were on his heels.

Because, it being George and Lonny, they were.

Running as fast as he could manage through the slippery streets, Tad could hear them shouting back and forth. This was bad. He could usually lose the big ones through small holes in broken fences, steep hills and mounds, or bunches of trees if he could find them—hedges best of all.

Except Big George was a canny one. He'd grown up on the

streets like Tad. His tree-trunk legs drove faster than was natural for a man his size and never seemed to tire.

Lonny? He just never gave up.

Isabella was dead. *Gasp*. Fat Bristol saying Simon was dead. *Gasp*. Why was everyone dying?

The park far behind now, Tad wasn't seeing any help on the streets. No walls or culverts or skinny gaps that might fit him in this district. Nothing to cut them off from him. And his legs were getting wobbly, not having had a bite to eat all day.

Lonny would catch him in the end unless he found a place to hide.

He ran and ran until his lungs burned hot and his legs were stumbling under him. He could still hear them behind, fallen back a bit but now matching his weak pace. They'd surely see him tiring.

He lurched onto the river walk. Over the wall, just yards below, was the dark flow of the Thames.

"Come on . . . boy." He heard the approach of Lonny's voice over hard breaths. "Come on. It's not . . . what you think. Isabella took a fall, son, that's all. A fall on the ice. We were supposed to meet, the three of us . . . so I could reward you and Isabella. That fancy Lord Brummell and the fancy princess . . . they wanted you sent off. I told 'em no unless you were well taken care of. Then, it's so tragic, Isabella slipped and fell. But you can have her share now. You deserve it, son. She'd want that. Just . . . come along now. No more running."

Tad looked back over his shoulder at Lonny, just twenty yards away. "If that's all it is," he gasped back, "why've you got George with you?"

Lonny didn't answer but kept coming at him.

Tad could see George off to the left, cutting him off from running back into the heart of the city. Both George and Lonny continued moving toward him like they were cornering a rat. Lonny's smile under his drooping eye had the glassy look of a cat

Tad had once seen, crushed in the street after being run over by a wagon.

Soulless.

"Sweet Mother Mary," he whispered. Then he turned and jumped the wall toward the icy black waters of the river below.

36

THE OLD BAILEY

Fully robed, leaning into a biting wind, William marched up Bailey Street, his briefcase containing his wig and papers clutched in his left hand.

A large crowd lapped about the entryway to the stone face of The Old Bailey. William had expected them. The press had trumpeted the case for days, every article damning Captain Tuttle and his defense team and Lady Jameson's family as charlatans and thieves. It was a terrible crime that a man like the captain was sold as entertainment at six pence a paper. William's anger helped him shoulder through the crowd to reach the constable barring entry to any more spectators.

"I'm counsel for the defense," William said, knowing that he needn't specify the case.

The constable let him through with a disapproving gaze.

On the first day of most trials, William rode a flurry of nerves and anticipation. "*Demons taunting failure; angels promising success*," he'd described it to Edmund. It was extraordinary. The first time he experienced it, he'd known this would be his profession for life.

Yet this morning the sensation was absent. Instead, all that filled him was a cold fear that a man's life was at stake and he had no great hope of saving it.

The towering courtroom chamber was roiling with the buzz of the crowded upper and lower galleries. The box reserved for waiting defendants was empty, as there would be no other matters heard during the three-day trial scheduled. Neither the judge nor Sir Barnabas had yet made their entrances, though juniors and court clerks were arranging exhibits and papers at counsels' tables.

William located Obadiah in the lower-level gallery and gave him a nod, which Obadiah returned. Then he walked to the space at counsel table reserved for himself and Edmund to prepare.

Only moments passed before Edmund took the seat beside him, dropping a copy of the *Gazette* on counsel table. "Trial starting and it's the first day we're not the top article in the rags."

"Oh?" William said as he arranged his papers, cross-examination on top. "What catastrophe has shouldered us from the lead?"

"A murder in St. James's Park. Someone who worked in Carlton House."

"Murder on the king's doorstep? It's little wonder it got the headline. Leave it. I'll read it later."

"Have you decided who they'll put up first?" Edmund asked.

"My opinion hasn't changed. Crew members from the *Padget*. Then, if they've managed to arrange it, perhaps a member of the French ship's crew. They have to establish the taking of the French ship first thing."

"Then the arresting constable?"

"Perhaps. Which is when we'll learn if good Judge Raleigh will allow in evidence of the shooting."

"Um-hmm. Do you think we'll have any surprises?"

"If I could predict them, they wouldn't be surprises," William said. "Now leave me a minute more to prepare."

He must sound like it, but he wasn't really annoyed at his junior. Edmund was only talking from nerves. William glanced about the spectators in the gallery, confirming what he'd already known: Madeleine was not in attendance. Renewed worry rose in his stomach.

"Mr. Snopes!"

Recognizing the voice, William looked in that direction slowly.

Sir Barnabas had arrived. It looked like half the London bar was along to attend him. William nodded at the KC, unsmiling, before looking back to his papers.

"All rise before the Honorable Judge Cecil S. Raleigh!" the bailiff called.

Bewigged, stern-faced Justice Raleigh entered the courtroom at a brisk step and marched to his bench seat on the dais. "Sit down, sit down," he called out. "This will be an unusually long trial, so unless counsel have any matters for the court's attention, I wish to get right to it. The jury has been screened to eliminate any with knowledge of that regrettable penny dreadful. Are there any objections to bringing them in now?"

"I have one matter for my lord's consideration," Sir Barnabas said, rising. "I wonder if we might discuss it in your lordship's chambers?"

Judge Raleigh nodded, annoyed. "We won't be making a habit of this, will we, Sir Barnabas?"

"Of course not, my lord."

The chamber just beyond the courtroom was emptied of all clerks and other personnel. Judge Raleigh made a point of not sitting. "What is it?" he asked impatiently as the door closed behind William.

"My lord," Sir Barnabas began, "there is the matter of the injured boy."

"Murdered boy," William corrected.

"I've already ruled that that matter won't be tried today," the judge said emphatically.

"Yes, my lord. But we anticipate that Mr. Snopes will nevertheless inquire about the event in order to sway the jury. It will divert this case into irrelevant and highly prejudicial grounds."

"My lord," William instantly rejoined, "Sir Barnabas hopes to censor us before even knowing what evidence we wish to introduce. Certainly, there are circumstances in which the cold-blooded murder of an innocent child would bear on the allegations against Captain Tuttle."

"There he goes again, my lord. Playing to passion."

"I'm not a juror, Sir Barnabas," the magistrate said with a huff. "I'm not easily swayed by lurid language. But your colleague makes a point, Mr. Snopes. The shooting has no relevance to this piracy trial. It will stay out of my courtroom."

"Your Honor," William pleaded, "at least withhold judgment on the matter until more evidence is presented. To allow context for possible admissibility of the boy's fate."

"I see no circumstance where that evidence could be relevant to the piracy charges. That's my decision."

William left the chambers for the counsel table trying to hide his dejection. Nevertheless, Edmund noticed immediately.

"It's the Simon Ladner evidence, isn't it?"

"Yes," William whispered. "It's been quashed. For now."

The bailiff brought in the twelve men of the jury. From their dress and bearing, they were, as usual, from the middle classes. William recognized at least one from a prior jury he'd faced—not an unusual prospect, given the prestige attached to being selected a juror. A schoolteacher, William recalled. Four others had the appearance of shopkeepers or tradesmen. There could be a constable or a soldier among them as well. All would have heard of the case. Many would already hold opinions, most naturally leaning toward supporting the Crown.

Hopefully they could still be swayed.

Captain Tuttle was brought in next. William nearly ground his teeth at his pale appearance, though the man seemed to be trying to muster an air of strength as he'd been instructed.

"William?" a voice called from the bar nearest counsel table.

He turned. Father Thomas stood there. How he'd gotten so close when he should have been confined to the gallery, William had no idea. William stood and walked to his side.

The Father reached out over the bar to give William a bear hug.

Mortified, William accepted the embrace for several seconds before firmly detaching himself. Behind him, he heard the rising murmurs of the gallery and, presumably, the jury box.

"My prayers will be with you and the good Captain Tuttle," Father Thomas said overly loud.

"*Mr. Snopes!*" the magistrate called out.

It was overdone, but William was grateful. Even if it only warmed the ice in a single juror, it was worth it.

"I'm sorry, my lord," he said, bowing to the magistrate before returning to his seat.

"Gentlemen of the jury," the magistrate began, fixing the twelve in a gaze perilous with gravity, "the matter which you are about to judge . . ."

The magistrate's opening description of the case was as predisposed toward guilt as any William had sat through. Or at least it seemed so to him. He longed to stand and demand a rebuttal but knew that none would be permitted. He had to content himself with smiling at his papers as though the good judge were declaring his client to be a reasonable candidate for apostleship.

"Sir Barnabas," the judge said in conclusion, turning to William's opponent, "please proceed."

"Thank you, my lord. The Crown calls Pierre Gourdon, the former captain of the *Charlemagne*."

Edmund turned to William, saying low, "You win on the first bet, sir."

The presentation of the French captain first in his case was a good choice by Sir Barnabas. The man's English was excellent, his recollections vivid.

"They swooped upon my ship, firing as they came," the witness testified. "We were startled and unprepared. They flew a British flag. '*What is this?*' my first mate exclaimed. '*We're not at war with the English.*' We could not believe it. It was so unmanly, attacking in this way."

"And did you overhear their leader once they boarded you?" Sir Barnabas asked.

"Oui. I was amidships when the captain of the *Padget* boarded and I demanded an explanation."

"What did the English captain say?"

"'*Your cargo is ours, Frenchman. Man your boats. We're sinking your ship.*' The seas were high. I said that it would be the death of my entire crew, so far from shore in such weather."

"And did the English captain relent?"

"Only because his own crew appeared ready to mutiny if he did not."

"So your ship was spared."

"Oui."

"Is the English captain here in the courtroom today?"

"Oui." The witness pointed to Captain Tuttle. "There the pirate is."

"Objection." William rose. "I believe the matter of whether Captain Tuttle is or is not a pirate is to be decided by this good jury rather than our French guest."

The judge shook his head. "I'll not censor the witness. Overruled."

"A final question, Captain Gourdon," Sir Barnabas picked up. "Did the Englishman offer any explanation for his taking the cargo of a French ship when our two countries are not at war?"

"Oui. He said, '*Tell your French friends that the war with Napoleon isn't over where the* Padget *sails.*'"

"They're making this about revenge?" Edmund leaned over to whisper to William. "Revenge for what?"

"It doesn't matter," William whispered in return. "The point they're making is that Captain Tuttle made no mention of a Letter of Marque to justify his actions."

"Your witness, Counsel," Sir Barnabas announced.

William stood. "Captain Gourdon, how many of your crew were killed in the encounter with Captain Tuttle?"

"None," the witness replied low.

"Could you speak up a bit, Captain Gourdon?"

"None."

"Thank you. How many wounded?"

"None."

"None? Not even the grazing of a musket ball? A sliver, perhaps?"

"Objection," Sir Barnabas called.

"Sustained," Judge Raleigh answered. "Restrain your sarcasm, Mr. Snopes."

"Thank you, my lord. Captain Gourdon, no one injured, correct?"

"Yes."

"Your ship was spared, and you were permitted to sail away?"

"Oui."

"Does all that strike you as unusual in a *pirate attack*?"

"We did not resist."

"Why not?"

"Because I could not believe we were actually being pirated. We thought there was some other reason the English ship had shot a cannonball across our bow."

"A *cannonball*? Just a moment ago, you said the *Padget* swooped upon you, *'firing as they came.'* In fact, it was a single cannon shot across your bow, was it not?"

"Oui," the witness replied.

"Is it your understanding that it's common in pirate attacks for the attacker to at least confiscate the targeted ship as well as her cargo?"

"So I have heard. I have never encountered a pirate attack in my time at sea."

"Did you think at the time, perhaps, that you were being boarded as a policing action?"

"A what?"

274

"A policing action. An effort to enforce a legal right. Isn't it correct that you believed the *Padget* was challenging you as a policing action and *that* was the true reason you didn't resist? After all, monsieur, you were carrying illegal cargo, weren't you?"

"Objection!" Sir Barnabas bellowed.

"Sustained," the judge called. "Mr. Snopes, the French crew is not on trial here. And I will judge the legalities in this courtroom, not you."

"Monsieur," William picked up instantly, "what exactly *was* in your hold?"

"Tea."

"Acquired from where?"

The Frenchman hesitated. "China."

"You are aware, aren't you, that the British East India Company has contracts and a Royal Charter establishing a monopoly on the tea trade in that region?"

The witness muttered something.

"I'm sorry, Captain Gourdon. You've grown quiet again. Could you please repeat that?"

The witness's face radiated hostility. "Just because you claim such rights does not make it true," he said.

"Oh, then you disagree with the legality of the British East India Company's position?"

"Everyone knows those agreements were forced on China by the British."

"Really? Are you aware, Captain Gourdon, that the British Crown wholeheartedly supports the East India Company's position?"

"I suppose."

"Are you saying, monsieur, that our English sovereign, King George III, reigning through his son the Prince Regent George, supports illegal trade by its citizens?"

The witness didn't answer.

"I'll take that as a yes. Isn't it true, sir, that Captain Tuttle, when he boarded the *Charlemagne*, told you that he was taking the cargo because it was smuggled tea, illegally obtained and shipped in violation of the East India Company's monopoly, and that he had sanction from the British Crown for the taking of the cargo in the form of a Letter of Marque?"

"No!" the witness said, then shrank back. "No. He said what I told you he said."

"Repeat what you claim Captain Tuttle said."

"Pardon?"

"Please repeat what you say Captain Tuttle said when he boarded the *Charlemagne*."

The witness took a breath. "'*Tell your French friends that the war with Napoleon isn't over where the* Padget *sails*.'"

"You said it perfectly, monsieur. I wrote it down," William said, picking up a sheet of paper. "You repeated it the second time exactly as you had the first, word for word. Are you good at memorization?"

"Uh, I don't know."

"I'll wager you are. Particularly at memorizing a statement provided you by prosecuting counsel perhaps?"

"*Objection!*"

"Sustained. Unless you have proof of any such allegations, Mr. Snopes, you will keep them to yourself."

"Of course, my lord. No further questions."

As William sat, Sir Barnabas leaned across counsel table and snarled low, "So that's how it will be, Mr. Snopes?"

"Exactly as you served it up, Sir Barnabas," William responded.

When he leaned back in his chair, William saw that Edmund was restraining a satisfied grin.

"It will get much more difficult," he whispered to his junior. "And you know our greatest peril awaits us in Captain Tuttle's testimony and cross-examination."

William's gaze rose over Edmund's head. He noticed that Lord Beau Brummell had arrived, seated alone in the gallery in a private box reserved for dignitaries.

276

He felt a momentary surprise. Not at his presence but at the lord's face. Especially given the lord's encouragement at the ball.

Though it was a distance away, William thought he discerned displeasure at William's cross-examination of the witness.

THE OLD BAILEY

"But, Mr. Smythe," Edmund pressed, "it's true, is it not, that at no time did you hear Captain Tuttle express any particular personal animus or hostility toward the French people?"

The *Padget* sailor smoothed his oiled hair with a thick hand. "Aye, that's true."

"And isn't it also true," Edmund went on, "that Captain Tuttle informed the crew that they would be sailing under a Letter of Marque from the British Crown?"

"Well, he said it. Never saw it, though."

"Captain Tuttle never allowed you to see the Letter itself?"

"That's what I'm sayin', aye."

"Did you ask to see the Letter?"

"No."

"Why not?"

"Well, I guess the cap'n seemed a straight one."

"He seemed honest to you?"

"Yah."

"Treated the crew well?"

"As you say."

"And isn't it true that another reason Captain Tuttle may have refrained from showing you the Letter was that you cannot read?"

"Could be."

"No further questions."

Sir Barnabas stood. "Captain Tuttle will shortly testify, Mr. Smythe, that he had a Letter of Marque but that it was stolen the hour that you reached London Harbor. Does that seem a likely thing to have happened?"

The sailor hesitated. "Well, I don't see how it could've. Cap'n's quarters are next to our'n. If someone went into the cap'n's cabin that didn't belong, any of the crew awake belowdecks would've seen 'em."

"Is there anyone among the crew you believe capable of such an act of thievery?"

"No. I mean, it was a good crew. No real troublemakers."

"Thank you." Sir Barnabas turned to address the judge. "My lord, I suggest we break for the day. It's likely that the prosecution will rest in the morning."

The judge nodded. "Very well. Mr. Smythe, you're excused. We will reconvene at nine." The gavel fell with a *bang*.

William watched the crowd in the gallery shuffle out as the jury followed the bailiff to their exit. He looked over each juror carefully.

After the monotony of two more of the French crew repeating Captain Gourdon's testimony, and nine *Padget* crew members saying nearly the same as Mr. Smythe, any juror would be sliding toward slumber. But Sir Barnabas knew, as William did too, that monotony had its purpose. It would take powerful evidence to shake the deeply set impressions created this first day.

A messenger approached the bar. "Edmund Shaw?" he called. The junior went to him.

"Mr. Snopes," Edmund said after reading the message, "I need to run an important errand. Can I meet you back at your office at Gray's after supper?"

"Of course. You're prepared for tomorrow's examinations? You do recall the order of witnesses?"

"Yes, sir. After you take Captain Tuttle's testimony, you'll also take that of Sergeant Rhodes, whom you met on the *Padget*'s deck—and who should be arriving at the courtroom by midday, accompanied by the constables tasked to deliver him. Then I'll be questioning our three witnesses from the *Padget* crew."

"That's it, thank you," William replied. "Please return from your errand as soon after dinner as possible in case there's need for further consultation this evening."

"Very well."

Obadiah appeared just as Edmund rushed out. "What did you think of the first day, sir?"

William considered his sense of mild satisfaction. "Edmund did a fine job with the last of Sir Barnabas's *Padget* witnesses," he said. "Yet we won't win the case by challenging the reading skills of the crew. The jury is waiting on Captain Tuttle and anyone else who saw the Letter of Marque. It would surely help if Judge Raleigh allowed the testimony regarding the shooting of the boy. Painting the soldiers and constables as dangerous aggressors that night would make Captain Tuttle seem that much more trustworthy in his testimony."

"I agree, sir. But I don't think it's a bad jury. Only two were sleeping this afternoon, and all seemed sober. Still, they'll need more to side with our poor captain."

Indeed, William thought. Much more. Like word from the Bow Street Runners that they'd found Lonny and the thief confessed to a role in all this. Or Madeleine showing up with whatever evidence she'd gone chasing. Why would she race off like that? Why hadn't she told him what it was?

William gathered his papers—at the last grabbing the newspaper Edmund had brought that morning. *"Do your very best, pray it to be enough, then your work is done."* A simple saying that Aeron had used often years ago, particularly when William was wrestling with the most important decision of his young life.

He only wished his Irish mentor could be here now. He longed for the soft sibilance of his reassurances. The power of his humility.

Because, O God, William's heart cried, what he wouldn't surrender to win this case.

37

THE ROYAL MEWS
NORTH END OF CHARING CROSS
WESTMINSTER DISTRICT
LONDON

The stallion carrying Princess Charlotte came pounding in, dropping from a canter to a walk in just a few lengths to stop beside Lord Brummell, who stood near a fence, his hat in his hands.

Lord Brummell looked up at the princess as she patted the stallion. She was far from the beauty he'd thought her two years ago, or as people like Solicitor Bristol seemed to observe even now. Perhaps her charms had dimmed for him as the veneer of youthful innocence faded in his sight. Their arrangement these past years had dulled any assumptions he had of such virtue in the young woman. Or, perhaps, he'd simply never been so infatuated with youth as others were. He much preferred the seasoning of years.

"Do you think this was a good idea, Your Highness, summoning me in this way?"

"There's no one about. I saddled my horse myself. Have you read the papers?"

Always to the point. "Of course."

"Did you tell your man Bristol to murder the girl?"

Just what he'd expected was the purpose of this demanded appearance. "Of course not, Your Highness. I've given him no instructions other than those we both conveyed the night of the carriage ride."

"I thought it impossible for him to take us deeper down the rabbit hole, yet here we are," she fumed sharply. "And I having revealed myself to Bristol—on *your* advice."

"It seemed the correct course to cement Mr. Bristol's commitment and fealty. The man has a certain awe for your status, Your Highness, as well he should."

She ignored the vacuous compliment. "I told you at the time that it was foolhardy to repeat the same scheme at the docks with this *Padget* brig, no matter the profit we'd enjoyed on the first one. We've tempted the fates trying this a second time, and now we must deal with this killing."

Perhaps a reminder was in order. "At the time that we discussed this, Your Highness, you seemed as interested in replicating our profits as I was," he replied dryly. "Did I mishear you?"

Her eyes flashed. "Don't toy with that tongue of yours. I told you at the time that my father has leashed me to an allowance better suited to a gypsy than a princess. And you certainly didn't hesitate to proceed again. A few too many corsets and balls burdening your budget? Are the rumors of your bankruptcy serious?"

She was an excellent viper, wasn't she? Striking so close to the mark.

"The times and taxes have smitten us all," he smiled frostily. "But we gain nothing by sniping at each other."

Her eyes hadn't cooled. "So how do we weather this killing?"

"No one attributes the murder to anyone other than London's criminal elements."

"Perhaps now. But then a month ago there wasn't a whisper of piracy at the docks either. My confidence in you wanes, as it has in your Solicitor Bristol."

"It went well today at court," Brummell said, seeking to reassure. "Sir Barnabas is as good as always."

"And Mr. Snopes? How did he do?"

Brummell hesitated. She likely had her own sources observing at The Old Bailey, so he shouldn't sell the day's progress too hard.

"He has a certain style. But he has nothing of substance to present. All the jury heard was the undenied taking of the French ship by the *Padget* and the absence of any proof of a Letter of Marque."

"Tell me, Lord Brummell, are you really so confident that Solicitor Bristol will protect us if things become difficult?"

"Oh yes."

"Really? And why?"

"Because of the awe I mentioned, and his longing for status. He would go to any length for a knighthood, which I'm sure you could arrange if necessary. But also because he has no means to do otherwise. Neither you nor I have had any contact with his employees. Neither you nor I have been seen arriving with him at any of the social events where I've arranged for him to be invited. Even the invitations themselves have been tendered through surrogates. To all the world, Mr. Bristol and we two are passing ships in a broad sea. A sea in which Bristol lacks friends of power and influence."

She looked away. "I hope you're correct. If this should ignite, I doubt the flames could reach high enough to engulf my tower."

But they would certainly reach mine, you gutter snipe, Lord Brummell thought, smiling.

"Shall I see you at the Thackerys' ball tonight?" he asked.

"Yes."

"I'll be leaving the event a bit early for some matters I need to supervise, but we could at least go together. Would you like me to pick you up in my carriage?"

"I think I'll go alone tonight," the princess said.

Severing connections. The response wasn't lost on Lord Brummell. "Of course, Your Highness. I'll see you there."

The princess kicked the stallion and rode away without looking back.

OFFICE OF BARRISTER WILLIAM SNOPES
GRAY'S INN

William watched Obadiah and Father Thomas, seated near his desk, eating ravenously of the roasted chicken and potatoes Suzanne had delivered to his office. He'd managed a few bites but wasn't terribly hungry himself. Trials were always the death of his appetite. This one more than any before.

"When did Edmund say he'd be back from his errand, Mr. Snopes?" Obadiah asked.

"He didn't," William replied, railing at the reminder. Another of his assistants for the trial scattered. He should have demanded to know where Edmund was off to.

They spoke for a while about the coming morning's skirmishes.

"Keep an eye on that juror in the back row," Obadiah suggested. "The straight-backed, serious-looking one. If he's not a prig with the other jurors, he may well be selected their foreman. His view of the charges is a bit of a mystery, but he's listening well."

"Tell me if you see anything in particular that moves him," William said.

"I will. And, Father Thomas, I think your greetings of Mr. Snopes have caught the attention of at least two of the jurors. One looks puzzled. The other, perhaps, approving."

"'The arms are fair, when the intent of bearing them is just,'" Father Thomas intoned.

Obadiah looked at the Father quizzically. "That's no Scripture I've ever heard."

"Shakespeare," William said. "*Henry IV*, if I'm right. No biblical jewels for us tonight, Thomas?"

"I'm saving it for Captain Tuttle," Father Thomas said through a mouthful of chicken, then looked at William. "'Give not that which is holy unto the dogs, neither cast ye your pearls before swine, lest they trample them under their feet.'" He glanced at Obadiah. "No offense is meant for you in that, Obadiah."

Obadiah shrugged. "None taken, sir."

"Thank you again for seeing Captain Tuttle tonight, Thomas," William said, meaning it. "I've arranged my visit for eight, near the changing of the prison guard. They've given permission for your visit at nine. One hour of final preparation should be enough. I hope you can brace up his spirits."

"I believe I can," Father Thomas said. "Or I'd stay away from the poor soul."

<hr />

NEWGATE PRISON

"That's the sum of it, Captain," William said. "Remain calm. Answer truthfully. Look to the jury when you answer. Don't argue with Sir Barnabas—leave that to me. You'll do very well."

The captain looked immune to encouragement. "We're losing, aren't we?"

William gave his best smile. "Not based on today's evidence. Captain, please understand that we've barely begun. This first day has cleared the throat. We've at least two more days and much to say on the topic of your innocence."

"Please, sir. Don't lie to a man on the eve of his death."

If only he could reassure the captain, buried all these weeks in the depths of this ungodly place. He could shout of certain victory in his best advocate's voice. But how could he make such an unsupportable promise without losing credibility, just on the eve of the captain's testimony?

Instead, William overcame his natural reticence and reached through the bars to grip the captain's shoulders. "Harold, lies are unnatural things. Bad ones fall apart like sodden paper. Good ones are hard to conjure and wearying to sustain. I don't know why someone is expending such energy to perpetuate their lies about you and the Letter of Marque, but I've learned in my practice that all falsehoods fail in the end. The challenge is ensuring they do so in the time of our need. I'm doing everything in my power to achieve that in the courtroom. All I ask is that you stay faithful for a few days more."

Captain Tuttle looked to the cell floor at his feet. "If lies are so unnatural, then remind me what truth is in this world, Mr. Snopes, and how it can be hidden so. I've forgotten."

"Father Thomas will tell you from his profession that it's God's most fundamental trait. The *essence* of who He is. In the courtroom, truth is tool and brick: powerful to wield and the only foundation for real justice. Anyone telling you otherwise is a liar, a modern Narcissus, or self-deluded."

Footsteps sounded on the stairs, growing louder until Father Thomas descended, then emerged into the torchlight.

"Am I too early?" he asked.

"No," William said. "We were just finishing."

William said his good-byes and turned to go, fervently hoping the Father could reinvigorate the captain.

The man was ready to collapse before even reaching the dock. Any improvement would require divine intervention.

Father Thomas's field now.

An hour later, William was back at Gray's Inn. His hope was disappointed that Edmund would be there or at least have left a note. He dropped wearily behind his desk.

The newspaper lay beside his papers. He picked it up to read the article Edmund had mentioned about the murder in St. James's Park. He got no further than the second line.

> *"The poor victim, twenty-two-year-old Isabella Stratton, resided at Carlton House, where she was employed as an assistant for the care of our sovereign King George III . . ."*

He hesitated only a moment before rising and grabbing his coat on the way to the door.

38

ST. JAMES'S PARK

In the dark, hands in his pockets against the cold, William traced the ground at his feet. Wind shushed through pine branches overhead as his steps took him to a private corner of the park—not hidden exactly but sheltered from the commonest walking paths.

He reached the quiet corner, amid oak and more pine. The *Gazette* had described this as where the murdered girl, Isabella, was found by constables. The paper had painted the scene. Strangled. Still warm when they'd discovered her. Lying with a bag close by as though she was to be transported away. Likely dead less than an hour.

He looked about at the ground in the starlight. For someone who had been strangled, there was no sign of a scuffle. Nor any indication she'd been dragged to this site forcefully.

William looked up.

Carlton House, the royal residence where William had seen the girl himself, was just up a nearby trail and a few ascending stairs away. Apparently, Isabella was a resident there as well. She was one of several caring for the insane king.

Extraordinary. Why would the girl have been out in the chill at the late hour? Such an out-of-the-way spot could only have been an intended destination. Which implied she was murdered by someone she'd planned to meet. Few would take a meeting if anticipating harm, so she couldn't have expected danger from the rendezvous.

He watched his breath drift away. Despite the hour, despite the approaching dawn of another day at trial, his compulsion to be here remained intense. It was . . . *odd*, the death of this girl so shortly after he'd crossed paths with her at the Lord Privy Seal's office.

No, odd didn't capture it. There were no coincidental occurrences, not of this type. Her fate must be part of the maelstrom surrounding the captain's case. Did she know something about the captain's Letter of Marque, real or forged? Was she part of the scheme circling the *Padget*?

Pieces to the puzzle of the case kept dropping at his feet as he waded deeper into the trial. Lonny McPherson's interest in Simon Ladner. The murdered cabin boy.

Isabella, an attendant in Carlton House, dying the night before trial.

Then the cold—the park—were gone.

He had an idea. Conjecture without evidence. But with symmetry to firm up the conjecture.

William began humming. He hadn't done so for so long. This time it was a violin piece from Paganini, playing as he rushed through the snow and ice back toward his office.

As the strings joined his thoughts in a stirring of his blood, he wondered if he'd get any sleep tonight.

OFFICE OF MANDY BRISTOL
MAYFAIR DISTRICT
LONDON

Mandy's nerves tingled, seated at the desk in the front foyer of his office, occasionally wiping perspiration from his forehead. On a client chair in the corner sat a man dressed in a plain brown shirt and trousers, a cloth mask over his head, covering all but his eyes.

There was a knock at the door.

"Come in!" Mandy called.

Lonny McPherson stepped through the door, grinning brightly. "Evening, Mr. Bristol. I—" He stopped. The grin disappeared as his head swiveled toward the man in the corner. "Who in the devil is this now?"

"You weren't seen coming here, were you, Lonny?" Mandy demanded.

"No. No footpads or thieves, not a soul. Now tell me what's goin' on. Who the blazes is this?"

The figure shook his head, looking to Mandy, who on cue raised a hand, slamming it to the desk.

"Pay attention to me, Lonny! Tell me who told you to kill the girl!"

Lonny looked back and forth between Mandy and the mask.

"I'm not gonna talk in front of . . . whoever this is."

"You'll talk, Lonny!" Mandy shouted. "You'll talk. And you'd better tell the truth."

"You want to talk, then tell him to take off that cloth."

"He won't do that. Now answer me. *Who told you to kill the girl?*"

Lonny hesitated, looking off-center. "Isabella dear got testy, God's honest truth. Threatened to give the whole scheme away. She was going to talk. What was I to do?"

Relief spread through Mandy that Lonny hadn't tried to implicate him. "Why didn't you come to me and get instructions?"

"I'd already given her your money. She pocketed it and the next day come back, asking for a meeting at the park. When I got there, she said she had to have more. I begged her. I pleaded with her. She put her back to me and said she was goin' to the authorities. What choice did I have?"

"You should have come to me first."

"Ahh, you wouldn't have wanted to know, Mr. Bristol. Just get it done, that's what you always want. Well, it's done. Had no choice about the methods."

Mandy let loose a quiet lungful of air. "What about the boy?"

"Tad? He's relocated. Like you asked."

Mandy looked at the hooded figure. The figure nodded back.

"All right, Lonny," Mandy said. "Now listen carefully. You and yours have to disappear for a while—just like Tad. Leave town if you must. But there must be no possibility of any of you being picked up during this trial. Especially with the death of Isabella, there must be no way Snopes can question any of you."

"I'd already done as much with me and mine—staying low, that is. Until I got your message, we'd all been tucked safely away." Lonny raised his chin higher. "But even if they got me, I'd tell 'em nothing. You know that."

To save your neck, you'd tell them everything and more, Mandy thought behind his smile. *Even if it meant sending your mother to the rope.* "Good, Lonny. You'll be paid for the time underground."

"How much?"

"Sufficiently."

"Excellent, Governor." He held out his hand.

"After. Go now, Lonny. We'll not speak again for some time."

Lonny looked prepared to argue the point, yet the presence of the hooded man seemed to weaken his resolve. He rubbed the scar over his grotesque eye. Then, reluctantly, he headed out the door.

As Lonny's steps retreated down the staircase, Mandy let out an audible sigh. "Is that acceptable, Lord Brummell?"

Lord Brummell removed his mask. "Yes, Mandy. For the present. Now you will do the same."

He hadn't heard right. "Me?"

"Yes. You'll leave town until this trial is over."

"But my practice!"

"It will have to wait. Mr. Snopes may get the court's permission to subpoena you."

Like Lonny before him, Mandy considered arguing the point. He'd never done so with Brummell before. His heart wavered. Then he let out another heaving sigh. "If you wish it, Lord Brummell," Mandy said submissively.

"I do. In fact, I wish it tonight."

SOHO
WEST END, LONDON

Edmund stood at the mouth of the alleyway just a few blocks from Leicester Square. He knew these blocks, though not well. A gambling house he used to frequent was only a few streets farther east. Maybe that was why Hardacre, an even more dedicated gambler than himself, had picked this area in which to meet.

But the man, curse him, was *hours late*. If it wasn't so important, if his hopes hadn't been raised so high, Edmund would have left long ago.

"*Eddie!*"

Hardacre was striding down the lane in the dark at last, his face shadowed. When he got within reach, Edmund looked him over carefully.

"You're very late, Phineas."

"Sorry. Hard to get away. And I wanted to be sure of things tonight."

"Well, I was disappointed at your note," Edmund replied. "I'd almost finished writing my penny dreadful. Ready to go to press. Got a special chapter on how you cheated Striker Bosworth last year. You'd love reading it."

The journalist glowered. "Don't rub it in. It took some time, that's all. Asking around without raising suspicion isn't so easy, and I don't want to lose my job." He looked about. "Let's get in here." He gestured with his head toward the alley. "Out of the street."

They walked to the midpoint in the alley before stopping.

"So, what've you got," Edmund demanded. "I've got trial work to finish and it's very late."

"One of them that put pressure on the *Gazette* to run stories trashing your Mr. Snopes said he's willing to meet with you. He's even willing to discuss some kind of accommodation about your trial."

Edmund's hopes rose, but he kept it from his face. "Who is it?"

"I got to him through a go-between. I've got no names."

"I need a name."

"I can't give you a name. Not now."

"All right. But we're running out of time. When do we meet?"

"*Now!*" a voice rumbled.

The club blow to the back of Edmund's head was like the kick of a horse. The second blow to his face as it struck the pavement was the slam of a flat iron.

"That's what you get for trying to push me around, Edmund, lad," he distantly heard Hardacre bluster.

The last clear sound Edmund heard was his own grunt of pain, heaved after a savage kick to his ribs.

39

THE OLD BAILEY

"My lordship, the prosecution calls the accused Captain Harold Tuttle to the stand."

William tried to settle himself for what was coming. It wasn't easy.

Edmund nowhere to be seen. Madeleine still missing. The startling murder of the Isabella girl. His tumble into conjectures—ones he'd dare not use at trial until he could piece the story together fully with supporting evidence.

It all rendered a painful sense that, even if he had some theories at last, the case still raced beyond his control.

William watched his client take the stand. Captain Harold Tuttle, pale and shrunken too slender for his clothes, could barely raise his legs to climb into the witness box.

Look at the poor man. Perhaps he should strike now with his ideas. *Don't be foolish.* A premature attack could wound rather than kill. A glancing blow could anger the judge further and alert Sir Barnabas without convincing the jury of anything but that they were grasping at straws. He'd been right to not even share his thoughts with Captain Tuttle yet for fear of raising his hopes too soon.

No, he must hope that the Bow Street Runners will come through and find Lonny McPherson, or Madeleine return with whatever she was digging for. And, of course, he still had Sergeant Rhodes to surprise Sir Barnabas with, if the judge relented and permitted him to take the stand.

William took in the glower of Magistrate Raleigh. Glanced at Obadiah's wife, Suzanne, sitting in the gallery, who returned a kind smile. Saw Beau Brummell occupying his special box. Looked once more in vain for Madeleine.

Clear your mind, he admonished himself. *Pay attention.*

"Captain Tuttle . . ." Sir Barnabas began his examination.

"I wish to go back again, Captain, to your description of the hour of your capture in the upper pond of the Thames."

Remarkable, William thought. Sir Barnabas didn't look the least fatigued after being on his feet for hours, with only a few breaks in all that time. Still pounding on Captain Tuttle's weary frame like a butcher tenderizing a cut of meat.

"You say that moments before your arrest, you'd looked at this Letter of Marque in your cabin?"

"That's correct."

"What purpose could that serve, sir? In the hour that you were docking in London?"

"No particular purpose. It's just that we were finishing a long and difficult voyage and I wanted to see it once more before we docked."

"I see. So you opened the drawer of your desk where you kept the Letter and took it out?"

"Yes."

"Read it again?"

"Yes."

"Then put it back and locked the drawer?"

"That's right."

"And no one other than yourself had a key to the drawer?"

"Correct."

"And later, with the constables present, you returned to the desk drawer and unlocked it?"

"Yes."

"And when you arrived in your cabin to do so, the drawer was still locked and showed no signs of having been forced open?"

"Right."

"Yet the Letter was now gone?"

"That's correct."

"Never to reappear, to this day."

"I'm afraid so."

"Would you agree with me, Captain Tuttle, that you've described an impossibility?"

"I don't understand."

"If no one had a key to your desk drawer other than yourself, and the drawer wasn't forced open, then the Letter occupying the drawer should still have been there when you took the constables to show them the Letter."

"That's right."

"Its absence was therefore an impossibility, sir, wouldn't you agree?"

"No, sir. It can't have been impossible. It happened."

"But you have no explanation."

Captain Tuttle grew quiet.

"You claim that your first mate had previously seen the Letter?"

"Yes."

"As well as, you say, a London solicitor of your choosing."

"Yes."

"Yet you also claim that both First Mate Ivars and the solicitor have disappeared."

"Not disappeared precisely. We just aren't able to bring them to testify at trial."

"Convenient, wouldn't you say?"

"Quite the opposite."

"Doesn't it seem more likely that these witnesses would not support your story about the existence of a Letter of Marque, Captain Tuttle, and that is the reason your counsel will not be bringing them to testify before this jury?"

"That's not true."

"You've also told this jury that mysterious investors provided you the Letter."

"Through their solicitor, correct. And they're not mysterious."

"Well, you've never seen them, have you, Captain?"

"No."

"Can't name them for us?"

"No."

"They too will not be testifying before this jury?"

"So far as I know."

"A missing letter. Mysterious investors. Are you given to hallucinations, Captain? A frequent user of opium, perhaps?"

"Objection!" William called, standing.

"Sustained," the judge grudgingly agreed. "Counsel will confine himself to traditional proof and not mere speculation."

"Of course, my lord. I have no further questions."

William stood instantly. "Captain Tuttle, did you serve in the king's Royal Navy before becoming a merchantman?"

"I did."

"For how many years?"

"Five. Under Admiral Cockburn."

"Did you see any action?"

"I did. At Martinique and in the Mediterranean."

"Is it true that you were mentioned in dispatches for bravery in action?"

"Yes, sir."

William paused to allow that much to sink in. "When you became captain of a merchant ship, why did you decide to join in the tea trade in China?"

"It was far more lucrative than our original plan for the *Padget*. We'd planned on trade in America."

"You've already described how you obtained a Letter of Marque to support your trade. From whom did you receive that?"

"As I said, from investors, through their solicitor."

"Did you accept the solicitor's word that the Letter was genuine?"

"No, sir. As I stated, I had my own solicitor review it first."

"And did your solicitor assure you that the Letter was genuine?"

"Objection!" Sir Barnabas called. "Hearsay!"

"My lord," William rejoined, "Sir Barnabas raised this topic in his own examination."

"But I didn't ask if anything was *said* by this imaginary solicitor to Captain Tuttle. Only that he'd examined the Letter!"

"Sustained," the judge intoned. "I'll have no such hearsay in my courtroom. Move on."

"Well," William said, then turned back to the captain, "after speaking with your solicitor regarding the genuineness of the Letter, did you sail for the Indian Sea with the belief you could take French cargo legally?"

"Your Honor!" Sir Barnabas shouted. "This is the same inquiry stated a different way."

"Agreed. Mr. Snopes, *move on*."

"Of course, my lord," he answered, glancing at the jury that had to now know—from his questions and Sir Barnabas's objections—that the captain was saying he got a positive opinion about the Letter's veracity. Hearsay still, but it would have to do. "Would you agree, Captain Tuttle, that if you had obtained your cargo of tea as a pirate, without the benefit of a Letter of Marque, it would have been foolish to return with the cargo to London?"

"Absolutely, sir."

"Why is that?"

"All cargo is subject to possible inspection at London Harbor."

"Given the East India Company's monopoly on the China tea trade, your cargo might have been subject to seizure then, correct?"

"Yes, sir."

While this point was important, it was also obvious and pedestrian. William glanced at the jury. They looked unmoved.

After two days of Sir Barnabas holding center stage, William was losing them. The KC was simply too good. As much as he might wish to hold back on his unprovable notions, either he showed *something* to the jurors to open their lidded eyes or even Sergeant Rhodes's testimony wouldn't shake them enough to consider Captain Tuttle's innocence.

William glanced to Father Thomas. He sat, eyes closed, apparently in prayer. It was a further sign, William thought, of his case's failing fortunes.

More caution would hang Captain Tuttle. Conjecture it must be.

William drew a deep breath. "Captain, who was the last person to whom you spoke on the deck of the *Padget*—before the arrival of the constables the evening you were arrested?"

"My First Mate Quint Ivars."

"I said the *last* person you spoke with."

The captain looked puzzled. "As I said, my first mate."

"Isn't it true, Captain, that the last person you spoke with was actually your cabin boy, Simon Ladner?"

Captain Tuttle stared for a moment. "Well, I guess that's true."

"How old was Simon Ladner?"

"Thirteen or fourteen, I believe."

"Describe the circumstances under which the boy was brought to serve on the *Padget*."

The captain explained.

"You didn't confirm your first mate's story about Simon Ladner's past, including his father's permission for the boy to sail, did you?"

"No."

"The Ladner boy was at your side shortly before the constables arrived, correct?"

"Yes."

"Which side?"

The captain looked puzzled once more. "My left. No, my right side."

"And you sent him to your cabin to retrieve your pistol before the authorities arrived to arrest you, correct?"

"Yes. While the ship was still docking. For my trip into town."

"And he returned with that pistol fully loaded?"

"Yes, sir, he did."

"Returned to your right side?"

"I suppose he did."

"Tell me, Captain Tuttle, into which pocket did you place the key to your desk—after you locked away the Letter of Marque for the final time?"

He thought a moment. "It would have been my right pocket, as I used the key with my right hand."

"The same side where the boy approached?"

"Yes."

"And you later confirmed that it was still in your right pocket after the constables boarded the vessel?"

"That's right. When I went to my cabin with them."

"Sir, do you know whether young Simon Ladner was, in fact, a practiced and expert pickpocket?"

"*Objection!*" Sir Barnabas roared, leaping to his feet.

The judge took him into his gaze. "And what is your objection, Counsel?"

"Mr. Snopes is introducing the purest speculation to confuse this jury, and in the process he's maligning a deceased child unable to defend himself."

"Am I to take from my learned colleague's comments," William replied calmly, "that the circumstances of young Simon Ladner's death are now on the table?"

Sir Barnabas's eyes widened. "Of course not! This is trickery of the lowest order. Just what I was led to expect from this barrister!"

Now they're awake, William thought, looking to the faces in the jury box.

"Gentlemen!" the judge called. "Into my chambers. Now!"

Behind closed doors, the judge turned on counsel—and particularly William—his face hot. "What is the meaning of this, Mr. Snopes?"

"My lord, I'm entitled to suggest alternatives to the jury other than Sir Barnabas's allegations for our inability to locate the Letter of Marque."

"Yes, but do you have any proof whatsoever to support this theory?"

"In fact, I do. But, my lord, I must have some opportunity to touch upon the Ladner boy's death to pursue it."

The magistrate shook his head. "You're tenacious, Mr. Snopes. I'll grant you that." He looked to Sir Barnabas. "What do you say to this?"

"My lord, the courtroom isn't a hall of mirrors for Mr. Snopes's amusement to confuse the jury. I'd like to know precisely what proof Mr. Snopes has that the key to Captain Tuttle's cabin drawer was pickpocketed and this fictitious letter stolen."

Of course you would. "And I'd prefer not to outline my case for my opponent," William responded.

The judge looked at William skeptically. "Your leash just got even tighter, Mr. Snopes. I will allow limited inquiry as to the circumstances of the boy's death to make your point during your case in chief, and on your present cross-examination of your client. But limited inquiry only. And, Mr. Snopes," he said with a glare, "you'd better have the evidence you claim."

They returned to the courtroom, William feeling half pleased and half as though the judge's leash had changed to a noose about his own neck.

Nevertheless, William renewed his attack. "Captain Tuttle, I ask again. Do you know whether young Simon Ladner was, in fact, a practiced and expert pickpocket?"

"I did not know that, no."

"Were you aware that he was the protégé of the master of a canon named Lonny McPherson?"

"No, sir."

"Do you know how or why this Lonny McPherson would have placed Simon Ladner on the *Padget* for her voyage to the Indian Sea?"

"No, I do not."

William's mind was moving only a bit faster than his lips. "Is it true, Captain, that the Ladner boy was shot and killed on the night the constables and soldiers seized your vessel?"

"Yes, it is. Right beside me. Almost immediately after Simon returned with the gun from my cabin."

"Who fired the fatal shot?"

"I don't know. I believe it came from a constable or soldier onshore."

"And afterwards, with this poor boy dead, who removed his body from the ship?"

"One of the soldiers or constables did, I suppose, as my crew wasn't permitted to leave."

"If the Letter of Marque was secreted on the boy's person, it would have been removed from the *Padget* along with his body."

"Yes."

"And presumably fallen into the hands of the soldier or constable who removed his body, yes?"

"Yes, sir."

William could see Sir Barnabas from the corner of his eye. He looked flushed but not yet panicked. "And the Letter has not been produced to this day?"

"That's correct."

"No further questions."

William took his seat, his shirt wet with perspiration. Now he'd done it. He'd taken a line he had no evidence to support. No Lonny. No bloodstained letter. He was improvising now, developing his theory in open court from the bits and pieces of things he knew.

Calming himself as Sir Barnabas finished with a few more questions, William realized that he cared little about what happened to himself now. If things went poorly, his fate, at the worst, paled next to that of Captain Tuttle's. But it was still a fact as clear as the glower on Judge Raleigh's face that if he failed to find the evidence he'd promised, his career as a barrister would end with this trial.

40

KELTIN FARM
ESSEX

A whipping wind raised moonlit snow devils on fields surrounding the road. Madeleine sat next to Roisin, who drove their wagon between low hedgerows, the women's scarves pulled up, the heads of their shaggy draft horses down. "We're to meet at the barn," Roisin muttered through the woolen cloth.

Shivering, Madeleine nodded back.

The farmhouse appeared after a long curve in the road. No candles shone through the windows. Roisin flipped the reins, and the horses picked up their pace as they neared the shelter of the darkened barn just beyond, its doors already flung open. She drove the horses inside and called "Whoa!" just as Madeleine heard footfalls crossing the hay-strewn floor, followed by the sound of the barn door shutting behind them.

A lantern lit. The American emerged from the darkness, holding the lantern high. Madeleine could make out others in the shadows and the shape of another wagon against a wall, filled deep with chests and boxes.

"Roisin, my darling," the American said, "this wasn't the party we arranged."

"Now, don't be gettin' flippant with me, Mr. Turner," Roisin said, tying off the reins and stepping down. "Hear the girl out. It's in your interest as much as hers."

Madeleine climbed down to face the man. She'd prepared herself for hours but still had to fight the tremor in her voice as she began to speak.

"The trial about my ship, the *Padget*. It started yesterday."

"I know," the American replied. "Everyone in London knows."

"There's a man we've been trying to find. He's important to our winning the trial."

"The very best of luck with that."

"I need your help in finding him."

"My help?"

"Yes. It's the first mate from the *Padget*, a man named Quint Ivars. He's disappeared. He has important testimony to offer."

"What have I got to do with it?"

"We've searched every merchant ship and company in London, and he's not signed on to any of them. I think he may have joined a smuggler's crew. It would have been in the last few weeks."

"Maybe he signed on with no crew at all."

"Maybe. But the *Padget* crew wasn't paid. He'd be needing work."

The American lowered the lantern, driving shadows across his face like a torn mask. "You'll understand that we don't get involved in legal affairs, Miss Jameson."

"If we don't find this man, we'll lose the case."

"Which will be a pity."

"More than a pity, Mr. Turner. There's not enough furniture or china or anything else left at Heathcote Estate to pay half of what you're owed. And that's if you beat my solicitor to it for the money we borrowed from him. If we don't win this case, you'll come away with nothing."

"Then, as I've already told you, there'll be a special kind of hell to pay."

She had no need to feign the anger and frustration rising in her. "Are you a businessman or a thug? If you want to be a highwayman, then sell your ship. If you want to be a trader, then help me. If we bring back this Quint Ivars, you'll get paid. If we don't, you won't. It's a simple proposition, even for an American."

Turner stood quiet, staring at Madeleine as though reevaluating her. He walked across the barn floor to one of the other men. Roisin drew close and put an arm around Madeleine.

When the American returned, he shook his head. "Given the time frame, there are only two possibilities I'd know anything about. Two of my competitors ply the waters of the eastern counties this time of year—though neither is bold enough to tangle with us here in Essex. If they're in those waters, one is likely north, the other south. Even if your first mate is aboard one of them and we can convince his ship's captain to give him up, it would be nigh impossible to locate both in time to get your man to London. Your luck's not been terribly good of late, has it, my lady? Nonetheless, north or south, you'll have to take your pick."

41

ABOARD THE AMERICAN'S SHIP
NORTH SEA OFF THE COAST OF SUSSEX COUNTY

In a steady, stabbing rain, the American smuggler's brig, the *Narragansett*, topped a wave's crest, creaked, then teetered over to slide to the bottom of the next swell only to begin again. Colder than she thought she'd ever been, Madeleine gripped a hatch cover to steady herself. Nausea accompanied her shivering as she strained to make sense of the careening waves, the snapping of sheets and canvas above her, and the horizon of land sliding in and out of view only a few miles distant.

"If you're going to be sick, my lady, it's best for all that you take it to the side."

She didn't look at the American, who'd arrived at her elbow. "I'll be fine, Mr. Turner," she said loudly over the wind and her chattering teeth. "I've never been on a ship in a storm, that's all."

The American shook his head. "This is no storm. These are your English seas in winter."

Bundled tight in a woolen sweater and topcoat, the American steadied himself with a hand gripping a rope ladder rising to the main gallant above them. Crew members passed by, heads down, unconcerned, tending to their tasks.

"That," the American said, pointing toward land, "is the shore of Sussex County, adjoining mine and Roisin's territory in Essex. Sussex is Geoffrey Singleton's run. I'd heard he was in these waters, finishing a trip from the Americas. We'll know soon enough if your choice to go south was the right one."

She'd chosen south when they'd reached the sea, hoping it would be easier to catch the other vessel sailing with the wind, particularly if the ship they sought was at anchor. She'd had several hours to think about it as Mr. Turner accompanied her back to his ship, riding together on a borrowed mare, leaving the crew members who'd accompanied him to finish distributing goods. It was the only notion she had for making a choice, though Madeleine knew that catching a ship was no guarantee that the first mate they sought would be aboard.

"Assuming Mr. Ivars is aboard Singleton's ship," Mr. Turner broke into her thoughts, "why do you think he'd agree to accompany you back to face the risks of trial?"

"I've got an idea on that score," she answered.

"It'd better be a good one." The American stared for several more seconds before saying, "Listen now, you should probably go belowdeck and get warm in my cabin. You'll be no good to me or anyone else if you're crippled by the cold."

"I'm all right."

"Really? You look about to drop. How long have you been awake?"

She thought a moment. "Since yesterday morning." And, she didn't add, she'd barely slept for days before that.

"Nearly twenty-five hours. Go. Use my cabin to rest. There's no shame in it. And no one will trouble you there."

She looked at the American, surprised at his insistence and sincerity. "But you'll come get me if you see anything?"

"Of course."

Madeleine allowed herself to be led to the cabin at the stern, where the captain closed the door and returned to the upper deck as soon as she was inside. In the shelter of the small cabin, she felt instant relief from the wind and rain, her body relishing release from the cold as she sat on the bed.

How absurd this is, she thought. Every hour that passed sent her farther from London, and further away from any hope of returning to trial in time. The chance that Mr. Ivars was even on the ship they were chasing was slim, and her plan to ensure his return to London carried no guarantee of success.

She lay down, closing her eyes. She imagined her cousin Harold's face, young and smiling, the cares of prison gone. He was always smiling and playful growing up—it was no wonder he'd been her favorite, and brother Devon's too. They were so much alike, Devon and Harold.

Sudden pain shot through her. "I'm really trying," she said aloud. Mother and beloved brother, both gone. How would she survive Harold's death as well?

Devon's voice filled her. *"There's no point to it, sister. See to yourself! Move on before they come for you too. You've done your best for us all and for Heathcote Manor. Start anew."*

"No," she whispered. "I'll see this through."

She felt William's arms, holding her as they waltzed. Felt again the haven of safety he'd been in the terrible seas of the ball.

Then her last bit of consciousness fled.

42

"Wake up, Lady Jameson."

Madeleine was shaken, roused from a dream of running and stumbling through black woods with wolves and other creatures close behind. Her eyes came open reluctantly.

Mr. Turner was leaning over her, his nose and cheeks bright red, his coat saturated.

"We've spotted a merchant ship at anchor near shore," he said. "Singleton's schooner."

The crushing truth of where she was came rushing back. "How long was I asleep?"

"Seven hours. Get up now. We're closing fast."

She followed the American on deck. The sun was up, the clouds parted, the freezing rain had stopped. Her ragged sleep in the captain's cabin had hardly been a rest at all, but still the cold air in her lungs brought Madeleine jarringly awake. They were much nearer shore now, sails stretched tight, rolling toward a three-masted schooner with the name *Spirit* painted on her bow. The ship was held by taut anchor lines about a hundred yards offshore.

The American moved among his crew, shouting orders while men aboard the *Spirit* watched their approach, including one with a telescope at its stern. The *Spirit*'s gunports, Madeleine saw worriedly, were open the length of the starboard hull. The mouths of cannons were drawn up, prepared to fire.

The *Narragansett* came about, anchoring against the wind a safe distance from the *Spirit*. Mr. Turner went to the prow, motioning Madeleine to follow.

"Geoffrey!" he shouted across the water separating the ships. "Request permission to come aboard!"

The man with the telescope shouted back, "What for?"

"It's private, Geoffrey. Come now. Our cannons are backed up. We're no danger."

Madeleine watched the captain of the *Spirit* confer with others surrounding him. After a moment, he cupped his hands to his mouth once more. "Come aboard, then! Three only."

The crew launched a dinghy over the *Narragansett*'s side, with Mr. Turner, his first mate, and Madeleine aboard. With long, sure strokes in the rocky seas, the first mate rowed the distance to the *Spirit* and brought them alongside.

A rope ladder was thrown over the schooner's side. Straining with fatigue, Madeleine led the climb, strong hands grabbing her arms as she neared the gunwale. When the first mate and the American were on board as well, a man dressed in heavy winter garb pushed through the sailors who'd helped them aboard. His face was narrow and pinched raw from the cold, his blue eyes lingering on Madeleine.

"Long time," he addressed the American with an accent Madeleine didn't recognize.

The American nodded. "Long time. And time's in low supply for us just now. Can we talk in your cabin?"

The captain looked at Madeleine again, then pointed to the stern. "You know the way."

Minutes later, alone in the cramped cabin, the American and his first mate stood close to the captain of the *Spirit*, speaking low enough so as not to be heard through the closed doors.

"Geoffrey, I'll get right to it. We're here about a member of your crew."

The captain shrugged. "Needing repairs? I might be convinced to lend you a carpenter, if you're prepared to pay and it's quickly done. Wait. You're not plagued, are you?"

"No. And we don't need repairs on the *Narragansett*. Did you pick up a seaman for this voyage out of London, one named Quint Ivars?"

Singleton leaned back. "Why would I tell you my crewmen's names?"

"Because he's fled to avoid testifying at a trial in London," Turner said. "In a case where I've got a financial stake. This man could make the difference in our winning the case. Come now, Geoffrey. I've handed you a lot of information over the years. Helped you avoid patrols. This isn't so much to ask."

Madeleine listened from behind the American, now ignored. Gusts of wind buffeted and rocked the ship like a metronome counting down the seconds being squandered. Madeleine held herself back from screaming her impatience.

Captain Singleton only shook his head. "You haven't given me *that* much information. Not nearly enough to turn on one of my own crew. How would it look to the rest?"

"This would be a new crewman, Geoffrey. Less than a fortnight aboard. You owe no loyalty to him."

"What kind of captain do you take me for? You've got some guts asking such a thing. Have you forgotten Belfast two seasons past? When you slipped out and left me to that boarding party ashore with nary a word of warning? We barely cleared the port."

"I scarcely learned about the raid before you did. Listen, Geoffrey, if you want to keep count . . ."

The last bonds in Madeleine burst. She elbowed the American aside to step between the men. "Captain Singleton," she addressed the surprise in his expression, "if this man is aboard your ship, we need to get him and leave and do so *now*. We'll also need help from any farmers you know ashore to arrange to rent horses to get us on our way. And if your crewman won't come with us of his own free will, we'll also need you to put him in chains for the trip back."

Singleton stared a moment before his head went back in a roar of laughter. "Who *is* this woman?" he gasped.

"Lady Madeleine Jameson of Heathcote Estate in Essex," Mr. Turner replied matter-of-factly. "She has a financial interest in this seaman we're looking for and the trial, just as I do."

Captain Singleton wiped tears from his eyes, sniffing as his laughter ended. "Well, my fine lady, shall I also arrange an audience for the three of you with the king? What do you say to tea and crumpets at noon? Garn, you're no better than the American here! Tell me why *you* think I'd hand you one of my men to satisfy your interests?"

"Because I'd pay you very well for your trouble."

"You'd pay, eh? *You'd pay*. Well, miss, there's not enough money—"

Madeleine withdrew her hand from a pocket. In it was a necklace with a large dark pearl that glinted in the dusty light of the cabin.

Singleton's eyes widened. Madeleine felt the American stiffen.

"Where did that come from?" Turner demanded.

"It was a gift from my brother, from Spain," Madeleine said. "And it's the last of my jewels. Captain Singleton, I believe this necklace to be worth a fair share of whatever's in your hold. It's yours if you do as we've asked."

Singleton looked from the necklace to Madeleine and back again. Madeleine saw Mr. Turner's hand stray to the pistol in his belt. She prayed it was to protect her and not to claim the necklace for a portion of her debt.

The captain turned and opened the cabin door to shout for his first mate. When the man appeared, he muttered to him, "Get the crewman we picked up just before we sailed."

The first mate left, returning moments later with a thin man with slicked down blond hair. As the first mate led the man into the cabin, the thin man looked about, perplexed and nervous.

"Captain, I—"

"What's your name, sailor?" Captain Singleton cut the man off.

"Logan Thompson, sir."

Singleton looked to Madeleine. "Is this the man you need to testify?"

"I'll need to see his upper left arm to know for certain. The man I seek has a tattoo of a schooner there."

"Show her your arm," Singleton ordered.

"What's this about? I don't—"

"Your arm, seaman. Or you'll be swimming ashore."

The seaman reluctantly removed his coat and rolled up his sleeve. Near his shoulder was a tattoo of a schooner in heavy blue-black lines.

"Yes," Madeleine said. "This man's real name is Quint Ivars."

Captain Singleton leaned close to the seaman's face. "This lady wants you to testify in a case in London . . . whatever your real name is. Are you willing to go?"

The seaman looked about again, this time as though searching for an escape hatch. "No, sir. I've no wish to leave the *Spirit*."

"I understand." Captain Singleton's eye went to the necklace still clutched in Madeleine's hand.

He reached out, took it, and turned to his first mate.

"Place this seaman in irons. He'll be going ashore in the custody of Mr. Turner and this fine lady."

43

THE SHORE OF SUSSEX

The stern lanterns of the *Spirit* were disappearing around a point, leaving the inlet to a panorama of high cresting waves and the anchored *Narragansett*. Reins on three horses, their manes long over winter coats, were held by one of the American's sailors. Two other sailors waited at the dinghy, now pulled high onto shore, that brought them from the *Narragansett*.

Mr. Turner, his first mate, and Madeleine surrounded the sailor from the *Spirit* whose hands were chained before him.

"I told you," Ivars complained, looking damp and miserable. "You don't need to do this. I'll testify as you want."

"I wish I could believe you, Mr. Ivars," Madeleine replied. "If you're now willing to testify, why did you deny your identity aboard the *Spirit*?"

"I was worried was all."

"Of what?"

"Of being arrested in London. Like Captain Tuttle was."

She watched his eyes that wouldn't meet her own. "Why seek work on a smuggler's ship after you left the *Padget*?"

"I couldn't find work elsewhere."

"I don't believe you. Most of your fellow crew members found

314

new berths. You left the *Padget* and went straightaway in search of a smuggler. Why?"

"I told you. With Captain Tuttle arrested, and watching the boy shot and all, I was just scared."

Mr. Turner, listening at Madeleine's side, shook his head. "I don't trust this one. Maybe a pull about in the cold inlet waters will loosen the truth from him."

The sailor went silent.

Madeleine's alarm was growing with each passing minute. But what good would it do to rush back with a witness who wouldn't tell the truth? She needed to penetrate those evasive eyes.

"What do you know about the *Padget* being seized?" she demanded.

"Nothing. I was as surprised as everyone else."

"Do you know a Mandy Bristol?"

"No."

"What do you know about the Crown giving Captain Tuttle authority for the taking of French ships?"

Ivars grew silent again.

"Did you see Captain Tuttle's Letter of Marque before the *Padget* sailed?"

Not a word.

One of the sailors from the dinghy came up the beach toward them. As he approached, Madeleine saw Quint Ivars's eyes widen.

"Captain?" the seaman addressed Mr. Turner.

"What is it?"

"May I speak with you, sir?"

They moved up the beach, speaking quietly. When they returned, the American pointed at Madeleine.

"Seaman Johnston, tell the lady what you just told me."

The sailor took off his wool cap, releasing a forelock to the blustery wind. "Miss, I know this man. I've sailed with him afore."

"When?"

"Three years past. Aboard a brig named the *Helen*, in the waters near Madagascar."

"That's a lie," Quint muttered. "I don't know this man."

"'Tweren't a lie," Seaman Johnston snarled. "You know it's true. Anyhow, I overheard what you were saying just now, about a ship being seized and all. Miss, the same thing happened to us."

"What do you mean?"

"On the *Helen*, our captain told us we were operating under papers from the Crown, allowing the takin' of French ships near the Cape. Captured a big cargo of tea from a French brig headed sou' by sou'-west. Then, when we got back to London, we all got seized by the Crown's men, ship and cargo and crew. Took our captain too. Just like you were saying."

"This man's a liar!" Quint shouted.

"Shut up," Turner growled, pushing him away. "Finish it, Johnston."

The sailor gripped his hat and nodded. "This here Quint? Called himself Pogue back then. And, miss, you spoke of a boy. Well, Pogue brought a boy on board when he come on the *Helen* too. Served as a cabin boy."

"What was the boy's name?" Madeleine asked.

"Billy Doyle. Hard worker, the boy was. Everybody liked 'im."

"What happened to the *Helen* in the end?" Madeleine asked, her heart quickening.

"They kept us all on board a day or two, with the captain elsewhere. Then they let us go, saying we'd be prosecuted for piracy if we said a word of what happened. I heard later our captain got sent off."

"Sent off?"

"Aye. Transported. To Sydney. Heard he agreed to it to keep from a piracy charge. And we never was paid for the voyage neither, miss."

The American stared at Seaman Johnston for a long while. Then he took Madeleine's arm and walked her up the beach.

Early starlight sparkled on the dark foamy waves as Mr. Turner leaned near to be heard. "Lady Jameson, it takes no barrister to know this information could help recover the ship and cargo tied to your captain's trial. Is your barrister up to making it work for us?"

"Yes," Madeleine answered, her mind racing. "Mr. Snopes is an alchemist. I agree that both Quint Ivars and your Johnston could be a boon to our case. We've three horses. I'd like Seaman Johnston to come with me back to London, along with Mr. Ivars."

Turner shook his head. "Johnston will never go to London to testify. You heard him say he'd risk prosecution if he spoke of his experience."

"You could order him to go."

"If I did, he'd simply abandon you somewhere on the road, or worse. And this Ivars, riding in chains? He'll never keep up the rapid pace you need. Nor, I fear, will you, exhausted as you are."

Madeleine wanted to shout her frustration at the resistance and continued delay. "What are you suggesting? That I give up?"

"No. I'm suggesting we first ensure that Ivars will give truthful testimony, and then I'll ride ahead and tell your barrister we're coming so he can prepare. These draft horses have seen better days. They'll not ride fast and will need rest from time to time. And we traveled far south before finding Singleton and his *Spirit*. But I believe I can make it to London by tomorrow afternoon. You'll follow with Ivars on the remaining two horses, hopefully only a few hours behind. Do you know how to use a pistol? If not, you'll have to pretend you do."

Madeleine's arms and legs ached. It hadn't fully dawned on her how hard it would be to complete the long tiring ride ahead through the relentless damp and chill.

"I know how to shoot," she assured him. "Without your Seaman

Johnston to tell his tale, though, we've only Mr. Ivars. How can we be sure that he tells the truth at trial? All of it? Including about the *Helen*?"

"I've got an idea on that score," the American replied, smiling grimly as he led her back down the beach toward Ivars and Johnston.

THE OLD BAILEY

"Where is Edmund?" William whispered, standing next to his solicitor at the bar. The third day of trial and still no word from his junior. Or Madeleine, for that matter.

Obadiah's eyes were clouded with his own worry. "I don't know, sir. I don't understand this."

"He's never liked this case. Could he have grown disgusted and left?"

"No, sir. You know that's not Edmund. He wouldn't do that in a thousand years."

"And you checked again this morning with the Bow Street Runners?"

"Yes, sir. They've got four men searching for Lonny McPherson. But they're saying it's as though he's left town or gone into hiding. Even the children in his canon seem to have disappeared from the streets."

As though he knew they were searching for him. William wanted to spit his anger. This was no good at all.

And sweet Madeleine . . . could she have been abducted?

While he was anchored to this trial, what was happening to everyone around him?

"What about my inquiry about possible forgers?"

"Your friend from the Bow Street Runners, Joel, said to tell you there's not a forger free in London who could pull off a document like a Letter of Marque well enough to fool an expert."

Father Thomas came to the bar, as he did every morning and afternoon to show his support for the captain's case.

"Thomas," William said, "Edmund is still missing. Could you help? Could you check the jails and hospitals? If Edmund's still in London, I've no other notion where to search."

"Of course, William."

In the back of the courtroom, a constable appeared. He looked in William's direction and nodded.

"They've brought Sergeant Rhodes," William explained to Obadiah.

"*All Rise!*"

William returned to his seat as the judge entered. He picked up his notes. Faced the jury box with anticipation. "The defense calls Sergeant Nathaniel Rhodes to testify," he called boldly, while beneath the table his toe tapped out the racing piano notes of Bach's Prelude and Fugue Number 1.

It was going to be just such a day.

Sergeant Rhodes, the soldier William recalled from their evening encounter on the *Padget*'s deck, was garbed in bright red, his tall gray cap resting on the bar that surrounded the witness stand. To strengthen the credibility of his testimony, William had spent longer than usual reviewing his credentials for the jury.

Now that had come to an end.

"All right, Sergeant Rhodes," William began his new tack. "Thank you for explaining your military experience. Now to the present. You're currently stationed at Portman Street Barracks, correct?"

"Yes, sir," the sergeant answered.

"Were you and other soldiers from your barracks assigned the duty, in February of this year, to seize the *Padget* and her captain and crew?"

"Yes, sir. Assisting London constables."

"Who was the head of that detail?"

"I was, sir."

"Did you carry out your duties?"

"Yes, sir, we did."

"Were you told why you were seizing the *Padget* and her crew?"

"Yes, sir. We were told that the *Padget* had committed piracy."

"Who informed you that the *Padget* had committed piracy?"

"Colonel Tollefson of Portman Barracks, sir."

"You carried out your instructions in the middle of the night, did you not?"

"We did, sir."

"Why at such a late hour?"

"I don't know, sir."

"And you awaited the arrival of the *Padget* at the Municipal docks on the Thames?"

"Yes, sir. For several nights."

"How many were you, soldiers and constables together?"

"Ten. Four constables and six soldiers."

The jury was leaning in. Maybe it was the uniform, or anticipation on the heels of the previous day's skirmishes, but either way they were paying attention.

Sweet heaven, please let it go well.

"And just as soon as the gangplank of the *Padget* reached shore, your detail marched to board her, isn't that true?"

"Yes."

"Guns in your hands?"

"Yes."

"Muskets and pistols?"

"Yes."

"Were there any crewmen visible on deck of the *Padget* as you boarded?"

"Only a few, sir, that I could see—including their captain near the gangplank."

"And as you were boarding the ship, gunfire broke out?"

"It did."

"And a young boy aboard the *Padget* was struck by that gunfire, wasn't he?"

"Yes, sir."

"The boy's name was Simon Ladner."

"Yes, I heard the name Simon used when they were trying to care for him, sir."

"Simon was killed, wasn't he?"

"Yes."

"And you chose not to investigate who among the soldiers had fired the shot, isn't that true?"

The soldier straightened. "Why, no, sir. I didn't investigate because I knew who fired the shot."

William went rigid. "You knew?"

"Yes, sir. The captain of the *Padget* fired the shot, sir. Captain Tuttle."

The room was swept with silence. William felt the walls collapsing upon him from all sides.

"Sergeant Rhodes, you are wrong," William heard himself say.

"Objection!" Sir Barnabas roared. "Is Mr. Snopes now testifying for the witness?"

"Sustained. Confine yourself to *questions*, Mr. Snopes," the judge called.

Through the pall of his thundering heart and suddenly cold limbs, William stared at the soldier. "Sergeant Rhodes, didn't we speak only ten days ago, on the deck of the *Padget*?"

"Yes, sir, we did."

"And didn't you tell me on that occasion that the fatal shot that killed young Simon Ladner was fired by someone from your own detail—but you failed to investigate who it was?"

"No, sir. I told you that it was Captain Tuttle."

He was too far in to allow this to stand unexamined. "How in the world could the captain have fired the shot at his own cabin boy?"

"Oh, it didn't appear intentional, sir. As we were approaching the gangplank, I saw that the captain held a pistol. I think our appearance startled him. I saw him drop the weapon, which fired when it hit the deck, striking the boy, sir. At least that's how it looked to me."

William glanced to Captain Tuttle in the dock. The captain had grown ashen and looked near to dropping.

Not this. A lava of rage began to flow. The shrill stirrings of a trumpet's call signaled no piece he recalled ever hearing before.

William leaned toward the witness.

"Have you spoken with anyone else about your recollection of that night, other than myself?"

"Only my superiors, sir."

"And what did you tell them?"

"Why, the same, sir."

"That would be pleasant to believe."

"OBJECTION!"

"Mr. Snopes!" the judge roared. "Another such comment and you will be cited for contempt."

"As you say, my lord. Sergeant Rhodes, did Sir Barnabas subpoena you to testify?"

"No. Only you compelled my appearance, sir."

"Do you know what a donkey looks like, Sergeant?"

"I don't understand."

"A donkey."

"Of course, sir."

"Do I appear to be such an animal to you?"

"*OBJECTION!*"

"Because"—William's voice rose over the mounting din inside the courtroom—"who, other than a donkey, would call you to testify in Captain Tuttle's defense, having been told that you would utter such a pack of lies to this jury?"

The gavel pounded again, again, again. The judge shouted for the courtroom to be cleared. Bailiffs descended on the gallery, the jury box, the floor.

William sat down in the midst of it, lost and oblivious to the chaos he'd birthed.

Minutes later, in the privacy of his chambers, Magistrate Raleigh pronounced, "Mr. Snopes, consider yourself in *contempt of this court.* If we weren't nearly through this trial, I'd have you jailed this afternoon. What do you have to say for yourself?"

William felt wrung out and unmoored. "I believe perjury has been suborned here, my lord."

"Are you accusing Sir Barnabas of such heinous misconduct?"

Perhaps. "No, my lord. But there are others with interests in the outcome of this proceeding."

"Who?"

"I don't fully know, sir."

"Unless you have *significant proof*, you'll keep your mouth shut on that topic in my courtroom. Wrap up your defense, Mr. Snopes, and let the jury rule. Then we'll schedule the hearing to determine your fate."

They returned to the courtroom. William looked to the grand clock high on the wall. Only eleven.

If he rested his case now, Captain Tuttle was doomed to the gallows. They had no hope except that Edmund would appear or Madeleine or the Bow Street Runners—someone with evidence that could rescue this sinking ship. And reaching that event required time, a substance rapidly running out for them.

He stepped over to the bar, motioning a pale-faced Obadiah to join him.

"I've been foolish to rely on this singular witness about the shooting," he explained to the solicitor. "Without authority to prosecute, I cared only that the soldiers shot the boy, not which one. Now we'll never find anyone else from the sheriff's detail or amid the constables in time to contradict this witness, nor can we trust that they'd do so. To gain time, I need you to bring the *Padget* witnesses we spoke with, those who have neither testified nor are already scheduled to testify. I need them here to put up as witnesses."

"But, sir, they hadn't much to say."

"I don't care."

"How many?"

"All."

Returning to his place at counsel table, refusing to look in Sir Barnabas's direction, William sifted through his papers as though preparing for a long day. Then he looked up at the despicable form of Sergeant Rhodes, once more in the witness box following their recess.

"Sergeant, I have a few more questions for you," he said.

45

THE OLD BAILEY

"Yes, Mr. Lockman," William intoned, "you completed your apprenticeship aboard the *Hermes*, but then served where?"

Sir Barnabas rose wearily to his feet and addressed the court. "My lord, since Sergeant Rhodes finished testifying, Mr. Snopes has called five witnesses in a row from the *Padget*, and not a soul among them had anything new for this jury's consideration."

"I quite agree," Judge Raleigh said.

William glanced at the clock. Still over an hour till evening recess. Worse still, Obadiah had signaled that he'd located no more *Padget* crewmen to testify. It was a wonder he'd found as many as he did.

The jury seemed stultified; two were simply asleep.

"I'm going to insist that you close your case unless you have more relevant evidence to share with this jury," the judge added.

"May we speak in chambers, your lordship?" William pleaded.

"We may," the judge granted grudgingly.

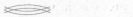

"Mr. Snopes's request is beyond preposterous," Sir Barnabas proclaimed, standing in the judge's chambers with his chin held high. "It is further contempt of your lordship and the jury."

William wanted to run Sir Barnabas through with a rapier at these words, though he knew he'd be arguing the same if their roles were reversed. "Your lordship," he began again, "it's not preposterous. I *do* have a witness pending, potentially critical to Captain Tuttle's defense."

"As I suspected," the judge said. "You *have* been wasting this court's time while hoping for the arrival of this mystery witness. We're concluding the third day of trial, Mr. Snopes. Why isn't he here by now?"

How did he describe Lonny McPherson? Or young Tad? Whomever or whatever evidence Madeleine had gone to find?

He chose to focus on McPherson. "The witness is . . . a fugitive, wanted by authorities for criminal offenses. I'm hoping he will be brought here at any hour today. I implore you, my lord. This is a *capital case*."

Judge Raleigh straightened his wig. "You are correct, Mr. Snopes. A capital case. And as the evidence stands, the jury would be derelict in its duty if it failed to render a guilty verdict against your client. I intend to tell them so in my final remarks." The magistrate shook his head. "No, I simply won't grant you more time. Your antics and delays have betrayed the shallowness of your defense. Now you ask me to push back these proceedings further on the promise of meaningful evidence from a criminal. Well, I won't force this jury to wait another twenty-four hours on your word that such a witness will dissuade them from the obvious conclusions."

The judge glanced at the pendulum clock that stood against a wall. "But it is half past four o'clock now. We'll adjourn for the day. Gentlemen, I'll allow you succinct closing remarks in the morning, after which time I will make my own. I'll see you both at nine."

Heart-stricken, William returned to the courtroom. The judge's explanation and dismissal of the jury were barely audible to him. He watched, distantly, the visitors and jury filing out, along with

Sir Barnabas and his herd of assistants. At the last, only Obadiah remained, seated in the empty lower gallery.

"Judge Raleigh won't relent, will he, sir?" Obadiah said. "He won't give you any more time."

"No, he won't," William replied. "And this once I can hardly blame him. We've been taunting him with ghosts and false witnesses and promises we haven't kept. The thin thread holding our case together is unraveling. Did you see the look on Captain Tuttle's face when the judge announced closing statements tomorrow? Once this jury rules and Raleigh sentences the captain to the gallows, all we'll have left will be an appeal to the king's pardon—unlikely after all of this."

Obadiah shook his head. "I can't believe it, sir. It shouldn't have turned out this way."

"Yet here we are." William began gathering his papers.

The courtroom doors opened. William looked up.

It was Father Thomas, his face gray. "I've found Edmund," he said. "Please. You must hurry."

WESTMINSTER INFIRMARY
LONDON

Soft sunlight came through the high stained-glass windows of the hospital ward. Edmund lay prone in a bed along one wall, his head bandaged, his left arm in a sling. One eye was black and swollen shut. His voice barely carried over a whisper.

"I met someone I knew, a journalist," Edmund was saying in barely a whisper. "He was supposed to be putting me in touch with another witness whom I thought showed promise. Instead, they attacked me. I would have gotten word to you sooner, sir, but just awoke this afternoon."

His junior's face filled William with worry. "Did you see them? Would you know if you saw them again?"

A spasm of pain crossed Edmund's face. He exhaled. "Other than the man I already knew, no. I was attacked ... from behind."

William strained to master his resurging anger. "You should have spoken with me before you went off chasing evidence like that," he said, not unkindly.

Though his face was already mottled purple, Edmund's shading deepened. "I thought I could manage it. As I said, I went to see someone I knew. A journalist who wrote some of the nasty articles about you and the lady. I demanded he tell me who was behind them. I was sure it would be those behind the captain's prosecution." His open eye closed. "If I'd gotten in even a single swing, I'd feel better about it all."

Obadiah shook his head. "Why attack Edmund for that inquiry? Why not me at the docks? Or you, Mr. Snopes, in Whitechapel?"

"Perhaps Edmund was closest to the truth," William answered. "Or maybe they waited until trial to throw off our efforts in court." Madeleine's face sprang to William's mind again, fueling fresh worry.

"How's trial going?" Edmund asked weakly.

"Fine," William said.

Edmund's eye opened a slit. "I see no evidence of that on Obadiah's face."

What point was there in further lies? "We've had some serious setbacks, Edmund," William acknowledged. "And now old Raleigh has said we must rest our case in the morning." He explained the state of the evidence, his recent conjectures, and the witness he'd hoped in vain might arrive.

A dour white-capped nurse arrived, a cloth in one hand and a tray in the other. William saw that the latter was filled with leeches.

"I must ask you fine gentlemen to leave the lad to rest," she said curtly. "At least for an hour or two."

William and Father Thomas rose. "Don't trouble yourself, Edmund. You focus on getting well."

"Is there nothing you can do to delay, sir?" Edmund squeezed out between swollen lips. "Any excuse?"

William smiled to hide his despondency. "Perhaps if I were to die in my sleep," he replied. "Though even then, it's likely Judge Raleigh would order me to make my closing statement before my own judgment was rendered."

46

ROAD TO LONDON
SUSSEX COUNTY

In the fading light of the winter afternoon, the horse in front of Madeleine swayed rhythmically. The patchwork of white on the roadsides melded into a dull blur of gray, then disappeared altogether. She began rolling forward, her reins slackening.

She barely registered as her hand, resting on the pistol the American had sent with her, slid gently away to her side.

Her horse stopped, causing a jolt. Madeleine stirred and caught herself. She squeezed her eyes to bring moisture and sat up straight.

Quint Ivars, her prisoner, stopped as well, pivoting in his saddle just ahead to survey her.

Madeleine grasped the pistol again.

Ivars kicked his horse, moving on.

Captain Turner had ridden on ahead many hours before, leaving them to crawl toward London at a snail's pace. It would be far into evening, or even into the next day, before they reached the city. She doubted she could stay awake to make it. It wasn't just fatigue, but the numbing chill that the steaming horse beneath her couldn't dispel. Even at this pace, she feared the horses would soon give out. Meanwhile, her prisoner would keep looking for an opportunity to escape.

She thought on it for a moment. Then, settling deeper into her saddle again, she allowed her eyes to flutter shut. Drifted forward.

Through the slit in her eyes, Ivars looked about again. Seeing her wavering, he kicked his horse gently, urging it toward the side of the road to let her pass.

She opened her eyes and raised the pistol, pointing it at the first mate. "My father taught me to hunt rabbits when I was six," Madeleine called out. "My proficiency pleased him very much. Do you think I'd miss a rabbit of your size from this distance?"

The first mate reined his horse back onto the road in front of her.

That might hold him a bit. But for how long?

The weary horses notwithstanding, she must risk speeding the pace.

"Faster," she ordered the first mate, then gave her own mare a kick.

47

FLAT OF WILLIAM SNOPES
SOMERS TOWN
LONDON

The cab rounded the corner, the driver drawing in the reins to halt the horses in front of the tobacconist's shop and William's flat. Burdened nearly to collapse with fatigue, William stepped from the cab into darkness, reaching up to pay the driver.

As the cab pulled away, William's hands began to shake. He took several long breaths and grasped them together to steady them. He'd chosen to return to his flat out of a desire for one comfortable night's sleep. At least the mob was finally gone, as Thomas had said. But now that he faced the flat, he was almost too weary to tackle the stairs to his rooms.

Standing a moment in the quiet, frosty street, William whispered a heartfelt prayer for a better tomorrow. He was just finishing when he heard a scuff of shoes on pavement.

William listened a moment, then looked about. "Is that you, Lonny?" he called. "You and your ape who did in Edmund so cowardly? Have you come for me now? Come into the open; I won't run away. Show your face. See what it's like to fight someone who's facing you."

Nothing stirred. It must have been an echo of his lacerated conscience for his taking this case. Shaking his head, William moved to the door, taking the steps to his flat like he was hiking up a mountain trail.

More thoughts crowded each step. He'd avoided political cases since Bristol's case in his youth. He should have stuck with that sentiment and never accepted the *Padget* affair. Then Madeleine and the captain could have hired a lawyer with the wisdom to convince them to accept Barnabas's offered arrangement. Madeleine would have lost her estate—but she was about to anyway. At least the captain would have had a chance, if he could survive transportation. What madness had led him to believe he could overcome Sir Barnabas, the Crown, *and* the investors—and whoever else might be behind this scheme? By taking the case and losing it in such grand style, all he'd achieved was the death of an innocent man.

Just beyond the last bend in the staircase ahead, he heard breathing.

Were they going to take him from both sides? He listened for the door to the street below to open.

"*Snopes?*" a voice called above him.

William didn't recognize it. He stepped tentatively up to the last landing.

On the floor atop the stairs sat a tall man, his thick shoulders slumped wearily.

"Who are you?" William commanded.

The man's voice was exhausted. "Can we talk inside?"

Too tired to protest, William edged past to open the door to his flat.

Inside, William lit a candle before turning his attention to the man, who had now dropped onto the sofa. In the dim light, he saw that he had long tangled hair falling nearly to his shoulders. His coat was stained, as were his tall boots. His eyes were bloodshot, his lips chapped from the cold.

"Who are you?" William insisted again.

"It wasn't easy finding you, Snopes. I arrived too late to catch you at the courthouse. It took some asking around to find your home. Sorry for my appearance. My horse gave out ten miles outside of London."

"I've let you into my flat," William said, his voice hardening. "Now I insist you tell me who you are or else be on your way."

The man coughed. "I'm an American," he said hoarsely. "Sent here with an urgent message."

"A message? From whom?"

"From Lady Jameson. She asked me to convey to you that she's captured the first mate of the *Padget*, Quint Ivars, and is on the road to London bringing him now."

A rush of blood returned life to William's aching limbs. "Is Madeleine all right?"

The American's eyebrows rose. "Madeleine? Yes. She should be. If Ivars hasn't overpowered her on the road."

His relief was overwhelming. Then he thought of the man's words. "Why were you with her?" he asked. "How do you know her?"

"We have a business arrangement."

"What kind of arrangement?"

"That's not your concern. But it means I've got an interest in the *Padget* and your case."

William thought a moment. His thoughts coalesced on the most likely explanation, one which brought a flare of anger. "You lent her money to acquire the ship, didn't you?"

The American stared back, clearly reading his reaction. "Do you want to know what Ivars has to say or don't you?"

"Yes, tell me."

"I only had time to hear part of the story, but the first mate was hired by a soldier to join the *Padget* crew and bring along a boy to steal a paper from the captain's desk when the ship returned to London. Ivars was supposed to help get the paper off the ship. They were paid a pretty big sum for the work."

"The paper was a Letter of Marque?"

"Yes."

Ivars's assistance was news indeed, the rest of it a confirmation of his conjecture. "The boy pickpocketed the captain's key as they landed, didn't he?" William asked. "And returned it after he stole the paper from the desk?"

"That's what Ivars claims, yes. But there's more. They'd done the same with another ship, the *Helen*, a few years before." The American went on to explain the seaman's story.

Both exuberance and devastating disappointment warred within William.

"It's almost worse to learn of this now," he said to the American, "because it's too late. The judge has told us that our case is closed. Even if Ivars arrives in time, the jury will deliberate tomorrow without hearing the first mate's testimony."

"That can't be. That's not justice. Your jury needs to hear this evidence."

"I agree. But I've exhausted every arrow in my quiver and more the past three days, trying to delay. The judge despises me."

"Come, you're a *barrister*. In fact, Lady Jameson insists you're one of the best."

Had she really said that? "Truly?" William responded.

"Yes. Don't tell me you're giving up so easily. There must be a way."

"Not unless I die in my sleep." He repeated the fatalistic statement he'd made to Edmund earlier.

As he finished those words, a vision came to him of Edmund in the infirmary.

The American stiffened, seeing the sudden change in William's face. "What is it? What are you thinking?"

William hesitated, silently staring at the floor, trying to decide if he was willing to do this. He'd need Father Thomas to make it work. But would the Father help him?

He at least had to try.

"I'm thinking, sir," he answered the American at last, "that a dear injured colleague of mine has taken a turn for the worse."

48

THE OLD BAILEY

"Why are you telling me this? Do you expect me to sanction a lie?" the Father protested at a vehement whisper. "You really expect me to join you in saying that Edmund is near death, when that doesn't appear to be true?"

Standing at the bar, William nodded. "Yes. That is why I'm telling you this. Either the judge or Sir Barnabas or both will *certainly* ask you to confirm my attestation to that fact. If you care whether Captain Tuttle lives or dies, you must answer them 'yes'."

"You're asking me to lie, William Snopes. Lie to a judge in a court of law, no less."

"Not really. How many times have you told me that '*in your sinful nature, you are daily partaking of death*'? You've insisted so to me for as long as I can remember. Doesn't that apply equally to Edmund?"

"You're twisting things again. Monstrously so."

"Thomas . . ." William paused, took a deep breath. "I can think of no other means to obtain a continuance than what I've proposed. Without a continuance, Captain Tuttle will surely be convicted and likely hanged. Don't tell me your scruples prevent you from a small deception that could save the life of an innocent man. Surely there's provision for that somewhere in the Bible."

"If you were half the barrister you believe yourself to be, you'd find a way to get the continuance without asking a priest to lie to a judge. This is no small matter to me, William, and no jest."

"Tell that to him." William pointed to Captain Tuttle, who was being escorted to the dock. Rings surrounded his hollowed eyes. His proud head looked near to teetering on his neck with weariness and despair.

"*All rise!*" the bailiff called.

The judge looked sprightly as he entered the courtroom. Pleased to have the trial nearly over, William guessed. Sir Barnabas appeared equally as energized at counsel table, a stack of notes before him belying the notion of a succinct closing statement. The jury seemed eager to be done as well. No one was slouching this morning, their collective attention seeming refreshed.

"Very well," the judge began as he sat. "We will now—"

"My lord," William called, rushing to stand at counsel table. "I'm very sorry, but I must beg the court's indulgence for a brief meeting in chambers."

Judge Raleigh looked as if he wanted to skin William alive. For a moment, William thought he would refuse. Then, with tight lips, he nodded.

On his way out of the courtroom, William looked over at Father Thompson. The priest's head was lowered, his eyes downcast.

"Now what do you want, *Mr. Snopes*?" the judge barked as soon as the chamber door was closed and himself seated, with Sir Barnabas standing stiffly near the door with arms crossed. "I expect you to keep this very brief."

"My lord," William said, "a tragic circumstance has arisen that forces me to ask for a short continuance of the trial."

The judge's head was already shaking. "What possible circumstance would lead you to believe I'd grant a continuance after our discussion yesterday?"

"It's my junior, Edmund Shaw, my lord. He was severely beaten by thugs two days past. I learned that he was in hospital only yesterday afternoon."

The judge leaned back in his chair. "Really? How severe is it?"

"Quite severe."

"Is he dying, Mr. Snopes?"

Instantly, Father Thomas's face came to mind. All the lectures, all the preaching. *"You'll go too far someday, William."* The Father's admonition. *"You'll stain both yourself and others in your zeal to win at any cost."*

William took a breath. "No, my lord. But I would like to be at his side as he recovers. The boy was an orphan. I'm like a father to him. He has no one else. I ask for a continuance to assist with his care."

The judge looked stunned. Sir Barnabas's posture conveyed absolute disbelief.

"This is a pack of lies, my lord," Barnabas snorted. "Mr. Snopes has manipulated this court for three days and is attempting to do so again. What proof does he have? For all we know, he's sent his junior on a holiday to support this absurd request."

"What proof *do* you have?" the judge asked William.

"Other than my word? I have the word of an Anglican priest, my lord. Father Thomas Neal."

"Where is this priest?"

"He's here at the trial. I can bring him back to chambers if your lordship requires it."

"I do."

William returned to the courtroom. Father Thomas sat in the gallery, lips tight together. William went to his side.

"The judge has asked you to come," he told the priest.

"And tell him what?"

"The truth."

Looking suspicious, the priest nodded. Somber, gripping a Bible in his hand, he followed William into chambers.

After William introduced Father Thomas to the magistrate, he said, "Father, please tell Judge Raleigh of Mr. Shaw's condition."

"Mr. Shaw was severely beaten the day before yesterday and rendered unconscious," Father Thomas replied. "At Mr. Snopes's request, I'd been searching for the boy, who is also one of my parishioners. I located him at the Westminster Infirmary."

"And Mr. Shaw's condition?"

"I'm not a physician, but his injuries appear to be quite serious."

"Would you say he's near to death?"

The Father closed his eyes, hesitating, as William held his breath. "No, your lordship. He will recover."

The judge nodded, then turned to William. "I can scarcely see how you can expect a continuance when your junior is expected to recover."

"But, my lord," Father Thomas spoke up, "there is a further consideration."

William's attention snapped back to the priest.

"And just what is that?" the judge asked.

"I happen to know—by Edmund Shaw's own confession to me—that Mr. Snopes's junior has an abominable gambling habit. In fact, he admitted to me privately last evening that one of the men who beat him was a fellow gambler. I believe there is a reasonable likelihood that, if not properly protected, if left alone, Mr. Shaw will be subject to attack again—perhaps even in the hospital as he lies unguarded."

Astonishing. William felt the judge's eyes turn to him.

"Is this true?" the judge asked, staring at William.

"I . . . I have suspected that my junior struggled with . . . some vices, my lord," he replied. "But I've not been previously informed of Mr. Shaw's weakness for gambling."

"Has he *any* family who can arrange for his protection?"

"No, my lord. As I said, he's an orphan, apprenticed under my watch."

Beyond belief, the judge had paused and was considering the request.

Sensing the turn, Sir Barnabas grew apoplectic. "My lord, if you're seriously considering this . . . this *preposterous excuse* for proceeding, I *demand* to see this Mr. Shaw for myself!"

It was a wonderful mistake. Immediately William nodded his assent. "I've no objection, your lordship," he said, knowing that the round trip would take too long to avoid dismissing the jury for much or all of the day, particularly in morning traffic.

"Very well," the judge grumbled. "We'll adjourn to permit Mr. Snopes to be at his junior's side to see to his protection. You may observe the young man as well if you wish to, Sir Barnabas. But I will allow twenty-four hours only. In that time, Mr. Snopes, you must make whatever arrangements are necessary for his care. Tomorrow you will be back here prepared to make your closing statement."

"Of course, my lord."

William accompanied Father Thomas from the chambers. As they stepped into the courtroom, his hand brushed the Father's. For an instant, he took it and gripped it hard.

"All rise!" the bailiff called once more.

William thought of the American, who'd left before dawn on William's horse to find Madeleine on the road and speed her arrival to London. This continuance had bought him a single day. Even if Madeleine and Quint Ivars arrived in that time, there still was no assurance the first mate would be allowed on the stand. In fact, the odds weighed heavily against it.

Yet, William reminded himself, less than half a day ago they were as good as through.

Under the circumstances, he decided as he gathered his papers, it would be unseemly and ungrateful to ask Father Thomas to join his prayers for more.

49

ROAD FROM SUSSEX TO LONDON

A loud *bang*. The world jumped beneath her.

Madeleine came suddenly awake.

A deep breath filled her lungs with chill air that brought a shiver. Early morning light washed over her. The reins were loose in her hands. She tugged on them to calm her pacing, frightened horse. As her mind cleared, she saw that they were beside a gravel road, bounded by fields of hay stubble.

Where was she? How had she gotten here?

"First Mate Quint Ivars," she said aloud. The man and his horse were nowhere to be seen.

On the ground lay her pistol, smoke curling from its barrel. It must have fallen from her grasp in her sleep and fired when it struck the earth. That and her mare's reaction had startled her awake.

She slid from the mare to retrieve the pistol. Weak as a baby, it took her half a dozen tries to return to the saddle.

Ahead, the road disappeared through a patch of tall oak. Her legs barely responded to her command when she kicked her horse's flank to go. The mare obeyed resentfully. The poor animal was as exhausted as Madeleine. She'd have to leave her at the next farm they passed.

Time meant nothing now. She could have been sleeping minutes or days. It no longer mattered. The last hope of winning her cousin's case was gone with Ivars's escape.

The horse walked slowly on toward London. It took all the strength of body and spirit that Madeleine could muster to even stay upright in the saddle.

LORD BRUMMELL'S RESIDENCE
LONDON

Alone in his library, Lord Brummell again opened the note, hand-delivered through the back entrance not half an hour before, and read:

> *"Your bumbling barrister has managed his continuance after all. Have you a plan for what's coming?"*

Crudely printed to avoid revealing its author, Lord Brummell had no doubt as to who'd sent it. The little princess, worried again. Was she ever not? The fact that she had reason this time didn't make it any more palatable to the lord.

What does Snopes have up his sleeve now?

Everything should be fully settled. Snopes's junior, stopped in his attempt to ferret out their contacts at the newspapers. The captain's solicitor, Mortimer, still in Edinburgh. Lady Jameson happily disappeared. Snopes finished with every available witness from the *Padget*, gaining nothing. Mandy and the McPherson fellow safely bundled away.

With all that had gone right the past four days, the jury should have received their summation and reached its inevitable verdict by now.

Then Snopes got his continuance.

What was he up to?

Ah, the princess was right—admit it. It would be foolish to make no plan for Snopes coming up with more evidence. But then plans required people to do his bidding—and Mandy and his lieutenants were in storage.

Though, he supposed, there was still one.

Brummell pulled out a blank sheet of stationery, lacking any name or address, and scribbled a hasty note. Satisfied, he summoned a servant.

"Take this to Portman Barracks in Marylebone. Ensure that it's delivered to a Sergeant Nathaniel Rhodes and to no one else. Stay as long as you must if he's not immediately available. And hurry."

50

ROAD TO LONDON

As the sun rose, the road grew busier about Madeleine, riding at her slow pace. Merchant wagons passed headed toward London; another rolled by hauling lumber. A troop of soldiers trundled past, marching the other direction at an easy jaunt. Several whistled at Madeleine until an officer shouted them down.

The high sun and relenting clouds warmed her early in the day, helping her stay awake. Now, in late afternoon, with the clouds dropping closer to earth, her eyes grew heavy again, demanding sleep.

The smell of coal fires was growing, the air becoming hazier. London must be near. Not that it mattered anymore. The trial was surely over, and she had little hope for the outcome. What could have happened to Mr. Turner? Maybe he'd met up with the first mate along the way and conjured a plan for both of their profits. The American probably promised to aid Mr. Ivars so he'd testify for the Crown, in exchange for recovering his loan from the *Padget*'s sale. Roisin was right. She never should have trusted the smuggler.

It was late afternoon, the road empty under dusky skies as it had been for over an hour, when a horse emerged from a copse of

TODD M. JOHNSON

sycamore ahead, coming her way. The animal was frothed with sweat, its tongue far out. It struggled to maintain an uneven trot. Madeleine squinted.

It was Quint Ivars.

Her mind cleared. Why was he coming back this direction? Why wasn't he already hidden in the maze of London?

Ivars saw her. His head swiveled, taking in the high hedges along the sides of the road that prevented him from reaching the surrounding fields. He flicked his reins. The exhausted horse grudgingly picked up its step.

He was charging her.

She should ride to the side of the road and let him pass. What purpose would it serve to try to stop him?

"Hi-yah!" She reined her mare sideways in front of the approaching animal and rider. "Stop, Mr. Ivars!" she shouted, expending the last of her strength.

The first mate yanked his reins to try to slip around her. Madeleine tugged on her own, backing the mare fully into his path once more.

He was twenty yards away when she remembered the discharged pistol in her pocket. Withdrawing it, she cocked it with both hands and raised it to the first mate's chest.

Ivars's eyes widened. He yanked on the reins, bringing his animal to a halt not ten feet away.

"You wouldn't shoot me, miss," the first mate growled.

"Perhaps not yesterday," she answered.

Over the first mate's shoulder, she glimpsed another rider emerge from the woods. His face was too distant at first, but she'd know that horse anywhere, even far away. It had a chestnut coat and black legs and mane. She first saw it the day the barrister visited her estate, two weeks and a hundred years ago.

It was William's handsome bay.

51

"Edmund, I feel so very close to understanding it all," William whispered. "We have so many pieces. Just not the assembled whole."

Asleep, Edmund didn't stir in his hospital bed. The young man's recovery was encouraging. He was breathing evenly, and the swelling had already subsided. Surely a sign of youth.

"All right then," William continued softly, leaning back in his chair. "Let's try again. The American says First Mate Ivars, if he makes it to the witness stand, will testify that he was hired by a soldier—I'd guess Sergeant Rhodes—to get a berth on the *Padget* and arrange for Simon Ladner to join him. Their true task, however, awaited their journey's end, when Simon was to steal the Letter in Captain Tuttle's desk as the ship docked in London, using his skill as one of McPherson's pickpockets. He then slipped away to the cabin for the Letter, returning the key afterward. The first mate helped, in some fashion, to shepherd the paper off the ship when the constables and soldiers arrived to arrest the captain and crew, as previously planned. Ivars likely forewarned his masters of the *Padget*'s coming arrival with a mail packet when the ship was in Gibraltar. Added to these facts is that this scheme had been carried out at least once before, presumably for the same bosses."

William paused. "Yet I still have no idea what was to be gained by it all."

Footsteps approached from behind.

"Why do you think they didn't destroy the Letter of Marque while still aboard the *Padget*, sir?"

William turned to greet his solicitor. "Obadiah. You needn't have come tonight."

"You'll need some rest for tomorrow, sir," Obadiah said, taking off his hat and sitting. "I'm glad to stay with Edmund awhile."

"I'll not need any rest if that American and Madeleine fail to arrive soon with Quint Ivars in tow. But to answer your question, there wasn't enough time, or seclusion, to destroy the Letter on board. They could do so at their leisure once ashore."

"Then how did they get it off the ship?"

"I suspect the original idea was for the first mate to plead for release of the boy when he and his crew mates were gaoled aboard the *Padget*, a plan ruined when the boy was accidentally killed. Perhaps the first mate sent the paper off the ship hidden on the boy's body. If Sergeant Rhodes was in control of the body and the document, he could have destroyed it later or placed it in the coffin for delivery to Mr. McPherson along with the boy."

"None of this tells us how they manufactured the Letter in the first place, or the scheme's ultimate purpose," Obadiah said. "Or how the poor murdered girl, Isabella, fits into it."

"Agreed. As things stand, until we understand the reason for all these things, we'll never deduce who's behind it. We'll need more help for that. With Simon Ladner dead, and Lonny McPherson disappeared, that help seems unlikely."

"Does it really matter, sir? Isn't the first mate's testimony about theft of the Letter enough to free Captain Tuttle?"

"Doubtful, Obadiah. Sir Barnabas will cross-examine the first mate and make him out a liar, especially after he admits to being brought here forcibly from a smuggler's ship to testify. He'll also confirm that Mr. Ivars has no way of knowing what he alleges he took, since he can't judge a true Letter of Marque from any other legal document. Barnabas will hammer at the paper not being produced and likely demand to admit evidence from the Lord Privy Seal's records showing no such letter was ever issued by the Crown. Add all this to the evidence damning the captain so far, and voilà—Ivars's testimony will smack of desperation or perjury. No, I believe we still must reveal the hands controlling these machinations if we're to prevail."

"The first mate's testimony will at least be a start, Mr. Snopes."

Obadiah's optimism, though never feigned, could still sometimes annoy. Tonight, William just smiled, which was surely Obadiah's goal.

"Yes, it's a start," William replied. "If he arrives, that is. Now, if you approve, I'll get home and hope that Madeleine and Mr. Ivars arrive *sometime* before early morning. We'll never get another day's continuance unless Father Thomas can pray up an earthquake to topple The Old Bailey. With or without the first mate, I'll be in that courtroom tomorrow at nine."

William left the infirmary to trudge the windy London streets. No moon or stars pierced the low clouds overhead. Occasionally he thought he heard footsteps following or tracing his route along the parallel alleyways, but when he stopped to listen, they disappeared. Hunched against the biting breeze, his mind grappled with all the unknowns: their inability to locate Lonny McPherson, the mystery of Mandy Bristol's role, their failure to locate Bristol's investors among those he hobnobbed with.

Mandy Bristol. William recalled his last visit to Bristol's office. The confrontation. The boy, Tad, appearing, and later standing in the street with tears in his eyes. A boy who seemed to be an assistant to Mandy, delivering court orders and appearing in his office—yet who had his own dark skills.

William's mind quickened with it all, swirling like a painted whirligig spinning to the opening of Vaňhal's Symphony in D.

Then it all stopped. Oh, how stupid he'd been.

William reached into his jacket pocket to confirm his new wallet was there, the wallet he'd purchased to replace the one he'd been unable to find since leaving Mandy's office.

"Simon Ladner isn't the only one related to Lonny McPherson," he said aloud to the empty street. "There's Tad too. Simon and Tad were pals: both pickpockets, both members of the same canon. That's why tough, street-hardened Tad was crying after hearing at Mandy's office that Simon was dead. And if Tad is working with Lonny McPherson . . ."

There was a sound in a nearby alleyway, of glass crushed underfoot, then footsteps running away.

William stared in that direction for a moment, broken from his reverie.

He should never have spoken aloud as he had. More stupidity.

With a shiver of concern, and still grappling with his new revelation, he hurried home.

52

FLAT OF WILLIAM SNOPES
SOMERS TOWN
LONDON

William awoke with painful slowness. He was lying on the couch, papers scattered across his chest and on the floor at his side. Pulling a blanket across his shoulders, he shuffled to the table where last night's teapot sat, icy cold. He pushed more papers and a stray shirt aside to light the brazier.

Thomas was right. He should hire a cleaning lady.

The pot settled, he sat again.

He'd pondered his midnight conclusion about Tad to a late hour, then continued to do so in his sleep, which was probably why he'd slept so poorly. Now an image of St. James's Park came to mind, from when he'd stood where the poor Isabella girl had been slain. Isabella, the girl who'd worked at Carlton House and was familiar with and had access to the Lord Privy Seal's books and records. Murdered.

And another puzzle piece settled gently into place.

There was no master forger. They had no need. Isabella prepared the Letter of Marque from templates at Carlton House—a simple task for a modestly trained forger. Even William could have done it. She'd similarly copied the prince regent's signature from myriad documents at her fingertips. Then she'd smuggled the letter out with the genuine seal already placed—again by her.

The explanation fit the facts.

Then why was she killed on the eve of trial? And what was their goal?

William was reaching for a teacup when the door rattled with a hard knock. The knocks grew more insistent as he stumbled to answer it.

The American stood on the upper landing. He gripped the arm of a slight, bleary-eyed man with dirty blond hair and beard. The American pushed him hard into the flat, past Snopes, then followed him in.

"Let me introduce Quint Ivars," the American said. "Mr. Ivars, this is Barrister Snopes."

William rubbed his eyes. "Where's Madeleine?"

"I left her at your solicitor's place."

"She's all right?"

"Exhausted. But she'll be fine."

"What time is it?" he asked, immensely relieved.

"Quarter past eight."

Quarter past eight? "I have to dress," William nearly shouted. "Do what you can to make this man presentable for the stand. There's a bowl of water by the window. Drag a razor over his face and see if you can find any clothes in this room that will fit him. We'll just have to talk with him in the cab ride to the courthouse."

THE OLD BAILEY

William strode out of the judge's chambers and into the courtroom, ahead of Judge Raleigh and Sir Barnabas.

They'd been arguing their positions for nearly half an hour with the judge. The jury looked taxed and impatient with yet another delay. In the courtroom, Father Thomas was seated, head lowered, eyes closed again. Obadiah, in the lower gallery, looked up, uncommonly worried. The perennial observer Lord Brummell, perched in his box seat, appeared oddly pale today. Suzanne, in the middle gallery, wore her usual encouraging smile.

But his gaze lingered longest on Madeleine, seated next to Suzanne. Pale, weak, strained.

But beautiful.

She noticed him and smiled. It brought a sudden draught of strength, though even in his relief he still harbored anger about her lie about the American smuggler.

Obadiah rose and came to the bar. "Sir, what did Judge Raleigh rule? Will he allow the first mate to testify?"

"Yes," William said.

Obadiah's expression of joy instantly faded. "Uh, at what price, sir?"

William sighed. "In exchange for the judge reopening the case and allowing Mr. Ivars to testify, I will accept the judge's contempt charge and resign from the bar without contest—unless the judge agrees that Mr. Ivars's testimony was necessary for the jury to render a fair verdict."

"Oh, sir, no . . ." Obadiah looked like a hammer had struck him. "That's no bargain at all. Why would the judge concede that? A day ago, the man wanted to have you horsewhipped."

"We have no assurance. But at least the jury will now hear the evidence."

"Why do you believe that Ivars will testify to the truth?"

William leaned closer. "Because the American said he promised the first mate that if he tells the truth, he'll be escorted from the courthouse to the American's ship for passage to America, escaping any further proceedings against him."

"And if he lies?"

"The same. Except the man's passage to America will go only half the distance."

"Shall we begin, Mr. Snopes?" the judge said, looking eager to speed his demise.

William resumed his place at counsel table.

"My lord, the defense calls First Mate Quint Ivars to the stand."

"All right, Mr. Ivars. You've explained your experience as a seaman," William summed up. "Now tell this jury what you were hired to do aboard the *Padget*."

Quint Ivars, looking as scruffy and scared as a cornered rabbit, held tight to the banister before him, not looking at the jury.

"I was brought aboard as first mate and physician's mate."

"No, Mr. Ivars," William said. "The jury knows the role Captain Tuttle hired you to perform aboard ship. Please inform them of the other role for which you were hired."

From the corner of his eyes, he noted that at least a few of the jury seemed to be shedding their indifference.

"I was hired to bring aboard a young boy, Simon Ladner."

"Hired by whom?"

"A soldier."

"What soldier?"

"Sergeant Rhodes."

"Would you repeat that a little louder, Mr. Ivars?"

"*Sergeant Rhodes.*"

"Thank you. And who was Simon Ladner?"

"A boy. About thirteen, when we sailed."

"Did this boy have a particular talent or skill?"

"Yes. I was told by the sergeant that he was a gifted pickpocket."

Rustling filled the jury box. William saw Sir Barnabas feigning indifference.

"Did you inform Captain Tuttle that the boy you'd brought aboard to serve as a cabin boy was a pickpocket?"

"No."

"What did you tell Captain Tuttle?"

"That he was the son of a friend, a cobbler from Whitechapel."

"And that was a lie?"

"Yes."

"What were you and Simon Ladner hired to do aboard the *Padget*?"

Hesitation.

"Take your time, Mr. Ivars. We only want the truth."

"Sergeant Rhodes said the boy was to take the captain's cabinet key and use it to steal a letter from the captain's cabin when we reached London at the end of the voyage."

"Take the key?"

"Pick the key, from the captain."

"What letter? A letter to a loved one?"

"No. A Letter of Marque."

The jury's stirring grew into whispers.

"Had you seen the Letter of Marque before the voyage began?"

"Yes. Captain Tuttle showed it to me."

"What was the purpose of stealing the Letter of Marque?"

"I don't know. Sergeant Rhodes didn't tell me."

"But he did pay you for the task, didn't he?"

"Yes."

"Speak up."

"*Yes*."

"How much?"

"Five hundred pounds for me. A hundred for the boy."

"And just what was your part in the theft?"

"I was to do my duties aboard the *Padget* until we finished our voyage. Then I was to make certain that Simon Ladner did his job and got safely ashore in London with the Letter."

"And you have no idea why the Letter of Marque was to be stolen from the *Padget* or who was behind the theft—other than Sergeant Rhodes's hiring of you, correct?"

"That's correct."

"Mr. Ivars, is it also true that this scheme you've described had been attempted at least once before?"

Again, Ivars hesitated before lowering his voice to answer. "Yes, it's true."

"How do you know?"

"Because the Ladner boy and me, we were hired for that one too."

The muttering amid the gallery rose until Judge Raleigh's gavel fell.

"And did you succeed on that first occasion?"

"Yes, we did."

"Your witness, Sir Barnabas," William ended.

Sir Barnabas rose like a lion to the kill.

"Where were you when Mr. Snopes located you as a witness for this proceeding?"

"I was aboard a ship."

"What kind of ship?"

"A . . . merchant ship."

"Did you come here voluntarily?"

"No."

"As I suspected. You're here against your will?"

"I guess so, yes."

"Under threat?"

"I don't know."

"Whose ill-fitting clothes are you wearing?"

"I borrowed them."

"From whom?"

He pointed to William.

"Of course. Now tell me, Mr. Ivars, you claim that Captain Tuttle showed you this purported Letter of Marque aboard the *Padget*. Had you ever seen a Letter of Marque before?"

"No."

"Then what Captain Tuttle showed you could easily have been a forgery."

"I suppose."

"Or simply no form of Letter of Marque at all."

"I suppose."

"And this boy. Wouldn't you agree that he may have been hired to retrieve this letter from Captain Tuttle in order that the captain could claim theft of the forgery before it could be examined by authorities?"

"I suppose so, sir."

"You've accused Sergeant Rhodes of gross corruption and dereliction of duty. Did you know that he is a decorated veteran who served in Spain?"

"No, sir."

"Did you serve?"

"Yes, sir."

"A seaman? No higher rank?"

"That's true, sir."

Sir Barnabas looked to the bench. "My lord, in view of this man's scurrilous testimony, and Mr. Snopes being permitted this surprise witness, I request leave to subpoena the Lord Privy Seal to testify."

"The attendant to the Crown's personal papers?" Judge Raleigh replied. "Sir Barnabas, I'm not certain I have the authority to do so. But, given the circumstances, I'm willing to attempt it if it's within my power."

Allowing a live witness to make the point would only dramatize the matter further. William stood. "My lord, I believe Sir Barnabas wishes the Lord Privy Seal to testify that there is no record in the Crown's papers of either the king or his regent issuing a Letter of Marque to Captain Tuttle prior to his voyage."

"That's correct," Sir Barnabas said, looking surprised at William's pronouncement before the jury.

"I would be happy to stipulate that that is the case," William said.

The judge looked stunned. "You will do so?"

"Yes, my lord."

"Sir Barnabas, do you agree?"

Sir Barnabas looked suspicious. "Yes, my lord."

"Very well. The jury will presume that there is no record in the Crown's papers of either the king or his regent issuing a Letter of Marque to Captain Tuttle before his voyage."

Sir Barnabas returned to the witness as William sat. "Mr. Ivars, you've alleged you do not know who ultimately wished for you and this boy to steal this so-called Letter."

"That's right."

"And since Simon Ladner is dead, he can't provide any helpful testimony either, can he?"

Ivars shook his head. "I suppose that would be true."

Sir Barnabas paused. "I'm sorry, Mr. Ivars. *Would* be true?"

"If he was dead, sir. It would be true if Simon Ladner was indeed dead. But he isn't, sir. Not so far as I know."

The gallery burst like a sudden storm. William looked to Captain Tuttle in the dock, whose face blossomed with disbelief and wonder. Sir Barnabas stood dumbfounded. Judge Raleigh, red-cheeked, pounded his gavel again. "*Silence!* Silence or I will clear this courtroom!"

Despite more gavel pounding, it took several minutes to return the courtroom to quiet again.

"This is preposterous." Sir Barnabas finally addressed the witness once more. "We've heard repeated testimony of eyewitnesses—Captain Tuttle and crewmen—who saw the boy shot."

Ivars shook his head again. "That was us, sir. Our way to get the boy and the Letter off the *Padget*. Sergeant Rhodes was to fire over the captain's head as the soldiers and constables were boarding. The boy had a ripe tomato under his tunic. He crushed it in his shirt as he went down. In moonlight, a tomato stain has the temper of blood."

"That's impossible!" Sir Barnabas cried. "Someone would have detected it!"

"No, sir. As the *Padget*'s physician's mate, I took charge of the boy. I brought his body to the top deck after telling the captain he was dead and handed him on to Sergeant Rhodes, who got him off the ship. The Letter was tucked in the boy's trousers."

"If this extraordinary story is true, then Mr. Snopes would have called the boy as a witness. Where is the boy now?"

"I don't know."

Shaken, Sir Barnabas looked to his coterie of juniors, who stared back, stymied. Sir Barnabas looked next to Judge Raleigh. "My lord, I have no more questions for this . . . this absurd witness."

The gallery had grown quiet, all attention centering on William.

As shocked as everyone else in the courtroom, what was he to do now?

"Mr. Snopes and Sir Barnabas," Judge Raleigh said, breaking the room's paralysis in a voice uncharacteristically low. "Into my chambers. *Now*."

"And you had no inkling of this testimony about the boy, Mr. Snopes?" the judge asked.

"I scarcely had time to interview Mr. Ivars before his testimony, so no," William answered.

Sir Barnabas nodded the same.

"And neither of you know where this Simon Ladner is at present?"

Each man agreed once more.

The judge stood and paced for long minutes before facing counsel.

"Mr. Snopes," he said, "I've been unimpressed with your antics in this trial. In my opinion, you've deliberately obfuscated the evidence in a manner unbecoming of an officer of the court. You've caused delay after delay. As matters stand, I'm not inclined to let you off the hook on my contempt findings. But I will admit that I don't know what to make of this first mate's testimony—whether bold lies, suborned perjury, or hinting of significant events. I can't allow these proceedings to go on forever. But I'm inclined to adjourn for the rest of the day and night. If you can locate this Simon Ladner witness in that time or produce any other witness who can help get to the bottom of Mr. Ivars's unexpected testimony, I'll permit them to be presented to the jury tomorrow morning. If you fail in that search, we will proceed to closing statements."

"But, my lord!" Sir Barnabas blurted out. "The interests of the Crown—"

"Will not be further prejudiced by a single day's delay. And yes, I know this is unusual, particularly as tomorrow is a Saturday. Nonetheless, I will impress upon the jury that their civic duty requires another day more of service, even if it forfeits a common day of rest. That is all."

53

WHITECHAPEL DISTRICT
LONDON

William stood in the midst of the group sheltered in a Whitechapel church from a growing rainstorm. The venue had been arranged by Father Thomas. Joel and Pidger and a third man from the Bow Street Runners had joined them—all that Joel could gather on short notice. Father Thomas had insisted on helping. Behind the group stood Madeleine, present despite William's strongest objections.

"Now we've each got a portion of Whitechapel to cover," William said. "It's too large an area and we've too little time to team together. You'll be searching and asking for Simon Ladner, who's nearly fifteen. And for Tad, about age eleven."

He described the boys' appearances: Simon from Captain Tuttle's recollection, Tad from his own. "Whitechapel was home for both boys. We assume the Ladner boy remained in London after his faked death aboard the *Padget*, though it's possible he's left town. Tad, the younger one, was last seen by me in Mayfair just before the start of trial. Given his age, it seems unlikely he would have left London. We'll search until midnight, then report back here. If you find either boy, blow the whistles I've given you as a signal to return."

The Bow Street Runners shuffled out, umbrellas in hand. Obadiah and Thomas followed, similarly equipped. This kind of search was old hat to the Runners, William knew, and he had no worries for them. He had more concern for Obadiah and Thomas in this rough part of town, though Thomas had worn his collar for whatever protection that might provide.

Alone now, he looked to Madeleine. Her face was pinched and drawn. He wondered that she was still on her feet. She also held an umbrella in one hand, a bag in the other.

"Lady Jameson, I hope you're not so foolish as to consider walking the streets of Whitechapel on a Friday evening alone. If you must, you can accompany me."

"What good would that do?" Madeleine protested dismissively. "We've too few people for this search as it is, and we've already lost hours organizing it. We need to search separately."

"If you refuse to remain here," William fumed, "then I'll be forced to stay behind to ensure that you do."

Her tired eyes smoldered. "You're still angry at me because I didn't tell you about the American smuggler and his loan."

"That has nothing to do with it."

"Really? You lie poorly for a barrister."

A dam crumbled in him. "Do you really want to discuss lying, my lady?"

Madeleine shook her head, a hint of shame coloring her cheeks. "I didn't lie. At my home, you asked if I'd done anything illegal and I hadn't. I didn't engage in smuggling, though I sympathize with some who do. Yes, I borrowed money from the American. That's all. I can borrow from whomever I please and the law has nothing to say about it."

"You knew what I was getting at with my question. If that smuggler's loan had come out at trial—if it still comes out—your cousin's case could topple, finally and irretrievably, and your estate along with it. You and your father may still be prosecuted for piracy yourselves, you know."

"If that happens, I'll have to accept it. But I didn't lie to you; I said what I needed to. Would you have represented us if I'd told you about the loan?"

It was a fair question. "I don't know," he answered.

"Exactly. What have you done this entire case? The same as in all your cases, I imagine. What was necessary to save lives and property for those who could not defend themselves. You've sailed the waters in which you found yourself, weighing your needs against right and wrong, setting your own limits rather than simply hewing to others. Well, I did the same, to save my estate, my family, my community. Have we acted so differently?"

"You know it's different."

"I do not."

"You could at least have told me after the ball."

"And why then?"

That blow struck hardest of all. He recalled the glaze in her eyes as the carriage drew away from the ball, out into the streets. The extra miles they rode until she had full possession of herself again. Talking of family and friends, present, gone, or left behind, to raise her spirits.

Because we left the ball more than client and lawyer, he wanted to say. At least he'd thought so. Perhaps he'd been wrong.

"Please stay here, Lady Jameson," he begged again.

She looked uncertain. Her eyes fell. "We're only wasting time. Go then. I'll be here when you return."

William stormed away, through the church door and into the street, raising his umbrella against the windblown spray.

No matter what she said, he wasn't another version of Mandy Bristol, William thought as he hurried. He didn't manufacture witnesses to line his and his clients' pockets. In this case he'd done and said only as necessary to salvage a verdict for an innocent man.

He'd even done as Father Thomas had insisted and told the truth of Edmund's condition.

Her words to him *were* different. Different because she'd lied to him. She'd lied . . . *to him*. And she'd never corrected her wrong.

Would he care so if she were only a client?

He pushed the argument out of his mind as he headed toward the only part of Whitechapel he knew well: the area surrounding the undertakers' shops he'd visited once before.

54

LORD BRUMMELL'S RESIDENCE
LONDON

"Sergeant Rhodes, I'm afraid this must be done."

Dressed in civilian clothes, the sergeant stood straight-backed in the center of Lord Brummell's study. Like a toy soldier out of uniform, Lord Brummell thought.

"Impressive library you have here, my lord," the sergeant remarked.

"Sergeant, time is of the essence."

"So I gather. But it's no playacting you're asking for, like on that ship or in the courtroom. You've never before asked me to do anything like this."

"Yet it must be done. This Snopes character has gone from nuisance to hindrance to a serious hazard. That includes for you too, Sergeant—your name featured prominently in yesterday's testimony."

"But you said he has no evidence, other than his word."

"True. But they're out searching for evidence as we speak."

"Can they find it?"

"The only witnesses who might assist them have been sent out of the city."

"You're sure?"

"Yes."

"Then why do you want this done?"

"Because at every step of this trial I've been equally sure, or have been reassured, that there was no risk. Each time that's proved untrue. There's only one irreplaceable part in the captain's defense. That is William Snopes."

"And you believe he's searching in Whitechapel?"

"It's the only place that makes sense."

"And that he's there himself?"

"Yes. I'd make a sizable wager he's participating in the search for a witness. You do recall what he looks like from your encounter on the *Padget* and the witness stand, don't you?"

"I do. I also think I'd recognize his walk from his visit to the ship. Light-footed, a bit springy. But if I'm to do this, it would have to appear like a hoisting gone bad."

"A hoisting?"

"A mugging. A theft."

Lord Brummell nodded.

"And I want to be paid enough to leave the ranks. I want to go to America."

"I'd welcome it, Sergeant Rhodes. Rest assured, I'll pay you amply enough for a fresh start."

"Yes, you will." The sergeant turned to go, then stopped in front of one of the shelves to take down a book. "Byron," he said, glancing at the spine. "I've not read this one." He slipped the small volume into his pocket. "I'll take this as a down payment."

55

STREETS OF WHITECHAPEL
LONDON

Stepping around another large puddle, Madeleine's legs chafed in the rough men's trousers she wore, just as the cap covering her hair squeezed her forehead. Suzanne Cummings had tried mightily to dissuade her from secretly borrowing Obadiah's clothes before she left for a cab to Whitechapel. In the end she'd allowed it, when Madeleine pointed out that she'd be in much greater danger if she tried to walk the streets in women's attire.

Suzanne was becoming a close friend. She needed friends. She'd lost all those she thought she had before, perhaps including William.

The hat protected her face from the driving rain, but after spending hours out of doors, the rest of her felt the wet. Even her riding boots, mostly hidden beneath her trousers, were soaked through.

She turned another corner and walked on.

Her argument with William weighed heavily. She hadn't wanted to admit it under his interrogation, but no, she hadn't told him the full truth. But didn't he see that that was before she'd begun to know him? Before she'd watched him work so marvelously hard on Harold's behalf?

Before he'd rescued her from the ball . . .

Hadn't he become another new friend?

Along nearly every street, she'd found one or two people to stop and ask about the boys. Many were women, and Madeleine had no wish to know their business, out in the night like this. When she explained her search for lost relatives, nearly all had tried to help. Madeleine had even ventured nervously into a few pubs, speaking only to those she was sure weren't already inebriated. All had shaken their heads in response to her inquiries.

Madeleine stopped and looked about. Had she already been at this corner? Just ahead, a smallish figure was walking away. It was the first child she'd seen on the streets.

She hurried, catching up and grabbing the figure's shoulder. "Excuse me . . ."

The man who turned had a beard down to his knees. "Whaddya want?"

She shook her head, disappointed, and moved on.

Twice she believed she'd seen one of the other searchers a block or so in the distance. She'd headed another direction each time, not wanting to be discovered helping.

She reached another street corner. To her right, the road sloped upward, taking her to higher ground. Feeling the need to get off the low and grimier streets, she turned that direction.

This was growing intolerable. William had hoped the knowledgeable Whitechapel undertaker who'd helped before might direct him to someone likely to know either Simon or Tad. Fifty shillings had gotten him addresses that proved useless. The same with the pub manager who'd been so helpful only weeks before.

At last, William had begun to simply knock on doors. Half

answered his knocks. Some offered advice on children they'd seen. None recognized the names or faces he described.

Finally, in desperation, he'd dived into alleys. More people were there, some engaged in pursuits he wouldn't approach. Others were too intoxicated to answer his questions. A few listened but couldn't help.

William emerged onto a main street again. Looked about. The streets began to rise here, toward a higher area not squarely in his assigned walk.

He decided to turn that direction.

Sergeant Nathaniel Rhodes fingered the garrote in his right pocket and the knife in his left. It would have been ridiculous to search the entirety of the district blind. Except he knew this place much better than the Snopes character or any of the rest of them. He'd spent a fair amount of time here, visiting the pubs around the nearby docks.

Over the course of three hours, he'd asked at a dozen establishments. Six had been visited by folks asking questions about Simon and Tad. Two gave a fair description of Snopes. With that help, it'd been like following a string—moving along the barrister's route, asking if people had been questioned by a man with a barrister's tongue.

A figure appeared on Highchapel Road, up a distance from where he was walking. The stride looked familiar. Nathaniel turned that direction.

Another ten minutes and he reached the heights. There were fewer establishments here, fewer buildings to try to get his bearings as to where Snopes might have gone.

He kept walking, hoping for a little luck in coming upon the man's path.

And then there it was: a man looking out of place, walking

almost timidly, half a block ahead. Hands in his pockets. Drenched coat. Bowler hat.

Nathaniel smiled to himself as he picked up his pace.

The man began to turn in his direction.

The sergeant quickly ducked into the space of a recessed door.

Madeleine finally reached the summit, yet the higher elevation didn't better her view of the district. Mostly endless rooftops stretched out in the sad, dark neighborhood below.

She walked on.

Footsteps sounded behind her. She thought she'd heard them before, but now she was sure.

She turned about, expecting to see one of her fellow searchers.

No one was there. She listened. Nothing.

Just her nerves. She moved on uneasily.

Light spilled onto the wet street from another pub ahead. She went inside.

The place was nearly empty. She'd wait a minute to calm down.

Taking a seat, she closed her eyes. Perhaps she'd done all she could. She'd heard no whistles, but maybe one of the others had gotten lucky and she just hadn't heard.

It was time to return to the church. Once there, she'd try to get a moment alone with William, to clear the air.

Nathaniel waited a count of ten, then stepped back onto the sidewalk and moved on.

There the man was again. Still walking ahead at his methodical pace. Only this time, Snopes walked only another quarter block before suddenly disappearing into a pub.

This would work. Nathaniel positioned himself near the pub's door, settling against the brick wall to wait.

371

Madeleine stepped out through the pub's door. Standing again in the rain, she looked both to her left and right.

A man leaned against the wall only a few yards away. His hand clutched something in his pocket. His cap was pulled down. The light sprawling through the door of the pub was bright enough that she could make out his face.

Fear engulfed her at the murder in his eyes.

The man hesitated an instant. Then he rushed, and would have reached her, except that a foot slipped from his awkward lunge and he stumbled to the ground.

She ran. This man was no mugger. He wanted her dead.

She turned at the curb, her own boots slipping on the wet cobblestones. The man's strides, awkward at first, had settled into a measured pace. A faster pace than hers.

She took another corner. Ahead, a small park of ash and sycamore came into view. She ran into the deep shadows beneath them, her eyes straining in the blackness and rain for a place to hide.

There was nothing. She hurried through the park and out the other side.

The footfalls behind her had quieted on the soft soil of the park. Now they returned, closer than before.

Madeleine turned onto another empty road.

"This way!" a high-pitched voice called.

Her eyes went to the sound.

The voice had come from a narrow alley just across the street.

The thudding footsteps were now only ten yards behind. She ran toward the alley.

The rain relented in the gap between buildings that was scarcely twice the width of her shoulders. Ahead, she made out a figure hurrying away from her.

Why had she come this way? She was trapped!

"In here! Follow me," a voice called from the darkness ahead.

She hurried farther in. Only half a dozen strides more until she reached the alley's end.

The walls surrounded her on three sides. At her feet, a narrow culvert dipped down, its mouth nearly filled with the rush of flowing rainwater.

She looked back.

The man chasing her was only steps away.

She might fit into the culvert. The man never would.

Dropping to her chest, she slid into the water-gorged dark.

A hand grabbed her ankle. Another joined it. Fist over fist, they began hauling her back out of the culvert.

She screamed and kicked.

Her shoe came loose.

She slid free.

The water rushed downward, pulling Madeleine through the pipe like a waterfall plunging in absolute dark. Spitting mouthfuls in an effort to breathe, her body careened from side to side in its tumbling flow. Terror-filled seconds passed as she plummeted in the water's grasp. Until . . .

She was suddenly floating through air as though she'd been expelled from a giant's mouth. She dropped for an instant, rolling and weightless. Then her back struck hard on solid ground where she lay unmoving.

Water continued splashing over her from the pipe overhead, just above her feet. Stunned and feeling lifeless, she stared at the cascade. After several long seconds, she regained enough will to roll to one side and escape its icy flow.

Even so, she remained there, unable to do more than catch her breath.

"Miss? Are you okay?"

She turned her head.

She was lying in a high-ceilinged storm sewer. In thin, dancing light she saw several pipes like the one she'd been ejected from, emptying streams at intervals along the walls.

The words had been uttered by a boy, nearly a young man, seated a few yards away and holding a torch. He looked as drenched and cold as she felt herself to be.

He must have been the one who called her into the culvert, she reasoned as her mind began to calm.

"Thank you," Madeleine managed, sitting up as her teeth began to chatter.

How had her rescuer been so near in her need? "Have you been following me?" she asked.

He nodded. "You've been askin' about for me, haven't you, miss?"

"Yes. You're Tad?"

"No," the boy answered. "Lonny murdered him. Him and Isabella."

Even cold, battered and miserable, she still felt the horror of what the boy might have seen to have that knowledge. Then the truth dawned on her.

She stood and moved carefully closer. The boy didn't object or move away. She stopped within a few feet of him where she sat down once more.

After a few minutes, she spoke again. "If you're not Tad, are you Simon?"

The boy didn't answer. He didn't need to.

"Simon, do you know why we've been looking for you?"

"It's the trial, ain't it?"

"Yes, the trial."

They sat silently for a moment before Madeleine asked, "How do we get out of here, Simon? We'll need dry clothes soon or we'll freeze to death."

"I've got some blankets, torches, matches and such stashed in a few places down here. There's a pile just over there."

She rose and retrieved a tattered blanket for herself from the pile where Simon had pointed, draping it over her shoulders. Taking another, she returned to sit by the boy, placing the second blanket over his back.

When she was settled, the boy spoke. "If I don't go and talk at your trial, they're going to kill me, ain't they?"

Madeleine heard the urgency and fear in the question as her shivering relented and her mind grew clearer. "We won't let them do that, Simon."

"But it's true, ain't it? Don't lie to me now, miss. I gotta know."

She turned to face him. "Yes, Simon. If we don't protect you, someday I think they will try."

He nodded, his eyes focused on the dank floor. "Then I suppose I've got no choice, have I?"

"I suppose not," she said. Then she stood and reached out a hand.

56

PARISH CHURCH, WHITECHAPEL
LONDON

"I'm sorry I couldn't find them," Father Thomas was saying.

The rain had stopped. William sat next to the priest on the outside steps of the church, two torches lit to either side.

"It's all right, Thomas," he said. "Everyone has tried."

"She's a clever and resourceful woman," Thomas added. "You needn't worry. Madeleine will be here any minute. I'm certain of it."

Yes. With strength he couldn't have imagined. But this was Whitechapel. He ached to know she was safe.

The Bow Street Runners had returned at midnight—without finding Tad or Simon—then gone out again when it became clear that Madeleine wasn't returning. William and Obadiah had insisted on doing the same, while Father Thomas remained behind in case she did return.

But they'd had no luck locating her either. Not a trace.

Once, wandering in the dark, William thought he'd heard a faint whistle. But it was too far away to make out with certainty. He'd continued his search, only returning to the church a few minutes earlier, telling himself during the last mile back that she was surely waiting for them. Obadiah had come in shortly after.

But she wasn't waiting for them. She was nowhere in the streets. The despair in his chest was unbearable.

"What's that?" Father Thomas suddenly whispered. "Did you hear that?"

William heard nothing. He looked about, straining to see in the dark.

Five figures emerged, with Joel in the lead. Pidger and his other Bow Street companion were at the back.

Between them walked Madeleine and a boy.

William rushed to her. Her clothes were damp under a ratty woolen cloth, and she was missing a shoe. He took off his coat and wrapped it tightly around her.

She muttered a throaty "Thanks," then said, "This is Simon Ladner."

William turned to the boy, scarcely caring in the wake of his receding worry. "It's very good to meet you, Mr. Ladner."

Simon stared back. "You're the barrister fellow?"

"I am. And I'm very glad you're safe."

"'Course you are. You want me to talk at your trial."

William shook his head. "No, son. Because I'd feared that Lonny or others had done you harm."

The boy plumbed William's eyes in the torchlight, then looked back at Madeleine. "Can I believe him, miss?"

Madeleine nodded. "You can."

"You trust him yourself?"

"Yes. With my life."

William was warmed by her words as Simon looked back to him.

"All right then," the boy said. "There's somewhere I need to take you."

57

THE OLD BAILEY

William floated on a cloud of exhaustion. A disjointed Beethoven piece careened behind his eyes—a monstrous amalgamation of the Fifth and Eighth. He surveyed the courtroom gallery. Madeleine was there—she would have come from her deathbed. Suzanne. Father Thomas. Lord Brummell, surprisingly having abandoned his box to stand next to the bar, speaking with Sir Barnabas and looking oddly wretched.

Then he noted another figure who surprised him far more.

Seated in the front row of the lower gallery was the Lord Privy Seal.

"Sir?" Obadiah called.

William turned about and joined the solicitor at the bar.

"Sir, I've made all the arrangements."

"Good."

"You're sure this will work, sir?"

"As certain as a Londoner of rainy weather."

The bailiff called the courtroom to order. Judge Raleigh marched in. When he'd taken his seat, he addressed William, his face showing genuine curiosity for the first time.

"Does the defense have any new witnesses to present?"

"It does, my lord. The defense calls Simon Ladner to the stand."

There was no murmur of surprise in the gallery or jury box. Only an odd and serious silence as the blond-haired figure entered, sinuously, with the stretched form of a boy on the cusp of manhood. His face was unreadable. He seemed uncomfortable until he'd entered the witness box and was able to stand with his back to a wall.

"Simon Ladner?" William began.

"Yes, sir."

"You're not dead."

The ice broke, laughter erupting in the gallery and jury box.

"No, sir."

"Were you a cabin boy aboard the *Padget* until February of this year?"

"I was."

"Where have you been since you left the *Padget*?"

"In York, sir."

"Why?"

"I was sent there by my boss."

"The captain of the *Padget*?"

"Not that boss, sir."

"Who, then?"

"Lonny McPherson. The boss of my crew, sir."

"Your crew? Are you referring to Mr. McPherson's canon of pickpockets?"

The boy hesitated. "Yes, sir."

"Why did Mr. McPherson send you away?"

"He wanted me away until the *Padget* got taken care of, sir."

"Taken care of?"

"Yes, sir."

"What did that mean?"

"I don't know for sure, sir."

William raised himself up on his toes. "Isn't it true, young Mr. Ladner, that you were placed on the *Padget* for the express purpose of using your pickpocket skills to steal a document from Captain Tuttle's cabin the night of your return from the Indian Sea?"

"Yes, sir."

"And did you do so?"

"Yes."

"Did you know what that document was?"

"Not clearly, sir. I can't read. Except I was taught how to cipher its title, sir. To be sure I had the right one."

"What was that title?"

"A Letter of Marque, sir."

Gallery whispers grew. The gavel fell.

"Did you carry out this scheme?"

"Yes."

"And did you then feign being shot so that you and the document could be removed from the *Padget* safely and the document passed on to others?"

"Yes."

"And who received the document?"

"It was taken by a soldier."

"Sergeant Rhodes from the detail that boarded that night?"

"I don't know his name, sir."

"Could you recognize him if you saw him again?"

"I believe so, yes."

"This wasn't the first time you participated in this type of scheme, was it?"

"No, sir."

"Isn't it true that, when you were age eleven, you were placed aboard the English merchant *Helen* as a cabin boy with the very same purpose?"

"Yes."

"And did you steal a Letter of Marque held by the captain of the *Helen* on that occasion?"

"I did."

"Passing it on to the same soldier?"

"Yes."

"All under orders from Lonny McPherson?"

"Yes."

"Why have you come forward to testify to this now, Mr. Ladner?"

"Because I think they're going to kill me, sir."

"Who?"

"Lonny . . . uh, Mr. McPherson, sir."

"Why do you believe that?"

"Because of what they did to Tad."

"Tad?"

"Tad Stocker."

"Who is Tad Stocker?"

"He was my best friend in the crew. They were training him to replace me, sir. I was getting too old for the setup. They chased him into the Thames."

William was suddenly drained to his bones and in danger of collapse. *Swallow that, King's Counsel!* his mind exclaimed. He gestured to Sir Barnabas. "Your witness."

Sir Barnabas looked to the lower gallery, where Lord Brummell was seated. Then he stood. "My lord. May we speak in chambers?"

The judge stared at Sir Barnabas curiously. "All right," he ruled.

"And I ask leave for someone other than counsel to join us."

Judge Raleigh looked perplexed. "Who would that be?"

"Lord Beau Brummell, sir."

JUDGE RALEIGH'S CHAMBERS

"My lord," Lord Brummell began, addressing the judge among the seated participants, "I find myself in an awkward position."

"As do we all," the judge said sympathetically. "But I scarcely know how you factor into this."

"My lord, I met early this morning with our Prince Regent George in a private session. In that session, Prince George asked me to appear as an intermediary for the Crown, granting me some latitude to speak on his behalf."

The judge's eyes widened. "That's . . . unusual."

"I agree. Yet this case presents much that is unusual. As a loyal subject to the Crown, and being privileged to know the prince as a friend, I've kept Prince Regent George fully up to date regarding the particulars of this case. Yesterday I voiced my concerns to the prince about the testimony of Mr. Ivars and the direction the evidence has taken. It became clear to me—and Prince George shares this impression—that the matter of Captain Tuttle's conduct and his guilt of the charge of piracy have become muddled at best. That perhaps there is even an element of injustice in continuing this proceeding."

"It's true we are in perilously strange waters, Lord Brummell," the judge said. "This court recognizes the Crown's deep interest in this matter as one of international importance. But to intervene in this fashion is unprecedented. What precisely are you and the Crown proposing, sir?"

"My lord, the prince and I believe there's been too much doubt raised by the recent testimony to proceed with so serious a criminal charge as piracy against Captain Tuttle, carrying as it does the risk of hanging. We propose, rather, that the charges be dropped to minor trade offenses, punishable by fine or brief imprisonment. Dependent, of course, upon the captain agreeing to the return of the cargo to the French."

"That's a most generous resolution." The magistrate looked to William. "What do you say, Mr. Snopes?"

William shook his head. "Wholly unacceptable, my lord."

"How dare you, Counsel!" Sir Barnabas declared, taking to his feet. "Have you any idea the gift being offered you? I'm shocked the Crown would extend it at all. You must realize that your first mate and this guttersnipe Ladner have done nothing more than tell a story that lacks characters or even an ending. We're left speculating that this Lonny McPherson fellow engineered the theft of a document—but to what end? To set up a legal charge which would return the cargo to the French? Who profits from that? Who are the masterminds behind this perverse canvas you're trying to paint? I'll crush Ladner in my cross-examination."

"I know you will," William agreed.

Sir Barnabas looked stunned. "You know? Then why are you turning down the Crown's offer?"

"Because I have someone to fill the holes in Simon Ladner's story. And he will identify everyone who was involved."

"Who's that?"

William turned to Judge Raleigh. "The defense wishes to next call Tad Stocker to the stand."

In the abrupt silence that followed, William noticed, for the first time, that one of Sir Barnabas's juniors had accompanied them into chambers, sitting in the back and writing notes on a small lap desk. With William's announcement, Sir Barnabas gestured to the junior, who rose and hurried from chambers.

"This Tad is the friend Simon Ladner mentioned?" Judge Raleigh inquired. "I thought the Ladner boy said his friend had been killed."

"He said that persons unnamed had chased him into the river, presumably intent upon killing him. In fact, the boy survived the attempt on his life. When we located him last night, Simon at first adhered to the story that Tad was dead. After a bit, he trusted sufficiently to confide in us. Only then did he tell us the truth and lead us to his friend. But Tad Stocker is very much alive."

"And he will testify to what exactly?"

"That for the past two years, he's been trained to replace Simon Ladner in this Letter of Marque scheme, before there was an attempt to end his life. He will testify who was behind it and the methods they used. He will, my lord, complete Sir Barnabas's rhetorical canvas."

"*Everyone* behind it?"

"Yes, sir. If the court will permit his testimony."

William saw Lord Brummell out of the corner of his eye. Wonderfully dressed as usual. Spotless coat. Colorful cravat. All framing a face that was ghostly pale.

They all sat in silence for a long moment, the judge appearing desperately torn. William watched the clock with each second growing more concerned where the judge would turn.

The judge straightened. "Mr. Snopes, I realize that the evidence now emerging improves your case. However, I struggle with allowing more witnesses when you have deliberately declined the Crown's offer, which could put this case to a just rest. If you persist in this decision, I'm forced, in these circumstances, to rule that—"

The door opened again. The scribing junior had returned. He passed a note to Sir Barnabas.

"My lord," the prosecutor spoke up, looking to the judge, "uh, I should inform the court that, like Lord Brummell, as counsel for the Crown I've been reporting to the prince regent. This morning, Prince Regent George had the Lord Privy Seal present in the gallery. My junior has just returned from updating him regarding our discussions and has informed me by this note that Mr. Snopes has been requested at a meeting."

"A meeting? In the middle of trial?"

"Yes, my lord. A meeting alone. Mr. Snopes has kindly been asked to attend to Prince Regent George at Carlton House."

"When?"

"Immediately, my lord. Immediately."

58

The prince regent was dressed splendidly, seated behind a massive desk in a room more than twice as large as William's entire flat. He reminded William of Beau Brummell himself, which was not surprising. Even as divorced from social gossip as William was, he knew that Lord Brummell and the prince regent were friends. Enough so that Lord Brummell provided much of the prince's fashion direction.

The most obvious difference between the two men was girth. Beau Brummell had retained his youthful stature. The prince regent had long since moved on.

"I've been kept closely informed of the trial, Mr. Snopes," the prince regent said. "Even your detractors say you've done a marvelous job with little evidence."

"I'll take that as a compliment, Your Highness, though that deficit in evidence is about to be rectified."

"So I was told. I've no wish to delay trial longer than I must, so let me get directly to the point of my summoning you. I'm aware of your falling out with your father, Lord Snopes, and your rejection of the wealth and status he might have gifted you. As a result, I'm compelled to ask: are you a loyal subject of England?"

"I am."

"Do you support the Crown?"

"I do, so long as it comports itself justly and fairly."

"Not a Whig like your junior, Mr. Shaw?"

"You're well informed, Your Highness. No. I'm not a Whig. I do not share Edmund's objections to the Crown. Though I admit to ambivalence about some in England's upper classes. Ambivalence which this case has only heightened."

"I see. Very well, then. As a loyal subject, I must ask you to accept the offer I conveyed through Lord Brummell."

"I can't do that."

"Why not? I can ensure your client spends no time in jail. The charges of piracy will be dropped. He will emerge a free man."

"He will emerge a damaged man, with no reputation at all. My other clients, Lady Jameson and her father, will lose their ship and cargo, and so be bankrupt. There's no justice in that, Your Highness."

The prince regent settled deeper into his chair. "What do you believe you know that would justify a more generous offer?"

"Everything."

"Explain yourself."

"I know how the scheme worked, who was involved, and how long it's gone on."

"Tell me what you believe to be the facts."

"First, Your Highness, Captain Tuttle was in fact provided a valid Letter of Marque, from the office of the Lord Privy Seal."

"Impossible. I never signed such a document."

"That's true, so I assume the document wasn't strictly legal. But it was prepared in this house, in the office of the Lord Privy Seal, and authenticated with your seal."

"How?"

"By a young girl employed in this house to care for your ailing father. Her name was Isabella Stratton."

"And how did she manage to create such a document?"

"Given access to your house, it wasn't difficult, Your Highness. What's required is the proper paper and an ability to use another such document as a template and, most importantly, access to your seal. You have facsimiles of many Letters of Marque in this house issued during the late war with Napoleon, and Isabella was trained by a master of a London canon at picking locks to access them. Isabella prepared the Letters she required, sealed them, then secretly took them out of Carlton House late at night to her boss, who waited for her in St. James's Park. From there they were carried to another messenger, most recently Tad Stocker, who took them to the office of a solicitor in Mayfair, where Tad slid them under the door."

"You believe all this?"

"I do. In fact, it is my belief that Letters of Marque weren't the only official documents prepared and secreted from this house under seal by Miss Stratton. Tad Stocker took a peek at some he carried. His reading skill was limited, but I've pieced together from his memory that there were corporate charters, taxation waivers, and at least one bill of divorce."

"What do you believe was done with these documents?"

"They were sold. They were quite valuable for those who couldn't obtain the Crown's favor otherwise. The marketing of these documents has gone on for at least four years."

The prince regent shook his head. "And the Letters of Marque, you say there was more than one?"

"At least two. But those papers weren't sold. They were provided to captains eager to conduct trade in the Far East, foisted off as tickets to take cargo from French vessels, enabling the captains to avoid the cost of purchasing their own trade cargo. The ships were the *Helen* and the *Padget*. Their captains sailed to the Indian Sea, captured cargo, then returned—only to have that cargo and their ships impounded at the docks."

"What good would it do the thieves to have the cargo impounded?"

"Because it was part of a process much more lucrative than simply selling a Letter of Marque to the captains. Rather than pocket a paltry sum for the Letters, this scheme gained the bosses thousands of pounds of tea plus the ships themselves. The bosses tendered the Letters of Marque with a meaningless commission agreement to the captains, then, when the ships returned to the London docks, arranged for soldiers and constables—most uninvolved in the scheme other than receiving handsome pay for silence—to immediately impound the ships and cargos. In that same moment, young Simon Ladner was poised to steal the Letters themselves, which represented the only evidence that the captains had been acting under a genuine belief that they had the authority of law.

"The crews were jailed belowdecks, where they couldn't spread word of the impoundments, and the captains secretly imprisoned at Newgate, with the aid of bribes to the clerks there, silencing and isolating them as well. All reporting of the events by the London papers was suppressed. It was at that point that the captains were presented with their ultimatums: either agree to transportation or suffer a dangerous trial, followed by the trials of their innocent crewmen. The captain of the *Helen* accepted the offer. I'm sure I'll be able to confirm that his indictment and guilty plea were taken quietly at court before he was shipped off—leaving the bosses of this scheme to sell the cargo and the ship, with a suitable share paid to the French Crown. Then they started the process again with Captain Tuttle and the *Padget*."

"Wait there. Now you're saying that *King Louis* shared in this scheme?"

"Why else was there no outcry among the French when the first ship, the *Helen*, was seized and sold? I have no immediate proof, but I believe the French Crown agreed to this arrangement to help fill its own empty coffers, which had been used up by Napoleon during the lengthy wars preceding reinstatement of the French king."

William leaned back in his chair and scrutinized the prince regent. "But you know all this, don't you, Your Highness? It's written on your face. I haven't surprised you a bit."

The prince regent stared back a moment longer. "That's not entirely true. You've surprised me *a bit*, Mr. Snopes. But, yes, I'd learned much of what you're relating already. However, I knew none of it when we began the prosecution of your Captain Tuttle. But on your visit to Carlton House, you so impressed the Lord Privy Seal with your vehement insistence of your client's innocence that he requested, even demanded, to do his own investigation. I permitted it. He was able to learn of the marketing of other Crown documents and traced the source of the thefts to your young Miss Stratton, by then already deceased. Still, it wasn't until the *Padget*'s first mate testified the other day that we were able to put some remaining facts in order, particularly about the Letters of Marque. Which is why the Lord Privy Seal was present in your courtroom today."

"Then do you know who all was involved?"

"Please tell me your thoughts on that matter as well."

William nodded. "A career criminal named Lonny McPherson chose from among his pickpocket canon Simon Ladner and Tad Stocker for their respective roles. Isabella was one of his group as well. Given where Isabella was found murdered, I suspect that Lonny had a role in that also—perhaps to keep her quiet on the eve of trial. Tad has told us that he delivered the documents to the office of Solicitor Mandy Bristol, who must have served as liaison between the captains and his investors—the real bosses in this."

"And who were those real bosses?"

"Two persons deeply in debt and requiring cash. Lord Beau Brummell. And your daughter, Your Highness. Princess Charlotte."

The prince regent raised his face until he was looking down

his nose at William as though appraising a racehorse for a bet. "Why do you believe Lord Brummell and my daughter were involved?"

"Because Tad did errands and chores for Mandy Bristol and overheard the solicitor and Lord Brummell speaking about aspects of the plan during a meeting at Mandy Bristol's office—after Lord Brummell arrived secretly up a back staircase. Also, because Tad saw Lord Brummell and your daughter share a cab with Mandy Bristol to a social event only a week or more ago."

"That's scarcely proof enough of my daughter's involvement."

"There is more, Your Highness. Lonny McPherson told Tad on the night he nearly killed the boy that your daughter and Lord Brummell were in charge of the scheme."

For the first time, William saw real concern appear on the prince regent's face. That last statement was news to him. Or he suspected it but was crestfallen that William had proof.

"What is it that you want, Mr. Snopes?" he finally asked softly. "Money? A KC? Because I will tell you that if news of this got out, your junior and his Whigs might well succeed in toppling the Crown."

"I know," William said. "I thought long about that consequence. I confess I considered that there might be some justice in it. Yet after as much personal meditation and prayer as I could fit into a long and sleepless night, I've thought better of it. In fact, avoiding that occurrence is the reason I've shared this information with no one else."

"No one?"

"Not even my clients. They know nothing more than has been testified to in open court to date."

"Then what is it you want? I can have the charges of piracy against your client fully dismissed. Would that suffice?"

"That won't do."

"Isn't that what you've sought?"

"No. Dropping charges will leave behind a mystery that will

taint my clients and their families forever. I want the case to go to the jury for determination."

"Impossible! Then you'd be forced to present the evidence you've shared with me to avoid a guilty verdict, and it would all be in the public realm!"

"No. I want your Lord Privy Seal to voluntarily take the stand this afternoon and testify that, after diligent search, he's finally located the administrative record in his office which confirms that you did, in fact, issue a Letter of Marque to Captain Tuttle in November of 1816. Then I want Sir Barnabas, on behalf of the Crown, to rest his case—declining to make a final statement to the jury. I will make my own statement proclaiming Captain Tuttle's innocence, after which Judge Raleigh will instruct the jury, based on the Lord Privy Seal's unequivocal testimony, that it should find Captain Tuttle not guilty. The jury will certainly oblige. The captain's reputation will be restored, as will that of Lady Jameson and her father. Particularly after you bring sufficient pressure on the London papers to make the acquittal and exoneration a headline story for at least a week."

The prince regent pondered a moment, then nodded. "That is acceptable."

"Good. I also want the *Padget* returned to my clients with its cargo intact, along with damages commensurate with their suffering. You must also secretly communicate with the French king that neither he nor the owners of the French vessel must attempt any further effort to recover the *Padget*'s cargo, or the French Crown will face public claims as well."

"You spoke of damages to your clients. How much in damages?"

"I'm not prepared to say. You'll have to trust me to be fair."

The prince regent cleared his throat. "I'm not accustomed to placing such trust in barristers. Is that *all*?"

"No. Then there is the matter of my fees."

"Of course."

"And I want no charges brought against the boys, Tad and Simon. I'll arrange for their care. And I must know what will happen to the malefactors. If you've deduced some of these crimes the past few days, I suspect you've already given that some thought."

"Before I respond, do I take it that you agree Sir Barnabas had no role in these schemes?"

"I do. As much as I railed against some of his tactics, his surprise at the critical evidence was sincere. I intend to confirm that belief, but I think I'll find that he had no role in the impoundment of the *Helen* or the secret charging of the captain and so didn't realize the seizure of the *Padget* was a replay of an illegal scheme."

The prince regent sighed. "I fully agree. As to the remaining persons involved, I have thoughts about punishments commensurate with the crimes. Trials in open court risk releasing evidence that must not become public fare. We'll capture Lonny McPherson eventually, but he already has a dozen capital crimes which can be charged. The man can only be hanged once."

William nodded. "I understand. Sergeant Rhodes?"

"If he hasn't fled already, he'll be court-martialed for his actions in a closed military proceeding."

"Mandy Bristol?"

"What do you think appropriate?"

An image of the long-gone Tyburn gallows came to mind, though he had no proof that Bristol had engaged in the portion of the crimes warranting capital punishment. "Transportation would do nicely," he said grudgingly. "I imagine Mr. Bristol will agree, given the alternative of a lengthy stint in Newgate."

"As you wish."

"What of Lord Brummell?"

"Mr. Snopes," the prince regent said, "once again I must ask: what would you have me do? If everything you say is true—and it is now difficult to believe otherwise—I can't openly try him for his crimes, for the reasons we've discussed. And he can't simply disappear; he's too enmeshed in society." The prince regent paused. "Have you given some thought to Lord Brummell's punishment?"

"I have, Your Highness. I believe you should require Lord Brummell to write a full confession, to be kept in the royal vaults for one hundred years—only to be released before that time has passed if necessary, to use it as evidence for prosecution in the event he violates the terms of your punishment. I would like to retain a copy of that confession as well."

"What punishment do you envision?"

"Exile from England forever. Modestly paid employment as a government clerk in Tasmania perhaps, where, should he live long enough, he will be permitted to retire."

The prince regent shrugged. "That's a kindness after what he's done."

"Perhaps. I imagine that fashions are abysmal in Tasmania, which will prove the severest punishment for the man. In any event, I see no alternative."

"Very well. We've left the matter of my daughter for last."

William looked to the floor. "No matter the leverage I may have, Your Highness, I can't bring myself to insist on a father imposing punishment of my choosing on his own daughter."

"Thank you, Mr. Snopes," the prince regent said with a sigh. "Thank you very much. Apart from my personal feelings, I face the same dilemma openly punishing Charlotte for her crimes as I do Lord Brummell, yet I will admit that the Lord Privy Seal's research and yours implicate her in great wrongdoing. I can't bring myself to believe she had a hand in the murder of the poor girl Isabella. She was kind once, though a point of contention between her mother and me. I've convinced myself that hers were crimes of greed that spun in directions she couldn't control, driven perhaps by restrictions I've placed on her marriage and the tight purse I've imposed. In that light, I've considered an imprisonment of a different sort for someone who treasures money and society. I have in mind marriage to a certain aging baron in

Silesia, a man of stultifying tastes who despises ostentation and travel."

William stood. "I accept that, Your Highness. Now I need to get back to court. Will you inform Judge Raleigh of the arrangements, so far as they require the court's involvement?"

"I will send someone immediately, Mr. Snopes, as well as begin to fulfill the remaining terms we discussed."

"Thank you." William hesitated. "There is one last thing, Your Highness."

"What is that, Mr. Snopes?"

"Forgive me," William began, "but it must be said. I'm aware of what difficult financial times these are for England and for the Crown as well. I pray that that hasn't colored your own judgment in these matters."

The prince regent's face grew red. "What are you insinuating, Mr. Snopes?"

"As I informed a colleague recently, I don't insinuate, Your Highness. I prefer to speak right to the heart of matters."

He drew on his last energy to project the conviction he usually reserved for juries.

"I have unresolved concerns, Your Highness, about the role Lord Brummell has played in these matters, as a liaison to yourself and to Sir Barnabas as well. Should I ever learn that you joined in these terrible crimes, either by your action or purposeful inaction—crimes nearly ruinous to innocent people and the death of one—then I'll pursue you and the Crown itself with all the skill and experience I possibly can bring to bear. Good day, Your Highness."

59

HEATHCOTE ESTATE
ESSEX

William trotted his bay up the drive to the manor house in the fresh air of an early spring. Not enough time had passed for great improvements since his last visit before trial. Nor, he knew, had enough funds yet arrived from the Crown to pay for significant work, though they were promised for the coming week. But the dew-sparkled grounds gave off the heady smell of freshly cut grass. And he noticed, even in a matter of a few weeks, the drive had been repaired. It seemed a small but determined gesture.

Miss Kendall took William to the study. Captain Tuttle was there, seated before flames in the fireplace. He rose and gave William a broad smile. William saw, happily, how much he'd already improved.

"Forgive my visit without notice or invitation, Captain," William said. "It was a sudden decision."

"Not at all. I'm just glad you have time to visit so soon after the trial."

"I've seen no notice in the papers of your betrothal."

Harold smiled. "Rebekah's parents still disapprove. But I think I'm winning them over. It won't hurt to collect my portion of the *Padget*'s profits."

"Are you visiting your cousin?"

"It's a bit more open-ended than that. Since the acquittal and the impending sale of the *Padget*'s cargo, I've accepted my cousin's invitation to stay at the manor for a while to help out. At least while I decide how to proceed with the *Padget* in the future. Have you put your own affairs at Gray's Inn in order? Can you stay a few days at least?"

"I can't stay. But I can happily report that the judge has vacated his contempt order—expunged it entirely, in fact, at the Crown's urging. We've also received assurances that the funds promised by the Crown to compensate us all will be arriving soon. And it seems that a wealth of new clients are finding my door."

"Clients who can pay with more than future promises, I hope?"

"I believe so, though I haven't accepted any quite yet."

"Planning a rest?"

William hesitated. "No. It's just that I have some decisions of my own to make first."

The captain nodded and smiled knowingly. "Is that so? Perhaps you'd like to greet Madeleine, then. She'll be very pleased by your visit. She's in the back gardens, down by the brook."

William gladly accepted the gesture and left out a back door.

A path led through beds still dormant from winter but already showing glimmers of hope. The detritus of the long cold was being cleared away by a few staff working there. Shapes of past and future glory could be seen breaking through the garden's surface.

He took the path down to the arched bridge over the brook, then passed beyond to rows of hedges. He made out Madeleine ahead, working on patches of some lower gardens. She was wearing the work clothes he remembered from his first visit. Kneeling, her back to him, he got near without her noticing.

"Lady Jameson?"

She turned.

He was instantly struck again by the openness of her smile—as though the jury's verdict had been a reprieve for her spirit as well.

Her braided hair and everything else about her were, as always, so unconsciously natural. He helped her rise.

"Once again, you arrive unannounced, Mr. Snopes."

"Once again, I find you indistinguishable from your staff."

She laughed. "I actually can dress better, especially if I'm fore-warned."

"I've no doubt. You forget I accompanied you to a ball. But I think I may prefer you this way."

"There's so much to be done. Harold has promised to stay and help me get it in order, but even so, I can't afford enough help to begin to satisfy my ambitions yet. But you must see it in summer. The estate will look like it hasn't for years."

"I'm sure its beauty won't disappoint, Lady Jameson," he said, not looking away.

Her cheeks reddened. "I think, Mr. Snopes, that you may call me Madeleine now."

He bowed. "William, at your service."

An awkward silence grew.

William spoke first. "Uh, Madeleine, I owe you an apology."

"You don't, William. I breached your trust by not telling you the entire truth of my situation. I was just too stubborn to admit it at the church in Whitechapel."

"You did what was required for the best of reasons. I'm sorry I blamed you so. You acted . . . as I would have acted in your place."

"I appreciate your forgiveness."

He felt her gaze and smile on him like a beating sun and knew that if he waited, he'd certainly lose his nerve and turn away before expressing what he'd really come to say.

"Madeleine," he began again, "I have ambitions of my own. As I shared with your cousin a moment ago, clients are finding my door with matters the likes of which I've never entertained before. Claims of fraud implicating a duke. A banker alleged to have spied in the late war. But I've held them all off, not wanting to make business decisions until I'd settled other matters."

She nodded but remained silent.

He took a deep breath of the faint fragrance of the nascent garden. "I haven't told you much about my life, other than that I left home when I was young. Too young to make decisions of importance with any wisdom. Leaving was the right decision; I believe that. But it's meant a lonely life. Not that I've minded too much. I love what I'm doing, mostly. I love the law and all it's capable of at its best. I love London and mentoring Edmund and Obadiah. It's always seemed enough. Until now."

Madeleine raised a hand to interrupt. "William, if I understand your purpose, will you please let me say something first?"

"All right," William said hesitantly.

"Did you see my father when you rode in?"

"No."

"I'm sure he was there, sitting at the window of his front room. He sits and looks out on an estate that he sustained all his life, even as it withered and nearly died around him, died as much of his family had done. I've spent years trying to save Heathcote Manor, struggling not to succumb to an utter loss of every faith I ever held. Now that is passing, and thanks to you and Harold, I believe I can save the estate. I want to finish that job before I consider dedicating myself to anything else. Before he dies, I want my father to see the manor as it was. Can you understand that?"

"I can," William said, knowing her meaning and forcing a smile in return.

She paused. "There's more I want to share with you. I had a visit yesterday from the American."

A twinge of uncommon jealousy rose in him. "You did?"

"I did. A surprising visit, since I'd told him that it would still be some weeks before I can finish repaying his loan. He didn't care. He came to ask for my hand."

William stood mute. He never thought he'd feel such crushing disappointment again.

"I told him no."

"You did?"

"Yes. He's a better man than he cares to admit, but he's not a man I'd marry. For the reasons I just shared. But for more as well."

He watched her face, wondering if he really understood her. "What you hope to achieve here doesn't require isolation, does it?"

"No. But it will require someone centered here, in the countryside. Just as your growing practice will, I suspect, demand that your life be centered in London and its courts. At least for a time."

This was so foreign to him. A path never taken. A cause he couldn't argue to persuasion.

"It seems you've already thought this through," he said sadly.

"I have. I've also thought a great deal about you."

William looked toward the woods where he now knew he'd first loved her. Seeing her that night beyond the flames, framed by the dark, the rain, and her crumbling home. Refusing to surrender. This was a singular woman. He would wait two lifetimes for her, so long as he was certain there was a chance.

"Are you saying such single-minded dedication won't be necessary forever, Madeleine?"

"It won't, William. Not so very long, I hope. Nor does it require solitude. Tell me, was it so long a ride here today?"

"No. It was . . . refreshing. I wouldn't mind taking it often."

"Good. And I enjoy a good ride into London. Perhaps to stay with Obadiah and Suzie again." She smiled in that way that nearly overcame him the first time he'd seen her smile so in Obadiah's home. "Promise me something, William."

"What's that?"

"Promise me that you won't forsake your habit of visiting without notice. It allows me the hope, any time and any day, of seeing you ride up the drive on that beautiful bay again."

Epilogue

LATE SPRING, 1818

OFFICE OF BARRISTER WILLIAM SNOPES
GRAY'S INN
LONDON

Edmund strode into William's office. William noticed that he still limped, though it was better each day. In his hand was a sheet that he was reading closely.

"Have you seen this, Mr. Snopes?" Edmund asked.

"Seen what?"

"This brief. The one alluding to the charge of spying involving Count Mountcrest."

"Yes, I have seen it."

"What do you make of it?"

"Very interesting. I think the case against him is weak."

"Intriguing."

There was a rap on the doorframe behind Edmund. Father Thomas stood there. "Am I interrupting?" he called.

"Often," William replied. "But not at present. What can we do for you?"

"I was considering lunch. I thought perhaps someone might wish to join me."

"Can't," Edmund replied. "My boss works me like a slave."

"I'd be game," William said, "but I was asked by Obadiah to wait for him. He said he was coming by with a new client."

There was the sound of footfalls up the hall beyond the office. Obadiah appeared behind Father Thomas with Suzanne on his arm.

"It appears to be a party," Edmund said. "I haven't the time for it."

"No, wait, Edmund," Obadiah declared, then looked to William. "I've brought the new client, sir."

Worried, William addressed Suzanne. "Are you in legal trouble?"

She smiled. "No. If I was, I'd have hired a solicitor with fewer future time constraints." She patted her belly.

Father Thomas was already grinning as Edmund threw his arms around Obadiah. "Don't be a fool, Mr. Snopes!" he cried. "Get your head out of the law books."

The light dawned. William stood and came around the desk to embrace Suzanne.

"I'm so pleased, Suzie. Really, I am. When will we meet the new client face-to-face?"

She smiled. "November, Mr. Snopes."

"In time for a Christmas christening by Thomas. This is wonderful news."

"We could only drop by for a moment," Obadiah said. "We've errands to run, preparing for the new arrival."

"Then you are free for lunch," Father Thomas said to William.

"I suppose I am."

Obadiah and Suzanne said their good-byes over a final round of congratulations. Edmund retreated to his office as William retrieved a hat.

William thought a moment. "Have you ever tried The Peacock, Thomas?"

"I haven't."

"Excellent tea."

"Good," the Father said. "Because I've brought some tracts for you to look over."

"Railing about the legal profession?"

"The same! Perhaps you've already read them, then."

"Mr. Snopes," Edmund called from his office. "We *will* go over the count's matter when you return, correct, sir?"

William gazed out the window at the spring sunshine that warmed the office air. It was a day for Bach: music that was light, melodic, gallant. He felt the first tremors of a piece as he turned back to his junior.

"Yes, Edmund. I can't think of anything I'd like more."

ACKNOWLEDGMENTS

Thanks to Bethany House and my editors for their continuing input and support.

Thanks to Jim for his reading and comments.

And thanks again to my family of manuscript readers and listeners: my lovely daughter, Elizabeth (Libby), my wonderful son, Ian, and my extraordinary and patient wife, Catherine.

You echo in every good thing my characters say and do.

About the Author

Todd M. Johnson is the author of acclaimed novels *Fatal Trust* and *Critical Reaction*. He has practiced as an attorney for over thirty years, specializing as a trial lawyer. A graduate of Princeton University and the University of Minnesota Law School, Todd taught for two years as adjunct professor of international law and served as a U.S. diplomat in Hong Kong. He lives near Minneapolis with his wife, Cathy. They have two children, Ian and Elizabeth. To learn more, visit www.authortoddmjohnson.com.

Sign Up for Todd's Newsletter

Keep up to date with Todd's news on book releases and events by signing up for his email list at authortoddmjohnson.com.

More from Todd M. Johnson

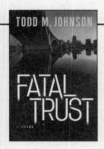

Defense Attorney Ian Wells is struggling to build a law practice while caring for his sick mother. When a new client offers a huge sum to take on a simple trust fund case, he can't afford to say no. But when the investigation leads to a decades-old mystery linking the trust to dangerous criminals, he realizes this case could cost him his career.

Fatal Trust

You May Also Like . . .

Laura Callaway daily walks the windswept Cornwall coast, known for many shipwrecks but few survivors. And when a man with curious wounds and an odd accent is washed ashore, she cares for him while the mystery surrounding him grows. Can their budding attraction survive, and can he be returned to his rightful home when danger pursues them from every side?

A Castaway in Cornwall by Julie Klassen
julieklassen.com

Fleeing to the beautiful Isles of Scilly, Lady Elizabeth Sinclair stumbles upon dangerous secrets left behind by her cottage's former occupant and agrees to help the missing girl's brother, Oliver Tremayne, find his sister. As the two work together, they uncover ancient legends, pirate wrecks, betrayal, and the most mysterious phenomenon of all: love.

The Nature of a Lady by Roseanna M. White
THE SECRETS OF THE ISLES #1
roseannamwhite.com

In search of her father's lost goods, Adria encounters an eccentric old woman who has filled Foxglove Manor with dangerous secrets that may cost Adria her life. Centuries later, when the senior residents of Foxglove under her care start sharing chilling stories of the past, Kailey will have to risk it all to banish the past's demons, including her own.

On the Cliffs of Foxglove Manor by Jaime Jo Wright
jaimewrightbooks.com

◆ BETHANYHOUSE

Beneath a Thousand Apple Trees

Janie DeVos

LYRICAL PRESS
Kensington Publishing Corp.
www.kensingtonbooks.com

LYRICAL PRESS BOOKS are published by

Kensington Publishing Corp.
119 West 40th Street
New York, NY 10018

All Kensington titles, imprints, and distributed lines are available at special quantity discounts for bulk purchases for sales promotion, premiums, fund-raising, educational, or institutional use.

Special book excerpts or customized printings can also be created to fit specific needs. For details, write or phone the office of the Kensington Sales Manager: Kensington Publishing Corp., 119 West 40th Street, New York, NY 10018. Attn. Sales Department. Phone: 1-800-221-2647.

Lyrical Press and Lyrical Press logo Reg. U.S. Pat. & TM Off.

First Electronic Edition: August 2016
eISBN-13: 978-1-60183-681-6
eISBN-10: 1-60183-681-3

First Print Edition: August 2016
ISBN-13: 978-1-60183-682-3
ISBN-10: 1-60183-682-1

Printed in the United States of America

This book is dedicated to two of the strongest women I am privileged to know: Cindy Lindsey, and Gertrude Huskins, whose dignity and amazing grace are constants, even when life strikes its cruelest blows. *May the years ahead be as gentle as Appalachian days in May.*

Acknowledgments

The writing of this book would have been impossible had it not been for a large number of exceedingly wise and patient—and I emphasize *patient*—people. Many hours were spent with them as they shared stories with me about the realities of growing up in such a beautiful, but often harsh and unforgiving place as the Appalachian Mountains. In order to survive, these wonderful people have always relied on each other, and, in order to write this book, I, too, had to rely on them. In their usual way, they were there for me, and I am forever grateful.

First, I'd like to thank Bill Carson, proprietor of The Orchard at Altapass. For hours, we sat on the deck of his country store overlooking his massive apple orchard as he patiently and painstakingly explained what goes into the running of an orchard. Every part of my novel pertaining to anything apple-related is because of the time and interest Mr. Carson took in my project. Many thanks, Bill. I'd write another story about apples just to sit on your deck with you again.

Next, I'd like to thank Keith Woody and Ricky Hollifield, members of the world-renowned family of chair makers who run Woody's Chair Shop in Spruce Pine, NC. I'd also like to posthumously thank their mentor, Arval Woody, whose beautiful rockers grace the Smithsonian Institute, as well as the Kennedy Library, in Washington, DC. My novel's characters, Prescott Guinn and Salvatore Lupari, both furniture makers, came to life because of Mr. Woody's and Mr. Hollifield's furniture-making expertise. My deepest gratitude to both of you.

I'm also indebted to Mr. Tim Parker, of Parker Forest Products. Without his personal guided tour through his timber mill, I would never have been able to adequately explain my character Rachel's terrible injury suffered at her father's mill, nor describe the day-today business of running one. Thank you, Tim. Letting you test drive my new Jeep was small payment for your tour.

Lastly, I'd like to thank Calvin Hall, whose family has graced these mountains for hundreds of years. As we sat on Calvin's front porch, looking off into the distance at the leaning, vine-covered cabin his grandfather built in the 1800s, I learned about the enormous courage and resilience of these amazing people, not to mention their undiluted dedication to their land and their people. Thank you, Calvin, for making me feel like one of your clan.

There are many others who contributed to this novel but in the interest of saving space for the actual story itself, I will just add a very broad but heartfelt thank you. You know who you are, as I do, and because of you, *Beneath a Thousand Apple Trees* was born.

PART 1

Rachel

CHAPTER 1

1916, Howling Cut, NC

I wasn't born with a bad right foot. Instead, I'd been dealt a bad hand when an accident at Papa's timber mill crippled me. The man known as the *off-bearer* was busy stacking boards that had just been cut by the spinning, sharp-toothed saw and didn't see me walk up beside him. With his mind a million miles away, he was simply repeating the tedious pulling-off-and-stacking motion of yet another board when he turned and dropped it on my foot.

It seemed to happen in slow motion. The off-bearer, who was a stoic Irishman named Rusty Flaherty, saw me standing there just a fraction of a second after he'd let the board go, and the look of horror on his face was one I would never forget, and which froze me in place. I was lucky, they said, because it had narrowly missed my head. But I wasn't lucky *enough*, for even though Papa immediately threw me in the wagon and hauled me over to Doc Pardie's house, my foot had never healed right.

The doctor wouldn't operate because I was only four and "still had growin' to do, and there ain't any use but to wait 'til she's done a-doin' it," he'd told my father. I heard Papa tell Mama later that he wouldn't have let Doc do it anyway, since he smelled like he'd "dived into a bottle of one hundred proof. Maybe it'll just straighten out on its own," he'd said, without too much conviction in his voice. And it had healed, just not straight enough or strong enough, and there'd never been enough money to do anything to correct it.

I walked with a pronounced limp, and the fact that I was short and small-boned only helped to accentuate it. I'd been given the offensive name of Laggin' Leg early on, and each time I was called by it, I wished the darn pine had, indeed, clobbered me in the head. But, as Grandma was quick to remind me when I came home in tears, I must have been saved from certain death for a reason, and "that which doesn't kill us makes us stronger," she'd point out, while pointing at *me* to emphasize *her* point.

That's all well and good, I thought, *but I just wish the good Lord had warned me to stand on the other side of Mr. Flaherty, and found someone else to make a point with.*

The first time someone referred to me as Laggin' Leg was when I was six. It was during Sunday school class as I walked back to my seat after reciting the first five verses of John. I'd proudly made it through my recital without omitting one word, and Mrs. Jacobson was in the midst of telling the class that I was "a true disciple of the Lord's," when nine-year-old Ray Coons deliberately stuck his foot out in front of me. Suddenly, I went from walking proudly with my chin up, to lying on the floor with a split in it. The whole class—all thirteen of them—fell into fits of laughter, while stars danced before my eyes as though they were having a celestial recital on the scuffed pine floor where I lay staring in dazed confusion.

"Ray Coons!" Mrs. Jacobson scolded as she quickly walked over to me. "I saw that!"

"Why, Miz Jacobson, I didn't do nothin'," Ray innocently objected. "She's just a cripple, that's all. She can't walk too good. She's got that laggin' leg o' hers, and she falls all the time, don't ya, girl?" Ray looked at me as though he'd cut my throat if I didn't concede that the fall had been my fault. I didn't—couldn't—say a word, however, as I was too busy trying to refill my lungs with air; the fall had knocked all of it out of me. And the wracking sobs that had followed only made the possibility of my breathing again that much more unlikely.

The episode left me with two things: a scar on my chin from the gash that required four stitches (which Doc Pardie sewed during a rare moment of sobriety), and the cruel new nickname. I hid in the back of the loft in the barn after receiving my stitches until Grandma coaxed me out with the smell of a cheese biscuit. I think she'd given me time to process the event—and to get hungry enough to make cheese biscuits more important. I came down the ladder and turned around, facing her.

Looking at her was like looking at an older version of myself, except for the fact that she had thick, medium-length, coal-black hair, with just a few streaks of gray blended throughout. My hair, however, was long and curly, and the same insignificant color brown as a withered maple leaf, just like my father's. But Grandma and I had the same build, same face, and the same brilliant blue eyes; "Carolina blue," she always called them. As we stood looking at each other, she pulled pieces of straw from my hair, then rather roughly rubbed away the telltale tracks of some dried up tears. I knew she wasn't mad at me for crying, but was angry with whoever had been the cause of it.

The wind whistled through the gaps in the plank siding on the north side of the barn, creating an eerie tune and causing me to shiver. Our town, Howling Cut, had been named for just that very reason—the eerie, howling sound the wind made when it rushed down the mountains and through one of the logging roads or "cuts" in the forests which surrounded us. And the place was living up to its name at the moment. Grandma handed me the biscuit and pulled the collar of my worn-out brown coat closed, trying in vain to keep the cold out.

"I can't keep life from hurtin' ya, Rachel," she said. "Alls I can do is learn ya to be tough enough to stand up to it."

She pulled me close to her and I could smell the smoke from our wood stove when I laid my face against her breast. She sighed after a long moment, held me away from her, and I caught the glint of tears that threatened to spill over from the reddened pockets of her lower lids.

"C'mon. We're gettin' as cold as our supper is." Turning, she led the way out of the barn.

CHAPTER 2

Secrets in the Laurel

Big Grandma, Gertrude Cooper—Grandma's mother—lived with us until her passing when I was seven years old. She'd come to live with us when my great-grandfather, Earl Cooper, died and I was four. The two had lived in a cabin that was much farther up the mountain than ours, making my great-grandparents' cabin practically inaccessible to anyone that didn't have a darn good reason for undertaking the long haul up there. Once my great-grandfather had passed away, Big Grandma felt the solitude and isolation far more than she ever had before, thus, she'd packed up most of what she had, gave the rest to the church—including the cabin—and moved in with us. Her small cabin was left to the ravages of creeping vines and thick laurel that quickly took over the place and created a well-hidden and safe haven for a couple of turkeys, a family of mice, and a rat snake, all of whom must have taken into consideration the fine accommodations and reluctantly agreed to live and let live. And there were two others who found the perfect use for the abandoned home place—Myra Jenkins and John Vespie.

John was a married man, but forgot that small fact every Wednesday at noon. On those afternoons, John and Myra would casually leave the bank in town together, where they were both employed, he being the bank manager and she his secretary, and they'd make the rough trek up the old logging road in John's fancy Model T Ford (one of only two in town) to my great-grandparents' cabin. Their story was always the same: John had a standing date with his son for an afternoon of fishing on the river and, being the gentleman that he was, he was kindly dropping Myra off at her ailing mother's so that the dear and unselfish daughter could tend to the soon-to-be-departed woman's few remaining needs. Little did the town know that Myra's mother had died when she was twelve, and that Myra, being the result of a tryst between her mother and a timber man who'd long since come and gone, had been brought up by a strict and overly protective spinster aunt who lived two towns over in Honeycutt.

John had discovered the wonderful windfall of Big Grandma's deserted cabin when the church pastor happened to mention "the Holy Spirit–driven generosity of Sister Gertrude." Unfortunately, Pastor Franks said, the cabin was too high up and too far off the beaten path to be useful to the church. John, however, immediately thought of a wonderful use for it. Thus, Wednesday afternoons ended up being a blessed union for two of the most faithful of Pastor Franks's flock.

Their well-kept secret lasted two years, until one unfortunate Wednesday afternoon when John Vespie's wife, Edna, and son, Little John, came in to the bank to see if John Sr. would like to take them for an early supper at the diner. When asked where her husband was, the bank manager's assistant, Mr. Humphrey, stupidly replied that he was fishing with their son—their one-and-only son, who happened to be standing right before him. So, the already-suspicious Mrs. Vespie easily put two and two together, and figured the two absent bank employees were together. Unsurprisingly, Myra Jenkins put in her resignation the next morning, and left town that afternoon.

Nothing more was heard from the disgraced woman, but it was a miracle to see how suddenly and humbly John J. Vespie became a deeply devoted lamb of the church. And show his devotion he did when it came time to ante-up for the offering plate each Sunday. Some said he was trying to buy his way back into the good graces of the church, and God, Himself. And I suppose he figured he had a lot of amends-making to do, for he never missed a Sunday's service thereafter, nor slacked on his enormous tithing. Soon enough, the money seemed to make up for his indiscretions for no one, the preacher included, had any more to say about his "momentary dance with the devil" after the church got its long-awaited and much-prayed-for roof later that year. And Mrs. Vespie's face got a little less dour looking and a little haughtier looking instead when she finally got the mansion that she'd always dreamed of. And it had nothing to do with the one that was being prepared for her in heaven.

Big Grandma laughed about it and said that that poor old cabin had seen more life in it in the last two years since John and Myra had been sneaking around than it had had in the last twenty when she and my great-grandfather had lived there.

Being seven at the time, though, I wasn't privy to all the ins and outs of what was going on at Big Grandma's old place, or in the town, either. And, truthfully, the little I'd heard hadn't much interested me. But, something that *did* interest me and that I was well aware of, even at that young age, concerned Big Grandma herself. What she was fascinated me and lured me to her, yet, at the same time, caused me to keep a certain reverent distance from her. For my great-grandmother was the Wart Buyer.

CHAPTER 3

The Wart Buyer

There was a certain awe and respect that went with the title of Wart Buyer. Perhaps it had something to do with a secret fascination with witchery, although a Wart Buyer was certainly not a witch. She was, however, thought of as a healer, although my great-grandmother never claimed to be such. But I know that when Big Grandma treated Minna George for the warts on her hand, Minna swore up and down that Big Grandma had also healed her rheumatism. And then there was Tycee Burns. She claimed that after Big Grandma got rid of the ugly wart on her forehead that she no longer had the paralyzing headaches either.

I didn't know if one thing was really connected to another, but I did know that Big Grandma held a lot of people's secrets, and they were as closely guarded as the ancient secret of *how* the healing of a wart actually took place. People respected Big Grandma's ability to hold that knowledge close to her, and so they entrusted more knowledge, of the personal kind, to her care. Far more than she probably wanted, needed, or knew what to do with. Simply because she held the enigmatic title of Wart Buyer, she had a certain aura of mystique and power, and was set on a level that was higher and demanded more respect than your every day, run-of-the-mill mountain folks.

Anyone that knew something that others did not was placed on a pedestal built on the foundation of folklore, myths, superstition, and magic. The Wart Buyer was highly revered. In people's minds, she had done something worthy of being given that role. The million-dollar question, though, was what? *What* had the Wart Buyer done to be set so far apart from the rest? The answer never came, of course. But, regardless, people treated all Wart Buyers with great reverence, and entrusted their greatest secrets, hopes, and dreams to them.

There could only be one person in the family who bought warts. And, until she (for it was usually a woman in the role) figured it was time to pass the secret knowledge of wart buying down, that person would remain the sole purchaser. The only way this ancient practice could be accomplished, Big Grandma explained to me (while carefully keeping from me the secret of *how* it actually worked), was that the one with the wart had to agree to sell the wart. Only then would the process work. If the seller was a non-believer, or joked about the reality of such a remedy working, then there could be no deal made. But, once the deal was agreed upon, then Big Grandma would take a penny out of a mason jar filled with them, and rub the wart gently but thoroughly with it. Then she gave the seller the penny and he or she was instructed to never, ever spend it, but to tuck it safely away instead. If the penny was used or lost, the wart would return. And that was true. I saw it happen, just as I saw warts miraculously disappear a few days after the ritual was performed. Since there could only be one wart buyer in a family, *when* the torch would be passed down was a decision only the present buyer could make. It was usually near the end of the buyer's life, though. Then, the newly designated Wart Buyer kept the secret to herself until it was time for *that* buyer to pass it on to the next one selected.

Grandma Willa was called into Big Grandma's room three weeks before she passed. "Close the door, darlin'," the dying woman rasped. I wanted to go in, too. I wanted to know what seriousness was being discussed, but I knew I wasn't allowed. I pressed my ear to the door but could only make out the words "knowed," "rubbed," and "copper." Mama came up the porch steps with Doc Pardie, who, as usual, looked like he'd spent the night out in the pasture with the goats, and I quickly sat back down in my rocker, appearing to be thoroughly engrossed in my *ABCs* primer book. Grandma came out of the bedroom then and quietly closed the door. I could tell she'd been crying, which was a rare thing for her to do. Quickly, she brushed away the remaining wetness, nodded curtly at Pardie, and mumbled something to the effect that "there wasn't much he could do, so just let her be." Then Grandma brusquely announced that she had to snap the beans or supper wouldn't get on the table until midnight. I called after her to see if I could help, but my mother told me to stay put; then she and the doctor went in to see Big Grandma. I looked back at the kitchen door but realized, even at that young age, that Grandma needed to be alone. And I realized something else then, too; that something large had shifted in those fifteen minutes behind closed doors. There'd been a passing of the torch, and my Grandma Willa was now the Wart Buyer.

CHAPTER 4

A Slow Unveiling

There were two reasons that I always opened Christmas presents slowly. The first reason was because we received only a couple; usually one from my parents, and another small something from Grandma. Without fail, I'd sit on the floor by Grandma's rocker and observe everyone's joy, or lack thereof, in what my parents had given to each of us. I watched their faces closely, trying to measure their expressions as being sincerely happy, or just a polite show of approval. On the one hand, we were glad we had anything to open. But, as we lay awake the night before, the hope was still out there that the gifts awaiting us under the tree would be the ones each of us had dreamed of. When Mama would ask us what we wanted for Christmas, we knew in our hearts that it was a ritual for her to do the asking, but the getting was a whole different story.

A bigger mill had opened up in the town of Flat Top, in the next county over, and though that would seem far enough away not to bother Papa's business, it wasn't. It was just the other side of the mountain—the mountain we were on—and Flat Top was the closest town to Howling Cut. The Hollis family ran the mill there, and they built up their business through whatever means were necessary; whether it be through the use of bribery, blackmail, or bullying. One way or another, they "won" the business, and the end result was that our mill lost most of our long-time customers, including two furniture stores. The changes that hit us were never more apparent than they were on Christmas morning, when a sparse number of gifts awaited their unveiling beneath our garland-draped tree. So, I opened the present from my parents slowly, to savor it, to keep hoping for those last few remaining seconds before the brown paper was finally pulled off... *Yes! Hallelujah!* Indeed it *was* what I'd been hoping and praying for (and bargaining with God over), for the weeks leading up to *the* day! But that whispering voice inside, the one that makes us face the truth for what it is, told me that a Christmas present of my heart's desire was a thing of the past, a luxury only for those who still had two furniture stores as customers.

And the second reason that I opened my gifts slowly was because of what faced us afterward. I knew that once the paper was off, flattened out and put away to be used again on someone else's package next year, and the last of the Christmas fruit cake had been eaten, we would be forced to look into the eyes of the bleakest, blackest, wickedest thing that always came this time every year. And that wicked thing had a name: Winter.

CHAPTER 5

The Killing Time

When I was almost nine, Mama gave birth to twin boys. When they were finally pushed out into this world, the quietness that filled the room was deafening. It took a few good slaps to get Albert breathing, and though it took less to get Walter to suck his first lungful of air, his breathing was never very ambitious. They were scrawny and sickly from the get-go, and Grandma figured they wouldn't make it to winter. They both did, however, but by the time the wind whipped and bit its way into the middle of January, bringing the worst case of influenza with it, the twins just didn't have enough strength to see it through. Albert went first; then Walter followed four days later.

Because the ground was frozen, we had to put the poor little things into Old Man Tyne's root cellar. He had been the undertaker for longer than anyone could remember, so it just seemed like the logical thing to do. Papa quietly carried each one over to Tyne's place in the back of the wagon, while Mama rested after sleepless nights of poultice making, praying, and carrying each baby, hoping that keeping them upright might help to drain the fluid out of their rattling lungs. Once, when she had been awake for more than two days straight, trying to will the life into her dying sons, I saw her desperately shaking Albert, demanding that the fluid drain out of his wheezing lungs. Grandma gently, but firmly, took the baby from her, telling her she'd shake the child to death before the sickness had a hand in it. Mama didn't say anything. With the most frighteningly vacant look in her eyes, she walked out into a freezing rain. I stood at the window and watched her go into the barn. She didn't come out for hours. Papa finally went out to get her, to let her know that Albert had flown off with the angels, and a keening, howling sound issued forth from that old barn the likes of which I hoped I'd never hear again. Only I did. Four days later, Mama's howling accompanied the screeching wind in a macabre January song.

CHAPTER 6

The Darkest Night

Several weeks after the twins passed, Mama woke Prescott, Merry Beth, and me in the middle of a bitterly cold night. "C'mon," she whispered. "Get dressed, and be quiet about it!" Her long, thick, dark hair hung down like wild ropes about her face. Not only had it not been pinned up into a loose bun on the top of her head, which was her usual style, but it hadn't been brushed either. Her eyes looked like a horse's at branding time, which made her appear like some wild specter, invading the gentle dreams of unsuspecting children.

"Where we goin', Mama?" Prescott asked in a thick, sleepy voice.

"You'll knows when we get there. It's a surprise," she said, though not in that liltingly light tone that announced a happy event to come.

"Can't it wait 'til mornin'?" I asked, not convinced that it would really be any better when morning came, but by then Grandma and Papa would be awake, and if things were amiss, which I definitely felt they were, then perhaps they'd intervene.

"Hush, now!" Mama warned. And no one asked another question. We just stuffed our feet into our shoes, grabbed our coats, and climbed down the ladder from our loft, leaving both Papa and Grandma asleep, snoring and unknowing in their bedrooms.

Mama ushered us into the barn, where, apparently, she had already made the preparations for a trip; for Natty, our mare, was hitched up to the wagon, and a battered suitcase rested in the back corner of it.

"Where're we goin', Mama? I'm cold!" Merry Beth cried, pressing herself into a corner of the barn in an effort to stay out of whatever was about to take place—an event that she just knew, even at the age of six, could have no good attached to it.

"Get in," Mama ordered. And Merry Beth did. We all did. "Now, no one say a word. Do ya hear me? Not a sound!"

We sat huddled together, shaking more out of fear than from the cold as Mama quietly led the horse out of the barn, talking in whispers to keep it quiet and calm as we walked by the chicken coop, then the withered and empty vegetable patch, and finally past our house's front door. When we reached the halfway point on our dirt driveway, she quickly climbed up onto the driver's seat, and with a soft slap of the reins, guided the wagon down to the sawmill road below our house, then took a right, off into the night.

"Where we goin'?" Merry whispered.

"I don't know. But someplace long enough to need a suitcase," I whispered back. "Where ya think, Pres?" I inquired of our brother, who was the only one of us peering over the side of the wagon, while Merry and I stayed down and tucked up against its side, and each other's.

Prescott didn't answer. He just stood, gripping the side of the wagon and looking out, while his dark blond hair whipped in the wind like a strange banner. Finally, he gave up trying to figure it out. The cold won, and fear won, and he lined himself up by us in the bottom of the wagon.

We traveled quite a few miles, and had dozed off and on, but we were jarred fully awake when Natty finally stopped. "C'mon," Mama said, jumping down from her seat and knocking on the side of the wagon where we were huddled. We poked our sleepy heads up over the side like baby birds surveying a new world around us. And we were amazed to find that we were in the front yard of Alice Gentry's house.

Alice Gentry had been Mama's Sunday school teacher when Mama was a young girl living in Marion, a town down the mountain to the south. She had two grown children; a daughter, Polly, and a son, Herbert, both of whom were married and lived in parts unknown to me. Mrs. Gentry had lost her husband of forty-one years to "poor blood" the summer before last and we'd come to her house for his wake. She now lived alone, except for a fat black-and-white cat named Elsa.

"What're we doin' *here*?" Prescott cried.

Mama didn't answer. She just stood at the back of the wagon and waited for us to climb out. There wasn't a sign of life in Mrs. Gentry's house, but it *was* the middle of the night, so that didn't seem out of place, although we did. Mama turned and marched up to the front door, and told us to follow her. Then she gave three sharp raps on the faded blue frame of the screened door. After a few seconds, she repeated this again, and by the time she'd begun the third sequence of knocking, a pinpoint of light could be seen in the far left window and then footsteps sounded.

"Who's there?" asked a sleep-fuzzy but frightened voice.

"It's Anna Guinn, Miz Gentry, and my young'uns."

"Who . . . what?! Anna?! What in the world . . ." Mrs. Gentry opened her wooden front door but not the screened door. "What in heaven's name are y'all doin' out this time of night? And *here*!" She held up her lamp to examine the scene more fully and I was able to see her vaguely familiar, bent, gray-haired form, as well.

"I need to leave 'em with you, Miz Gentry. I need to leave 'em for a while," Mama said in an urgent and unusually high-pitched voice. It was a desperate voice. One none of us recognized. Prescott and I exchanged startled looks and I heard a frightened whimper sneak out of Merry Beth's throat.

"Get in here where it's warm." Mrs. Gentry held open the screened door and looked at Mama questioningly but said nothing. Instead, she walked over to her sideboard and lit a second oil lamp, then handed it to Prescott. "Go on into the kitchen, children," she directed. "There's part of a sweet potato pie on the table."

We were glad for the warm, lamp lit house and our escape—if only for a few minutes—from Mama's company. But, most of all, we were very grateful for the reassuring, even solidness of Mrs. Gentry.

The pie was left untouched as the three of us pressed our ears against the heavy kitchen door. "Anna, sit down," we heard Mrs. Gentry say. There was a thick silence as we waited for Mama to sit down.

"Anna, tell me what's happened, child?" Mrs. Gentry probed. Her voice soothed like a cool cloth on a fevered forehead.

"There's something in the house killin' 'em, Miz Gentry," Mama whispered. "I just know that come spring there won't be a one of 'em left, if they stays there." She half cried, and we heard her move in the room.

"Lord a-mercy, Anna," Mrs. Gentry replied softly. We heard footsteps again, and the creaking of a cabinet door opening, then the clinking of glasses. "Sit down and drink this," she instructed.

"I don't drink spirits!" Mama protested.

"You do tonight," Mrs. Gentry responded.

A moment later Mama coughed. There were several minutes of absolute quiet then. It was almost like Mrs. Gentry was waiting for Mama's thinking to shift, to calm, to clear.

"Anna, you can't possibly believe that any of your children died because of something in that cabin. It's just a part of God's plan, honey—" she continued, but Mama broke her off.

"Miz Gentry, the devil's disciples do terrible deeds on this Earth. I knows," she said, in a low, frightening sounding voice, "there's somethin' evil in that house, and in me! Can't be no other explainin' it."

"Lord, child! Surely you can't believe that was any of your doin'. If you think you're partnerin' up with the devil on this, then so's the whole town. They's all the devil's minions. Shoot, Anna, there's been more of our young'uns—and old'uns, too, for that matter—killed by the grippe than killed in all the wars we've been in. Lord, child! I can't believe what I'm hearin'!"

Mama rose and swayed as she eased her way toward the door. "I got to leave 'em," she whispered. "I got no other choice."

"What about Willa and Calvin, Anna? Why in the world can't they take care of 'em while you go visitin' somewheres for a time? It'd be good for you, honey. Good for you and the young'uns, alike."

"It ain't just me, Miz Gentry. It's the house, too. I don't know which infected the other; the house titched me, or I titched the house. Either way, it ain't good inside of there. It ain't good inside of *me*!"

With those last words, we heard the heavy front door creak open, followed by the screen. We heard Mrs. Gentry's voice fading as she followed Mama out the door, "Anna, for heaven's sake. Calvin won't . . ."

For several minutes there was absolute silence in the kitchen with the exception of our heavy breathing. It was as though we'd been holding our breath and now we were breathing hard in an attempt to make up for lost time.

Finally, we heard one set of footsteps approaching the kitchen door. We scrambled backward and quickly found seats at the table. The untouched pie was a clear sign that no eating had taken place.

"Children," Mrs. Gentry began as she sat down in the vacant chair at the table. "I know you heard what we've been sayin'. I know it's hard to understand, but I think your Mama is plum wore out. Just crazy tired and sad. Sorrow can do funny things to the mind, and sometimes it just makes clear thinkin' an impossible thing to do. What's say y'all spend a couple of days here and let her rest a spell?"

We nodded but no one said a word. The words Mrs. Gentry spoke, however, were both comforting and reassuring, and they were all we had at this moment. We had nothing else to hang on to, for everything in our lives had just shifted. The frigid wind rattled the windows as violently as Mama had just rattled our world.

CHAPTER 7

The Wait

The snow came so hard and so fast the next day that Mrs. Gentry worried about us all being buried alive. We knew she didn't really mean it, although several years before, all the chickens in the coop at the Baxters' had, indeed, been buried alive when the roof caved in after the record snowfall of nineteen inches in a day's time. We felt like those chickens must have, though, when the old roof on Mrs. Gentry's house creaked and groaned in protest at the increasing weight. I envisioned Papa finding us in the spring as they pulled up the splintered boards of the roof only to discover all of us underneath just as flat as my paper dolls.

We knew that Mrs. Gentry wanted to get us home. She figured that Papa and Grandma Willa would be frantic if Mama didn't tell them where we were, and Mrs. Gentry had no phone to call home to let them know. But even if she did have a phone, the weight of the snow on top of the vulnerable lines would have brought them down anyway. There was nothing that could be done about getting out for the time being, and no way of telling anyone where we were. We'd look out at the trunk of a walnut tree in her front yard every now and then, and try to measure the amount of snow that had fallen by measuring its increasing climb toward the letters *H G* about four feet up on the trunk, which had been carved many years before by Mrs. Gentry's son Herbert. The snow continued its path upward toward the letters, and, from the looks of the low hanging gray clouds, it appeared that the storm had enough left in it to make sure the snow covered the old carving and beyond.

Merry and I helped with some household chores, while Prescott kept the back door cleared as best he could so that he could continue bringing in more firewood to save us from freezing to death. Between clearing and hauling, he began whittling a piece of hickory into a stretched-out dog. I knew he felt as I did; if we didn't stay busy doing something—*anything*—we'd go crazy with the wanderings our thoughts would take. Yet, I found that I didn't want to speak much to anyone, save Prescott every now and then. We'd find a moment by ourselves to discuss the grim possibilities awaiting us in the days, months, or years ahead. And, somehow, the fact that Prescott worried along with me was a comfort. We didn't want to let Merry hear our conversations, and, frankly, we knew she didn't want to hear what we had to say, anyway. She'd convinced herself that all was well, and acted as though everything was perfectly normal. And I wondered if it was a blessing or a curse that she could create such a safe and unrealistic cocoon around herself. She showed no concern or fear over our present situation. On the contrary, she seemed to enjoy the attention Mrs. Gentry gave her. Even with Merry's grating chatter, it *felt* so quiet in the house. I knew Mrs. Gentry's pleasant small talk was forced, which made the atmosphere even heavier and lonelier than did the quiet in its pitiful attempt at normalcy.

On the third day after the storm began, it stopped as abruptly as it had started. The sun came out and transformed our surroundings into a crystallized land. Prescott had to climb out of the front window, for the wind had blown so much snow against the doors that it was impossible to push them open. We had run out of firewood from the porch the night before, and the large heap behind the shed was buried deep in snow, so the cabin was almost colder than it was outside. Prescott grabbed the snow shovel and began the backbreaking task of bailing us out. Once the door was clear enough, we pushed while he pulled, and when the door was forced open all of us came out onto the porch, breathing deeply of the chilled fresh air and looking around in amazement at our altered white world.

Softly, Prescott said, "Miz Gentry, when you think we'uns can go on home?"

Mrs. Gentry let out a sigh and looked as though the question had been an expected—and dreaded—one. "Honey, I don't rightly know. We could try to make it on out of here in a couple of days, once the snow has melted some on the road, I guess. But it might be best if we just wait it out 'til your Papa comes to fetch y'all."

"We can't do that, Miz Gentry!" I spoke up. "I bet Mama didn't tell him where she took us, and I bet he and Grandma are worryin' themselves to death. We gotta get on out of here, even if it means we're doin' it by ourselves and walkin'."

"Rachel, honey, you can't go and take to the trail on foot. Why, there's coyotes and wolves out there, and they's as hungry as . . . well . . . bears!"

I started to cry and she pulled me into her small, fragile frame. "There, there, chil'," she soothed. "We'll figure somethin' out. What's say we give it just a wee bit of time, and then see what's what?"

That seemed to satisfy all of us, for we nodded and uh-huh'ed our acceptance of the plan. The truth of the matter, though, was we wondered if we were going to have to face the possibility of Papa and Grandma not coming for us as soon as the roads would allow. Perhaps, once they'd gotten over the shock that Mama had gotten rid of us, and they'd gotten used to fewer mouths to feed and fewer lives to worry over, maybe they'd found that they preferred it that way.

CHAPTER 8

Farewell, Safe Harbor

In the early morning hours of what was to be our fourth day at Mrs. Gentry's, there came a pounding on the door. We all sat up in bed—Merry and me in Polly's old feather bed, and Prescott in Herbert's old room next to ours. Mrs. Gentry hurried out of her room, while pushing her right arm through her flannel robe and firmly telling us to stay put. As she approached the front door, she glanced up at the shotgun hung above the frame as if to reconfirm that it was there for the using.

"Who is it?" she demanded in a tone that was several octaves lower than her normal voice's pitch.

"Miz Gentry, it's Calvin Guinn. Are my young'uns in there?"

The three of us jumped out of our beds and were out in the living room before he even finished his sentence. We knew that voice! We'd waited for that voice! And it now spoke to us through the dead-bolted front door. Mrs. Gentry unlocked it and we flew into Papa's arms. I suddenly heard someone weeping and realized that it was my strong, never-flinching brother. I'd never seen him cry before, and it came out as almost a groaning whine. It was animalistic in its sound; in its rawness and pain. Looking back on it much later, I realized that Prescott had been even more heavily burdened and frightened by the abandonment than Merry or I. Surely the road of uncertainty that perhaps lay ahead of us would be traveled with him in the lead; providing for us, protecting us, and, hardest of all, loving us, not as a young, carefree brother does, but patiently and compassionately, as a parent is expected to do. He was barely twelve, and those slight, thin shoulders had borne the weight of enough worry in those several days to fill up a boy's entire childhood.

Papa seemed to understand this, and uttered reassurances as he kissed him repeatedly, just as he did Merry and me, but the difference was that Papa had never kissed Prescott before, not that I had seen anyway, and that moment of tender affection and understanding between them spoke many unsaid words. Once the hugging and kissing and crying had stopped, we all looked wrung out and exhausted. Finding it hard to catch my breath, I watched Papa with desperate eyes. The next words he might speak would shape our lives ahead.

"We're goin' home." His words were quiet, but firm.

Oh, Lord God of all that's good and right! Sweeter words were never spoken. We were going home! We were wanted, missed, and loved—at least by Papa. We were Calvin Guinn's children, and we were staying that way.

"Children, go gather your things," Mrs. Gentry instructed, exhaling quite loudly as she did so. "And close your bedroom doors so's your Papa and I can have a few minutes to talk before you head on."

We did as we were told, but no one said anything about not pressing our ears to the door. We figured that their words involved us, so the conversation should be ours to hear, too.

"Where's Anna?" Mrs. Gentry asked in a demanding way.

"She's in Morganton, at the state hospital there. She's done gone soft in the head, Miz Gentry. She came home the mornin' she left the young'uns with you, and she picked up Walter and Albert's blankets, walked out to the barn and wouldn't come out of there for nothin'. She wouldn't say a word, neither. Nary a one. I first tried askin' her what she'd done with the young'uns, but she just stared off into space all stone-like. I got real panicky then, and started hollerin' that she'd damned well—pardon the word, Miz Gentry—better take me to 'em, or she'd be askin' the devil himself for a coolin' drink of water before the day was through. She just kept a-starin'. I tried callin' that Doc Pardie, but he was too much into the cups to come out to help, so Willa finally got her to drink a calmin' elixir, and then Anna slept a full day and a half. When she woke up she still wouldn't, or couldn't, talk; just kept a-starin' at the wall, or whatever she was lookin' at and finding so damned—pardon the word, Miz Gentry— so interestin'.

"Finally, Pardie come and looked her over. Said she needed some

serious help to get her fixed up. Said she needed to be over in Morganton. Lord, but we had a time gettin' her there. Guess the words
"state hospital" burrowed through to that convoluted brain of hers,
and she started a-screamin' and a-kickin' and swearing to Jesus
Christ Himself, that she wasn't goin'. I told her I'd divorce her if she
didn't. And I also told her I'd beat the tar outta her and *then* divorce
her if she didn't tell me where my young'uns was. So, she's there in
the crazy ward, and I'm here in your kitchen to fetch my young'uns."

"Lord, Lord, Lord!" Mrs. Gentry said, shaking her head. "All this
death and dyin' and craziness. Dear God in Heaven! I know it was
hard on ya, but ya did the right thing—both in the threats and in the
decision to take her away."

"Oh, no, Miz Gentry, those weren't no *threats*. Those was *facts*!
If'n she didn't tell me where the kids was, I was gonna beat her 'til
she sprouted wings and flew over here to get 'em herself. Now, don't
get me wrong; I ain't never lifted a hand to her—to no woman, for
that matter. But no woman has ever tried givin' my young'uns away
neither."

"Thank the good Lord it didn't come to that, Calvin," she said
kindly, shaking her head again and gently patting my father's arm,
which hung rigidly down at his side with his fist clenched. "She's
where she needs to be," she assured him once more. Then, "Children,
are you ready?" she called.

We left Mrs. Gentry's simple, snow-swept cabin with a mixture
of feelings. On the one hand, it had been a place of uncertainty, filled
with terrifying questions about our future, about our place in the
hearts of the family we so loved. And, yet, it had been a harbor of
calm and stability. A place where one could just be quiet and still
while being comfortably cocooned in the safe company of a woman
whose only seeming frailty was that of an aging body, but not of the
mind, nor the spirit, and, most especially, not the heart.

CHAPTER 9

Answers in a Cup

Mama stayed in the hospital for nine months, and returned a week before my tenth birthday. People at the Glorious Salvation Baptist Church knew she was coming home just in time for my birthday, and they connected the two events as being wonderfully divine. "The good Lord's a-bringin' your mama home fer your birthday, chil'," someone would point out. "And I *know* that's what you must 'a been wishin' fer!" No, what I'd been wishing for was the red-and-blue plaid coat with the lovely—albeit fake—red fur collar on display in Taft's front window. Lord, but I wanted that coat! But the Lord saw fit to bring me a new set of mittens instead (actually, it was courtesy of Grandma's knitting needles, and not the good Lord), and a purportedly good-as-new, powdered-up-pretty, all-too-familiar-looking-but-now-a stranger-to-me mother the day before my special celebration.

Papa had taken the buggy (a most rare occurrence, especially given the fact that it had seen far better days) instead of the wagon, and gone to fetch her in Morganton. He'd left just as the sun had begun to rise over the ridge. Wearing his Sunday suit of worn black wool, and carrying two paper-wrapped ham biscuits for his dinner, he'd climbed into the buggy and headed out. I came walking out of the bedroom several minutes later. Grandma turned from the window over the kitchen sink and told me to sit down and have a cup of coffee with her. Grandma had never offered me coffee before, claiming it'd stunt my growth, but I guess she figured if I was old enough to have to handle a mother who had no handle on things, then I was old enough to drink coffee. I poured it from the pot myself, while Grandma, having taken a seat at the table, stared into her cup as if she were reading tea leaves. She drank her coffee black, so I intended to do the same. However, upon my first taste of it, I knew that Grandma and I took different roads there. After going out to the springhouse and retrieving the small bottle of cream, I added a good dose of it, then two generous spoonfuls of sugar, only to add one more after another test sip from my cup, until I finally had my coffee fixed to my great liking. I was afraid to spill it and be thought of as a little girl—surely too young to indulge in such a grown-up concoction—so, I held the old Dogwood-patterned china cup with both hands and softly slurped the rich drink.

"Lord, chil'," Grandma said, coming out of her deep thoughts. "Don't you know it ain't polite to slurp like that?!"

"It's hot," I countered.

"Then let it set a spell an' cool before you try to drink it," she chided, then went back to staring into her cup.

"What's wrong, Grandma?" I finally had the courage to ask. I knew the answer, but I still felt the need to ask it to see if her fears and doubts mirrored my own.

"I was just wonderin' how your mama's gonna do, being home and all," she said.

"Do you think she'll be . . . well . . . all right? Happy?" I asked, with my voice fading out so softly at the end of my question that Grandma had to lean in toward me to hear it.

"Well, them doctors told your Pa that she's herself again," she said. "The only question is which self; the one before the twins died, or the one after?"

She went back to staring into her coffee cup. And it seemed as good a place as any to look for answers, so I stared down into mine.

CHAPTER 10

A Heart Shift

We heard the buggy pulling up to the house just before dark. Everyone had stayed close to the house, even though it was Saturday. With a mixture of anticipation and trepidation weighing heavily on all of our minds, no one was their usual carefree self on this clear but chilly mid-October day. Instead, we were quiet and withdrawn, or, if we had to interact, our dialog was succinct and sometimes even curt. It was apparent that everyone was on edge about the answers that would soon be given to questions we'd asked ourselves— and each other—over the months leading up to this day. We found ourselves glancing out the windows time and time again, straining our eyes to their limits in an attempt to look as far down the sawmill road as we could in order to announce Papa and Mama approaching. We all felt we needed a moment to prepare ourselves, to take that necessary deep breath, and plan the first few words out of our mouths before she stepped from the buggy.

While I watched and waited, I silently rehearsed the many questions I wanted to ask: "Why did you do it? If losing the twins broke you, why was giving us away the means to mend you? How would that help?" And, most importantly: "Do you love us again, or was it that you never did to begin with?"

I so badly wanted to ask those questions, but I knew I couldn't. In truth, I wasn't ready to. So, I decided to play it safe and say a few polite words—nothing accusatory or offensive. But I was afraid that once I opened my mouth, the floodgates would burst open, too, allowing the depth and intensity of my anger and sadness to come boiling and roiling out. If that were to happen, then it would inevitably lead us to that thing which terrified me the most: hearing her answers to all of my many questions.

When they finally arrived, we heard them before we saw them. We were just finishing up our supper of leftover vegetable soup when the telltale squeaking of the buggy's wheels heralded their arrival. I was very aware of the fact that only Merry Beth excitedly jumped up and ran out to greet them, though I wasn't surprised. There was an undeniable bond between my mother and little sister—one that the rest of the family didn't share with either of them. Merry Beth was developing into a miniature version of our mother—certainly on the outside, and I had started to believe that perhaps on the inside, as well. For I'd seen small but undeniable indications every now and then that led me to believe that Merry Beth might very well be the apple that didn't fall far from the maternal tree.

In her usual fashion, Merry Beth had defended Mama's actions, and had explained Mama's abandonment as an event that, though hard to understand, was in some way warranted. She'd told both Prescott and me that she was sure "Mama hadn't meant nothin' mean by leavin' us with Miz Gentry. Maybe it was just somethin' mamas had to do once in a while." I tried to explain the truth about it time and again, and Prescott had as well, but nothing we said seemed to penetrate her fortress-like defense of Mama. One afternoon, Grandma overheard the volleying back and forth between Merry's pathetic excuses and our frustrated and snide remarks in response, and she walked out of the kitchen, drying her hands on a faded-pink dishtowel, and told Merry Beth to go feed the chickens. Merry Beth told Grandma that they'd already been fed, but Grandma said that we needed extra big eggs for a cake she was planning on baking, and the chickens might give us what we needed with a little extra feed. It was an obvious ploy to get Merry Beth out of earshot, and once she was, Grandma tore into us with a fury I'd never seen in her before, much less aimed at us.

"What the devil is wrong with you two?" she angrily asked. "Don't you know that there'll be no healing in this place if there ain't forgivin' first?"

"Seems to me that's a tall order," Prescott replied, which startled me because I'd never seen him speak so belligerently to Grandma.

Her head actually snapped back, as though she'd been slapped.

But then she quickly walked up to him, looked him fiercely in the eyes, and said in a frighteningly hard, monotone voice, "Son, that woman may be your mama, but she was my daughter first. Don't forget that. She hurt all three of you—*all* of us—I know. And don't think she don't know, too. But something crawled into that woman's soul when her babies died, and she couldn't conquer it. It was a monster, and a thief—a thief of her time with her children who are still here. And it was a monster that changed her into someone we didn't know, someone who couldn't do nothin' but hide in the corner of a barn and howl like a wounded animal, and give her own children away rather than have them stolen away, one after another. That monster, that thief, has a name, and it's one I don't never, *ever*, want you two to forget, because it crawled inside of you two as well, and it's still a-living there now. And its name is Grief. If you don't kill it with forgiveness and love, and lots of it, it'll continue to eat this family alive, until none of us are left to feed it.

Prescott and I were stunned. We were shocked by the anger of her words. I realized much later on that it was an anger born of the deep hurt that filled her. But there was also the agonizing frustration of not being able to fix any of it, or any of us. Grandma had held it all in until it could no longer stay contained, and we were witness to the cracking of her solid, strong, resilient self when it finally came crashing down in an avalanche of emotions.

She seemed as stunned as we were. The three of us just stood there for several seconds staring at each other, until Prescott, unable to hold her gaze any longer, looked down at his mud-spattered shoes and muttered, "Sorry, Grandma."

And, still watching her, I followed with a softly uttered, "Me, too."

Tears that had welled up and begun to slip out of Grandma's reddened blue eyes were quickly swiped away with her pink dishtowel; then she curtly nodded her acceptance of our feeble apologies and stiffly began to clear our supper dishes. As she did, I noticed that her frame seemed suddenly smaller and that her shoulders were slightly hunched over, whereas they never had been before. On the contrary, she was a stickler for good posture and was constantly correcting me on mine. She'd told me that even though I had a limp, if I held myself tall and straight, it would be less noticeable, and whatever small limp remained wouldn't count much if the rest of me didn't seem overly concerned or affected by it. But, as she walked back into the kitchen that afternoon, she looked as though she carried the weight of the world on her shoulders, and the fear, sorrow, and anger that made up that weight was taking a toll both physically and emotionally on her.

My thoughts were startled back to the present as Grandma cleared my soup bowl from in front of me. "Let me help you, Grandma," I offered, quickly rising from the table. Doing the detestable job of washing dishes would buy me a bit more time before I had to face my mother of many faces.

"No, Rachel. You and Prescott go say hello to your ma," she directed. I wondered if she was just trying to give Prescott and me a few minutes alone with our mother first before she went out to see her, or if Grandma needed that tiny extra slice of time to ready herself, too.

We heard faint and muffled voices and footsteps on the front porch. We turned to face the front door, and as we did, Grandma reached out and placed her hands on top of Prescott's and mine, both of which gripped the edge of the table tightly. "She needs you both," she said, "now more than ever before." That one sentence, made up of a total of only nine words, totally dispelled any small notion that I might have had that the mother we had once counted on, leaned on, looked to, and loved was very likely no longer there. And, even if she was, I knew that she would never have enough power to undo that deathblow image I had of her telling Mrs. Gentry that she was leaving us. In that one desperate act, she had fractured the almost indestructible bond between a mother and child. And though I knew she would always be my mother, and that I would always care for her, I also knew that the once warm and kind, fiercely protective "Mama" I had been given at birth was forever gone . . . along with my unconditional love for her.

CHAPTER 11

A Snake in the
Garden of Ginseng

Leonard Lomax had just celebrated twenty-five years as owner of the apple orchard when he passed away. And it was all on account of ginseng picking. It wasn't the picking of the plant that actually caused his demise, but the coiled and concealed copperhead that did him in. Mr. Lomax was a huge, jolly man who played Santa Claus in Howling Cut's Christmas parade each year. There was a lot to like about the man, but not his frugality. One had to be careful when buying apples in bulk from him for he always stuck a few wormy ones down in the middle of the bag or bushel so they couldn't be seen. A lot of applesauce and apple butter came from those apples, and I was always afraid to look too closely at either for fear of what some of those lumps might actually be.

Maybree, his wife, was a dried-up-looking, pious little thing, and it was always curious to me that a man as big and jolly as Mr. Lomax had seen something worth making a wife out of in her. Perhaps she had hidden talents, and perhaps they were what made Mr. Lomax so jolly. But, from all appearances, she was quiet and somber and had no time for pleasantries or foolishness of any kind. She worked the counter in the apple orchard's fruit and gift shop, and she always tucked a handwritten Bible verse in the bag of a customer's purchase. They sold peppermint sticks—the thick, soft kind—and whenever I had a penny, I walked to the orchard store for that treat most dear to my heart. On my birthday, which landed on October twenty-sixth, I always took any pennies I might have received and made a beeline to the store. I knew it was my last chance to get one or two of the coveted treats before they closed for the season. Taft's Mercantile carried peppermints, too, but they were in town which was much further from our house than the orchard. Taft's brand was more expensive, too.

The last day of Mr. Lomax's life was the last day of September. It was picture perfect for ginseng picking, with brilliant Carolina blue skies and just a hint of coolness to the air. Mr. Lomax was eagerly pulling a thick area of the patch when he reached down and *bam!* A copperhead, startled out of a perfectly pleasant nap beside a sun-warmed rock, bit Mr. Lomax on his left index finger. The thing slithered away, but Mr. Lomax, never one to miss an opportunity to make a dollar, sucked the poison from his finger, spat good several times, wrapped it in his monogrammed handkerchief (dutifully embroidered by Maybree), and continued the hunt for the green gold. He comforted himself by saying that he'd never heard of anyone dying from the bite of a copperhead. But what he didn't say to himself was that those who had been bitten were wise enough or afraid enough to go see Dr. Pardie immediately, and if not the doctor, than at least one of the midwives in town who would concoct a poultice of snakeweed to draw the hot poison out of the wound.

By the time Mr. Lomax returned home some hours later, his hand was almost the size of a melon and red streaks were shooting up his arm. Mrs. Lomax put him to bed immediately and started to go call the doctor from the phone at Walcott's Dairy, a mile away, but Mr. Lomax's breathing became so shallow she was afraid to leave him. Finally, once Mr. Lomax had fallen asleep (or unconscious) and his breathing seemed a little better, Maybree jumped into the wagon and hurried off to use the phone. But, while she sat with the phone pressed tightly to her ear, praying that Doc Pardie wasn't too inebriated to answer, the hand of divine intervention stopped Mr. Lomax's hand from throbbing when it stopped his beating heart, too.

Folks gathered around Maybree Lomax with all of the compassion and attention one would expect from a small mountain town. It was the right time for death, given the fact that the weather was cooler, the holidays were just around the corner, and everyone was ready for some excitement. Everyone wanted to be involved, so plenty of cakes and casseroles were baked and delivered to the Lomax house for shared suffering, as well as a sharing of all of the grisly details they could squeeze out of anyone who knew anything, or who was clever enough to make things up as they went along. Just as long as it was believable sounding and gory enough, no one really cared what the truth was or wasn't. Statements issued forth from timid church ladies like, "Don't tell me! I can't bear to hear any more!" However, each one sat glued to her chair, leaning ever closer to the teller of the version being offered at the moment. And she stayed through to the story's end, only leaving when she was sure that no other juicy details could be tweezed out. Then she would dab her eyes and nose in proper grieving style, and say something to the effect that it was just too hard to hear, and would everyone please excuse her as she needed to see about things in the kitchen.

Maybree, and one of her fellow parishioners, Linda Fox, prepared the diminished body for the viewing and laid it out in the Lomaxes' parlor. Finally, a "lovely, lovely!" funeral was held at the Glorious Salvation Baptist Church.

The preacher, Pastor Jasper Dukes, was a firm believer in scaring the sin out of every one of his parishioners. For over an hour he promised that ". . . the flamin' fars of Hell-lah will be a'waitin' those who don't bow down before the Lord God Almighty"—*and him,* I thought to myself—"and profess each and every sin-ah and beg for Jeeezus' sweet salvation!" I glanced down the pew to see ninety-seven-year-old Joyce Baynard's head bowed and her chin resting on her chest. I figured she was either deaf or had a conscience that was clear enough to allow for a little nap during his fire-breathing sermon. But she did wake up in time to holler a loud and sure "Amen!" at just the right time nearing the end of the pastor's performance. I muttered an obligatory but unenthusiastic "Amen" too, as I was busy wondering who'd take me to town for my birthday peppermints next month since Mrs. Lomax was closing the store. Over the next few weeks, the orchard would harvest and sell all its apples, and once that was done, the place would be put up for sale.

CHAPTER 12

Hail the Floundering Hero

Everyone wondered what would become of the apple orchard, and it took a year to find out. A distant cousin of Maybree's, Mr. Gilbert Harris, had been doing odd jobs down in Macon, Georgia, since returning from his tour of duty in WWI, late in September of 1918. He'd been blinded in his left eye after an unfortunate accident involving the lid of a pressure cooker that blew off, striking him on the left side of his face during the cooking of a pot roast on board a naval battleship patrolling the waters off of France. Very few people were told the true version, though, and were instead given a well-spun, highly detailed story of unselfish bravery and disregard for his own life in order to save the badly injured captain of their ship during a particularly heavy artillery bombardment. According to Gilbert's story, the captain "was hit fair in the head" during "that epic battle of the sea." Glorious but grisly scenes were described of how he'd attempted to drag his wounded leader inside the mess hall as a scene of carnage raged on around them. Then, just as he had his captain halfway through the doorway, the brave Gilbert Harris took one for his country.

After the war, Mr. Gilbert Harris found that war heroes were plentiful, and though they were graciously welcomed back to their motherland with confetti-strewn parades and colorful speeches, all too soon their heroic deeds were filed away in scrapbooks in attics, and it was back to business as usual. If Mr. Harris had dreams of grandeur about being given the world on a silver platter for his sacrifices, he was quickly and painfully set straight. Time and time again, he was turned down for jobs. The excuse was repeated over and over that the "position had just been filled." But the truth of the matter—and Gilbert began to get the picture—was that business owners were concerned about frightening off their customers with the new heroic clerk who closely resembled Mary Shelley's Frankenstein, with the large, vertical scar running down his face, along with a drooping, sightless, milk-blue left eye accompanying it. So Mr. Harris did odd jobs around town for the next two years—jobs which offered meager pay and even less respect. Finally, after a long day of tobacco picking, Mr. Harris took the much-disliked graveyard shift running a printing press in the back room of a new-to-town printing company. The printing, he soon found out, was of a felonious nature, and fearing that he'd wind up in the state pen, or worse, he literally walked away three weeks later. He didn't give notice. He just left one morning at the end of his overnight shift without saying a word. He knew that they knew what he knew, and he worried that the shop owners would see to it that he was headed back to sea, but this time with an anchor tied to *him* and not to a United States battleship. So, he packed up his family before noon that day, and moved his thirteen-year-old son Jackson, nine-year-old daughter Harriet, wife Lydia, their mutt Tootie, the cat Peepers, and some of their household belongings in their wagon and headed north to his brother Lyle's home in Akins, South Carolina. Over a second helping of banana pudding two nights later, Lyle informed him of the odd death several weeks before of their uncle-by-marriage, poor old snake bitten Leonard Lomax, and the apple orchard that their grieving Aunt Maybree had no interest in keeping now that her beloved Lenny was gone.

Gilbert found it hard to sleep that night and by the next morning he had a newfound direction in life; that of being the future apple orchard owner and shop proprietor. The next morning the Harris family piled into their overly stuffed wagon and Gilbert slapped the reins and let out an enthusiastic "Yah!" to spur on their tired old horse. Off they set for Howling Cut, North Carolina, as the reddish gray dust from the South Carolina dirt road kicked up and out behind them, nicely covering their past.

CHAPTER 13

The Birthday Redeemer

The note taped to the jar on the candy counter in Taft's Mercantile said the peppermints were two cents apiece, and since I only had three cents I could only get a stick and a half. And they weren't selling halves.

"I'll take one, please," I said in a downtrodden voice.

Mrs. Taft tucked one in a small brown paper bag (minus the Bible verse), and rang up the sale. I thanked her, walked off with the bag, and waited for Papa to come out of the feed store. I'd thought about going over there to see if he could make up the difference by giving me the extra penny, but knowing that times were so very hard and that the peppermints at Taft's just weren't like the orchard's most delectable soft ones, I resigned myself to the single stick. Then I settled down on the sidewalk to savor it next to our wagon, which was lined up between two others on Pickney Street, the dusty main thoroughfare in our town.

As I sat there licking and waiting for Papa, I rolled my newly acquired age of eleven around in my head, and it felt good. I liked it. I also reviewed the birthday gifts I'd received that morning. First, Grandma had given me a hair comb; one that she said had been her grandmother's and that I was now old enough, and responsible enough, to wear. The comb had little blue and green crystals in the frame, and they twinkled like jewels in the mid-morning sun. Mama and Daddy had given me the expected pair of new black shoes—to be worn on Sundays, and special occasions only, one of which, they agreed, was today. Prescott offered up his gift next, which was a well-worn comic book with the next to the last page missing, but he volunteered to fill me in once I reached that part. I didn't want to diminish the generosity of his gift by telling him that I'd read all of his comic books at least twice, so I'd be able to fill in the blanks myself. Instead, I told him how nice it was that he should give one to me. Finally, a piece of candy was pulled from Merry Beth's pocket; one she had saved from a little birthday party she'd been to at her friend's house the week before. After pulling the lint off the sour lemon ball, I quickly devoured it. All in all, it hadn't been a bad birthday, and I felt real appreciation and tenderness toward them all for their gifts, knowing that little sacrifices had been made in order to give them. Yet, at the same time, there was a touch of resentment toward Mama as I knew things would have been different—that I, too, might have had a small party—if she'd felt strong enough to have arranged one. Though Mama had been back for a year, she still seemed weak and tired. Rarely did we see a flash of her old self; the one that balanced strength and independence with a beautiful, vibrant femininity. And when she did give us a glimpse of that person I so deeply missed, I learned not to get my hopes up and expect that version of her to remain. It always slipped away, returning to that place of separateness and quiet in which she chose to live most of the time. I had heard Grandma saying quietly to her in the kitchen two days before, as they stood at the sink washing the supper dishes, that they still had time to bake a cake and some cookies and have a few of my friends over if Mama felt up to it. But Mama had muttered an even softer "let's not," and the subject had not been brought up again.

While mulling this over, and trying (but with great difficulty) to convince myself that Mama was doing the best she could at the moment and that I really didn't want a party anyway, a slow moving, overly loaded wagon grabbed my attention as it rambled into town from the south end of Pickney Street. A wiry black dog in the back was heatedly barking back at a golden retriever that ran along the wagon's side. Finally, the barbershop owner, Fred Stiles, called to his retriever, Moe, and the dog ran back into Fred's shop.

A badly scarred, tired-looking man was driving the wagon, and an even more tired-looking woman sat next to him. As they moved past me, I saw a dark-haired boy, perhaps a little older than me, and a dark-haired younger girl, with her arm slung around the now quietly panting dog, sitting on a faded, blue-flowered beige couch in the bed of the wagon. The boy looked over at me as I was busy studying them—him, mostly—and we looked hard at each other for a brief second before my peppermint stick was roughly yanked out of my hand.

"Looky here! It's Laggin' Leg!" said a familiar, taunting voice from behind me.

Ray Coons sneered down at me. I hated Ray. I hated him with every fiber of my being for creating my torturous nickname. I jumped up to grab my candy and when I did, Ray laughed and pushed me, causing me to fall off of the sidewalk and into a pile of horse dung that Natty, our very own horse, had dropped as she stood hooked to our wagon waiting patiently for Papa to return. At the moment, however, she stomped and stepped nervously about after the commotion of the barking dogs and my fall. More concerned about being stomped on by her shoed hooves than anything else at the moment, I scrambled out from underneath her and limped away as quickly as I could. I looked around for further assault from Ray, but he had hurriedly run down the street before anyone else could point him out as the culprit. As I leaned against the front of Taft's, trying to stop shaking and trying even harder to make myself small and invisible, I realized that my hair smelled awful, and felt heavy, too. It was pushed back in a strange way from the right side of my face and when I reached up to untangle it I felt a large glob of horse dung caked all through it. Snarled in the mess was Grandma's comb. I pulled it from my hair, then began to cry as I realized that one of its teeth had been broken off. Walking over to the horses' watering trough, I worked the old handle of the rusted pump and held the ancient comb beneath the lukewarm water, trying to wash away the stinking, nauseating remnants of Natty's deposit. The final blow came, though, when I realized that one of the comb's green crystals was missing, too, which turned my soft crying into hard, breath-sucking sobbing. Regardless of the fact that it was nearly impossible to breathe, I bent over and held my matted, filthy hair beneath the flowing water. Finally, when I'd done all I could, I hoisted my dirty and damaged self up and over into our wagon's bed, lying down so that no one could see me or further torture me on this, my most special day.

Suddenly, Natty snorted and my eyes snapped open. Realizing that I must have fallen asleep and was now staring up into a blinding noonday sun, I quickly shut them and rolled over onto my left side. I was busy watching the orbs of light dance behind my eyelids when suddenly I heard a soft, scraping, papery sound come from above and to my right. Turning my head toward the sound, I saw a hand pulling back from the wagon's seat. Fearing it was Ray Coons again, I lay quietly, not breathing, and prayed to God that Ray would not see me tucked in the back. After a minute of stillness, I cautiously sat up and looked on the seat.

There, lying on the passenger's side of the wagon's bench lay a small, brown paper bag. I reached out and poked at it, afraid something alive, slithery, and poisonous might be lying in wait inside. But when nothing poked pack, I gingerly picked it up with two fingers and placed it down by me in the wagon's bed. Inside, glistening and wonderful and delivered from some heavenly birthday angel above, were two brand new, beautiful peppermints sticks. My mouth formed into a perfect surprised *O*, then quickly but timidly I peeked out over the side of the wagon. Settling back onto the faded blue-flowered couch in the bed of the strangers' wagon was the dark-haired boy. In his hand was another brown paper bag. He looked up at me as though he knew I must be watching, and seeing that I was, he opened his bag, pulled out a peppermint stick, smiled the most beautiful smile I'd ever received and promptly stuck it in his mouth.

I laughed out loud in response, and then, while never taking my eyes off of him, I reached into my own bag and promptly stuck a peppermint into my own waiting mouth. I saw his shoulders rise and fall in a slight chuckle. He seemed pleased by my surprise and delight. I couldn't know if it seemed like a little thing to him, this kindness he'd shown me, but it was a large and indescribable moment for me. With his one small act of compassion and sympathy, this boy had created his own place in my heart. He was my ally and friend, and I instantly loved him. Now all I needed to know was his name.

CHAPTER 14

Into the Mist

The end of 1921 and most of 1922 were an ongoing process of trying to regain and maintain some semblance of normalcy in our lives, as normal as our family could hope to be, anyway. We'd all been affected by Mama's actions. She kept pretty much to herself, and because of that, our garden had never been more bountiful, our clothes had never been kept as spotlessly clean and well pressed, and our family's cemetery had never had such a frequently revolving array of fresh flowers gracing each headstone as it did with Mama's almost obsessive care of it. She involved herself in her chores as enthusiastically as most parents involve themselves in their children's lives. The space that she'd created between herself and the family was apparently a comfortable place for her to be. And, so, we mostly gave it to her. Merry Beth, however, seemed intent on pleasing Mama, perhaps in the hope of keeping her happy enough to not try giving us away again. Merry's chores were always finished before Mama could issue a second request to do them, and she constantly made, found, or, on rare occasion, bought little gifts for Mama. It was both pathetic and irritating to watch my little sister's attempts at trying to win Mama's affection and approval.

Prescott, on the other hand, continued to be so angry with our mother that he found things to do away from home as much as possible. Cutting firewood for a couple of widows who lived close by, as well as painting, mending fences, and working in their gardens, gave him legitimate reasons for being gone all day, most every day. But all of that changed when Mama told him on his fourteenth birthday that he was far too old to continue sharing the loft with Merry and me. Thus, Prescott—and Papa, whenever available—began construction on the addition that would be his new bedroom. He worked feverishly throughout the warm weather months, and well into the cold ones until his hands shook from the freezing temperatures as he tried to hold a nail steady while hammering.

When Papa allowed, Prescott accompanied him to the sawmill to help cut logs for the addition, and he even undertook some simple carpentry work, building several simple but sturdy pieces of furniture for his room, including a desk, chair, and frame, head-, and footboards for his bed. Prescott carved a beautiful wolf in the headboard, and even though he was a novice, he was actually very good. But sometimes the materials just weren't available at the mill and with every delay, Prescott showed growing impatience for the maddening interruption of his beloved project. The widows, however, were glad for those delays, and Prescott was mollified by the small income the extra work brought.

Mama's sympathetic decision to allow Prescott the space he needed—both literally and figuratively—brought about a shift in Prescott's attitude toward her. He seemed to find some peace for himself, and, apparently, some forgiveness for her, for the heaviness that had permeated the air around them ever since she'd returned home gave way to an easier relationship between them. It struck me as ironic that it was Mama's idea to build on to our home and, consequently, build up the relationship with her son when she had come so very close to completely tearing both apart.

Papa went about his usual routine at the sawmill, with business getting better it seemed, for our bill at Taft's was paid regularly. There was plenty of sugar, flour and coffee in the cabinets; and our clothing didn't fall off of us before enough money was scraped together to purchase more, or to buy new material so that it could be made. Papa, not wanting to upset Mama in any way, tried overly hard to do for her and please her. It seemed as though the guilt of having to threaten her with a divorce in order to learn our whereabouts ate at him. He loved Mama, that much was clear, but the whys and wherefores of that love were way beyond what I could understand. It seemed to me that the threats he'd been forced to make had been well deserved. But, apparently, Papa was so affected by the intensity of his anger toward this fractured woman whom he'd promised to always love, cherish, and protect that he continued to try to make it up to her.

On their eighteenth wedding anniversary, Papa presented Mama with a brand new buggy. Dark green with gold fringe running along the edge of the carriage's top, it was the most beautiful conveyance I'd ever seen. Mama *ooohed* and *ahhhhed* over it, while I stood back in disbelief. There was something about the whole scene that was unsettling to me, and I didn't know what to say. Grandma, on the other hand, trying to see the good in things as usual, said it'd be wonderful to take a Sunday drive in it, and if they'd like to do that after church service, she'd be glad to put on a pot of chicken and dumplings for our dinner. Merry immediately jumped up onto the driver's seat and said she thought that'd be fun and could they ride over to see our cousins' new colt. Grandma told her that she'd be staying put with Prescott and me, and helping her bake a carrot cake that afternoon. As we rode to church in the new buggy, two questions plagued me: Why had Papa been given, while I had not, the blessing of a heart that loved so deeply that forgiveness was given automatically and completely? And how had Papa been able to afford the buggy?

Grandma's relationship with Mama had done its own share of shifting and was as complicated as everyone else's, although Grandma had said numerous times that things behind us should be left there. But it wasn't as easy as that, not even for her. She had never been an overly demonstrative woman, but was even less so with Mama now. There was a touch of sharpness in the way Grandma spoke to her, and looked at her, and rarely did a smile accompany Grandma's words or reach her eyes. The space between the two women was the widest and saddest of all in some respects, and I just figured it was because Grandma was mad at Mama for what she'd done. It never occurred to me that Grandma might have actually been mad at herself.

My relationship with Mama was quite different from the others', though. Simply put, it had flatlined. My anger and hurt had dimmed over time, but I was left with a heart that had little feeling in it for her. And the little bit that was there bordered on indifference. I viewed her as weak and broken, and I had little tolerance for her. Had I been brutally honest with myself, however, I would have admitted that I was scared to death that the apparent cracks in her soul might have been passed on to me. I wouldn't even let myself consider the matter, though—at least not consciously. It was just easier and more comfortable to distance myself from her. I knew that the Bible told us to judge not, lest we be judged, but I didn't care. And I thought that Jesus had some nerve expecting me to forgive and forget all when He'd had the mother of all mothers. *She'd* never abandoned *Him*!

One of the things we were most grateful for during that time was that no family deaths were recorded in our Bible. We did lose one friend, however: Delford Mays. He wasn't a close friend, but he was a member of our "church family," so we were required to feel sad about it. Personally speaking, I wasn't. Delford had a terrible habit of adjusting his crotch whenever he was passing the time of day with someone—as long as it was a female someone—and he didn't particularly care who that someone might be: young, old, or in between. Making matters even more repulsive was the fact that his breath always smelled like onions. I asked Grandma about his crotch-grabbing habits one Sunday as we rode home from church, and she said that "Delford was trying to convince everyone he had more down there than in his durn head!"

"Mama!" my mother admonished.

"Well, it's the truth, Anna," she countered, with a twinkle in her bright blue eyes. "That man is still tryin' to get hitched, and to let his possible bride-to-be know that she's in for a good ol' time."

"Lord, Mama!" my mother sighed, exasperated.

"He sure ain't shy about it neither," Grandma continued. "He does it in front of everyone—including the preacher's wife! Guess he's not discountin' anyone as a possibility!" Then she snorted with great laughter. We all laughed with her, even Mama.

Delford was only forty-four years old when he suffered a heart attack while working on a story for our town's weekly paper, *The Update.* Ironically, the article he was writing was entitled, "The Road Home," a piece about the return of our servicemen and -women following their tours of duty. Many a remark was made about *that* little irony of life, and not all of the quips were complimentary of the way Delford had lived his. Not everyone was so sure that the road he had taken home went north instead of south. "He never did like the heat, poor ol' thing," Mrs. Alvina Brown laughingly remarked, "bein' heavy and all." More snickering and unchristian-like comments from the Christian ladies followed that statement.

So, considering that we still had a roof over our heads, food on the table and in the feed troughs, wood for our stove and fireplace, a fancy buggy in the barn, and all family members could be counted alive, it hadn't been a bad year at all.

I turned twelve that October, and I actually received the birthday present I'd asked for—a brassiere. As humiliating as it was to ask for such a thing, it was a necessary item, especially when trying to jump rope at school.

I figured my folks must have felt sorry to be giving me so mundane a gift, though, because tucked beneath the undergarment, hidden in a soft green silk pouch, was a lovely little pearl bracelet. Quickly tucking the bra into the pocket of my flannel robe, I set my attention to my new bracelet and thanked Mama and Papa with joy.

"The 'thanks' goes to Grandma, honey," Mama corrected. "She's the one responsible for the bracelet. It belonged to her."

I looked over at Grandma, and she pretended to be thoroughly involved in folding up my discarded wrapping paper. "Thanks, Grandma," I said, smiling with deep appreciation. Though a bra was what I most needed, it was one of the least desired items I'd ever asked for. Grandma's beautiful and generous gift was a wonderful and welcome surprise. It saved my birthday for me that year.

"Every *young woman* should have a piece of pearl jewelry," she answered, giving my new age status a little extra emphasis, along with a knowing smile. She knew that the much-needed bra was an obvious indicator that my body was changing, but Grandma was also aware that my thoughts were changing, too.

One day two weeks earlier, Grandma and I were in the barn milking our cows, Tess and Minnie, and I asked her if she'd heard any more about the goings-on with the Harris family (whose boy was the ever-fondly-and-frequently-thought-of "peppermint boy"). We knew that the family had gone into partnership with Maybree Lomax and her apple orchard, and were now the proprietors in residence since Maybree had moved in with an old maid sister in Hardeeville, South Carolina.

They'd worked hard in the months following their arrival, fixing up the orchard's store, the adjacent home, and the struggling orchard itself, but Mother Nature had given the family an early lesson in who was truly in control when she zapped the newly budding old apple trees with the terrible spring blizzard of twenty-two. Injury was heavily added to insult when three days of howling winds followed, coupled with relentless single-digit temperatures. The cold didn't settle down into the valleys because of the winds, and because the orchard grew up the sides of three mountains, the frigid winds attacked the trees with demonic force. It was the granddaddy of all freezes, killing or damaging quite a few of the old apple trees and their offspring in the orchard. The cold also killed an enormous number of the county's trees and vegetation, countless animals, as well as five people in and around Howling Cut. I couldn't help but wonder if the Harris clan felt they'd made a colossal mistake in going into the hugely difficult, not to mention enormously risky, business of running an apple orchard.

Although the Harris children were obviously school-aged, they hadn't set foot in our one room schoolhouse yet. I *had* seen them outside of the Howling Cut First Methodist Church on several Sunday mornings, though, as it was just down the road from our church. The boy—Jackson, I'd learned his name was—had waved to me twice. I didn't wave back, though, as I didn't want questions or comments from my family. Mostly, I didn't want my parents to know there had been some trouble in town with Ray Coons, even though it had been a year before. And I didn't want to explain Jackson's involvement.

My family, however, figured he was waving to them all and they waved in return. But Grandma's head snapped around to look at me, as though she understood that his wave was directed at me, and she smiled an amused, knowing smile. *Knowing what?* I irritably wondered. But Grandma just knew a lot about . . . well . . . a lot. She was, after all, the Wart Buyer. So, when I asked her what news she'd heard about the Harris family as we milked the cows, she answered that she had not gotten "any more particulars on 'em," and then she turned away from Minnie's udder to smile broadly at me, looking as though she'd just heard something quite funny come out of my mouth.

Lordy, I thought, *I'm only askin' a dad-burned question.* But, the grin on Grandma's face made me uncomfortable enough that I abruptly jumped up from the milking stool, hurriedly grabbed the bucket from underneath Tess, which caused a good amount of its contents to slosh out, and announced that the cow had given all she could for the day. Grandma's amused cackling burned my ears far more than the north wind as I hurried out of the barn and crossed the yard heading for the kitchen door.

About a week after my birthday, as I walked back to the kitchen after gathering enough eggs from the henhouse for our breakfast, I saw a gentle veil descend over our yard. It danced and floated like a coy spirit, evasive in its movements. The early morning fog, born of the rain the evening before, gently played down around Mama's freshly hung laundry and me. I stood still and watched it for a moment, wondering how it must feel to be that free. How it must feel to be able to come and go and be, and do those things you were simply moved to do. And I swore then and there that I would go and be and do the things *I* chose to. But I knew that in order to find out exactly what my choices might be, I would need to venture out and away— perhaps far away—from this place.

The realization shot through me with a frightening and powerful jolt, and I quickly moved on toward the house. Then I ran. I knew that the eggs had to make it with shells intact to the kitchen counter, but standing there feeling the weight of my future waft in and out and around me struck an inexplicable fear in me. Perhaps it was because I suddenly knew that there was no "forever" in my life in regards to this place. Or perhaps it was because I suddenly understood how quickly the ideas of yesterday could be changed and rearranged by a simple night's sleep, by swirling fog, a trip to the henhouse, or by just standing still in one's own backyard.

"Rachel! Slow down with them eggs!" Mama scolded from the back porch. "You'll break every single one of 'em."

Looking at Mama as I slowed my pace caused the tightness in my stomach to begin loosening up. Not because the sight of her reassured me. On the contrary, it made me that much more determined to move on one day, freely, boundlessly, into the mist of my future. Wherever and whatever that might be.

CHAPTER 15

The Moon Man

The next Saturday morning, the first in November, Grandma hitched Natty up to the wagon and placed a basket in the bed of it.

"Where you goin', Grandma?" I asked as I approached her from the door of the barn while she tucked a light blue-and-white checked dishtowel more securely in and around the food in the basket. I could smell some of the ham biscuits from this morning's breakfast, as well as the blackberry pie she'd made last night, which I'd assumed we'd have after dinner today.

"I'm goin' to see Samuel Harold. You know, the Moon Man." She smiled. "It's his birthday," she added in an off-handed way as she turned back to her task.

"The Moon Man! Who's the Moon Man?" I quickly moved up beside her. She had my undivided attention.

"*Samuel Harold.* You know, chil', the *Moon* Man!" she emphasized, as if doing so would clear things right up for me. She placed two jars of bread-and-butter pickles, a jar of pickled beets, and one of split runner beans into an old crate that she had braced against the wicker basket.

"I don't know him," I stated.

She turned and stared at me in the oddest way for several seconds as if processing this newly acquired bit of information, and then told me to run into the house and tell someone that I was going with her. Strangely enough, she told me to tell someone other than Mama, and to beat it back to the wagon in a hurry. The fact that Grandma wanted me to avoid letting Mama in on our plans was utterly delicious to me.

I ran into the house to find that Mama was taking stock of the jars of food in the pantry, so I ran up the ladder to the loft where Merry was sitting before the vanity's mirror working on braiding her thick dark hair. When I told her I was going with Grandma, Merry Beth said she wanted to go, too, as I'd expected, and started toward the ladder. The discussion ended quickly enough, though, when I pointed to her feet and told her to put on her thickest snake boots for there were plenty of them where we were going. I knew she hated the reptiles with a passion, and my tactics for dissuading her from going worked perfectly; she abruptly turned back around, went back to her braiding, and offered up the excuse that if she went with us there'd be no one else around to help Mama with the cooking. Issuing a compliment on how considerate she was of others, I made a hasty retreat down the ladder, and hightailed it out to the wagon, where Grandma was waiting and ready. I pulled myself up onto the seat next to her, and then, leaning forward, she picked up the reins and slapped them against Natty's back. We lurched forward as the wagon rolled out of the barn.

"Who's the Moon Man, Grandma, and where're we goin'?" I asked again once we turned onto the sawmill road. I figured that since I was now part of this mysterious mission, I had the right to know.

"Samuel Harold, like I said before," Grandma firmly stated. "Don't ask any more questions right now, Rachel. Let's just listen to the world go about its business around us for a spell, while we go on about ours."

After that, I kept my questions to myself, loving the whole idea that just Grandma and I were headed to parts unknown, to see a man who was also unknown—to me, anyway. Soon I would be privy to the world of one Samuel Harold, a.k.a. The Moon Man, and I couldn't help feeling excited. But, at the same time, there was an unexplainable feeling of anxiousness, too. After all, I was with my Grandma, a strong and reliable force in my life, so what was there to fear?

It was just so uncharacteristic of her to be so cryptic about something, and because this was behavior I'd rarely seen in her before, and it was in relation to some aspect of her life that I had no knowledge of either, it gave me a very unfamiliar feeling of being uncomfortable in her presence. I just didn't know what to think, much less to say, so abiding by her request, I said nothing more for a long while. Instead,

I just watched the dirt road weave and wind and lead us onward into unexplored territory.

We crossed the Titan Mountain pass, which was about seven miles north of us. Then we took a series of switchbacks, and crossed Lightner's Creek, the Bolsey River Bridge, and came out on the river road. I had only come this way one other time in my life and that was to attend my second cousin's wedding at a small Methodist church nearby.

I glanced over at Grandma, and watched the wind whip loose the strands of her hair from the knot at the base of her neck. She must have felt me watching her for she glanced over at me and gave me a smile—one that seemed a little nervous, I thought. There was apprehension there, and as quickly as the smile came, it was gone; then she redirected her focus back to the curving road, and her own thoughts.

A couple of hours after we'd set out, we turned left onto a well-rutted and worn path that was just past the Bolsey River Gristmill. Giant oak, maple, and hickory trees encroached on the ancient-looking trail, blocking out the dim November sunlight with their heavy branches, many of which were adorned with browning yellow and red leaves. Some of the branches hung down low enough to knock us off the wagon's seat. I scooted closer to Grandma, and she mumbled something about the trees having grown so much over the years, which made me wonder just how *many* years she'd been coming to this isolated, dark place. We traveled about a half-mile further down the old path until we came around a bend and into view of one of the strangest sights I'd ever seen before.

In the middle of a clearing stood a very old, rather small log cabin that had been weather-darkened to a deep molasses brown. Over the front doorway was a plaque with the Lord's Prayer handwritten in what had once been bright blue paint, with two simple crosses painted in now-faded white on each side of the words. But it wasn't the cabin with its religious signs that made the scene strange, it was the trees, or rather what was *in* the trees. For there, hanging from and amid the branches were hundreds of hand-cut and carved wooden or metal crescent moons, in all shapes, sizes, and colors. Some had faces painted or carved on them, while others were plain and somehow frighteningly beautiful in their own simplicity. They hung from the tree branches with fishing line, so that it seemed as if they floated on their own. They spun, bounced, and swirled in the chilly November wind, then calmed in their movement between the gusts to a gentle swinging and swaying.

"What are they doin' here, Grandma?" I asked in a breathy whisper. *And what are we doin' here*, I silently asked myself.

"Keepin' haints out," she answered.

Warding off ghosts was not the answer I'd hoped to hear. That was not one of the calming, reassuring answers that I could usually count on from her. This was an answer that almost began to make me sorry I had come along for the ride . . . almost, but not quite.

"How many are hauntin' this place, Grandma?" I whispered.

"Only one, that I knows of anyway," she answered.

"Who is it?" I asked.

"Your granddaddy, chil'."

I immediately looked at the plaque over the front door, and when I understood the reason for it, started reciting the Lord's Prayer to myself: *Our Father, who art in Heaven, hallowed be Thy name. Thy kingdom come . . .* This was as good a time for it as there ever had been in the history of mankind. *Oh, God, oh, Jesus! Oh, God, oh Jesus (and any others that might want to jump right in here to help me!)*, I prayed, *I swear on my family's Bible that if you'll keep that ghost—my granddaddy!—away from me, I'll try to like Mama better again, and I'll not wish bad things on Ray Coons. Well, I won't wish for things to happen to him that could kill him, anyway. And I'll never touch my breasts—or anyplace lower—under my sheets at night again.*

I was so scared I couldn't even ask why my granddaddy (who'd died before Mama was born) was haunting this, of all places. And, most importantly, why was he haunting *any place* at all?

Suddenly, a shotgun blast snapped me out of my holy supplications, and caused Natty to buck and try to turn around.

"Whoa, Nat! Whoa!" Grandma called to the startled horse, while pulling on the reins in quick response. As no other shot was forthcoming, Grandma loudly called out, "Sam, it's Willa. Willa Holton! Come out here, old dog, where I can see ya."

"Great day in the morning!" An excited voice exclaimed from around the back of the cabin. "Willa? Is it truly you, gal? Sweet Savior! Hold on, I'm a-comin'!"

And, with that, a rather thin but strong-looking man of medium height came into view with a shotgun in his right hand and a long, fat, dead rattlesnake in the other. He had thick, mostly gray hair, but with golden blond streaks running through it, and his eyes were an intense rich brown. I wasn't sure which one I should be more afraid of, but I was pretty sure it was the old man given that the snake's head was gone. I leaned into Grandma, who patted my knee reassuringly, and then yelled back to the man in a high-spirited, animated way: "Samuel Harold. Look at the likes of you! My land, but you're lookin' fairly good for a man who's a celebratin' sixty-two years today!"

"Ah, Willa, my gal. Is it my birthday? I hadn't thought about it." He lowered his eyes and shook his head in a reflective, where-have-the-years-gone kind of way. Then he looked back at Grandma, and displaying a handsome smile that boasted a full set of teeth, he said, "Come down here and give this old man a squeeze!"

Grandma actually did as she was bidden and it was a moment I knew I'd never forget. The years seemed to fall away from her as she slipped over the side of the wagon. And with a most submissively feminine act of compliance, this woman of unbendable strength and wisdom, a woman who almost always managed to keep her feelings in check, gave in to this stranger's appeal and went without hesitation into his outstretched arms. "There's a first time for everything," I'd heard her say countless times. I knew that this was certainly one of those "first times," and, perhaps, the last time that I'd ever see my grandmother so unabashedly caught up in such an intimate moment.

They spoke softly and it was obvious that their words were only for each other. Strain though I might, I couldn't make out full sentences and just caught a murmured "good" or "missed" and several "blessings" in their quietly private conversation.

There was something about their meeting that was both joyful and sad. I didn't understand the *why* of any of it, because I didn't know their story yet, but it was clear to see that there was indeed a story, and it was one that was not an open book for the world to read. I knew I was privy to a scene that was one of the later chapters from a tale that had begun a long time ago; one that deeply involved these two lives, but that had somehow brought them to this near-conclusion of moon-filled trees, ghosts (of many kinds, I was sure), and rare, yet emotion-filled words. These were all part of a deep and cherished understanding between them. I felt confused by it, and awkward, yet absolutely fascinated as I witnessed the latest moment in their story.

"Sam, this is Rachel, my eldest granddaughter. You've heard me talk a lot about her," she said, suddenly self-conscious as though she'd just remembered I was there—and watching them.

"Great day in the mornin'! Rachel!" he said, looking at me as though I'd come from one of his hanging moons. "My God, but you look like your grandma! All except the color of your hair, 'a course."

I smiled, pleased to be compared to her, and muttered a soft "hello," and "thank you."

A rising wind made the moons dance and swirl in an agitated way. "Let's go on in," Sam said, looking up at the sky and sniffing at the same time. "I smell rain, and it's comin' in quick."

"Well, help me with the food I brought ya, Sam. There's a pie in there that'll be ruined if we don't get 'er in quick-like."

With that, I followed the Moon Man and Grandma over to the wagon, and grabbing the crate and wicker basket, we hurried inside.

I glanced up at the hand-painted plaque with the Lord's Prayer on it before stepping inside, hoping it would ward off any ghosts that might otherwise be lurking in the corners, not to mention large spiders or the family of the beheaded rattler. From the outside there didn't appear to be any gaps between the logs, but varmints still had a way of finding their way in to seek the warmth of a fireplace, not to mention the occasional crumb that the Moon Man might carelessly drop. But upon entering, I realized that the cabin was well cared for and far neater than I'd expected.

Just inside the door was a lovely old oak hall tree. It had delicate, richly detailed carvings of birds and flowers adorning the top edge, and centered below was an oval beveled mirror. Though darkened by age, the piece was elegantly beautiful and free of any smudges or dust. There were wooden hooks to each side of the mirror and an oil-skin jacket and hat were hung from one, while neatly placed on the floor below were galoshes that were well-worn but wiped free of mud. The Moon Man hung our coats on the hall tree's empty hook and then we followed him into his sparsely furnished but pleasant and warm living room. There were two matching wing-backed chairs that were done in a faded but still handsome green-and-red plaid, and between them was a small, round table where a Bible and a copy of the Sears catalog rested. Before the large fireplace, which was made from river rock of varying hues, lay a long, thin old cat that had not moved at all since we'd come in. I immediately went to the golden animal and bent down to pet it. It quickly raised its head and then laid it back down as if satisfied that I meant no harm, but offered, instead, a much-desired stroking.

"That's Thomas," the Moon Man said. "He's an old one, he is. Must be near 'bout twenty years old now. He's blinder 'n a bat, and deaf as a doorknob, but he's still good company. Don't ask for much other than a meal now 'n then, and a warm place to wait out the winter. I'm thinkin' this may be his last one, though. He's been sleepin' more 'n usual and not eating enough to keep a flea goin'."

I somehow understood that the loss of this animal would affect the man deeply. Though they were both independent creatures, they relied upon each other for their basic needs: the cat for food and shelter, and the man for companionship. There was no question that when the time came for one to be without the other, it would be painfully felt.

"What happened to Roscoe?" Grandma asked, looking around as if maybe she'd just overlooked him when she'd first come inside.

"Lost him a few months ago," replied Sam. "He broke his leg one day while out gallivantin' around and it never did heal right. Poor old feller limped around for some weeks while that darn leg festered and festered. I finally put the dog out of his misery," he said, glancing up at the rifle he kept over the front door.

"I'm sorry, Sam. I remember when you found him under the bridge at Fork Crossing. Darn cute, he was. He grew into a mighty fine hunter. Mighty fine." She patted Sam's arm. "Now, how 'bout if I make us some coffee?" She moved into the small kitchen that was off to the left.

"I'll help you, Grandma," I said, following her in.

"Rachel, take the pie out of the basket and we'll have a little celebration for Sam's birthday. Sam, it's your special day, so sit down and relax." He didn't argue. Instead, after putting another log on the fire, he pulled out a chair from the kitchen table and sat down as requested, then watched us move around the small space with a look of absolute pleasure on his face.

"It's been some time since I had two beautiful gals in my kitchen, and with a pretty pie, to boot. Will wonders never cease?"

Grandma reached up into a cabinet to the left of the sink and retrieved a jar of coffee. Sitting on the counter below was a percolator. Grandma handed me the pot. "Run to the pump out back and fill this up," she instructed, nodding her head toward a door that was just to the right of the sink's counter. I opened the door and stepped out onto a covered, fairly narrow back porch. There was a stack of firewood that ran the length of the porch, which was ten feet or so long, and a low roof, which the stack of wood nearly touched. It took up most of the width of the porch and I had just enough room to keep out of the light rain that fell while I looked around to see where the pump was located. It was about a dozen yards away, off to the left, so I gave the yard a quick survey, recalling the fact that the Moon Man had been out back with the rattler when we'd first arrived. I didn't see anything more threatening than an old washtub next to the pump, a broken wagon wheel, and an old soot-blackened metal barrel. I hurried over to the pump, filled the pot, and ran back onto the porch without getting too terribly soaked.

As I neared the back door, I looked through its window and saw Sam standing there facing Grandma. His left arm circled her waist, while his right hand reached up to tuck a wisp of hair that had escaped her bun back behind her ear. Then, bringing his face down close to hers, he gently kissed her lips for several seconds, while his right arm completed the circle around her. Her hands came to rest on his chest. I thought for a second she might push him away from her, but she didn't. Her hands rested on him in a familiar, practiced way. It was clear that she'd done this before. *They'd* done this before. I knew I was watching something that I shouldn't. I knew it was a moment that was solely intended for the two of them. But I was transfixed. I stood there watching a woman I'd known so well—at least I'd thought I did—act in a way that made her bizarrely unfamiliar to me. It frightened me and intrigued me, and, for some reason I didn't understand, it saddened me.

I walked loudly on the porch to let them know I was back from my short errand and they moved apart, busying themselves with china plates and cups that he handed her from the cabinet.

"Here's the water," I managed, though I couldn't bring myself to look either one of them in the eye. That seemed all right with them, however, as neither one seemed to want to make eye contact with me.

Sam placed the china on the table, while Grandma started the coffee perking. "Put the pie on the table, Rachel," she said as she pushed a candle down into the flakey crust. She'd asked me to take the candle from a kitchen drawer back at our house when I'd run in to let Merry know I was going with her. It was half the size it had originally been, but it had also lit quite a few birthday cakes and pies over the last year. It was never left to burn long, just long enough for the birthday celebrant to make his or her special annual wish. So, after closing his eyes for a brief moment, he opened them, blew with unnecessary gusto, and the candle blinked out immediately, saving the short remains to grace a couple more birthday desserts to come.

"Now, Sam," Grandma started, handing him the knife, "cut the first slice, dear." The way she said the affectionate term so kindly and tenderly, it seemed as though she were talking to a child. But then Samuel Harold looked as delighted as a child as he stepped back from the pie after eagerly blowing out the candle's flame.

Grandma picked up one of the china plates as Sam began cutting the pie into sections. The china had scalloped edges (and a small chip, I noticed), and there were small deep pink roses painted in a circular pattern in the center of the ivory-colored plate. The small china cups were the same ivory color, and in the bottom of each was a rose that matched those on the plates. It was a beautiful, delicate old set, and I wondered if it had been some couple's wedding present. As if reading my mind, Sam volunteered, "These belonged to my folks. They didn't have a whole lot"—he smiled wistfully—"but what they had was worth savin'."

We talked about simple things for a while as we ate the pie and drank the rich, hot coffee. We talked about weather, how cold it was getting already and how the Farmer's Almanac predicted a hard winter. We talked about the new cow Sam had gotten, and whether or not he'd get another cat once Thomas was gone. Then the conversation turned to illegal alcohol, which had been brewed for generations in the western mountains of North Carolina, and long before Prohibition had been enacted. Most of the counties had been dry or alcohol-free since they'd been formed, but that didn't mean that all of the residents' homes were.

The mountain folks had depended on the homemade liquor to put meat on the table, bullets in their guns, clothes on their children's backs, and sugar in their coffee (not to mention in their stills) for so long now that it just seemed to be an accepted—if illegal—way of life. But it was a risky business, to say the least, and frequently paid those employed in it with deadly wages.

Many a man on both sides of the law had shaken hands with the Grim Reaper while trying to protect a still or tear one down. And there were so many lawmen that were actually on the side of the 'shiners that it was difficult to tell who were really good guys or bad guys on any given day. It was an often-hostile game of cat and mouse, and all bets were off as to who was really winning.

"Charles Pottman was gunned down last week after runnin' his shine over to Tennessee. Madison County Sheriff's office got 'em. Dang fool didn't even have anythin' on him. He'd done delivered it all, but he thought havin' 'em chase him in his brand new Dodge automobile was as fun as a barrel of monkeys. Stupid son of a bitch."

"Watch your mouth, Samuel Harold," Grandma scolded. "Tender ears a-sittin' here," she reminded him.

"S'cuse me," he humbly replied. Then, "Them deputies on their horses took the short cut through the woods at Harney's place, and caught up with Charles when they came out on the dirt road on the other side of the ol' man's tobacco fields. They just stood in the road waitin' for Charles, and here he comes, just a-flyin'. Well, he slams on his brakes cause he can't get around 'em, with them standin' in the road 'n all, and, besides, he wants to let the ol' boys have a good look at his new car. But when he got out, being as drunk as he was and not thinkin', he went to pull his wallet out of his coat pocket in the hopes of bribin' them officers into forgettin' they'd seen him that night. The law, thinkin' he was pulling out a gun, shot his ass—s'cuse me—dead. Then the deputies tied their horses to the back bumper of Charlie's car, laid him out in the back seat, and drove him on back to his Mama's house. They parked in the poor woman's front yard! The coroner's office was sent for to come and declare him dead—like they didn't already know it, and his poor ol' Mama a-settin' there and knowin' it, too! Lord, God, but that woman about come undone. She started rantin' and ravin', and carryin' on so, and no one could do anything to calm that poor ol' thing down. The damnedest part of it all was that one of the deputies finally gave her a swig of whiskey from his *own* flask to settle her down. And here they goes and kills her son over the same concoction they used to quiet the half-crazed woman down. Beats all, I swear. It surely beats all."

Grandma had responded throughout the story with the occasional and properly placed "Oh no!" and "Do tell!" and "What a shame!" until Sam was through.

We stayed for a short while longer; then Grandma said she reckoned we'd better start back as it was getting late and she wanted to be home before dark. "Gotta help Anna with supper," she explained, "and, I don't intend upon bein' a bear's."

I helped Grandma wash up the dishes, and then Sam walked us out. As he did, I looked back at poor old Thomas, who'd managed to make it over to a bowl of food left out for him, and I knew I'd most likely never see him again. I wondered if I'd ever see the Moon Man again. And I wasn't quite sure which way I hoped it worked out. There had been too many unexpected feelings running through me that day, and I needed some time to process them all, to gauge what all I was feeling, even if I didn't understand exactly why. I just knew that I'd spent a good part of this day in the company of a man who obviously meant a great deal to my grandmother. I wondered where my mother fit into this, and especially my grandfather. Why was his spirit haunting such a nice seeming man (if indeed he was), forcing Sam to go to extremes to ward off my grandfather's unwanted, post-mortem presence?

Sam gave me a hug goodbye, and, as I was pulling away from him, he gently caught my chin between his right thumb and index finger and told me I had my grandmother's eyes. "There's a strong, good spirit behind 'em," he said. "I reckon that you'll be a force to be reckoned with." He laughed. Whether it was his play on words that amused him, or whether it was imagining those who would be the unlucky recipients of my reckoning, I wasn't sure. But being compared to my grandmother was enough.

I climbed up into the wagon while Grandma and Sam put the empty basket and crate in the back. They spoke quietly to each other, but I could hear them saying the typical end-of-a-visit kind of things, and a minute later Grandma was helped up onto the seat beside me.

"Don't stay away so long, Willa. I do miss ya, ol' gal."

"I'll come when I can, Sam. You take care of yourself, you hear? Use Parker Boone's phone down at his store and call Taft's Mercantile if you need me. They'll get a message on over to me if'n it's an emergency."

"Don't fret, Willa. I'm right as rain out here. Go on with ya now, before it gets any later."

And with that, Grandma bid him good-bye, and I did as well. Then she slapped the reins against Natty's back and we jerked forward to begin our long trek home. As we made our way down the path through the long zigzagging line of ancient trees, Grandma asked me what I thought of Sam.

"Who is he, Grandma? Who is he, *really*?" I searched her face for truths, for answers, and I had a feeling that some of them might make my insides tighten up.

"He's the man who killed my husband, your grandfather, Rachel."

I stared at her as she stared at the road. And yes, indeed, my insides tightened up, for I realized that what she was about to tell me might very well change the rest of my life.

PART 2

Willa

CHAPTER 16

Late September, 1881, Upper Bolsey River, NC

Willa ran past the barn and into the grove of walnut trees beyond. There were no stars out, she noted, which made it harder for her to see, but it also made it harder for Malcolm to see. She stumbled over a protruding tree root but immediately got up and pushed on. There wasn't a moment to waste over worrying about her kneecap, which had taken the full impact from the fall. She'd have to forget that for now and just focus on getting into the deepest part of the woods beyond.

She could hear breaking twigs and the slashing of tree branches as Malcolm hurriedly plowed through them trying to get to her. There was no mistaking that it was him for he had been close on her heels when she'd first taken off. But due to the fierce love and protectiveness of her mutt Bailey, who had gone after Malcolm with as crazy a look in its eyes as Malcolm had in his, Willa was able to break away from her raging husband. He'd had a shovel in his hand, had threatened her with it, and as he swung the makeshift weapon at her head, Bailey had bounded out of the darkness with teeth bared and leaped at Malcolm's arm. She'd taken that moment as her opportunity for flight, and not looking back for fear of losing one precious second, she'd screamed for Bailey to come, but was only answered with a heavy, dull sounding *THUNK* as Malcolm turned his rage on the dog. A pitiful yelp issued forth and then her dog was silent. *Don't think about it, now. It'll only slow you down. He's just stunned, that's all,*

62 • *Janie DeVos*

and is heading for his hiding spot beneath the porch. But she knew better. Her loyal companion would never have given up his fight for her life. On this black night, however, he'd given up his life for her fight.

Willa still heard Malcolm coming. She ran hard to keep ahead of him, but he was gaining ground. Suddenly, she heard a crash and the footfalls stopped for a moment; then he let out a string of filthy words. Willa knew he must have fallen and was thankful for the additional distance it put between them, but all too soon she heard the whipping and cracking of thin branches as he began the hunt again, and, judging by the sound of his faster than ever footfalls, he was doing so with an unearthly, wicked determination.

Willa came out on the far side of the woods and abruptly stopped on the crumbling lip of the high bank. *It's too dark to see the river,* she thought, precariously leaning over the bank's edge and focusing hard in a vain attempt at making out the rushing water below. The water didn't scare her but the deadly boulders did. However, her violent husband scared her even more. *I can swim but he can't,* she thought. So, figuring her odds were better with the boulders than with Malcolm, she jumped. The cold water hit her about as hard as Malcolm's shovel had, and the wind was knocked out of her. With her heart beating so loudly from both fear and cold that she could barely hear the strong rapids ahead, Willa began swimming downstream. She was well aware the rapids were there, though, along with the bone-breaking boulders. And she knew they would likely kill her. But, as she watched Malcolm navigate the shoreline in an attempt to catch up with her, she knew the river would be a kinder death, for there would be no evil involved, no cruelty. It would simply be an outmatched meeting with Mother Nature's power.

Willa stopped trying to swim and just let the strong current take her. She couldn't get her breath back. The shock of the cold had forced it from her lungs, but it was her fear that kept it at bay. She was hyperventilating, which only caused her panic to increase, making it impossible to make it to the shore even though she desperately wanted to. She couldn't see Malcolm anymore. *He's lost sight of me, and given up,* she thought. *How easy it would be for me to do the same.* She was exhausted and weak. Her strength was gone. The only thing that remained was a hollowness that was black and cold and calling. And then the blackness swallowed her whole, as her head crashed against a rock that jutted up in the rapids.

CHAPTER 17

Beginnings

The movement around Willa startled her awake, which resulted in excruciating pain shooting through her head. Malcolm must have hit the left side of her head soundly with the shovel, she thought, clamping her teeth together in response to the pounding. She lay still, waiting for it to ease, and realized that she was cocooned in soft and comfortable warmth. She needed to open her eyes and figure out where she was, but she needed to do so carefully and slowly without letting anyone who might be there with her know that she was now awake. *Thank you, blessed sweet Jesus,* Willa thought, as she pulled in a deep breath. *At least I can breathe again.* Carefully she cracked open her right eye to assess her surroundings. And as she did the thought flashed through her mind that depending on where she was, she might be sorry she'd somehow managed to survive her midnight swim.

Through blurry sight, she saw a gigantic bear leering down at her. Survival instincts took over once more, and Willa jumped out of bed, frantically twisting around, looking for a way out. Quickly glancing at the bear again, she realized that there wasn't a body attached to the mounted head, and her adrenaline rush began to dissipate, causing her shaking legs to fold beneath her. There was nothing to grab onto and Willa crumpled down into a heap on the oak floor.

"Good God, woman! Whatcha tryin' to do? Finish yourself off?" A male's voice came from above her. She looked up at him, but her concussion made it impossible to see him very clearly. Willa knew it wasn't Malcolm, though. Her husband's voice was gravelly and hard; *like his heart*, she thought. This stranger's voice, though low in pitch, was gentler sounding, although at the moment it was urgently insisting that she return to bed and rest.

Two strong hands reached down and grasped Willa underneath her arms, then lifted her up from the floor and helped her back into bed. And she let him. He pulled the covers over her body, which was now clothed in a man's nightshirt, she realized, and moved the lantern off the nightstand and away from her light-sensitive eyes. *Here I am,* she thought, *in a strange man's cabin—and bed!—at the mercy of his whims. I'm in the middle of . . . God only knows where . . .* but she thanked her maker that she was wherever this warm, comfortable place might be. She'd rather take her chances with a stranger, in his cabin, than be back at her own home, surrounded by the familiar, including her abusive, battering husband. Both she and her unborn baby might actually have a chance for survival, she thought. However, once she—*they*, she had to think in those terms now—did return home, all bets were off. *But we can't go back. How do we go back when death may well greet us at the door? Or has death already stolen one of us?* she wondered, for she hadn't felt the baby move. Not since running away from Malcolm. How long ago was that? Willa, still exhausted, needed sleep now far more than answers, and drifted off into that peaceful place of nothingness.

She quietly awoke to sunlight pouring through the window. She saw the stranger through the open bedroom door, sitting at the kitchen table restringing a snowshoe, but he caught the movement as Willa swung her legs over the side of the bed and slowly began to try to sit up. Immediately, he jumped up and came to her.

"How ya feelin', miss?" he inquired softly. Willa was alert enough now to see the concern in his intense brown eyes. Relieved that she was finally able to see him and everything else clearly again, she gave herself a moment to look closely at the man. His hair was a thick, wavy gold, and his smile was bright and genuine. Of medium height and build, he looked as though he was quick and agile, and his movements had confirmed that in the way he'd lightly and smoothly moved to her side to assist her.

"Let me try puttin' my body fully upright," she replied, "and I'll let you know then." With that, she carefully began the task of standing up, and, with the man's hand under her arm for support, Willa drew herself up and stood there, albeit swaying, but she stood nonetheless. The man cautiously let go of her but stayed close in case her legs couldn't hold her up.

"I need water and the outhouse," she said, "and I'm not sure which one first. My mouth is as dry as cotton, but my bladder couldn't hold a drop. Best show me to the outhouse first, I guess. Oh, um . . . would you have a coat I can throw over myself?" she self-consciously asked. Her legs were still too shaky to worry about getting back into her own clothes at the moment, but she couldn't parade around in his nightshirt, injured or not. The man grabbed a black wool cape from the hall closet, wrapped her in it, then took Willa's arm and guided her out the back door.

A worn path ran through the middle of the backyard and beyond to the outhouse, which was about a hundred yards from the house. As they made their way, Willa looked back at the log cabin she'd been sheltered in for . . . how long? The cabin was rather small and weathered brown. A large river-rock chimney shot upward from the middle of the house, which made her recall that one side of the fireplace faced the small living room, while the other side of it opened to the bedroom she'd been staying in. Then Willa turned back around and took note of a garden that lay just ahead and to the right, with a few remaining vegetables in it that were more than ready to be harvested. To the left was a fenced-in chicken coop, with several hens and a rooster picking at potential edibles in the dirt. And just beyond the garden, Willa saw a dark gray, soot-streaked smokehouse. Finally, they came to a narrow footbridge that spanned a full, broad creek, and Willa could see the outhouse standing in a small clearing just beyond. In stark contrast to the weathered building was a bright smattering of black-eyed susans, mountain honeysuckle, and echinacea coloring the sun-washed ground.

"Where exactly are we?" she asked, while holding tightly to the railing as she crossed the bridge. "And how long have I been here?"

"You've been here for two days now," the man replied, following closely behind her. "We're at my place on Bolsey Creek, a branch of the bigger river of the same name."

"I know the river well," Willa replied. "I live on a northern branch of it. It's just lovely here, though. Where I live is more rugged and . . . I don't know . . . kind of stark-like." She looked around, feeling an unaccustomed peacefulness in this simple, unassuming place.

"It's home, miss, and has been since my grandpap first laid a claim here. He had a hundred and five acres to begin with, but sold most of it off over time. You might say he wasn't a very good business man, and was an even worse farmer," he laughed. "I've managed to hang on to the remaining twelve, though sometimes even that seems to be too much. My farmin's about as good as his was." He smiled.

"Well, it's just beautiful, Mr . . . ah . . . I'm sorry, I don't know your name."

"It's Harold, Miss. That ain't the first, though, it's the last. My name's Samuel Cornelius Harold. Sure is an important soundin' name for a man who ain't so important." He smiled easily again.

"I wouldn't say that. You saved my life, Mr. Harold . . . or was it Samuel?" She frowned. "I'm sorry. I guess I'm still not quite right."

"It's Samuel Harold, miss, and you're doin' just fine." With that, they reached the outhouse, and after checking to make sure no animals of any kind had found shelter within the dark shack, Sam walked politely away; far enough to allow her the privacy she needed, but close enough to hear her if she called for him.

Several minutes later, they began walking back up the same narrow path that they'd come down. When they reached the creek, Sam pulled a small tin cup from his overall's pocket, squatted down and scooped up a cup full of the creek's cold water for her. Willa gulped the water down, not caring that streams of it ran down both sides of her mouth. Then, squatting down at the bank's edge, she drank two more cups full of the cold water before finally stopping long enough to gaze at her reflection. A quiet little pool had been damned off from the rest of the creek with a deposit of small logs and broken branches, courtesy of a family of thick-pelted beavers. She lowered her face to the pool and began scrubbing away the last remaining vestiges of dirt and dried blood, and, as she did, she became painfully aware of a very tender area just above her left temple. Turning her face so that she could better see her injury, she spotted a jagged line of red, sutured flesh that was about two inches long. She gently cleaned it with more of the creek water.

"I remember feelin' like my head exploded when I was in the water. And that's about all. What happened after that, Mr. Harold? How did I make it to your place?"

"I'd headed north on the river to set a couple more traps in an area that'd seen a lot of action in it lately. As I was settin' one of them up,

I saw you go divin' into the drink. I thought, is she crazy? Has she had too much 'shine? That's when I saw that man followin' you on the bank. God, but I almost run into him! There wasn't any moonlight, and we just about collided into one another. I couldn't understand how he didn't hear me walkin' so near to him, but then I guess I'm used to hearin' sounds over the rush of the river. Not everyone is, though. I knew he was real trouble, and I wasn't prepared to be on the other end of it. And I had a bad feelin' he wasn't there to help you out any. So, as quiet as I could, I got behind a big old oak tree, and watched *him* watchin' for *you*. There's one thing I'm good at that not all men are, and that's seeing in the dark. I'm used to it, with trappin' an' all. I could see him lookin' for you, but I knew he couldn't see me watchin' him. So I waited and let him get a little ahead of me, just to be sure he wasn't gonna catch me. And then I followed. Guess after a spell he either got tired of followin' ya down the river, or, more likely, he just couldn't keep you in his sight, so he gave up. Probably figured you'd drown, if you hadn't already. He turned around an' went back the way he came.

"Soon as he was gone, I hurried on down the river, lookin' for ya. And, lo and behold, there ya were, about a quarter mile down. You was hung up on the rocks—wedged between two good-sized boulders, actually, and it was hard to see you. Your head was bleedin' something fierce, but through the mercy of God Almighty, you had turned face up when you'd been conked on the head by one of them rocks. If you hadn't, you'd-a-drowned. Another thing lucky was that the rock didn't hit you on the temple, but got you just above. I fished you out, with you a-thrashin' a bit and sayin' somethin' about 'shovels.' You was somewheres else, that's for sure. I drug you up on the bank, got you into my wagon, and hurried back to my place. I knew the darkness was on my side, but the light would be on that man's, and he'd come back a-lookin' for ya. That was two days ago."

"And were you the one that did the sewin' on my head?"

"Naw. I was afraid I'd scar you worse than you might be otherwise. Besides, I was havin' trouble rousing you. So I fetched Doc Newton. I hated to leave you, but I was afraid you might bleed to death if I didn't. So I raced over to his place, a couple of miles from here, and he come right back with me.

"Miss, I don't mean to meddle in your business, but if you don't mind my askin', who was that man lookin' for you?"

Willa couldn't look Sam in the eye to answer his awkward question. Self-consciously looking down at her water-stained, worn out shoes, which she'd slipped on before leaving the cabin, she said, "I'm ashamed to say he's my husband; has been for the better part of a year now. Knowin' him, he'll keep lookin' for me, wanting to make sure I'm as cold and blue as he's hoping I am, so I'll make my stay a very short one, Mr. Harold."

"Miss, that man—that so-called husband of yours—ain't gonna find you here, no way, no how. Lordy, woman, we're so far back in this holler that even *I* get lost tryin' to find my way back home again." He laughed, clearly trying to reassure her, to make her feel safe and protected, as well as bring some levity to a most sad and serious situation.

"Mr. Harold, I can't tell you how grateful I am for all you've done. I . . . well . . . I don't know what would . . ."

"I did what I bet you'd do if you saw what I seen that night."

"You'd lose that bet, Mr. Harold."

He looked hard at her and said, "I don't think so, Miss. I surely don't. Someone that has blue lightnin' for eyes don't back down too easy. No, ma'am."

She smiled at him, then turned to continue walking down the path. After a minute filled with a comfortable quiet, Sam said, "Miss, I'd be grateful if you'd do two things for me. The first thing is to call me Samuel or Sam. My dad was as mean as a bobcat, and the name *Mr. Harold*—not to mention every belt I see—only reminds me of him. That's why I wear only overalls or suspenders." He laughed, but she could tell it was forced. "And the other thing you can do for me is to tell me your name."

"My name's Willa. And as far as my name goes, that's all you need to know. I'm pleased to make your acquaintance, Sam." She reached her hand out to shake his. Suddenly, she began to laugh as she realized the absurdity of her attempt at proper etiquette. After all they'd already been through and she was *pleased to make his acquaintance*? She threw her head back and laughed; at the ridiculousness of herself, her seemingly impossible situation, and with the miracle of being alive. But most of all, she laughed with joy over the fact that her baby was busy kicking away at her insides. *And with the strength of a mule.*

CHAPTER 18

The Best-Laid Plans

Her six weeks with Sam flew like the golden oak and red maple leaves that swirled down in the stiff autumn breezes from the towering trees in Sam's front and side yards. There were a few more blackberries to be found up on Buckeye Ridge, so Willa took a white enameled bowl and headed up to just below the crest of it. During the course of a conversation, Sam had let it slip that his birthday was coming up in a couple of days. And, during the course of another conversation—cleverly instigated by Willa—she'd found out that his favorite dessert was blackberry pie. So, she'd decided to surprise him with one for his birthday, along with a new cap she'd quickly and secretly sewn out of an old wool blanket that had seen far better days before hungry moths had found it. There had been enough of the blanket left to allow Willa to make a new and warmer dress for herself, as well. The one that she'd floated down the river in was still wearable, but the cooler days made it impractical.

The wool cap Willa designed for Sam had long flaps that hung down to cover his ears, for as the wind had increased in its velocity and frigid bite, so had Sam's complaints about his aching ears. After coming in from long hours of working in the mica or emerald mines (depending on who was hiring), or trapping around the creeks and rivers, not to mention panning for gold in them, too, Sam suffered from ears red and raw from exposure and wind burn.

During those long days alone, she busied herself with cleaning the cabin, washing and mending Sam's clothing, clearing out and canning the remains of his garden, and re-stuffing a corn shuck mattress (which Sam was now using for his bed in the loft upstairs). She cooked stews or roasts from fresh game he'd trapped or shot, while salting to preserve the rest of the meat, or fried up a mess of trout that she'd caught and cleaned for their supper. Sam embraced the blessings of a smart, resourceful, and capable woman, and was not short on words of praise and thanks. His kindness and appreciation of her work made the doing of it a pleasure for her instead of a chore. It was exactly the opposite of the way it had been with Malcolm.

Although it sickened her to do it, she forced herself to think about him, and the future that lay ahead for both her and their baby. No! It wasn't *his* baby. She couldn't think of the child as such. In *no* way would this child be brought up to think, act, react, or live its life in such a cruel and loveless way. It wouldn't be fair to this child or the world either, for that matter. So the biggest question that hung over Willa's head was how she could protect her baby from Malcolm, and protect the world from another like him. Without question, she knew she couldn't seek refuge at her parents' home, which was just a couple of hours north of Sam's. Malcolm would have already checked to see if she was back there, of that she was certain, and he would continue going over there again and again until he found her. She wouldn't put her mother and father in harm's way, for wherever he might finally find her living (hiding out, actually), only the good Lord knew what would happen to those giving her shelter. Malcolm felt that he owned her, that when the justice of the peace had handed them a signed marriage certificate, he had also given Malcolm a receipt for the bill of sale for his new bride. Living with him had been hell since the first night. The man had two sides to him, and before the ink was dry on their marriage certificate, her kind, thoughtful, and handsome new husband had turned into an unjustifiably jealous and brutal man.

The thought that her baby would have to endure years, if not a lifetime, of being a target of his terrifying temper made her course of action crystal clear: She had to keep the father and child away from each other. Neither could know the other existed. And in order to accomplish that, Willa had to put a lot of distance between them. More miles meant a greater likelihood of his never finding them, and the faster she could get away, the better. For she knew without a whisper of a doubt that if her husband found her at Sam's he'd kill them all before taking his next breath. Willa knew that she was going to have to travel fast and hard, and head north into Tennessee, or Virginia, and she would need to move before the winter storms began. But to do so she would need two more favors of Sam; she had to ask that he take her to the stage coach depot in Marion, and, as humiliating as it was, ask to borrow the ticket fare, with the promise of paying him back, of course. Then, she and her unborn baby would be on the first outbound coach.

CHAPTER 19

In the Cards

Willa wore her old cotton dress while she washed the wool one in the creek. She'd done the washing just two days before so there were only a handful of things to be laundered, but she wanted to leave things as tidy and neat for Sam as she could before she left. She didn't have enough laundry to make it worth the trouble of hauling and heating water for the washtub, so she decided to do the wash in the creek.

It was a perfect Indian summer day, and the mid-morning sun beat down on Willa while she slapped the clothes against a small boulder. Before too long, Willa was drowsy and as limp as the clothing that she hung over the branches of a laurel bush to dry. She knew it wouldn't take the clothes long, but long enough to allow for a nap, so she lay back on the brown grass of the bank to sleep.

It's hard to believe I've been here for six weeks, she thought. The idea of leaving caused a physical ache in her chest, especially considering the conversation that had taken place between her and Sam the night before, but she knew she had to depart immediately. The area had already seen a storm come through, which dropped two inches of snow, but the ground had been warm enough still to melt it off, though that wouldn't be the case for much longer. As it stood today, the stagecoaches were the only mode of commercial transportation in the area, but she knew that before long the building of the railroad that was already underway in the western mountains of North Carolina would change that, would change a lot of things, actually. Life in these isolated Blue Ridge Mountains would never be the same when the tracks were complete. They would bring the world to this place, to these people, and she wasn't sure how she felt about the invasion. *But,* she laughed ironically to herself, *the outside world is where I'm hoping to escape to tomorrow. Ah, well, I guess everything and every place can make a person want to run from it, or to it.*

The sadness of her departure, combined with the fear of heading into an unknown place and having to find work there to support both her and the baby tightened the muscles in her stomach. Lying there, she tried to push the worries from her mind and relax by listening to the rhythmic sound of the flowing creek. Finally, she was lulled into a soft sleep . . .

She stood on the top of a mountain looking out at the snow-covered valley below. Off to the left, poking up through the whiteness, were small, dark trunks with gnarly, stark branches that reached up toward a bright blue sky as if wanting to be noticed, lifted up and held by supreme, ethereal hands. The more mature trees in the apple orchard stood sentinel over a quiet, sleeping land. Three crows caw-cawed their way over her in flight, and she lifted her right hand in greeting. How she wished she could soar up with them and go wherever the air's currents might dictate. Instead, she tucked her hand back into the pocket of her dark wool cape and began walking through the snow-covered meadow. The cold air was bone-dry, and her mouth was dry from it, so she reached down and cupped a handful of snow. Bringing it to her mouth, she felt its good coldness. Odd. It was so hard. But it was freshly fallen, with no tracks from any animal packing it down, so why was it so hard and metallic tasting? Why was . . .

Willa's eyes snapped open and she stared up at Malcolm as he stood above her, straddling her, and pointing a shotgun down at her with the end of the cold barrel pressed painfully against her lips. "Don't ya move, bitch," Malcolm said in a low and deadly voice. He pushed the gun more firmly against her mouth, and it felt as though her front teeth would shatter before a bullet could do the damage.

"Did ya really think I wouldn't find you, girl? D'ya think I'm some damn *fool*? I walked down that whole damn river the night you jumped in, and then started back up it when I couldn't find you at the ford. You think I *wouldn't* find you?" His words grew higher in pitch, along with his rage. "I knew you'd gotten out somewhere, and I been looking around ever since. Been asking around, too. No one could say they'd seen you, though. But then, as *luck* would have it, I was playing cards, and Doc Newton—from right around here—joins in. Hadn't seen the doc in a while, so just trying to pass the time o' day with him between games, I ask him what news he's got, and he proceeds to tell me a bunch of bullshit, like I really give a damn. But then he gets to the part about sewing up a gal's head some weeks before that looked a lot like my wife.

"Remember, Willa, he'd seen you in town with me a year or so ago? We run into him at the store while spending the money I'd won off of him playing poker the night before. Anyway, I played all dumb-like. Said I'd been away a while, playing cards down in Morganton, and when I come back you was gone. Told him you had kin up this way, and you'd likely gone on to see your cousin. Then real casual-like I ask him exactly *where* he saw you. He was good about directions, I'll tell you. If there's one thing you gotta know, Willa, a man ain't gonna cover for a no-good slut, especially if she's an associate's wife."

If Willa hadn't been paralyzed with fear, she would have laughed at that last remark—"associate," indeed!

"So, here I am and here you are. And what I want to know is, who is that son of a bitch you been playing house with? When I came up here through the clearing this morning, there you two were, standing outside that smokehouse of his, and talking all close and sweet-like. Been shacking up, Willa? Huh? What you thinking, gal, that I wouldn't hunt you down, dead or not? I'm here to reclaim what's rightfully mine. And you *is* mine, and I'm taking you back home with me. But first I'm gonna remind you of what you should have been taking care of at home—tending to *my* business, and not his!"

Malcolm, still pointing the gun at her with his right hand, let go with his left, and reached across to his right hip to unsheathe the hunting knife he always carried. Then he pulled the shotgun away from her face as he immediately knelt down, straddling her thighs. He unbuttoned the front of his wool pants—pants she'd made for him—and holding the razor-sharp blade against her throat, he pressed home the point that he'd kill her quickly if she tried to fight him. As he did, she felt the warmth of her own blood run down the side of her throat.

"Try screaming and I'll cut your voice cords before you can close your mouth." With that earnest threat, paired with the knife painfully breaking her skin, Willa bit down on her tongue in order to squelch the scream that wanted to escape. Now she could taste her own blood as well as feel it.

"Spread your legs, or I'll stab each one of 'em 'til you do."

Willa, terrified, did as she was told, and as soon as she did, Malcolm pushed her dress up over her belly—the belly that carried the seed of this insane man. Then he brutally rammed into her. Unable to stop herself, she instinctively tried to sit up to move away from the pain. But she was no match for his strength, and his knife cut even deeper into her throat. He pushed her back down and continued pounding into her body with an intense and agonizing anger, and she felt as though she was being torn apart. *Hang on,* she urged herself. *Hang on. I've got to for the baby's sake. Just lie here and maybe he won't kill us both.*

The truth of the matter was that she could have easily let go, and most likely would have had she been the only casualty of his vicious assault. She could have fought back with the force of her own immeasurable pent up anger and sadness, humiliation, and disappointment. Then, without any doubt, she would have received release, for Malcolm would have won, physically speaking, anyway. Through her death she would have won her freedom and slipped off to that place of peace and solace, where worries and pain no longer existed. She'd have soared away from this darkness and into that place of light. That was where she wanted to be.

How important is it for my child to have a chance at this life, if he or she has to endure the things I've had to, she wondered. *Wouldn't it be kinder and fairer to let this child take the journey from darkness to light with me?* And with that question came a definitive answer: *her* baby had a right to live! With that conviction, Willa forced herself to lie there, remaining as still as she could in order to prevent any further harm than had already been inflicted. It was one of the hardest things she had ever done. However, she could not stop herself from reacting in one small way—she spat directly into his face. Enraged even further than he already was, he retaliated by slamming his right fist into her jaw.

Suddenly, the morning sun directly behind Malcolm was blocked out by the silhouette of Sam. With a rifle pressed up against the back of Malcolm's head, Sam ordered him to move.

"Drop the knife real easy-like, and get the hell off of her."

Malcolm sat up slowly, with the knife still gripped in his outstretched hand. No fear moved across his face. On the contrary, he smiled a small, insane smile and a dangerous gleam lit his eyes. Then, moving with predator-like speed, he tried one last savage act, moving to slam the knife down into her chest. It was a final attempt to keep Willa for himself, even though he knew it meant the death of them both, but it was a price Malcolm was willing to pay. Suddenly a thunderous explosion shattered the morning air. It was a boom to awaken the dead and quiet the living, and it stopped the downward thrust of the knife just a couple of inches above Willa's heart. The deafening sound of the gunshot reverberated off of one mountainside then another as Malcolm's body, with only half of his head remaining intact, slumped over Willa. And the river of his blood washed her and their unborn baby in a macabre kind of baptism.

CHAPTER 20

Ties that Bind

Sam pulled the mangled remains of Malcolm off of Willa, who had begun screaming hysterically once she realized what had happened.

"Get up, Willa!" Sam ordered. "We got to get you washed off!" He did not have to tell her twice. Sam pulled her to her feet and she stumbled into the frigid creek below. She fully immersed herself in the rushing water, attempting to rinse away the blood, brain matter, hair, and bone fragments that had once made up the hard and ruthless features of her husband. Scooping up handfuls of sand from the creek bottom, she scrubbed her hair, face, and clothing with it. "Hurry!" she screamed at Sam, who was also scrubbing at the sickening remains sticking to her. "Wash him off of me!" Her teeth chattered both from the cold and shock, and after several more minutes of harsh scrubbing, Sam put his arm around her waist and, half pushing and half carrying her, forced her up onto the creek's bank and toward the cabin.

"We can't leave him here like that!" she cried.

"I won't. I want to get you inside and then I'll come back and tend to him."

Willa grunted as if in agreement, however her uncontrollable shaking rendered her incapable of saying any more.

Sam built up the low-burning fire in the hearth while instructing Willa to get into a pair of his heavy wool pants and shirt. After doing so, she wrapped herself in the quilt from her bed and came back to the fire. Sam had built up the fire in the wood stove, too, and the coffee pot was re-warming the remains from their breakfast. Sitting down on the floor in front of the fireplace, Willa stared into the flames.

"Soon as that's warm," Sam said, indicating the warming coffee pot with a nod of his head, "you drink it. There's a bottle of brandy in the cupboard, to the left of the molasses. You put a double-shot in that mug, Willa."

"I don't drink, and you know it, Sam."

"This ain't drinking for the sake of drinking, Willa! We gotta get you to stop shaking, and to get some warmth back in your body. I'll pour it down your throat if you won't. Shock is tryin' to set in, and you're—we're—gonna be in trouble if you can't stop it from takin' over.

"We're already in trouble, Sam," Willa replied. "We just killed a man."

"No, *ma'am!*" Sam forcefully replied. "I was the only one that did any killin' today!"

"Don't matter, Sam," Willa continued, while still staring at the flames. "It don't matter who pulled the trigger. We're both involved, and we're both in a hell of a lot a trouble. My last name is Holton, Sam. I never did say it to you before. And the man you just killed weren't just my husband, but Malcolm Holton, whose grandfather is Beaumont "Buddy" Malcolm Holton. *Senator* Buddy Holton. My husband's grandfather is a North Carolina state senator, Sam. We're both courtin' a hangman's noose." Though she spoke the words in a whisper, Sam clearly understood the weight behind them, and she was sure they shook Sam's world to its core.

CHAPTER 21

Fractured Lives

Sam sat on a filthy cot in the county jail, and wondered if the next person to visit his cell would be Deputy Burke, with some kind of food—food that even the mice were hesitant to eat—or Sheriff Buchanan, with a signed death warrant.

After getting Willa tended to, Sam had put Malcolm in the back of his wagon and headed into town. That had been five days ago. He'd stopped in front of the sheriff's office and told Sheriff Buchanan to come out to his wagon. He'd had to tell him who Malcolm was when the sheriff looked over the side. "Holy Mother of Jesus!" he'd exclaimed, paling as he did so. Even though he was a deacon at the First Baptist Church of Bolsey River, Sam couldn't figure out if it was the appropriate response to seeing the mangled man, or not. But he definitely knew that the cursing which ensued was not. Suddenly, the sheriff seemed to calm down, and, with the strangest smile on his face, made some senseless remark about the fact that Sam may have just helped him win another term. Sam hadn't a clue as to what he meant, and he didn't bother to ask for he had more serious issues to concern himself with. Sheriff Buchanan had then quickly ushered Sam into his office while the deputy drove the wagon over to McCrea's Funeral Home. There Malcolm would remain until the senator could be notified and arrangements made.

Sam asked himself again whether he should have just thrown the son of a bitch down an old mine shaft; the mountains were riddled with them. He knew that the chances of anyone finding Malcolm would have been slim to none, but Sam also knew that it wasn't quite as simple as that. What made things so complicated was the fact that Doc Newton had seen Willa at his cabin. *And that was my own stupid fault,* Sam thought bitterly. *If I'd just sewn her up myself this whole nightmare wouldn't have happened. Our options would have been better, that's for sure, but I was worried about her head then and not our necks. Stupid, stupid, stupid! I should have thought things through before involving anyone else.*

Now he sat wondering what would happen to Willa. He hadn't been able to talk to her since he'd been incarcerated, although Sam knew she'd come by on two different occasions. She'd been turned away both times, though, for he was able to hear her muffled conversation with the deputy in the sheriff's office, which was directly below his cell on the first floor. The first time she'd come had been the day after he'd turned himself in, and he'd shouted out the window to her as she was mounting his mule to leave, telling her that he was all right. She'd quickly looked up at the barred second story window and shouted back that she'd get him out of there somehow and to stay strong.

The deputy came out of the sheriff's office like a shot and issued a very heated warning to her, saying that if she didn't move on immediately or if she ever attempted to communicate with Sam again without permission that she'd be down at the end of the hall from him with a gag in her mouth, and a long sentence ahead of her for obstructing justice and disturbing the peace. Sam had felt the deputy's wrath more severely however, for he'd come up to Sam's cell after chasing Willa away and beaten him thoroughly with a small wooden bat.

Two days later, she'd returned to town again. "Now Miz Holton, it's like I said to you the other day," Deputy Burke began as he stood in the doorway blocking Willa from even entering the sheriff's office, much less the jailhouse beyond. "We can't have you comparin' stories and workin' things out, now can we?" he'd condescendingly asked. "Why, there's no tellin' what you two could concoct, not to mention the fact that we don't want you smugglin' anything *in* to help Sam *out*, now do we?" His insipid smile exposed the gap where once an incisor tooth had been, and he spoke to her as if she were a stupid child, or a stupid woman, which seemed to be about one and the same to the deputy. "If'n I let you go visitin' Sam, why I'd have to search you, and I imagine that wouldn't sit too well with you, *or* Sam, now would it?" The lecherous glint in his eye was unmistakable. He laughed and his enormous belly shook as she reacted to his offensive implications by taking a step back from him.

He stinks, Willa thought, *and his hair's as greasy as a skillet full of bacon. Lord, when's the last time that man washed?* His hair was black but the thought ran through her mind that it might actually be brown without the grime in it. Willa bit down on her tongue to stifle the retort that came so close to being fired back at him. It wouldn't do to end up in jail, too. There wouldn't be a thing she could do to help Sam, though she was at a loss as to what she could do to help him at this point, even being a free woman.

"Deputy, I just want to see that Sam's all right," Willa responded. Deputy Burke was known to be a rough handler, especially of female inmates, but he was known to be abusive with men, too. She prayed he wasn't hurting Sam in any way.

"Why, gal, are you suggestin' that we'd hurt a hair on his head? Besides, what do you care? He ain't your husband, which makes me wonder if that cockamamie story he done told the sheriff is really what happened out there at his place."

Although Willa hadn't been present when Sam had given his statement to the sheriff, she was sure that Sam had told him the truth. There wasn't any reason to do otherwise. "I can assure you, deputy, it is *exactly* what happened." Then she not only regained the step she'd taken away from him just moments before, but took several more toward him until her face was just inches from his.

"Deputy Burke," she began in a heated whisper. "I been told what takes place in this jail, and that Ida Portnoy's son is a result of such. She didn't seem to be pregnant when she came in, but lo and behold, she had a child ten months after first being incarcerated and she'd only been out for three. Heard tell she had to convince her husband that it was an unusually long pregnancy. Watch what you do, deputy, or as God is my witness, I'd as soon hang from the nearest locust tree then let you hurt anyone else again—Sam Harold most especially."

"You threatenin' me, woman?" The deputy was almost nose to nose with her.

"No, sir," Willa replied in a deadly even tone. "I'm swearin' it on every one of the graves that fills up my family's cemetery. You'll be in worse shape than Malcolm if you lift a finger to Sam." With that, Willa mounted the mule, slapped the reins on its rump, and trotted away.

Once she rounded the bend and was out of view, she let it all go. The tears that had run silently down her cheeks as she rode down the town's main street were now accompanied by deep sobbing that expressed all of the sorrow that had been building up since Malcolm was killed and Sam had turned himself in. As guilty as it made Willa feel, she felt no sadness over the loss of her husband. She did, however, feel absolute despair over the possibility of losing Sam, and the deepest guilt at the likelihood that he would lose virtually everything he had, perhaps even his life, simply because she'd come into his.

Bittersweet memories worked their way through her anguished sobs and Willa thought back to when she and Sam had first admitted their growing feelings for each other. It had been the afternoon before Malcolm showed up. She'd told Sam of her plans to take the stagecoach out of Marion, and when she'd finished, he'd run his hands through his wavy blond hair and his dark brown eyes had stared long and hard at her.

"Don't leave, Willa. Please. I don't . . . Please don't go," he'd responded in a low, emotion-filled voice before turning toward the cabin's front door and saying he needed to check something in the smokehouse. She couldn't help but smile at his endearing awkwardness. And she didn't miss the fact that the smokehouse was out back, and he always went through the kitchen door to work in it. He walked back into the house less than a minute later, and without saying a word, but looking as though something had been decided inside of him, he firmly but gently grasped her upper arms. Looking hard into her eyes, he pulled her to him.

Though Sam was not a terribly large man, wiry by some people's thinking, he was hard as a rock. Years of living alone and working the land, without a brood of children to help, had done that for him. His hands were capable and calloused. His shoulders were sturdy and strong. He smelled of the cedar wood which lined his closet and scented every piece of his clothing, and he smelled like the coffee he'd been drinking while she explained her plans to him.

Sam spoke softly against her right ear, though the words were hoarse sounding and urgent, and she knew what they'd be even before they were said, "I've started loving you, woman," he gruffly admitted. "Don't go. Please."

"My feelings are growing for you, too, Sam. As wrong as it is," she quietly admitted, dropping her forehead to rest against his chest.

"God help us." Her voice cracked with the pain and truth of her feelings.

"Willa, look at me," Sam demanded, holding her away from him. "This can't be wrong. I don't believe that. It feels too *right*. This is what God intended a man and a woman to feel for each other, and mean to each other."

"A man and *wife*," she corrected.

"Damn the rules, Willa! I'm not convinced that isn't just man's way of controlling things, and not the good Lord's way of wanting things. Sometimes I think we set our lives out in the way *we* see fit, not in the way God would. Can you honestly say that you believe God thinks it's all right to be beaten by your husband? Do you believe God thinks it's okay for a man to gamble every last penny away that he has, leaving his wife and family to starve or freeze to death? I surely don't believe He does. Just because a preacher and a signed marriage paper say things are all proper-like, don't make 'em so! You deserve more, Willa. Much more. There's not an ounce of me that's sorry that I got involved with you, or this situation. And I never will be. I'm just sorry that it wasn't sooner. Divorce him, Willa, and be with me. There'd be no shame in it. The only shame there'd be is if you stayed with a man that hurts you like he does. Then you'd be doing nothing less than saying it was okay for him to abuse you!"

Willa moved back into Sam's arms again and finally allowed herself to let go of many unshed tears. After only a moment, though, she stepped away from him and said, "I have to think about it, but from the angle I'm seeing things, there doesn't seem to be any solution for a good outcome."

But Willa *was* tempted to do what Sam wanted her to, though she knew that they'd pay a terrible price. Even if she could get away from Malcolm, she and Sam would be ostracized by those they'd known all their lives. They'd be pariahs in their communities, and they'd end up hating each other for it. Try as they might to ignore the pain and the loneliness of being outcasts, the resentment they'd eventually feel toward each other would eat away at them.

But all of Willa's wants and needs paled in comparison to those of her child. She was willing to give up whatever was necessary in order to provide a life of security and happiness for her son or daughter.

She knew with absolute certainty that she couldn't raise her child in the malignant atmosphere of a home where Malcolm lived. But she also knew that she couldn't let the baby's life start out under a cloud of shame. And to divorce her husband and immediately take up with another man would bring disgrace to this baby from the moment it drew its first breath. She couldn't be with either man, and that knowledge helped Willa make a difficult decision easier. She would raise the baby on her own, wherever that might be.

She worried greatly about being found, and the possible actions that Willa's grandfather-in-law had the power to take. *Oh dear God, what if the senator tries to take my baby from me? To raise as a rightful heir?* Willa quickly pushed that thought from her mind. She knew there were more immediate things to worry about, and she was convinced that by leaving both Sam and Malcolm, in the end it would save them all. However, unquestionably, it would shatter Sam's heart, and her own in doing so. *We'll heal in time*, she tried to assure herself. But she knew that it would be a long, long time in coming. If ever.

Not long after Sam had gotten her back to the cabin after killing Malcolm, he'd told her he had to go take care of things. She heard him drive the wagon out of the barn and assumed he was going to pick up Malcolm's body to bury him. But once the sun began to dip below the tree line with no sign of him, she began to worry about what might have happened to cause such a delay. *Perhaps he decided to bury Malcolm much further away*, she told herself. *But even so he ought to have returned by now.* Willa became almost frantically worried, but knew she had to try to calm down or risk hurting the baby. Trying to change her focus, she thought about starting some supper, but even the idea of food was nauseating, so Willa decided instead to busy herself by doing a little mending. She went into the bedroom to retrieve the wicker basket of Sam's clothing that she'd placed in the corner just the night before, and as she grasped the handles of the basket to carry it out to the living room, she glanced down and saw a neatly folded note that had not been there earlier. She immediately realized that Sam must have placed it there for her before he'd left to take care of the grisly chore. With shaking hands, Willa carried the paper over to the window to better see it in the streaking golden light of the fading day.

My dearest, Willa;
I've taken Malcolm to town. If I don't turn myself in,
they'll come after me, and I don't want you taking the blame

for something I did. Maybe if I explain what happened they won't hang me for it. Stay at the cabin for as long as you want. Forever, I hope. Raise the baby there. You know how I feel about you. But I can't help but think that you wish you'd never laid eyes on me. That troubles me more than knowing I kilt a man. I don't regret having done it, Willa. I don't regret any of it.
  Your loving Sam.

By the time the sun had risen the next morning, Willa had put two miles behind her and the mule, with four yet to go before she reached town, and, hopefully, Sam. But, after five days and two long trips back and forth to town, she still hadn't gained any ground.

CHAPTER 22

Hanging in the Balance

Willa had no idea if she would fare any better in her third attempt at seeing Sam, but she had to try. There wasn't a choice. The trip to town was difficult in places. The road wasn't actually a road at all, but a well-worn narrow path. There were spots where only ten feet separated the steep mountainside and the deep ravine below, with the Bolsey River running through it. But if there was a chance that she could help Sam, then she'd come back again and again. So far, though, she'd only been able to talk with the deputy. She needed to talk with the sheriff, but he'd been out on other business both times she'd attempted it. So far she'd gotten nothing from her efforts but blisters on her buttocks and thighs from the ill-fitting saddle she used on Sam's mule. By far, she would have preferred to take the wagon, but the deputy had told her that both it and Sam's horse had been confiscated as "evidence." Willa was willing to bet, however, that the "evidence" was providing someone with a more comfortable ride than the one she had with the mule and the over-sized saddle.

It had been frustrating not being able to talk with the sheriff. The deputy was a dangerous fool, and the chance of getting any help through him was nil. He'd told Willa that since it was an election year, the sheriff was mighty glad to have another solved "murder" case under his belt. And that since the books were closed on it, there was no reason for him to interview her. But when she'd tried to explain (quite firmly) that Sam had *not* committed murder, but had had to kill Malcolm in order to save her, he'd made some asinine remark about Willa being lucky to still be a free woman, and that perhaps they ought to lock her up as an accomplice. However, since they had a confession from Sam, she was off the hook, and she'd be smart to be on her way and get out of their way.

As Willa came around the bend and began her approach into the heart of town, she looked down the dusty main road. But just to the left of the sheriff's office and jailhouse some movement caught her eye: There, in a small grassy lot, four large men were busy fitting and hammering together heavy planks of wood to finish off the building of a gallows. Willa immediately understood that was the place where Samuel Harold's neck would be stretched until it snapped and death mercifully claimed him.

CHAPTER 23

A Ballot Cast

Willa whipped the rump of the stubborn mule harder than she'd ever hit an animal before and the mule responded to the lashing with a surprised braying, followed by more speed. The hood of Sam's old cloak blew back off her head, and wisps of her thick black hair flew wildly about her face. Her eyes were as big as the mule's when she pulled the reins in hard in front of the gallows.

"Who're they hangin'?" she urgently asked, terrified of the coming answer.

"That feller that done kilt the senator's grandson. Sam . . . somethin'-or-other," replied one of the largest men, looking back over his shoulder as he lifted another plank up to the waiting man who was finishing the gallows' railing. Willa began to tremble as she watched another man fastening one of the hinges on the trap door.

"When?" Willa cried, forcing her eyes back to the man who had answered her.

"Tomorrow mornin', after sun-up. Guess they's a-waitin' until thar's enough light so that everyone can see real good," he drawled, looking over at the other workers and encouraging their amused laughter.

"Where's the sheriff?" Willa demanded.

"Just got back in his office. You gonna ask for a front row seat?" He grinned, showing many black spaces in his mouth where there used to be teeth. The others laughed again at his demented humor.

Willa did not bother to answer, but dug her heels into the sides of the mule instead, urging him over to one of the hitching posts that sporadically lined the street. After tying the animal to it, she hurriedly walked into the sheriff's office.

Sheriff Buchanan was sitting at his desk with a brown paper bag spread out before him, sucking on the bone of what had once been the leg of a chicken. Shattered white eggshell pieces lay haphazardly discarded on both the bag and his desk. As soon as the door opened and he saw that it was not his idiotic deputy, or anyone else he was familiar with, the sheriff hurriedly set the gnawed bone down, stood up and wiped his greasy mouth on the back of his shirt's dingy white sleeve.

"Can I help you?" he asked, rubbing his hands down the front of his black pants in a disgusting attempt to be rid of the grease that covered his hands, too. There was no smile accompanying his inquiry for he was clearly annoyed to have been interrupted.

"Sheriff, my name is Willa Holton, and my husband is . . . *was* Malcolm Holton. I just been told you're planning on executing Sam Harold tomorrow for the killin', but you'll be doing wrong when you do! I know *exactly* what took place, Sheriff, I was there. And had Mr. Harold not done what he done when he done it, then I wouldn't be telling you what I'm about to tell you 'cause I wouldn't have lived to stand here and tell it!" She sucked in a deep breath and then rushed on again with what exactly had taken place, all the while hoping to God that her version was a perfect match to Sam's.

After Willa had gotten started, and the sheriff realized there wasn't going to be any stopping her until she'd gotten out all that she had to, he breathed an exasperated sigh and sat back down. Leaning way back, he began rocking in his chair as though he was patiently listening to the nonsense of a small child while working an annoying piece of chicken loose with his little finger between two of his upper back teeth.

His condescension did not go unnoticed and Willa stopped in mid-sentence, took another deep breath and tried to slow her speech down enough so that she didn't sound like a hysterical woman.

"Sheriff, Sam saved me from bein' stabbed to death by my husband. Is that not self-defense? There's a law that allows a person to protect himself, isn't there?"

"Yes, ma'am, there most certainly is. The only problem, though, is that Mr. Harold wasn't bein' threatened, you was. So why didn't you do the shootin', ''stead of the defendant?"

"I had no gun, sheriff. Sam told Malcolm to get away from me. He had no intention of killing him! But when Malcolm tried to stab me, Sam did what he had to do. He saved my life, sheriff!

"Now, Miz Holton. I find it awfully hard to believe that your husband would forfeit his life in order to take yours. That's crazy talk! I ain't met a man yet that had the balls . . . ah, 'scuse me, Miz Holton . . . the nerve to argue with the barrel of a gun. But ya know, seein' as how things ended up for your husband, it kind of makes me wonder if your husband was just gettin' in the way of somethin' that maybe you and Mr. Harold had goin' on." The smile accompanying his accusation was made all the more disgusting by food trapped between his front teeth.

"Sheriff, how *dare* you imply that there was anything goin' on between Sam and me that shouldn't have been! As God is my witness, we didn't do nothin' that our churches, families, and friends would have been ashamed of us for. And I resent your suggesting as much. And I'll tell you another thing, sir. When Sam is hanging from the gallows tomorrow, I'm gonna be praying to God in Heaven, and every angel He's got with Him, to let the fires of hell lick you good for the rest of eternity. I know why you're doin' what you're doin', and it has nothing to do with the innocence or guilt of anyone. It has to do with votes, and being called *Sheriff* for four more years. I saw the notice on the board outside. I know the election's comin' up and that it'll look real good to hang a 'criminal as dangerous as Sam!'"

Willa was about to choke on a throat full of tears. There was nothing more to be said, anyway. She'd said all that she could, so she turned around and left the office, slamming the door so hard that the tintype of the sheriff's mother (which hung on the wall behind "her precious puddin's" bald head), fell to the floor with a resounding *crash!*

"*Mama!*" the sheriff cried, quickly retrieving the tintype. Wiping away some particles of dust and reassuring himself that no damage had been done, he kissed the woman's sour, wrinkled face and gently returned her picture to its rightful place on the wall above him.

CHAPTER 24

The Peace of Letting Go

After Willa left the sheriff's office, she went to the town's jewelry store and sold her gold wedding band. Then she took a portion of the small amount she'd made from the sale and checked into the Pine Bridge Hotel. After freshening up from treating herself to a five-cent bath, she went into the hotel's dining room, found a small table in the back near the fireplace and ordered the day's special, which was leg of lamb with mint, roasted potatoes, buttered carrots, biscuits with butter, and blackberry pie for dessert. She'd paled when the waiter brought Sam's favorite dessert to her table and asked that he please wrap it so she could take it with her. Then a thought hit her and she quickly amended her request, asking that a second piece of pie be wrapped up as well, and to place both of them back in the kitchen for safekeeping until she returned. He'd graciously done as she asked, and she tipped him more than she should have, but his small kindness was so needed.

She'd felt a little stronger once she'd left the restaurant, even though she'd left much of the meal untouched. But she'd had to make herself eat something in order to keep her strength up, and the baby's strength, as well. The baby reassured Willa daily as to its health by its frequent strong kicking which beat at her insides like an internal drum. At this moment in time, though, she was keeping her strength up for Sam, most of all. He would need her tomorrow as he'd never needed anyone before. And she would be there. He would see her, feel her love and gratitude, and, perhaps, in the last fading moments of his life, know that his selfless actions to save her had not been in vain. She would stand there, proud and strong for him, in the knowledge that they knew the truth of what had taken place, and that it was a truth that neither one of them would deny or would run away from. On the contrary, they both would look others in the eye without guilt or shame. And she would be standing with Sam, sharing that conviction. Willa would not allow him to face his death alone.

She took a long walk along the river until she felt composed and as ready as she could be to do one of the hardest things she would ever have to do in her life. Then, after stopping back by the hotel's restaurant and retrieving the pieces of pie, Willa finally crossed the street to the sheriff's office to see if she might be allowed to spend a few minutes with Sam to say good-bye.

When Willa walked into the office, she found the deputy staring down at a report on the desk, one which he was fully engrossed in, it seemed, for he didn't even look up when she closed the door firmly behind her. But then she heard his snoring and realized that he was sound asleep with his chin resting comfortably on his flabby chest. "Good evening, deputy," Willa called out, startling him awake. But in his effort to straighten up and look as though he was alert and busy, he nearly fell off the chair beneath him. Willa played the innocent and apologized for interrupting his work, then asked if she might spend just a few moments with Sam.

The deputy immediately began to deny her the opportunity but she lifted the bag that held the wedges of pie out in front of her, opened it and let the aroma of buttery crust and sweet filling fill the air around them. She quickly explained that she'd brought one for Sam, and knowing that the deputy was putting in long hours, had brought one for him, as well. Reminding herself that this was her only chance to see Sam, she forced out words of apology for the threat she'd made against him some days before, telling the deputy that she knew that he "surely understood the weak constitution of a woman," and that she'd spoken out in a moment of near hysterics. Since then, however, she'd "resigned herself to Sam's sad, but unavoidable fate."

"Well," the deputy began while licking his thick lips. "I don't see nothin' wrong in lettin' our prisoner have a little sweet from his sweet before his neck is stretched too thin to allow him to swallow," he said, laughing at his own sick wit. Then he held his fat hand out to her, waiting to receive his payment in pie for his Christian act of kindness. Pie or not, though, the deputy insisted that she remain outside of Sam's cell in the narrow, putrid-smelling hallway. And he insisted on staying within earshot during their visit.

Sam was watching a hawk outside his window as it swirled and glided on the air's current when the deputy and Willa arrived at his cell door. "I saw you walkin' up to the sheriff's office," he said to her as he turned from the window and approached his cell door.

"No touchin', you two," Deputy Burke instructed. "If'n I sees either one of yous a-reachin' through them cell bars, I'll kick the lady out of here faster'n you can say 'neck snap!' " he laughed, showing the dark gaps in his mouth. But the look both Willa and Sam gave the deputy for his cruel humor was enough to cause him to duck his head slightly and waddle off to a chair at the end of the hallway.

"How are you, Sam?" Willa asked.

"I'm all right, Willa. Are you doin' okay?" he inquired, searching her face for the truth.

"Ever the one to worry about others, aren't you, Sam? Were you always this way?"

"I s'pose so," he replied with a small smile.

"Have they hurt you at all?" she asked, glancing over at the deputy.

"Naw, I'm fine, Willa. Really, I am," he assured her. But the fading purple bruises on the left side of his face were visible enough even in the low lighting in the cell. She realized he must have been badly beaten earlier in the week. "Don't get me wrong, gal, you're sure a sight for sore eyes, but you shouldn't have come. There's not a thing you can do for me, Willa, and it's not good for you or the wee one to be doin' all of this running back and forth to town on that durn mule."

"That baby's as strong as the mule is, Sam." She smiled, trying to reassure him. "Shoot, seems the more I do, the more the babe likes it. And it lets me know by pounding on my insides."

"What're you gonna do after I'm . . . after tomorrow, Willa? Will you stay at the cabin like I told you to do in my note?"

"I'm still thinkin' on it, Sam. I'm going to miss you something terrible, and I think that staying there is only going to make the missin' worse," she replied, praying that God would keep the tears gathering in her throat at bay.

"Willa, now listen to me. This is important," he whispered, and reached his hand out to grab hers as he did so.

"Boy!" The deputy stood up immediately and called out to Sam in warning. "You try takin' her hand one more time, and she gives you hers, I'm gonna come over there and beat both of 'em with this club 'til there ain't nothin' left of your right and her left but bloody stubs. You get what I'm sayin' to ya?" he threatened.

"It won't happen again," Sam assured him.

Willa watched the man regain his seat, then, without touching but leaning in closer, she asked, "What is it, Sam? What do you need to tell me?"

Sam glanced over at the deputy, who had turned his attention back to the last few bites of pie. "Willa," Sam began, speaking more softly than before. "There's an old leather satchel back at the cabin. It belonged to my grandfather." Then, lowering his voice so that the deputy couldn't hear him, he said, "Look under the board that's the third one out from the foot of the bed. Pry it up, it's loose. It's under there."

"I can't *hearrr* youuu," said the deputy in a singsong voice. "You speak up, boy, with whatever it is that needs sayin', you understand me?" the deputy ordered.

"Yes, sir," Sam agreed, then turned back to Willa and in a loud voice continued. "In that satchel is my family's Bible. I want you to have it. And I've left a letter inside for you, too. I left it there when I wrote the other one for you. Just in case. Okay?"

"All right, Sam, I'll get it. Oh, Sam, I'm . . ." She couldn't hold it back any longer and began to cry. And cry hard. "I'm sorry, Sam. I wanted to be strong for you. And here I am . . . I'm so sorry."

Willa hated how weak she was being. Sam needed her to be strong, to hold it together, to hold *them* together, but Sam seemed so calm in the face of death. She looked at him closely and saw resignation and acceptance in him. Through that letting go, he'd been given the gift of peace.

"I don't know what to do without you, Sam. I just don't know."

"You will, Willa. It'll come to you. You'll know. Stay at the cabin, like I told you. The way will be made clear to you. Don't do nothin' but rest and take care of yourself and the baby until you know what to do and where to go, if you're thinkin' you have to go somewhere else. Promise me," he urged.

"I promise, Sam. I'll stay for a little while anyway. Until I know . . ." Willa acquiesced.

"Good." He seemed to exhale as he said it, as though he'd been holding his breath until she agreed to stay, and it was a great relief when she finally had. "And another thing, Willa, I don't want you to be here in the mornin'. You hear me! I want you gone tonight. Hurry up and leave now, and you'll get home not too long after dark. I don't want you here when they . . . I don't want you seein' me that a-way. Do you understand?" Finally, Sam seemed on the verge of tears.

"All right, Sam. I'll do whatever you want me to do. I want to be here for you, Sam, so you don't have to go through this alone. But if supporting you means not being here, then I'll do that, too."

"Go now, darlin'. Head on home. And, Willa, girl, I love you. And I will into the next life." Without thinking, he put his hand back through the cell bars, and Willa, not caring if the deputy beat her hand or not, reached back, taking the hand of the man she'd loved and lost so quickly. How unfair life was, she thought.

"I love you, too. Be there for me when I cross over some day, Sam. I'll be looking for you, before looking for God, Jesus, or anyone else! I love you, too," she reaffirmed once more, before she began to cry again.

"Go on, now," Sam said, releasing her hand and turning back toward the window where he'd been watching the freedom of the hawk's flight. "I want to watch the end of the day." And that was the last Willa heard Sam say.

"Good bye, Sam," she whimpered. Then, without giving the deputy the satisfaction of ushering her out, she fled down the stairs and out of the building.

CHAPTER 25

The Means to a Beginning

Willa rode the mule hard down the main street and out of town. And she never looked back. There was nothing to look back for unless she wanted to see the completed gallows throwing its long shadow in the late afternoon sun, eerily stretching toward the jail as if impatiently attempting to reach its waiting victim. The thought made her whip the mule into an even harder run. Willa reached back and removed the comb from her hair. It was one her grandmother had given to her on her eleventh birthday, and she'd had it in her hair the night she'd run away from Malcolm. She wore it today, wanting to look nice for Sam, but now she needed to let her hair fly free. *She* needed to fly free and away from this God-forsaken place.

As quickly as she let her thick black hair fall loose, it was picked up by the wind and blew out behind her like long, wicked fingers. Finally, after rounding the bend so that Bolsey was out of sight, Willa slowed the heaving mule to a trot and guided it over to the river off to their right. Sliding off of the sweating beast, Willa led it down the bank and let it quench its thirst. She stroked it as it did, and whispered an apology for riding it like hell's demon. Leaning against its dark skin, she felt the sheen of hot moisture covering the animal but she didn't care, she needed the contact of another living thing, so she laid her head against its still heaving shoulder as it drank. And while it did, Willa sobbed. She cried for all she'd lost, and for those things she had thought she'd have but never would. And she cried for the bleak-seeming future awaiting the fragile life she carried. Finally, exhausted and spent, Willa knelt down at the river's edge, where she washed her face and drank deeply. Then glancing toward the west and seeing that the sun was going down quickly, she led the mule back up onto the road and continued the lonely journey home.

Willa reached Sam's cabin about an hour after nightfall. She felt more exhausted than she'd ever felt in her life. She lit one of the oil lamps and set it on the kitchen table, then went into Sam's room. Willa looked around, needing to feel his presence, his essence, and slowly touched some of his things. First, she went to his flannel shirt, which she removed from the peg it hung from on the wall. She held it close to her body, inhaling his familiar masculine scent as she did so. Next, she lifted the lid on a large hickory box he'd made, which held, among other things, his father's pocket watch, his mother's wedding ring, and a small gold cross (which Willa assumed was his mother's, too). She also found a small tintype of a very young Sam, perhaps nine years old, standing between a handsome couple who were most likely his mother and father.

Lowering the lid, Willa spotted Sam's heavy wool work jacket hanging across the back of a chair in the corner of his room. The cuff's hem had come loose on the left sleeve, she noticed, lifting it to inspect it. *Well, no need to fix it for him now,* she thought, and with that sharp reminder, she dropped the sleeve and sank down on his bed, still holding his flannel shirt against her. Willa lay back, only intending to rest for a few minutes before forcing herself to eat something, but she fell into an exhausted sleep.

Sometime during the middle of the night Willa was startled awake by the baby's kicking. "I know, little one, you're hungry," she murmured and forced herself up out of bed. Walking out into the kitchen, she watched the play of shadows move across the walls and ceilings from the breeze that stirred the lamp's dwindling flame. She'd only left the window cracked but the night was cold. Winter was rapidly approaching, although the weather had been unusually warm, even through the afternoon of the day before.

Yes, the day before, Willa thought. *Sam dies today. Oh, God!*

Willa closed the kitchen window, then reached up to pull together the red plaid curtains, and as she did she glanced outside and saw the season's first snowflakes floating down in the ghostly glow of a muted moon. They came down lightly, as if in no hurry, but Willa realized that she must hurry if she were to leave the area before the storms paralyzed all travel. The time of snow was upon her, and should she decide to go somewhere north from here, the going could be treacherous. But what would she be running from now? Her situation had changed with Malcolm's death. How ironic life was, Willa thought. Her life-threatening situation had been solved by Sam, who would now die to pay for removing that threat from her life. Willa turned to the woodstove and got it lit. She needed to heat the cabin, as well as her small supper. Something warm in her stomach might help her feel a little better.

She began warming some coffee still left in the pot and placed two biscuits in the oven. Then, returning to the bedroom, she went to the washstand and poured some ice-cold water into the washbowl and began rinsing away some of the road's dust and grime from her face and hands. The water was shockingly cold. Willa reached for the towel hanging from the washstand, and glanced at the floor through the veil of droplets cascading down her face. *Sam's satchel! Under the floorboards,* she suddenly remembered. *If ever there was a time to need a Bible, it was now.* However, she was so mad at God that she wasn't sure if she would feel any relief from reading the old and familiar passages. But Sam's letter was in there, too. Grabbing a butter knife and the oil lamp, Willa counted three floorboards from the foot of the bed, then knelt down and began prying up the wood. After a minute the board popped up, and moving it to the side, Willa reached into the gap and felt around on the dirt floor below. Suddenly, her hand brushed up against leather. Grasping it, she lifted the heavy bag out. Carrying both the lamp and satchel, she moved back into the kitchen and placed them on the table. Then grabbing a china cup from the cupboard, Willa poured the remains of the thick, black coffee and sat down to read the letter and perhaps a verse or two from the Book of Psalms.

Willa inspected the lovely tool work on the beautiful old bag, wiping away some of the dirt clinging to it as she did. Age and oil had turned the leather a deep walnut brown. Not including its long shoulder strap, the bag measured about two feet by two feet, and the initials A.H. were hand-tooled into the hide on the flap. Willa knew that Sam's grandfather, who'd also been a trapper and miner, had been named Augustus Harold. She whispered his name out loud. It made him more real to her, almost brought him into the room as company. She ran her hand over the beautifully carved letters which somehow made her feel closer to Sam, and to his family. Then she brought her face down and smelled the dark leather. It was bitter from the oil that had been rubbed into it to keep the hide soft and pliable.

Finally, Willa opened the flap and reached inside, but her hand did not meet the hard leather binding of a book as she'd expected, but loose papers instead. Mystified, Willa turned the bag upside-down, and shook the contents out on the kitchen table. There, piled in a heap, were dollar bills, many dollar bills, most of which were tens and twenties, with a few fifties mixed in. Poking out from beneath some of them was the corner of a folded white piece of paper. Pulling it out, Willa saw her name written in Sam's now-familiar handwriting. She opened the letter and began to read.

> *My dearest Willa,*
>
> *By now I am either in prison or dead. I'm sorry it turned out the way it did. I don't know of no other way it could have though. Take this money—there's over $6,800.00 here—and make a good life for yourself. It's all I got, but it'll get you started here or wherever you choose to be. I love you, Willa, and I'd have done anything to be there with you and the baby. But what's done is done, and it had to be that way, I guess. I pray God you'll be happy and the baby will grow up to be strong and beautiful like its mama—if it's a girl—or strong and kind if it's a boy. With you raising it, it's got a real good chance at being someone special.*
>
> *Your Sam.*

Willa clutched the letter to her breast and stared at the money. She knew Sam had lived simply. This cabin was the one his parents had built soon after they'd married, the place where they had raised him. And Sam remained in it even after influenza had killed both his mother and father. He hunted or grew most everything he ate, and his clothing was simple and basic. No, Sam had not squandered the money that he'd earned from trapping and mining, and perhaps some of it had been gifted to him upon his parents' deaths. He'd been putting it away, Willa guessed, until the right woman came along and he could start a family. Overwhelming sadness weighed her down once more, and she laid her head on the table. "Thank you, Sam," she whispered. "Thank you, dear one. Thank you! But what now? Where do I go and what do I do?"

The wind outside had risen. She needed some of that freshness, she thought. Cold or not, she needed to feel it. Willa felt as though she'd been holding her breath for over a week and she needed to exhale as intensely as the wind was doing. So she went outside, and stood in the front yard, feeling it, listening to it. It was colder than she'd thought it would be, and it bit into her. *It's not yet December and it cuts like a knife,* she thought. Suddenly, something familiar echoed down inside of her. *What is it,* Willa asked herself. *What is familiar? What am I trying to remember?* And then it hit her. It was so clear and so perfect and so right! It was the place she needed to go. A place that was close to her parents, a place she loved but had not seen for so long because Malcolm had isolated her from them, from everyone. Yet it was a place that was far enough from them that no one would know her, nor have heard through the town's gossip the shame that she'd brought upon her kin when her husband was killed at the hands of the man she'd been living with. *A kind and gentle man, who saved my life—twice! And provided shelter and safety for me, as well as a future for my child.* Yes, *that* was the answer! *That* was the place to go! Tomorrow morning, she would pack her few things and leave this place, a place that would remind her each and every day of Sam, and the pain of losing him.

But first, she would go back into the town of Bolsey River one last time. She needed a wagon, for she couldn't keep riding the mule. It was too dangerous for the baby. She needed to visit Sam's grave. She owed him that much. She had promised she wouldn't be there for the execution, but she'd said nothing about going back when it was over. After saying a final goodbye, she and her baby would head north and then west; toward newfound hope and new beginnings. To a new life in Howling Cut, North Carolina.

CHAPTER 26

A Wayward Son

Willa rode into town mid-morning. She had sat at the kitchen table after getting very little sleep, and finished the last of a pot of coffee as she listened for the old mantle clock to gong eight times. When that finally happened, Willa donned her cape, mounted the mule and rode back into Bolsey for the last time.

She'd spent much of the rest of the night and the first part of the morning packing the little she had, and going through a few of Sam's personal possessions. She'd felt funny doing so, but she wanted something of his—apart from the money—to take with her. She selected three things: A small book of poetry by Emerson, which Sam had, on occasion, read to her and the small gold cross and old tintype of Sam and his parents from the hickory box. She'd considered taking the box itself, but the size of it made it cumbersome and heavy, so regretfully, she left it behind.

All Willa owned was packed away in a large carpetbag she'd found in the cabin's only closet. The carpet it'd been sewn from was of a blue and red paisley print, with gold piping along the edges. She wondered if the rug had been in Sam's cabin at one time. No matter, she was glad to have it now for she needed an easy and practical way to carry her belongings. She wished the colors were more subdued, however, for she didn't want to bring any attention to the bag: Sam's money was hidden in its lining. Using a sharp knife, she'd cut a slit in the thin material early that morning, and had hidden most of it inside. Then she'd sewn it up, using extra care to mend it along the same seam she'd ripped open so the stitches were barely noticeable. Once she had seen Sam's resting place, she'd take the poor old mule to the livery stable and see about getting a wagon for her trip to Howling Cut. She just hoped Sam's confiscated wagon wouldn't be the one offered for she was afraid feathers would fly. It would already be hers if Sam had had any say in the matter. On the other hand, she'd be happy to have it back—as she would anything of Sam's—so she'd probably just pay the asking price and be done with it.

She rounded the bend and the town came into view. She immediately looked over at the jailhouse and saw no one standing anywhere near the gallows, which meant that the business of killing Sam was over and done with, and the town's folk had returned to their normal activities. She was sickened by the lonely sight of the scaffolding, but also relieved that she hadn't come upon the sight of a man's—*her* man's—lifeless body, swaying in the cold breeze while birds picked and poked their way through to his bones. Just the thought of it made her nauseous, and she forced herself to breathe deeply and move her thoughts on to the matters at hand. She knew that the cemetery for those executed, as well as the town's paupers, was just behind the jailhouse, so pulling the reins in that direction, she urged the tired mule toward it. When she rounded the side of the building, the neglected and overgrown cemetery spread out before her.

Headstones were askew or had completely fallen over as the growth of tree roots, extreme weather, age, and vandals had left their destruction. Each stone was actually a small white or gray slate, with the deceased's first initial and last name, as well as the date of his or her death, chiseled into it. Willa realized that Sam would not have a marker at this early date so she immediately scanned the area for a fresh grave. And there it was, just off to her left in a small corner of the cemetery.

Whimpering like a small, sad child, Willa dismounted from the mule and, taking the carpetbag with her, hurried over to the plot. She knelt down at what she guessed was the foot of it, though she really couldn't be sure, and began to weep quietly. After several minutes, Willa wiped her eyes and began speaking to the gentle man who lay in quiet slumber beneath the cold, brown earth. She told him she'd found the money, thanked him for it, then told him where she was going. She told him she loved him and always would, and that his dying for her would not be in vain. She swore it to God, and every one of His heavenly angels. She promised to raise the child to know about him and his selfless love, and the gifts that he'd given to them both and paid dearly for. And she promised to try to live a life of happiness and to keep him close to her heart always. She'd just pushed herself up to leave when she heard a somewhat familiar voice behind her say hello. Turning, she saw that it was the waiter from the hotel restaurant.

"Oh, uh, hello," Willa self-consciously answered, and immediately began brushing the mud and dirt off her cape.

"Hello, miss," said the young waiter again. "I'm sorry to interrupt your . . . well, uh . . . interrupt you, but are you all right?" he timidly inquired.

"Yes, thank you, Mr . . . Mr.? I'm sorry, I don't know your name," Willa said rather distractedly, as she finished brushing at her soiled clothing.

"It's Henry Camp, miss, of the Camps just to the south of here in Maytree. Do you know 'em?" he asked.

"No, I'm sorry, I don't." Willa shook her head. "I'm really not from here, but I . . . well . . . just stopped by to see a friend," she explained, with a sad half smile.

"A friend? Your friend is buried in *here*?" he asked, sounding surprised that this fine-looking woman cared deeply for someone who was buried in a criminal's or pauper's grave.

Willa nodded and looked down at the fresh grave. "What time was the hanging this morning?" she quietly asked.

"Ended up there wasn't no hangin'." He actually sounded a little disappointed. "I was deliverin' the mornin's milk to folks around town—that's my other job, workin' for Tiller's Dairy—and I'd hurried to be done in time to see the hang . . ." He trailed off, embarrassed, appearing to realize that it sounded as though he'd looked forward to the event; the event which was to end the life of someone who mattered very much to this young woman.

Willa stared at him in confusion. "No one was . . ." Willa began, taking a step forward and tightly clasping his arm. "*Did you say no one was hanged today?*" Her voice escalated with desperate hope.

"That's right, miss, no one," Camp repeated, pulling back from her a little. Her intense reaction to his simple statement made him uncomfortable.

"Then who's buried there?" she cried, still holding his arm with one hand but turning to point at the fresh grave with her other.

"Why, I'm not sure, miss, other than the fact that I saw the wagon from McCrea's Funeral Home arrive a couple of hours ago with a coffin. And whoever was in it got buried in a hurry," he quickly explained. "I was over at the restaurant doing my lunch prep, so I just watched it from there."

"And you don't know who it was?" Willa pressed.

"No, I don't. And no one else at the restaurant did either. But I do know that if there had been someone hanged, they wouldn't have needed McCrea's. The sheriff woulda just hired a couple o' guys to dig a pauper's grave to put the body in—'less, o' course, the poor sap's family come to claim him. But seein' as how there wasn't nobody's family hangin' 'round—oh, pardon the expression, miss—I figured McCrea's was buryin' a payin' customer."

"Thank you, Henry! Oh, thank you!" Willa's broadly smiling mouth firmly planted a kiss on the surprised young man's cheek; then she abruptly turned and walked away, leaving him staring after her in curious amazement. With a torrent of questions running through her brain, Willa hurriedly led her mule to a hitching post in front of the sheriff's office, securely tied it, grabbed her carpetbag, and walked through the door.

Sheriff Buchanan was actually in attendance for a change, and after looking up to see Willa enter, sighed audibly, then went back to perusing the newspaper that lay open on his desk.

"Where is he?" Willa wasted no time in asking.

"Where's who?" the sheriff indifferently replied, turning the page and feigning complete interest in an article on women's parasols.

"You know damn well who I mean, Sheriff. Where's Sam Harold?" she insisted, gripping the edge of his desk and leaning over toward him, fighting to keep herself under control.

"Tsk, tsk, Miz Holton! No need to use such strong language, and in a public servant's office, no less!" he scolded.

Willa took a deep breath knowing that any verbal pushing on her part would only result in his pushing back, and since he was the one wearing the badge, and she was nothing but a lowly widowed woman, she knew who'd win that game.

"Sheriff," she began again, trying to soften her voice a bit. "Please be kind enough—sympathetic enough—to tell me what took place this morning. Please, Sheriff." And as much as she hated herself for it, her voice cracked with emotion.

"The deputy took him away," the sheriff simply stated.

"Sam?" Willa quickly clarified.

"No, Miz Holton, the Archangel Gabriel! Yes, woman, Sam Harold, for *God's sake*," he loudly snapped. "Here." He pulled a yellow sheet of paper out of the desk's top drawer and tossed it across to Willa. Snatching it up, she immediately saw it was a telegram.

```
To Sheriff Buchanan:
    Received your telegram re: grandson's
death. STOP. The one who killed that son
of a bitch should be canonized. STOP. Do
NOT execute. STOP. Signed, Senator
Beaumont Holton. STOP.
```

"Oh my God," Willa exclaimed, sinking down onto the chair in front of the desk. "Oh my God," she repeated softly. Tears had filled her eyes but she quickly brushed them away. "Where'd your deputy take him, Sheriff? Did you release him somewhere?" she asked.

"Now, c'mon, Miz Holton, you know damn well that I couldn't just let him go. Why, how would that look to the townsfolk? How would that make *me* look? Why, I'd look like an old soft fool. And—"

"And it's election year," Willa angrily finished, clearly understanding the sheriff's motives.

"Why, yes, ma'am, it sure is." He smiled. "And I'm planning on keepin' my job." Then, leaning forward, he added, "And that means keepin' folks around here happy. And 'happy' means keepin' the streets clean of garbage, the man-made kind, and man himself. Why, hells bells, gal, you don't think I could have let him walk, do ya? Shoot, the folks 'round here would have had my hide, if I hadn't done somethin' with his."

"And what did you do, sheriff?" she asked, terrified.

"Well, Miz Holton, it really ain't none of your business, now is it, considering you ain't one of my constituents. But seein' as how you's so upset an' all, I'll tell ya. Mr. Harold was sentenced bright and early this morning, then I placed him in the care of my deputy, and sent him on over to a place that'll keep him, ah . . . tied up for a while." He smiled at his choice of words. "And that's where that 'friend' of yours will stay until he's an old, old man." concluded the sheriff.

"You can't sentence him, Sheriff Buchanan! Who gave you the authority to do so?" Willa was furious.

"Now hold on, Miz Holton. I never did say I was the one doin' the sentencing, now did I?" the sheriff asked in the calmest, most smug way.

Still infuriated, but trying to keep her head about her, Willa calmly asked, "Then who did, sheriff?"

"Ya know, it's an amazin' thing how much a person can get done when he's got friends in high places, or, in this case, a brother-in-law in a high place. Mine happens to be a judge here in town, Miz Holton, and he had a problem, too, a-lettin' a murderer go simply because some half-assed state senator—and a Democrat, to boot—thought I should. The telegram didn't go so far as to say let him go, so we didn't. It just said not to kill him, so we didn't!" he spat, clearly angry that the hanging had not taken place this morning.

"Your brother-in-law is apparently up for reelection, too, isn't he, Sheriff?"

"Now, now, Miz Holton, that's beside the point. As elected men of the law, we both felt it was our duty to uphold that law, and do what was right for the welfare of the good folks of Bolsey. And like it or not, that meant seein' that your 'friend' paid a hefty price for killin' a man. There ain't no gettin' 'round the fact that Mr. Harold blew half of Mr. Holton's head clear to Tennessee. And because of that, that fella of yours is a-goin' away for a long, long time. And whether or not he ever comes back is for the good Lord to decide—oh, an' the parole board. Now, if you'll excuse me, miss, I've got a town to run." And with those closing words, he swiveled around in his chair and stood up to escort her out the door.

Willa was momentarily at a loss for words. She quickly found her voice, though, when she realized the sheriff was dismissing her. If she didn't find out more now, chances were she never would.

"Where'd you have him taken, Sheriff? *Where?*" She asked, fear evident in her voice.

He grabbed her elbow in a forceful grip and guided her quickly to the door, but Willa dug her heels in and grabbing the doorframe with her free left hand, repeated her question: "Where'd you take him?"

Pulling the door open, the sheriff yanked her loose from the frame and shoved her out the door, then replied with a sadistic gleam in his eye, "He's on his way to Salisbury Prison, the state pen in Hickory.

It's the old Confederate Prison. It's a rough one, Miz Holton, but I think the accommodations are rather fittin'. He's gonna be there 'til you're at least a grandma, if not a great-grandma. And there ain't a damn thing you can do about it!" And with that, he started to shut the door, but then remembered one last thing he wanted to say, "Oh, and Miz Holton, they don't let women in for any visitin', so you can bet your little bonnet you won't be a-seein' him for a very long time, if ever again. Now, have a *nice* day." Smiling a most vicious smile at her, he once again started to slam the door, but Willa blocked it.

"One last thing, Sheriff; who was just buried out back today?"

"Why, your murdered husband, ma'am," he answered, surprise lacing his voice, as though it was only logical she would have figured that one out. "It seemed a shame not to use one perfectly good brand new grave. And seein' as how his family didn't care to come get the poor fella, the grave your 'friend' should have filled was the perfect answer. You know, ma'am, we could have tossed him in the river, but we're God-fearin' around these parts. God-fearing!" he reemphasized, again smiling viciously as he did so. And with that, he slammed his office door in Willa's face.

Frozen with anger and fear, Willa stared at the door for a moment. Knowing there was nothing more that she could do—at this time, anyway—she returned to the mule, secured her bag to the saddle and mounted. She'd worry about purchasing a wagon in the next town she came to; she needed to be gone from this malignant place as fast as possible. As she rode past the graveyard, with the newly turned earth marking the resting place of a husband she could only think of with loathing and disgust, she gently but firmly bumped her heels against the mule's sides and turned her back forever on the town of Bolsey River.

PART 3

Rachel

CHAPTER 27

November 5, 1922, Howling Cut, NC

Grandma and I took our time on the way home from Sam's as she continued telling me more about our family's history, and answering my many questions. Grandma had said I was old enough to not only hear about it but understand it, and the fact that she felt that way made me sit up a little taller in the seat beside her and attempt to weigh the newfound information from a more mature point of view. I knew that her story would be replayed in my mind over and over again until I could digest it to the point that it became part of the fabric of my life. I wanted it to feel comfortable and familiar. Mama, however, had never been able to do that—to accept the fact that the father she'd never known had been a man whose sole purpose in life, it seemed, was to bring pain to everyone who had the misfortune of meeting up with him. Even his own family had disowned him by the time he was in his late teens.

The Holton clan had been a family with a fair amount of wealth, and an even greater amount of respect in their community, the burgeoning town of Gastonia, North Carolina. Malcolm's father, Davis, had been a highly regarded lawyer. Davis's father, Beaumont, was an attorney as well, but had climbed the ladder of success to even greater heights by winning the seat of mayor of their town, and had even bigger political aspirations in mind. Malcolm, however, had been a blemish on the family's otherwise sterling name. A black sheep almost from the beginning, he'd been in trouble from the time he was big enough to put a crate below a neighbor's open window, hoist himself through it, and steal nineteen dollars in cash, a red coral cameo brooch, and a pair of emerald and diamond cufflinks. He sold the goods to some older teenage thieves, who, in turn, took them to the next town over and sold them for an even greater amount. But the event that put an unbridgeable distance between the boy Malcolm and his family was the death of Malcolm's younger brother Benjamin.

The two had gone with some other boys over to Blue Lake one hot June morning. The friends had fished for wide-mouth bass, followed by diving from a rock outcropping into the deepest and coolest part of the lake. Eventually, the two other boys with the Holtons decided to try another, less-frequented part of the lake, so grabbing their poles, they headed over to a cove on the lake's southeast side. Malcolm, who was sixteen at the time, stayed behind with fifteen-year-old Benny, drying off and dozing in the sun on the lush grass of the lake's bank. At one point, as they lay there in that soft and fuzzy state of half-wakefulness, Benny mentioned that he planned on asking Ruthie Jemmison to the upcoming Fourth of July dance on the town's square. Benny had an aching crush on Ruthie, and Malcolm knew it. However, out of meanness, or maybe a secret shared passion for the little blond-haired, green-eyed beauty, Malcolm had beat Benny to it and had asked Ruthie just the day before. The girl had accepted. Malcolm, who had been waiting for just the right time to inform his brother of the news, smiled with cruel delight as he watched a bevy of emotions wash over his usually passive and quiet brother's face. After a stunned moment, Benny jumped up and challenged his far bigger brother, and the two came to blows. As they fought, Malcolm intentionally drove Benny closer to the edge of the rock outcropping, and finally, with one right-fisted blasting blow, he shattered Benny's nose and sent him over the side into the darkening lake below.

The two friends heard Malcolm yelling for their help, and running back as hard as they could, they found him in a nearly hysterical state. They finally made out enough to get some idea of what had happened: Malcolm claimed they'd been having some fun, just wrestling with each other, when Benny had slipped off the outcropping, hitting his head as he did, and falling into the lake. Malcolm told them he'd immediately jumped in after him but had been unable to find the boy in the deep, murky water, and that it had been a good ten minutes or so since his fall. As plausible as his story sounded, there was one fact that seemed to tell a far different version of it; and that one fact was that Malcolm's hair was dripping wet, while his clothes were only slightly damp. There was just something off, and the boys knew it. Not wanting to waste precious time, however, they did not question him. Instead, the older of the two friends jumped in to see if he could spot Benny in the depths below. But after several futile minutes, he climbed out and all three went for help.

The lake swarmed with dozens of people who joined in the search. But, it wasn't until three days later, when a bloated and blue Benjamin Wayne Holton resurfaced on Blue Lake, that the final chapter of the boy's short life was closed. Though no charges were ever brought against Malcolm, and it was written in the books that accidental drowning was the cause of Benny's death, the boys who had accompanied the Holton brothers to the lake that awful day were more than willing to tell their side of the story to willing listeners. Unsurprisingly, a great cloud of suspicion followed Malcolm thereafter. And no one was more suspicious of the troubled boy's part in Benny's death than his own family. Finally, less than a year later, with pockets filled with money made from selling off quite a bit of expensive jewelry he'd taken from the Widow Waltrap's home, Malcolm headed toward Asheville to begin his professional life—one befitting his nature and his need for dangerous escapades, as well as dangerous company. Malcolm became a professional gambler.

As it happened, one of the games Malcolm joined in with was in a little saloon called The Painted Horse, in a town named Spring Creek, just outside of Howling Cut. The saloon owner was none other than Willa's own father, Earl Cooper, and it just so happened that on that fateful afternoon, Willa had stopped by on instructions from her mother to ask Earl for a dollar with which to get some black thread and cornmeal. Once in town, Willa had headed directly over to her father's saloon to retrieve the money, and it was then that she met the tall, darkly handsome stranger. Malcolm was taking a break from his eight game losing streak of seven-card stud, and was standing at the bar downing his second whiskey of the afternoon, when the raven-haired, blue-eyed beauty came hurrying in, waiting for her father to finish helping another of his customers.

Willa stood there awkwardly as Malcolm gave her a good looking-over. Although very aware of the stranger's perusal, she pretended not to notice, which made it all the more obvious that she did. Finally, amused by her attempt to ignore him, he moved closer to her, introduced himself and made small talk about how windy a day it had been, how nice the town's people seemed. Hoping to evoke some pity, Malcolm mentioned being new to town and knowing no one. Looking into the stranger's dark gray eyes and feeling compassion for this person who was so alone, Willa was easily hooked.

A two-week period of whirlwind courting followed, but was cut short because Malcolm's money was running out. He knew that in order to keep Willa, he'd better wed her quick before the truth was found out about his "temporary state of financial instability," which was how he referred to his ever-increasing debt to an ever-increasing number of people in various places. Naive, young, restless, and in love, Willa accepted his proposal immediately, and they married the following weekend in the Baptist church she'd been raised in. The simple, homespun wedding was followed by a honeymoon in Asheville.

But the honeymoon ended almost immediately when Malcolm's money ran out, and Willa was forced to take in laundry while her husband took his anger and frustration out on her. As Willa was quick to learn, Malcolm lost far more than he won. They left Asheville in the middle of the night a couple of months later, owing more money than they'd ever be able to repay, and headed toward Upper Bolsey River. There, Malcolm built a small cabin on a piece of land which his father had given to him soon before he'd left Gastonia. The land had been part of a larger parcel of unused land that had been in the family for many years. No one in the family had ever had any use for it, until Malcolm became a problem and an embarrassment to them. The vacant land seemed to offer the perfect solution to the Holtons; Malcolm would have land of his own and be far enough away to keep him out of their lives. Upon handing Malcolm the quitclaim deed, his father had informed him that should he ever come back to Gastonia, he would delve more deeply into the events surrounding the death of his beloved son, Benjamin. The threat worked, as did the "gift" of land, and the family was rid of the thorn in its side. Malcolm, in turn, had the perfect place to build a new life with his bride, for it was isolated enough to hide from those he owed money. And it was also far enough off the beaten path that few were likely to see the telltale signs of the beatings his new bride had to bear.

So, as life would have it, the good and kind Samuel Harold ended up spending twenty-one years in Salisbury Prison for the slaying of the vicious and cruel Malcolm Holton. And those years had been spent at hard labor and enduring endless abuse. There were days he wished to God that some angel from above would come down with that hangman's noose, after all, just to free him from the hell he'd been sentenced to. Constant beatings, little to no food, a cell that was either as hot as a coal furnace or as cold as an ice cave eventually wore Sam down to the point of fracturing. He'd been able to hold it together longer than most, but was nearly driven past the breaking point of both life and sanity the day he'd been beaten about the head and body with a lead pipe for helping a man whose legs had turned to mush from working a twelve-hour day laying railroad ties in ninety-seven-degree weather. The man had been sixty-one years old, and suffered from poor health as it was. But there was little medical help for convicts, and even less compassion, so many of those sentenced to hard labor—which was the majority of them—died from being worked to death. The state turned a blind eye to the mistreatment for there were plenty of others to fill the bunks of those that had departed for their heavenly reward, or, as most believed, to begin serving a far harsher eternal sentence in a place that made Salisbury, North Carolina in July feel like Fargo, North Dakota in January.

The only things that brought comfort to the man who had saved my grandmother's life were the letters they wrote to each other. Those had been his saving grace. And though it might have been less torturous to just move on since the pain of knowing that he would never have her cut like a knife, there was nothing for him to move on to. The road ahead looked as endlessly bleak and desolate as the train tracks, he thought, as he gazed down the steel and wood path, while eating his noontime ration of deer jerky and hardtack. Though he knew the tracks led to many wonderful *somewheres*, they never would for him, at least not until he was old and gray. And that terrible realization broke his spirit down as thoroughly and painfully as the prison guards' beatings broke down his body.

Finally, after twenty-one years, two months, and seventeen days, Sam was awakened by one of the less malicious guards who told him the state parole board had figured his sentence had been justifiably served. Sam was handed the clothing he had been brought in wearing (which was now about four sizes too big), a brand new silver dollar, and the door to freedom. And even though it was a door he'd been longing for, he wasn't quite sure what he'd find on the other side of it. Fortunately for him, he found his cabin still standing, though many new tenants of the furry and venomous sort had long since taken up residence. But after some serious cleaning and repairing, Sam settled back into his old home place and returned to his old way of life of hunting, trapping, and mining.

All had been going along fairly peacefully, until one particularly dark night, when there was absolutely no moon, and he'd gone out to see why his mule, horse, and cow were making such a ruckus in the barn. As he'd hurried across the yard, he saw the soft white outline of a free-floating . . . *something*. His head told him it couldn't be a man, but the shape of it told his eyes different. And to make things worse— much, much worse—his eyes told him that the white, gliding shape looked eerily like Malcolm Holton. As much as he wanted to forget the man, his image would stay forever burned into his memory. He figured it had something to do with the fact that he'd killed him, for that, in and of itself, still haunted the gentle Samuel Harold. It mattered not that the man had left Sam little choice, that Malcolm would have killed Willa that day by the river. No matter how justifiable Sam's actions had been, he'd paid a dear price for them, and continued to do so, for there was no harsher judge and jury for his actions than Sam, himself.

Grandma had asked repeatedly why Sam hung crescent moons in his trees, and Sam had repeatedly refused to tell her, until the time Grandma swore she wouldn't come back to see him unless he did. That greatest of all threats finally broke Sam's resolve never to tell her, so he finally admitted to seeing Malcolm numerous times; adding that it only seemed to happen when there was no moon. So Sam began to make and hang moons. And he noticed that the occurrences became less and less frequent as his trees became fuller and fuller of the bizarre lunar works of art. I asked Grandma if she believed Sam's crazy-sounding tale, and she said that it really didn't matter what *she* believed; Sam believed it and that was all that mattered. "Could be," she'd continued, "that guilt haunts him more than any spirit does." I asked her if his guilt was why the two of them had never gotten to-gether—never married and started anew. She'd said it was, but Sam also felt that being married to a convict was almost as bad, if not ac-tually worse, than being a convict.

Another hurdle was the fact that my mother hated Sam. She hated the man who had killed the father she'd never known. It didn't matter that Grandma tried explaining how cruel and brutal Malcolm had been, or that if she'd been raised by Malcolm, chances were that she would have suffered the same abuse as Grandma. Nothing she said made a difference in Mama's stubborn opinion. She'd convinced herself that if her father had had the chance to know his daughter, he'd have been a changed man. After repeated attempts to make Mama understand the painful truth of the situation, Grandma gave up. And by doing so, she knew that she was also giving up any chance at a future with Sam. However, it wasn't just a matter of changing Mama's mind; it was also a matter of changing Sam's. And after years of trying unsuccessfully to do so, she'd given up and let things be.

After all, she figured, the best years of their lives had come and gone. And her daughter was a force she just couldn't combat. There were two facts about Mama that Grandma had to come to terms with: Mama would never, ever accept Sam, and Mama had inherited Malcolm's unstable mind. But while Malcolm was cold, brutal, and calculating, Mama was easily frightened, fragile, and weak, and could easily slip into the kind of darkness that was destructive to both herself and her family. I felt a physical coldness penetrate my body as a reaction to my grandmother's painfully honest words. But the sad truth of the matter was that I understood her assessment of my mother for I had experienced the depth of that black hole that she could crawl into. I'd seen just how bottomless it could be. And I prayed to God that I wasn't cut from that same dark cloth.

As we got closer to home, Grandma grew quiet. The book of her past was gently closed, and we both stared silently ahead, watching for our house to come into view. We didn't need to remind each other that Mama would be watching for us, and that knowledge made us stop looking at the past and start thinking about the possible ugliness of the immediate future. I had to admit that I'd worried about Mama's reaction to my going with Grandma. After all, she'd had no say in it and had only learned of my going through Merry's sketchy recitation of my even sketchier message. As if reading my mind, Grandma mumbled something to the effect that Mama would be madder 'n a cat in a full bathtub. She would know the story had finally been told to me, and she would be none too happy about it. But when we finally walked into the house that evening, Mama wasn't standing by the window as expected, but was sitting in a living room chair instead, seemingly unconcerned with our whereabouts and quite involved with some embroidery.

"I took your supper off the stove, or it would have burned up by now. It's waitin' on the table," she said, hardly glancing up from her sewing.

"Thank you, daughter," Grandma responded, as we both walked straight toward the kitchen door without looking too closely at her.

"You had a visitor," Mama said casually. Grandma stopped short and I ran into her back.

"Who did, Anna, Rachel or me?" Grandma turned to inquire.

"You did. It was Lydia Harris; that woman whose husband has the orchard now. She had her daughter with her. Harriet—that's her name—has a mess o' warts on her left hand, and Miz Harris was told you're the Wart Buyer 'round here," Mama said, still not looking up from her needlework.

"Well, did you tell her to come back tomorrow?"

"No, I told her you'd gone off somewhere, and I didn't know when or even *if* you'd be coming back," she answered, finally looking up from her task and pinning us with a hard, cold glare.

"That's silly, Anna. I hope you told her you were teasing." Grandma forced a chuckle.

"Old woman," Mama venomously spat, suddenly standing up and forcefully throwing her sewing into the chair. "Don't you come in here a-tellin' me what I ought to be tellin' anyone else! You're a crazy ol' fool. And if you're wantin' to go a-gallavantin' around the countryside on a fool's errand, then be my guest. But next time you do, you leave my daughter behind!"

"I'm old enough to go where I want, Mama, and I wanted to go with her," I interjected, disliking the fact that I was being discussed in the third person. I also felt the need to defend Grandma's decision to take me with her. "And I'll go again. I like Samuel Harold." And with that bold declaration, the room went deadly silent.

"Rachel," Mama started in a low, deep voice. It was a voice I'd heard before, and a chill began to creep up my spine. She took three steps toward us, and though she stood much taller than either Grandma or me, she seemed especially tall then. Her dark eyes flashed. "If you ever speak the name of that servant of Satan's again, I swear on everything I deem holy, I'll cut that tongue out of your mouth, and you'll never speak his name or anyone else's again!" And with that terrifying oath, she closed the distance between her and my grandmother, and leaning down into her face until their noses almost touched, hissed, "And I'll cut more than that out of you!"

Without another word, she crossed the room to her bedroom, and upon opening the door, I caught a glimpse of my father snoring away in ignorant bliss on their bed. Then, turning around to quietly close the door behind her, Mama looked up at Grandma and me, and her mouth turned up into the eeriest wisp of a smile. Beneath it was a blackness, born of anger or illness, which I wasn't sure, and I couldn't breathe for a few seconds. Apparently, Grandma had been witness to it before, though, for she sounded amazingly composed and firm, even motherly, as she calmly replied, "Get some sleep, Anna. You'll feel better in the mornin'." Then she put her hand firmly on my shoulder and turned me toward the kitchen, murmuring something about eating our supper before it got any colder. As I numbly moved through the kitchen door, I suddenly realized with an awful clarity that I knew exactly what my grandfather must have been like, and *looked* like, for I had just seen the incarnation of the father in the daughter.

CHAPTER 28

News from the Orchard

Mrs. Harris had returned the Saturday following our trip to Sam's, and had Harriet in tow. Since there was no school, Papa had taken Prescott with him to the sawmill. Mama had been in the garden burying cabbages upside-down to keep them from spoiling until we needed them, and Grandma, Merry, and I were busy sorting turkey feathers when our visitors arrived.

We'd starting raising turkeys several years before, when things had been at their leanest. And even though our household finances had drastically improved, we still had turkeys a-plenty. Grandma had learned how lucrative the turkey business could be while raising my mother, and had continued with it until the grandchildren came along. Then she got busy helping to raise us.

We sold the majority of our turkeys at Thanksgiving, of course, and did so at ten to twelve cents per pound. And we also made money by selling their feathers. Mrs. Sweetser ran a millinery in town; making hats of all sorts and sizes, and she loved using both turkey and peacock feathers for the trimming. So, we sorted feathers by size, color, and quality. The poor quality feathers were used to stuff pillows and mattresses, and any we had left over after filling our own immediate needs were sold to Mr. Taft for stock in his store. We also sold him turkey eggs. But we sacrificed one of the fattest birds of the bunch for our own Thanksgiving dinner. I never could stand to watch the execution, but the following morning, while feeding the survivors who'd been thin enough or fast enough to escape the axe, I quickly figured out which poor tom or hen had been the centerpiece on our bountiful table the afternoon before.

We heard our latest dog, Alfie (a bloodhound mix), barking up a storm, then heard Mama's muffled voice telling the dog to hush, followed by muffled conversation. Merry and I went out to the porch and looked off to the side of our house where our garden was, and saw Mama with the new arrivals standing on the edge of it.

The woman and girl looked familiar to me, and I knew it must be Mrs. Harris and Harriet. "Let's go in," I heard Mama say. "She's inside, and will be glad to help y'all, I'm sure," she finished, undoubtedly referring to Grandma. All three turned toward the house, and saw us standing on the porch, watching them.

The young girl was about ten like Merry, but the woman's age was far more difficult to gauge. Common sense told me that she couldn't be that old, with a child that young—two, actually, though I hadn't seen the boy for a couple of months. Last time was outside the Methodist church, and one other time as he came out of the feed store with a couple of sacks thrown over his shoulder. I'd been riding out of town with Papa after running some errands when I saw him. My stomach dropped just a bit, and I wished we were just arriving. I wondered what I might have said or done to get a conversation started between the two of us—Jack was his name, I remembered. Perhaps I'd have said something amusing and he'd repeat that same smile he'd flashed at me on my birthday, the year before. I'd try almost anything to see that smile.

Now, here were Jack's mother and sister. *Why couldn't the boy have had the warts,* I thought. What a golden opportunity it would have been to start a conversation, take a walk, or, most importantly, get him to smile at me again.

"Rachel, Merry, this here's Miz Harris and her daughter, Harriet. Harriet's right 'tween you two in age," Mama informed Merry and me. I softly said my hellos, while Merry, without a second's hesitation, brightly jumped from the porch and said to Harriet, "You wanna see our new horse? She was born four days ago!" And after a soft "Okay" from Harriet, the two girls ran off and disappeared into the darkness of the barn.

"C'mon in, Lydia," (apparently their muffled conversation in the garden had put them on a first name basis with each other). "I just

made an applesauce cake last—" Mama abruptly cut off her words
and stopped walking, realizing she'd just put her foot in her mouth.
Where she'd blundered was offering her guest a piece of a cake that
had been made with apples that had not come from Mrs. Harris's orchard. Mama looked properly embarrassed. I'd never seen anyone go
from white to red so fast, and I wondered if she might faint.

"I'm sorry, Lydia, I didn't mean to . . . I have oatmeal cookies or . . ."

"It's fine, Anna. It's all right. If we had some good apples to sell
then I might be a touch out o' sorts with you for not buyin' 'em from
us. But with the orchard so run down to begin with, and that freeze
on top of it, why it's no wonder we ain't got anything worth eatin',
much less sellin'. Don't you go feelin' bad about gettin' apples at Taft's,
if that's where you're gettin' 'em. Don't know of any place closer 'n
that, do you?"

"No, that's about it, not countin' a few apples someone might
grow for themselves. How long y'all figure 'til you get things growin' good again?" Mama gently inquired. It never ceased to amaze me
how much more sympathetic and soft she could be with other people
than with her own family, the ones most affected by her emotions.

"We're thinkin' next year's crop may be all right. But I don't
know if we can make it another year without some return. Honestly,
I don't rightly know how we've been able to make it through this
one. Somehow we have, though. The Lord is good is 'bout all I can
say," Mrs. Harris finished quietly. She stopped looking at Mama and
glanced down at the ground instead as if suddenly self-conscious that
she'd told us so much about their dire situation.

Grandma came out of the house at the perfect time to change the
subject. She joined me at the porch railing as Mama and Mrs. Harris
started up the steps. "Mornin'!" Grandma greeted.

"Mornin'!" Mrs. Harris returned cheerfully, looking relieved.
"I'm Lydia Harris, Mrs. Holton. I heared you was the Wart Buyer
'round here."

"Yes'm," Grandma confirmed. "Who's needin' to be rid of 'em?"

"Harriet, my girl," Mrs. Harris said. "She's gone back with your
granddaughter to see your new pony. I'll call her—"

"No, now, let the young'uns get a little acquainted. If you'll set a
spell, you 'n I'll do the same. I been wantin' to meet you folks. Sit
down, sit down," she insisted, after taking a seat herself in one of the
wooden rockers. "I want to hear what's been goin' on at the orchard;

how y'all been gettin' along, and who all you got over there workin' with you."

Mrs. Harris began by telling us about her husband, Gilbert, being a veteran and the trouble he'd had getting a job once he was back from the war. Then how serendipitous it had been when they'd heard about the orchard needing someone to take it over. "It was like a sign from God. We figured Howlin' Cut was where we needed to be," she declared, glancing skyward toward "He who'd made it all possible." She talked about what bad shape the orchard was in. The first reason was obvious; it had been totally neglected for a good year, and it was just as obvious that little care or upkeep had been given to it prior to that. Grandma quickly pointed out how miserly the previous owner, Mr. Lomax, had been, and that he'd never hired enough people to help with the running of the place. Mrs. Harris agreed that his extreme frugalness had harmed the orchard greatly, with the irony being that the man who was too tightfisted to let money go had ended up robbing himself of much to be gained. Vines had taken over many of the trees, so they only produced a fraction of what they were capable of. And the apples that *were* able to grow appeared in the treetops in a never-ending battle to escape being strangled out.

They discussed the deadly freeze that had hit soon after the Harrises' arrival, and then moved on to more interesting matters (in my estimation, anyway).

"How's your boy doin', Lydia?" Grandma asked, quickly glancing over at me as she did. Mrs. Harris had insisted Grandma call her by her first name, just as she'd asked Mama to do. I had the feeling that Mrs. Harris desperately needed some friends. She seemed almost relieved to be sitting and talking with us. I had let most of what the woman was saying go in one ear and out the other until I heard Grandma's question about "the boy." Then my attention was quickly redirected back to their conversation. (*Finally! Now we're gettin' somewhere!*)

"Why, he's doin' all right, I s'pose," Mrs. Harris answered. "I feel a bit sorry for him though, 'cause he's a-wantin' to get back in to school somethin' awful, but he's not been able to go on account of all the work needin' doin' at the orchard. Not to mention in the store. We're tryin' to make it so that he can go back next year. He's workin' real hard, too, tryin' to make that happen. He's a good boy, and smart. *Lord*, how he's smart! He's taken to that orchard like a fish to water. Readin' up on things all the time, and tellin' his daddy how things oughta be done. I'm right proud of him, to tell the truth. I told my husband that I don't care if the orchard goes to seed, Jack—and Harriet—is goin' to school next year. They ain't gonna end up like me or their daddy, with hardly any learnin', and a whole lot of poor to show for it," she said with absolute conviction. "My young'uns are gonna have a lot better chance at good things in this world than me or Gilbert ever did."

"What grades will your young'uns be in?" Mama asked.

"Well, let's see . . ." Mrs. Harris closed her eyes as she calculated. "Jack is fourteen, and Harriet's eleven. I don't know where the teacher'll think they oughta be, though. Guess it's gonna depend on what they know. I think Jack'll be alright, 'cause he reads a lot, like I said before. But Harriet, she's too busy ridin' Mr. Smythe's nice little mare next door, or getting underfoot when we're tryin' to work in the orchard. She just can't hardly make herself sit still to put any learnin' in that head o' hers. Oh, well, guess that's why there's a teacher in that school house yonder." She laughed. "Maybe she'll get Harriet to settle down some."

"A hickory stick's good for settlin' young'uns down, too," added Grandma. The adults laughed and nodded in agreement, but I was too busy thinking about the possibility of having Jack in class with me next year. But that would mean ten months of waiting. And ten months of wondering who he might decide was worth smiling at in our class.

CHAPTER 29

Three Things to Keep

Lydia Harris brought Harriet to Grandma several times between
November and spring of the following year, which was 1923. I
had never met anyone who complained of having so many warts,
though the truth of the matter was Mrs. Harris came for companionship more than anything else. I heard Grandma talking about it one
evening after supper as she and Mama stood at the sink doing the
dishes. Mrs. Harris had stopped by with her daughter in the middle of
the afternoon, and because it was a fairly cold day, with several
inches of snow on the ground, Mama thought it was odd to make the
trek in their well-worn wagon through difficult, if not downright dangerous, conditions for such an unimportant reason.

"She's just needin' company is about all," Grandma had stated.
"Now I'm getting rid of warts that aren't even there yet. The woman
says, 'See thar, Willa. Ain't that one just under the skin?' And not
wanting to make her feel bad or unwelcome, or letting her know I see
through the excuse to just come over for some company, I say, 'Well,
Lydia, I can't say as I do, but you never know, so let's go ahead with
a little rubbin' of the spot.' That seems to satisfy her until the next time
she needs someone to talk to, or tell her secrets to, and she has more of
those than warts." Grandma seemed to understand the woman's loneliness and isolation, and so she tried to remedy the situation by treating
a few nonexistent warts while providing some much-needed company. More than once the thought crossed my mind that Mrs. Harris
seemed to prefer Grandma's company over Mama's, even though
Mrs. Harris was far closer to Mama's age. *But then, who can blame*

her, I thought. And then felt bad about thinking such a thing. After all, Mama couldn't help being who she was. But the rest of us couldn't help feeling the way we did about her, either.

Early one evening, not long before the sun went down and our supper was being put on the table, Mrs. Harris came by. Usually she had Harriet with her, and they came much earlier in the day. This time was different somehow, and I knew it just by looking at her face. I happened to be coming back from the springhouse with a bottle of milk when I saw her wagon pull off the sawmill road and into our driveway. I waited until she'd brought her mule to a stop and stepped out.

"Evenin', Miz Harris," I greeted.

"Evenin', Rachel. Is your grandma about?"

"Yes, ma'am. She's in the kitchen putting supper on. Come on in," I said unnecessarily, for the woman was already walking toward the porch steps.

"Come in, Lydia!" I heard Grandma call to her when Mrs. Harris had cracked open the front door and announced her presence. "What're you doing out this late, honey?" I heard Grandma ask as I walked through the front door behind Mrs. Harris. "Don't tell me you got a wart needs removin' this late in the day?"

"No, no, Willa. It's nothing like that," Lydia quickly corrected. "I just need to talk to you about something, that's all." She was always coming over to talk about something, so Grandma continued slicing the ham, while Mama continued mashing potatoes in the pot she'd boiled them in.

"It's, kind of . . . um . . . could we maybe talk somewhere . . . private, Willa?"

"Sure, honey," she said, looking more closely at Mrs. Harris's face and deciding that whatever she needed to say should be discussed away from the rest of us. The woman looked more worn out than usual. Sadly, I would have thought that would be nearly impossible.

"Rachel, carry this to the table and finish helping your mama," she said, handing me the ham. "Come on, Lydia, let's talk in my room." Lydia led the way and Grandma followed, shutting the door behind them.

It was quiet in the kitchen as I helped Mama. Merry was engrossed in homework, Prescott was in his bedroom with the door shut, uninterested in what was going on, and Papa wasn't home yet from the mill.

He'd been keeping longer hours and working odd hours, too. But he'd told Mama when she'd complained one time that to keep up with competition he had to do things differently, and they weren't always changes that suited everyone. Times were hard for almost everyone we knew, but we'd somehow managed to keep our heads above water, even with the Hollises running their successful and expanding mill on the other side of the mountain. They continued to build a fortune with the help of the furniture stores that had once been Papa's best customers, as well as plenty of other clients that were just too afraid of them not to give them their business. Papa's work was far superior, but fear drove many people in the direction of his competition. Papa had hung on, though, and he'd attributed it to his faith in God, and good old-fashioned hard work (never mind that his prices were far cheaper than the Hollises' were).

So, Mama and I joined Merry by the fire and waited for Grandma and Mrs. Harris to finish their talk, or Papa to come through the front door. He'd be hungry, no doubt, and we'd eat as soon as he washed up, regardless of whether Lydia and Grandma had come up for air.

About thirty minutes later, Grandma's bedroom door opened and the two women walked out.

"Sorry to keep you folks from your supper," Mrs. Harris apologized after seeing that our supper sat ready but untouched. Though she smiled as she spoke to us, it was fairly apparent that she'd been crying for her eyes still glistened and her face was splotchy red.

"It's fine, Lydia. It's fine. You sure you can get home okay? It's dark now," Grandma said.

"Yes, yes. I'll be fine. It's not too far and I could drive the road blindfolded," she laughed in an attempt at sounding light, though the short clipped laugh sounded more like a bark.

"Well, if you're sure, then," Grandma said, walking her to the door.

"I'm sorry to have bothered you with this, Willa," Mrs. Harris said as she walked out the door. "I just didn't know who else to talk to about it."

"I'm glad you told me, Lydia. It's gonna be fine. Have faith. It's gonna be all right. 'Night, now," she finished, and slowly but firmly closed the door to Lydia and the night.

We all sat there staring and waiting; waiting to hear what had brought this overly tired, obviously upset woman out at dusk and in the cold. Just her looks alone told us her news could not have been good.

"Well?" Grandma said, looking at each of us but offering up no explanation. "Are you ready to eat or are you waiting 'til Calvin comes in?" It was obvious she wanted to move away from the subject of Lydia.

"Mama, what did Lydia want?" Mama asked. "What in the world would have brought her out this time of night?"

"Daughter, let's let it be for right now. I'm about worn out. I don't think Calvin will care one bit if we start without him, do you?" She sounded as tired as Mrs. Harris had looked. "There's not a bit o' air left in this old lady's balloon," she quipped, though that admission worried me greatly. I could not remember the last time I'd heard Grandma admit she was tired.

"No, it's fine, let's start," my mother agreed, looking rather concerned as she did so. "Are you all right, Mama? Did Lydia say somethin' to upset you?"

"No, no, child. Can't a body ever be tired without everybody thinkin' the worst? Lydia can be . . . well . . . Lydia. And I'm just ready for the day to end so's I can have a little quiet time to myself." And with that last statement, Grandma slowly walked over to the dining room table and sat down. I'd never seen her look that faded and worn out, with the exception of the evening when she'd heatedly reprimanded Prescott and me for talking so negatively about Mama as we waited for her return from the hospital. Her uncharacteristic behavior on both nights was equally disturbing.

We ate our dinner in relative silence as each of us thought of countless possibilities that might be plaguing Mrs. Harris. Grandma didn't say one word except an occasional "Uh-huh," or "Is that right?" in response to our feeble attempts at some light dinner conversation. She closed herself off in her bedroom after asking Merry and me to help Mama with the dishes. As soon as she was out of earshot, Prescott was quick to guess that maybe the Harrises had lost the orchard. Perhaps, he'd suggested, Mrs. Lomax had been disillusioned enough to say she was selling the whole thing for the best offer to come along. She still had the majority ownership at fifty-one percent, so that was a real possibility. But Mama didn't think that was the case. After all, getting someone to purchase a large, struggling orchard was easier said than done. After a few more guesses around the table, which carried over to a sink full of dirty dishes, everyone got involved with other things.

But I couldn't get Mrs. Harris's visit out of my mind. And I was still wide awake wondering when I heard Papa come through the front door. The clock had chimed ten times not too long before, so I knew he was later than usual. I heard Mama move back into the kitchen from her chair beside the fireplace. She could finally fix Daddy a plate and finish putting the food away. I could hear their murmurings, but could not make out their conversation, so I drifted off into my own thoughts again. I remembered Grandma saying that Lydia Harris had "more secrets than warts," and I wondered how one person could have so many. I knew not a one of them, of course, for Grandma would never ever divulge any. She was, after all, a Wart Buyer, and was privy to information that could never to be repeated or used in any way. I truly believed that the good God above couldn't have pried it out of her. But Wart Buyer or not, my grandmother had always had a strong conviction that you kept people's confidences, under almost any circumstance, with the exception possibly being that it meant life or death for someone. And even then, I wasn't sure that Grandma wouldn't stop and think it through before spilling the beans. Actually, there were three things Grandma staunchly believed one *must* keep: your dignity, a promise, and a secret you were entrusted with. And if you didn't, then she would say you were "lower than a hog in deep mud."

With that last thought, I rolled over to try to get some sleep and forget about Mrs. Harris and her many secrets. There was no reason to lie awake guessing over what this latest one might be. I doubted Mrs. Harris would divulge whatever it was that ailed her body, mind, or spirit. But I knew the odds were far greater that she would give up her secrets before my tight-lipped, wart-buying grandmother ever did.

CHAPTER 30

Jack

There was only a month and a half of school left before summer break when early one April morning, Jack Harris stepped into our one-room schoolhouse, and into our lives. Our previous teacher, Mrs. Jacobson, had been married late in the fall the year before and moved with her new husband to Biloxi, Mississippi. Her replacement was a soft-spoken, slender young man with thinning light brown hair by the name of Percival Gary. Grandma had said that considering he'd been given the name of Percival, one would expect him to be as tough as nails fighting to defend himself. Mama had scolded her and told her that someone's name had nothing to do with his nature. Grandma said that she agreed with her, but that didn't mean the whole world did. And she concluded the subject by saying that she bet he could have made life much simpler for himself by reversing the first and last names. No one could argue her point.

"Ah, welcome, Mr. Harris," Mr. Gary greeted Jack as he rather self-consciously stood just inside the door of our room. "Have a seat anywhere and I'll be with you shortly to determine exactly what you'll be studying."

Jack glanced my way as he started toward an empty seat and immediately turned back to take a better look at me as recognition dawned. Saying nothing, however, he moved past me to an available desk behind the despised Ray Coons.

The Coons family had never been liked, and for far more reasons than just the fact that Ray tormented me over my disfigured foot. They were a family that had come from nothing, and they didn't seem to expect more than that for themselves. They were lazy, as well as mean. But, my family did more than just dislike the Coons, they resented them, too, for Ray's daddy, Wyatt, had taken a job at the Hollises' sawmill a couple of years before. It wasn't that my father could blame the man, really; he was just trying to make a living for his family. But it was the snide and often cutting remarks that Wyatt had thrown at Papa when they'd had occasion to run into each other in town that caused my father to have a deep dislike of the man.

"I swear, Anna, that man is just itchin' to start a brawl with me," Papa stated tiredly one evening after many long hours at the mill. "I saw him in town this mornin' when I went in for some new wrenches. He bragged that they'd picked up the Moore's Furniture account—from all the way over in Johnson City—and that they's so busy they had to employ another two men. Hell, I only got two and *a half* men—me and Nathan Street, who's so old I don't dare let him go 'cause no one else would want him. And the half part bein' Prescott, who's only there part-time. But there just ain't enough work to employ him full-time."

"He needs to finish school anyway," Mama reassured him. "But we're doin' alright, Calvin." She seemed content with the fact that we had more than we'd had many times in the past. And as long as she could buy the lace she loved or a new pair of shoes for herself now and then, she was manageable. *Things* pacified Mama, and as much I hated to admit it, that hurt me. I felt that *people*—namely *family*—should be what filled a person up, or made a person feel content and secure, not *things*. But Mama saw *things* differently, I realized. "We got plenty of food, some livestock, including three horses, not to mention that fine buggy, and some decent clothes," she continued. "Why, we've had far less, without a doubt. Honestly, we ain't got much to complain about. Not much a'tall." And, after offering up that confirmation of what she saw as the important things in life, Mama got up from the table where she'd been keeping him company while he ate his late supper, and retrieved the rest of the collards from the stove for him. Papa stared down into his plate, absorbed in unspoken thoughts, and finished his meal.

Mr. Gary worked with Jack most of the day in order to determine what Jack's grade level was. As it turned out, the fifteen-year-old was as advanced with his reading as many seventeen-year-olds, and Mr. Gary was both delighted and dismayed. First, he was delighted that this bright and capable student required very little catching up to put him at a grade level that was appropriate for his age. But he was dismayed because it wouldn't be long before Jack would surpass all that he could offer him at any grade level. As it turned out, Mr. Gary ended up bringing many of his own college books and workbooks to class and letting Jack study them; he needed very little guidance even with the advanced materials. Jack seemed most drawn to the business and economic books, and it was hard to pry him away from them, even when it was time for recess or lunch.

On the day of Jack's arrival, the class took lunch outside to sit in the weakening autumn sun. "How do I know you?" he asked, sitting down by me at one of the picnic tables. "Other than seein' you ride by our church every Sunday."

"The peppermints," I answered, "that day in town nearly two years ago. You bought me peppermints."

"Oh, yeah! Right," he said, drawing out the "right" so that it sounded like "Riiiiight." "You're the peppermint girl!" He grinned at finally being able to place me. The brisk wind blew my paper sack off the table, and inside was a freshly laundered white hanky I didn't want to lose. Jumping up and hobbling quickly to catch up with it, I was finally able to step on the bag with my good left foot. I could feel Jack's eyes on me during my pathetic attempt to chase it down, and I could feel myself growing red even before I turned around and confirmed it.

"What's wrong with your foot?" he asked without hesitation once I'd sat back down, face aflame.

"There was an accident, when I was four, at Papa's sawmill," I stared down at my paper bag. The wind kicked up again, and blew curling strands of my long brown hair across my mouth. I reached up and drew them away, then, after taking in a deep, bracing breath, I turned and boldly looked at him. "It won't get any better," I stated flatly, looking into his brown eyes. It was the first chance I'd had to really look at them, and they were unlike any eye color I'd ever seen before. They were a lovely golden brown, kind of like dark honey.

"I'm sorry," he answered quietly. And when he did, I felt that there was no pity attached. It was a different thing entirely that came from him. It was true sadness that I would have to bear my disability forever. And in a small and gentle show of compassion, he reached up and drew away another wayward strand of my wild hair, and tucked it behind my ear.

"We have to get back to class," I said, suddenly self-conscious about his attention. "Mr. Gary just called us in."

"See you later, peppermint girl," he said with a smile, although it wasn't quite the same one that I remembered so well. This one was more thoughtful, less big and bright. Beautiful though it was, it was softer, more muted, rather than being an outward display of joy or delight. I waited for a moment, hoping to see it broaden, but he redirected his attention instead and stood up, grabbed his lunch pail, and walked back into the schoolhouse for the afternoon's lessons.

The remaining weeks flew by without much more interaction with Jack. He'd become friendly with Prescott, our cousin Peter, and Frank Tilley, who lived a mountain over but made it to school every day, no matter how inclement the weather was or how treacherous the roads and passes could be. The four spent long hours hunting, fishing, throwing horseshoes, or playing ball with some of the other boys in the area. But sometimes Prescott had to forego play and help Papa at the sawmill and when that was the case, the remaining three ventured off into the warm and wild woods of the ancient Appalachian Mountains, enjoying their fleeting days of youth with innocent abandon.

CHAPTER 31

A Merry Fourth of July

Taft's Mercantile's annual Fourth of July picnic of 1924 was nearly canceled due to the rare occurrence of a tornado that suddenly appeared north of town just two hours before the first eager picnickers were due to arrive. The destructive force carved out a path through the largely uninhabited woods and steep land on the outskirts of town. Then it finally moved due east toward Silver Mountain. Once there, it did little damage with one exception; it blew through the farm of Mildred and Oscar Lentz, overturning their silo, picking up their brand new John Deere tractor, then dropping it in their neighbor's pond, and stranding their prize-winning heifer on top of their two-story barn. It was a good thing Oscar had over-ridden Mildred's objection to replacing the barn's deteriorating roof the year before because the sound structure held, saving the life of the high-flying heifer, not to mention two horses, one mule, twelve chickens, and Mildred's prized possession, a Model T Ford, that were all safely tucked inside the undamaged barn. After the newspaper had been called, and a dozen or more photos of the cow on the roof had been taken for posterity, as well as the next day's edition, the cow was removed by using a winch-and-pulley system. Needless to say, there was much to talk about at that year's picnic, and the tornado was a topic that was always included in every Fourth of July picnic thereafter.

We arrived at the lake just shortly before noon and immediately surveyed the social situation. Prescott joined Peter Guinn and Frank Hardy, who were already swimming. Papa struck up a conversation with Luther Grange, who was one of Papa's best friends and a deacon at our church. Lydia Harris found Grandma. Mama got involved with setting out the deviled eggs, pole beans, and peanut butter pie we'd brought as our contribution, while Merry Beth ran down to the shore after spotting Corrine in the shallows. I walked over to talk with Patricia Truman, who was a classmate, as well as a member of our church. She was a bland, spindly little thing, with thin medium-length blond hair and round black-rimmed glasses that did very little to help with her severe case of astigmatism. To be perfectly honest about things, she was blind as a bat, but looked like a surprised owl due to her greatly magnified eyes. I felt sorry for her, and I could certainly identify with the pain she felt at being laughed at and ridiculed, or, perhaps even worse, being totally ignored.

Patricia (not *Patty*—she was always quick to correct) was eating a piece of watermelon Mr. Taft had given her from a platter he was passing around to every family in attendance. Watermelon juice had escaped the left corner of her mouth and dripped unattractively from her chin. "Hi, Patricia, good melon?" I asked, looking around as I did to take in who had already arrived and with whom.

"Uh-huh," Patricia absently confirmed. "Is your brother here?" she inquired, cutting right to the chase. It was no secret that she had a crush on Prescott, and had for the last year. As far as he was concerned, though, she didn't exist. He not only didn't look *at* her, but far worse, he looked *past* her. The one who would have eagerly returned her affections was, ironically, Ray Coons's younger—and much kinder—brother, Ronnie. Ray was merciless with her, constantly tormenting her about her glasses. Through his cruelty she had earned the nickname "bug eyes." And, because Ray was bigger than everyone in class, he bullied all the others into joining his teasing.

Fortunately for me, but unfortunately for Patricia, most of Ray's teasing was centered on her, mostly because Patricia let it show how much he bothered her, whereas I refused to. Her crying and ranting only fueled Ray's sadistic taunting, and just like the hound that smells the injured prey's blood, it sent him into a frenzy of the cruelest kind of teasing. On several occasions, Patricia had left school in hiccupping sobs (which only gave Ray more fodder for his incessant tormenting), and walked the three miles back home alone just to be away from him.

Ronnie had tried to get his older brother to stop by actually stepping in front of Ray while he was in the middle of one of his taunts. Mr. Gary had excused himself to take care of "nature calling," and that's when the attack had begun. All the poor girl had done was sneeze, but it was enough to bring Ray's attention to her. Hesitantly, yet courageously, Ronnie stood up, walked over to Ray and timidly asked him to leave her alone. First it stunned and then infuriated Ray. No one, but *no one*, told him what to do, especially his snotty-nosed younger brother, and certainly not with the whole class watching. Ray retaliated by letting the accusations fly about Ronnie still wetting the bed even though he was twelve, and waking up in a compromising pubescent physical condition every morning after murmuring things about Patricia in his sleep. Had there been a hole to dive into, Ronnie would have done so. Instead, he ordered Ray to shut his "damn mouth," which ended with Ray shutting Ronnie's mouth, and for exactly six weeks. The break inflicted by Ray's right fist to the left side of Ronnie's jaw fractured it, which resulted in his jaw being wired shut.

Into the melee jumped Prescott, and, grabbing Ray by the back of his shirt, he pulled him off of Ronnie; then, with the help of Jack, Prescott dragged Ray out to the watering trough in the front yard of the school house and thrust his face under until he spat out the word "Uncle!" along with a strangling mouthful of water. Thus, Prescott had become more than just a crush, he'd also become Patricia's hero, and Jack was not too far behind. Not too far at all. What the girl couldn't quite understand, though, was that Prescott was not defending *her*, but rather Ronnie. Prescott liked the younger boy and made it quite clear that *that* was the true impetus for his getting involved. And even though there was a part of Prescott that might have felt compelled to defend the owl-eyed, hiccuping little girl, it was against some unwritten but well understood law that teenage boys would never admit such a thing.

As I shared the bench with Patricia, munching on a half-burned corn muffin her much-too-thin mother had baked, I scanned the area of the lake where I'd seen Prescott with the other boys earlier, and finally spotted my brother on a large floating platform about twenty yards offshore. People were diving from it, or lying back and enjoying the sun on a day that had gone from potentially disastrous to clear, hot, and beautiful. And as I watched those I'd grown up with, gone to school with, and worshipped God with, one I knew better than the rest came climbing up the platform's ladder. Her dripping tangled mass of black hair spread out like a spider's web across her thin cotton blouse, which clearly showed her unrestricted, newly budded, twelve-year-old nipples beneath. The beautiful woman-child gracefully walked out to the edge of the platform, stood for a moment, then reacted to something someone said by throwing her head back in a rich and easy laugh. With absolute abandon, she raised her arms and dove back into the water, then Merry Beth resurfaced and was instantly and familiarly pulled in close by Jack Harris, who'd been waiting in the water for her. Then he gave my little sister the gift that I had been waiting for, and longing for—Jack smiled his beautiful, glorious smile at her.

CHAPTER 32

Those We Think We Know

I avoided Merry Beth the rest of that afternoon by acting as though I was thoroughly involved in helping the older women with the food, as well as watching over the younger children as they played near the lake's edge. It was a good thing not one of them got into trouble under my less-than-watchful eye, for my mind was a million miles away, wondering just how Jack and Merry might have become so "familiar" with each other. I'd never seen them talk much in school, and she'd never mentioned him to me. On the way home, however, I just couldn't stand another minute of not knowing so I asked her straight out how she'd gotten to know him.

"I've been over to the orchard a couple of times," Merry vaguely answered. "You know how Grandma's gone over there to help Mrs. Harris set up the gift shop. Well, I'd visit Harriet then . . . and Jack some, too."

She looked at me hard as she said the last half of her sentence, as though daring me to challenge her. But I didn't want anyone to know I was as interested in him as I was, and, for some inexplicable reason, I especially didn't want Merry to know. There had never been much sibling rivalry between us, but I felt an unfamiliar and uncomfortable dose of it then. She and I were so different from each other, with her being so much more outgoing, and mischievous, while I was quieter— shyer, really—and more serious. The difference had never been an issue before; in fact, we seemed to balance each other out in some way, but that balance seemed to shift now. It occurred to me that perhaps

Grandma had said something to Merry. After all, Grandma knew. But as soon as the thought entered my head, it went right back out for I knew that secrets were always safe with her.

The apple orchard opened for business by the end of August, but on a smaller scale than when the Lomaxes ran it. According to the Harrises, it would be running at one hundred percent by the summer of 1925, but at least the gift shop was open and some of their trees were bearing fruit again. The apples were plenty fine for cooking, baking, and sauce making, and some were good enough for just plain eating. We were happy for the Harris clan, knowing the blows they'd taken getting things up and running, and I was happy to be getting my favorite peppermint sticks again. Mrs. Harris had taken careful note when I explained in detail about the type I had been unable to get since the orchard's closing, and she made a special effort to re-stock them.

Merry Beth often rode our younger horse Mack over to the orchard on the pretense of seeing Harriet. But it was no secret to anyone anymore that she gave her undivided attention to Jack. According to Lydia, Jack treated her like a little sister, "Just another nuisance," she laughed, when telling Grandma about how Harriet and Merry followed Jack around like playful pups, annoying him to no end. Mama objected to her going alone, to which Merry would respond by saying that anyone was welcome to accompany her, but most often supper still needed to be fixed and other chores completed, thus my adventurous little sister happily made the trek herself.

Papa was none too pleased about Merry's solo trips to the orchard. And he was especially upset when Mama told him over his noon dinner that she had given Merry permission to sleep over there that night to celebrate Harriet's birthday. "There's plenty for her to do here," he admonished, while sopping up chicken gravy with a slice of hot bread. "And anything that she can't do *here* but can do *there* can't be any good for anybody!" he pointed out, using his soggy bread to punctuate each syllable of his statement.

"Now, Calvin, tomorrow's Harriet's birthday," Mama said, trying to smooth his feathers. "Besides, don't you remember? I was just a wee bit older than Merry when you and I met."

"Yes, Anna, I remember. I remember it well," he said, grimacing. "And that's what's got me so damn worried!"

"Calvin!" Mama protested, though I wasn't sure exactly why. Was it simply because Papa was being difficult about letting Merry grow up, or was it because of the memories that had just been resurrected in both Mama's and Papa's middle-aged minds, embarrassing my mother to the roots of her still-black hair, and increasing my father's gray ones? Either way, it caused Mama to become almost flustered and head off to the kitchen mumbling something about helping Grandma with the dishes.

"Ya know as well as I do, woman," he called after her as he rose from the table, "a lot can happen to a girl that age—a girl that looks too damn much like a woman for her own good—or *ours*," he amended, shaking his head.

Grandma, who had wisely stayed quiet, acted like she was minding her own business as she stood at the kitchen counter wrapping up the leftovers. But when Papa poked his head through the door to say he was heading back to the mill and wouldn't be home until late, she speared him with a piercing look—one I'd never seen her give my father before. The only reason I noticed it was because I happened to look up at her as I was walking back into the kitchen after retrieving the remainder of a bowl of okra and tomatoes. And the look she shot him was like bright blue fire and ice.

"Thanks for dinner, Willa," he said quietly, suddenly finding something quite interesting on the top of his shoes. As he turned to go, she uttered a chilly goodbye and mumbled something under her breath that was too faint for any of us to hear. I didn't need to hear her words, though, to know something was off between them. The look she gave him spoke volumes. They were at odds with each other over something, and I knew that it went much further than any possible goings-on with my sister in the apple orchard.

All evening, Grandma seemed restless. First she tried to knit, but gave up on that rather quickly and turned to reading a well-worn copy of *Little Women* instead. Even the antics of Jo March couldn't keep Grandma's attention, so she told Mama and me that she was calling it an early night (even though it was apparent that sleep was the farthest thing from her mind), and went into her bedroom, shutting the door solidly behind her.

Prescott had wanted to return to the mill with Papa, but Papa said that there wasn't enough for him to do, which left Prescott working on another lovely carving of a nativity scene he planned to sell in the orchard's gift store. He'd already sold half a dozen, and Mrs. Harris had ordered ten more. She sold the handcrafted Christmas favorite at a dollar and a half, keeping fifty cents for the store, and Prescott was thrilled. It had become apparent that this was his God-given talent.

I often wondered what mine was, but still wasn't sure I'd figured it out. Mr. Gary, however, had assured me that I *did* have a talent, and one, he said, that was "indeed rare for women." My newly recognized skill was my ability with numbers. I was good at math. And I was good with reading comprehension, too. Mr. Gary said I would be a natural in business, and told me that he could truly see me heading up a woman's necessaries shop someday, or perhaps a boarding house, both of which I knew would bore me to tears. However, the fact that I was told I had the makings of being a good businesswoman made me feel far better about myself than if he'd told me I had a lovely voice, or could bake like no one's business.

Though we were well into the twentieth century, few women were acknowledged as being capable of handling business, and that fact not only amazed me but infuriated me. I knew, beyond a shadow of a doubt, that had it not been for the ingenuity, and calm, rational thinking of the women in my community (and worldwide, too, I figured), most of us would have starved or frozen to death, or died from infections, diseases, or wounds. And there would have been so much infighting and chaos that the social structure would have broken down completely.

Men might give the sweat and blood to build nations, but women were often the driving forces behind them. Many a night, while tucked between the covers with the women they loved—or, at least lusted after—men were told just how things were going to be. Many a town and institution was built; legislation was written up and signed; businesses boomed or went bust because women dangled that one trump card that only they can play. But the irony of it all was that the one obstacle women couldn't overcome was the men they'd helped to seat in positions of power, but who denied those of "the weaker sex" the right to the same opportunities.

CHAPTER 33

Moonshine on the Mountain

March, 1925

The pounding on the door came soon after we'd gone to bed. And our hearts echoed the loud beating as we jumped up in a mixed state of alarm and half sleep. It was getting late, but Papa was still at the mill, so seventeen-year-old Prescott grabbed the rifle from over the doorframe and pulled the door open. Grandma stood in front of my frightened mother, who held on to an equally frightened Merry Beth, while I stood off to the side.

Luther Grange, Papa's friend from church, stood at the door looking nearly as shook up as the rest of us. "I'm sorry to disturb you folks, but I've got to talk to you, Miz Holton," he said, looking past Prescott toward Grandma.

"Come in, Luther. It's cold out there," she urged.

"No, ma'am, I think you better come out here," he insisted.

Doing as he asked, she pulled her shawl closer around her neck and moved toward the door. "Y'all stay here," she said, as Prescott and I started to follow. Mama, however, remained frozen in place, and Merry hadn't moved a muscle either.

"We want to kn—" Prescott responded.

"No! Stay here," Grandma demanded. She closed the door and Prescott and I immediately held our ears to it, but the pine was thick and we couldn't hear anything coming from the other side. Not a minute later, Grandma quickly walked back in.

"I'm goin' with Luther," she said, heading straight for her bed-room. We talked to her through the closed bedroom door as she hur-riedly dressed.

"Where? Has somethin' happened to Cal? What's happening?" Mama cried.

"I'm goin', too!" Prescott said.

"No, you're not, Prescott! And nothin's happened to Calvin, Anna! You need to stay here with the children. I'll be back shortly." The way she said it left no doubt that she wouldn't put up with a challenge from any of us, although I still tried.

"But Grandma, we—" I began to argue but was quickly cut off.

"Stay put! And I *mean* it," she snapped, flinging open the bed-room door and immediately heading out the front. As she turned to pull the door shut, she pinned us with her ice-blue eyes and restated the words once more with absolute finality, "Stay here."

"I'm followin' them," I urgently whispered to Prescott as soon as the door closed. Without saying another word, and ignoring my mother's high-pitched, frightened protestations, I got dressed and hurried out the kitchen door with Prescott right behind me. Without taking the time to saddle up, I mounted Mack, Prescott mounted his horse, Sampson, and we exited the barn and followed the settling dust kicked up by Luther's wagon on the sawmill road.

We hung back a ways and stayed off the road, traveling out of sight by staying close to the tree line, so Luther and Grandma were unaware that we'd followed them. Before long, the orchard was in sight in the valley below. And sure enough, that's where they turned in. Several lamps were hung up on nails or pegs out back in a large shed, and we could see the movement of several people in and around the area. Directing our horses to follow the wagon, but still staying far enough behind to keep out of sight, we wound our way down the curving road to the orchard below.

"What's goin' on, Prescott? What're all those folks doin' here this time of night?" My throat was dry from the road's dust as well as nerves, and my voice sounded thick.

"They gotta be makin' moonshine," he flatly stated. "That's the only thing you hide in the dark to do, 'less it's huntin' or screw—" He stopped himself.

We were getting close to the orchard's gift store and, because the shed was directly behind it, we decided to hide in the shadow of a large, ancient apple tree that was diagonally across the road. There we sat, waiting to see what was taking place, and exactly who all was involved.

We strained our eyes, scanning the area for the familiar figure of our father, but we didn't see him. We could, however, see several people moving around. I didn't recognize any of them, although standing just outside the ring of light cast by one of the lamps stood a man who did look a bit familiar. Suddenly, he turned toward the light and I could clearly make out a long, jagged scar that ran down the side of his face. It was Jack's father, Gilbert Harris. We could hear the men's voices, and they spoke in hurried, anxious sounding tones.

Suddenly, I saw Grandma and Luther move out of the shadow of the gift shop toward the men. All action around the shed ceased as the two approached, but within a couple of seconds those frozen in place became reanimated upon recognizing my grandmother and Mr. Grange. And one of those was my father, who stepped out from the darkness of the interior of the shed. Prescott and I immediately moved over to the side of the gift shop where we could hear better but remain unseen.

"God in heaven, Willa! What're *you* doin' here? Damn it, Luther, why'd you bring her?" Papa anxiously asked, stepping off the porch.

"Since I couldn't talk sense to you earlier, Cal, I figured maybe she could. Like I told you before, trouble's comin'. Maybe you'll listen to her, because you sure ain't listenin' to me! I told ya; my wife's cousin is married to that deputy and the law knows what's goin' on. Someone tipped 'em off and they're plannin' on catchin' you in the act! You gotta get outta here *now*!"

"Calvin, you get in that wagon of yours an' you follow us outta here. You understand me!" Grandma didn't mince words. She was beyond angry. Her words were clipped and spoken in low, hard tones, not like she was trying to be quiet, but like she was holding herself together and controlling an anger that waited right below the surface. The men standing around her either muttered too quietly for Grandma to hear, or stared down at the ground trying to avoid becoming the focus of her anger.

"We're finally finishin' up, Willa, and I plan on seein' it through. We got just—"

But he never got the chance to finish. Suddenly, a shot rang out from the orchard below, immediately followed by a voice within the trees shouting, "*This is the law! Hands in the air! No one move!*"

None of the bootleggers had been hit by the warning shot, and they began to scatter. However, one of the men made the grievous error of standing his ground and returning fire. In response, tiny explosions from the deputies' guns blinked orange among the trees as they took serious aim at the scattering men, several of whom were reaching for their own weapons. The deputies' bullets met solid marks, including the forehead of Gene Roscoe. He was killed instantly. Then one of the bootleggers' bullets connected with a deputy's leg, missing a main artery but shattering his left knee. Papa had separated himself from Grandma and Luther, perhaps to lessen the chance of making them targets, or maybe to return to the shed to retrieve his own weapon. Either way, it was a serious mistake, and as soon as he was back in the illumination from the lamps, he was cut down by a bullet to his stomach. Papa went down hard, hitting his head on the second step of the shed's porch.

"*Papa!*" I yelled, jumping up as I did so, but Prescott grabbed me by the back of my coat and pulled me down hard.

"Shut up! Are you crazy? Stay down!" he ordered. "There ain't no use in us getting' kilt. If we run out there now, the law won't be able to tell who we are or which side we're on. And neither will the 'shiners. We'll end up with holes in us from both sides!" So we stayed pressed tightly against the building while the chaos continued.

Grandma started to go to Papa, too, but was pulled away by Luther, who dragged her back to the relative safety of the side of the gift shop, exactly the spot where we were crouched down. "Oh, dear God!" Grandma exclaimed, stopping dead in her tracks when she saw us. Then she stumbled forward, hurrying to cover us, while just a step behind her, Luther's exclamation was softer in sound but stronger in words.

"Help me shield them!" Grandma cried. Finally, what seemed like an hour later, but was probably no more than another minute or so, the orchard went deathly quiet. The bootleggers who had survived had escaped into the blackness of the orchard, and those who remained were either wounded, some critically so, or already dead.

Sheriff Donald Weldon came lumbering up the hill in front of the shed, with his rifle still aimed and ready. Following close behind him were Deputies Lawson and Platt, while another deputy stayed behind with the injured one just inside the tree line below. As they began to carefully survey the scene, Grandma and Luther came out from the side of the gift store with Prescott and me close behind. Immediately the lawmen cocked and pointed their weapons at us, but upon seeing our arms raised up in the sign of surrender, and hearing Luther shout, *"Don't shoot, Donald! Don't nobody shoot!"* they relaxed their fingers, which lay trembling against the triggers.

"God Almighty, Willa! What the *hell* are you all doin' here?" Sheriff Weldon angrily asked. His gun, though still pointed in our direction, had been lowered, so that if he fired we'd lose our kneecaps, instead of our lives. Lawson and Platt followed suit.

"We come to bring him home," Grandma answered, hurrying straight past the lawmen and over to Papa. His breathing was rapid and shallow, and beads of sweat covered his forehead. "Hold on, Calvin! Hold on, son! We're gonna get you patched up and you'll be right as rain." I knelt down by her and softly spoke reassuring words to him, while Prescott went around to Papa's other side. He was at a complete loss as to what he could do to help our dying father, so Prescott just paced back and forth alongside him, raking his fingers through his hair, all the while repeating, "Oh, Pa! Why'd ya *do* it, Pa? Why'd ya have to *do* it?"

Pulling his shirt up from the waistband of his breeches, Grandma surveyed his wound. Though it was small, it was in a place that usually required the service of an undertaker rather than a doctor. With no time to waste, she used her teeth to start a rip in her shawl, then began tearing it into long black strips. "Bring me some of that whiskey," she demanded. Immediately Deputy Platt brought a jug of it to her. "Pour it into the wound," she instructed, "and one of y'all bring me a lamp. I can't see nothin'!" As Platt poured the alcohol in and around the small bullet hole, the half moan, half scream that issued forth from my father, though chilling, reassured us that he was still with us, and I begged God, and my fading father, that he would live. Papa lapsed into blessed oblivion then, and Grandma continued to carefully work on him, now moving even more quickly. Using a large section of the shawl, Grandma bunched it up to staunch the flow of blood and to keep the wound as clean as possible. Then she had Prescott gently put Pa in a sitting position so that she could examine his back to see if the bullet had exited. Once she confirmed that it had, she used the long strips of her shawl to wrap around his middle and secured the makeshift bandage in place with a sound knot. "Get him in the wagon," she ordered. "I got to get him someplace warm and clean, and with good light so's I can tend to him better." Immediately Platt moved to lift Papa under the arms, while Lawson took his legs. Though the two men had just killed, or, at the very least, wounded others, they lifted Papa as gently as they would their own newborn children, then quickly but carefully placed him into Luther's wagon bed.

Prescott tied Mack and Sampson to the back of the wagon Papa had arrived in, and drove behind us, while Grandma and I sat in Luther's wagon bed tending to Papa while Luther quickly but carefully drove us home. Halfway there, my father opened his eyes and looked directly at me. I was holding his left hand, and wiping the sweat off of his brow with the other. He uttered two words then, "Sweet girl," clenching my hand tightly as he did. Then Papa released it, as he, too, was being released, and he died with his head in my lap, his sightless eyes ironically reflecting the ghostly blue-and-white hue of the moon's shine.

CHAPTER 34

The River Home

One morning in June, exactly three months to the day after Papa was killed, Mama walked up to the family cemetery and graced each grave with butter-yellow daylilies, as well as peach and red tulips. Though the mass of flowers she'd picked left her garden nearly bare, the cemetery became a kaleidoscope of bright, beautiful colors. Once she was finished with that, she gathered up a week's worth of our laundry and said she was going down to the river with the two burlap sacks.

It was rare for her to wash at the river anymore as she preferred using the large washtub filled with warm water to help prevent her hands from chapping. She always hated chapped hands, and applied cream multiple times a day to prevent them from becoming red and raw.

She seemed distant and distracted, but that wasn't unusual for her. At those times, we gave her space, knowing it was just easier to do that than to expect her to give us any particular reason why she was a little off that day. So, when she headed out the door, I let her go without any hesitation. But, by late afternoon, when she'd still not returned, I mentioned the strangeness of it to Grandma, and said I'd walk down to the river to check on her. Prescott, overhearing me as he finished washing up at the kitchen sink, said that, no, he'd go and hurried out the door, but Grandma and I followed him.

My brother found our laundry on the bank, but not seeing Mama, he dove in and found her almost immediately. He struggled to bring her to the surface though, for she had filled both laundry bags with baseball-size river rocks and tied them around her waist before apparently pushing herself off of the end of the large boulder that jutted out over a deeper part of the river. Using his pocket knife to cut the cordage from around her, Prescott was finally able to bring Mama back up and over to the bank of the river.

We knelt down beside her and wept. But no one asked why she had done it. We all knew the answer to that. And we also knew that all that had weighed her down in life had been washed away on the river's current, and there was a certain comforting peace in the knowledge. Three days later, we buried her body between those she so desperately longed for; between Papa and the twins.

Though we never would have admitted it out loud, an unfamiliar but welcome sense of calm and relief settled over our home even though Grandma, Prescott, and I continued our daily struggle for financial survival. Though stressful, it was a healthy chaos that filled the walls of our cabin, as compared to the chaos that had been created by madness. And though there were times when the reality and the tragedy of the loss of our mother was as painfully felt as a staggering blow to the stomach, we stayed so busy just trying to keep our household going that it left little time to dwell on the sadness and the "what-ifs" of the past.

Merry, on the other hand, found her own ways of dealing with her emotions. She became the unofficial keeper of the family's cemetery. She was good about keeping freshly cut flowers on our loved ones' graves, with the lushest and brightest blooms always reserved for Mama. But she would go on to behave in a way that was contrary to what folks usually do when they're mourning. And though I realized that it might just be a passing thing, it worried me greatly that Merry was cut from the same bolt of defective cloth that Malcolm and Mama had been.

PART 4

Willa and Rachel

CHAPTER 35

January 1927, Howling Cut, NC

"Mr. Mercer wants more gravy," I said to Grandma as I came through the kitchen door, using my right elbow to push it open while both hands held on to an empty but still heavy bowl of what had been mashed potatoes.

"Well, tell him he's done eaten all we had, so if he wants more, then he needs to come on in here and fix it himself," she complained. "I still have all their dishes to clean, not to mention bread to bake for their breakfast tomorrow. Lord, those men can pack it away. When did that Mercer fella say he was movin' on, anyway? That one's about to do me in! He's bigger 'n a house 'n louder than cicadas in August." We both laughed, if for no other reason than we were just too worn out to complain anymore.

Though we were constantly tired and often complained about the endless demands of our boarders, the truth of the matter was that we were awfully glad to have them—even gluttonous, voluble Herman Mercer.

The laying of the railroad through Howling Cut and the Blue Ridge Mountains had been our family's saving grace. For over ten years, the iron horse had been huffing and puffing up mountains, down valleys, and through gorges, and with each run it made, it seemed to bring new opportunity with it. The sad truth of the matter was that Papa could have made a far better living for himself—for us all—had he used a little good old-fashioned common sense, and taken advantage of the new age of mass transportation to find markets for our sawmill. As the rails were laid, people were moving in, which meant houses, office buildings, churches, and stores were needed in order to make these once isolated places new and, hopefully, prosperous towns. And it took building materials to build those towns, much of which we could have supplied. But Papa had simply gotten worn out and worn down, and the temptation of quick and easy money was too much for him to pass up. He'd grown tired of coming home with near-empty pockets, and lying awake night after night worrying about losing his last decent paying customers to the Hollis mill. Then, out of the blue, Gilbert Harris had come to town, and dealing with bout after bout of bad luck with the orchard, the two had plenty to commiserate over. Night after night in the back room at the mill, they'd planned their apple brandy business. Eventually, they brought their well-thought-out plan to life under the cloak of darkness, within the struggling apple orchard.

As hard as Prescott worked, he was just eighteen and still learning the business. It was too early to tell whether or not he could make the mill any more successful than our father had. We did not have much hope, because the Hollis Mill was still going strong, but we tried to stay positive.

In the meantime, Grandma and I knew we had to do something to keep our family clothed, sheltered, and fed. Thus, we took advantage when opportunity knocked, and we answered the door to men asking about the availability of a room to rent while they performed the backbreaking labor of building up our town. There were those, too, who worked in the rich mica and feldspar mines. The mines produced enough material to give the world its fill of pottery, china, wallpaper, lampshades, and more, once the trains were able to transport the minerals in and out quickly. Laborers were in great demand, and so was the need for places to house them all.

Using lumber from the mill, Prescott, Luther Grange, and two good Samaritans from our church built two additional bedrooms on to our home. As soon as they were completed, I rode into town, put a sign in the window of Taft's advertising three bedrooms for rent (our parents' was available, too, of course), and we filled them before the sun went down. We could have easily filled a half dozen more, as well.

We offered a pleasant alternative to those hard-working men who preferred accommodations that felt similar to their own homes, as opposed to the cramped and dirty camps. Each camp cabin housed far more varmints in it than men. And man and creature alike half froze in the winter and nearly succumbed to heat stroke in the hottest months of the summer.

We provided a hearty breakfast and supper six days a week, as well as breakfast on Sunday, clean beds, laundry service once a week, and, probably most important of all, an understanding ear when a man wanted to talk about loved ones back home. The one thing that ailed these strong, determined men most was homesickness. Many of those building our country's railroads were immigrants; they came all the way from Russia, Italy, and Germany in search of their share of this land's promised milk and honey. The boarders paid us a fair amount and overpaid us in compliments. They also helped around the house when something needed repairing, which was a bonus for us. Prescott, however, had a difficult time adjusting to their presence.

My brother worked endless days and many nights in our struggling mill, his only help coming from the now-ancient Nathan Street, who worked as much as his dimming eyesight allowed. Coming home bone-tired to an often noisy and crowded house seemed to keep Prescott in a perpetual bad mood. We tried to be patient with him and overlook his often surly, quick-tempered responses to us, but there was little we could do to help lighten his mood. Grandma and I felt a great deal of sadness over Prescott's unhappy lot in life, and we'd both told him that there would be no dishonor or blame cast upon him if he chose to turn his back on the mill forever and forge a new path for himself. He always responded the same way: "I just might have to do that." Yet he continued getting up before dawn each day with a stubborn determination to turn things around.

There was one, however, who seemed to revel in our family's new circumstances, and that was our uninhibited, flirtatious Merry Beth. At fourteen, she was something to behold, if one could get a hold of her. She was never still for long and her attention shifted from place to place just as quickly as the rest of her did. She could be exasperating and infuriating, selfish, and shallow, but with her dark bright eyes, thick jet-black hair, and rich, melodious laugh, men made allowances for her as they never would have for anyone else, their own mothers and sisters included.

At any given time, there were five or six boarders in our home, and Merry found their company most exciting. When it was warm enough, she could be found swimming in the river with one or more of them, which meant I was forced into the role of chaperone. I never quite understood why society's rules of etiquette seemed more properly adhered to with me standing guard. After all, I was only sixteen, and in that "delicately impressionable" age bracket, too. But people treated me as if I were older than I actually was, and, in truth, I felt as if there had been some additional years piled on top of the ones I'd actually lived.

As patient and understanding as we all tried to be with our restless and rebellious Merry Beth, her behavior infuriated all of us at times, but none more so than Prescott. A wall of resentment had risen between them, and I knew it would get harder and harder to tear down as the two of them got older and angrier.

Though there was no arguing the fact that Merry's flirtations with the boarders were both trying and inconvenient, ironically, there was also a silver lining to that cloud. The time spent with them meant less time for her to keep company with Ray Coons.

Following Papa's tragic death, we found out more and more details about his moonshining. And with each newfound bit of information, our family's horror, anger, and anguish deepened. As it turned out, the one who had indirectly been the cause of the "tip off" in the orchard raid had been none other Merry Beth, herself.

Merry Beth had often used visiting Harriet as a ruse, when in fact she was meeting boys at one of the abandoned sapphire mines, ridge tops, or some other isolated place. As I feared, she'd often spent time with Jack not long after that Fourth of July picnic by the lake. On one occasion, Jack had confided to Merry that his daddy was moonshining in order to keep them afloat. He had not, however, mentioned our father's involvement in it.

Apparently, almost as quickly as the words came out of his mouth, Jack regretted them, for he knew that there could be devastating consequences if Merry ever said anything about it. So, Jack did the only thing he could do at that point, and swore her to secrecy, praying to God above that she would use more discretion and sense in keeping her mouth shut than he had. Revealing the secret could easily be the end of the main source of his family's income, he explained, without adding that it could be for her family as well. And Merry *had* kept it quiet, until Jack's maturity had caused his eyesight to clear, allowing him to see Merry's narcissistic ways.

He'd told her kindly and gently enough that it had been fun while it lasted but that he needed to get serious about his future. She realized he had not mentioned her in relationship to that future of his, but that omission only seemed to encourage her rather than drive her away. Her determination to have and keep him was thrown into high gear, and she went after him with a vengeance.

When it was clear to even her that her efforts were in vain, she turned on him, and she did so in the most effective way possible—by taking up with the boy he hated, and spilling his darkest secret: his daddy's moonshining business. Thus, while whispering deep and often dark secrets during clandestine meetings with Ray Coons, Merry just happened to let it slip that Jack's father was moonshining. It was all the jealous boy needed: he left the long abandoned mining cave that afternoon with the taste of Merry in his mouth, and the knowledge of just how he could repay Jack for the affection his Merry still felt for the son of a bitch.

That evening, he took a look around the apple orchard, keeping well out of sight and, lo and behold, about thirty minutes after he arrived, along came none other than Calvin Guinn. Still staying behind the tree line, Ray watched as Jack's and Merry's fathers worked together in the shed distilling what he surmised to be applejack or brandy, for no one used the cover of darkness to make vinegar or soft cider. And even had that been a possibility, knowing what he knew, thanks to his little hellion dark-haired beauty, he put two and two together and figured that Calvin had joined Gilbert Harris in his illicit operation.

It all made sense to him then, for he'd heard his own daddy, Wyatt, wonder often enough how Guinn could stay in the timber business when seventy-five of his customers were gone, and the twenty-five percent that remained "weren't payin' enough to keep the roof on a henhouse!" On the other hand, the Hollis Timber Mill had been doing well, thanks in great part to the addition of Guinn's longtime customers. But regardless of business being so good that the mill had more hands working than ever before, Ray's daddy was about to lose his job on account of being drunk too often while on it. Now, with Ray's newfound information—which he'd immediately relay to his father—he knew his daddy's job would be secure. The Hollis mill would finally be able to have its long-sought-after monopoly in the three-county area once Calvin Guinn went down. And this monopoly meant keeping the business they'd taken away from the Guinn mill. It was no secret that one of the furniture companies was planning on giving its business back to the Guinns. His quality was better, they'd said. And the Hollises knew that once one customer left, the others were sure to follow. Fred Hollis, owner and slave driver, had actually discussed burning the Guinn mill down, but he was afraid he'd be the first they'd look at, so he'd talked to Wyatt Coons about striking the match. But Wyatt, though bad to the bone, was a coward. So, he'd encouraged his own son to play with matches, and Ray had told him he'd think about it. Now, though, there was a beautiful light at the end of this tunnel, he thought, and, oh, how it shined! Just as bright as the moon, he laughed to himself. Repeating to his daddy what he had just learned was going to leave the sweetest taste in his mouth—maybe even sweeter than the taste of Merry Beth Guinn.

CHAPTER 36

Apple Jack

The night of the raid at the orchard, Gilbert Harris was one who'd escaped into the woods. He was caught the following evening, two towns over, stealing a hen out of the yard of James Harvey, who kept the would-be thief at gunpoint in the wagon while his son drove them to the sheriff's office in Clovis Creek. He was returned to the jurisdiction of Howling Creek after his three-month sentence for being a chicken thief was served, and then the book was really thrown at him. Whether it was due to the fact that he was a relative newcomer to town, or whether he had been judged from the get-go as a real bad apple because of the horrific scar on his face, no one knew, but his penalty for bootlegging was severe. The fact that one of the deputies had been wounded in the confrontation only made things worse for Gilbert, even though he had not been the triggerman. Oftentimes, lawmen turned a blind eye to the goings on of the whiskey-making trade, especially if those involved were kin, or if they could earn a little on the side for doing so. However, there they felt no loyalty to Gilbert Harris, for he hadn't been "generous enough" to those in charge who could make sure that things ran smoothly. Thus, Gilbert paid dearly—sixteen years of hard labor in Central Prison, over in Raleigh, which left seventeen-year-old Jack in charge of a ruined apple orchard and a family that was nearly ruined, as well.

Jack had more than the self-taught knowledge of running an apple orchard, however; he had courage and determination. He also had an innate set of values and ethics, and a firm conviction that since he was now the head of the family, he had to do better by them. He vowed there would not be one night when any of them went to bed hungry, and he also made it his mission to improve their standing in a community that had never warmly welcomed them, much less extended hands in genuine friendship.

Mrs. Harris wanted to pack Harriet, Jack, and herself up immediately after Gilbert was sentenced and move closer to the prison (and any place where they wouldn't be known). But Jack felt as though the family's name had to be salvaged, and he insisted that they stay put and attempt to make a legal livelihood out of what seemed to be an ill-fated orchard.

The biggest problem he had to contend with was not the orchard itself, but Maybree Lomax, who, understandably, wanted to see a solid return on her investment with the Harris family. Jack wrote to her and informed her of the situation, of which she was completely aware already. The grapevine remained up and running even though she lived a long way off. She still had her finger on the pulse of the place, and knew that things had gone from grim to virtually impossible at her old orchard. So, in trying to cut her losses, she gave the Harris clan an ultimatum: Show a profit in two years' time, or they would forfeit all they'd put into the orchard.

Jack took up Maybree's demands as if it had been a gauntlet thrown, and hired his friends Peter Guinn and Frank Hardy. Then he worked like he had the devil on his heels. Long hard days and nights were spent out in the orchard pruning, removing vines, grafting trees, cutting the grass around with scythes, and picking and packaging the fruit. The list of must-dos, and have-tos was endless. Meanwhile, Harriet and Lydia were forced to be more resourceful than ever before. They worked in the gift store during the days, and at night baked pies and cakes, crocheted doilies, hot pads, baby blankets, cold-weather caps, and gloves as additional inventory for the store. It was inventory that didn't rely on Mother Nature to bring it to fruition. After barely finishing a small plate of supper, the exhausted Harris clan would fall asleep, usually before they could even get undressed. Work was hard, life was harder, and the return was small. But they kept at it for they had no other place to go.

I hadn't seen Jack, except in town several times, and at the annual Fourth of July picnics of both '26 and '27. Though I hadn't been ignoring him, I just hadn't made it a point to sit down and talk to him. If the truth be known, I wasn't ready to. I was afraid that the things

Jack might tell me would make me hate *him*, and, for some odd reason, I just didn't want to hate Jack. Perhaps, I thought, it was because few things in life made me feel as warm inside as Jack Harris did. Even after all that had transpired. I just didn't want to lose that. I didn't want to lose any more than I already had.

On my seventeenth birthday, I went over to the orchard's gift shop for my annual peppermint sticks. Though I told myself that the candy was my only objective in going over there, had I been honest, I would have admitted that I just couldn't stand the not knowing anymore. I needed some answers. And enough time had gone by that the wounds weren't quite as sore, and I was finally ready to hear what needed to be told.

When I rode up on Mack, I saw Jack and Frank out in the orchard. Because it was late October, apple picking was well underway. I tied the horse to a hitching post in front of the gift shop and walked in. Only Harriet was inside, and she was sitting at an old desk in the back office, thoroughly engrossed in eating a piece of pie. The jingling of the door's hanging bells startled her, and she immediately jumped up.

"Mornin', Rachel." she called, hurrying out of the office and resuming her post behind the counter, while self-consciously wiping away crumbs from her mouth. "I was just havin' a piece of pie that's too old to sell, but still good to eat. Want a slice?" I had seen Harriet several times when she and Lydia stopped by the house. The night of the raid was a topic we all avoided, however.

"Oh, no thanks, Harriet. I just came by for some peppermint sticks," I said, while looking past her and through the window to the orchard beyond. I could see Jack pointing toward something in the orchard while several men batted at the branches with bamboo poles, knocking the apples off into baskets below.

"Have y'all hired some extra hands?" I asked, still looking past her shoulder at the scene beyond.

"Yes," she said, turning around. "It's the busiest time for us, and we've got to get these apples picked, packed, and shipped. It actually turned out better this year than we'd hoped. Jack's done a fine job, Rachel," she said, sounding far more serious and mature than a fifteen-year-old girl should.

Harriet went on to explain that Jack had hired some of the immigrants who wanted to make extra money to send back home to waiting relatives. So, after working at their various jobs during the day,

158 · *Janie DeVos*

men with varying dialects, skills, and ambitions spent several hours harvesting apples. They worked at the orchard on Sundays, too.

Jack was shipping the apples to various parts of the country by train, and he'd gotten some buyers' and distributors' attention by his sincere intention to bring them the best product and price. And the buyers and distributors had seen a true and deep sincerity in the tall, golden-eyed young man with the firm handshake.

"We're gettin' our crop to places all over by train, and locally by wagon and truck. Jack's payin' a percentage of what we net to the extra fellas helpin' us. And, you know, Rachel," she said, looking back over her shoulder once again, "they's a pretty good lot, sure enough. I think sometimes people just don't give 'em a chance, especially when they can't understand 'em. She shrugged and turned back to me with a smile.

"How goes it at the mill, and with your boarders, Rachel? I swear you and I haven't really talked much since school last year. Shame we had to quit. I liked it, especially the history part," Harriet said, adding a sigh for emphasis.

"I actually finished school," I explained. "I was so close to getting my diploma, but . . . well, you know . . . with the way things went . . . I just couldn't go back to school like before. Anyway, that Mr. Gary tutored me and I passed the final exam," I said. "Mr. Gary tried to help Prescott, too, but he . . . well, he just didn't care about it," I finished quietly. "Oh, and things at home and the mill are goin' okay." In truth, however, the business at the mill was terrible. But to admit it was equivalent to admitting defeat, so I just let it go at that.

"The boarders are good. Most of them are immigrants, and they're very helpful around the house. One man, Salvatore Lupari, is especially good at woodworking. You should see the chair he made for the head of our dining room table when that giant Mr. Mercer broke our old one in two, sittin' down too hard. Lord, when I heard him hit the floor, I came running in from the kitchen and there he was, sprawled out on the floor. I thought he'd had a heart attack! Then *I* nearly did when I saw what he'd done to our poor ol' chair. I swear." I laughed, shaking my head. It felt good to be talking and laughing with another girl close to my age. It felt good to be out and about, instead of being in front of the stove, washtub, or ironing board. And it felt good to be sucking on a peppermint stick like I was five years old again, without a care in the world, for a few minutes.

Through the window I saw Jack walk past the shed that had been the scene of the blackest night of my life. On this day, however, the shed housed orchard tools, bushel baskets, and crates. And with the sun shining down on it, and the orchard in general, the place was washed in a light that seemed to lessen the awful stain on it.

Coming through the backdoor, Jack did a double take after he happened to glance up at me while engrossed in studying a machine part he held in his hand. "Rachel," he said softly as he stopped walking. He looked at me with a mixture of pleasure and uncomfortable surprise. "Rachel, how are you?" It was the usual polite greeting, yet his meaning was deeper and we both knew it.

"I'm fine, Jack. You doing all right?" I returned.

"Yeah, I'm doin' okay. Busy this time of year. That's good, though. How're things over at your place? Those boarders behavin'?" He smiled. Though they could sometimes be a rough and rowdy bunch, our boarders were gentlemanly enough in our home and in our presence.

"They are." I returned the smile, then changed the subject: "I hadn't had a chance to tell Harriet how nice this place is lookin'. You've all worked hard. It shows."

"Things are some better." He nodded, looking around as if surveying the store, and I saw a subtle yet noticeable look of pride on his face. "The railroad's makin' a big difference. Our biggest problem is not having enough of a harvest for what customers are callin' for. I'm hoping that'll change before long, though. Frank, Peter, and some of them foreigner fellas have been the savin' grace of this place." He pronounced *foreigner* as *FURiner*. "Without their help," he continued, "we'd be peddlin' someone else's melons back in Georgia." He laughed, although I knew there was more than a grain of truth to his words. *And it still might be the case, too, if the weather doesn't cooperate,* I thought. *Or the workers are moved out by either of their two biggest employers: the government or the railroad. Or if the fearful locals decide to move them out first.*

"What all you got growin' now, Jack?" I asked, curious.

"C'mon. I'll show you." He turned back toward the door.

As I started to follow him, Harriet said, "Rachel, we're having a little autumn dance on Halloween. We're charging a nickel admission, but you can come in for free, can't she, Jack?" She turned and looked at him. Smiling, he nodded, and she continued, "It's a covered dish thing, but we'll have soft cider, pies, some fellas playing music and a few contests, like bobbin' for apples, and such. We're puttin' pennies and a few nickels in some of 'em, too, so a person can win back what he spends to get in! Try to come," she urged.

It didn't escape me that she made a point of saying that the cider they were serving was the *soft* sort. I understood. "I'll bring a casserole of some kind." Then, after thanking her for inviting me, I turned to Jack, who waited patiently by the backdoor, and we walked out into the orchard.

"It's a nice day," I said, breathing in the distinctive autumn air and looking around at the bright splashes of color scattered across the Blue Ridge Mountains. Intermittently, spires of smoke billowed upward as folks burned mounds of gathered leaves, piles of trash, or remnants from their worn-out gardens that wouldn't benefit their compost piles. Fires in hearths and wood-burning stoves added to the number of curling, smoky columns.

"It sure is," Jack agreed. There was an awkward moment of silence between us as we moved into the front line of apple trees. It really wasn't the quiet that made us both uncomfortable, but everything that needed to be said and figuring out just exactly how to get started.

"What kind of apples are these?" I asked, stopping to look around at the various trees.

"We got a pretty good crop of Goldens; the ladies like those for cookin'—though you probably know that." He smiled. I smiled back, wondering if he included me in that group because he saw me as a woman now, or merely because he assumed I knew how to cook. "We also got Black Bens; they're the pretty ones, though they ain't—they're not," he corrected himself, "the best eatin' one. 'Course we got Reds, and Staymans, for sauce, and I'm trying to get that York apple to grow good again. That's the one I got high hopes for, but we'll see," he finished.

"You've got a lot of good apples growing, Jack!"

"Naw, Rachel, I got a few good trees of a lot of different types. So many got damaged or kilt in the freeze, or by apple scab, and the rest was neglected almost to the point of no return. But we've worked our asses—pardon me, Rachel—we've worked our fingers to the bone and our backs to the point of breakin' and I'm startin' to see this place turn around. Between you 'n me, I've got high hopes for it. Real high hopes."

"I have faith that you'll do it, Jack," I said, touching his arm and stopping to look at him. "I think you've got enough determination to make up for the lack of experience. What you need to learn, you will. You've never been afraid to ask a question. I remember that from class." We both smiled, remembering a less complicated time.

"I need for people to have faith in me. Even when I'm not sure I have it myself," he admitted softly.

We walked on in silence for a minute, then, "I'm sorry about your mama, Rachel." The words seemed to come out as if he were exhaling. It was as though he'd been holding them back, but had wanted to say them for quite some time. "I don't know what else to say other than that. I've thought about comin' over to see you to tell you how bad I felt about it all, but . . . I just wasn't sure if you wanted me to. It's a terrible shame. I just don't know—" He shook his head. "How's your grandma doin' with all of this, if you don't mind my askin'?"

"She's all right, considering."

"She's not feelin' guilty, like she could have stopped it, or changed it, is she?"

"No, Grandma knows there's nothin' she could have done to stop her. Mama was just . . . I don't know . . . disturbed. She hadn't been right for a very long time."

"And with Calvin, too? Willa knows there wasn't anything she could have done any different to stop that either, right? My mama said your grandma tried talkin' to him again just the night before the raid, but he wouldn't—"

"Wait! What do you mean, Jack?" I stopped and grabbed him firmly by the arm. "She talked to him about *what*?"

"About the moonshinin', Rachel! Surely you know that she knew!" Then seeing the expression on my face, he amended, "Oh, Lord. No you didn't. Oh, God."

"Tell me everything, Jack," I said in a low but level voice. Somehow, the cat he'd just let out of the bag was one I'd seen poking its head up for some time. Flashbacks of Lydia coming over to have private talks with Grandma, some of which left her in a disturbed mood, played through my mind.

"My mother knew they were doing it—making the stuff. She tried to stop my pa, but he wouldn't. Said we'd starve to death if he did. Apparently, your daddy felt the same way. They had me out there helpin' 'em a time or two, though I never did like it. Your daddy said he was makin' more 'n a month than he'd made in a year at the mill. Said he needed to keep the money comin' in to help keep y'all afloat, and to keep your mama happy—said she liked the pretty things in life, that she'd seen enough of the ugly."

"Haven't we all?" I spat.

"Yeah, we have, Rachel. But some let the bad things in life wear 'em down until they're so low they can't get up again. And others let the few good things in life lift 'em up enough to keep them going. I feel that way about the orchard. I see the poor little leaves that are struggling to grow on a lot of these damaged trees, and even though I can look around and see lots of dead trees, too, I think there's enough of them in here that are bound and determined to survive, and I think they're trying to tell me to do the same. It's like saying if they can do it, so can my family." He turned away from me and started walking again. "We can either live to see the good things in life, or die from the conviction that there aren't enough of them to keep us goin'."

I didn't say anything for a while. I just wasn't sure how I felt about all he'd said, much less how to respond to it, so I veered onto another subject. "How's your daddy farin'? Is he okay?"

"We've gotten a few letters from him. The most recent one said he'd been workin' on a chain gang putting some roads in. Said the prison has its own fields of corn, potatoes, and such, and that he liked that work the best. Other than havin' fresh vegetables for part of the year, though, the food is really bad. Said there're worms in the meat, and the worms are the only part of the meat he could recognize." He tried to smile but it didn't mask the pain in his eyes.

We walked on in silence. I was so angry about Papa's carryings-on, and Grandma's knowledge of it, that I was afraid to bring it up again. And, in truth, I was furious that Jack's daddy had pulled mine into something he'd never had a hand in before. And then the thought struck me; how did I know Papa hadn't? Who taught who to moonshine? I had to know.

"Jack, who knew how to get the stills up an' runnin'? Who knew how to make the stuff?"

"Your daddy, Rachel. He told my daddy that he'd learned from his granddaddy."

"Like a cherished family tradition," I said sarcastically under my breath. Then, "I've got to go, Jack. It's gettin' late." I turned around to head back toward the gift shop.

"Let me walk you back," he said, turning around, too.

"No, Jack. There's no need. I'm . . . fine. I really am," I said, but unconvincingly so. But before he could say another word, I walked away from him and out of the orchard as fast as I was able. Jack stayed where he was, but I could feel him watching me and it made me so self-conscious that I was sure my limping became more pronounced.

I said a hurried good-bye to Harriet, who was sorting some inventory behind the counter in the shop. "Don't forget your peppermints, Rachel," she said, holding the bag out to me. "And don't forget about the fall festival!"

"I'll do my best to come, Harriet. Bye." I couldn't get home quick enough. I had questions, lots of them. And I knew who needed to answer the majority of them.

CHAPTER 37

Onions and Lightnin'

By the time I returned home, Grandma was in the midst of getting the boarders' supper ready. I put my bag of peppermints inside of my dresser drawer, and got busy helping her.

"Where you been, child? I coulda used you to kill a couple o' those chickens a little bit ago. Macy Taft come by and told me that Sam's neighbor called. Said he's under the weather. His breathin' ain't good." (I noticed Grandma was reverting back to folksy words like *ain't*. She only did that when she was hurrying or upset or, as in this case, both.) 'Stead of goin' over in a couple o' weeks for his birthday," she continued, "I'm goin' over tomorrow after I get finished with breakfast to tend to him. Lydia's comin' to help you and Merry with supper.

"Speakin' of birthdays," she said, smiling and turning to look at me more closely. "I finally got your present finished. Go look on my bed. Sorry I didn't get a chance to wrap it, honey."

I told her it was fine that she hadn't wrapped my gift, and apologized about being late to help with dinner. Then I questioned her more about Sam's condition. Not knowing any more than she'd already told me, she said to take another minute to see if I liked my present before I got involved in the messy business of frying chicken.

I walked into her bedroom and there, lying on her bed, was a powder blue chiffon dress, with a creamy lace bodice and lace sleeves. The neckline was cut in a sweetheart style, and the long, tight-fitting sleeves had a lovely pearl button at each wrist. Around the waist was a deep blue ribbon that created a dramatic separation between the lace bodice and the drop of the three-quarter-length skirt. Another dark blue ribbon trimmed the hem. It was far from being a little girl's dress; it was exquisitely made from fine and expensive material, and was meant to be worn by a young woman. I held it up in front of me and stared at myself in the long oval mirror. And for the first time I truly liked what I saw: My long curly brown hair had grown a little darker over the years, so it looked like coffee with a little cream in it, and the richness made my intense blue eyes stand out even more. Small in stature, I had filled out enough in the right places. Although I would never be as exotic looking as Merry Beth, with her dark eyes, thick blue-black hair, and voluptuousness, I was content to look as I did. And that was in great part due to my grandmother, whom I favored in so many ways—both inside and out.

Suddenly, I felt ashamed of the anger I'd felt for this generous, strong, and loving woman. I stopped to think about one of the questions Jack had asked me, "How's your grandmother doin'?" I'd dismissed the question with a vague, "She's doing alright, considering." But was she really? Or was she just holding herself together in order to hold the rest of our family together? I hadn't given that thought any consideration before, and my lack of sensitivity toward my grandmother made me feel deeply ashamed of myself. We needed to talk—about a lot of things, and not just about those things that were in my heart, but in hers, as well.

I carried the dress into my bedroom and hung it up. Then I went into the kitchen, walked up behind Grandma as she stood at the sink draining a steaming pot of boiled beets, wrapped my arms around her waist and rested by cheek against her back. "Thank you, Grandma," I whispered. "It's the most beautiful dress I've ever seen. When did you ever have the time to sew it?" My voice returned to normal as she pulled my hands from her middle, and turned around to look at me with the most pleased smile upon her tired, aging face.

"A minute here and a minute there," she replied. "I'm glad you like it, honey. You're well old enough to wear a dress like that. High time you had one." I knew she was thinking back to my last couple of birthdays. With so many changes, uncertainties, and sadness in our home, none of us had felt like doing much celebrating. But now, although times were still very lean, we managed to find some joy in life again. "I ordered the material from Mrs. Taft a few months ago. Our chickens been generous with their egg layin' this year. They're the ones that paid for most of it. I had the lace in my trunk. It was a piece your mama had, but never got around to doing anything with. I think she'd like that we used it, don't you?" she asked, and I noticed a wave of deep sadness cross her face.

"I know she would. Yes. She would," I nodded firmly. "Grandma, I'd like to go with you tomorrow to see Sam." Even with the wonderful gift dousing my anger, I still needed to sort things out with her, and this was a rare chance to do it without any interruptions.

"Well, since tomorrow's Saturday, an' some of the men will probably head to parts unknown 'til Sunday evening, cookin' will be easier. I s'pose it'd be alright. Merry and Lydia should be able to hold down the fort. Yes. Alright," she said again, as if she'd just finished running through the usual Saturday routine in her mind, and confirming that all would go well without both of us. "We'll leave at eight o'clock. The men'll have to eat early and fast, or they'll have to cook their own biscuits and clean up their mess. Bet knowin' that, they'll be done and out of the house by seven forty-five." We both laughed and then I helped her carry platters of chicken, beets, pole beans, rice, and gravy and biscuits to the men congregating at our dining room table.

Just as Grandma had promised, we left at eight sharp, and we took Mama's beloved buggy instead of the wagon. Though Grandma much preferred the latter, it looked like rain, and the carriage afforded us more protection from the weather with the small roof over the driver's seat. Besides, Grandma packed some food as well as medicinal herbal concoctions to take with us, and she didn't want to take a chance that they'd be ruined in a downpour.

We crossed the Titan Mountains, and as we did the wind picked up. Grandma gave up the battle trying to keep her sunbonnet in place, and allowed the wind to whip loose strands of her black and white hair from the bun at the nape of her neck. When the sun did manage to escape the cover of the clouds, Grandma turned her face toward its small warmth in a young, carefree kind of way. Even with all of the worry and despair in this woman's life, she allowed herself momentary reprieves by enjoying the simple things in life. As much as I disliked having to interrupt one of those rare moments, I knew this was the time to talk to her about Papa's bootlegging.

"Grandma, how long did you know about Papa's moonshinin'?" I asked, my tone hushed.

"Long enough, Rachel. Too long, really," she answered honestly and immediately. So quickly, as a matter of fact, that it seemed as though she'd been waiting for the question to be asked, and did not seem the least bit surprised that I'd somehow learned of her knowledge.

"Was there nothing you could have done to stop it—stop him?" I heard my voice click up an octave, and I made myself take a deep breath for I didn't want emotion to interfere with our straightforward conversation.

"Child! Try tellin' a man to stop doing what he has to do in order to put food on the table for his family! Lord, Rachel, do you really think he liked the lying or the sneaking around? It tore the man up. I tried talking to him when Lydia first told me how he and Gilbert had gone an' gotten themselves involved with it, but I was just wasting my words. For one thing, the money it brought in helped to keep the mill running. It takes money to make money, you know. Had your Pap not done what he did, well . . . only the good Lord knows where we'd all be right now," she finished. "Like it or not, the makin' and sellin' of alcohol has been going on in these parts for a long time now. And if it hadn't, there'd be fewer mouths to feed, less to feed them with, and a lot more graves to be tending. During those years when weather either burned up or froze out everybody's crops, mountain men and their moonshining saw us all through. It's not what most of them would have chosen to do, but it was what most of them *had* to do. And their families survived because of it."

"Well, if Papa needed the moonshinin' money to keep the mill going, how're Prescott and Nathan managing?" I responded.

"They hardly ain't, Rachel!" She sounded surprised I hadn't realized it. Then, "And I haven't figured it out yet as to how we're gonna keep on goin'. Maybe it'd be for the best if we just shut it down." I could see the resignation in her eyes when she glanced over at me. And it scared me to the core. It wasn't just the fact that we were so close to losing the mill that struck terror in me, it was the fact that this unbreakable, determined woman, who had never given up on anything or anybody for as long as I'd known her, was nearly ready to admit defeat.

"I'll start goin' to the mill, Grandma, to see if there's anything I can do. At least I'll look at the books and see if we can't cut some expenses somewhere to keep us going for a bit longer." She nodded her approval, although I wondered if it was just to placate me. Neither of us said anything more as Grandma focused her full attention on navigating the steep trail as we continued to make our way down the muddy, slippery slope before us.

Lightner's Creek was high and running swiftly, and Grandma said that the area must have seen a good amount of rain for it to be that full and fast. We maneuvered around areas on the road that had been badly washed out, and around downed limbs, as well. When we finally turned down Sam's road, the encroaching trees that I remembered so well were still there, but even those strong, ancient, and gnarled sentinels had incurred some damage. When we reached Sam's cabin, we saw that one of the giant oaks that had displayed many of his handcrafted moons had been sliced vertically in two. And the moons which had swayed and spun so freely from the limbs lay on the ground among the debris of the remains of the tree. There was damage to Sam's roof, as well. Quite a few of the old wooden shakes had been ripped away by strong winds and were scattered about the yard.

"My God!" Grandma whispered as she surveyed the damage. "My God, where's Sam!" She reined in Natty, and bounded off her seat with the agility of a young woman, and hurried up to Sam's door. Trying the old doorknob, she found it was unlocked, but it was swollen and stuck from the dampness in the air. Tugging at it with great determination, she finally pulled it open, but almost fell backward when the door at last gave up the fight.

"Sam! Sam! Are you here?" she urgently called as she rushed into the cabin while I gathered her carpetbag with all of its concoctions, as well as some of the food, and hurriedly followed her inside. I found her sitting on the edge of Sam's bed, leaning over and softly talking to the pale and withered shadow of the man I'd met years before.

"What's happened, Grandma? What's wrong with him?" I had come up behind her.

"Ask *me*, gal! I ain't dead yet!" Sam answered, and I could see a touch of a twinkle in his dark eyes. But the effort of talking brought on a sickeningly thick, rib-shattering cough.

"Shh, shh, now," Grandma said, gently patting his shoulder, "you don't need to talk any more than necessary. Any talkin' that needs doin', I'll do it. But you do need to tell me, Sam, what ails you, dear? What's happened?"

"We got the beginnings of what looked to be a bad storm," he began before another fit of coughing interrupted him. Then continuing, "I went to the henhouse to get some eggs for my breakfast for the next mornin', figurin' it might be even worse by then. Soon as I got what I needed and was walkin' back to the house, damn if a limb off that ol' maple tree didn't go a-crashin' down right on me. Damn th"—he coughed again—"damn thing knocked me out for a while, and I guess bein' out in the el'ments for too long did the damage. I was okay when I saw my neighbor the other day—well, better than I am now anyway—but she was worried. Guess she knew I was sicker than I figured I was. She come by to check on me yesterday, and she said she thought I seemed worse, but things really went downhill last night. I got real bad." His voice faded off, but whether it was from fatigue or fear of what the outcome might be, I wasn't sure.

"She did right to call Taft's, Sam. You know I'd want to know." Grandma's voice was thick. I looked over at her and saw she was about as choked up as Sam was, but in her case, emotion was the cause. "Now shut up, old man, and let me listen to your lungs. Breathe in and out, normal-like." She laid her right ear against his heaving chest, listened for several moments, then said, "We'll be right back, Sam. I need to brew up some medicine for you. You got lung fever." I knew that *lung fever* was the old-timers' way of saying that Sam had pneumonia. And I also knew that much of the time it was deadly.

I followed Grandma into the kitchen and waited for instructions from her. "Go out to Sam's cellar, Rachel—you'll see the door to it out yonder—bring me a half dozen onions."

I went outside to the cellar door, pulled it open and traversed the steep steps down into its darkness, hearing the scurrying of disturbed creatures as I did. After a moment, my eyes adjusted to the dim light coming from the open cellar door and I could make out several baskets, barrels, and cases on the dirt floor, as well as countless jars, jugs, and bottles lined up on plank shelves. Hurriedly looking into the baskets, I found potatoes, carrots, and finally the onions. Using my ankle-length wool skirt as a makeshift apron, I picked out six large ones, then awkwardly navigated the steps back out into daylight.

In the kitchen, Grandma had already gotten a good fire going in the wood stove. After we peeled and sliced the onions, she melted some bacon grease in a large black iron skillet then added the slices, as well as some sugar and a very small amount of water. She cooked the onions until they were well caramelized, then set them aside to cool slightly. While they did, she poked around in her carpetbag until she found a roll of rather thin cotton material, which I recognized as being a large piece of an old sheet of ours, and she quickly rolled it out on the kitchen table. Taking a pair of scissors from her bag, she cut a large square from it, and then another long, very wide strip. "Bring the pan," she directed. I did as she asked, and we returned to Sam's bedroom.

"Sam, this onion poultice will feel good to ya, and it's sure to help your breathin'. It's a might warm, but it ain't gonna burn ya. Sit up for me now, dear. I need to get your shirt off." When Sam protested that he was freezing, she told him she'd get him good and warm, and he let her remove his flannel shirt. While he remained sitting up, she took the wide piece of cloth, folded it in two, and laid it on the bed behind him, positioning the ends out to each side of him. After she had Sam lie back down, she took the smaller square of cloth and laid it directly over his chest. "Spoon them onions on top," she told me. As soon as I finished that, Grandma took the ends of cloth that were laying to each side of Sam, and wrapped them over the mound of onions. "Rachel, I forgot to get 'em. Grab me two large pins out of my bag, honey."

I quickly did so, then pinned the strips' ends securely and the poultice stayed in place.

"Sam, do you have any moonshine?" Grandma asked. "Any liquor at all?" He wasn't as alert as he had been when we first came in, and he mumbled something we couldn't make out. He was falling asleep, or perhaps unconscious.

"We gotta break the fever, Rachel. The onions will help his congestion, but the fever will kill him as quick or quicker. Start looking in all the cabinets. We need to find some alcohol."

"Grandma, I saw jugs and such in the cellar! I'll be right back!" I ran to the cellar again, and down its dark steps as quickly as I dared. Then, with too little light to allow me to read the handwritten labels pasted on each jar, jug and bottle, I began pulling cork stoppers out, or unscrewing the caps and smelling the contents inside. When I uncorked the fifth jug, the overwhelming smell nearly knocked me over. There was no mistaking what it was—white lightning.

"Here, Grandma!" I thrust the jug at her as she rose from peering into one of the low kitchen cabinets. She immediately grabbed a glass from an upper cabinet and a small towel from a drawer by the sink, then told me to come with her, and we hurried back to Sam's side.

"Pour a fair amount on this towel," she instructed. "Drench it good." Both of us reacted to the moonshine's overwhelming smell by drawing back from it as I poured a good amount into the towel she had loosely bundled in her hand. "Now fill that glass about a quarter full.

"Sam! Sam! Listen to me," she said, turning her attention to him. "You've got to drink this 'shine. We gotta burn that fire outta you! You hear me! You drink this down, or I'll get it in you another way!" Slipping her left arm behind him, she helped him sit up. Then taking the glass of liquor from me, she began pouring it into his mouth in small doses. Like a baby bird opening its mouth to be fed, Sam opened his and submissively took his "medicine." He coughed after each swig, but he'd no sooner stop than Grandma would get him to swallow another mouthful.

"You tryin' to get me drunk, or drown me?" Sam weakly asked, though it was clear that the potency of the alcohol had cleared the fog for him slightly and a little spark of the old Sam shone through.

"I'm trying to save you. Now hush and do what I'm tellin' ya to do!" she barked, but the encouraged smile that lit up her face was un-mistakable. He was fighting for his life, and that, more than poultices or moonshine, could save him. "Start spongin' him down with that towel, Rachel," and I did—first his back, while Grandma still had him sitting up, then his arms, hands, shoulders, neck, face, and feet. When I had thoroughly bathed those areas, Grandma said that she'd tend to the rest of him, and I quietly left Sam's room.

During the middle of the night, Sam's fever broke. I had fallen asleep on one of the red and green wingback chairs in the living room, and woke up as Grandma stirred around in the kitchen.

"How long was I asleep, Grandma? I'm sorry! What can I do?" I asked, while stiffly but quickly uncurling myself from the position I'd been in for quite some time. "How is he?"

"It's alright, honey. You stay put. The fever broke a little while ago. And his lungs are sounding a bit better. He's still coughing, but at least he's coughing stuff up. He's sleepin' some, and more soundly, too. You did real good, Rachel. Real good. Go on back to sleep now, but go in that spare bedroom. There's a small cot in there."

"I'm okay, Grandma, but you need sleep too. Have you had any?"

"I've dozed off 'n on some in a chair by Sam's bed. I still need to keep a good eye on him. He's gettin' close to the tree line, but he ain't outta the woods yet." She smiled. But as exhausted as her smile was, and as cautious as her words were, there was still relief in both. Sam, she felt, would make it.

"Rachel, I'm thinkin' about bringin' Sam back with us. If he'll go, that is. It's gonna take some time for him to recuperate, and he's gonna need some help doing it. I'd stay, but I can't be gone from the work at our house. Lydia can't stay there, and Merry isn't much help, so I've got to get back or we'll lose our boarding business. How do you feel about that? And how do you think Prescott will feel? To tell the truth, Merry's opinion on things doesn't concern me much." I was surprised at her frankness, but I recognized it for what it was; it was the truth in a time when large decisions had to be made, and when lives would change because of them.

Without hesitation I responded. "Bring him home, Grandma. It's where he belongs. It's where he's *always* belonged."

CHAPTER 38

A Mill Reincarnated

It took quite a bit of convincing before Sam agreed to come home with us. One of his biggest concerns was that Malcolm's spirit would follow us, although he'd admitted that he hadn't seen it in a long time.

My grandmother sat on the edge of the chair by Sam's bed and took his hand in hers, "Sam, honey, you've got to leave the past behind now. It's not only time for you to be free of Malcolm, but for Malcolm to be free of you. Don't you see; he'll stay here as long as you do. Have you ever thought that maybe he isn't just haunting you, but haunting the place where he was killed, too?" Squeezing his hand firmly, and with tears collecting in both her throat and eyes, she continued: "When are we gonna stop lettin' things keep us apart, Sam? You left prison a long time ago, but you've built another one for yourself here. When's enough, enough? Do you have to die to set yourself free?" And with the thought of losing one or the other to death when they'd both worked so hard at keeping each other alive, Sam gently patted her hand and agreed to come home with her.

We bundled Sam up that afternoon and settled him as comfortably as possible in the buggy, then, tying his horse, Milo, at the back, we headed out.

We arrived home near suppertime, and God bless Lydia Harris, she was still there and cooking up a large pot of spaghetti sauce with none other than our Italian-born boarder, Salvatore Lupari, who stood at the stove enthusiastically instructing her in the making of the authentic recipe. "Willa! Rachel!" she cried when we walked in the kitchen door. "Thank God you're home. We were gettin' truly worried and I was gonna call Taft's tomorrow to find out what was goin' on."

"Well, we're home now, Lydia, and all is well. Salvatore, we need you to help bring Mr. Harold in. Let's put him in the little back room off the kitchen here. It'll be warm and easy for him." She was referring to our old pantry, which had been converted into a tiny additional bedroom for a boarder. It was the last room we offered for rent, as it was small and often stuffy, but for Sam's recovery, it was perfect.

The days that followed brought many changes. Sam continued to regain his health and it was wonderful seeing light and energy returning to the gentle man. Grandma fussed over him more than I'd seen her fuss over anyone in a long time. Her ministrations reminded me of the fierce battle she'd led, trying to keep my infant twin brothers alive, as well as the vigilant care she gave me when my foot was shattered. She told me years later that her greatest worry had been that my foot would become gangrenous.

Sam seemed to bask in the attention, though he often told her to "stop your silly fussin'!" He fooled no one, though. We all saw the invincible bond they shared, and as Sam's strength increased, so did their small outward displays of affection for each other, with a frequent kiss on the cheek, a peck on the lips, or with the simple holding of hands. They often took walks along the river in the warm months, and a very long time milking the cows in the barn during the cold ones.

My siblings' reaction to Sam was divided. Merry, for the most part, ignored him, and continued to be out and about doing God only knew what for many hours of the day. She seemed to try to avoid Sam, never sitting and talking with him, or involving herself with a puzzle he might be working on, or helping him with chores when another set of hands would be helpful. I figured that Merry knew Sam could see through her like thin tissue paper. There was no fooling him as far as what her goings-on were, and she could clearly sense his disapproval, but he knew it wasn't his place to say anything about it.

Prescott, on the other hand, was far more accepting than I thought he might be, but only after the first week. He missed our father terribly, and when Sam came into our home, I think my brother felt he might foolishly try to fill the position of patriarch, which no one, to my brother's way of thinking, could ever do. But once he saw no threat of that from Sam, but realized Sam was trying to be a friend more than a substitute father or grandfather, Prescott relaxed a little. And when he did, he found they had much in common.

Sam and Prescott spent many a night whittling animals and people from simple scraps of wood. They often used the flared-end pieces from the butts of logs that had been sawed off, and the works of art the two men created were nothing less than amazing. They taught each other, or learned as they went. And together they came up with new and wonderful tools with which to create more intricately worked pieces. I loved watching the bond grow between the men, but it concerned me that Prescott spent more time with his woodworking than he did at our still-failing mill.

In late April of 1928, the Harrises decided to open the orchard for business a little early with a spring dance. The Halloween party had gone so well, and they'd sold so much in their gift shop, that Lydia and Harriet worked long and hard through the winter making more fine crafts to restock the store with. Prescott and Sam pitched in, too, with their exquisite woodcarvings, and the entire household looked forward to going—boarders included. I was more excited than anyone knew for I'd had to miss the fall party because of Sam's arrival and the time-consuming care involved in getting him back on his feet.

I took every opportunity to try different styles with my hair, and though the 1920s "bob" was a sleek, tomboyish look for many young women my age, it seemed more appropriate for girls in New York, Boston, or Atlanta. My hair reached down to the middle of my back, and I normally wore it in one neat braid, which was often pinned up in a circle at the back of my head. For the party, however, I planned to wear it loose with some spring flowers pinned above my ear. Cream-colored dogwood blossoms were easy enough to find, as were blue irises, and the soft, delicate combination of flowers would be the perfect accessory to the beautiful dress Grandma had made for my seventeenth birthday. The upcoming party at the orchard was the perfect—and first—opportunity I'd had to wear it, and that alone was enough to make me look forward to the event.

But my daydreaming about the party, or anything else pleasant for that matter, was constantly interrupted by worry over the fact that our mill was almost bankrupt and we'd be forced to close its door very soon. It weighed heavily on my mind throughout the day, and even wove its way into my dreams at night. I couldn't get away from it.

We had so few customers left, the amount they spent with us hardly made it worthwhile to keep the mill open and pay the expensive overhead. I came once a month or so to do the accounting work, so the spiraling down of our once lucrative business was clearly shown in black and white in our books. I studied our accounts, trying to figure out a way of cutting even more expenses, but the fact remained we were just too short on customers. There'd been talk that some of our former clients were returning after receiving unsatisfactory merchandise from the Hollis mill. But after Papa's death, they remained "former," and the Hollis mill continued to prosper. Our mill had replaced the power of the waterwheel with electricity some years ago, and the power bill alone was almost more than we could manage each month. I figured at the rate we were going, we'd be closed in six months' time, if not before. I hated to insist we close the mill down, for it wasn't just our family that depended on the mill for a living, meager though it was, but so did Nathan Oliver (our one full-time employee), and his family. Nathan was in his early seventies by then and suffered from arthritis. We knew it was only a matter of time before he would be forced to give up his job, but we hated to close before Nathan gave up. There was something symbolic and inspiring about his determination and loyalty, and his dogged spirit helped to keep us going, at least for the moment.

Sometimes, in the later hours of the evening, when the boarders had either gone to sleep or found a quiet corner to read, Prescott and I talked about our options with the mill, and the reality that we'd be forced to close up soon if things didn't turn around, and turn around in a big way. "I think I might be on to somethin', Rach," Prescott said one evening. "I have some ideas about the mill."

"Well, for heaven's sakes share them with me, Prescott. We need to do something and fast." But before he could explain, Sam walked in from the back porch with an armful of firewood. After laying the wood by the fireplace, he returned to the kitchen and asked if we minded him joining us.

"Prescott," he began, after we'd told him we'd be glad for his company, "what would you think about me comin' with ya to the mill in the mornin'? I've been wantin' to see it, and waitin' for you to invite me over, but since it looks like I've got to invite myself, well, then . . . how's about it?"

"Sam, you know you could have come by anytime. I never figured there was a need to give you any invitation. I just figured you didn't care about it," Prescott said, looking both surprised and a little embarrassed.

"Well, then, I'll be ready at seven sharp. See you in the mornin'." And with that, Sam bid us both goodnight and retired to his room.

Early the next morning, Sam and Prescott left for the mill. While they were gone, Grandma and I washed and ironed clothing that the boarders were wearing for the party that night. We also took a couple of hours in the middle of the afternoon to indulge in long baths and wash our hair. Years before, Papa had added a bathroom onto our house in another attempt to please Mama. The truth was that everyone was pleased about it, especially when nature called in the middle of the night, in the dead of winter.

By four o'clock that afternoon, Sam returned from the mill and quickly cleaned up. "How did it go today?" I heard Grandma ask as they sat in the living room waiting for Merry and me to finish getting dressed.

"My Lord, Willa—" Sam began just as I walked into the room. All conversation ceased when I did, and Sam immediately stood up in respectful gentlemanly fashion. He let out a soft whistle of approval. "Rachel, if I didn't know better, I'd think I was lookin' at your grandma more 'n forty years ago. I swear! It's like seein' a ghost!"

"Well, she ain't my ghost," Grandma said, " 'cuz I'm still here and breathin'!" Then directing her attention back to me, she continued, "Rachel, honey, you *do* look beautiful. You're all growed up." And she looked at me as if that was truly hard to fathom. "The dress is just perfect on you."

Feeling a little awkward but also very pleased, I mumbled thanks to them both, then took a seat in one of the chairs near the fire. "So go on, Sam," I said. "How was it at the mill today? With all I've had going on, I haven't been down there for some weeks now. Not since I went to straighten the books out, and then I was just in and out of the office."

"And you haven't been down either, Willa? You don't know what Prescott's been doing?" he asked, looking surprised. Her brows knit together in a perplexed frown, and she shook her head in answer as Sam continued. "Ladies, we'll be going right by there on the way to the party. What say we leave now? What I need to show you won't take long." We tried to hurry Merry along, but she said wasn't ready and would ride over to the orchard with Prescott when he got home and cleaned up. He was late coming in from the mill, but was due at any moment, so the three of us piled into the buggy and headed down the sawmill road. We wondered if we'd pass him as he headed home, but he was obviously still at work for we could see dim light shining through the transom windows of the building when we pulled up.

We walked in through the front door and called out to Prescott, but found that the main part of the building was empty and fairly dark. We walked by the log carriage and the saw, then went deeper into the building—past the mill's office, the bathroom, and the room where employees ate—until we came to a large warehouse-sized room where our inventory of cut logs was stored. The door to it was open and this was where the light seen through the transom windows was coming from. Sam stepped aside, allowing Grandma and me to enter first.

The sight that opened out before us caused a collective gasp to issue forth from Grandma and me. There, filling the room, was furniture, all beautifully crafted and carved. There were chairs, tables, nightstands, and end tables. And the most beautiful, elaborately carved fireplace mantle I'd ever seen. At work on a small chair was Prescott, and as he saw us walk in, his hand froze in mid-air just as he was bringing down a mallet to pound a wooden peg into the seat. Toward the back of the room was Salvatore Lupari, smoothing down a freshly cut table leg with a piece of glass.

"Prescott! Oh, my God. When did you start building these pieces?" I asked, walking through the maze of furniture and touching the simple yet exquisitely worked pieces. Although they were predominantly colonial in design with the expected turnings and scallops that were so characteristic of that style, there was also some added flair to many of the pieces. Scrollwork and carvings, depicting scenes of birds in flight and flowers adorned some, while other pieces had beautiful inlays of various types of wood. These magnificently unique additions brought the old and respected colonial design to a different level.

"Salvatore taught me how to make the furniture, Rachel. A couple of other fellas who Salvatore knows help us some, too. They're from the *old country*—Italy and Germany—and they're really skilled crafts-men. They come in the evenings sometimes. That's when we do all of this," he said with a sweep of his hand. "And they work for as long as they can, but it ain't often, and it ain't enough. I haven't been able to pay 'em and won't be able to until we can start sellin' this stuff." When I didn't say anything, he misconstrued my silence as a sign of disapproval and quickly said, "Hell, Rachel, we have so much un-used and unsold material from the mill here that it's a shame to let it go to waste."

"It's wonderful, Prescott." I said in an awed whisper. "I had no idea. I'm sorry I didn't know about all of this. It never occurred to me to come back into the warehouse to see what was going on." I shook my head in continued disbelief.

"Prescott," Grandma began, "you've got a talent that would be a crime and sin not to use. We'll help you in any way we can to get this furniture makin' of yours off the ground. What are ya lackin' ta do that, son? What is it you need?"

"Before anything else, I need to pay Salvatore, and them other fellas, not to mention regular and overtime pay for poor ol' Nathan. Now that we have quite a few pieces, I need to get word around about what we're doin' so we can sell this stuff."

"If you paid 'em by the piece, Prescott, what do you figure you'd be owin' by now?" Grandma asked. It was an odd question, and I wasn't sure where she was going with it. She was standing close to Sam, and they kept whispering to each other, but I was out of earshot.

"Dunno, Grandma," Prescott said, looking down with furrowed brows as if trying to mentally calculate it, but there were too many figures to add up without an adding machine.

"Well, figure it out, son. Sam and I are going to help you. We've got some money—it's Sam's actually." Sam jumped in, disagreeing with her, but she immediately told him to hush and continued. "We'll pay the workers, and figure out some way of getting the word out."

"I can do that," I piped in. "I can take care of that part of it." I had an epiphany that came out of the blue like a bolt of lightning on a clear day.

"Well, then, that's all taken care of. Now c'mon, let's go danc-in'," Grandma said and turned to leave. Sam followed her around the maze of furniture and out the warehouse door.

"Where ya s'pose they're gettin' the money?" Prescott asked with a look of absolute disbelief on his face. Actually, he looked almost pale. But I knew it was just the result of finally letting us in on his well-kept secret, and being thoroughly amazed and relieved that we not only approved, but already had ideas about how his vision could be realized.

"I'm not sure," I said, "but I have a feeling that a satchel beneath some floorboards from a long time ago has something to do with it." At his confused look, I just laughed and told him to hurry home to fetch Merry, and meet us at the orchard. Then I ran through the mill to catch up with Grandma and Sam outside, and as I did, I thought about a letter I needed to write first thing in the morning to a very important future customer: Calvin Coolidge.

CHAPTER 39

Moon Shine and Moonshine

By the time we got to the orchard, the spring dance was in full swing. The building that housed the gift store had plenty of space for a band, as well as chairs that people had brought or the orchard had provided. Along the north and south walls bordering the dance area were long tables filled with everything from coconut cake and fried chicken to deviled eggs. I brought a buttermilk pie and set that, along with a bowl of potato salad, courtesy of Grandma, on one of the tables. The floor literally vibrated as Edgar and Arthur Pritchard played the fiddle and mandolin, respectively, while Curtis Hurley's fingers plucked the strings of his five-string banjo in wonderful accompaniment to Matthew Glen on guitar.

They were in the middle of playing a reel called "Geese in the Bog," and I immediately spotted Ronnie Coons dancing with Patricia Truman. He looked like an eager little puppy trying to impress her, while she seemed rather bored, or did, at least, until she saw me and realized that Prescott was most likely there, as well. Suddenly, Patricia came alive and threw herself into the reel, weaving in and out with Ronnie and the other dancers as they completed another figure-eight pattern on the well-worn oak floor. Each time she turned toward Grandma, Sam, and me, she craned her neck to see if Prescott was among our group. By the time the song ended without Prescott's appearance, she literally seemed to droop, and Ronnie seemed to take it as an indication that she was worn out from dancing because he headed for the refreshment table. Patricia made a beeline to where we were standing near the gift store's counter saying our hellos to

Harriet and Lydia, as they waited to show any potential customers their knitted caps, gloves, or doilies.

"Prescott here tonight?" Patricia asked, as nonchalantly as possible.

"Not yet, but he should be along any minute." My answer brought renewed animation to the bland-faced girl. Only tonight, as I took a good look at her, I saw that she had grown into her spindly, awkward body and become a softly attractive young woman. Her wheat-colored hair was darker than it had been as a child, which took away that washed-out look she'd always had. Gone were her round black-rimmed glasses, and in their place were gold wire ones. And the rose-colored dress she wore seemed to add a soft glow to her fair skin and hazel eyes. "You look pretty, Patricia. That's a nice dress, and I like your hair done up like that. Prescott'll like it, too." She lit up and blushed, and the shade was identical to that of her dress. Suddenly, Ronnie appeared at her side. "Here's yer punch," he slurred, and it was obvious he'd had more than punch.

"Mr. Coons!" Patricia began, "Have you lost yourself and indulged in the drink 'o demons," she accused, her choice of words sounding suspiciously like some from Pastor Dukes' sermon two weeks before.

"Ah, sugar," Ronnie started to explain, but as he did he lost his balance and stumbled into her with enough weight to push her back against the counter.

"Go home, Ronnie," Grandma said, "before you make a real fool of yourself."

"Too late for that," Ronnie laughed. "I been one since I was born. C'mon, honey," he began again, reaching for Patricia's arm, "let's have us another dance."

Suddenly a large hand reached between Patricia and me, grasped Ronnie's upper left arm and pulled him away from Patricia. "You need to go home, Ronnie," Jack Harris said firmly. "You've had enough of both the drink and the dance. Go on home." The look he gave Ronnie Coons left no room for argument, and Ronnie swore under his breath, then staggered out the side door near the band.

"You alright, Patricia?" Jack asked, genuinely concerned.

"'Course I am," she answered with a look that was a mixture of both embarrassment and delight at being the center of attention with two handsome young men.

"Good. Evenin', Rachel, Miz Holton," he nodded, then looked at Sam a little awkwardly. Suddenly I realized that they hadn't met.

"Oh, Jack, forgive me. This is Sam Harold. He's a friend . . . a friend of our family," I quickly finished. As the men shook hands, the band began playing a waltz.

"Dance with me, Rachel?" Jack asked.

"I don't dance, Jack. You know, my foot . . ." I said softly, looking down self-consciously.

For a moment, Jack seemed to not understand, then understanding dawned on his face. "Rachel, you can dance as good as anybody. C'mon, I'll show ya." And without giving me an opportunity to protest again, he pulled me out onto the dance floor. Instead of holding me away at arm's length as was customary, Jack held me close and firmly. At first I thought he wasn't familiar with the proper positions that dancers always took in a waltz. But then I realized, as we began to move in rhythm to the music, that he held me as he did so that we moved. I moved—fluidly and smoothly. I danced without a limp. With ease and grace, we circled the dance floor. "You look beautiful, Rachel," he whispered against my ear. "Let's take a walk in the orchard after our dance. The moon's full, and it's not too chilly out."

After a glass of punch, we wove our way through the crowd to the backdoor and out into the orchard. The moon cascaded through the gnarled trees, lighting them in a soft blue-gray haze. Somehow, they seemed warm and welcoming, instead of sinister and forbidding, and we wandered among them as just a hint of the first apple blossom perfume touched the air.

"I'm glad you came," Jack began. "I wasn't sure you would, since you didn't come to the one in the fall. I figured maybe you thought it was better not to have anything to do with us.

"I don't resent you or any of your family, Jack. I know now that our fathers did what they had to do. They loved us more 'n the law, you could say. It took me some time to come to terms with it all, but I have. Grandma helped. I didn't come to the fall dance 'cause I couldn't. The boarders take a lot of our time, and adding to that, Sam came to live with us and he was real sick." I went on to explain much of what had taken place during the last six months, and finished with our discovery at the sawmill earlier that evening.

"So, what're you gonna do to get the furniture business started?" Jack asked after quietly listening to my story.

"I'm gonna have Prescott and Salvatore build the most beautiful, elaborately carved walnut bench to send to President Coolidge in memory of his son, who died of blood poisoning several years ago. Did you know that? His son, Calvin, Jr., played tennis without socks and his shoes gave him a blister that got infected. He died from blood poisoning from a blister! Anyway, I'm gonna get Prescott to start on it tomorrow."

"I hope something good comes of it, Rachel. I really do."

"How goes it with the orchard, Jack? How're your trees doing?"

"There doing all right, really. Comin' along better 'n better. Naturally Maybree Lomax is pleased. But I need to get an edge on the competition. I need to do more than sell some bushels here and there, and to more than families. The business needs to grow just like the trees, Rachel, and I'm trying to figure out the best way of doing it." As he finished, we reached the edge of the orchard and I began to step out of the dimness of the trees and back into the light that spilled out from the gift shop's windows.

"Wait," Jack said, grabbing my hand while we were still hidden in the shadows. "I need to ask you something." I took a step back toward him, standing nearly as close as when we waltzed. "Rachel, would you let me court you?" he asked, and his penetrating, dark eyes reflected the light from the windows, making them seem to emit a golden light of their own.

"Jack, I-I . . ." I awkwardly began. "I don't know. Didn't you and Merry have a . . . ? Weren't you two . . . ?" I wasn't sure how to phrase it. I wasn't quite sure what to ask. I had seen the flirting between them, and I knew that if I'd seen that, there was likely much more that I hadn't seen—things that took place in private.

"As God is my witness, Rachel, I never touched her. Not in that way, anyway. I know she wanted to, but I knew I'd regret it. As tempting as she is, there's something . . . well, there's something about her that stopped me. I know she's your sister, Rachel, and I don't mean to say anything against her, or that would hurt you, but there's something not quite right about her sometimes. I don't know." I nodded in understanding. "She just gets this look in her eyes that's really far away, almost wild-like, and then, at other times, almost empty. There never was anything serious going on with us."

"All right then, Jack," I said.

"All right then, what?" he asked. But before I could answer he narrowed the small gap between us, putting his left hand on the small of my back and pulling me close to him. Then lightly taking my chin between his thumb and index finger, he pulled my face to his and gently ran his tongue around my lips until I naturally responded to him by opening my mouth and meeting his tongue. It was a moment of joy and excitement for me, and, oddly enough, unexpected comfort. I realized then that this was something I had always felt would happen, from the moment I first saw Jack in town after the confrontation with Ray. It just felt right. Tonight we had danced together, moved together, and kissed as intimately as if we'd done it through many lifetimes. Finally, I pulled away from him, telling him that I needed to get back inside before anyone grew concerned. But I knew better. I knew that should my wise and wonderful grandmother realize that both Jack and I were nowhere to be found, she would know that I was exactly where I should be.

As Jack and I walked up toward the back door of the gift shop, I saw Ronnie and Ray Coons standing with a group, just outside the side door of the building. There was only one small window on that side, so very little light was emitted. However, the light from the full moon illuminated the group clearly and we could see that mason jars of what we knew had to be homemade brew were being passed around. Suddenly, I heard a deep, sultry laugh, and didn't have to see the source to know that it was Merry Beth. Taking a step into the middle of the circle of men, she took a mason jar from a young man I didn't know.

"Oh, Jack!" We were holding hands and I pulled him to an abrupt stop. "There's Merry," I said softly. "I need to get her." I let go of his hand and hurriedly walked over to them with Jack close behind.

"Merry! Come inside with me. We'll eat something." I reached out and firmly grabbed her by her forearm. She looked up, startled to see me appear at her side.

"She ain't goin' nowhere," Ray Coons slurred, roughly pulling my hand off of her.

"She is, Ray! She's comin' in with me!"

"And the rest of y'all are leavin'," Jack said to the group. "It's getting late and you need to be on your way. We'll be closing things down pretty soon." His words were polite enough, even though there was an underlying anger in the tone of them. I knew he was trying to defuse a potentially bad situation as calmly as he could.

"C'mon, Merry," I said, taking her arm again and gently pulling her toward me.

"No! I'm stayin' with him!" she said, pulling her arm free and stepping backward to Ray. "Loosen up and have a drink with the rest of us. Me and Ray's gettin' married, and we're toastin' the happy occasion!"

I took a step back myself, as if I'd been slapped, and felt the solidness of Jack behind me. Her words stunned me to the point that I couldn't do anything but shake my head and repeat, "No, no, no!" over and over.

"Yes, yes, *yes*!" she mocked. Then leaning into me she hissed, "You're just jealous, Laggin' Leg. Ya'd give anything if the men paid as much attention to you as they do to me!" Her eyes, wild and feverish, looked exactly like another pair of eyes I'd seen many years before on a frigid night when we were roused from the warmth of our beds and our security had been taken from us. The moon lit Merry Beth's face in a blue, eerie glow, and I watched in horror as she almost seemed to transform into our mother. I knew with a sickening certainty that the same cracks and fractures that had plagued our mother, and her father Malcolm, were part of my beautiful little sister's nature, as well.

"Don't do it, Merry," I cried, ignoring the offensive things she said to me. I knew she wasn't in her right mind and that it went well beyond just being drunk. "At least come home tonight and sleep on it. Decide what you really want to do in the morning."

"Get the hell out of our way, ya sorry, limpin' Laggin' Leg . . ." Ray slurred, wedging his way between us. But before he could finish his verbal assault, Jack grabbed Ray by the front of his brown-and-orange plaid flannel shirt and slammed him up against the side of the building. The window casing shook with the force of it.

"I'm telling you now," he said in a deadly whisper, "if you ever call Rachel that name again, I'm gonna knock every one of those filthy teeth outta your mouth, Ray. So help me, God, you'll be drinkin' moonshine out of a straw, and every meal you take, too. Don't come near her again! Do you understand me, Ray? Do you *understand?*" And as he asked the question, he pulled Ray away from the building, then slammed him roughly against it again to emphasize his words. Jack released him then and Ray, though a little stunned, pushed himself away from the wall of the building and Jack's wrath.

"I'll kill you some other time, you son of a bitch," Ray threatened, "when you ain't expectin' it, and when you ain't got a ton o' people around to help ya. You better be lookin' over your shoulder all the time, boy." Then, "C'mon, Merry, let's get out of here and find us a justice of the peace." He looked at me and smiled spitefully, knowing there wasn't a thing I could do to stop them. Then they turned and walked away. I followed them, begging her not to go, grabbing at her arm to stop her, but she pried my hand off and kept shouting for me to leave her alone. Finally, Jack pulled me away.

"Let her go, Rachel. Just let her go." Jack placed himself between Ray, Merry Beth, and me.

"But she's barely sixteen, Jack! You're just sixteen, Merry!" I cried, craning my neck around Jack's broad shoulders to see Merry retreating. "And not with Ray, Merry! Dear God in Heaven, not Ray! He'll hurt you! He'll . . ." I was sobbing to the point of hardly being able to talk. Jack pulled me into his chest, trying to calm and comfort me, while Ray and Merry hurried away.

They melted into the shadows, but a moment later we watched as they galloped by on Ray's enormous dark gray horse. Merry, sitting behind him with her arms wrapped around his waist, looked over at me with a smile that was both victorious and frighteningly vicious. And as I watched her ride off into the night with her black hair whipping around and behind her like angry serpents, she looked like Medusa's daughter.

CHAPTER 40

The Betrayal

We didn't hear from Merry again for the next six months. But our lives got so busy with work that we only thought of her every hour instead of every minute. Prescott followed my suggestion, building a beautiful walnut bench in memory of Calvin Coolidge, Jr., and it was packed up in a straw-filled pine crate and sent by train to Washington, DC. I worked for a week on a letter to accompany the gift, keeping it simple and to the point, stating that *"even in the smallest of places, the Coolidges' grief and loss was felt."*

True to Grandma and Sam's word, they gifted Prescott with fifteen hundred dollars to pay the furniture workers, as well as guarantee them a steady income for at least a while to come. The money they so generously gave him had, indeed, been that which was under the floorboards in the satchel at Sam's house so many years ago. Grandma had used five hundred dollars of it when she arrived in Howling Cut. She'd purchased a bunch of turkey hens and a couple of toms, as well as the cabin that she raised Mama in (and that my parents had later raised Prescott, Merry Beth, and me in), but she'd saved the bulk of it for Sam in case he was ever released. Although he tried to make her keep it, she refused, saying she'd used enough of it already, and that because of it, she'd been able to start out fresh when she'd left Bolsey River. "You done enough, Sam. Far more than enough!" she said, gently scolding him. But the unmistakable look of deep gratitude and love was there in her eyes, all the same.

The gift of Sam's money—and Grandma's, as he was quick to

correct—also enabled us to give old Nathan a small retirement check. His arthritis gave him no choice but to retire and our modest gift was greatly appreciated by him. He didn't stay away for long, though. Often he came in mid-morning, not to work, but for the company. He missed the mill and his work, but most of all, he missed our family. So we set up a comfortable chair near the pot-bellied stove in the warehouse area, where the furniture making took place, and he watched with great enthusiasm as our company grew, ever offering well-intended advice that we appreciated. We made it known that had it not been for Nathan's loyalty through the blackest of black times, those at work in the mill today would be employed elsewhere. Needless to say, there was a great deal of respect and appreciation for Nathan.

I knew that the chance of gaining any true recognition or future business as a result of the Coolidge gift was a long shot, so I placed well-designed ads in newspapers from Asheville to Wilmington, as well as strategic cities all up and down the eastern seaboard, from Washington to the booming state of Florida.

One late morning, a couple of months after our bench had arrived at the White House, Prescott came riding in on Sampson looking as if the devil, himself, were on his heels. It was too early for dinner, and even if it had not been, Prescott was getting so busy with furniture orders from responses to our ads that he was taking his dinner in a pail to the mill most days and not returning until late in the evening. On this day, however, he rode into our yard, dismounted before the poor, lathered horse had even stopped and ran through the front door waving a paper in our startled faces.

"What's happened, Prescott?" I anxiously asked, as I wiped vinegar off my hands. It was a canning day for Grandma and me, and we were in the midst of making bread-and-butter pickles with the many cucumbers from our garden. Sam had also seen Prescott arrive in a flurry and had hurried in from where he was working on a chicken coop repair.

As all three of us stood there looking alarmed, Prescott thrust a heavy-bond, cream-colored sheet of paper at me. "Look!" he said breathlessly. "Read it out loud to everyone!" On the top was the seal of the President of the United States, and the words in the body of the letter were not typed but handwritten. In disbelief I began to read aloud:

Dear Mr. Guinn,

We received your exquisite bench last week, and it goes without saying that my family and I are deeply touched and eternally grateful for your thoughtful and lavish gift. The bench has been placed beneath a willow tree that Calvin, Jr. especially admired, and we know he would have been very pleased with your beautiful piece and its placement of it there.

My family and I have been truly humbled by the outpouring of care and concern from the American people, and our burden of grief has been lessened because of it.

Thank you again for your kindness. May God bless you and your family.

Your humble servant,
Calvin Coolidge

"My, lord! Prescott," Grandma said from behind me. There was an unmistakable catch in her throat. Clearing it, she went on, "You've done us all proud. Now, the very next thing you need to make is a frame fittin' enough to hold a letter from the president." He agreed as I passed it around for everyone to look at. They held it gingerly at the edges, then, after everyone had had a turn looking at it, Grandma told us to come eat. Prescott decided to stay and shared more news with us from his busy morning.

"I got another order for half a dozen chairs for the courthouse in Wilmington. Seems they love the curvature of the backs. The secretary who put in the order said the employees aren't going home with backaches each day. I kinda wonder though if the chairs they were using were s'posed to be uncomfortable to keep 'em awake so they'd get the work done faster!" We laughed with him. It felt good.

"It was good gettin' the phone in," Prescott continued. "We're not having to wait for letters to hear what folks want and when. Sure's made a difference." He slathered butter over his warm cornbread and dunked it into his steaming plate of beef stew. "If things continue bein' as busy as they've been, I'm thinkin' about hirin' on another man or two. Take a look at the books, Rachel, and see what you think." I assured him that I would, and said I'd do it the next day before heading to Asheville.

"But tomorrow's Sunday," Grandma said. "Aren't you goin' to church first before headin' out?"

I told her I didn't think God would mind much if I missed a service now and then. And being a far less rigid member of the church than many others, she agreed with me.

I did want to check the books to see if it was a financially sound move to hire another couple of men, but my main reason for going to the mill before meeting up with Jack was that I'd left a small gift for him in my desk. The trip to Asheville was, undoubtedly, going to cost Jack a fair amount, and there'd been countless other lovely excursions he'd taken us on, as well. Our outings were not always costly, but often they took a little time and effort to plan. This trip, however, promised to be quite lavish, and I knew that great thought and planning had gone into it. It was all on account of my eighteenth birthday, which was in two days. And although Jack was giving me this trip as my gift, I wanted to give him one, too, in appreciation, and I wanted to do so while we were away.

My gift to him was a beautiful cherry box I'd had Prescott make. He'd carved Jack's initials into the rich cherry wood; I'd had to ask Lydia what his middle name was because he'd never told me. It was Donald, after her father. So, it was Jackson Donald Harris. The letters *JDH* were carved into the box's lid with great care and skill.

Excusing myself from the table, I returned to the kitchen so that I could finish up the pickles and begin making sauerkraut from the cabbages. I had much to finish before I could even begin to get ready for my overnight trip with Jack. As I stood at the kitchen window, washing canning jars and admiring the orange-red leaves of an October Glory maple tree, I thought about some of the things Jack and I had done together during the six months we'd been courting.

When weather permitted, we would pack up Jack's wagon with a picnic lunch and go to an outdoor concert in our town's small square, or go fishing and swimming in the beautifully untouched areas of the river or small lakes around us. And when money permitted, we would take Mama's beloved buggy to the restaurant in our town's hotel for a lovely supper. Howling Cut remained a small logging town, however, so once in a while we enjoyed the cultural offerings of some of the larger towns around us; like Morganton, Marion, and even Johnson City, TN, once, for a horserace. The following night, however, we had tickets to a play in Asheville, and it would be our first overnight trip together. It was a special occasion, because it was my birthday, so Jack splurged on a room for each of us at the grand Grove Park

Hotel, and bought tickets for the wildly popular George and Ira Gershwin play *Rosalie.*

As I arranged some of the new jars of pickles on one of the shelves in a cabinet by the kitchen door, I could hear Sam and Prescott talking in the dining room. "You can start anytime, Sam. I'll get one of the guys to show you what's what. I think I'll just start ya out with the froe. That new Presbyterian church needs shingles for its roof, and I don't have a guy right now that I can spare to get 'em cut. Your comin' on board is surely good timing."

"Did I hear right?" I asked, coming through the kitchen door. "Is Sam becoming an employee of Guinn Timber Products?" The name had been changed from "timber mill" to "timber products" in order to broaden the scope of our business in people's minds, and it had worked. But among ourselves, we still referred to it as "the mill."

"Looks that way, Rachel." Sam smiled broadly. "Looks like I'll be starting first thing next week."

"That's wonderful, Sam! Good for you!" I smiled at both of them and I wasn't sure who looked more pleased; Sam, Prescott, or me. I did know, however, that the idea of Sam working at the mill just felt right, and apparently the two of them felt the same way.

I left for the mill in Mama's buggy about seven the next morning. In the distance, the sky was dark and thunder heralded the coming of a cold front. The leaves were glorious in their vivid colors, and as the wind began to blow, they swirled up like mini tornados from the ground, while those still clinging desperately to the last vestiges of life waved from the swaying branches above. It was a magical time of year in the mountains, and autumn seemed like a final gift from the earth before it became starkly bare and quiet.

Entering the mill, I walked through the dark saw room, and the memory of a tiny foot being crushed swirled through my mind as I walked by the exact spot where the accident had occurred. It happened a lot—reliving it—and I felt the pain for a split second as I did. But I pushed it out of my mind as I concentrated on what I needed to do in my office: I'd take a look at the company's ledger very quickly, grab Jack's gift, and then head over to pick him up in the buggy.

I walked into the office and turned on the small desk lamp. The room was particularly dark with the approaching storm, and my small desk lamp did little more than cast a circle of light on the center of my desk. Swinging my cape off my shoulders, I turned to hang it up on the peg on the back of my office door and came face to face with Ray Coons, who was pressed against the wall behind it. He was dimly illuminated by the desk lamp, but I caught a glimpse of a knife in his left hand as the light glinted off it. With his other hand, he grabbed me around the neck and pulled me into him. He placed the cold steel against my jugular vein, and hissed into my ear, "Scream, move, do anything, and I'll cut your throat right now." Forcing myself to remain completely still, I said nothing and he went on. "Now, little ol' laggin' leg girl, you're gonna open that safe of yours for me, ain't cha?" He turned me slightly toward it and I could see several tools lying on the floor in front of the safe. The filing cabinet next to it was open, and folders, as well as the papers they contained, were scattered in a mess beneath.

Ray stepped behind me and, keeping the knife pressed against my throat, guided me over to the safe. "Now do yer thing, bitch. You get it open for me, and I'll kill you quick-like. You fool around any, and I'll start cuttin' ya piece by piece. You understand?" Choking back a sob, I nodded, then squatted down and began turning the lock's number dial to the right. My hands shook as I worked at the combination and Ray continued his threats, but I finally opened it. Inside lay the result of years of struggle, pain, loss, and determination.

Ray reached past me and pulled out the bundles of stacked bills. Next week was payday, as well as the week we paid our bills. I would have taken this money in for deposit next week before issuing checks. Somehow Ray knew the safe would have more money than usual. Somehow he had known. Someone must . . . Merry Beth! Merry Beth had to have told him the usual routine of the business. Papa had always talked openly about the running of the place, and we had adhered to his same routine. I had to know if she was involved.

"Where's Merry Beth?" My voice shook as I asked.

"Why, she's playin' the good wife at home," he sneered. I closed my eyes when he said the word "wife."

"What's the problem, bitch? Don't ya like the idea of me as your brother-in-law? Or, could it possibly be that you were holdin' out hope that you might be lucky enough to get some of what Merry Beth's gettin' daily? Well, hell fire, gal, there's plenty o' me to go around!"

And with that, I felt the small black buttons on the back of my black and white striped satin blouse popping off as Ray ran the knife underneath each one. Oh, God, no! *No, no, no!*

"Please, Ray, please . . ." I started to rise and when I did, he pulled me backward by the hair and I landed on my back—hard. Ray climbed on top of me, straddling me, and then, pinning me down with his right forearm while still gripping the knife in that hand, he leaned over so our faces were almost touching and I could smell the stench of whiskey on his breath.

"Lemme taste ya," he whispered, and covered my mouth with his, trying to force his tongue between my lips. I kept my mouth pinched closed, and that only infuriated him. "If you don't open your mouth, I swear to God I'm gonna open it for ya and cut your tongue out!" I had no choice, so I opened my mouth but only slightly. He gouged his tongue fully into my mouth and I could feel the bile rising up my throat. At that point, I knew I had to move.

Trying to remain calm and cooperative was not going to help me, and Ray was already pulling up my black skirt and yanking at my bloomers. The button at the undergarment's waistband popped off and Ray awkwardly began pulling them down with one hand, while trying to keep control of the knife at my neck with the other. I knew it was hard for him to do both at the same time though, so I took advantage of the awkward moment. Bringing my hands up, I clawed at his face like a wild animal. I sliced open the lid of his left eye, and gouged a chunk out of the bridge of his nose. During my attack, he dropped his knife as he instinctively tried to protect his face, but just as I was pushing hard against his chest to get him off of me, I felt a fist shatter my jaw. Spots of black-and-white light danced before me as I fought to remain conscious. The pain was excruciating and I was sure that he'd broken it, but I continued to claw and push at him anyway. He grabbed the hair at the crown of my head, and slammed my head against the floor several times, stunning me to the point that more spots of light danced before my eyes. Then he pulled my head back so that my throat was perfectly exposed. Cold steel bit into my neck, and it felt as though I'd been stung by a yellow-jacket wasp. I could feel a small stream of blood snaking down my throat, and I prayed to God that if the end was coming, it would come quickly.

Fumbling with the buttons on his trousers, Ray got them open, then deciding it was easier than trying to get my undergarment off me, he quickly cut open the crotch of my bloomers, while just barely avoiding doing the same thing to my flesh. Ray repositioned himself between my legs then, and keeping me pinned down with his forearm, rammed into me with all of his strength. The pain was searing, and I bit my tongue to keep from screaming. I wouldn't give him the satisfaction of knowing how badly.

"You're gonna die now, you son of a bitch. You're done." Jack had suddenly appeared behind Ray, as did a shotgun to the back of his head. The words were spoken so chillingly low that it almost seemed as if the person I knew as Jack was no longer there, but had been replaced instead with a cold and deadly twin. His eyes were dark, much darker than they were supposed to be, and his face was frighteningly pale and tight. I knew in that second that I was seeing hatred in its purest form.

"Don't do it, Jack! Don't! They'll take you from me. The law'll take you, Jack. Just like it took Sam!"

My words, my voice, seemed to bring the Jack I knew back from the edge. Looking as if he'd been in a dark room and was now being blinded by the light, Jack blinked several times, then shouted, "Get off her! Now!" Ray pushed himself up, zipping his pants as he did so, then turned around to face Jack. There was hatred on Ray's face, just as there was on Jack's, but there was also fear in Ray's eyes. While still keeping him in the gun's sights, Jack circled around him to stand by me as I straightened my clothing and stood up on wobbling legs. "Can you reach in my back pocket, Rachel, and get that hanky? Hold it against your neck. You're bleedin' pretty good. Hold it tightly." He'd kept his eyes and the gun on Ray as he talked to me and I retrieved the handkerchief. But once I had it firmly placed against my neck, he directed his words at Ray again. "Sit down on that chair." He jerked his head toward a straight-back leather chair that was positioned in front of my desk for the occasional visitor. "Rachel, I need some thick twine or rope."

I hurried out of my office and found a roll of twine in the parts room down the hall.

"Good," Jack said when I returned with it. "Now, Rachel; tie each one of his wrists to an arm of the chair. Then tie his ankles to the legs. If you move a muscle, Ray, I swear to God, I'll shoot it. And I'll tell you the truth, I'm wantin' to pull the trigger real bad and I'm lookin' for any ol' excuse to do it." As soon as I had Ray bound so tightly that I wondered if I'd cut off his circulation, Jack quickly called the sheriff's office, told them what had happened and where to find Ray. Then after putting me in the buggy to get me to Dr. John-son's (the new doctor who'd replaced the now deceased Dr. Pardie), Jack gave my horse a stinging slap with the reins and the loyal old animal flew down the sawmill road as if he was Pegasus incarnate, wings and all.

CHAPTER 41

And Justice for All

The only reason I'd come out of the attack alive and fairly unscathed was because Jack had decided to accompany his family to church that fateful day. It just seemed logical to have them drop him off at my house following the service in order to save me the trouble of picking him up for our trip to Asheville, so he planned to get to my house before I could leave for his. However, as the Harrises had passed the mill on the way to the Methodist Church, Harriet had spotted the buggy parked at the side of the building and pointed it out to Jack. He'd turned the reins over to his mother, and grabbing his travel satchel from the back of the wagon, jumped out, waved goodbye, and walked up to the front door of the mill. As he was about to let himself in, however, he noticed an unfamiliar horse tied up behind the left side of the building, which struck him as odd. Feeling there was surely a simple explanation—perhaps a worker putting in some overtime—he let himself into the building, but did so quietly, nonetheless. When he walked in, however, he saw no lights coming from the warehouse end of the building, but instead heard the pounding coming from the direction of my office as Ray slammed my head against the floor. So, taking no chances, he armed himself with the shotgun he knew Prescott kept on a top shelf in a front closet, then crept down the hall toward the sound of the banging, peeking into several doors' windows as he did so, until he came upon the brutal scene playing out in my office.

That had been nearly two months ago, and now the hallway outside of the courtroom was full of would-be spectators milling around, waiting for the courtroom's doors to open. But Jack and I were with the prosecutor behind closed doors in one of the adjacent rooms discussing the case. Ray Coons, it seemed, had accepted a plea deal before court could reconvene for the afternoon's session. After taking a good look at the hard faces of the jurors who'd been seated that morning, his defense attorney had advised him that it was now or never in making a deal, and that, under the circumstances, with two well-respected eyewitnesses to the crime, it would behoove him to think things through. And Ray had done just that, agreeing that the certainty of a long time in a prison cell beat the possibility of a long stretch of his neck.

The judge, who was known for being a no-nonsense man of the court, was informed of the new development in his chambers while in the middle of his favorite deviled egg salad sandwich. Judge Lucas T. Fletcher told the clerk to have everyone back in the courtroom a half an hour later than usual so that he could speak with both prosecutor and defense attorneys before court resumed. After he had done so, court reconvened and the jury was excused. Once they'd taken leave of the standing-room-only courtroom, Ray Coons was brought before the bench, handcuffed and shackled, and ready for sentencing.

As I waited outside with Jack, Grandma, Sam, and Prescott, I couldn't stop fidgeting. I picked at a hangnail and then picked lint off of my new navy blue suit. It was the first suit I'd owned and I felt good in it. I just wished that I was wearing it any place other than where I was at the moment.

Pacing back and forth, I repeated over and over in my mind the things I planned to say to the judge. I wanted a long sentence for Ray. I knew he deserved that. I was, however, relieved that he wasn't going to hang. Rape and attempted murder were dealt with harshly in the state, but the thought that my testimony would cause his death—though perhaps justified—would haunt me forever and I knew it. I lay awake nights before the trial wondering if I would begin making wooden moons to hang in the trees in front of the house, just in case Ray's spirit got the notion to torment me from beyond. However, with Ray's plea deal being accepted, it looked like my conscience would remain free and clear, and my trees would, too.

"Darlin'," Jack said to me, taking my elbow and ushering me toward the courtroom's doors. "They've just called you. You need to go say your piece now. I'm right here with you. You're strong, and he's not gonna break you. He couldn't before, and he can't now." As soon as we entered, Jack released my arm and stepped aside. I glanced over at Ray Coons for the briefest moment, then, taking a deep breath and lifting my chin with the solid conviction of what I was about to do, I limped down the aisle to the podium and the awaiting judge.

Ray was sentenced to twenty-five to life and was hurried out of the courtroom less than half an hour after we'd gotten started. After my request that Ray receive a fair but harsh sentence, Ray's pitiful mother came before the court, pleading that her son be shown "compassion and mercy so that he might still have time to make somethin' of hisself before he has to account to the highest court of all for his doin's."

Her words fell on deaf ears, however, for after she was done, the judge sentenced him to the longest prison sentence he had the power to impose. Ray's filthy, straggly light brown hair fell into his eyes when his head dropped dejectedly upon hearing the sentence. He never looked up again. Instead, two deputies, one on each side, escorted him through the courtroom's side doors and up to his holding cell on the floor above. In a week he would be transported to Central Prison, the same prison where Jack's father, Gilbert Harris, was now serving out his lengthy sentence; a sentence Ray had helped to bring about. Central Prison wasn't too far from Salisbury, the old Confederate prison where Sam had spent over twenty years of his life for killing a man who had brutalized my grandmother in exactly the same way Ray had brutalized me. And even though the three stories and crimes were unrelated, there was enough of an intertwining irony to them that it seemed as if justice was truly being served for us all.

PART 5

Rachel

CHAPTER 42

The Different Somethings

"I promise I won't forget to bring it back to you!" I said to Grandma, for what seemed like the twentieth time. Jack and I were finally going to Asheville, and but instead of seeing the play we'd missed in the fall, which had long since closed, we had tickets for *Mourning Becomes Electra*, and I'd promised Grandma I'd bring the playbill back for her.

"You sure you got everything, now?" she asked, for what seemed like the twentieth time. I knew that I was just a little on edge. After all, Jack and I were getting married at noon, and then leaving for Asheville following a small reception at the orchard. I'd spent the week before getting my clothes ready, as well as finishing up some business at the mill that needed my attention before I could comfortably turn my mind to nothing and no one other than Jack and me.

Apparently, sending the bench to President Coolidge had not only been a thoughtful but clever thing to do, for people who had taken a small rest upon the walnut bench beneath the willow tree at the White House found it to be comfortable, as well as handsome, and orders for fifty-six more had come in. Two senators wanted full dining room sets, and other people in the world of politics wanted various pieces as well. Word of mouth is the best form of advertising, and that was certainly proving to be true with the Coolidge bench. As I finished packing my trousseau, I thought back to the months leading up to this one day. As it turned out, Jack had been planning on proposing to me during my birthday trip to Asheville. But under the circumstances, we'd postponed the trip and Jack had put off his proposal.

Four months ago—a week after Ray's sentencing—Jack and I had taken a walk through the apple orchard. It was Christmas Eve day, and I'd gone over to the Harrises' house with a fruitcake I'd baked for them. After coffee and cake, Jack told me he wanted to show me something in the barn. "It's freezing, Jack! And I'm just getting warmed up after my cold ride over here," I laughed, as he pulled me up from my comfortable place in front of the woodstove.

"C'mon. I have a surprise for you. I was gonna bring it over tomorrow, but since you're here now . . ." We entered the dark barn, but soon my eyes adjusted and I saw that Harriet's easy-going bay horse (given the uninspired name of Baybay) was hitched up to a beautiful new sleigh. "Merry Christmas," he whispered, wrapping his arms around me from behind as I admired the rig. "I had the sleigh made for you over at an ironworks place in Bristol, Tennessee. They delivered it late last week."

"Oh, Jack! I can't believe . . . Oh . . . I just love it!" I cried, moving away from him and hurrying over to the sleigh to inspect it. It wasn't large, just big enough for two. And it was painted a beautiful deep red, white, and gold. It truly looked like a smaller version of Santa's sleigh. It was a sleigh that was just the perfect size for Mrs. Claus, I thought. Suddenly I remembered the gift I had for him, which was a beautiful pair of onyx cufflinks. "But Jack, I have your gift back at my house. Knowing y'all are coming for dinner tomorrow, I just thought I'd give it to you then."

"Then I'll get it then!" He laughed. "Now, let's go for a ride!" Clearly, he was totally enjoying the moment. He circled my waist with his large hands and lifted me up into the sleigh. A crocheted afghan made from the softest cream, green, and crimson-colored yarns lay neatly folded on the far side of the seat. At Jack's prompting, I lifted the edge of the beautiful throw and read the inscription that was embroidered in dark green thread on a small cream-colored satin square sewn into the corner: *Merry Christmas, Rachel. Harriet and Lydia Harris, 1928.* After exclaiming my absolute delight with it, I spread the afghan over our legs and we headed out onto the enormous white blanket that covered the land.

We zigzagged our way down the winding paths around the perimeter of the orchard, and though it was cold, it was clear, and the brightness of the sun on the freshly fallen snow created a dazzling winter world around us. Small icicles hung from the apple trees like lovely prism ornaments, while holly bushes, bearing the red berry that symbolizes Christmas, grew in sporadic clusters along the path. Every now and then, the vibrant crimson color of a cardinal could be seen in one of the trees, or the brown furry tail of a rabbit appeared as it hopped its way across the orchard in search of a meal. It was a world of crystallized splendor, of quiet contentment, and I felt a complete sense of happiness and well-being flow through me.

A short while later, Jack pulled the sleigh over and I assumed he wanted to point something out to me, but he jumped out and reached up to help me down, too. "Where're we goin'?" I asked, intrigued. There was nothing around us except the sleeping orchard, but Jack just took my hand and led me down into it.

We reached a very old and gnarled tree, and, with Jack still holding my hand, he stopped, leaned against it, and said in a quiet, almost reverent way, "Rachel, this orchard is my future. It's where I'm meant to be. I know it. It's worked its way into my blood, and it's become almost like a part of me." Looking around at the orchard that rose up the hills and rolled down into the valley surrounding us, he shook his head as though it was hard to understand how this place could have taken such a hold of him. "But it's not what I love most in this world," he continued, focusing back on my face and looking directly into my eyes. It was as though he wanted me to see the depth of their truth in his eyes. "Rachel, I love you far beyond any of this. I have for a long time now. Without you here, sharing this with me, then all of this loses it importance, its meaning. I don't just want to carve out a living; I want to build a life for us here, beneath these thousand apple trees," he turned, sweeping his hand across the expanse of land, indicating its vastness. "If you're not in the center of this," he said, "I'll continue to work it, but I know I'll quit loving it.

"Marry me, Rachel. I love you. I need you with me..." His words drifted off as he bent down to kiss me. As his lips touched mine, I responded with a mutually deep and gentle kiss.

When we finally pulled our lips apart, I whispered, "I'll marry you, Jack. Yes, I'll marry you." I laid my head against his chest and heard what sounded like a very soft exhale, a sigh of relief.

"Good." Exhale. "That's good," he repeated. Then he rested his chin on the top of my head and I felt him exhale a third time. I wondered if he'd been holding his breath until he'd heard my answer.

"It's late," Grandma said, poking her head into my bedroom and pulling me back into the present. It was eleven fifteen, and the wedding was to be at the Methodist church Jack and his family attended. We'd decided to make it the church we'd attend, as well, and the church's minister, Reverend Hamlyn, was officiating the ceremony.

The day was sunny, golden and blue, and it would have been perfect had it not been for the persistent and painful emotional injury inflicted by Merry Beth's actions.

No one had seen her since the time of Ray's attack on me. We'd looked for her with the help of Ronnie Coons as our guide, and finally found the cabin where she and Ray had lived. It was isolated, which did not surprise me, and it was horrible, which surprised me even less. It was filthy and nearly devoid of furniture. Old and torn curtains covered the windows, and a battered table with two equally worn chairs stood in the tiny kitchen area. In the one bedroom, pressed snuggly up against one wall, was a rope bed that had seen far better days. A small nightstand stood by it, with an oil lamp on top. There were several wooden pegs along one wall and I spotted a couple of pieces of Merry Beth's old clothing hanging from them. The pantry off the kitchen—a kitchen with no running water—was pitifully bare, and there were just a few pieces of firewood remaining on the cabin's rickety back porch. As I stood there looking around and thinking that I would never be able to fathom why Merry had chosen this abusive, desolate, and poverty-ridden road she traveled, I thought of Mama's irrational and troubled mind, and realized that the apple had truly fallen close to the tree.

We never did find her, although Prescott talked to one of the neighbors—distant though he was—who said the couple had talked about heading to San Francisco once Merry's "inheritance" came in. We knew what that "inheritance" really was, and it still hurt me beyond words that Merry would have shared the terrible responsibility if our family had lost the business because of Ray's theft. And she would have also played a direct role—although perhaps unwittingly so—in my death. Her betrayal was almost a physically painful thing and I did not want it to weigh me down on this special day. So, as hard as it was, I pushed the terrible memories from my mind and got back to the wonderful task at hand, marrying Jack Harris.

I was closing up my trunk when Grandma walked in with my wedding gown. She had made it for me. We'd allowed ourselves the extravagance of purchasing some heavy cream-colored satin and lace through a special order from Taft's. As she helped me dress, we went over all of the ancient rituals that brides have adhered to through the ages, checking to make sure we had covered each one: The dress was my "something new." My "something blue" were small sapphire and gold earrings Grandma had given to me, which her mother had given to her. Lydia Harris loaned us her family Bible, to be used in the ceremony, and that filled the part of the "something borrowed." I had told Grandma some days before that the earrings could double for my "something old," but she told me she had something special to fill that particular role, but would give it to me when I was getting dressed for the wedding. Then, just before putting on my veil, she reached into her dress pocket, pulled out a large gold locket with my new initials engraved on the front, and had me lift my hair while she fastened it into place.

"It's not the locket that's old, Rachel," she said, turning me around to see how it looked. "It's what's inside. But you can't open it until after the ceremony."

Thanking her for yet another lovely gift, I promised to wait to see what lay inside, and allowed her to finish helping me dress.

"Now, let me have a good look at ya." Her inspection started at the top; from the lace veil that would not cover my face but would rest lightly on my head and flow down to my waist; to my lace sleeves, with the satin-covered buttons at the wrists; to my high-necked lace bodice which ended in a point at my waistline, both in front and in back. Then her inspection moved to the satin skirt portion of my dress, which cascaded down to the tips of my matching satin shoes in front, while the back of the skirt trailed outward in a short train.

"You're beautiful, Rachel." She smiled a rich, broad smile that told me I truly must be so. "Are you ready?" I was too emotional to answer, so I stepped up to her, hugged her tightly and nodded my head against her cheek in answer. "Then, let's go," she said, though the words were hoarsely whispered. But neither of us moved. We just stood there holding on to each other, knowing that our lives would never be the same, but knowing that the directions they were taking were the right ones.

Before letting her go, I whispered, "I love you, Grandma." The words were spoken so softly and sweetly that even to my own ears they sounded like they'd come from a little girl.

"I love you, too, honey. Always have, and always, always will." Finally, she patted my back, turned away from me while rapidly wiping away an escaping tear, then opened my door and called out to Prescott to come take my trunk out to the buggy.

CHAPTER 43

Something Old

A soft snow fell outside the warmed window, and I could see my reflection cast by the brightly burning fireplace behind me and the small table lamp on the nightstand beside me. It was not unusual to have snow this late in April, but it was still an unexpected surprise. It had started soon after we'd departed Howling Cut after the reception, and continued to fall after we arrived at the Grove Park Inn, in Asheville.

The day had been perfect . . . well, almost. Had Merry Beth been there to share the day with us, *then* it would have been perfect. I sighed and leaned my forehead against the window. How wonderful the wedding and reception had been otherwise. Prescott had given me away, and prior to that, Sam had escorted Grandma down to their rightful seats up front. Standing by a long table crowded with various delicious foods during the reception, I'd heard Sam tell Grandma that the next time he "walked her down the aisle, they would be the ones gettin' rice pelted at 'em." Grandma looked surprised and pleased, and actually blushed at his statement. Perhaps, I thought, he's finally free of the chains that bound him for so long—namely guilt, and the conviction that Grandma deserved better. At sixty-seven, he was still handsome, with a thick shock of gold and silver hair, and dark-brown eyes that sparkled, especially when he looked at Grandma. And Grandma was still capable of turning a few heads with her now shoulder-length, naturally bobbed salt-and-pepper hair and vivid Carolina-blue eyes. Their looks were very different, but they balanced each other well.

Now came the hard part: coming together with Jack—physically and mentally—the way I so wanted to. I wanted him to know how deeply he was loved, and to do that I needed to show him in the most intimate and ancient way. But every time I thought about it, all I could remember was the pain and revulsion I'd felt as Ray had plunged himself into me. Each time I thought of it, I began to shake. And I was afraid it wasn't just from the memory, but from the fear of having the same thing happen over and over, even though it would be with Jack. *Would I freeze up each and every time,* I wondered, *with no chance of ever thawing out?*

"It's beautiful, isn't it?" Jack had come to the window to stand beside me, wrapping his left arm around my waist. I felt myself tense up when he did, and I silently admonished myself for it. The last thing I wanted was to make my husband feel like he wasn't.

"Rachel. Turn around. Look at me." Self-consciously, I did so. He had thoughtfully given me a few minutes alone (making up some transparent excuse about needing to ask the hotel clerk at the front desk about dinner reservations) while I got out of my traveling suit—the blue one I'd worn at the courthouse—and into my lovely peach-colored negligee (a gift from Lydia Harris, no less). Now he was seeing me in it for the first time, and I felt terribly vulnerable. "You're terrified, aren't you?" he gently asked. All I could do was nod my head for fear that I'd start crying. "Is it because of what happened with Ray?" Jack asked. Again, I just nodded. "Rachel, what Ray did to you is not what a man does to a woman he loves. What he did was violent and cruel. That's not what making love is. I will never force you to do anything you don't want to do—or aren't ready to do. Rachel, do you trust me?" I whispered yes so softly that he asked me to repeat myself. "Good. That's enough for now," he continued. "Just come lie down with me. I won't ask you to do anything but to just lie next to me. Would that be all right?" he asked, tilting my chin up and looking directly into my eyes.

"Yes," I whispered.

Tenderly lifting me into his arms, he carried me over to the turned down bed, and laid me on it as carefully as he would a small child. Jack watched me closely as he lay down by me, pulling me close to him. I snuggled my head onto his chest as he toyed with my long curly hair, and gently stroked my back as we talked about the day, the people who'd celebrated with us, and the many amusing and heart-warming things that had taken place. We laughed. We kissed. We talked. And with the help of my patient, kind, and naturally skilled husband, I relaxed. Then, slowly, all conversation ceased, and we came together in a way that only love can make right. And as we reached that wonderful, intense release, I finally knew what being complete, whole and truly free felt like.

I slipped out of bed soon after daybreak, and slid on the large dress shirt Jack had worn the day before. I glanced back as I did and smiled at my snoring husband's contented face. Nothing could have awakened him . . . well, one thing maybe, but it would have to wait. I quietly crept over to the embers in the fireplace, placed another couple of logs into it from a cast-iron container sitting to the side, and knelt in front of the building flames to examine the contents of the gold locket, which I'd not removed the night before. Prying open the small catch, I found a tightly folded piece of paper lying within. There was writing on both sides and I curiously began to read the note that was written in my grandmother's lovely script:

> *My dearest Rachel,*
>
> *I have waited a long time to write this letter, but there was never any doubt in my mind that it would be written to someone other than you.*
>
> *The people who become the guardians of these words have been chosen for their unusual strength, wisdom, unselfishness and courage. And you possess all of these qualities. Thus it is only natural that you should become the next Wart Buyer.*
>
> *I do not have to wait until my dying breath to pass the secret on to you, for it is my choice as to when the torch is passed. Furthermore, now that you have become a Harris, there will be no conflict of having two wart buyers in one family. So, I hand over the responsibility to you with great love and confidence. May you fulfill the promise of keeping people's secrets locked away in your heart, as all wart buyers have done before you.*
>
> *When it comes time for you to pass these words on, may your choice be as easy as mine was for me.*
>
> *Now, the Wart Buyer's secret for getting rid of warts is . . .*

I quietly laughed at the unbelievable simplicity of the remedy. As I reread the letter in order to commit to memory everything she'd written, it did not go unnoticed that she had reemphasized those three things she staunchly believed one must learn to keep: dignity, promises, and secrets. And I realized that these things were as important to the Wart Buyer's customer as was the remedy. Throughout my life she had repeated these three things over and over to me. And, now, she felt that I truly understood their value and the importance of living by them.

There was one last thing to do before returning to the warmth of my bed, and the warmth of my new husband. Balling the letter up, I tossed it into the fireplace and locked the first secret away in my heart.

EPILOGUE

The Harrises

Howling Cut, 1933

"Kathryn Willa! Do not take a bite out of an apple and put it back!" I said, closing the orchard's ledger and rising from my desk as I tried to smother a laugh. My three-year-old daughter, Kathryn Willa, looked at me for a brief moment before defiantly resuming her relentless dig through a small bushel of apples. She was a true combination of Jack and me, with Jack's dark hair and my facial structure, but her green eyes were hers alone. "Kathryn!" I admonished again, as I stepped around my nearly two-year-old son who slept atop a folded quilt inside an apple basket. Scooping her up, I nuzzled my nose into her sweet-smelling little neck. "Let's leave the few good apples alone and see what your daddy's up to, shall we?"

We walked out the back door of the orchard's gift store and stood looking out at the lush, fruit-bearing trees below. Hearing voices just off to the right, I turned and saw Jack handing an empty bushel and bamboo pole to a new man he'd hired just that morning, and watched as he explained the method of gathering the fruit. Kathryn, or "Kate," as she was most often called, heard and saw him, too, and began wriggling in an effort to be put down. Shouting a high-pitched version of *Daddy*, she went careening down the small hillside and slammed into his legs, knocking herself back onto her bottom. Apple picking was immediately forgotten as Jack lifted her high above his head while she squealed her delight.

Life had been good to us and I was never more aware of it than I was at this special time of the day, as the sun set low on the mountains and ribbons of peach, gold, and purple melded into the darkening sky. Another day's chapter was at an end, adding to a story I was happy to be a part of.

On the hillside directly across from me, and above the highest tree line in the orchard, men were finishing up their day's work on the new two-story house that Jack and I were having built for our expanding family. I rubbed my growing belly and laughed, thinking about the fact that in just a few months another little Harris would, undoubtedly, wreak havoc in our lives. Out of the corner of my eye, I spotted Lydia gathering up a few pieces of clothing from the clothesline behind the old house. It was the original orchard home, and the one that she would be staying in. In our nearly completed new home, Jack and I would be close enough to be there for my aging and oftentimes needy mother-in-law, but we would also have the privacy that any young family needs. Lydia seemed a bit put out by our plans at first, but then she started thinking about "wonderful ways to redecorate *her* home," and suddenly the whole situation greatly appealed to her. I laughed to myself at her recent obsession with fabric possibilities, and paint selections. At last she had a little bit of money to be frivolous, and I was delighted for her.

Our two families were doing well, and I stayed involved with both sides. I still tended to the books at the mill, but shortly after our marriage, I took over the accounting at the orchard, as well. Lydia was never very good at it and she far preferred working in the gift shop. Harriet was in Asheville in nursing school and Jack was too busy with the other aspects of running an orchard to be concerned with the accounting part of it. So, by default, the task fell to me. I didn't mind, though. I loved the work, and loved being involved with both businesses.

Prescott had continued to build a solid and highly respected furniture and timber business. And that respect had served him well, for he had been able to keep the place going even when the stock market crashed. Though it was a dark time in our country, the country folks had survived well. And a lot of our survival was attributed to the fact that we had been self-sustaining and self-reliant all along. Because we grew, made, traded, or raised most everything we could ever need, the Great Depression was not felt too greatly by the Appalachian Mountain people.

However, fewer people were ordering furniture, so Prescott and I put our heads together. Depression or not, the railroad was moving forward and it needed tracks in order to continue doing so. With tracks came the endless need of wooden ties, and we were able to secure a large government contract for the continuous production of them. The Hollis Mill wasn't as fortunate, or, perhaps, their reputation for shady, borderline-legitimate dealings finally caught up with them, and they shut their doors permanently in the summer of 1931.

The apple orchard had found a way to survive, too, through the simple fact that babies need to eat. Those little mouths out in the rural areas continued to get their usual sustenance from their families' gardens, cows' milk and cream, and their hens' eggs. The city folks, however, relied almost entirely on store-bought products and they fed their babies, even if they could not afford to eat themselves. Fortunately for us, one of the products the city folks still bought was Gerber's baby food applesauce. Several months into the Depression, I boarded a train out of Howling Cut, complete with a lovely hand-selected bag of our best apples, and headed for Fremont, Michigan, and a meeting with Mr. Daniel Gerber, himself. An agreement was reached with the nice man, and an even nicer contract was signed, and our York apples—the same apple that Jack had told me he had "high hopes for" years before—became the main ingredient in babies' applesauce in cities across America. Because of that gem of an apple, we were able to buy out Maybree Lomax's share of the orchard, giving the Harris family full ownership.

Sam, true to his word, walked down the aisle with Grandma, with rice pelting them, just three months after Jack and I were married. Grandma used the excuse that it just didn't seem proper to be running a boarding house with a bunch of single men living in it, and her being unmarried. So, Sam, in a "valiant effort to save her reputation," as he was so fond of saying, did the right thing and married her. But the reality was that they were foolish about each other, and to be around them was to be around two people who acted like young teenagers in love. At long last, their love had prevailed.

As far as Merry Beth went, I had only seen her one time, and that was at the baptism of Kathryn. As Jack held the baby still for Reverend Hamlyn's sprinkling of holy water, I glanced out the side window of the church just beyond Jack's shoulder and saw my sister standing a good ways back from the window, still close enough to see, but too far away to be a part of our family again. She looked disheveled and much too old for her age, and my heart broke for her—and for our loss of her. I didn't do or say anything at the moment, although I quickly walked outside in search of her afterward, but she was nowhere to be found. I never did tell anyone. I figured she didn't want anyone to know or she would have come in.

As a matter of fact, there were a lot of secrets that were bound to me by then. Some heavier than others, and some harder to hold, but I would always hold them close, protecting them, until one day they would be buried, along with me, beneath our beloved apple trees.

Author's Note

Wart Buyers really do exist, and the use of a copper penny in the ancient art of ridding a person of warts is factual, although how and why it works is a well-guarded mystery. I have taken an author's liberty in embellishing the depth of the Wart Buyer's practices to include being the recipient and keeper of people's secrets. However, for the steadfast, often-isolated people of the Blue Ridge Mountains, where storytelling was the means by which traditions and memories were kept alive, I can't help but think that many confidences have, indeed, been whispered to Wart Buyers as they faithfully tended those who turned to them. May they always hold their secrets close to the heart.

Read on for an excerpt from Janie DeVos's next novel about the Harris family, *The Art of Breathing,* coming in February, 2017.

My parents, Jack and Rachel Harris, built the white two-story house I grew up in on the edge of their enormous apple orchard. My home wasn't far from my great-grandmother's place, which she'd bought as a young woman in the 1880s, and where my grandmother and mother had been born. The town was so small that most everyone was related in some way, even if they were "distant, distant somethings," and if they weren't related then you could bet your last dollar they knew each other well—well enough to know things they probably shouldn't.

I was the first of Jack and Rachel's three children, and I looked like a perfect combination of the two. My hair was dark brown, like Daddy's, and my nose was the female version of his straight and strong one, but the rest of my facial structure was much like Mama's. We both had light eyes, as well, but hers were a true "Carolina blue," just like the sky on an October day, whereas mine were as green as the grass in June.

My brother, Andrew, was sixteen months younger than I, and nearly a carbon copy of me. Though he'd grown into a ruggedly handsome young man, he'd been a beautiful, almost delicate-looking baby. I thought he was pretty and called him such, although my toddler's attempt to say the word "pretty" came out sounding like "Ditty," and the name stuck.

Our sister, Emily Nell, came into the world two years after Ditty, and she was fierce and fearless from the start. I heard Mama once say that she was startled when she first laid eyes on Emily Nell because she reminded her so much of her own sister, my wayward aunt, Merry Beth, whom I'd never met. According to Mama, both had raven black hair, and it grew as fast and wild as a wisteria vine. And, apparently, both of their spirits were just as wild. I'd questioned Mama about my aunt a few times but it wasn't a conversation she wanted to get into, and she always said that Merry Beth had ended up going down the wrong road with the wrong ride; then Mama would conveniently find something else to distract us both.

When Emily Nell was two years old, she caught a cold that just wouldn't go away. It was early January, and we were experiencing record cold that winter. The house was warm enough, but even so, the north winds crept through every tiny space it could find in the walls, relentlessly working to bring the below zero temperatures into our home. Daddy kept the kerosene heaters full, and the fireplaces blazed, but even so, Emily Nell developed pneumonia. For nearly a week, the roads were impassible because of the thick layer of ice that covered them like glaze on a coffeecake.

Finally, my parents knew they had no choice if there was any chance of saving her. They wrapped my raggedly breathing baby sister as warmly as they could, and took her to the hospital in Marion, slip-sliding down the mountain roads as they did so, all the while praying to God that they would not all die before they could attempt to save my sister. They arrived at the hospital in one piece, and the doctors used every medication and technique available to them at the time, but Emily Nell was just too far gone. She died there in Mama's arms three days later. It was the darkest period that I've ever seen my family go through. Even though I was only six years old at the time, I'll always remember the black grief that gripped our family as deeply and as painfully as the north wind did that winter.

But spring unfailingly returned, as did all of the seasons over and over again, and through those years, my parents expanded their apple orchard as often as they could. They had a standing contract with Gerber Baby Food products, not to mention with several restaurants in Cabot and nearby Asheville, and every year, it seemed, more of my parents' apples were in demand. But the spring freeze of '44 had damaged many of the trees, and that year my parents were forced to purchase apples from orchards further south in order to fulfill their contracts. Over the following two years, they'd had to purchase more trees, as well as more land, leaving less money to help with my college expenses. So I worked long hours as a short order cook at Woolworth's Five and Dime, in Durham, to help make ends meet.

I'd decided to study nursing at Watts Hospital School of Nursing, just as my father's sister, my Aunt Harriet, had done, and I met Geoffrey Cavanaugh during his final year of law school at Duke. One late frigid January evening in 1948, I had just begun to degrease the grill after a twelve-hour shift when a highly intoxicated Geoffrey, along with several of his fellow law school friends, staggered in. Silently scolding myself for not having locked the door before starting on the grill, I grabbed an order pad and walked to the middle of the counter where the four inebriated men had made themselves at home on the red leather stools.

"What can I get y'all?" I asked, with pencil and pad at the ready. But the men were in their own world, laughing at things only they found humorous, and slurring any word that had more than one syllable. I waited another minute for the men to pull themselves together, but when they still couldn't, I firmly told them that I had work to do and asked them to leave. However, one of the men, Marshall Tanner, who was shorter and stockier than the other three, did not take too kindly to being told what to do, especially by one he considered as insignificant as a short order cook. Making matters worse, he noticed through his bourbon-soaked brain that I had a deep southern drawl, which had been especially apparent when I referred to them as "y'all." I learned later that Marshall was from Washington, DC, and the son of a Pulitzer Prize–nominated journalist for *The Post*; and his air of superiority came to the surface full force when he declared that I had all the telltale signs of being the daughter of an ignorant cabbage farmer.

"Easy there, Tanner," Geoffrey immediately interceded, rising from his stool and moving to stand behind him, then slapping him on the back much too forcefully to have been a friendly gesture. "The poor girl is just trying to get out of here, that's all. No need to insult her. As a matter of fact, you really owe her an apology."

Wanting nothing more than to finish up and get out of there, I quickly denied any need for an apology, but Geoffrey clamped his hand down on that tender area between the shoulder and neck, and applied just enough pressure that Marshall croaked out a very disingenuous and humiliated, "I'm sorry!"

"There now, don't you feel better?" Geoffrey asked the red-faced young man, patting the place he'd squeezed. Then, "Let's go. Let the young lady close up. We'll get a bite over at Dusky's." The four of them started for the door, but not before Geoffrey laid an extravagant tip of five dollars on the counter and said, "Sorry for the trouble, pretty lady. I'll be seeing you." Then, smiling broadly at me, he opened the door and, with a great flourish, bowed while sweeping his hand out before him in a grandiose gesture that allowed the other three to exit before him. When he straightened up, he looked at me and winked, and, in return, I smiled a soft, grateful smile; then he, too, walked out.

I quickly went to the door and locked it while my eyes remained on the handsome young man with the dark blond hair as he rejoined his group. Abruptly, I turned away, but I wished I'd done so a half second sooner, for Geoffrey had turned around just in time to catch me watching him, as if he was sure I would be. Smiling, he lifted his hand in a wave before he walked out of the circle of light cast down from a street lamp and faded into the darkness.

Janie DeVos, a native of Coral Gables, Florida, worked in the advertising industry in the late 1980s, but left the field in 2000 to turn her love of writing into a full-time career. DeVos started her freelance writing company, Rainy Day Creations, and became a copywriter for several greeting card companies. In 2002, her national-award-winning poem *How High Can You Fly?* was published as a children's picture book through River Road Press, and a second hard cover picture book, *The Path Winds Home*, soon followed.

In 2007, Ms. DeVos's third children's picture book, *Barthello's Wing*, was published through East End Publishing, and was included in Scholastic Books' North American school book fairs. To date it has sold over 90,000 copies.

Ms. DeVos gave up city life to live in the beautiful Blue Ridge Mountains of North Carolina in 2007. And though she continued to write for children, including the publication of her fourth children's book, *The Shopkeeper's Bear*, in 2012, she found that her writing interests began to change as she became more embedded in the lives and the traditions of the mountain people.

Ms. DeVos has made numerous appearances in schools, libraries, and bookstores, and has been a keynote speaker as well as a selected author for special events, including the Miami Book Fair International and the Carolina Literary Festival.

Janie DeVos continues work on her newest women's fiction novel while enjoying her not-so-quiet life with her husband and three howling basset hounds in a log cabin on top of a mountain.

Made in the USA
Middletown, DE
25 February 2018